The World's Finest Mystery and Crime Stories

First Annual Collection

Forge Books by Ed Gorman

(as E. J. Gorman)
The First Lady
The Marilyn Tapes
Senatorial Privilege

(as editor)
*The World's Finest Mystery and Crime Stories:
First Annual Collection*

The World's Finest Mystery and Crime Stories

Edited by Ed Gorman

A TOM DOHERTY ASSOCIATES BOOK

NEW YORK

THE WORLD'S FINEST MYSTERY AND CRIME STORIES: FIRST ANNUAL COLLECTION

Edited by James Frenkel
Design by Ellen Cipriano

A Forge Book
Published by Tom Doherty Associates, LLC
175 Fifth Avenue
New York, NY 10010

www.tor.com

Forge® is a registered trademark of Tom Doherty Associates, LLC.

ISBN 0-312-87480-4 (hardcover)
ISBN 0-312-87479-0 (trade paperback)

First Edition: September 2000

Printed in the United States of America

0 9 8 7 6 5 4 3 2 1

*Dedicated to the memory
of Howard Browne*

—E. G.

Thanks to Martin H. Greenberg, Larry Segriff, John Helfers, the doughty band at Tekno Books, to Jon Lutz, and Ed Hoch for their helpful and informative front-end summaries of the field, and, of course, to my editor at Tom Doherty Associates, Jim Frenkel, and his able assistant, Kris O'Higgins.

—ED GORMAN

"Unchained Melody" by Doug Allyn. Copyright © 1999 by Doug Allyn. First published in *Ellery Queen's Mystery Magazine,* January 1999. Reprinted by permission of the author and his agent, James Allen, Literary Agent.

"Something Simple" by Rob Kantner. Copyright © 1999 by Rob Kantner. First published in *Alfred Hitchcock's Mystery Magazine,* June 1999. Reprinted by permission of the author.

"The Circle of Ink" by Edward D. Hoch. Copyright © 1999 by Edward D. Hoch. Ellery Queen characters copyright © 1999 by Fredric Dannay and Manfred B. Lee Literary Properties Trust. First published in *Ellery Queen's Mystery Magazine,* September/October 1999. Reprinted by permission of the author.

"The Death Cat of Hester Street" by Carol Gorman. Copyright © 1999 by Carol Gorman. First published in *Cat Crimes Through Time.* Reprinted by permission of the author.

"Dark Times" by Peter Crowther. Copyright © 1999 by Peter Crowther. First published in *Subterranean Gallery.* Reprinted by permission of the author.

"Those That Trespass" by Peter Tremayne. Copyright © 1999 by Peter Tremayne. First published in *Chronicles of Crime,* Vol. II. Reprinted by permission of the author and his agents, A. M. Heath & Company.

"Blitzed" by Phil Lovesey. Copyright © 1999 by Phil Lovesey. First published in *Ellery Queen's Mystery Magazine,* June 1999. Reprinted by permission of the author and his agents, Gregory and Radice, Agents.

"For Services Rendered" by Jeffery Deaver. Copyright © 1999 by Jeffery Deaver. First published in *Ellery Queen's Mystery Magazine,* November 1999. Reprinted by permission of the author and his agents, Gelfman-Schneider Literary Agency, Inc.

"The Tinder Box" by Minette Walters. Copyright © 1999 by Minette Walters. First published in *Ellery Queen's Mystery Magazine,* December 1999. Reprinted by permission of the author and her agents, Gregory and Radice, Agents.

"Symptoms of Loss" by Jerry Sykes. Copyright © 1999 by Jerry Sykes. First published in *Crimewave,* June 1999. Reprinted by permission of the author.

"Taking Care of Frank" by Antony Mann. Copyright © 1999 by Antony Mann. First published in *Crimewave,* June 1999. Reprinted by permission of the author.

"Styx and Bones" by Edward Bryant. Copyright © 1999 by Edward Bryant. First published in *999,* edited by Al Sarrantonio. Reprinted by permission of the author.

"Not Long Now" by Carol Anne Davis. Copyright © 1999 by Carol Anne Davis. First published in *QWF Magazine.* Reprinted by permission of the author.

"The Shortest Distance" by Mat Coward. Copyright © 1999 by Mat Coward. First published in *Shots,* Winter 1999. Reprinted by permission of the author.

Contents

The Year in Mystery and Crime Fiction: 1999

Jon L. Breen

Call 1999 crime fiction's Year of Retrospection. Not only because the end of a century naturally encourages nostalgia, reevaluation, and list-making but also because the historical mystery continued to increase in prominence, including both popular and critical success. Well over half of my favorite books this year were set partly or entirely in the past, and early awards nominees reflect a similar trend.

A favorite object of fictional retrospection, possibly inspired by the success of Steven Spielberg's great 1998 film *Saving Private Ryan* but more likely coincidental, was the twentieth century's two world wars and their effects on those who lived through them.

It was also a year of looking back at the unmatched contribution to twentieth-century mystery fiction of Ellery Queen (the team of Frederic Dannay and Manfred B. Lee). To commemorate the seventieth anniversary of *The Roman Hat Mystery* (1929), the debut of author and sleuth Queen, Crippen & Landru (P.O. Box 9315, Norfolk, VA 23505) published *The Tragedy of Errors*, half a gathering of uncollected Queen stories (including a final novel outline by Dannay) and half a collection of essays and remembrances of the team by friends, family members, fans, and fellow writers. *Ellery Queen's Mystery Magazine* commemorated the anniversary in its September/October issue with (among other features) Queen pastiches by Edward D. Hoch and the present writer.

BESTS OF THE YEARS

In the spirit of looking backward, and with the present series of best-of-year volumes taking on new scope and ambition along with a new publisher, a look at the history of annual best-mystery volumes seems in order.

Early efforts in the line proved short-lived. The earliest example seems to be *Best Detective Stories of the Year 1928* (1929; published in the United States as *Best English Detective Stories: First Series*), edited by Father Ronald Knox and H. Harrington. Incorporated in its introduction were Knox's famous (and at least half serious) ten rules for writing detective fiction: no supernatural, no intuition, all clues on the table, etc. As an added feature, and one true to its period, Knox identifies at exactly what point in each story the reader who wants to solve the case ahead of the detective should stop to ponder the clues. Though Knox and Harrington included such famous names as Agatha Christie, Maurice Leblanc, E. Phillips Oppenheim, and Baroness Orczy among their contributors, many of the others (K. R. G. Browne, Charlotte Dockstader, Gladys St. John-Loe) are unlikely to ring a bell with even the most encyclopedic buff. *Best Detective Stories of the Year 1929* (1930; U.S. title *Best English Detective Stories of 1929*), anonymously edited, followed with a more star-studded lineup (Anthony Berkeley and G. K. Chesterton plus Leblanc, Oppenheim, and two by Christie), but there the series ended. The anonymously edited *Best Mystery Stories of the Year 1932* (1933) was published only in Britain, though including both British and American authors, and had no sequels. The British publishers Faber & Faber would do many more anthologies with *Best* in the title, but no more confined to a single year.

An American counterpart also lasted a mere two years. Prolific detective novelist and pioneering how-to writer Carolyn Wells edited *The Best American Mystery Stories of the Year, Volume 1* (1931), comprised mostly of stories from 1930 but with a few from 1929. Her second volume (1932) was entirely made up of 1931 stories. Among the familiar contributors to one or both of the volumes were Ben Ames Williams, Melville Davisson Post, Ben Hecht, Gelett Burgess, Clarence Budington Kelland, Lawrence G. Blochman, MacKinlay Kantor, Irvin S. Cobb, Octavus Roy Cohen, Ernest Haycox, and Wilbur Daniel Steele. As these names would suggest, Wells drew most of her tales from the slicks—of the forty selections over two years, the leading sources were *Collier's* (nine stories), *The Saturday Evening Post* (eight), and *American* (five). But Wells was sensitive enough to the changing fashions in detection to feature *Black Mask* stories by Dashiell Hammett in both volumes.

It was not until 1946 that a more durable best volume was introduced. By a route I'll describe later, the present series can trace its lineage to David C. Cooke's *Best Detective Stories of the Year*. One merit of best volumes, the way they represent and illuminate the mystery fashions of their time, is illustrated by the story Cooke chose to lead off the collection. The name G. T. Fleming-Roberts will resonate with pulp magazine collectors but might be unfamiliar to most mystery fans. (His only entry in Allen J. Hubin's comprehensive bibliography is for a couple of Secret Agent X pulp stories published under the house name Brant House.) "Married to Murder" is a terrific novelette, tightly and cleverly plotted in a style somewhat reminiscent of a *Suspense* radio show, and typical of its time. It may also remind you of later stage mysteries like Anthony Shaffer's *Sleuth*. Other contributors to Cooke's first tour are more familiar, including Q. Patrick, Bruno Fischer, and Day Keene.

Though the slicks figure in Cooke's first selection—there are stories from both *The Saturday Evening Post* and *Cosmopolitan*—the pulps now loom much larger, with entries drawn from *Detective Tales, Doc Savage, Detective Story Magazine, Black Mask, The Shadow,* and others. Cooke made no selections from the top specialty publication (then and now), *Ellery Queen's Mystery Magazine*, but he would remedy that in later volumes of the series.

The second volume was *Best Detective Stories of the Year 1947*, comprising stories published in 1946. The year of publication would be featured in the title through 1956. The 1957 volume was called *Best Detective Stories of the*

Year: 12th Annual Collection, a pattern that would be followed through Cooke's last annual selection, the 14th (1959). During his tenure, the pulps completed their vanishing act and the digests (notably *EQMM* and its hardboiled competition *Manhunt*) became the primary source of stories. *The Saturday Evening Post* and other slicks still provided a few of the stories.

In *Best of the Best Detective Stories* (1960), Cooke bade farewell to the series with one selection from each of the fourteen volumes plus a single story, Gilbert Ralston's "Bottle of Death," to represent 1959, leaving that year more or less in series limbo.

Brett Halliday took over as editor for two volumes, the 16th (1961) and 17th (1962). The creator of private eye Mike Shayne, at that time fronting his own digest-sized mystery magazine, hobbled himself somewhat by excluding stories from *EQMM.* Though the grounds seemed reasonable—that magazine's own annual series could be expected to siphon off the best stories—Halliday failed to recognize that *EQMM*'s second best were generally superior to most of the stories he drew from other publications. His first selection included nine from *Alfred Hitchcock's Mystery Magazine,* four from *Mike Shayne Mystery Magazine,* one from *Bestseller Mystery Magazine,* and three from *Manhunt,* the seminal fifties digest that was by then on its last legs. The slicks were still in the picture, with a single story from *The Saturday Evening Post,* one from the Sunday supplement *This Week* (a frequent market for big-name writers of the time), and one from *The Dude.* Halliday's second collection was almost all from the digests, with the short-lived *Ed McBain's Mystery Book* the principal source.

The 18th collection (1963) was a watershed in the series. Taking over as editor was Anthony Boucher, the esteemed mystery critic of the *New York Times,* who was also renowned as a mystery, fantasy, and science fiction writer and editor. He brought *EQMM* back into the fold, working closely with editor Fred Dannay to determine which stories he could have and which would be tapped for the magazine's own annuals. In correspondence with Dannay, he indicated his efforts to keep continuity by including at least some stories from *Mike Shayne Mystery Magazine* and the difficulty of finding worthy ones to reprint. Boucher's first annual saw the first contribution from the famous/infamous men's magazine *Playboy,* which would become the most frequent slick-magazine source in the years to come. By the 22nd volume, Boucher, an editor of broad and sophisticated taste, was casting his literary net far enough to include two stories from *The New Yorker.*

With his first volume, Boucher added a new feature that gave the series an added reference value, taking it beyond being just a collection of good stories: The "Yearbook of the Detective Story" included a bibliography of anthologies, single-author collections, and critical works; a listing of award winners; a necrology; and an honor roll of the best stories published during the year. Boucher continued through the 23rd annual, published in 1968, the year of his death, by which time he was too ill to provide the Yearbook feature beyond an abbreviated honor roll.

In 1961 and 1962, I lived only a few blocks from Anthony Boucher in

Berkeley, though our only link consists of his listing two of my stories in that final honor roll.

With the death of Boucher, 1968 fell into series limbo. The 24th annual (1970) covered the stories of 1969 with a new editor: Allen J. Hubin, founder of the pioneering mystery fanzine *The Armchair Detective*, Boucher's successor as *New York Times* mystery critic, and (in later years) the genre's principal bibliographer. Hubin had the industry and good sense to continue Boucher's Yearbook feature during his six-year stint as editor.

Hubin also edited *Best of the Best Detective Stories 25th Anniversary Collection* (1971), made up of twenty-four stories from earlier volumes in the series plus an alphabetical checklist of all the selected stories to date. (Most prolific contributors: Ellery Queen with eleven, Jack Ritchie with ten, and Richard Deming, Craig Rice, and Edward D. Hoch with six each.) In introducing *Best of the Best*, Hubin noted some of the changes in the series over the quarter century: on the down side "a certain loss of innocence," on the upside, thanks to Boucher's taste, an increase in humor.

Beginning with *Best Detective Stories of the Year—1971*, the series reverted to putting the year of publication in the title, though the selected stories actually represented the previous year. The 1976 volume introduced another new editor, the series' fifth: Edward D. Hoch, the most prolific writer of short stories of his time and arguably the best spinner of formal puzzles at any length. Hoch continued and expanded the Yearbook feature.

After the 1981 volume, the 35th annual, Dutton decided to discontinue the series. The enterprising Hoch found a new publisher and by necessity changed the title to one more reflective of the annual's scope, which was never limited purely to detective stories. *The Year's Best Mystery and Suspense Stories 1982*, published by Walker, launched a series identical but for title to Dutton's. It continued through 1995, just short of a half-century after Cooke's first compilation.

Other editors were attracted to the best-of-the-year format. Beginning with *The Best American Mystery Stories 1997* (Houghton Mifflin), containing stories published in 1996, series editor Otto Penzler has collaborated with celebrity guest editors including (so far) Robert B. Parker, Sue Grafton, and Ed McBain.

The present series can be traced to a trial balloon, a first annual not followed by a second: *Under the Gun: Mystery Scene Presents the Best Suspense and Mystery* (NAL/Dutton, 1990), edited by Ed Gorman, Bob Randisi, and Martin H. Greenberg. Gathering stories from 1988 with a few from 1987, it included an introduction by editor Randisi designating 1988 the Year of the Woman, thus creating a precedent for the present introduction writer. *Year's 25 Finest Crime and Mystery Stories: First Annual Edition* (1992), credited to the editors of *Mystery Scene* magazine, actually gathered stories from 1989, 1990, and 1991, but subsequent volumes drew on one year at a time. With the sixth volume, the editors Gorman and Greenberg were named. (The sixth volume also had a celebrity guest editor in Joan Hess.) The first seven were published by Carroll & Graf, the eighth by Subterranean Press, bringing us to the volume you hold in your hand, bigger and better than ever with a new title, a new look, a new publisher, a new century, a new millennium, a new paradigm, a new and improved dirt-fighting formula—excuse me, I get carried away sometimes.

What are now the sources of stories for these best-of-year volumes? More rarely the slicks, and of course there are no pulps. The surviving digests (*EQMM* and *AHMM*) still provide good stories as do a healthy number of other pro and semipro fiction magazines. A new player unknown in the days of Wells or Cooke, even of Boucher or Hubin, is the original anthology of stories.

But what about that link I promised between this volume and the series David C. Cooke began back in 1946? Easy. Beginning with the fifth annual *Year's 25 Finest* (1996), the series began to incorporate Edward D. Hoch's Yearbook feature from the Dutton and Walker series, extending one part of Anthony Boucher's enduring legacy to the crime fiction field.

A final question: Are the best really the best? In one way or another, directly or indirectly, most of the editors of these volumes admitted that the word *best* was a misnomer. If an author or his agents asked too large a price for reprint of a story, the editors would have to pass. If two excellent stories were too similar in theme or structure, only one would be chosen. If a given writer turned out half a dozen great stories in a year, the natural decision would be to select one of them. The need to include big names was one sel-dom-acknowledged factor. Note that the second volumes edited by Cooke, Halliday, and Hubin all had notably more star power on the table of contents pages than their first efforts. Was this a coincidence or the result of nudges from the publisher to up the marquee value?

To sum it up: Rather than representing an objective or consensus eval-uation, the best volumes have actually been one or two people's subjective selection of the stories they enjoyed most of those they read during the year that offered sufficient name value, contained an attractive balance and vari-ety, and were available to reprint at a price within the volume's budget. Whatever these compilations were, they made and continue to make an important contribution to both readers and scholars of crime fiction.

BEST NOVELS OF THE YEAR 1999

Now my own annual disclaimer, which at least doesn't have a budgetary component: No one person can cover the whole crime-mystery-suspense output of a given year. The fifteen books that follow are the ones I liked most among those I reviewed in *EQMM* over the course of 1999, augmented by a little focused catch-up reading at the end of the year.

A continuing theme of several of these books is the effect on combatants and noncombatants alike of living through a war, present to a greater or lesser degree in the titles by Airth, Crais, Crombie, Dickinson, Linscott, Parry, and Robinson. You'll find four of the five Edgar best-novel nominees on the list below, and the fifth never came my way, so my kudos to the committee on their unusually fine (i.e., like mine) taste—even if they did overlook the best book of the year.

AIRTH, RENNIE. *River of Darkness* (Viking Penguin). Airth's Edgar nominee invigorates a tired subgenre (the inverted cop-vs.-crazy-serial-killer thriller) with a vivid and moving evocation of post–World War I Britain.

BURKE, JAN. *Bones* (Simon & Schuster). Another Edgar nominee that combined menace, detection, extensive research into forensic anthropology and dog training, and a clever (fairly clued) secondary whodunit involving the accomplice of the all-too-known villain who stalks journalist Irene Kelly.

COLLINS, MAX ALLAN. *Majic Man* (NAL). Private eye Nate Heller takes on another real-life twentieth-century mystery, the Roswell flying saucer incident, and as usual provides a credible and inventive solution. (The prolific Collins produced another winning historical in *The Titanic Murders* [Berkley], which makes a sleuth of doomed mystery writer Jacques Futrelle.)

CONNELLY, MICHAEL. *Angels Flight* (Little, Brown). Harry Bosch looks for the killer of a civil rights attorney in the latest from one of the finest current police series—and a book that makes creative use of several Los Angeles landmarks.

CRAIS, ROBERT. *L.A. Requiem* (Doubleday). In another complex and rewarding novel that captures the essence of Southern California, Los Angeles private eye Elvis Cole probes the mystery of his taciturn partner Joe Pike. A deserving Edgar nominee.

CROMBIE, DEBORAH. *Kissed a Sad Goodbye* (Bantam). What does a present-day mutilation murder have to do with the experiences of a child evacuee from London during World War II? I've said before and will say again that Crombie is much the best of the American women writing British police novels.

DAVIS, LINDSEY. *Three Hands in the Fountain* (Mysterious). Learn all about the Roman water system in this latest case for the always amusing Marcus Didius Falco. (Charges that Falco is a modern man fitted for a toga are somewhat beside the point: Any historical novel reflects the time in which it is written at least as much as the time in which it is set. I'll admit the Yorkshire slang is a little distracting, though.)

DICKINSON, PETER. *Some Deaths Before Dying* (Mysterious). A dying woman in her nineties, wasted in body but clear of mind, enlists the help of her nurse to solve the mystery of her late husband's duelling pistols. For me, this superb novel was the book of the year—and its author among the half-dozen finest crime writers of the past quarter-century.

GERRITSEN, TESS. *Gravity* (Pocket Books). This semi–science fictional medical thriller, about a mysterious malady afflicting astronauts on an international space station, was one of the year's highlights for pure suspense.

GORMAN, ED. *The Day the Music Died* (Carroll & Graf). Black River Falls, Iowa, of the late 1950s comes to vivid life in the first of a new series about small-town private eye Sam McCain and the eccentric judge who employs him.

KEATING, H. R. F. *Bribery, Corruption Also* (St. Martin's). Will Inspector Ghote relocate from Bombay to his wife's hometown of Calcutta? One of the most thoughtful and least conventional in a consistently surprising series.

LINSCOTT, GILLIAN. *Absent Friends* (St. Martin's). British suffragist Nell Bray stands for Parliament in still another book to illuminate post–World War I Britain.

McBAIN, ED. *The Big Bad City* (Simon & Schuster). More than forty years after *Cop Hater* introduced the 87th Precinct, McBain offers one of the very best in the series, including a memorable villain known as the Cookie Boy.

PARRY, OWEN. *Faded Coat of Blue* (Avon). The first case for Union Army Captain Abel Jones, beautifully written and exhaustively researched, is one of the best historical mysteries I've ever read and second only to Dickinson for my choice of novel of the year. (Is this a first or the work of a previously published writer? Either way, its failure to gain an Edgar nomination in some category is one of the true-life mysteries of the year.)

ROBINSON, PETER. *In a Dry Season* (Bantam). Alan Banks's present-day investigation of some old bones alternates with an account of the British World War II homefront in a rich and rewarding Edgar-nominated novel.

SUBGENRES

There were plenty of other 1999 novels worthy of recommendation.

Jan Burke's Irene Kelly was not the only journalist sleuth in good form. Moving from the print to the TV side, R. D. Zimmerman's Twin Cities reporter Todd Mills interviews a handsome film star who may or may not be gay in *Innuendo* (Delacorte). A TV weatherman is featured in Dick Francis's *Second Wind* (Putnam), a return to novel-writing after the previous year's short-story collection was reported to mark his retirement.

Fans of the formal puzzle should seek out Jennifer Rowe's *Suspect* and *Something Wicked* (Ballantine)—the Australian Agatha Christie maintains her title despite the change of central character from amateur sleuth Verity Birdwood to cop Tessa Vance. Puzzle buffs and Japanophiles will enjoy Akimitsu Takagi's *The Informer* (Soho), only the third of this writer's novels to be translated into English—and I hope there will be more. Pure detection intersects with the supernatural in Barbara Michaels's *Other Worlds* (HarperCollins), featuring an otherworldly sleuthing club whose members include Conan Doyle and Houdini.

Among the many historical detectives in action were Anne Perry's Charlotte and Thomas Pitt in *Bedford Square* (Ballantine); musician Benjamin January of antebellum New Orleans in Barbara Hambly's *Graveyard Dust* (Bantam); Carolyn Roe's blind physician Isaac of Girona in *An Antidote for Avarice* (Berkley); the Canterbury Pilgrims in P. C. Doherty's *Ghostly Murders* (St. Martin's); and John Maddox Roberts's Decius Caecilius Metellus (a Roman sleuth by no means outclassed by the creations of Steven Saylor and Lindsey Davis) in *Saturnalia* (St. Martin's).

Apart from Collins, Crais, and Gorman on my list of fifteen, the fictional private eyes were well represented by newcomer Payton Sherwood in Russell Atwood's *East of A* (Ballantine) and (with an asterisk) by Harry James Denton in Steven Womack's *Dirty Money* (Fawcett), worth recommending as a good novel albeit a severe letdown strictly as a *mystery* novel.

As the presence of Airth, Connelly, Crombie, Keating, McBain, and Robinson on my list of fifteen suggests, professional cops made the best showing of the year. The procedural form had at least one notable new practitioner: Scholar/anthologist Paula L. Woods introduced L.A. policewoman Charlotte Justice in *Inner City Clues* (Norton). Also featured in good cases were Faye Kellerman's Peter Decker in *Jupiter's Bones* (Morrow), Reginald Hill's Dalziel and Pascoe in *Arms and the Women* (Delacorte), Tony Hillerman's Leaphorn and Chee in *Hunting Badger* (HarperCollins), and especially Ian Rankin's John Rebus in *Dead Souls* (St. Martin's), a novel that justifies both its 400-page length and the jigsaw motif of its jacket. If your sense of humor is as perverse as mine, you might also enjoy a much shorter example of Brit Noir, Ken Bruen's *A White Arrest* (Dufour), a satirical, antiprocedural, antidetective story about the hunt for a serial killer of cricketers.

Four writers noted for their humor (among other virtues) had strong offerings: two with quite different farcical/satirical looks at the Hollywood scene, K. K. Beck with *The Revenge of Kali-Ra* (Mysterious) and Elmore Leonard with *Be Cool* (Delacorte); two with humorously observed treatments of more serious subject matter, Katherine Hall Page with *The Body in the Bookcase* (Morrow) and Catherine Aird with *Stiff News* (St. Martin's).

If you can't get enough of fictional lawyers, I can recommend O. J. Simpson prosecutor Christopher Darden's first novel, written with veteran pro Dick Lochte, *The Trials of Nikki Hill* (Warner), and Barry Siegel's *Actual Innocence* (Ballantine), the second case for defender Greg Monarch.

Among the amateur sleuths, Paula Thomas-Graham's Veronica Chase occupies a three-way marketing niche in *Blue Blood* (Simon & Schuster): female, African-American, and (for the Amanda Cross crowd) an Ivy-League academic. In *Murder Is the Deal of the Day* (St. Martin's), Robert J. Randisi and Christine Matthews offer a fresh variation on the husband-and-wife detecting team in St. Louis TV-shopping-show-anchor Claire Hunt and her bookdealer husband, Gil. Sara Hoskinson Frommer's small-town sleuth Jane Spencer solves the case of *The Vanishing Violinist* (St. Martin's).

SHORT STORIES

A mystery book dealer of my acquaintance tells me that his customers prefer single-author short story collections to anthologies of stories by different writers, an ironic observation in that single-author collections have always been a tougher sell to the major commercial publishers. Still, thanks in large part to the efforts of some specialist publishers, single-author collections continue to appear at an unprecedented rate. For the full story, see Ed Hoch's bibliography, but I'll mention some I found to be highlights: Doug Allyn's *All Creatures Dark and Dangerous* (Crippen & Landru), O'Neil DeNoux's *La-Stanza: New Orleans Police Stories* (Pontalba Press, 4417 Dryades Street, New

Orleans, LA 70115), Nancy Pickard's *Storm Warnings* (Five Star, P.O. Box 159, Thorndike, ME 04986), Ed Gorman's *Famous Blue Raincoat* (Crippen & Landru), and Janwillem van de Wetering's *The Amsterdam Cops* (Soho). Collection of the year, though, was *The Investigations of Avram Davidson* (St. Martin's), gathering the best mystery and crime fiction of an undervalued master of the short story regardless of genre.

As for the anthologies, both original and reprint compilations were plentiful, perpetrated by all the usual suspects: Ashley, Gorman, Greenberg, Penzler, Jakubowski, Ripley, Dziemianowicz, et al. (Again, see Ed Hoch's bibliography.) Coincidentally, two successful pastiche collections—1987's *The New Adventures of Sherlock Holmes* (Carroll & Graf), edited by Martin H. Greenberg, Carol-Lynn Waugh, and Jon L. Lellenberg; and 1988's *Raymond Chandler's Philip Marlowe* (ibooks/Pocket Books), edited by Byron Preiss—were reissued with new stories added.

REFERENCE BOOKS AND SECONDARY SOURCES

It was a banner year for reference sources, not all of them in book form. Two invaluable CD-ROMs updated and offered improved access to a couple of standard print references: Allen J. Hubin's *Crime Fiction III: A Comprehensive Bibliography 1749–1995,* updating by five years the most recent book edition of this authoritative work, and William G. Contento's *Mystery Short Fiction Miscellany: An Index*, which updates and augments his 1990 volume *Index to Crime and Mystery Anthologies* (with Martin H. Greenberg). As an example of their usefulness, the two CD-ROMs combined gave me the fullest list of Sherlock Holmes pastiches, short and long, I've ever seen. Publisher of both is Locus Press, P.O. Box 13305, Oakland, CA 94661.

It was also a notable year for biography. Tom Nolan's *Ross Macdonald: A Biography* (Scribner) did a fine job of capturing a fascinating and difficult subject. A volume not yet published in the United States created a stir throughout the book world: Graham Lord's *Dick Francis: A Racing Life* (London: Little, Brown) claimed that the retired jockey's novels were at least partly and maybe primarily written by his wife.

Which leads me to an embarrassing gaffe by one of the contributors to the superb one-volume *Oxford Companion to Crime & Mystery Writing* (Oxford University Press), edited by Rosemary Herbert with Catherine Aird and John M. Reilly. The author of the article "Celebrity Crime and Mystery Writers" proclaimed, "While almost all celebrity mysteries are ghostwritten, there are exceptions—for example, no one suggests that Dick Francis, a famous steeplechase jockey before the publication of his first novel, *Dead Cert* (1962), does not write his own books." I confess, I did it—wrote the article, not the books.

A SENSE OF HISTORY

Mystery fiction continues to honor its past. Dashiell Hammett became the second crime fiction writer, following Raymond Chandler, to have his *Complete Novels* collected by Library of America, in a single volume with notes by Steven Marcus. Some of Hammet's short stories, along with his fragmentary first stab at *The Thin Man,* were gathered in *Nightmare Town* (Knopf), with a fine introduction by Hammett biographer William F. Nolan.

It's one thing to keep the famous names in print—Hammett, Chandler, Rex Stout, Margery Allingham, Ngaio Marsh, Agatha Christie—and quite another to revive less familiar bylines simply because they produced quality works that a present-day audience might enjoy. That's why the program of Rue Morgue Press (P.O. Box 4119, Boulder, CO 80306) to reprint such writers as Elizabeth Dean, Manning Coles, and the team of Constance and Gwenyth Little is so admirable. Of special note in their program is Joanna Cannan, a first-rate but relatively little-known writer in the Golden Age tradition, most of whose work has never even been published in the United States. In 1999, Rue Morgue provided a first American edition of her *They Rang Up the Police* (1939) and a reprint of *Death at the Dog* (1941). Most of the Rue Morgue books have fresh introductions by publishers Tom and Enid Schantz, whose mystery bookshop (also called Rue Morgue) puts out one of the most entertaining and informative customer newsletters in the business.

Also doing a singular service is Five Star, which publishes, along with its short-story collections, first hardcover editions of noted paperback originals, including Thomas H. Cook's 1980 Edgar nominee, *Blood Innocents,* a splendid police novel in the Lawrence Sanders *Deadly Sins* tradition.

AT THE MOVIES

Among its other virtues, 1999 was a banner year for big-screen mystery. First consider the Edgar nominees: the droll small-town crime story *Cookie's Fortune,* directed by Robert Altman from a script by Anne Rapp; the British gangster farce *Lock, Stock and Two Smoking Barrels,* written and directed by Guy Ritchie; the wonderfully inventive and purely cinematic German film *Run, Lola, Run,* written and directed by Tom Tykwer; the somewhat controversial (to fans of the book) but enthralling and beautifully photographed adaptation of Patricia Highsmith's *The Talented Mr. Ripley,* directed by Anthony Minghella from his own screenplay; and Julie Taymor's visually remarkable *Titus,* about as good a screen version as one could hope for of one of Shakespeare's lesser works, *Titus Andronicus.*

Worthwhile films all, but in this unusual year it's possible to make another list of five nearly as good that were bypassed by the Edgar committee. The leading Oscar contender *American Beauty,* written by Alan Ball and directed by Sam Mendes, is, among other things, a cleverly calibrated whodunit. To fill out the second five, consider the revenge drama *The Limey,* directed by Steven Soderbergh from Lem Dobbs's script; *The Bone Collector,* adapted by Jeremy Iacone from Jeffery Deaver's novel and directed by Philip Noyce; and a couple of choice supernatural thrillers, M. Night Shyamalan's *Sixth Sense* and David Koepp's *Stir of Echoes,* from Richard Matheson's novel. Still left out in the cold are the beautifully acted and photographed *Snow Falling on Cedars,* directed by Scott Hicks from Ronald Bass's adaptation of David Guterson's novel, and the historically controversial but effective dramatization of the Ruben Carter case, *The Hurricane,* directed by Norman Jewison from a script by Armyan Bernstein and Dan Gordon.

Are movies better than ever? Probably not, but 1999's crime films were a bumper crop. And finally, speaking of film, a couple of observations about recent trends:

Though some writers create compelling fistfights, car chases, and other physical action, the movies generally do them better; verbal combat and plot movement make better reading.

With so many series these days resembling soap operas, maybe it's time to revive the Patrick Quentin novels about Peter and Iris Duluth, who, clearly ahead of their time, went through all sorts of personal miseries (alcoholism, mental illness, amnesia, divorce, adultery) over the course of nine novels between 1936 and 1954.

AWARD WINNERS FOR 1998

Edgar Allan Poe Awards

(MYSTERY WRITERS OF AMERICA)

Best novel: Robert Claril, *Mr. White's Confession* (Picador)

Best first novel by an American author: Steve Hamilton, *Cold Day in Paradise* (St. Martin's)

Best original paperback: Rick Riordan, *The Widower's Two-Step* (Bantam)

Best fact crime book: Carlton Stowers, *To the Last Breath* (St. Martin's)

Best critical/biographical work: Robin Winks and Maureen Corrigan, editors, *Mystery and Suspense Writers* (Scribner)

Best short story: Tom Franklin, "Poachers" (*The Texas Review,* Fall/Winter 1998)

Best young adult mystery: Nancy Werlin, *The Killer's Cousin* (Delacorte)

Best children's mystery: Wendelin Van Draanen, *Sammy Keyes and the Hotel Thief* (Knopf)

Best episode in a television series: Rene Balcer and Richard Sweren, *Law & Order:* "Bad Girl" (NBC)

Best television feature or miniseries: Charles Kipps, *Law & Order:* "Exiled" (NBC)

Best motion picture: Scott Frank, *Out of Sight* (Universal)

Best play: John Pielmeier, *Voices in the Dark* (produced in New Brunswick, New Jersey, 1998)

Grand master: P. D. James

Robert L. Fish award (best first story): Bryn Bonner, "Clarity" (*EQMM*, May 1998)

Ellery Queen award: Sara Ann Freed

Raven: Steven Bochco

Agatha Awards

(MALICE DOMESTIC MYSTERY CONVENTION)

Best novel: Kate Ross, *The Devil in Music* (Viking)

Best first novel: Sujata Massey, *The Salaryman's Wife* (Broadway Books)

Best short story: M. D. Lake, "Tea For Two" (*Funny Bones,* Signet)

Best nonfiction: Willetta Heising, *Detecting Men Pocket Guide* (Purple Moon)

Anthony Awards

(BOUCHERCON WORLD MYSTERY CONVENTION)

Best novel: Michael Connelly, *Blood Work* (Little, Brown)

Best first novel: William Kent Krueger, *Iron Lake* (Pocket Books)

Best paperback original: Laura Lippman, *Butcher's Hill* (Avon)

Best short story: Barbara D'Amato, "Of Course, You Know That Chocolate Is a Vegetable" (*EQMM*, November 1998)

Best critical/biographical: *Deadly Pleasures Magazine,* edited by George Easter

Lifetime achievement: Len and June Moffatt

Shamus Awards

(PRIVATE EYE WRITERS OF AMERICA)

Best novel: Bill Pronzini, *Boobytrap* (Carroll & Graf)

Best first novel: Steve Hamilton, *A Cold Day in Paradise* (St. Martin's)

Best original paperback novel: Steven Womack, *Murder Manual* (Fawcett)

Best short story: Warren Murphy, "Another Day, Another Dollar" (*Murder on the Run,* Berkley)

Lifetime achievement: Maxine O'Callaghan

Dagger Awards

(CRIME WRITERS' ASSOCIATION, GREAT BRITAIN)

Gold Dagger: Robert Wilson, *A Small Death in Lisbon* (HarperCollins)

Silver Dagger: Adrian Matthews, *Vienna Blood* (Cape)

John Creasey Award (best first novel): Dan Fesperman, *Life in the Dark*

(No Exit)

Best short story: Anthony Mann, "Taking Care of Frank" (*Crimewave 2*, TTA Press)

Best nonfiction: Brian Cathcart, *The Case of Stephen Lawrence* (Viking)

Diamond Dagger: Margaret Yorke

Ellis Peters Historical Dagger: Lindsey Davis, *Two for the Lions* (Century)

Macavity Awards

(MYSTERY READERS INTERNATIONAL)

Best novel: Michael Connelly, *Blood Work* (Little, Brown)

Best first novel: Jerrilyn Farmer, *Sympathy for the Devil* (Avon)

Best critical/biographical work: Jean Swanson and Dean James, *Killer Books* (Berkley)

Best short story: Barbara D'Amato, "Of Course, You Know That Chocolate Is a Vegetable" (*EQMM*, November 1998)

Arthur Ellis Awards

(CRIME WRITERS OF CANADA)

Best novel: Nora Kelly, *Old Wounds* (HarperCollins Canada)

Best first novel: Liz Brady, *Sudden Blow* (Second Story)

Best true crime: Derek Finkle, *No Claim to Mercy* (Penguin Canada)

Best short story: Scott MacKay, "Last Inning" (*EQMM*)

Derrick Murdoch Award for lifetime achievement: Ted Wood

Hammett Prize

(INTERNATIONAL CRIME WRITERS)

William Hoffman, *Tidewater Blood* (Algonquin)

A 1999 Yearbook of Mystery and Crime

Edward D. Hoch

Collections and Single Stories

ALLINGHAM, MARGERY. *Room to Let*. Norfolk, VA: Crippen & Landru. A 25-page booklet containing a 1947 radio play, printed in a limited edition for friends of the publisher.

ALLYN, DOUG. *All Creatures Dark and Dangerous*. Norfolk, VA: Crippen & Landru. Seven novelettes from EQMM, 1995–98, about veterinarian Dr. Dave Westbrook.

———. *Saint Margaret's Kitten*. Norfolk, VA: Crippen & Landru. A short historical mystery from *Cat Crimes Through Time*, included as a pamphlet in the limited edition of Allyn's *All Creatures Dark and Dangerous*.

AMES, MEL D. *Amazon: The Complete 13 Adventures of Detective-Lieutenant Cathy Carruthers*. Oakville, Ontario, Canada: Mosaic Press. Thirteen stories and novelettes, eleven from *Mike Shayne Mystery Magazine*, 1980–84. Introduction by Charles E. Fritch, afterword by Peter Sellers.

BANGS, JOHN KENDRICK. *Sherlock Holmes Again*. New York: The Mysterious Bookshop. A limited-edition pamphlet containing the first separate publication of a 1899 parody.

BARRETT, LYNNE. *The Secret Names of Women*. Ithaca, NY: Carnegie Mellon University Press/Cornell University Press Services. Eight mainstream stories, including Barrett's 1990 Edgar-winner from *EQMM*, "Elvis Lives."

BLOCK, LAWRENCE. *The Collected Mystery Stories*. London: Orion. Seventy-one of Block's short stories, fourteen previously uncollected, omitting the twenty-four early pulp stories collected in *One Night Stands*.

———. *Make a Prison*. Norfolk, VA: Crippen & Landru. A short-short crime tale from *Science Fiction Stories* (1/59) included as a pamphlet in the limited edition of Block's collection *One Night Stands*.

———. *One Night Stands*. Norfolk, VA: Crippen & Landru. A limited edition of twenty-four stories from various mystery magazines, 1958–62, not previously collected. Introduction by the author.

BOUCHER, ANTHONY. *The Compleat Boucher*. Framingham, MA: The NESFA Press. All forty-five of Boucher's fantasy and science fiction stories, one previously unpublished, including several mystery fantasies. Edited by James A. Mann.

BOYER, RICK. *A Sherlockian Quartet*. Alexander, NC: Alexander Books. Boyer's Sherlockian novel *The Giant Rat of Sumatra*, plus three new shorter pastiches.

BRACKETT, LEIGH. *No Good from a Corpse*. Tucson, AZ: Dennis McMillan Publications. Brackett's first (1944) novel, together with all eight of her mystery novelettes and short stories, 1943–57. Introduction by Ray Bradbury, afterword by Michael Connelly.

CARR, JOHN DICKSON. *The Detective in Fiction & Harem-Scarem*. Norfolk, VA: Crippen & Landru. A booklet containing a brief article from *The Writer* (6/32) plus an uncollected short-short story from the *London Evening Mail* (3/24/39), distributed to attendees at Malice Domestic XI.

CHAMPION DE CRESPIGNY, ROSE. *Norton Vyse: Psychic*. Ashcroft, British Columbia, Canada: Ash-Tree Press. Six stories about an occult detective, from *The Premier Magazine*, 1919. Edited and introduced by Jack Adrian.

DeNOUX, O'NEIL. *LaStanza: New Orleans Police Stories*. New Orleans: Pontalba. Seventeen stories about homicide detective Dino LaStanza, six new.

ELLROY, JAMES. *Crime Wave: Reportage and Fiction from the Underside of L.A.* New York: Vintage Books. Three novelettes and eight articles, all from GQ magazine, 1993–99.

EVOE (EDMUND GEORGE VALPY KNOX). *Me, or The Strange Episode of the Reincarnated Greek*. New York: The Mysterious Bookshop. A limited edition pamphlet containing the first separate publication of a 1923 Sherlockian parody.

FORREST, GEORGE F. *The Adventure of the Diamond Necklace*. New York: The Mysterious Bookshop. A limited edition pamphlet containing a single brief Sherlockian parody from the collection *Misfits* (1905).

FRANKLIN, TOM. *Poachers*. New York: Morrow. Ten mainstream stories from various literary quarterlies, set mainly in the rural South, including the title novelette from *The Texas Review*, winner of the Mystery Writers of America Edgar Award for 1998.

FREEMAN, R. AUSTIN. *The Dead Hand and Other Uncollected Stories*. Shelburne, Ontario, Canada: The Battered Silicon Dispatch Box. Twenty-four stories and four essays. Edited and introduced by Douglas G. Greene and Tony Medawar. Volume 9 of the Freeman Omnibus Edition.

———. *Dr. Thorndyke's Short Stories*, Shelburne, Ontario, Canada: The Battered Silicon Dispatch Box. The first collection of all forty Thorndyke short stories in a single volume. Introduction by Norman Donaldson. Volume 2 of the Freeman Omnibus Edition.

GEORGE, ELIZABETH. *The Evidence Exposed*. London: Hodder & Stoughton. Three novelettes, one new.

GORES, JOE. *Speak of the Devil*. Unity, ME: Five Star. Fourteen stories, 1958–91, some fantasy.

GORMAN, ED. *Famous Blue Raincoat*. Norfolk, VA: Crippen & Landru. Twelve stories, 1996–99, five from *EQMM*.

———. *Mom and Dad at Home*. Norfolk, VA: Crippen & Landru. A single story from a 1999 anthology, included as a pamphlet in the limited edition of *Famous Blue Raincoat*.

GOULART, RON. *Murder in Studio 221B*. New York: The Mysterious Bookshop. A limited edition pamphlet containing a single new Sherlockian pastiche.

HAMMETT, DASHIELL. *Nightmare Town*. New York: Knopf. Twenty stories and novelettes, including an early abandoned version of *The Thin Man*. Edited by Kirby McCauley, Martin H. Greenberg, and Ed Gorman. Introduction by William F. Nolan.

HARVEY, JOHN. *Now's the Time*. London: Slow Dancer Press. Eleven stories, two new, about Detective Charlie Resnick.

HENRY, O. *The Sleuths*. New York: The Mysterious Bookshop. A limited edition pamphlet in the Mysterious Sherlock Holmes series, reprinting a single story from the collection *Sixes and Sevens* (1911).

HOCH, EDWARD D. *The Adventure of the Cipher in the Sand*. New York: The Mysterious Bookshop. A single new pastiche in a limited edition pamphlet, part of the Mysterious Sherlock Holmes series.

HURD, DOUGLAS. *Ten Minutes to Turn the Devil*. London: Little, Brown. Short adventure-intrigue stories by a Member of Parliament.

KAMINSKY, STUART M. *Hidden and Other Stories*. Unity, ME: Five Star. Sixteen stories from various sources, 1965–95, one fantasy.

KLINGER, LESLIE. *The Adventure of the Wooden Box*. New York: The Mysterious Bookshop. A single Sherlockian pastiche in a limited edition pamphlet, first published in *Baker Street West 1* (1999).

LIMA, JOEL. *Sherlock Holmes and the Mysterious Card*. New York: The Mysterious Bookshop. A single new pastiche in a limited edition pamphlet.

LOVISI, GARY. *Dirty Dogs*. Brooklyn, NY: Gryphon Publications. Twelve stories about tough Detective Vic Powers.

MCBAIN, ED. *Driving Lessons*. London: Orion. A single new 20,000-word novella.

———. *I Saw Mommy Killing Santa Claus*. New York: The Mysterious Bookshop. A new crime story in a pamphlet for clients of a New York bookstore.

MICHAELS, BARBARA. *Other Worlds*. New York: HarperCollins. Two connected mystery-fantasy novellas in which a club of sleuths from the past investigate psychic mysteries.

MOSLEY, WALTER. *Walkin' the Dog*. Boston: Little, Brown. Twelve new adventures of Socrates Fortlow, ex-con.

PAUL, BARBARA. *Jack Be Quick and Other Crime Stories*. Unity, ME: Five Star. Nine stories, 1976–98, from various sources.

PHILLIPS, GARY. *The Desecrator*. Mission Viejo, CA: A.S.A.P. Publishing. A single story about a black private eye and an essay by the author on black detectives in fiction.

PICKARD, NANCY. *Storm Warnings*. Unity, ME: Five Star. Nine stories, one fantasy, from various sources, 1989–97.

QUEEN, ELLERY. *The Tragedy of Errors*. Norfolk, VA: Crippen & Landru. A detailed plot synopsis by Frederic Dannay of the final, unwritten Queen novel, together with six uncollected short stories, 1956–75, and twenty-two essays, tributes, and memoirs by family members, friends, and current mystery writers.

RANKIN, IAN. *Death Is Not the End*. London: Orion. A single new 20,000-word Inspector Rebus novella (1998).

RHEA, NICHOLAS. *Constable in the Farmyard*. London: Robert Hale. More adventures of a Yorkshire constable on the trail of rural crime.

ROBERTS, GILLIAN. *Where's the Harm?* Unity, ME: Five Star. Twelve stories from various sources.

SELLERS, PETER. *Whistling Past the Graveyard*. Oakville, Ontario, Canada: Mosaic Press. Thirteen crime and horror stories, five new, some fantasy. Introduction by Don Hutchison.

STRAUB, PETER, *Pork Pie Hat*. London: Orion. First separate edition of a 1994 novella.

VACHSS, ANDREW. *Everybody Pays*. New York: Vintage Crime/Black Lizard. The title novella and thirty-seven short stories, some previously published.

VAN BELKOM, EDO. *Death Drives a Semi*. Kingston, Ontario, Canada: Quarry Press. Twenty mystery, fantasy, and horror stories from various sources.

VAN DE WETERING, JANWILLEM. *The Amsterdam Cops: Collected Stories*. New York: Soho Press. Thirteen stories, two newly translated into English.

"VON DIME, N.O.T." *The Pinke Murder Case*. New York: The Mysterious Bookshop. A brief parody of S. S. Van Dine first published in Britain in 1930.

"WATSON, A. CONAN, M.D." *A Pragmatic Enigma*. New York: The Mysterious Bookshop. A single story by John Kendrick Bangs in a limited edition Mysterious Sherlock Holmes pamphlet, reprinted from *Potted Fiction* (1908).

WESTLAKE, DONALD E. *A Good Story and Other Stories*. Unity, ME: Five Star. Eighteen stories, 1958–97, from *Playboy* and other sources. Nine previously collected.

WILHELM, KATE. *The Casebook of Constance and Charlie: Volume 2*. New York: St. Martin's. Two novels, a novella, and two stories from *EQMM*.

Anthologies

ASHLEY, MIKE, ed. *Royal Whodunnits*. New York: Carroll & Graf. Twenty-six new mysteries involving kings, queens, emperors, and royal families through history.

BLOCK, LAWRENCE, ed. *Death Cruise: Crime Stories on the Open Seas*. Nashville: Cumberland House. Twenty stories, sixteen new, mainly by members of the International Association of Crime Writers.

————. *Master's Choice*. New York: Berkley. Nine mystery writers choose a story of their own paired with a story by a writer who inspired them.

CHIZMAR, RICHARD, AND WILLIAM SCHAFER, eds. *Subterranean Gallery*. Burton, MI: Subterranean. Twenty new stories of dark crime and horror.

COWARD, MAT, AND ANDY COX, eds. *Crimewave 2: Deepest Red*. Witcham, England: TTA Press. Thirteen new stories and one reprint, including Antony Mann's "Taking Care of Frank," winner of the Gold Dagger Award from Britain's Crime Writers' Association.

DZIEMIANOWICZ, STEFAN, BOB ADEY, ED GORMAN, AND MARTIN H. GREENBERG, eds. *Murder Most Scottish*. New York: Barnes & Noble Books. A novel by Bill Knox and nineteen stories, one new, from various sources.

DZIEMIANOWICZ, STEFAN, DENISE LITTLE, AND ROBERT WEINBERG, eds. *Mistresses of the Dark*. New York: Barnes & Noble Books. Twenty-five macabre stories and novelettes by well-known women writers, some criminous, some fantasy, from a variety of sources.

DZIEMIANOWICZ, STEFAN, ROBERT WEINBERG, AND MARTIN H. GREENBERG, eds. *100 Hilarious Little Howlers*. New York: Barnes & Noble Books. Humorous short-short stories, about a dozen criminous.

EDWARDS, MARTIN, ed. *Missing Persons*. London: Constable. Fifteen new stories and one reprint in the annual anthology from the Crime Writers' Association. Introduction by Ian Rankin.

EIDELBERG, ROBERT, ed. *Detectives: Stories for Thinking, Solving, and Writing*. New York: AMSCO School Publications. A high school textbook containing twenty-four classic and modern stories and plays.

GORMAN, ED, MARTIN H. GREENBERG, AND BILL PRONZINI, eds. *Pure Pulp.* New York: Carroll & Graf. Twenty-four stories and novelettes, 1944–84, plus a 1962 novel by Peter Rabe.

GREENBERG, MARTIN H., JON L. LELLENBERG, AND CAROL-LYNN WAUGH, eds. *More Holmes for the Holidays.* New York: Berkley. Eleven new Christmas stories about Sherlock Holmes.

GREENBERG, MARTIN H., CAROL-LYNN ROSSEL WAUGH, AND JON L. LELLENBERG, eds. *The New Adventures of Sherlock Holmes.* New York: Carroll & Graf. An expanded edition of a 1987 anthology, with three new stories added.

JAHN, MICHAEL, DORIAN YEAGER, AND BARBARA PAUL. *A New York State of Crime.* Toronto: Worldwide Mystery. Reprints of two novels by Jahn and Yeager, plus a new short story by Paul.

JAKUBOWSKI, MAXIM, ed. *Chronicles of Crime: The Second Ellis Peters Memorial Anthology of Historical Crime.* London: Headline. Nineteen new historical mysteries.

KELLERMAN, JONATHAN, ed. *Diagnosis Dead.* New York: Pocket Books. Fourteen new stories in an anthology from Mystery Writers of America.

MARKS, JEFFREY, presented by. *Canine Christmas.* New York: Ballantine. Fifteen new mysteries involving dogs at Christmas.

MARON, MARGARET, presented by. *Malice Domestic 8.* New York: Avon. Thirteen new stories in an annual anthology of traditional mysteries.

MATERA, LIA, ed. *Irreconcilable Differences.* New York: HarperCollins. Twenty new mysteries of relationships gone wrong.

MCBAIN, ED, AND OTTO PENZLER, eds. *The Best American Mystery Stories 1999.* Boston: Houghton Mifflin. Nineteen stories, with notes by the contributors.

MORGAN, JILL M., AND MARTIN H. GREENBERG, eds. *Till Death Do Us Part.* New York: Berkley. Eighteen new stories by mystery writers in collaboration with their spouses.

PENZLER, OTTO, ed. *Murder and Obsession.* New York: Delacorte. Fifteen new stories, one previously published in a limited edition.

PICKARD, NANCY, ed. *The First Lady Murders.* New York: Pocket Star Books. Twenty new mysteries involving the wives of American presidents.

———. *Mom, Apple Pie & Murder.* New York: Berkley. Sixteen new stories, with apple recipes from several of the authors.

PREISS, BYRON, ed. *Raymond Chandler's Philip Marlowe.* New York: ibooks/Pocket Books. An expanded edition of a 1988 anthology, with two new stories and an introduction by Robert B. Parker added.

RANDISI, ROBERT J., ed. *First Cases, Volume 3: New and Classic Tales of Detection.* New York: Signet. Fourteen stories, two new, recounting the first cases of popular series sleuths, 1949–99.

RAPHAEL, LAWRENCE W., ed. *Mystery Midrash: An Anthology of Jewish Mystery & Detective Fiction.* Woodstock, VT: Jewish Lights Publishing. Thirteen stories, some new. Preface by Joel Siegel.

RIPLEY, MIKE, AND MAXIM JAKUBOWSKI, eds. *Fresh Blood 3.* London: Do Not Press. Fifteen new stories in the third volume of a British anthology series.

SMITH, MARTIN CRUZ, ed. *Death by Espionage: Intriguing Stories of Betrayal and Deception.* Nashville: Cumberland House. Twenty stories, eleven new, in an anthology from the

International Association of Crime Writers.

A Suitcase of Suspense. London: MQ Publications. A small cardboard "suitcase" with three paperbound books: *Classic Detective Stories, Classic Murder Stories,* and *Classic Mystery Stories*, containing in all twenty-two stories, some fantasy, 1843–1980. (No editor listed.)

Tannert, Mary, and Henry Kratz, eds. *Early German and Austrian Detective Fiction: An Anthology*. Jefferson, NC: McFarland. Six stories and novelettes, 1828–1909, newly translated by the editors.

Weir, Charlene, George Baxt, and Maxine O'Callaghan. *Murder at the Movies*. Toronto: Worldwide Mystery. Reprints of two novels by Weir and Baxt, plus a new short story by O'Callaghan.

Wheat, Carolyn, ed. *Murder on Route 66*. New York: Berkley. Sixteen new stories set along the famous American highway.

White, Tony, ed. *Britpulp!* London: Sceptre/Hodder & Stoughton. Twenty-two stories "from the literary underground," all but five new, several criminous.

Nonfiction

Auerbach, Nina. *Daphne Du Maurier: Haunted Heiress*. Philadelphia: University of Pennsylvania Press. A new biography of the author of *Rebecca*.

Auiler, Dan. *Hitchcock's Notebooks: An Authorized and Illustrated Look Inside the Creative Mind of Alfred Hitchcock*. New York: Avon/Spire. A detailed study of the screenplays, storyboards, and correspondence behind many of Hitchcock's films.

Blades, Joe, ed. *Two Voices: Crime Writers in Conversations with Their Characters*. New York: Ballantine. A 99-page promotional booklet in which thirteen Ballantine mystery writers carry on imaginary conversations with their creations.

Cade, Jared. *Agatha Christie and the Eleven Missing Days*. New York: Dufour Editions. Deals with the mystery writer's 1926 disappearance.

Canick, Michael. *Clayton Rawson: Magic and Mystery*. New York: Volcanick Press. A 34-page illustrated booklet containing a brief biography with sections on Rawson as artist, magician, writer, editor, and master of ceremonies, together with a full bibliography of his novels, short stories, and nonfiction.

Condon, Paul, and Jim Sangster. *The Complete Hitchcock*. London: Virgin. A companion to all the director's films.

Derie, Kate, ed. *The Deadly Directory 2000*. Berkeley, CA: Deadly Serious Press. A guide to the world of mystery fiction, including booksellers, magazines, websites, awards, conferences, and more.

Foord, Peter, and Richard Williams. *Collins Crime Club: A Checklist of the First Editions. Compiled by Peter Foord and Richard Williams, with a guide to their value by Chris Peers, Ralph Spurrier and Jamie Sturgeon*. Scunthorpe, England: Dragonby Press. A 60-page booklet listing 2,028 first-edition Collins Crime Club books with 143 additional titles, together with their value. Introduction by Ralph Spurrier.

Gorman, Ed, and Martin H. Greenberg, eds. *Speaking of Murder, Volume II: Interviews with Masters of Mystery and Suspense*. New York: Berkley Prime Crime. Interviews with twenty-two popular mystery writers.

Grossman, Jo, and Robert Weibezahl, eds. *A Taste of Murder*. New York: Dell. Recipes from well-known mystery writers.

HAUT, WOODY. *Neon Noir: Hardboiled Films and Fiction from the 1960's to the Present*. London: Serpent's Tail. A study of recent works of noir.

HERBERT, ROSEMARY, ed. *The Oxford Companion to Crime & Mystery Writing*. New York: Oxford University Press. An alphabetical compilation of 666 entries on every phase of mystery writing by some 250 experts in the field.

JAMES, P. D. *Time to Be in Earnest: A Fragment of Autobiography*. London: Faber & Faber. A memoir and journal kept by the author from August 1997 to August 1998.

KENDRICK, STEPHEN. *Holy Clues: The Gospel According to Sherlock Holmes*. New York: Pantheon. A minister finds value in the awareness and observation of the Sherlock Holmes stories.

LORD, GRAHAM. *Dick Francis: A Racing Life*. London: Little, Brown. A biography of the author, which first revealed his wife Mary's collaborative role in his novels.

MCDERMID, VAL. *A Suitable Job for a Woman*. Scottsdale, AZ: Poisoned Pen. First American edition of a study of female sleuths. New introduction by Nevada Barr.

MURPHY, BRUCE F. *The Encyclopedia of Murder and Mystery*. New York: St. Martin's. Over 1,500 entries on authors, characters, individual works, subgenres, plot devices, etc.

NOLAN, TOM. *Ross Macdonald: A Biography*. New York: Scribner. A life of the famed creator of private eye Lew Archer. Introduction by Sue Grafton.

PENZLER, OTTO. *Earl Derr Biggers' Charlie Chan*. New York: The Mysterious Bookshop. A 24-page booklet on collecting mystery fiction.

———. *Cornell Woolrich, Part I*. New York: The Mysterious Bookshop. A 36-page booklet on collecting mystery fiction.

———. *Ian Fleming's James Bond*. New York: The Mysterious Bookshop. A 36-page booklet, first of a series on collecting mystery fiction.

———. *Mickey Spillane*. New York: The Mysterious Bookshop. A 35-page booklet on collecting mystery fiction.

———. *S. S. Van Dine*. New York: The Mysterious Bookshop. A 36-page booklet on collecting mystery fiction.

QUEEN, ELLERY. *Selected Facsimile Pages (in Reduced Size) of a Draft of The Tragedy of Errors*. Norfolk, VA: Crippen & Landru. A 17-page booklet printed as a supplement to the limited edition of *The Tragedy of Errors*, showing Frederic Dannay's extensive notes and revisions.

SAYERS, DOROTHY L. *The Letters of Dorothy L. Sayers, 1944–1950: A Noble Daring*. Cambridge, England: The Dorothy L. Sayers Society. Volume three of a projected four volumes, chosen and edited by Barbara Reynolds, preface by P. D. James.

SILET, CHARLES L. P. *Talking Murder: Interviews with 20 Mystery Writers*. Princeton, NJ: Ontario Review. Fifteen interviews reprinted mainly from *The Armchair Detective* and *Mystery Scene*, 1992–99, together with five new ones.

STASHOWER, DANIEL. *Teller of Tales: The Life of Arthur Conan Doyle*. New York: Henry Holt. A new biography of Sherlock Holmes's creator.

STEWART, RICHARD F. *End Game*. Shelburne, Ontario, Canada: The Battered Silicon Dispatch Box. A survey of writings about Charles Dickens's unfinished novel, *The Mystery of Edwin Drood*.

WALTON, PRISCILLA, AND MANINA JONES. *Detective Agency: Women Re-Writing the Hard-*

boiled Tradition. Los Angeles: University of California Press. A study of how women writers are changing the traditional tough mystery.

WRIGHT, ERIC. *Always Give a Penny to a Blind Man.* Toronto: Key Porter Books. A memoir of the British/Canadian mystery writer's early life.

Necrology

ADAMS, JOEY (1911–1999). Well-known comedian who contributed to mystery magazines and published a single mystery novel and accompanying short story, *You Could Die Laughing & The Swingers* (1968).

ARNOTE, RALPH (1926–1998). Author of four novels, 1992–98, about Detective Willy Hanson.

AVALLONE, MICHAEL (1924–1999). Well-known author of more than two hundred novels, about half under his own name and thirty about private eye Ed Noon, beginning with *The Tall Dolores* (1953). Other novels appeared as by "Nick Carter," "Priscilla Dalton," "Mark Dane," "Jean-Anne de Pre," "Dora Highland," "Stuart Jason," "Steve Michaels," "Dorthea Nile," "Edwina Noone," "Sidney Stuart," and "Max Walker."

BARBER, FRANK DOUGLAS (1916?–1999). British author of a single suspense novel, *The Last White Man* (1981).

BARR, ROBERT (1909–1999). British journalist and television writer who published a pair of mystery novels in the early 1970s. (Not to be confused with an earlier Robert Barr who died in 1912.)

BATTISON, BRIAN (1939–1998). British author of three police procedurals, beginning with *The Christmas Bow Mystery* (1994).

BECKER, STEPHEN (1927–1999). Author of seven mystery and suspense novels, notably *A Covenant with Death* (1964).

BENTON, KENNETH (1909–1999). British author of eight mystery and spy thrillers, notably *Spy in Chancery* (1972), and chairman of Britain's Crime Writers' Association, 1975–76.

BIOY-CASARES, ALDOLFO (1914–1999). Well-known Argentine fantasy and mystery writer, best known in America for his 1975 mystery, *A Plan for Escape*, and his 1942 collaboration with Jorge Luis Borges, *Six Problems for Don Isidro Parodi*, published here in 1981.

BLANC, SUZANNE (1915–1999). Author of four detective novels, starting with her Edgar-winning *The Green Stone* (1961).

BLANK, MARTIN (1926?–1998). Chicago writer, active in Mystery Writers of America, whose first novel was *Shadowchase* (1989).

BOWLES, PAUL (1910–1999). Mainstream author whose work includes two criminous short stories in his collection *The Hours After Noon* (1959).

BOYCE, CHRIS (1943–1999). Scottish science-fiction writer who also published suspense novels, starting with *Blooding Mr. Naylor* (1990).

BRADLEY, MARION ZIMMER (1930–1999). Well-known science fiction and fantasy writer who published at least eight gothic mystery novels starting in 1965.

BROWNE, HOWARD (1908–1999). Screenwriter and author of eight novels, four originally published as by "John Evans," including the classic Paul Pine mysteries *Halo in Blood* (1946), *Halo for Satan* (1948), *Halo in Brass* (1949), and *The Taste of Ashes* (1957).

COPP, DEWITT S. (1919–1999). Author of three intrigue novels under his own name and others as "Sam Picard" and "Nick Carter."

COULSON, ROBERT STRATTON "BUCK" (1928–1999). As "Thomas Stratton," in collaboration with Gene DeWeese, he wrote two novelizations of the *Man from UNCLE* TV series, both published in 1967.

DAVIS, MEANS (1904–1999). Pseudonym of author and journalist Augusta Tucker Townsend, who published three mystery novels in the 1930s.

DIMONA, JOSEPH (1923?–1999). Screenwriter and author of five mystery-thrillers, notably *Last Man at Arlington* (1973).

DUNCAN, ROBERT L. (1927–1999). Author of TV and film scripts as well as more than two dozen novels, many criminous. Three novels appeared as by "James Hall Roberts" and one, written with his wife, Wanda, as by "W. R. Duncan."

EHRLICHMAN, JOHN (1925–1999). Former aide to President Nixon, who published three suspense novels after leaving the White House.

ESHLEMAN, JOHN M. (1914–1999). Author of two mysteries, 1953–54.

EVERSON, DAVID (1941–1999). Associate chancellor of the University of Illinois at Springfield, author of several paperback mysteries about detective Robert Miles, starting with *Recount* (1987).

FALK, LEE (1915–1999). Creator of comic strip heroes Mandrake the Magician and The Phantom, who published seven paperback novels about The Phantom during the 1970s. (Others in the series were ghosted by Ron Goulart and Basil Copper.)

GEIS, DARLENE (1917–1999). Author of novels for young readers, including *The Mystery of the Thirteenth Floor* (1953).

GOFF, IVAN (1910–1999). Coauthor with Ben Roberts of a three-act play, *Portrait in Black* (1948), and numerous television crime shows including *Charlie's Angels,* which they created.

HANLEY, CLIFFORD (1922–1999). British author of a single crime novel under his own name and nine others, notably *It's Different Abroad* (1963), as by "Henry Calvin."

HENDERSON, DON (1921–1999). British author of a single suspense novel, *Bomb Two* (1983).

HIGGINS, GEORGE V. (1939–1999). Well-known author of some two dozen novels, mainly criminous, starting with *The Friends of Eddie Coyle* (1972).

HITTLEMAN, CARL K. (1907–1999). Author of a single film novelization, *36 Hours* (1965).

ISRAEL, CHARLES E. (1920–1999). Author of three suspense novels including *The Mark* (1958).

KALLEN, LUCILLE (1922–1999). Television comedy writer who published five novels about sleuth C. B. Greenfield, 1979–86.

KARP, DAVID (1922–1999). Edgar-winning television writer who wrote eight suspense novels under his own name and one as by "Wallace Ware."

KENT, SIR HAROLD (1903–1999). British lawyer and government official who published two mystery novels in the early 1930s, *The Tenant of Smugglers' Rock* and *The Black Castle.*

KNOX, BILL (1928–1999). Scottish author of more than sixty mystery novels, mainly police procedurals, under his own name and as "ROBERT MACLEOD." Many of the

"MacLeod" books were published in America as by "Noah Webster" or "Michael Kirk."

KONSALIK, HEINZ G. (1921–1999). German author of a single suspense novel, *Strike Force Ten* (1979).

LE BRETON, AUGUSTE (1913–1999). French author of several mystery and crime novels, one of which was the basis for the film *Rififi*.

MACSHANE, FRANK (1927?–1999). Author of *The Life of Raymond Chandler* (1976) and other literary biographies.

MARTIN, MALACHI (1921?–1999). British/American writer and former Jesuit priest who wrote a thriller, *Hostage to the Devil*, about exorcism, in 1976.

McCONNELL, FRANK D. (1942–1999). Author of critical works in the science fiction field, who also published five mystery novels about a pair of private eyes, one an ex-nun.

McCUTCHEON, HUGH (1909–1999). Prolific Scottish author of nearly thirty crime novels, some published as by "Hugh Davie-Martin." He also wrote as "Grisela Wilding."

McGAUGHEY, NEIL (1951–1999). Mystery reviewer who wrote four novels about a mystery reviewer sleuth.

MESSICK, HANK (1922–1999). True crime author of a single paperback crime novel, *Syndicate Wife* (1975).

MILLER, TONY (1927?–1999). Screenwriter and author of a single paperback crime novel, *Night Calls* (1989).

MOORE, BRIAN (1921–1999). Highly regarded mainstream writer whose novels often used criminous elements to explore moral issues. At least eight of the Moore novels are criminous, and under the pseudonyms of "Michael Bryan" and "Bernard Mara" he published five other, more traditional crime novels early in his career. His screenplays include Hitchcock's *Torn Curtain* (1966).

NOWINSON, DAVID (1910–1999). Radio and TV writer who contributed stories to *The Shadow* and *Ten Detective Aces* pulp magazines, as well as originating the Photocrime feature in *Look* magazine.

OSMOND, ANDREW (1938–1999). British Foreign Office official who collaborated with Douglas Hurd on four political thrillers starting with *Send Him Victorious* (1968). He also collaborated with Richard Reid Harris on *The Fun House* (1974) and published two solo thrillers.

PERKINS, WILDER (1921?–1999). Author of two historical mystery novels beginning with *Hoare and the Portsmouth Atrocities* (1998) and three stories for *Alfred Hitchcock's Mystery Magazine*.

PERRIN, NEIL H. (1922–1999). Author of two Canadian paperbacks (1949), whose real name was Danny Halperin. He later became a London journalist.

POLONSKY, ABRAHAM (1910–1999). Well-known screenwriter who collaborated with the late Mitchell A. Wilson on a single mystery novel, *The Goose Is Cooked* (1940), as by "Emmett Hogarth."

POTTS, JEAN (1910–1999). Author of fourteen novels, 1954–75, beginning with the Edgar-winning *Go, Lovely Rose*.

PUZO, MARIO (1920–1999). Famed best-selling author of *The Godfather* (1969), *The Last*

Don (1996), and other novels, including a 1967 paperback under the pen name "Mario Cleri."

RAE, CATHERINE M. (1914–1999). Author of four romantic suspense novels, starting with *Brownstone Facade* (1988).

RURYK, JEAN (?–1999) Pseudonym of Canadian mystery writer Jean Shepherd, author of three novels about sixtyish widow Cat Wilde, beginning with *Chicken Little Was Right* (1994).

RUSSELL, A. J. (ANDREW JOSEPH) (1915?–1999). TV writer who published two crime novels, 1975–77.

RUSSELL, RAY (1924–1999). Horror writer and editor whose work included three mystery fantasy novels, notably *Incubus* (1976).

SAKURAI, HAJIME (1943?–1999). Japanese book illustrator who turned to writing mystery fiction in 1989 under the pseudonym "Ikki Kazama."

SCOTT, HARDIMAN (1920–1999). British author of five suspense-intrigue novels, 1982–87, who also published a 1951 novel as "Peter Fielding."

SIBLEY, CELESTINE (1917–1999). Atlanta newspaper columnist who wrote a single mystery novel, *The Malignant Hearts,* in 1958 and returned to mystery writing in the 1990s with four additional novels about newspaperwoman Kate Kincaid Mulcay.

SIMS, GEORGE (1923–1999). British rare book dealer and author of a dozen mystery novels, 1964–84, notably *The End of the Web* (1976).

SMITH, JANET ADAM (1905–1999). British literary editor who wrote two biographies, *John Buchan* (1965) and *John Buchan and His World* (1979).

STERNIG, LARRY (1908–1999). Author of a score or more stories in *Mike Shayne, Detective Story Magazine,* and other mystery pulps, who later became a successful literary agent.

TARG, WILLIAM (1907–1999). Well-known editor and bookman who wrote two suspense novels, *The Case of Mr. Cassidy* (1939, with Louis Herman) and *Secret Lives* (1983).

TARLOW, RICKI (?–1999). Short story writer, active in the New York chapter of Mystery Writers of America for more than thirty years.

TEILHET, HILDEGARDE TOLMAN (1906–1999). Author of six solo mystery novels, one as by "Hildegarde Tolman," plus three others in collaboration with her husband, the late Darwin Teilhet.

THORP, RODERICK (1936–1999). Mainstream novelist who published at least three mystery-suspense novels, notably *The Detective* (1966) and *Nothing Lasts Forever* (1979), basis for the film *Die Hard.*

TOWNEND, PETER (1935–1999). British author of four suspense novels under his own name and one other as "Peter Gascoigne."

VEIGA, JOSE J. (1915–1999). Brazilian author and editor who published one crime novel in America, *The Three Trials of Manirema* (1970).

WALLACE, IAN (1912–1998). Pseudonym of John Wallace Pritchard, author of seven science fiction mysteries.

WEST, MORRIS L. (1916–1999). Well-known mainstream novelist whose work included more than a dozen suspense novels, notably *Proteus* (1979). Two of his novels were originally published as by "Michael East."

WEST, W. J. (1942–1999). British author of *The Quest For Graham Greene* (1997), revealing Greene's friendship with thriller writer James Hadley Chase.

WOODRUFF, PHILIP (1906–1999). British author of two suspense novels, 1945–48, who went on to write a classic history of British India under his real name of Philip Mason.

Anne Perry

Heroes

ANNE PERRY has made Victorian England so much her own that one hesitates to read anything else on the subject because it might dull or lessen the period to which Perry has given such vivid color. From the start with *The Cater Street Hangman*, Anne Perry has given us Victorian England with all the real angst and poetry left in. The Thomas Pitt and the William Monk series are alike in their steadfast re-creation of their time. In her more recent novels, *Traitor's Gate, Cain His Brother,* and *Pentecost Alley*, Perry has expanded the range of her books so that the portraits of Victoria's time are richer than ever. While her excellent novels have won her all sorts of well-deserved awards, she should also be lauded for her shorter work. She is a first-rate practitioner of the short story, and readers hope that there will soon be a collection of her shorter works to prove it. This story first appeared in *Murder and Obsession*.

Heroes

Anne Perry

Nights were always the worst, and in winter they lasted from dusk at about four o'clock until dawn again toward eight the following morning. Sometimes star shells lit the sky, showing the black zigzags of the trenches stretching as far as the eye could see to left and right. Apparently now they went right across France and Belgium all the way from the Alps to the Channel. But Joseph was only concerned with this short stretch of the Ypres Salient.

In the gloom near him someone coughed, a deep, hacking sound coming from down in the chest. They were in the support line, farthest from the front, the most complex of the three rows of trenches. Here were the kitchens, the latrines and the stores and mortar positions. Fifteen-foot shafts led to caves about five paces wide and high enough for most men to stand upright. Joseph made his way in the half dark now, the slippery wood under his boots and his hands feeling the mud walls, held up by timber and wire. There was an awful lot of water. One of the sumps must be blocked.

There was a glow of light ahead and a moment later he was in the comparative warmth of the dugout. There were two candles burning and the brazier gave off heat and a sharp smell of soot. The air was blue with tobacco smoke, and a pile of boots and greatcoats steamed a little. Two officers sat on canvas chairs talking together. One of them recited a joke—gallows humor, and they both laughed. A gramophone sat silent on a camp table, and a small pile of records of the latest music-hall songs was carefully protected in a tin box.

"Hello, Chaplain," one of them said cheerfully. "How's God these days?"

"Gone home on sick leave," the other answered quickly, before Joseph could reply. There was disgust in his voice, but no intended irreverence. Death was too close here for men to mock faith.

"Have a seat," the first offered, waving toward a third chair. "Morris got it today. Killed outright. That bloody sniper again."

"He's somewhere out there, just about opposite us," the second said grimly. "One of those blighters the other day claimed he'd got forty-three for sure."

"I can believe it," Joseph answered, accepting the seat. He knew better than most what the casualties were. It was his job to comfort the terrified, the dying, to carry stretchers, often to write letters to the bereaved. Sometimes he thought it was harder than actually fighting, but he refused to stay back in the comparative safety of the field hospitals and depots. This was where he was most needed.

"Thought about setting up a trench raid," the major said slowly, weighing his words and looking at Joseph. "Good for morale. Make it seem as if we were actually doing something. But our chances of getting the blighter are pretty small. Only lose a lot of men for nothing. Feel even worse afterward."

The captain did not add anything. They all knew morale was sinking. Losses were high, the news bad. Word of terrible slaughter seeped through from the Somme and Verdun and all along the line right to the sea. Physical hardship took its toll, the dirt, the cold, and the alternation between boredom and terror. The winter of 1916 lay ahead.

"Cigarette?" the major held out his pack to Joseph.

"No thanks," Joseph declined with a smile. "Got any tea going?"

They poured him a mugful, strong and bitter, but hot. He drank it, and half an hour later made his way forward to the open air again and the travel trench. A star shell exploded high and bright. Automatically he ducked, keeping his head below the rim. They were about four feet deep, and in order not to provide a target, a man had to move in a half crouch. There was a rattle of machine-gun fire out ahead and, closer to, a thud as a rat was dislodged and fell into the mud beside the duckboards.

Other men were moving about close to him. The normal order of things was reversed here. Nothing much happened during the day. Trench repair work was done, munitions shifted, weapons cleaned, a little rest taken. Most of the activity was at night, most of the death.

" 'Lo, Chaplain," a voice whispered in the dark. "Say a prayer we get that bloody sniper, will you?"

"Maybe God's a Jerry?" someone suggested in the dark.

"Don't be stupid!" a third retorted derisively. "Everyone knows God's an Englishman! Didn't they teach you nothing at school?"

There was a burst of laughter. Joseph joined in. He promised to offer up the appropriate prayers and moved on forward. He had known many of the men all his life. They came from the same Northumbrian town as he did, or the surrounding villages. They had gone to school together, nicked apples from the same trees, fished in the same rivers, and walked the same lanes.

It was a little after six when he reached the firing trench beyond whose sandbag parapet lay no-man's-land with its four or five hundred yards of mud, barbed wire, and shell holes. Half a dozen burnt tree stumps looked in the sudden flares like men. Those gray wraiths could be fog, or gas.

Funny that in summer this blood- and horror-soaked soil could still bloom with honeysuckle, forget-me-nots, and wild larkspur, and most of all with poppies. You would think nothing would ever grow there again.

More star shells went up, lighting the ground, the jagged scars of the trenches black, the men on the fire steps with rifles on their shoulders illuminated for a few, blinding moments. Sniper shots rang out.

Joseph stood still. He knew the terror of the night watch out beyond the parapet, crawling around in the mud. Some of them would be at the head of saps out from the trench, most would be in shell holes, surrounded by heavy barricades of wire. Their purpose was to check enemy patrols for unusual movement, any signs of increased activity, as if there might be an attack planned.

More star shells lit the sky. It was beginning to rain. A crackle of machine-gun fire, and heavier artillery somewhere over to the left. Then the sharp whine of sniper fire, again and again.

Joseph shuddered. He thought of the men out there, beyond his vision, and prayed for strength to endure with them in their pain, not to try to deaden himself to it.

There were shouts somewhere ahead, heavy shells now, shrapnel bursting. There was a flurry of movement, flares, and a man came sliding over the parapet, shouting for help.

Joseph plunged forward, sliding in the mud, grabbing for the wooden props to hold himself up. Another flare of light. He saw quite clearly Captain Holt lurching toward him, another man over his shoulder, deadweight.

"He's hurt!" Holt gasped. "Pretty badly. One of the night patrol. Panicked. Just about got us all killed." He eased the man down into Joseph's arms and let his rifle slide forward, bayonet covered in an old sock to hide its gleam. His face was grotesque in the lantern light, smeared with mud and a wide streak of blood over the burnt cork that blackened it, as all night patrol had.

Others were coming to help. There was still a terrible noise of fire going on and the occasional flare.

The man in Joseph's arms did not stir. His body was limp and it was difficult to support him. Joseph felt the wetness and the smell of blood. Wordlessly others materialized out of the gloom and took the weight.

"Is he alive?" Holt said urgently. "There was a hell of a lot of shot up there." His voice was shaking, almost on the edge of control.

"Don't know," Joseph answered. "We'll get him back to the bunker and see. You've done all you can." He knew how desperate men felt when they risked their lives to save another man and did not succeed. A kind of despair set in, a sense of very personal failure, almost a guilt for having survived themselves. "Are you hurt?"

"Not much," Holt answered. "Couple of grazes."

"Better have them dressed, before they get poisoned," Joseph advised, his feet slipping on the wet boards and banging his shoulder against a jutting post. The whole trench wall was crooked, giving way under the weight of mud. The founds had eroded.

The man helping him swore.

Awkwardly carrying the wounded man, they staggered back through the travel line to the support trench and into the light and shelter of a bunker.

Holt looked dreadful. Beneath the cork and blood his face was ashen. He was soaked with rain and mud and there were dark patches of blood across his back and shoulders.

Someone gave him a cigarette. Back here it was safe to strike a match. He drew in smoke deeply. "Thanks," he murmured, still staring at the wounded man.

Joseph looked down at him now, and it was only too plain where the blood had come from. It was young Ashton. He knew him quite well. He had been at school with his older brother.

The soldier who had helped carry him in let out a cry of dismay, strangled in his throat. It was Mordaff, Ashton's closest friend, and he could see what Joseph now could also. Ashton was dead, his chest torn open, the blood no longer pumping, and a bullet hole through his head.

"I'm sorry," Holt said quietly. "I did what I could. I can't have got to him in time. He panicked."

Mordaff jerked his head up. "He never would!" The cry was desperate, a shout of denial against a shame too great to be borne. "Not Will!"

Holt stiffened. "I'm sorry," he said hoarsely. "It happens."

"Not with Will Ashton, it don't!" Mordaff retorted, his eyes blazing, pupils circled with white in the candlelight, his face gray. He had been in the front line two weeks now, a long stretch without a break from the ceaseless tension, filth, cold, and intermittent silence and noise. He was nineteen.

"You'd better go and get that arm dressed, and your side," Joseph said to Holt. He made his voice firm, as to a child.

Holt glanced again at the body of Ashton, then up at Joseph.

"Don't stand there bleeding," Joseph ordered. "You did all you could. There's nothing else. I'll look after Mordaff."

"I tried!" Holt repeated. "There's nothing but mud and darkness and wire, and bullets coming in all directions." There was a sharp thread of terror under his shell-thin veneer of control. He had seen too many men die. "It's enough to make anyone lose his nerve. You want to be a hero—you mean to be—and then it overwhelms you—"

"Not Will!" Mordaff said again, his voice choking off in a sob.

Holt looked at Joseph again, then staggered out.

Joseph turned to Mordaff. He had done this before, too many times, tried to comfort men who had just seen childhood friends blown to pieces, or killed by a sniper's bullet, looking as if they should still be alive, perfect except for the small, blue hole through the brain. There was little to say. Most men found talk of God meaningless at that moment. They were shocked, fighting against belief and yet seeing all the terrible waste and loss of the truth in front of them. Usually it was best just to stay with them, let them speak about the past, what the friend had been like, times they had shared, just as if he were only wounded and would be back, at the end of the war, in some world one could only imagine, in England, perhaps on a summer day with sunlight on the grass, birds singing, a quiet riverbank somewhere, the sound of laughter, and women's voices.

Mordaff refused to be comforted. He accepted Ashton's death; the physical reality of that was too clear to deny, and he had seen too many other men he knew killed in the year and a half he had been in Belgium. But he could not, would not accept that Ashton had panicked. He knew what panic out there cost, how many other lives it jeopardized. It was the ultimate failure.

"How am I going to tell his mam?" he begged Joseph. "It'll be all I can do to tell her he's dead! His pa'll never get over it. That proud of him, they were. He's the only boy. Three sisters he had, Mary, Lizzie, and Alice. Thought he was the greatest lad in the world. I can't tell 'em he panicked! He couldn't have, Chaplain! He just wouldn't!"

Joseph did not know what to say. How could people at home in England even begin to imagine what it was like in the mud and noise out here? But he knew how deep shame burned. A lifetime could be consumed by it.

"Maybe he just lost sense of direction," he said gently. "He wouldn't be the first." War changed men. People did panic. Mordaff knew that, and half his horror was because it could be true. But Joseph did not say so. "I'll write to his family," he went on. "There's a lot of good to say about him. I could send pages. I'll not need to tell them much about tonight."

"Will you?" Mordaff was eager. "Thanks . . . thanks, Chaplain. Can I stay with him . . . until they come for him?"

"Yes, of course," Joseph agreed. "I'm going forward anyway. Get yourself a hot cup of tea. See you in an hour or so."

He left Mordaff squatting on the earth floor beside Ashton's body and fumbled his way back over the slimy duckboards toward the travel line, then forward again to the front and the crack of gunfire and the occasional high flare of a star shell.

He did not see Mordaff again, but he thought nothing of it. He could have passed twenty men he knew and not recognized them, muffled in greatcoats, heads bent as they moved, rattling along the duckboards, or standing on the fire steps, rifles to shoulder, trying to see in the gloom for something to aim at.

Now and again he heard a cough, or the scamper of rats' feet and the splash of rain and mud. He spent a little time with two men swapping jokes, joining in their laughter. It was black humor, self-mocking, but he did not miss the courage in it, or the fellowship, the need to release emotion in some sane and human way.

About midnight the rain stopped.

A little after five the night patrol came scrambling through the wire, whispered passwords to the sentries, then came tumbling over the parapet of sandbags down into the trench, shivering with cold and relief. One of them had caught a shot in the arm.

Joseph went back with them to the support line. In one of the dugouts a gramophone was playing a music-hall song. A couple of men sang along with it; one of them had a beautiful voice, a soft, lyric tenor. It was a silly song, trivial, but it sounded almost like a hymn out here, a praise of life.

A couple of hours and the day would begin: endless, methodical duties of housekeeping, mindless routine, but it was better than doing nothing.

There was still a sporadic crackle of machine-gun fire and the whine of sniper bullets.

An hour till dawn.

Joseph was sitting on an upturned ration case when Sergeant Renshaw came into the bunker, pulling the gas curtain aside to peer in.

"Chaplain?"

Joseph looked up. He could see bad news in the man's face.

"I'm afraid Mordaff got it tonight," he said, coming in and letting the curtain fall again. "Sorry. Don't really know what happened. Ashton's death seems to have . . . well, he lost his nerve. More or less went over the top all by himself. Suppose he was determined to go and give Fritz a bloody nose, on Ashton's account. Stupid bastard! Sorry, Chaplain."

He did not need to explain himself, or to apologize. Joseph knew exactly the fury and the grief he felt at such a futile waste. To this was added a sense of guilt that he had not stopped it. He should have realized Mordaff was so close to breaking. He should have seen it. That was his job.

He stood up slowly. "Thanks for telling me, Sergeant. Where is he?"

"He's gone, Chaplain." Renshaw remained near the doorway. "You can't help 'im now."

"I know that. I just want to . . . I don't know . . . apologize to him. I let him down. I didn't understand he was . . . so . . ."

"You can't be everybody's keeper," Renshaw said gently. "Too many of us. It's not been a bad night otherwise. Got a trench raid coming off soon. Just wish we could get that damn sniper across the way there." He scraped a match and lit his cigarette. "But morale's good. That was a brave thing Captain Holt did out there. He wanted the chance to do something to hearten the men. He saw it and took it. Pity about Ashton, but that doesn't alter Holt's courage. Could see him, you know, by the star shells. Right out there beyond the last wire, bent double, carrying Ashton on his back. Poor devil went crazy. Running around like a fool. Have got the whole patrol killed if Holt hadn't gone after him. Hell of a job getting him back. Fell a couple of times. Reckon that's worth a mention in dispatches, at least. Heartens the men, knowing our officers have got that kind of spirit."

"Yes . . . I'm sure," Joseph agreed. He could only think of Ashton's white face, and Mordaff's desperate denial, and how Ashton's mother would feel, and the rest of his family. "I think I'll go and see Mordaff just the same."

"Right you are," Renshaw conceded reluctantly, standing aside for Joseph to pass.

Mordaff lay in the support trench just outside the bunker two hundred yards to the west. He looked even younger than he had in life, as if he were asleep. His face was oddly calm, even though it was smeared with mud. Someone had tried to clean most of it off in a kind of dignity, so that at least he was recognizable. There was a large wound in the left side of his forehead. It was bigger than most sniper wounds. He must have been a lot closer.

Joseph stood in the first paling of the darkness and looked at him by candlelight from the open bunker curtain. He had been so alive only a few hours ago, so full of anger and loyalty and dismay. What had made him throw his life away in a useless gesture? Joseph racked his mind for some sign that should have warned him Mordaff was so close to breaking, but he could not see it even now.

There was a cough a few feet away, and the tramp of boots on duckboards. The men were stood down, just one sentry per platoon left. They had returned for breakfast. If he thought about it he could smell cooking.

Now would be the time to ask around and find out what had happened to Mordaff.

He made his way to the field kitchen. It was packed with men, some standing to be close to the stoves and catch a bit of their warmth, others choosing to sit, albeit further away. They had survived the night. They were laughing and telling stories, most of them unfit for delicate ears, but Joseph was too used to it to take any offense. Now and then someone new would apologize for such language in front of a chaplain, but most knew he understood too well.

"Yeah," one answered his question through a mouthful of bread and jam. "He came and asked me if I saw what happened to Ashton. Very cut up, he was."

"And what did you tell him?" Joseph asked.

The man swallowed. "Told him Ashton seemed fine to me when he went over. Just like anyone else, nervous . . . but, then, only a fool isn't scared to go over the top!"

Joseph thanked him and moved on. He needed to know who else was on the patrol.

"Captain Holt," the next man told him, a ring of pride in his voice. Word had got around about Holt's courage. Everyone stood a little taller because of it, felt a little braver, more confident. "We'll pay Fritz back for that," he added. "Next raid—you'll see."

There was a chorus of agreement.

"Who else?" Joseph pressed.

"Seagrove, Noakes, Willis," a thin man replied, standing up. "Want some breakfast, Chaplain? Anything you like, on the house—as long as it's bread and jam and half a cup of tea. But you're not particular, are you? Not one of those fussy eaters who'll only take kippers and toast?"

"What I wouldn't give for a fresh Craster kipper," another sighed, a far-away look in his eyes. "I can smell them in my dreams."

Someone told him good-naturedly to shut up.

"Went over the top beside me," Willis said when Joseph found him quarter of an hour later. "All blacked up like the rest of us. Seemed okay to me then. Lost him in no-man's land. Had a hell of a job with the wire. As bloody usual, it wasn't where we'd been told. Got through all right, then Fritz opened up to us. Star shells all over the sky." He sniffed and then coughed violently. When he had control of himself again, he continued. "Then I saw someone outlined against the flares, arms high, like a wild man, running around. He was going toward the German lines, shouting something. Couldn't hear what in the noise."

Joseph did not interrupt. It was now broad daylight and beginning to drizzle again. Around them men were starting the duties of the day: digging, filling sandbags, carrying ammunition, strengthening the wire, resetting duckboards. Men took an hour's work, an hour's sentry duty, and an hour's rest.

Near them somebody was expending his entire vocabulary of curses against lice. Two more were planning elaborate schemes to hold the water at bay.

"Of course that lit us up like a target, didn't it!" Willis went on. "Sniper fire and machine guns all over the place. Even a couple of shells. How none of us got hit I'll never know. Perhaps the row woke God up, and He came back on duty!" He laughed hollowly. "Sorry, Chaplain. Didn't mean it. I'm just so damn sorry poor Ashton got it. Holt just came out of nowhere and ran after him. Obsessed with being a hero, or he'd not even have tried. I can see him in my mind's eye floundering through the mud. If Ashton hadn't got caught in the wire he'd never have got him."

"Caught in the wire?" Joseph asked, memory pricking at him.

"Yeah. Ashton must have run right into the wire, because he stopped sudden—teetering, like—and fell over. A hell of a barrage came over just after that. We all threw ourselves down."

"What happened then?" Joseph said urgently, a slow, sick thought taking shape in his mind.

"When it died down I looked up again, and there was Holt staggering back with poor Ashton across his shoulders. Hell of a job he had carrying him, even though he's bigger than Ashton—well, taller, anyway. Up to his knees in mud, he was, shot and shell all over, sky lit up like a Christmas tree. Of course we gave him what covering fire we could. Maybe it helped." He coughed again. "Reckon he'll be mentioned in dispatches, Chaplain? He deserves it." There was admiration in his voice, a lift of hope.

Joseph forced himself to answer. "I should think so." The words were stiff.

"Well, if he isn't, the men'll want to know why!" Willis said fiercely. "Bloody hero, he is."

Joseph thanked him and went to find Seagrove and Noakes. They told him pretty much the same story.

"You going to have him recommended?" Noakes asked. "He earned it this time. Mordaff came and we said just the same to him. Reckon he wanted the Captain given a medal. He made us say it over and over again, exactly what happened."

"That's right," Seagrove nodded, leaning on a sandbag.

"You told him the same?" Joseph asked. "About the wire, and Ashton getting caught in it?"

"Yes, of course. If he hadn't got caught by the legs he'd have gone straight on and landed up in Fritz's lap, poor devil."

"Thank you."

"Welcome, Chaplain. You going to write up Captain Holt?"

Joseph did not answer, but turned away, sick at heart.

He did not need to look again, but he trudged all the way back to the field hospital anyway. It would be his job to say the services for both Ashton and Mordaff. The graves would be already dug.

He looked at Ashton's body again, looked carefully at his trousers. They were stained with mud, but there were no tears in them, no marks of wire. The fabric was perfect.

He straightened up.

"I'm sorry," he said quietly to the dead man. "Rest in peace." And he turned and walked away.

He went back to where he had left Mordaff's body, but it had been removed. Half an hour more took him to where it also was laid out. He touched the cold hand and looked at the brow. He would ask. He would be sure. But in his mind he already was. He needed time to know what he must do about it. The men would be going over the top on another trench raid soon. Today morale was high. They had a hero in their number, a man who would risk his own life to bring back a soldier who had lost his nerve and panicked. Led by someone like that, they were equal to Fritz any day. Was one pistol bullet, one family's shame, worth all that?

What were they fighting for anyway? The issues were so very big, and at the same time so very small and immediate.

He found Captain Holt alone just after dusk, standing on the duckboards below the parapet, near one of the firing steps.

"Oh, it's you, Chaplain. Ready for another night?"

"It'll come, whether I am or not," Joseph replied.

Holt gave a short bark of laughter. "That doesn't sound like you. Tired of the firing line, are you? You've been up here a couple of weeks; you should be in turn for a step back any day. Me too, thank God."

Joseph faced forward, peering through the gloom toward no-man's-land and the German lines beyond. He was shaking. He must control himself. This must be done in the silence, before the shooting started up again. Then he might not get away with it.

"Pity about that sniper over there," he remarked. "He's taken out a lot of our men."

"Damnable," Holt agreed. "Can't get a line on him, though. Keeps his own head well down."

"Oh, yes," Joseph nodded. "We'd never get him from here. It needs a man to go over in the dark and find him."

"Not a good idea, Chaplain. He'd not come back. Not advocating suicide, are you?"

Joseph chose his words very carefully and kept his voice as unemotional as he could.

"I wouldn't have put it like that," he answered. "But he has cost us a lot of men. Mordaff today, you know?"

"Yes . . . I heard. Pity."

"Except that wasn't the sniper, of course. But the men think it was, so it comes to the same thing, as far as morale is concerned."

"Don't know what you mean, Chaplain." There was a slight hesitation in Holt's voice in the darkness.

"Wasn't a rifle wound, it was a pistol," Joseph replied. "You can tell the difference, if you're actually looking for it."

"Then he was a fool to be that close to German lines," Holt said, facing forward over the parapet and the mud. "Lost his nerve, I'm afraid."

"Like Ashton," Joseph said. "Can understand that, up there in no-man's-land, mud everywhere, wire catching hold of you, tearing at you, stopping you from moving. Terrible thing to be caught in the wire with the star shells lighting up the night. Makes you a sitting target. Takes an exceptional man not to panic, in those circumstances . . . a hero."

Holt did not answer.

There was silence ahead of them, only the dull thump of feet and a squelch of duckboards in mud behind, and the trickle of water along the bottom of the trench.

"I expect you know what it feels like," Joseph went on. "I notice you have some pretty bad tears in your trousers, even one in your blouse. Haven't had time to mend them yet."

"I daresay I got caught in a bit of wire out there last night," Holt said stiffly. He shifted his weight from one foot to the other.

"I'm sure you did," Joseph agreed with him. "Ashton didn't. His clothes were muddy, but no wire tears."

There were several minutes of silence. A group of men passed by behind them, muttering words of greeting. When they were gone the darkness closed in again. Someone threw up a star shell and there was a crackle of machine-gun fire.

"I wouldn't repeat that, if I were you, Chaplain," Holt said at last. "You might make people think unpleasant things, doubts. And right at the moment morale is high. We need that. We've had a hard time recently. We're going over the top in a trench raid soon. Morale is important . . . trust. I'm sure you know that, maybe even better than I do. That's your job, isn't it? Morale, spiritual welfare of the men?"

"Yes . . . spiritual welfare is a good way of putting it. Remember what it is we are fighting for, and that it is worth all that it costs . . . even this." Joseph gestured in the dark to all that surrounded them.

More star shells went up, illuminating the night for a few garish moments, then a greater darkness closed in.

"We need our heroes," Holt said very clearly. "You should know that. Any man who would tear them down would be very unpopular, even if he said he was doing it in the name of truth, or justice, or whatever it was he believed in. He would do a lot of harm, Chaplain. I expect you can see that . . ."

"Oh, yes," Joseph agreed. "To have their hero shown to be a coward who laid the blame for his panic on another man, and let him be buried in shame, and then committed murder to hide that, would devastate men who are already wretched and exhausted by war."

"You are perfectly right." Holt sounded as if he were smiling. "A very wise man, Chaplain. Good of the regiment first. The right sort of loyalty."

"I could prove it," Joseph said very carefully.

"But you won't. Think what it would do to the men."

Joseph turned a little to face the parapet. He stood up onto the fire step and looked forward over the dark expanse of mud and wire.

"We should take that sniper out. That would be a very heroic thing to do. Good thing to try, even if you didn't succeed. You'd deserve a mention in dispatches for that, possibly a medal."

"It would be posthumous!" Holt said bitterly.

"Possibly. But you might succeed and come back. It would be so daring, Fritz would never expect it," Joseph pointed out.

"Then you do it, Chaplain!" Holt said sarcastically.

"It wouldn't help you, Captain. Even if I die, I have written a full account of what I have learned today, to be opened should anything happen to me. On the other hand, if you were to mount such a raid, whether you returned or not, I should destroy it."

There was silence again, except for the distant crack of sniper fire a thousand yards away and the drip of mud.

"Do you understand me, Captain Holt?"

Holt turned slowly. A star shell lit his face for an instant. His voice was hoarse.

"You're sending me to my death!"

"I'm letting you be the hero you're pretending to be and Ashton really was," Joseph answered. "The hero the men need. Thousands of us have died out here, no one knows how many more there will be. Others will be maimed or blinded. It isn't whether you die or not, it's how well."

A shell exploded a dozen yards from them. Both men ducked, crouching automatically.

Silence again.

Slowly Joseph unbent.

Holt lifted his head. "You're a hard man, Chaplain. I misjudged you."

"Spiritual care, Captain," Joseph said quietly. "You wanted the men to think you a hero, to admire you. Now you're going to justify that and become one."

Holt stood still, looking toward him in the gloom, then slowly he turned and began to walk away, his feet sliding on the wet duckboards. Then he climbed up the next fire step and up over the parapet.

Joseph stood still and prayed.

David Morrell

Rio Grande Gothic

Adventure fiction of the serious kind has no better friend than DAVID MORRELL. In the tradition of the great John Buchan and Geoffrey Household, Morrell has restored well-written, intelligent, and moral adventure fiction to its proper place on the best-seller lists. He is equally adept at horror fiction, bringing to it the same skills of humanity and wisdom one finds in his adventure work. Here is a stunning story that ranks with the very best the author of *First Blood, The Totem,* and *The Brotherhood of the Rose* has to offer. This story first appeared in *999*.

Rio Grande Gothic

David Morrell

When Romero finally noticed the shoes on the road, he realized that he had actually been seeing them for several days. Driving into town along Old Pecos Trail, passing the adobe-walled Santa Fe Woman's Club on the left, approaching the pueblo-style Baptist church on the right, he reached the crest of the hill, saw the jogging shoes on the yellow median line, and steered his police car onto the dirt shoulder of the road.

Frowning, he got out and hitched his thumbs onto his heavy gun belt, oblivious to the roar of passing traffic, focusing on the jogging shoes. They were laced together, a Nike label on the back. One was on its side, showing how worn its tread was. But they hadn't been in the middle of the road yesterday, Romero thought. No, yesterday, it had been a pair of leather sandals. He remembered having been vaguely aware of them. And the day before yesterday? Had it been a pair of women's high heels? His recollection wasn't clear, but there had been *some* kind of shoes—of that he was certain. What the . . . ?

After waiting for a break in traffic, Romero crossed to the median and stared down at the jogging shoes as if straining to decipher a riddle. A pickup truck crested the hill too fast to see him and slow down, the wind it created ruffling his blue uniform. He barely paid attention, preoccupied by the shoes. But when a second truck sped over the hill, he realized that he had better get off the road. He withdrew his nightstick from his gun belt, thrust it under the tied laces, and lifted. Feeling the weight of the shoes dangling from the nightstick, he waited for a minivan to speed past, then returned to his police car, unlocked its trunk, and dropped the shoes into it. Probably that was what had happened to the other shoes, he decided. A sanitation truck or someone working for the city must have stopped and cleared what looked like garbage. This was the middle of May. The tourist season would soon be in full swing.

It wasn't good to have visitors seeing junk on the road. I'll toss these shoes in the trash when I get back to the station, he decided.

The next pickup that rocketed over the hill was doing at least fifty. Romero scrambled into his cruiser, flicked on his siren, and stopped the truck just after it ran a red light at Cordova.

He was forty-two. He had been a Santa Fe policeman for fifteen years, but the thirty thousand dollars he earned each year wasn't enough for him to afford a house in Santa Fe's high-priced real estate market, so he lived in the neighboring town of Pecos, twenty miles northeast, where his parents and grandparents had lived before him. Indeed, he lived in the same house that his parents had owned before a drunk driver, speeding the wrong way on the Interstate, had hit their car head-on and killed them. The modest structure had once been in a quiet neighborhood, but six months earlier a supermarket had been built a block away, the resultant traffic noise and congestion blighting the area. Romero had married when he was twenty. His wife worked for an Allstate Insurance agent in Pecos. Their twenty-two-year-old son lived at home and wasn't employed. Each morning, Romero argued with him about looking for work. That was followed by a different argument in which Romero's wife complained that he was being too hard on the boy. Typically, he and his wife left the house not speaking to each other. Once trim and athletic, the star of his high school football team, Romero was puffy in his face and stomach from too much take-out food and too much time spent behind a steering wheel. This morning, he had noticed that his sideburns were turning gray.

By the time he finished with the speeding pickup truck, a house burglary he was sent to investigate, and a purse snatcher he managed to catch, Romero had forgotten about the shoes. A fight between two feuding neighbors who happened to cross paths with each other in a restaurant parking lot further distracted him. He completed his paperwork at the police station, attended an after-shift debriefing, and didn't need much convincing to go out for a beer with a fellow officer rather than muster the resolve to make the twenty-mile drive to the tensions of his home. He got in at ten, long after his wife and son had eaten. His son was out with friends. His wife was in bed. He ate leftover fajitas while watching a rerun of a situation comedy that hadn't been funny the first time.

The next morning, as he crested the hill by the Baptist church, he came to attention at the sight of a pair of loafers scattered along the median. After steering sharply onto the shoulder, he opened the door and held up his hands for traffic to stop while he went over, picked up the loafers, returned to the cruiser, and set them in the trunk beside the jogging shoes.

"Shoes?" his sergeant asked back at the station. "What are you talking about?"

"Over on Old Pecos Trail. Every morning, there's a pair of shoes," Romero said.

"They must have fallen off a garbage truck."

"Every morning? And only shoes, nothing else? Besides, the ones I found this morning were almost new."

"Maybe somebody was moving and they fell off the back of a pickup truck."

"Every morning?" Romero repeated. "These were Cole Hahns. Expensive loafers like that don't get thrown on top of a load of stuff in a pickup truck."

"What difference does it make? It's only shoes. Maybe somebody's kidding around."

"Sure," Romero said. "Somebody's kidding around."

"A practical joke," the sergeant said. "So people will wonder why the shoes are on the road. Hey, *you* wondered. The joke's working."

"Yeah," Romero said. "A practical joke."

The next morning, it was a battered pair of Timberland work boots. As Romero crested the hill by the Baptist church, he wasn't surprised to see them. In fact, the only thing he had been uncertain about was what type of footwear they would be.

If this is a practical joke, it's certainly working, he thought. Whoever's doing it is awfully persistent. Who . . .

The problem nagged at him all day. Between investigating a hit-and-run on St. Francis Drive and a break-in at an art gallery on Canyon Road, he returned to the crest of the hill on Old Pecos Trail several times, making sure that other shoes hadn't appeared. For all he knew, the joker was dumping the shoes during the daytime. If so, the plan Romero was thinking about would be worthless. But after the eighth time he returned and still didn't see more shoes, he told himself he had a chance.

The plan had the merit of simplicity. All it required was determination, and of that he had plenty. Besides, it would be a good reason to postpone going home. So after getting a Quarter Pounder and fries, a Coke and two large containers of coffee from McDonald's, he headed toward Old Pecos Trail as dusk thickened. He used his private car, a five-year-old, dark blue Jeep Cherokee—no sense in being conspicuous. He considered establishing his stakeout in the Baptist church's parking lot. That would give him a great view of Old Pecos Trail. But at night, with his car the only one in the lot, he'd be conspicuous. Across from the church, though, East Lupita Road intersected with Old Pecos Trail. It was a quiet residential area, and if he parked there, he couldn't be seen by anyone driving along Old Pecos. In contrast, he himself would have a good view of passing traffic.

It can work, he thought. There were streetlights on Old Pecos Trail but not on East Lupita. Sitting in darkness, munching on his Quarter Pounder and fries, using the caffeine in the Coke and the two coffees to keep himself alert, he concentrated on the illuminated crest of the hill. For a while, the headlights of passing cars were frequent and distracting. After each vehicle passed, he stared toward the area of the road that interested him, but no sooner did he focus on that spot than more headlights sped past, and he had to stare harder to see if anything had been dropped. He had his right hand ready to turn the ignition key and yank the gearshift into forward, his right foot primed to stomp the accelerator. To relax, he turned on the radio for fifteen-minute stretches, careful that he didn't weaken the battery. Then traffic became sporadic, making it easy to watch the road. But after an eleven o'clock news report in which the main item was about a fire in a store at the De Vargas mall, he realized the flaw in his plan. All that caffeine. The tension of straining to watch the road.

He had to go to the bathroom.

But I went when I picked up the food.

That was then. Those were two large coffees you drank.

Hey, I had to keep awake.

He squirmed. He tensed his abdominal muscles. He would have relieved himself into one of the beverage containers, but he had crumbled all three of them when he stuffed them into the bag that the Quarter Pounder and fries came in. His bladder ached. Headlights passed. No shoes were dropped. He pressed his thighs together. More headlights. No shoes. He turned his ignition key, switched on his headlights, and hurried toward the nearest public rest room, which was on St. Michael's Drive at an all-night gas station because at eleven-thirty most restaurants and take-out places were closed.

When he got back, two cowboy boots were on the road.

"It's almost one in the morning. Why are you coming home so late?"

Romero told his wife about the shoes.

"Shoes? Are you crazy?"

"Haven't you ever been curious about something?"

"Yeah, right now I'm curious why you think I'm stupid enough to believe you're coming home so late because of some old shoes you found on the road. Have you got a girlfriend, is that it?"

"You don't look so good," his sergeant said.

Romero shrugged despondently.

"You been out all night, partying?" the sergeant joked.

"Don't I wish."

The sergeant became serious. "What is it? More trouble at home?"

Romero almost told him the whole story, but remembering the sergeant's indifference when he'd earlier been told about the shoes, Romero knew he wouldn't get much sympathy. Maybe the opposite. "Yeah, more trouble at home."

After all, what he'd done last night was, he had to admit, a little strange. Using his free time to sit in a car for three hours, waiting for . . . If a practical joker wanted to keep tossing shoes on the road, so what? Let the guy waste his time. Why waste my own time trying to catch him? There were too many real crimes to be investigated. What am I going to charge the guy with? Littering?

Throughout his shift, Romero made a determined effort not to go near Old Pecos Trail. A couple of times during a busy day of interviewing witnesses about an assault, a break-in, another purse snatching, and a near-fatal car accident on Paseo de Peralta, he was close enough to have swung past Old Pecos Trail on his way from one incident to another, but he deliberately chose an alternate route. Time to change patterns, he told himself. Time to concentrate on what's important.

At the end of his shift, his lack of sleep the previous night caught up to him. He left work exhausted. Hoping for a quiet evening at home, he followed congested traffic through the dust of the eternal construction project on Cerrillos Road, reached Interstate 25, and headed north. Sunset on the Sangre de Cristo Mountains tinted them the blood color for which the early Spanish colonists had named them. In a half hour, I'll have my feet up and be drinking a beer, he thought. He passed the exit to St. Francis Drive. A sign told him that the next exit, the one for Old Pecos Trail, was two miles ahead. He blocked it from his mind, continued to admire the sunset, imagined the beer he was going to drink, and turned on the radio. A weather report told him that the high for the day had been seventy-five, typical for mid-May, but that a cold front was coming in and that the night temperature could drop as much as forty degrees, with a threat of frost in low-lying areas. The announcer suggested covering any recently purchased tender plants. The average frost-free day was May 15, but . . .

Romero took the Old Pecos Trail exit.

Just for the hell of it, he thought. Just to have a look and settle my curiosity. What can it hurt? As he crested the hill, he was surprised to notice that his heart was beating a little faster. Do I really expect to find more shoes? he asked himself. Is it going to annoy me that they were here all day and I didn't come over to check? Pressure built in his chest as that section came into view. He breathed deeply . . .

And exhaled when he saw that there wasn't anything on the road. There, he told himself. It was worth the detour. I proved that I'd have wasted my time if I drove over here during my shift. I can go home now without being bugged that I didn't satisfy my curiosity.

But all the time he and his wife sat watching television while they ate Kentucky Fried Chicken (their son was out with friends), Romero felt restless. He couldn't stop thinking that whoever was dumping the shoes would do so again. The bastard will think he's outsmarted me. You? What are you talking about? He doesn't have the faintest idea who you are. Well, he'll think he's outsmarted whoever's picking up the shoes. The difference is the same.

The beer that Romero had been looking forward to tasted like water.

And of course the next morning, damn it, there was a pair of women's tan pumps five yards away from each other along the median. Scowling, Romero blocked morning traffic, picked up the pumps, and set them in the trunk with the others. Where the hell is this guy getting the shoes? he thought. These pumps are almost new. So are the loafers I picked up the other day. Who throws out perfectly good shoes, even for a practical joke?

When Romero was done for the day, he phoned his wife to tell her, "I have to work late. One of the guys on the evening shift got sick. I'm filling in." He caught up on some paperwork he needed to do. Then he went to a nearby Pizza Hut and got a medium pepperoni with mushrooms and black olives, to go. He also got a large Coke and two large coffees, but this time he'd learned his lesson and came prepared with an empty plastic gallon jug that he could urinate in. More, he brought a Walkman and earphones so he wouldn't have to use the car's radio and worry about wearing down the battery.

Confident that he hadn't forgotten anything, he drove to the stakeout. Santa Fe had its share of dirt roads, and East Lupita was one of them. Flanked by chamisa bushes and Russian olive trees, it had widely spaced adobe houses and got very little traffic. Parked near the corner, Romero saw the church across from him, its bell tower reminding him of a pueblo mission. Beyond were the piñon-dotted Sun Mountain and Atalaya Ridge, the sunset as vividly blood-colored as it had been the previous evening.

Traffic passed. Studying it, he put on his headphones and switched the Walkman from CD to radio. After finding a call-in show (was the environment truly as threatened as ecologists claimed?), he sipped his Coke, dug into his pizza, and settled back to watch traffic.

An hour after dark, he realized that he had indeed forgotten something. The previous day's weather report had warned about low night temperatures, possibly even a frost, and now Romero felt a chill creep up his legs. He was grateful for the warm coffee. He hugged his chest, wishing that he'd brought a jacket. His breath vapor clouded the windshield so that he often had to use a handkerchief to clear it. He rolled down his window, and that helped control his breath vapor, but it also allowed more cold to enter the vehicle, making him shiver. Moonlight reflected off lingering snow on top of the mountains, especially at the ski basin, and that made him feel even colder. He turned on the Jeep and used its heater to warm him. All the while, he concentrated on the dwindling traffic.

Eleven o'clock, and still no shoes. He kept reminding himself that it had been about this hour two nights earlier when he had been forced to leave to find a rest room. When he had returned twenty minutes later, he had found the cowboy boots. If whoever was doing this followed a pattern, there was a good chance that something would happen in the next half hour.

Stay patient, he thought.

But as had happened two nights earlier, the Coke and the coffees finally had their effect. Fortunately, he had that problem taken care of. He grabbed the empty gallon jug from the seat beside him, twisted its cap off, positioned the jug beneath the steering wheel, and started to urinate, only to squint from the headlights of a car that approached behind him, reflecting in his rearview mirror.

His bladder muscles tensed, interrupting the flow of urine. Jesus, he thought. Although he was certain that the driver wouldn't be able to see what he was doing, he felt self-conscious enough that he quickly capped the jug and set it on the passenger floor.

Come on, he told the approaching car. He needed to urinate as bad as ever and urged the car to pass him, to turn onto Old Pecos Trail and leave, so he could grab the jug again.

The headlights stopped behind him.

What in God's name? Romero thought.

Then rooflights began to flash, and Romero realized that what was behind him was a police car. Ignoring his urgent need to urinate, he rolled down his window and placed his hands on top of the steering wheel, where the approaching officer, not knowing who was in the car or what he was getting into, would be relieved to see them.

Footsteps crunched on the dirt road. A blinding flashlight scanned the inside of Romero's car, assessing the empty pizza box, lingering over the yellow liquid in the plastic jug. "Sir, may I see your license and registration, please?"

Romero recognized the voice. "It's okay, Tony. It's me."

"Who . . . Gabe?"

The flashlight beam hurt Romero's eyes.

"*Gabe?*"

"The one and only."

"What the hell are you doing out here? We had several complaints about somebody suspicious sitting in a car, like he was casing the houses in the neighborhood."

"It's only me."

"Were you here two nights ago?"

"Yes."

"We had complaints then, too, but when we got here, the car was gone. What are you doing?" the officer repeated.

Trying not to squirm from the pressure in his abdomen, Romero said, "I'm on a stakeout."

"Nobody told me about any stakeout. What's going on that—"

Realizing how long it would take to explain the odd-sounding truth, Romero said, "They've been having some attempted break-ins over at the church. I'm watching to see if whoever's been doing it comes back."

"Man, sitting out here all night—this is some piss-poor assignment they gave you."

"You have no idea."

"Well, I'll leave before I draw any more attention to you. Good hunting."

"Thanks."

"And next time, tell the shift commander to let the rest of us know what's going on so we don't screw things up."

"I'll make a point of it."

The officer got back in his cruiser, turned off the flashing lights, passed Romero's car, waved, and steered onto Old Pecos Trail. Instantly, Romero grabbed the plastic jug and urinated for what seemed a minute and a half. When he finished and leaned back, sighing, his sense of relaxation lasted only as long as it took him to study Old Pecos Trail again.

The next thing, he scrambled out of his car and ran cursing toward a pair of men's shoes—they turned out to be Rockports—lying laced together in the middle of the road.

"Did you tell Tony Ortega you'd been ordered to stake out the Baptist church?" his sergeant demanded.

Romero reluctantly nodded.

"What kind of bullshit is that? Nobody put you on any stakeout. Sitting in a car all night, acting suspicious. You'd better have a damned good reason for—"

Romero didn't have a choice. "The shoes."

"What?"

"The shoes I keep finding on Old Pecos Trail."

His eyes wide, the sergeant listened to Romero's explanation. "You don't put in enough hours? You want to donate a couple nights free overtime on some crazy—"

"Hey, I know it's a little unusual."

"A *little*?"

"Whoever's dumping those shoes is playing some kind of game."

"And you want to play it with him."

"What?"

"He leaves the shoes. You take them. He leaves more shoes. You take them. You're playing his game."

"No, it isn't like that."

"Well, what *is* it like? Listen to me. Quit hanging around that street. Somebody might shoot you for a prowler."

When Romero finished his shift, he found a dozen old shoes piled in front of his locker. Somebody laughed in the lunchroom.

"I'm Officer Romero, ma'am, and I guess I made you a little nervous last night and two nights earlier. I was in my car, watching the church across the street. We had a report that somebody might try to break in. It seems you thought *I'm* the one who might try breaking in. I just wanted to assure you the neighborhood's perfectly safe with me parked out there."

"I'm Officer Romero, sir, and I guess I made you a little nervous last night and two nights earlier."

This time, he had everything under control. No more large Cokes and coffees, although he did keep his plastic jug, just in case. He made sure to bring a jacket, although the frost danger had finally passed and the night temperature was warmer. He was trying to eat better, too, munching on a *burrito grande con pollo* from Felipe's, the best Mexican takeout in town. He settled back and listened to the radio call-in show on the Walkman. The program was still on the environmental theme: "Hey, man, I used to be able to swim in the rivers when I was a kid. I used to be able to eat the fish I caught in them. I'd be nuts to do that now."

It was just after dark. The headlights of a car went past. No shoes. No problem. Romero was ready to be patient. He was in a rhythm. Noting would probably happen until it usually did—after eleven. The Walkman's earphones pinched his head. He took them off and readjusted them as headlights sped past, heading to the right, out of town. Simultaneously, a different pair of headlights rushed past, heading to the left, *into* town. Romero's window was down. Despite the sound of the engines, he heard a distinct *thunk*, then another. The vehicles were gone, and he gaped at two hiking boots on the road.

Holy . . .

Move! He twisted the ignition key and yanked the gearshift into drive. Breathless, he urged the car forward, its rear tires spewing stones and dirt, but as he reached Old Pecos Trail, he faced a hurried decision. Which driver had dropped the shoes? Which car? Right or left?

He didn't have any jurisdiction out of town. Left! His tires squealing on the pavement, he sped toward the receding taillights. The road dipped, then rose toward the stoplight at Cordova, which was red and which Romero hoped would stay that way, but as he sped closer to what he now saw was a pickup truck, the light changed to green, and the truck drove through the intersection.

Shit.

Romero had an emergency light on the passenger seat. Shaped like a dome, it was plugged into the cigarette lighter. He thrust it out the window and onto the roof, where its magnetic base held it in place. Turning it on, seeing the reflection of its flashing red light, he pressed harder on the accelerator. He sped through the intersection, rushed up behind the pickup truck, blared his horn, and nodded when the truck went slower, angling toward the side of the road.

Romero wasn't in uniform, but he did have his 9mm Beretta in a holster on his belt. He made sure that his badge was clipped onto the breast pocket of his denim jacket. He aimed his flashlight toward a load of rocks in the back of the truck, then carefully approached the driver. "License and registration, please."

"What seems to be the trouble, Officer?" The driver was Anglo, young, about twenty-three. Thin. With short sandy hair. Wearing a red-and-brown-checked work shirt. Even sitting, he was tall.

"You were going awfully fast coming over that hill by the church."

The young man glanced back, as if to remind himself that there'd been a hill.

"License and registration," Romero repeated.

"I'm sure I wasn't going more than the speed limit," the young man said. "It's forty there, isn't it?" He handed over his license and pulled the registration from a pouch on the sun visor above his head.

Romero read the name. "Luke Parsons."

"Yes, sir." The young man's voice was reedy, with a gentle politeness.

"P.O. Box 25, Dillon, New Mexico?" Romero asked.

"Yes, sir. That's about fifty miles north. Up past Espanola and Embudo and—"

"I know where Dillon is. What brings you down here?"

"Selling moss rocks at the roadside stand off the Interstate."

Romero nodded. The rocks in the back of the truck were valued locally for their use in landscaping, the lichenlike moss that speckled them turning pleasant muted colors after a rain. Hardscrabble vendors gathered them in the mountains and sold them, along with homemade birdhouses, self-planed roof-support beams, firewood, and vegetables in season, at a clearing off a country road that paralleled the Interstate.

"Awful far from Dillon to be selling moss rocks," Romero said.

"Have to go where the customers are. Really, what's this all a—"

"You're selling after dark?"

"I wait until dusk in case folks coming out of Harry's Road House or the steak house farther along decide to stop and buy something. Then I go over to Harry's and get something to eat. Love his barbecued vegetables."

This wasn't how Romero had expected the conversation to go. He had anticipated that the driver would look uneasy because he'd lost the game. But the young man's politeness was disarming.

"I want to talk to you about those shoes you threw out of the car. There's a heavy fine for—"

"Shoes?"

"You've been doing it for several days. I want to know why—"

"Officer, honestly, I haven't the faintest idea what you're talking about."

"The shoes I saw you throw onto the road."

"Believe me, whatever you saw happen, it wasn't me doing it. Why would I throw shoes on the road?"

The young man's blue eyes were direct, his candid look disarming. Damn it, Romero thought, I went after the wrong car.

Inwardly, he sighed.

He gave back the license and registration. "Sorry to bother you."

"No problem, Officer. I know you have to do your job."

"Going all the way back to Dillon tonight?"

"Yes, sir."

"As I said, it's a long way to travel to sell moss rocks."

"Well, we do what we have to do."

"That's for sure," Romero said. "Drive safely."

"I always do, Officer. Good night."

"Good night."

Romero drove back to the top of the hill, picked up the hiking shoes, and put them in the trunk of his car. It was about that time, a little before ten, that his son was killed.

He passed the crash site on the way home to Pecos. Seeing the flashing lights and the silhouettes of two ambulances and three police cars on the opposite section of the Interstate, grimacing at the twisted wrecks of two vehicles, he couldn't help thinking, Poor bastards. God help them. But God didn't, and by the time Romero got home, the medical examiner was showing the state police the wallet that he had taken from the mutilated body of what seemed to be a young Hispanic male.

Romero and his wife were arguing about his late hours when the phone rang.

"Answer it!" she yelled. "It's probably your damned girlfriend."

"I keep telling you I don't have a—" The phone rang again. "Yeah, hello."

"Gabe? This is Ray Becker with the state police. Sit down, would you?"

As Romero listened, he felt a cold ball grow inside him. He had never felt so numb, not even when he'd been told about the deaths of his parents.

His wife saw his stunned look. *"What is it?"*

Trembling, he managed to overcome his numbness enough to tell her. She screamed. She never stopped screaming until she collapsed.

. . .

Two weeks later, after the funeral, after Romero's wife went to visit her sister in Denver, after Romero tried going back to work (his sergeant advised against it, but Romero knew he'd go crazy just sitting around home), the dispatcher sent him back on a call that forced him to drive up Old Pecos Trail by the Baptist church. Bitterly, he remembered how fixated he had been on this spot not long ago. Instead of screwing around wondering about those shoes, I should have stayed home and paid attention to my son, he thought. Maybe I could have prevented what happened.

There weren't any shoes on the road.

There weren't any shoes on the road the next day or the day after that.

Romero's wife never came back from Denver.

"You have to get out more," his sergeant told him.

It was three months later, the middle Saturday of August. As a part of the impending divorce settlement and as a way of trying to stifle memories, Romero had sold the house in Pecos. With his share of the proceeds, he had moved to Santa Fe and risked a down payment on a modest house in the El Dorado subdivision. It didn't make a difference. He still had the sense of carrying a weight on his back.

"I hope you're not talking about dating."

"I'm just saying you can't stay holed up in this house all the time. You have to get out and do something. Distract yourself. While I think of it, you ought to be eating better. Look at the crap in this fridge. Stale milk, a twelve-pack of beer, and some leftover Chicken McNuggets."

"Most of the time I'm not hungry."

"With a fridge like this, I don't doubt it."

"I don't like cooking for myself."

"It's too much effort to make a salad? I tell you what. Saturdays, Maria and I go to the Farmers' Market. Tomorrow morning, you come with us. The vegetables don't come any fresher. Maybe if you had some decent food in this fridge, you'd—"

"What's wrong with me the Farmers' Market isn't going to cure."

"Hey, I'm knocking myself out trying to be a friend. The least you can do is humor me."

The Farmers' Market was near the old train station, past the tracks, in an open area the city had recently purchased called the Rail Yard. Farmers drove their loaded pickups in and parked in spaces they'd been assigned. Some set up tables and put up awnings. Others just sold from the back of their trucks. There were taste samples of everything from pies to salsa. A bluegrass band played in a corner. Somebody dressed up as a clown wandered through the crowd.

"See, it's not so bad," the sergeant said.

Romero walked listlessly past stands of cider, herbal remedies, free-range chicken, and sunflower sprouts. In a detached way, he had to admit, "Yeah, not so bad." All the years he'd worked for the police department, he'd never been here—another example of how he'd let his life pass him by. But instead of motivating him to learn from his mistakes, his regret only made him more depressed.

"How about some of these little pies?" the sergeant's wife asked. "You can keep them in the freezer and heat one up when you feel like it. They're only one or two servings, so you won't have any leftovers."

"Sure," Romero said, not caring. "Why not?" His dejected gaze drifted over the crowd.

"What kind?"

"Excuse me?"

"What kind? Peach or butter pecan?"

"It doesn't matter. Choose some for me."

His gaze settled on a stand that offered religious icons made out of corn husks layered over carved wood: Madonnas, manger scenes, and crosses. The skillfully formed images were painted and covered with a protective layer of vanish. It was a traditional Hispanic folk art, but what caught Romero's attention wasn't the attractiveness of the images but rather that an Anglo instead of a Hispanic was selling them as if he'd made them.

"This apple pie looks good, too," the sergeant's wife said.

"Fine." Assessing the tall, thin, sandy-haired man selling the icons, Romero added, "I know that guy from somewhere."

"What?" the sergeant's wife asked.

"Nothing. I'll be back in a second to get the pies." Remero made his way through the crowd. The young man's fair hair was extremely short. His thin face emphasized his cheekbones, making him look as if he'd been fasting. He had an aesthetic quality similar to that on the faces of the icons he was selling. Not that he looked ill. The opposite. His tan skin glowed.

His voice, too, seemed familiar. As Romero approached, he heard the reedy gentle tone with which the young man explained to a customer the intricate care with which the icons were created.

Romero waited until the customer walked off with her purchase.

"Yes, sir?"

"I know you from somewhere, but I just can't seem to place you."

"I wish I could help you, but I don't think we've met."

Romero noticed the small crystal that hung from a woven cord on the young man's neck. It had a hint of pale blue in it, as if borrowing some of the blue in the young man's eyes. "Maybe you're right. It's just that you seem so awfully—"

Movement to his right distracted him, a young man carrying a large basket of tomatoes from a pickup truck and setting it next to baskets of cucumbers, peppers, squash, carrots, and other vegetables on a stand next to this one.

But more than the movement distracted him. The young man was tall and thin, with short sandy hair and a lean aesthetic face. He had clear blue eyes that seemed to lend some of their color to the small crystal hanging from his neck. He wore faded jeans and a white T-shirt, the same as the young man to whom Romero had been talking. The white of the shirt emphasized his glowing tan.

"You *are* right," Romero told the first man. "We haven't met. Your brother's the one I met."

The newcomer looked puzzled.

"It's true, isn't it?" Romero asked. "The two of you are brothers? That's why I got confessed. But I still can't remember where—"

"Luke Parsons." The newcomer extended his hand.

"Gabe Romero."

The young man's forearm was sinewy, his handshake firm.

Romero needed all of his discipline and training not to react, his mind reeling as he remembered. Luke Parsons? Christ, this was the man he had spoken to the night his son had been killed and his life had fallen apart. To distract himself from his memories, he had come to this market, only to find someone who reminded him of what he was desperately trying to forget.

"And this is my brother Mark."

"Hello."

"Say, are you feeling all right?"

"Why? What do you—"

"You turned pale all of a sudden."

"It's nothing. I just haven't been eating well lately."

"Then you ought to try this." Luke Parsons pointed toward a small bottle filled with brown liquid.

Romero narrowed his eyes. "What is it?"

"Home-grown echinacea. If you've got a virus, this'll take care of you. Boosts your immune system."

"Thanks but—"

"When you feel how dramatically it picks you up—"

"You make it sound like drugs."

"God's drug. Nothing false. If it doesn't improve your well-being, we'll give you a refund."

"There you are," Romero's sergeant said. "I've been looking all over for are." He noticed the bottle in Romero's hands. "What's *that*?"

"Something called home-grown . . ." The word eluded him.

"Echinacea," Luke Parsons said.

"Sure," the sergeant's wife said. "I use it when we get colds. Boosts the immune system. Works like a charm. Lord, these tomatoes look wonderful."

As she started buying, Luke told Romero, "When your appetite's off, it can mean your body needs to be detoxified. These cabbage, broccoli, and cauliflower are good for that. Completely organic. No chemicals of any kind ever went near them. And you might try *this."* He handed Romero a small bottle of white liquid.

"Milk thistle," the sergeant's wife said, glancing at the bottle while selecting green peppers. "Cleans out the liver."

"Where on earth did you learn about this stuff?" the sergeant asked.

"Rosa down the street got interested in herbal remedies," she answered as the three of them crossed the train tracks carrying sacks of vegetables. "Hey, this is Santa Fe, the world's capital of alternate medicines and New Age religions. If you can't beat 'em, join 'em."

"Yeah, those crystals around their necks. They're New Agers for sure," Romero said. "Did you notice their belts were made of hemp? No leather. Nothing from animals."

"No fried chicken and take-out burgers for those guys." The sergeant gave Romero a pointed look. "They're as healthy as can be."

"All right, okay, I get it."

"Just make sure you eat your greens."

The odd part was that he actually did start feeling better. Physically, at least. His emotions were still as bleak as midnight, but as one of the self-help books he'd read had said, "One way to heal yourself is from the body to the soul." The echinacea (ten drops in a glass of water, the typed directions said) tasted bitter. The milk thistle tasted worse. The salads didn't fill him up. He still craved a pepperoni pizza. But he had to admit, the vegetables at the Farmers' Market were as good as any he'd come across. No surprise. The only vegetables he'd eaten before came from a supermarket, where they'd sat for God knew how long, and that didn't count all the time they'd been in a truck on the way to the store. They'd probably been picked before they were ready so they wouldn't ripen until they reached the supermarket, and then there was the issue of how many pesticides and herbicides they'd been doused with. He remembered a radio call-in show that had talked about poisons in food. The program had dealt with similar problems in the environment and—

Romero shivered.

That program had been the one he'd listened to in his car the night he'd been waiting for the shoes to drop and his son had been killed.

Screw it. If I'm going to feel this bad, I'm going to eat what I want.

It took him only fifteen minutes to drive in from El Dorado and get a big take-out order of ribs, fries, cole slaw, and plenty of barbecue sauce. He never ate in restaurants anymore. Too many people knew him. He couldn't muster the energy for small talk. Another fifteen minutes and he was back at home, watching a lawyer show, drinking beer, gnawing on ribs.

He was sick before the ten o'clock news.

"I swear, I'm keeping to my diet. Hey, don't look at me like that. I admit I had a couple of relapses, but I learned my lesson. I've never eaten more whole-some food in my life."

"Fifteen pounds. That health club I joined really sweats the weight off."

"Hi, Mark."

The tall, thin, sandy-haired young man behind the vegetables looked puzzled at him.

"What's wrong?" Romero asked. "I've been coming to this market every Saturday for the past six weeks. You don't recognize me by now?"

"You've confused me with my brother." The man had blue eyes, a hint of their color in the crystal around his neck. Jeans, a white T-shirt, a glowing tan, and the thin-faced, high-cheekboned aesthetic look of a saint.

"Well, I know you're not Luke. I'm sure I'd recognize *him*."

"My name is John." His tone was formal.

"Pleased to meet you. I'm Gabe Romero. Nobody told me there were *three* brothers."

"Actually—"

"Wait a minute. Let me guess. If there's a Mark, Luke, and John, there's got to be a Matthew, right? I bet there are *four* of you."

John's lips parted slightly, as if he wasn't accustomed to smiling. "Very good."

"No big deal. It's my business to deduce things," Romero joked.

"Oh? And what business is—" John straightened, his blues eyes as cold as a star, watching Luke come through the crowd. "You were told not to leave the stand."

"I'm sorry. I had to go to the bathroom."

"You should have gone before we started out."

"I did. But I can't help it if—"

"That's right. You can't help me if you're not here. We're almost out of squash. Bring another basket."

"I'm really sorry. It won't happen again."

Luke glanced self-consciously at Romero, then back at his brother, and went to get the squash.

"Are you planning to buy something?" John asked.

You don't exactly win friends and influence people, do you? Romero thought. "Yeah, I'll take a couple of those squash. I guess with the early frost that's predicted, these'll be the last of the tomatoes and peppers, huh?"

John simply looked at him.

"I'd better stock up," Romero said.

He had hoped that the passage of time would ease his numbness, but each season only reminded him. Christmas, New Year's, then Easter, and too soon after that, the middle of May. Oddly, he had never associated his son's death with the scene of the accident on the Interstate. Always the emotional connection was with that section of road by the Baptist church at the top of the hill on Old Pecos Trail. He readily admitted that it was masochism that made him drive by there so often as the anniversary of the death approached. He was so preoccupied that for a moment he was convinced that he had willed himself into reliving the sequence, that he was hallucinating as he crested the hill and for the first time in almost a year saw a pair of shoes on the road.

Rust-colored, ankle-high hiking boots. They so surprised him that he slowed down and stared. The close look made him notice something so alarming that he slammed on his brakes, barely registering the squeal of tires behind him as the car that followed almost hit the cruiser. Trembling, he got out, crouched, stared even more closely at the hiking boots, and rushed toward his two-way radio.

The shoes had feet in them.

As an approaching police car wailed and officers motioned for traffic to go past on the shoulder of the road, Romero stood with his sergeant, the police chief, and the medical examiner, watching the lab crew do its work. His cruiser remained where he had stopped it next to the shoes. A waist-high screen had been put up.

"I'll know more when we get the evidence to the lab," the medical examiner said, "but judging from the straight clean lines, I'm assuming that something like a power saw was used to sever the feet from the legs."

Romero bit his lower lip.

"Anything else you can tell us right away?" the police chief asked.

"There isn't any blood on the pavement, which means that the blood on the shoes and the stumps of the feet was dry before they were dropped here. The discoloration of the tissue suggests that at least twenty-four hours passed between the crime and the disposal."

"Anybody notice anything else?"

"The size of the shoes," Romero said.

They looked at him.

"Mine are tens. These look to be sevens or eights. My guess is, the victim was female."

. . .

The same police officers who had left the pile of old shoes in front of Romero's locker now praised his instincts. Although he had long since discarded the various shoes that he had collected in the trunk of the police car and of his private vehicle, no one blamed him. After all, so much time had gone by, who could have predicted that the shoes would be important? Still, he remembered what kind they had been, just as he remembered that he had started noticing them almost exactly a year ago, around the fifteenth of May.

But there was no guarantee that the person who had dropped the shoes a year ago was the person who had left the severed feet. All the investigating team could do was deal with the little evidence they had. As Romero suspected, the medical examiner eventually determined that the victim had indeed been a woman. Was the person responsible a tourist, someone who came back to Santa Fe each May? If so, would that person have committed similar crimes somewhere else? Inquiries to the FBI revealed that over the years numerous murders by amputation had been committed throughout the United States, but none matched the profile that the team was dealing with. What about missing persons reports? Those in New Mexico were eliminated, but as the search spread, it became clear that so many thousands of people disappeared in the United States each month that the investigation team would need more staff than it could ever hope to have.

Meanwhile, Romero was part of the team staking out that area of Old Pecos Trail. Each night, he used a night-vision telescope to watch from the roof of the Baptist church. After all, if the killer stayed to his pattern, other shoes would be dropped, and perhaps—God help us, Romero thought—they too would contain severed feet. If he saw anything suspicious, all he needed to do was focus on the car's license plate and then use his two-way radio to alert police cars hidden along Old Pecos Trail. But night after night, there was nothing to report.

A week later, a current model red Saturn with New Hampshire plates was found abandoned in an arroyo southeast of Albuquerque. The car was registered to a thirty-year-old woman named Susan Crowell, who had set out with her fiancé on a cross-country car tour three weeks earlier. Neither she nor her fiancé had contacted their friends and relatives in the past eight days.

May became June, then July. The Fourth of July pancake breakfast in the historic plaza was its usual success. Three weeks later, Spanish Market occupied the same space, local Hispanic artisans displaying their paintings, icons, and woodwork. Tourist attendance was down, the sensationalist publicity about the severed feet having discouraged some visitors from coming. But a month after that, the similar but larger Indian Market occurred, and memories were evidently short, for now the usual thirty thousand tourists thronged the plaza to admire Native American jewelry and pottery.

Romero was on duty for all of these events, making sure that everything proceeded in an orderly fashion. Still, no matter the tasks assigned to him, his mind was always back on Old Pecos Trail. Some nights, he couldn't stay away. He drove over to East Lupita, watched the passing headlights on Old Pecos Trail, and brooded. He didn't expect anything to happen, not as fall approached, but being there made him feel on top of things, helped focus his thoughts, and in an odd way gave him a sense of being close to his son. Sometimes, the presence of the church across the street made him pray.

One night, a familiar pickup truck filled with moss rocks drove by. Romero remembered it from the night his son had been killed and from so many summer Saturdays when he'd watched baskets of vegetables being carried from it to a stand at the Farmers' Market. He had never stopped associating it with the shoes. Granted, at the time he'd been certain that he'd stopped the wrong vehicle. He didn't have a reason to take the huge step of suspecting that Luke Parsons had anything to do with the murders of Susan Crowell and her fiancé. Nonetheless, he had told the investigation team about that night the previous year, and they had checked Luke out as thoroughly as possible. He and his three brothers lived with their father on a farm in the Rio Grande gorge north of Dillon. They were hard workers, kept to themselves, and stayed out of trouble.

Seeing the truck pass, Romero didn't have a reason to make it stop, but that didn't mean he couldn't follow it. He pulled onto Old Pecos Trail and kept the truck's taillights in view as it headed into town. It turned right at the state capitol building and proceeded along Paseo de Peralta until on the other side of town it steered into an Allsup's gas station.

Romero chose a pump near the pickup truck, got out of his Jeep, and pretended to be surprised by the man next to him.

"Luke, it's Gabe Romero. How are you?"

Then he *was* surprised, realizing his mistake. This wasn't Luke.

"*John?* I didn't recognize you."

The tall, thin, sandy-haired, somber-eyed young man assessed him. He lowered his eyes to the holstered pistol on Romero's hip. Romero had never worn it to the Farmers' Market. "I didn't realize you were a police officer."

"Does it matter?"

"Only that it's reassuring to know my vegetables are safe when you're around." John's stern features took the humor out of the joke.

"Or your moss rocks." Romero pointed toward the back of the truck. "Been selling them over on that country road by the Interstate? That's usually Luke's job."

"Well, he has other things to do."

"Yeah, now that I think of it, I haven't seen him at the market lately."

"Excuse me. It's been a long day. It's a long drive back."

"You bet. I didn't mean to keep you."

•   •   •

Luke wasn't at the Farmer's Market the next Saturday or the final one the week after that.

Late October. There'd been a killing frost the night before, and in the morning there was snow in the mountains. Since the Farmers' Market was closed for the year and Romero had his Saturday free, he thought, Why don't I take a little drive?

The sunlight was cold, crisp, and clear as Romero headed north along Highway 285. He crested the hill near the modernistic Sante Fe Opera House and descended from the juniper-and-piñon-dotted slopes of town into a multicolored desert, its draws and mesas stretching dramatically away toward white-capped mountains on each side. No wonder Hollywood made so many westerns here, he thought. He passed the Camel Rock Indian casino and the Cities of Gold Indian casino, reaching what had once been another eternal construction project, the huge interchange that led west to Los Alamos.

But instead of heading toward the atomic city, he continued north, passing through Espanola, and now the landscape changed again, the hills on each side coming closer, the narrow highway passing between the ridges of the Rio Grande gorge. WATCH OUT FOR FALLING ROCK, a sign said. Yeah, I intend to watch out, he thought. On his left, partially screened by leafless trees, was the legendary Rio Grande, narrow, taking its time in the fall, gliding around curves, bubbling over boulders. On the far side of the river was Embudo Station, an old stagecoach stop the historic buildings of which had been converted into a microbrewery and a restaurant.

He passed it, heading farther north, and now the gorge began to widen. Farms and vineyards appeared on both sides of the road, where silt from melting during the Ice Age had made the soil rich. He stopped in Dillon, took care that his handgun was concealed by his zipped-up windbreaker, and asked at the general store if anybody knew where he could find the Parsons farm.

Fifteen minutes later, he had the directions he wanted. But instead of going directly to the farm, he drove to a scenic view outside town and waited for a state police car to pull up beside him. During the morning's drive, he had used his cellular phone to contact the state police barracks farther north in Taos. After explaining who he was, he had persuaded the dispatcher to send a cruiser down to meet him.

"I don't anticipate trouble," Romero told the burly trooper as they stood outside their cars and watched the Rio Grande flow through a chasm beneath them. "But you never know."

"So what do you want me to do?"

"Just park at the side of the highway. Make sure I come back out of the farm."

"Your department didn't send you up here?"

"Self-initiative. I've got a hunch."

The trooper looked doubtful. "How long are you going to be in there?"

"Considering how unfriendly they are, not long. Fifteen minutes. I just want to get a sense of the place."

"If I get a call about an emergency down the road . . ."

"You'll have to go. But I'd appreciate it if you came back and made sure I left the property. On my way to Santa Fe, I'll stop at the general store in Dillon and leave word that I'm okay."

The state trooper still looked doubtful.

"I've been working on this case a long time," Romero said. "Please, I'd really appreciate the help."

The dirt road was just after a sign that read, TAOS, 20 MILES. It was on the left of the highway and led down a slope toward fertile bottomland. To the north and west, ridges bordered the valley. Well-maintained rail fences enclosed rich, black soil. The Parsonses were certainly hard workers, he had to admit. With cold weather about to arrive, the fields had been cleared, everything ready for spring.

The road headed west toward a barn and outbuildings, all of them neat-looking, their white appearing freshly painted. A simple wood frame house, also white, had a pitched metal roof that gleamed in the autumn sun. Beyond the house was the river, about thirty feet wide, with a raised footbridge leading across to leafless aspen trees and scrub brush trailing up a slope.

As he drove closer, Romero saw movement at the barn, someone getting off a ladder, putting down a paint can. Someone else appeared at the barn's open doors. A third person came out of the house. They were waiting in front of the house as Romero pulled up and stopped.

This was the first time he'd seen three of the brothers together, their tall, lean, sandy-haired, blue-eyed similarities even more striking. They wore the same denim coveralls with the same blue wool shirts underneath.

But Romero was well enough acquainted with them that he could tell one from another. The brother on the left, about nineteen, must be the one he had never met.

"I assume you're Matthew." Romero got out of the car and walked toward them, extending his hand.

No one made a move to shake hands with him.

"I don't see Luke," Romero said.

"He has things to do," John said.

Their features were pinched.

"Why did you come here?" Mark asked.

"I was driving up to Taos. While I was in the neighborhood, I thought I'd drop by and see if you had any vegetables for sale."

"You're not welcome."

"What kind of attitude is that? For somebody who's been as good a customer as I have, I thought you might be pleased to see me."

"Leave."

"But don't you want my business?"

"Matthew, go in the house and bring me the phone. I'm going to call the state police."

The young man nodded and turned toward the house.

"That's fine," Romero said. "I'll be on my way."

The trooper was at the highway when Romero drove out.

"Thanks for the backup."

"You'd better not thank me. I just got a call about you. Whatever you did in there, you really pissed them off. The dispatcher says, if you come back they want you arrested for trespassing."

". . . the city's attorney," the police chief said.

The man's handshake was unenthusiastic.

"And this is Mr. Daly, the attorney for Mr. Parsons," the chief said.

An even colder handshake.

"Mr. Parsons you've definitely met," the chief said.

Romero nodded to John.

"I'll get right to the point," Daly said. "You've been harassing my client, and we want it stopped."

"Harassing? Wait a minute. I haven't been harassing—"

"Detaining the family vehicle without just cause. Intimidating my client and his brothers at their various places of business. Following my client. Confronting him in public places. Invading his property and refusing to leave when asked to. You crowd him just about everywhere he goes, and we want it stopped or we'll sue both you and the city. Juries don't like rogue cops."

"Rogue cop? What are you talking about?"

"I didn't come here to debate this." Daly stood, motioning for John to do the same. "My client's completely in the right. This isn't a police state. You, your department, and the city have been warned. Any more incidents, and I'll call a press conference to let every potential juror know why we're filing the lawsuit."

With a final searing gaze, Daly left the room. John followed almost immediately but not before he gave Romero a victimized look that made Romero's face turn warm with anger.

The officer became silent.

The city attorney cleared his throat. "I don't suppose I have to tell you to stay away from him."

"But I haven't done anything wrong."

"Did you follow him? Did you go to his home? Did you ask the state police in Taos for backup when you entered the property?"

Romero looked away.

"You were out of your jurisdiction, acting completely on your own."

"These brothers have something to do with—"

"They were investigated and cleared."

"I can't explain. It's a feeling that keeps nagging at me."

"Well, *I* have a feeling," the attorney said. "If you don't stop exceeding your authority, you're going to be out of a job, not to mention in court trying to explain to a jury why you harassed a group of brothers who look like advertisements for hard work and family values. Matthew, Mark, Luke and John, for God sake. If it wouldn't look like an admission of guilt, I'd recommend your dismissal right now."

Romero got the worst assignments. If a snowstorm took out power at an intersection and traffic needed to be directed by hand, he was at the top of the list to do it. Anything that involved the outdoors and bad weather, he was the man. Obviously, the police chief was inviting him to quit.

But Romero had a secret defense. The heat that had flooded his face when John gave him that victimized look hadn't gone away. It had stayed and spread, possessing his body. Directing traffic in a foot of snow, with a raging storm and a wind chill near zero? No problem. Anger made him as warm as could be.

John Parsons had arrogantly assumed he'd won. Romero was going to pay him back. May 15. That was about the time the shoes had appeared two years ago, and the severed feet last year. The chief was planning some surveillance on that section of Old Pecos Trail, but nobody believed that if the killer planned to act again, he'd be stupid enough to be that predictable. For certain, Romero wasn't going to be predictable. He wasn't going to play John's game and risk his job by hanging around Old Pecos Trail so that John could drive by and claim that the harassment had started again. No, Old Pecos Trail didn't interest him anymore. On May 15, he was going to be somewhere else.

Outside Dillon. In the Rio Grande gorge.

He planned it for quite a while. First, he had to explain his absence. A vacation. He hadn't taken one last year. San Francisco. He'd never been there. It was supposed to be especially beautiful in the spring. The chief looked pleased, as if he hoped Romero would look for a job there.

Second, his quarry knew the kind of car he drove. He traded his five-year-old green Jeep for a three-year-old blue Ford Explorer.

Third, he needed equipment. The night-vision telescope he'd used to watch Old Pecos Trail from the top of the church had made darkness so vivid that he bought a similar model from a military surplus store. He went to a camera store and bought a powerful zoom lens for the 35mm camera he had at home. Food and water for several days. Outdoor clothing. Something to carry everything in. Hiking shoes sturdy enough to support all the weight.

His vacation started on May 13. When he'd last driven to Dillon, autumn had made the Rio Grande calm, but now the spring snowmelt widened and deepened it, cresting it into a rage. Green trees and shrubs bordered the foaming water as white-water rafters shot through roiling channels and jounced over hidden rocks. As he drove past the entrance to the Parsons farm, he worried that one of the brothers might drive out and notice him, but then he reminded himself that they didn't know this car. He stared to his left at the rich black land, the white buildings in the distance, and the glinting metal roof of the house. At the far edge of the farm, the river raged high enough that it almost snagged the raised footbridge.

He put a couple of miles between him and the farm before he stopped. On his left, a rest area underneath cottonwoods looked to be the perfect place. A few other cars were there, all of them empty. White-water rafters, he assumed. At the end of the day, someone would drive them back to get their vehicles. In all the coming and going, his car would be just one of many that were parked there. To guard against someone's wondering why the car was there all night and worrying that he had drowned, he left a note on his dashboard that read, "Hiking and camping along the river. Back in a couple of days."

He opened the rear hatch, put on the heavy backpack, secured its straps, locked the car, and walked down a rocky slope, disappearing among bushes. He had spent several evenings at home, practicing with the fully loaded knapsack, but his brick floors hadn't prepared him for the uneven terrain that he now labored over—rocks, holes, and fallen branches, each jarring step seeming to add weight to his backpack. More, he had practiced in the cool of evening, but now, in the heat of the day, with the temperature predicted to reach a high of eighty, he sweated profusely, his wet clothes clinging to him.

His pack weighed sixty pounds. Without it, he was sure he could have reached the river in ten minutes. Under the circumstances, he took twenty. Not bad, he thought, hearing the roar of the current. Emerging from the scrub brush, he was startled by how fast and high the water was, how humblingly powerful. It was so swift that it created a breeze, for which he was grateful as he set down his backpack and flexed his stiff shoulders. He drank from his canteen. The water had been cool when he had left the house but was now tepid, with a vague metallic taste.

Get to work, he told himself.

Without the backpack, the return walk to the car was swift. In a hurry, he unlocked the Explorer, removed another sack, relocked the car, and carried his second burden down the slope into the bushes, reaching the river five minutes sooner than he had earlier. The sack contained a small rubber raft, which after he used a pressurized cannister to inflate it had plenty of room for himself and his backpack. Making sure that the latter was securely attached, he studied the heaving water, took a deep breath, exhaled, and pushed it into the river.

Icy water splashed across him. If not for his daily workouts on exercise machines, he never would have had the strength to paddle so hard and fast, constantly switching sides, keeping the raft from spinning. But the river carried him downstream faster than he had anticipated. He was in the middle, but no matter how hard he fought, he didn't seem to be getting closer to the other side. He didn't know what scared him worse, being overturned or not reaching the opposite bank before the current carried him to the farm. Jesus, if they see me . . . He worked his arms to their maximum. Squinting to see through spray, he saw that the river curved to the left. The current on the far side wasn't as strong. Paddling in a frenzy, he felt the raft shoot close to the bank. Ten feet. Five. He braced himself. The moment the raft jolted against the shore, he scrambled over the front rim, landed on the muddy bank, almost fell into the water, righted himself, and dragged the raft onto the shore.

His backpack sat in water in the raft. Hurriedly, he freed the straps that secured it, then dragged it onto dry land. Water trickled out the bottom. He could only hope that the waterproof bags into which he had sealed his food, clothes, and equipment had done their job. Had anyone seen him? He scanned the ridge behind him and the shore across from him—they seemed deserted. He overturned the raft, dumped the water out of it, tugged the raft behind bushes, and concealed it. He set several large rocks in it to keep it from blowing away, then returned to the shore and satisfied himself that the raft couldn't be seen. But he couldn't linger. He hoisted his pack onto his shoulders, ignored the strain on his muscles, and started inland.

Three hours later, after following a trail that led along the back of the ridge that bordered the river, he finished the long, slow, difficult hike to the top. The scrub brush was sparse, the rocks unsteady under his waffle-soled boots. Fifteen yards from the summit, he lowered his backpack and flexed his arms and shoulders to ease their cramps. Sweat dripped from his face. He drank from his canteen, the water even more tepid, then sank to the rocks and crept upward. Cautiously, he peered over the top. Below were the white barn and outbuildings. Sunlight gleamed off the white house's pitched metal roof. Portions of the land were green from early crops, one of which Romero recognized even from a distance: lettuce. No one was in view. He found a hollow, eased into it, and dragged his backpack after him. Two rocks on the rim concealed the silhouette of his head when he peered down between them. River, field, farmhouse, barn, more fields. A perfect vantage point.

Still, no one was in view. Some of them are probably in Santa Fe, he thought. As long as nothing's happening, this is a good time to get settled. He removed his night-vision telescope, his camera, and his zoom lens from the backpack. The waterproof bags had worked—the equipment was dry. So were his food and his sleeping bag. The only items that had gotten wet were a spare shirt and pair of jeans that, ironically, he had brought with him in case he needed a dry change of clothes. He spread them out in the sun, took another look at the farm—no activity—and ravenously reached for his food. Cheddar cheese, wheat crackers, sliced carrots, and a dessert of dehydrated apricots made his mouth water as he chewed them.

．　．　．

Five o'clock. One of the brothers crossed from the house to the barn. Hard to tell at a distance, but through the camera's zoom lens, Romero thought he recognized Mark.

Six-thirty. Small down there, the pickup truck arrived. It got bigger as Romero adjusted the zoom lens and recognized John getting out. Mark came out of the barn. Matthew came out of the house. John look displeased about something. Mark said something. Matthew stayed silent. They entered the house.

Romero's heart beat faster with the satisfaction that he was watching his quarry and they didn't know it. But his exhilaration faded as dusk thickened, lights came on in the house, and nothing else happened. Without the sun, the air cooled rapidly. As frost came out of his mouth, he put on gloves and a jacket.

Maybe I'm wasting my time, he thought.

Like hell. It's not the fifteenth yet.

The temperature continued dropping. His legs cold despite the jeans he wore, he squirmed into the welcome warmth of his sleeping bag and chewed more cheese and crackers as he switched from the zoom lens to the night-vision telescope. The scope brightened the darkness, turning everything green. The lights in the windows were radiant. One of the brothers left the house, but the scope's definition was a little grainy, and Romero couldn't tell who it was. The person went into the barn and returned to the house ten minutes later.

One by one, the lights went off. The house was soon in darkness.

Looks like the show's over for a while, Romero thought. It gave him an opportunity to get out of his sleeping bag, work his way down the slope, and relieve himself behind a bush. When he returned, the house seemed as quiet as when he had gone away.

Again, he reminded himself, today's not important. Tomorrow might not be, either. But the *next* day's the fifteenth.

He checked that his handgun and his cellular phone were within easy reach (all the comforts of home), settled deeper into the sleeping bag, and refocused the night-vision scope on the farm below. Nothing.

The cold made his eyes feel heavy.

A door slammed.

Jerking his head up, Romero blinked to adjust his eyes to the bright morning light. He squirmed from his sleeping bag and used the camera's zoom lens to peer down at the farm. John, Mark, and Matthew had come out of the house. They marched toward the nearest field, the one that had lettuce in it. The green shoots glistened from the reflection of sunlight off melted frost. John looked as displeased as on the previous evening, speaking irritably to his brothers. Mark said something in return. Matthew said nothing.

Romero frowned. This was one too many times that he hadn't seen Luke. What had happened to him? Adjusting the zoom lens, he watched the group go into the barn. Another question nagged at him. The police report had said that the brothers worked for their father, that this was their father's land. But when Romero had come to the farm the previous fall, he hadn't seen the father.

Or yesterday.

Or this morning.

Where the hell was he? Was the father somehow responsible for the shoes and . . .

Were the father and Luke not on the farm because they were somewhere else, doing . . .

The more questions he had, the more his mind spun.

He tensed, seeing a glint of something reflect off melted frost on grass beside the barn door. Frowning harder, he saw the glint dart back and forth, as if alive. Oh, my Jesus, he thought, suddenly realizing what it was, pulling his camera away from the rim. He was on the western ridge, staring east. The sun above the opposite ridge had reflected off his zoom lens. If the light had reflected while the brothers were outside . . .

The cold air felt even colder. Leaving the camera and its zoom lens well below the rim, he warily eased his head up and studied the barn. Five minutes later, the three brothers emerged and began to do chores. Watching, Romero opened a plastic bag of Cheerios, Wheat Chex, raisins, and nuts that he'd mixed together, munching the trail mix, washing it down with water. From the drop in temperature the previous night, the water in his canteen was again cold. But the canteen was almost empty. He had brought two others, and they would last him for a while. Eventually, though, he was going to have to return to the river and use a filtration pump to refill the canteens. Iodine tablets would kill the bacteria.

By mid-afternoon, the brothers were all in one field, Matthew on a tractor, tilling the soil, while John and Mark picked up large rocks that the winter had forced to the surface, carrying them to the back of the pickup truck.

I'm wasting my time, he thought. They're just farmers, for God sake.

Then why did John try to get me fired?

He clenched his teeth. With the sun behind his back, it was safe to use the camera's zoom lens. He scanned the farm, staring furiously at the brothers. The evening was a replay of the previous one. By ten, the house was in darkness.

Just one more day, Romero thought. Tomorrow's the fifteenth. Tomorrow's what I came for.

· · ·

Pain jolted him into consciousness. A walloping burst of agony made his mind spin. A third cracking impact sent a flash of red behind his eyes. Stunned, he fought to overcome the shock of the attack and thrashed to get out of his sleeping bag. A blow across his shoulders knocked him sideways. Silhouetted against the starry sky, three figures surrounded him, their heavy breath frosty as they raised their clubs to strike him again. He grabbed his pistol and tried to free it from the sleeping bag, but a blow knocked it out of his numbed hand an instant before a club across his forehead made his ears ring and his eyes roll up.

He awoke slowly, his senses in chaos. Throbbing in his head. Blood on his face. The smell of it. Coppery. The nostril-irritating smell of stale straw under his left cheek. Shadows. Sunlight through cracks in a wall. The barn. Spinning. His stomach heaved.

The sour smell of vomit.

"Matthew, bring John," Mark said.

Rumbling footsteps ran out of the barn.

Romero passed out.

The next time he awoke, he was slumped in a corner, his back against a wall, his knees up, his head sagging, blood dripping onto his chest.

"We found your car," John said. "I see you changed models."

The echoing voice seemed to come from a distance, but when Romero looked blearily up, John was directly before him.

John read the note Romero had left on the dashboard. " 'Hiking and camping along the river. Back in a couple of days.' "

Romero noticed that his pistol was tucked under John's belt.

"What are we going to do?" Mark asked. "The police will come looking for him."

"So what?" John said. "We're in the right. We caught a man with a pistol who trespassed on our property at night. We defended ourselves and subdued him." John crumbled the note. "But the police won't come looking for him. They don't know he's here."

"You can't be sure," Mark said.

Matthew stood silently by the closed barn door.

"Of course, I can be sure," John said. "If this was a police operation, he wouldn't have needed this note. He wouldn't have been worried that someone would wonder about the abandoned car. In fact, he wouldn't have needed his car at all. The police would have driven him to the drop-off point. He's on his own."

Matthew fidgeted, continuing to watch.

"Isn't that right, Officer Romero?" John asked.

Fighting to control the spinning in his mind, Romero managed to get his voice to work. "How did you know I was up there?"

No one answered.

"It was the reflection from the camera lens, right?" Romero sounded as if his throat had been stuffed with gravel.

"Like the Holy Spirit on Pentecost," John said.

Romero's tongue was so thick he could barely speak. "I need water."

"I don't like this," Mark said. "Let him go."

John turned toward Matthew. "You heard him. He needs water."

Matthew hesitated, then opened the barn door and ran toward the house.

John returned his attention to Romero. "Why wouldn't you stop? Why did you have to be so persistent?"

"Where's Luke?"

"See, that's what I mean. You're so damnably persistent."

"We don't need to take this any further," Mark warned. "Put him in his car. Let him go. No harm's been done."

"Hasn't there?"

"You just said we were in the right to attack a stranger with a gun. After it was too late, we found out who he is. A judge would throw out an assault charge."

"He'd come back."

"Not necessarily."

"I guarantee it. Wouldn't you, Officer Romero? You'd come back."

Romero wiped blood from his face and didn't respond.

"Of course, you would," John said. "It's in your nature. And one day you'd see something you shouldn't. It may be you already have."

"Don't say anything more," Mark warned.

"You want to know what this is about?" John asked Romero.

Romero wiped more blood from his face.

"I think you should get what you want," John said.

"No," Mark said. "This can't go on anymore. I'm still not convinced he's here by himself. If the police are involved . . . It's too risky. It has to stop."

Footsteps rushed toward the barn. Only Romero looked as Matthew hurried inside, carrying a jug of water.

"Give it to him," John said.

Matthew warily approached, like someone apprehensive about a wild animal. He set the jug at Romero's feet and darted back.

"Thank you," Romero said.

Matthew didn't answer.

"Why don't you ever speak?" Romero asked.

Matthew didn't say anything.

Romero's skin prickled. "You can't."

Matthew looked away.

"Of course. Last fall when I was here, John told you to bring him the phone so he could call the state police. At the time, I didn't think anything of it." Romero waited for the swirling in his mind to stop. "I figured he was sending the weakest one of the group, so if I made trouble he and Mark could take care of it." Romero's lungs felt empty. He took several deep breaths. "But all the time I've been watching the house, you haven't said a word."

Matthew kept looking away.

"You're mute. That's why John told you to bring the phone. Because you couldn't call the state police yourself."

"Stop taunting my brother and drink the water," John said.

"I'm not taunting him. I just—"

"*Drink it.*"

Romero fumbled for the jug, raised it to his lips, and swallowed, not caring about the sour taste from having been sick, wanting only to clear the mucus from his mouth and the gravel in his throat.

John pulled a clean handkerchief from his windbreaker pocket and threw it to him. "Pour water on it. Wipe the blood from your face. We're not animals. There's no need to be without dignity."

Baffled by the courtesy, Romero did what he was told. The more they treated him like a human being, the more chance he had of getting away from here. He tried desperately to think of a way to talk himself out of this. "You're wrong about the police not being involved."

"Oh?" John raised his eyebrows, waiting for Romero to continue.

"This isn't official, sure. But I do have backup. I told my sergeant what I planned to do. The deal is, if I don't use my cell phone to call him every six hours, he'll know something's wrong. He and a couple of friends on the force will come here looking for me."

"My, my. Is that a fact."

"Yes."

"Then why don't you call him and tell him you're all right?"

"Because I'm *not* all right. Look, I have no idea what's going on here, and all of a sudden, believe me, it's the last thing I want to find out. I just want to get out of here."

The barn became terribly silent.

"I made a mistake." Romero struggled to his feet. "I won't make it again. I'll leave. This is the last time you'll see me." Off balance, he stepped out of the corner.

John studied him.

"As far as I'm concerned, this is the end of it." Romero took another step toward the door.

"I don't believe you."

Romero stepped past him.

"You're lying about the cell phone and about your sergeant," John said.

Romero kept walking. "If I don't call him soon—"

John blocked his way.

"—he'll come looking for me."

"And here he'll find you."

"Being held against my will."

"So we'll be charged with kidnapping?" John spread his hands. "Fine. We'll tell the jury we were only trying to scare you to keep you from continuing to stalk us. I'm willing to take the chance that they won't convict us."

"*What are you talking about?*" Mark said.

"Let's see if his friends really come to the rescue."

Oh, shit, Romero thought. He took a further step toward the door.

John pulled out Romero's pistol.

"No!" Mark said.

"Matthew, help Mark with the trapdoor."

"This has to stop!" Mark said. "*Wasn't what happened to Matthew and Luke enough?*"

Like a tightly wound spring that was suddenly released, John whirled and struck Mark with such force that he knocked him to the floor. "Since when do you run this family?"

Wiping blood from his mouth, Mark glared up at him. "I don't. *You* do."

"That's right. I'm the oldest. That's always been the rule. If you'd have been meant to run this family, you'd have been the firstborn."

Mark kept glaring.

"Do you want to turn against the rule?" John asked.

Mark lowered his eyes. "No."

"Then help Matthew with the trapdoor."

Romero's stomach fluttered. All the while John aimed the pistol at him, he watched Mark and Matthew go to the far left corner, where it took both of them to shift a barrel of grain out of the way. They lifted a trapdoor, and Romero couldn't help bleakly thinking that someone pushing from below wouldn't have a chance of moving it when the barrel was in place.

"Get down there," John said.

Romero felt dizzier. Fighting to repress the sensation, he knew that he had to do something before he felt any weaker.

If John wanted me dead, he'd have killed me by now.

Romero bolted for the outside door.

"Mark!"

Something whacked against Romero's legs, tripping him, slamming his face hard onto the floor.

Mark had thrown a club.

The three brothers grabbed him. Dazed, the most powerless he'd ever felt, he thrashed, unable to pull away from their hands, as they dragged him across the dusty floor and shoved him through the trapdoor. If he hadn't grasped the ladder, he'd have fallen.

"You don't want to be without water." John handed the jug down to him.

A chill breeze drifted from below. Terrified, Romero watched the trap-door being closed over him and heard the scrape of the barrel being shifted back into place.

God help me, he thought.

But he wasn't in darkness. Peering down, he saw a faint light and warily descended the ladder, moving awkwardly because of the jug he held. At the bottom, he found a short tunnel and proceeded along it. An earthy musty smell made his nostrils contract. The light became brighter as he neared its source in a small plywood-walled room that he saw had a wooden chair and table. The floor was made from plywood, also. The light came from a bare bulb attached to one of the sturdy beams in the ceiling. Stepping all the way in, he saw a cot on the left. A clean pillow and blanket were on it. To the right, a toilet seat was attached to a wooden box positioned above a deep hole in the ground. I'm going to lose my mind, he thought.

The breeze, weak now that the trapdoor was closed, came from a vent in an upper part of the farthest wall. Romero guessed that the duct would be long and that there would be baffles at the end so that, if Romero screamed for help, no one who happened to come onto the property would be able to hear him. The vent provided enough air that Romero wasn't worried about suffocating. There were plenty of other things to worry about, but at least not that.

The plywood of the floor and walls was discolored with age. Nonetheless, the pillow and the blanket had been stocked recently—when Romero raised them to his nose, there was a fresh laundry smell beneath the loamy odor that it had started absorbing.

The brothers couldn't have known I'd be here. They were expecting someone else.

Who?

Romero smelled something else. He told himself that it was only his imagination, but he couldn't help sensing that the walls were redolent with the sweaty stench of fear, as if many others had been imprisoned here.

His own fear made his mouth so dry that he took several deep swallows of water. Setting the jug on the table, he stared apprehensively at a door across from him. It was just a simple old wooden door, vertical planks held in place by horizontal boards nailed to the top, middle, and bottom, but it filled him with apprehension. He knew that he had to open it, that he had to learn if it gave him a way to escape, but he had a terrible premonition that something unspeakable waited on the other side. He told his legs to move. They refused. He told his right arm to reach for the doorknob. It, too, refused.

The spinning sensation in his mind was now aggravated by the short quick breaths he was taking. I'm hyperventilating, he realized, and struggled to return his breath rate to normal. Despite the coolness of the chamber, his face dripped sweat. In contrast, his mouth was drier than ever. He gulped more water.

Open the door.

His body reluctantly obeyed, his shaky legs taking him across the chamber, his trembling hand reaching for the doorknob. He pulled. Nothing happened, and for a moment he thought that the door was locked, but when he pulled harder, the door creaked slowly open, the loamy odor from inside reaching his nostrils before his eyes adjusted to the shadows in there.

For a terrible instant, he thought he was staring at bodies. He almost stumbled back, inwardly screaming, until a remnant of his sanity insisted that he stare harder, that what he was looking at were bulging burlap sacks.

And baskets.

And shelves of . . .

Vegetables.

Potatoes, beets, turnips, onions.

Jesus, this was the root cellar under the barn. Repelled by the musty odor, he searched for another door. He tapped the walls, hoping for a hollow sound that would tell him there was an open space, perhaps another room or even the outside, beyond it.

He found nothing to give him hope.

"Officer Romero?" The faint voice came from the direction of the trapdoor.

Romero stepped out of the root cellar and closed the door.

"Officer Romero?" The voice sounded like John's.

Romero left the chamber and stopped halfway along the corridor, not wanting to show himself. A beam of pale light came down through the open trapdoor. "What?"

"I've brought you something to eat."

A basket sat at the bottom of the ladder. Presumably John had lowered it by a rope and then pulled the rope back up before calling to Romero.

"I'm not hungry."

"If I were you, I'd eat. After all, you have no way of telling when I might bring you another meal."

Romero's empty stomach cramped.

"Also, you'll find a book in the basket, something for you to pass the time. D. H. Lawrence. Seems appropriate since he lived on a ranch a little to the north of us outside Taos. In fact, he's buried there."

"I don't give a shit. What do you intend to do with me?" Romero was startled by how shaky his voice sounded.

John didn't answer.

"If you let me go right now, I'll forget this happened. None of this has gone so far that it can't be undone."

The trapdoor was closed. The pale beam of light disappeared.

Above, there were scraping sounds as the barrel was put back into place.

Romero wanted to scream.

He picked up the basket and examined its contents. Bread, cheese, sliced carrots, two apples . . . and a book. It was a tattered blue hardback without a cover. The title on its spine read, *D. H. Lawrence: Selected Stories*. There was a bookmark at a story called "The Woman Who Rode Away." The pages in that section of the book had been so repeatedly turned that the upper corners were almost worn through.

The blows to Romero's head made him feel as if a spike had been driven into it. Breathing more rapidly, dizzier than ever, he went back to the chamber. He put the basket on the table, then sat on the cot and felt so weak that he wanted to lie down, but he told himself that he had to look at the story. One thing you could say for certain about John, he wasn't whimsical. The story was important.

Romero opened the book. For a harrowing moment, his vision doubled. He strained to focus his eyes, and as quickly as the problem had occurred, it went away, his vision again clear. But he knew what was happening. I've got a concussion.

I need to get to a hospital.

Damn it, concentrate.

"The Woman Who Rode Away."

The story was set in Mexico. It was about a woman married to a wealthy industrialist who owned bountiful silver mines in the Sierra Madre. She had a healthy son and daughter. Her husband adored her. She had every comfort she could imagine. But she couldn't stop feeling smothered, as if she was another of her husband's possessions, as if he and her children owned her. Each day, she spent more and more time staring longingly at the mountains. What's up there? she wondered. Surely it must be something wonderful. The secret villages. One day, she went out horseback riding and never came back.

Romero stopped reading. The shock of his injuries had drained him. He had trouble holding his throbbing head up. At the same time, his empty stomach cramped again. I have to keep up my strength, he thought. Forcing himself to stand, he went over to the basket of food, chewed on a carrot, and took a bite out of a freshly baked, thickly crusted chunk of bread. He swallowed more water and went back to the cot.

The break hadn't done any good. As exhausted as ever, he reopened the book.

The woman rode into the mountains. She had brought enough food for several days, and as she rode higher, she let her horse choose whatever trails it wanted. Higher and higher. Past pines and aspens and cottonwoods until, as the vegetation thinned and the altitude made her light-headed, Indians greeted her on the trail and asked where she was going. To the secret villages, she told them. To see their houses and to learn about their gods. The Indians escorted her into a lush valley that had trees, a river, and groups of low flat gleaming houses. There, the villagers welcomed her and promised to teach her.

Romero saw double again. Frightened, he struggled to control his vision. The concussion's getting worse, he thought. Fear made him weaker. He wanted to lie down, but he knew that, if he fell asleep, he might never wake up. Shout for help, he thought in a panic.

To whom? Nobody can hear me. Not even the brothers.

Rousing himself, he went over to the table, bit off another chunk of bread, ate a piece of apple, and sat down to finish the story. It was supposed to tell him something, he was sure, but so far he hadn't discovered what it was.

The woman had the sense of being in a dream. The villagers treated her well, bringing her flowers and clothes, food and drinks made of honey. She spent her days in a pleasant languor. She had never slept so long and deeply. Each evening, the pounding of drums was hypnotic. The seasons turned. Fall became winter. Snow fell. The sun was angry, the villagers said on the shortest day of the year. The moon must be given to the sun. They carried the woman to an altar, took off her clothes, and plunged a knife into her chest.

The shocking last page made Romero jerk his head up. The woman's death was all the more unnerving because she knew it was coming and she surrendered to it, didn't try to fight it, almost welcomed it. She seemed apart from herself, in a daze.

Romero shivered. As his eyelids drooped again, he thought about the honey drinks that the villagers had kept bringing her.

They must have been drugged.

Oh, shit, he thought. It took all of his willpower to raise his sagging head and peer toward the basket and the jug on the table.

The food and water are drugged.

A tingle of fear swept through him, the only sensation he could still feel. His head was so numb that it had stopped aching. His hands and feet didn't seem to be a part of him. I'm going to pass out, he thought sickly.

He started to lie back.

No.

Can't.

Don't.

Get your lazy ass off this cot. If you fall asleep, you'll die.

Mind spinning, he wavered to his feet. Stumbled toward the table. Banged against it. Almost knocked it over. Straightened. Lurched toward the toilet seat. Bent over it. Stuck his finger down his throat. Vomited the food and water he'd consumed.

He wavered into the corridor, staggered to the ladder, gripped it, turned, staggered back, reached the door to the root cellar, turned, and stumbled back to the ladder.

He did it again.

You have to keep walking.

And again.

You've got to stay on your feet.

His knees buckled. He forced them to straighten.

His vision turned gray. He stumbled onward, using his arms to guide him.

It was the hardest thing he had ever done. It took more discipline and determination than he knew he possessed. I won't give up, he kept saying. It became a mantra. I won't give up.

Time became a blur, delirium a constant. Somewhere in his long ordeal, his vision cleared, his legs became stronger. He allowed himself to hope, when his headache returned, the drug was wearing off. Instead of wavering, he walked.

And kept walking, pumping himself up. I have to be ready, he thought. As his mind became more alert, it nonetheless was seized by confusion. Why had John wanted him to read the story? Wasn't it the same as a warning not to eat the food and drink the water?

Or maybe it was an explanation of what was happening. A choice that was offered. Spare yourself the agony of panic. Eat from the bounty of the earth and surrender as the woman had done.

Like hell.

Romero dumped most of the water down the toilet seat. It helped to dissipate his vomit down there so that it wouldn't be obvious what he had done. He left a small piece of bread and a few carrot sticks. He bit into the apples and spit out the pieces, leaving cores. He took everything else into the root cellar and hid it in the darkest corner behind baskets of potatoes.

He checked his watch. It had been eleven in the morning when they had forced him down here. It was now almost midnight. Hearing the faint scrape of the barrel being moved, he lay down on the cot, closed his eyes, dangled an arm onto the floor, and tried to control his frantic breathing enough to look unconscious.

"Be careful. He might be bluffing."

"Most of the food's gone."

"Stay out of my line of fire."

Hands grabbed him, lifting. A deadweight, he felt himself being carried along the corridor. He murmured as if he didn't want to be wakened. After securing a harness around him, one brother went up the ladder and pulled on a rope while the other brothers lifted him. In the barn, as they took off the harness, he moved his head and murmured again.

"Let's see if he can stand," John said.

Romero allowed his eyelids to flicker.

"He's coming around," Mark said.

"Then he can help us."

They carried him into the open. He moved his head from side to side, as if aroused by the cold night air. They put him in the back of the pickup truck. Two brothers stayed with him while the other drove. The night was so cold that he allowed himself to shiver.

"Yeah, definitely coming around," John said.

The truck stopped. He was lifted out and carried into a field. Allowing his eyelids to open a little farther, Romero was amazed at how bright the moon was. He saw that the field was the same one that he had seen the brothers tilling and removing stones from the day before.

They set him on his feet.

He pretended to waver.

Heart pounding, he knew that he had to do something soon. Until now, he had felt helpless against the three of them. The barn had been too constricting a place in which to try to fight. He needed somewhere in the open, somewhere that allowed him to run. This field was going to have to be it. Because he knew without a doubt that this was where they intended to kill him.

"Put him on his knees," John said.

"It's still not too late to stop this," Mark said.

"Have you lost your faith?"

"I . . ."

"Answer me. Have you lost your faith?"

". . . No."

"Then put him on his knees."

Romero allowed himself to be lowered. His heart was beating so frantically that he feared it would burst against his ribs. A sharp stone hurt his knees. He couldn't allow himself to react.

They leaned him forward on his hands. Like an animal. His neck was exposed.

"Prove your faith, Mark."

Something scraped, a knife being pulled from a scabbard.

It glinted in the moonlight.

"Take it," John said.

"But—"

"Prove your faith."

A long tense pause.

"Yes," John said. "Lord, accept this sacrifice in thanks for the glory of your earth and the bounty that comes from it. The blood of—"

Feeling another sharp rock, this one beneath his palm, Romero gripped it, spun, and hurled it as strongly as he could at the head of the figure nearest him. The rock made a terrible crunching noise, the figure groaning and dropping, as Romero charged to his feet and yanked the knife from Mark's hands. He drove it into Mark's stomach and stormed toward the remaining brother, whom he recognized as John because of the pistol in his hand. But before Romero could strike him with the knife, John stumbled back, aiming, and Romero had no choice except to hurl the knife. It hit John, but whether it injured him, Romero couldn't tell. At least it made John stumble back farther, his aim wide, the gunshot plowing into the earth, and by then Romero was racing past the pickup truck, into the lane, toward the house.

John fired again. The bullet struck the pickup truck.

Running faster, propelled by fear, Romero saw the lights of the house ahead and veered to the left so he wouldn't be a silhouette. A third shot, a bullet buzzing past him, shattered a window in the house. He stretched his legs to the maximum. His chest heaved. As the house got larger before him, he heard the roar of the pickup truck behind him. I have to get off the lane. He veered farther to the left, scrambled over a rail fence, and raced across a field of chard, his panicked footsteps mashing the tender shoots.

Headlights gleamed behind him. The truck stopped. A fourth shot broke the silence of the valley. John obviously assumed that in this isolated area there was a good chance a neighbor wouldn't hear. Or care. Trouble with coyotes.

A fifth shot stung Romero's left shoulder. Breathing rapidly and hoarsely, he zigzagged. At the same time, he bent forward, running as fast as he could while staying low. He came to another fence, squirmed between its rails, and rushed into a further field, crushing further crops—radishes, he dimly thought.

The truck roared closer along the lane.

Another roar matched it, the roiling power of the Rio Grande as Romero raced nearer. The lights of the house were to his right now. He passed them, reaching the darkness at the back of the farm. The river thundered more loudly.

Almost there. If I can—

Headlights glaring, the truck raced to intercept him.

Another fence. Romero lunged between its rails so forcefully that he banged his injured shoulder, but he didn't care—moonlight showed him the path to the raised footbridge. He rushed along it, hearing the truck behind him. The churning river reflected the headlights, its fierce whitecaps beckoning. With a shout of triumph, he reached the footbridge. His frantic footsteps rumbled across it. Spray from the river slicked the boards. His feet slipped. The bridge swayed. Water splashed over it. He lost his balance, nearly tumbled into the river, but righted himself. A gunshot whistled past where he had been running before he fell. Abruptly, he was off the bridge, diving behind bushes, scurrying through the darkness on his right. John fired twice toward where Romero had entered the bushes as Romero dove to the ground farther to the right. Desperate not to make noise, he fought to slow his frenzied breathing.

His throat was raw. His chest ached. He touched his left shoulder and felt cold liquid mixed with warm: water and blood. He shivered. Couldn't stop shivering. The headlights of the truck showed John walking onto the footbridge. The pistol was in his right hand. Something else was in his left. It suddenly blazed. A powerful flashlight. It scanned the bushes. Romero pressed himself lower to the ground.

John proceeded across the bridge. "I've been counting the same as you have!" he shouted to be heard above the force of the current. "Eight shots! I checked the magazine before I got out of the truck. Seven more rounds, plus one in the firing chamber!"

Any moment the flashlight's glare would reach where Romero was hiding. He grabbed a rock, thanked God that it was his left shoulder that had been injured, and used his right arm to hurl the rock. It bounced off the bridge. As Romero scurried farther upriver, John swung the flashlight toward where he had been and fired.

This time, Romero didn't stop. Rocks against a pistol weren't going to work. He might get lucky, but he doubted it. John knew which direction he was in, and whenever Romero risked showing himself to throw another rock, John had a good chance of capturing him in the blaze of the flashlight and shooting him.

Keep going upriver, he told himself. Keep making John follow. Without aiming, he threw a rock in a high arc toward John but didn't trick him into firing without a target. Fine, Romero thought, scrambling through the murky bushes. Just as long as he keeps following.

The raft, he kept thinking. They found my campsite. They found my car. But did they find the raft?

In the darkness, it was hard to get his bearings. There had been a curve in the river, he remembered. Yes. And the ridge on this side angled down toward the water. He scurried fiercely, deliberately making so much noise that John was bound to hear and follow. He'll think I'm panicking, Romero thought. To add to the illusion, he threw another high arcing rock toward where John was stalking him.

A branch lanced his face. He didn't pay any attention. He just rushed onward, realized that the bank was curving, saw the shadow of the ridge angling down to the shore, and searched furiously through the bushes, tripping over the raft, nearly banging his head on one of the rocks that he had put in it to prevent a wind from blowing it away.

John's flashlight glinted behind him, probing the bushes.

Hurry!

Breathless, Romero took off his jacket, stuffed it with large rocks, set it on the rocks that were already in the raft, and dragged the raft toward the river. Downstream, John heard him and redirected the flashlight, but not before Romero ducked back into the bushes, watching the current suck the raft downstream. In the moonlight and the glint of the flashlight, the bulging jacket looked as if Romero were hunkered down in the raft, hoping not to be shot as the raft sped past.

John swung toward the river and fired. He fired again, the muzzle flash bright, the gunshots barely audible in the roar of the current, which also muted the noises that Romero made as he charged from the bushes and slammed against John, throwing his injured arm around John's throat while he used his other hand to grab John's gun arm.

The force of hitting John propelled them into the water. Instantly, the current gripped them, its violence as shocking as the cold. John's face was sucked under. Clinging to him, straining to keep him under, Romero also struggled with the river, its power thrusting him through the darkness. The current heaved him up, then dropped him. The cold was so fierce that already his body was becoming numb. Even so, he kept squeezing John's throat and struggling to get the pistol away from him. A huge tree limb scraped past. The current upended him. John broke the surface. Romero went under. John's hands pressed him down. Frenzied, Romero kicked. He thought he heard a scream as John let go of him and he broke to the surface. Five feet away, John fought to stay above the water and aim the pistol, Romero dove under. Hearing the shot, he used the force of the current to add to his effort as he thrust himself farther under water and erupted from the surface to John's right, grabbing John's gun arm, twisting it.

You son of a bitch, Romero thought. If I'm going to die, you're going with me. He dragged John under. They slammed against a boulder, the pain making Romero cry out under water. Gasping, he broke to the surface. Saw John ahead of him, aiming. Saw the headlights of the truck illuminating the footbridge. Saw the huge tree limb caught in the narrow space between the river and the bridge. Before John could fire, he slammed into the branch. John collided with it a moment later. Trapped in its arms, squeezed by the current, Romero reached for the pistol as John aimed it point-blank. Then John's face twisted into surprised agony as a boulder crashed down on him from the bridge and split his skull open.

Romero was barely aware of Matthew above him on the footbridge. He was too paralyzed with horror, watching blood stream down John's face. An instant later, a log hurtled along the river, struck John, and drove him harder against the tree branch. In the glare of the headlights, Romero thought he saw wood protruding from John's chest as he, the branch, and the log broke free of the bridge and swirled away in the current. Thrust along with him, Romero stretched his arms up, trying to claw at the bridge. He failed. Speeding under it, reaching the other side, he tensed in apprehension of the boulder that he would bang against and be knocked unconscious by when something snagged him. Hands. Matthew was on his stomach on the bridge, stretching as far down as he could, clutching Romero's shirt. Romero struggled to help him, trying not to look at Matthew's crushed forehead and right eye from where Romero had hit him with the rock. Gripping Matthew's arms, pulling himself up, Romero felt debris crash past his legs, and then he and Matthew were flat on the footbridge, breathing hoarsely, trying to stop trembling.

"I hate him," Matthew said.

For a moment, Romero was certain that his ears were playing tricks on him, that the gunshots and the roar of the water were making him hear sounds that weren't there.

"I hate him," Matthew repeated.

"My God, you can talk."

For the first time in twelve years, he later found out.

"I hate him," Matthew said. "Hatehimhatehimhatehimhatehim."

Relieving the pressure of silence that had built up for almost two thirds of his life, Matthew gibbered while they went to check Mark and found him dead, while they went to the house and Romero phoned the state police, while they put on warm clothes and Romero did what he could for Matthew's injury and they waited for the police to arrive, while the sun rose and the investigators swarmed throughout the farm. Matthew's hysterical litany became ever more speedy and shrill until a physician finally had to sedate him and he was taken away in an ambulance.

The state trooper whom Romero had asked for backup was part of the team. When Romero's police chief and sergeant heard what had happened, they drove up from Santa Fe. By then the excavations had started, and the bodies were showing up. What was left of them, anyway, after their blood had been drained into the fields and they'd been cut into pieces.

"Good God, how many?" the state trooper exclaimed as more and more body parts, most in extreme stages of decay, were found under the fields.

"As long as Matthew can remember, it's been happening," Romero said. "His mother died giving him birth. She's under one of the fields. The father died from a heart attack three years ago. They never told anybody. They just buried him out there someplace. Every year on the last average frost date, May fifteenth, they've sacrificed someone. Most of the time it was a homeless person, no one to be missed. But last year it was Susan Crowell and her fiancé. They had the bad luck of getting a flat tire right outside the farm. They walked down here and asked to use a phone. When John saw the out-of-state license plate . . ."

"But why?" the police chief asked in dismay as more body parts were discovered.

"To give life to the earth. That's what the D. H. Lawrence story was about. The fertility of the earth and the passage of the seasons. I guess that's as close as John was able to come to explaining to his victims why they had to die."

"What about the shoes?" the police chief asked. "I don't understand about the shoes."

"Luke dropped them."

"The fourth brother?"

"That's right. He's out there somewhere. He committed suicide."

The police chief looked sick.

"Throughout the spring, until the vegetables were ready for sale, Luke drove back and forth from the farm to Santa Fe to sell moss rocks. Each day, he drove along Old Pecos Trail. Twice a day, he passed the Baptist church. He was as psychologically tortured as Matthew, but John never suspected how close he was to cracking. That church became Luke's attempt for absolution. One day, he saw old shoes on the road next to the church."

"You mean he didn't drop the first ones?"

"No, they were somebody's idea of a prank. But they gave him an idea. He saw them as a sign from God. Two years ago, he started dropping the shoes of the victims. They'd always been a problem. Clothes will decay readily enough. But shoes take a lot longer. John told him to throw them in the trash somewhere in Santa Fe. Luke couldn't bring himself to do that any more than he could bring himself to go into the church and pray for his soul. But he could drop the shoes outside the church in the hopes that he'd be forgiven and that the family's victims would be granted salvation."

"And the next year, he dropped shoes with feet in them," the sergeant said.

"John had no idea that he'd taken them. When he heard what had happened, he kept him a prisoner here. One morning, Luke broke out, went into one of the fields, knelt down, and slit his throat from ear to ear."

The group became silent. In the background, amid a pile of upturned rich black soil, someone shouted that they'd found more body parts.

Romero was given paid sick leave. He saw a psychiatrist once a week for four years. On those occasions when people announced that they were vegetarians, he answered, "Yeah, I used to be one, but now I'm a carnivore." Of course, he couldn't subsist on meat alone. The human body required the vitamins and minerals that vegetables provided, and although Romero tried vitamin pills as a substitution, he found that he couldn't do without the bulk that vegetables provided. So he grudgingly ate them, but never without thinking of those delicious, incredibly large, shiny, healthy-looking tomatoes, cucumbers, peppers, squash, cabbage, beans, peas, carrots, and chard that the Parsons brothers had sold. Remembering what had fertilized them, he chewed and chewed, but the vegetables always stuck in his throat.

Ian Rankin

The Hanged Man

IAN RANKIN worked in a variety of unusual careers, including swineherd, viticulturalist, and folklore collector, before turning to writing more than a decade ago. The change has suited him well, and, more than a dozen novels later, he shows no signs of stopping. His wry short fiction has graced several year's-best anthologies and is a staple of *Ellery Queen's Mystery Magazine*. Usually his novels and stories center around John Rebus, a Scottish police inspector. They are becoming increasingly popular, having now been translated into Italian and Japanese. However, he doesn't need to rely on a series character to write gripping, tightly plotted mysteries. "The Hanged Man" is an excellent example of suspense writing at its finest. This story first appeared in the September/October issue of *Ellery Queen's Mystery Magazine*.

The Hanged Man

Ian Rankin

The killer wandered through the fairground.

It was a traveling fair, and this was its first night in Kirkcaldy. It was a Thursday evening in April. The fair wouldn't get really busy until the weekend, by which time it would be missing one of its minor, if well-established, attractions.

He'd already made one reconnaissance past the small white caravan with its chalkboard outside. Pinned to the board were a couple of faded letters from satisfied customers. A double-step led to the bead curtain. The door was tied open with baling twine. He didn't think there was anyone in there with her. If there was, she'd have closed the door. But all the same, he wanted to be careful. "Care" was his byword.

He called himself a killer. Which was to say that if anyone had asked him what he did for a living, he wouldn't have used any other term. He knew some in the profession thought "assassin" had a more glamorous ring to it. He'd looked it up in a dictionary, found it was to do with some old religious sect and derived from an Arabic word meaning "eater of hashish." He didn't believe in drugs himself; not so much as a half of lager before the job.

Some people preferred to call it a "hit," which made them "hit men." But he didn't *hit* people; he killed them stone dead. And there were other, more obscure euphemisms, but the bottom line was, he was a killer. And for today, the fair was his place of work, his hunting ground.

Not that it had taken a magic ball to find the subject. She'd be in that caravan right now, waiting for a punter. He'd give it ten more minutes, just so he could be sure she wasn't with someone—not a punter necessarily; maybe sharing a cuppa with a fellow traveler. Ten minutes: If no one came out or went in, he'd make himself her next and final customer.

Of course, if she was a real fortuneteller, she'd know he was coming and would have hightailed it out of town. But he thought she was here. He knew she was.

He pretended to watch three youths on the firing range. They made the elementary mistake of aiming along the barrel. The sights, of course, had been skewed; probably the barrel, too. And if they thought they were going to dislodge one of the moving targets by hitting it . . . well, best think again. Those targets would be weighted, reinforced. The odds were always on the side of the showman.

The fair stretched along the waterfront. There was a stiff breeze making some of the wooden structures creak. People pushed hair out of their eyes, or tucked chins into the collars of their jackets. The place wasn't busy, but it was busy enough. He didn't stand out, nothing memorable about him at all. His jeans, lumberjack shirt, and trainers were work clothes: At home he preferred a bit more style. But he was a long way from home today. His base was on the west coast, just down the Clyde from Glasgow. He didn't know anything about Fife at all. Kirkcaldy, what little he'd seen of it, wouldn't be lingering in his memory. He'd been to towns all over Scotland and the north of England. In his mind they formed a geography of violence. In Carlisle he'd used a knife, making it look like a drunken Saturday brawl. In Peterhead it had been a blow to the head and strangulation, with orders that the body shouldn't ever be found—a grand and a half to a fishing-boat captain had seen to that. In Airdrie, Arbroath, Ardrossan . . . he didn't always kill. Sometimes all that was needed was a brutal and public message. In those cases he became the postman, delivering the message to order.

He moved from the shooting range to another stall, where children tried to attach hoops to the prizes on a carousel. They were faring little better than their elders next door. No surprise, with most of the prizes oh-so-slightly exceeding the circumference of each hoop. When he checked his watch, he was surprised to find that the ten minutes had passed. A final look around, and he climbed the steps, tapped at the open door, and parted the bead curtain.

"Come in, love," she said. Gypsy Rosa, the sign outside called her. Palms read, your fortune foretold. Yet here she was, waiting for him.

"Close the door," she instructed. He saw that the twine holding it open was looped over a bent nail. He loosed it, and closed the door. The curtains were shut—which was ideal for his purpose—and, lacking any light from outside, the interior glowed from the half-dozen candles spaced around it. The surfaces had been draped with lengths of cheap black cloth. There was a black cloth over the table, too, with patterns of sun and moon embroidered into it. And there she sat, gesturing for him to squeeze his large frame into the banquette opposite. He nodded. He smiled. He looked at her.

She was middle-aged, her face lined and rouged. She'd been a looker in younger days, he could see that, but scarlet lipstick now made her mouth look too large and moist. She wore black muslin over her head, a gold band holding it in place. Her costume looked authentic enough: black lace, red silk, with astrological signs sewn into the arms. On the table sat a crystal ball, covered for now with a white handkerchief. The red fingernails of one hand tapped against a tarot deck. She asked him his name.

"Is that necessary?" he asked.

She shrugged. "It helps sometimes." They were like blind dates alone in a restaurant, the world outside ceasing to matter. Her eyes twinkled in the candlelight.

"My name's Mort," he told her.

She repeated the name, seeming amused by it.

"Short for Morton. My father was born there."

"It's also the French for death," she added.

"I didn't know," he lied.

She was smiling. "There's a lot you don't know, Mort. That's why you're here. A palm reading, is it?"

"What else do you offer?"

"The ball." She nodded toward it. "The cards."

He asked which she would recommend. In turn, she asked if this was his first visit to a psychic healer—that's what she called herself, "a psychic healer": "Because I heal souls," she added by way of explanation.

"I'm not sure I need healing," he argued.

"Oh, my dear, we all need some kind of healing. We're none of us *whole*. Look at you, for example."

He straightened in his chair, becoming aware for the first time that she was holding his right hand, palm upward, her fingers stroking his knuckles. She looked down at the palm, frowned a little in concentration.

"You're a visitor, aren't you, dear?"

"Yes."

"Here on business, I'd say."

"Yes." He was studying the palm with her, as though trying to read its foreign words.

"Mmm." She began running the tip of one finger down the well-defined lines which crisscrossed his palm. "Not ticklish?" she chuckled. He allowed her the briefest of smiles. Looking at her face, he noticed it seemed softer than it had when he'd first entered the caravan. He revised her age downward, felt slight pressure as she seemed to squeeze his hand, as if acknowledging the compliment.

"Doing all right for yourself, though," she informed him. "I mean, moneywise; no problems there. No, dear, your problems all stem from your particular line of work."

"My work?"

"You're not as relaxed about it as you used to be. Time was, you wouldn't have considered doing anything else. Easy money. But it doesn't feel like that anymore, does it?"

It felt warm in the caravan, stuffy, with no air getting in and all those candles burning. There was the metal weight pressed to his groin, the weight he'd always found so reassuring in times past. He told himself she was using cheap psychology. His accent wasn't local; he wore no wedding ring; his hands were clean and manicured. You could tell a lot about someone from such details.

"Shouldn't we agree on a price first?" he asked.

"Why should we do that, dear? I'm not a prostitute, am I?" He felt his ears reddening. "And besides, you can afford it, we both know you can. What's the point of letting money get in the way?" She was holding his hand in an ever tighter grip. She had strength, this one: He'd bear that in mind when the time came. He wouldn't play around, wouldn't string out her suffering. A quick squeeze of the trigger.

"I get the feeling," she said, "you're wondering why you're here. Would that be right?"

"I know exactly why I'm here."

"What? Here with me? Or here on this planet, living the life you've chosen?"

"Either . . . both." He spoke a little too quickly, could feel his pulse rate rising. He had to get it down again, had to be calm when the time came. Part of him said, *Do it now.* But another part said, *Hear her out.* He wriggled, trying to get comfortable.

"What I meant, though," she went on, "is you're not sure anymore why you do what you do. You've started to ask questions." She looked up at him. "The line of business you're in, I get the feeling you're just supposed to do what you're told. Is that right?" He nodded. "No talking back, no questions asked. You just do your work and wait for payday."

"I get paid upfront."

"Aren't you the lucky one?" She chuckled again. "But the money's not enough, is it? It can never recompense for not being happy or fulfilled."

"I could have got that from my girlfriend's *Cosmopolitan.*"

She smiled, then clapped her hands. "I'd like to try you with the cards. Are you game?"

"Is that what this is—a game?"

"You have your fun with words, dear. Euphemisms, that's all words are."

He tried not to gasp: It was as if she'd read his mind from earlier—all those euphemisms for "killer." She wasn't paying him any heed, was busy shuffling the outsized tarot deck. She asked him to touch the deck three times. Then she laid out the top three cards.

"Ah," she said, her fingers caressing the first one. "*Le soleil.* It means, the sun."

"I know what it means," he snapped.

She made a pout with her lips. "I thought you didn't know any French."

He was stuck for a moment. "There's a picture of the sun right there on the card," he said finally.

She nodded slowly. His breathing had quickened again.

"Second card," she said. "Death himself. *La mort.* Interesting that the French give it the feminine gender."

He looked at the picture of the skeleton. It was grinning, doing a little jig. On the ground beside it sat a lantern and an hourglass. The candle in the lantern had been snuffed out; the sand in the hourglass had all fallen through.

"Don't worry," she said, "it doesn't always portend a death."

"That's a relief," he said with a smile.

"The final card is intriguing—the hanged man. It can signify many things." She lifted it up so he could see it.

"And the three together?" he asked, curious now.

She held her hands as if in prayer. "I'm not sure," she said at last. "An unusual conjunction, to be sure."

"Death and the hanged man: a suicide maybe?"

She shrugged.

"Is the sex important? I mean, the fact that it is a man?"

She shook her head.

He licked his lips. "Maybe the ball would help," he suggested.

She looked at him, her eyes reflecting light from the candles. "You might be right." And she smiled. "Shall we?" As if they were but children, and the crystal ball little more than an illicit dare.

As she pulled the small glass globe toward them, he shifted again. The pistol barrel was chafing his thigh. He rubbed his jacket pocket, the one containing the silencer. He would have to hit her first, just to quiet her while he fitted the silencer to the gun.

Slowly, she lifted the handkerchief from the ball, as if raising the curtain on some miniaturized stage show. She leaned forward, peering into the glass, giving him a view of creped cleavage. Her hands flitted over the ball, not quite touching it. Had he been a gerontophile, there would have been a hint of the erotic to the act.

"Don't you go thinking that!" she snapped. Then, seeing the startled look on his face, she winked. "The ball often makes things clearer."

"What was I thinking?" he blurted out.

"You want me to say it out loud?"

He shook his head, looked into the ball, saw her face reflected there, stretched and distorted. And floating somewhere within was his own face, too, surrounded by licking flames.

"What do you see?" he asked, needing to know now.

"I see a man who is asking why he is here. One person has the answer, but he has yet to ask this person. He is worried about the thing he must do—rightly worried, in my opinion."

She looked up at him again. Her eyes were the color of polished oak. Tiny veins of blood seemed to pulse in the whites. He jerked back in his seat.

"You know, don't you?"

"Of course I know, Mort."

He nearly overturned the table as he got to his feet, pulling the gun from his waistband. "How?" he asked. "Who told you?"

She shook her head, not looking at the gun, apparently not interested in it. "It would happen one day. The moment you walked in, I felt it was you."

"You're not afraid." It was a statement rather than a question.

"Of course I'm afraid." But she didn't look it. "And a little sad, too."

He had the silencer out of his pocket, but was having trouble coordinating his hands. He'd practiced a hundred times in the dark and had never had this trouble before. He'd had victims like her, though: the ones who accepted, who were maybe even a little grateful.

"You know who wants you dead?" he asked.

She nodded. "I think so. I may have gotten the odd fortune wrong, but I've made precious few enemies in my life."

"He's a rich man."

"Very rich," she conceded. "Not all of it honest money. And I'm sure he's well used to getting what he wants." She slid the ball away, brought out the cards again, and began shuffling them. "So ask me your question."

He was screwing the silencer onto the end of the barrel. The pistol was loaded, he only had to slide the safety off. He licked his lips again. So hot in here, so dry . . .

"Why?" he asked. "Why does he want a fortuneteller dead?"

She got up, made to open the curtains.

"No," he commanded, pointing the gun at her, sliding off the safety. "Keep them closed."

"Afraid to shoot me in daylight?" When he didn't answer, she pulled open one curtain, then blew out the candles. He kept the pistol trained on her: a head shot, quick and always fatal. "I'll tell you," she said, sliding into her seat again. She motioned for him to sit. After a moment's hesitation, he did so, the pistol steady in his right hand. Wisps of smoke from the extinguished candles rose either side of her.

"We were young when we met," she began. "I was already working in a fairground—not this one. One night, he decided there had been enough of a courtship." She looked deep into his eyes, his own oak-colored eyes. "Oh yes, he's used to getting what he wants. You know what I'm saying?" she went on quietly. "There was no question of consent. I tried to have the baby in secret, but it's hard to keep secrets from a man like him, a man with money, someone people fear. My baby was stolen from me. I began traveling then, and I've been traveling ever since. But always with my ear to the ground, always hearing things." Her eyes were liquid now. "You see, I knew a time would come when my baby would grow old enough to begin asking questions. And I knew the baby's father would not want the truth to come out." She reached out a shaking hand, reached past the gun to touch his cheek. "I just didn't think he'd be so cruel."

"Cruel?"

"So cruel as to send his own son—our son— to do his killing."

He shot to his feet again, banged his fists against the wall of the caravan. Rested his head there and screwed shut his eyes, the oak-colored eyes—mirrors of her own—which had told her all she'd needed to know. He'd left the pistol on the table. She lifted it, surprised by its weight, and turned it in her hand.

"I'll kill him," he groaned. "I swear, I'll kill him for this."

With a smile, she slid the safety catch on, placed the gun back on the table. When he turned back to her, blinking away tears, she looked quite calm, almost serene, as if her faith in him had been rewarded at last. In her hand, she was holding a tarot card.

The hanged man.

"It will need to look like an accident," she said. "Either that or suicide."

Outside, the screams of frightened children: waltzers and big wheel and ghost train. One of his hands fell lightly on hers, the other reaching for his pistol.

"Mother," he said, with all the tenderness his parched soul could muster.

Carolyn G. Hart

Spooked

CAROLYN G. HART was already collecting accolades and awards for her cozy mystery series featuring bookstore owners Annie Laurance and Max Darling when she decided to strike out with a new series protagonist, Henrietta O'Dwyer Collins, a seventy-something reporter with one of the sharpest detecting minds since Miss Marple herself. Judging by the critical recognition, with one Agatha award and one Agatha nomination, the series is off to a grand start. A master at delving into the relationships and mores of southern towns, her audience continues to grow with each new novel. Henry O. appears in *Death in Lover's Lane* and in several stories in Hart's recently published collection of short fiction entitled *Crime On Her Mind*. This story first appeared in the March issue of *Ellery Queen's Mystery Magazine*.

Spooked

Carolyn G. Hart

The dust from the convoy rose in plumes. Gretchen stood on tiptoe, waving, waving.

A soldier leaned over the tailgate of the olive-drab troop carrier. The blazing July sun touched his crew cut with gold. He grinned as he tossed her a bubble gum. "Chew it for me, kid."

Gretchen wished she could run alongside, give him some of Grandmother Lotte's biscuits and honey. But his truck was twenty feet away and another one rumbled in front of her. She ran a few steps, called out, "Good luck. Good luck!" The knobby piece of gum was a precious lump in her hand.

She stood on the edge of the highway until the last truck passed. Grandmother said Highway 66 went all the way to California and the soldiers were on their way to big ships to sail across the ocean to fight the Japs. Gretchen wished she could do something for the war. Her brother Jimmy was a Marine, somewhere in the South Pacific. He'd survived Iwo Jima. Every month they sent him cookies, peanut butter and oatmeal raisin and spice, packed in popcorn. When they had enough precious sugar, they made Aunt Bill's candy, but Mom had to find the sugar in Tulsa. Mr. Hudson's general store here in town almost never had sacks of sugar. Every morning she and Grandmother sat in a front pew of the little frame church in the willows and prayed for Jimmy and for all the boys overseas and for Gretchen's mom working so hard at the defense plant in Tulsa. Her mom only came home about one weekend a month. Grandmother tried to save a special piece of meat when she could. Grandmother said her mom was thin as a rail and working too hard, but Gretchen knew it was important for her mom to work. They needed everybody to help, and Mom was proud that she put radio parts in the big B-24 Liberators.

Gretchen took a deep breath of the hot heavy air, still laced with dust, and walked across the street to the cafe. Ever since the war started, they'd been busy from early morning until they ran out of food, sometimes around five o'clock, never later than seven. Of course, they had special ration books for the cafe, but Grandmother said they couldn't use those points to get sugar for Jimmy. That wouldn't be right.

Gretchen shaded her eyes and looked at the plate-glass window. She still felt a kind of thrill when she saw the name painted in bright blue: Victory Cafe. A thrill, but also a tightness in her chest, the kind of feeling she once had when she climbed the big sycamore to get the calico kitten and a branch snapped beneath her feet. For an instant that seemed to last forever, she was falling. She whopped against a thick limb and held on tight. She remembered the sense of strangeness as she fell. And disbelief, the thought that this couldn't be happening to her. There was a strangeness in the cafe's new name. It had been Pfizer's Cafe for almost twenty years, but now it didn't do to be proud of being German. Now Grandmother didn't say much in the cafe because her accent was thick. She was careful not to say "ja" and she let Gretchen do most of the talking. Grandmother prayed for Jimmy and for her sister's family in Hamburg.

Gretchen tucked the bubblegum in the pocket of her pedal pushers. Grandmother wouldn't let her wear shorts even though it was so hot the cotton stuck to her legs. She glanced at the big thermometer hanging by the door. Ninety-eight degrees and just past one o'clock. They'd sure hit over a hundred today, just like every day for the past few weeks. They kept the front door propped open, hoping for a little breeze through the screen.

The cafe was almost as much her home as the boxy three-bedroom frame house a half-mile away down a dirt road. Her earliest memories were playing with paper dolls in a corner of the kitchen as her mother and grandmother worked hard and fast, fixing country breakfasts for truck drivers in a hurry to get to Tulsa and on to Oklahoma City and Amarillo with their big rigs. Every morning, grizzled old men from around the county gathered at Pfizer's for their newspapers and gossip as well as rashers of bacon, a short stack, and scrambled eggs. But everything changed with the war. Camp Crowder, just over the line in Missouri, brought in thousands of soldiers. Of course, they were busy training, but there were always plenty of khaki uniforms in the Victory Cafe now even though the menu wasn't what it had been before the war. Now they had meatless Tuesdays and Grandmother fixed huge batches of macaroni and cheese. Sometimes there wasn't any bacon, but they had scrambled eggs and grits and fried potatoes. Instead of roast beef, they had hash, the potatoes and meat bubbly in a vinegary sauce. But Grandmother never fixed red cabbage or sauerkraut anymore.

It was up to Gretchen to help her grandmother when her mom moved to Tulsa. She might only be twelve, but she was wiry and strong and she promised herself she'd never complain, not once, not ever, not for the duration. That's what everybody talked about, the duration until someday the war was over. On summer evenings she was too tired to play kick the can and it seemed a long-ago memory when she used to climb up into the maple tree, carrying a stack of movie magazines, and nestle with her back to the trunk and legs dangling.

She gave a swift, professional glance around the square room. The counter with red leatherette stools was to the left. The mirror behind the counter sparkled. She'd stood on a stool to polish it after lunch. Now it reflected her: black pigtails, a skinny face with blue eyes that often looked tired and worried, and a pink Ship 'n Shore blouse and green pedal pushers. Her blouse had started the day crisp and starched, but now it was limp and spattered with bacon grease.

Four tables sat in the center. Three wooden booths ran along the back wall and two booths to the right. The jukebox was tucked between the back booths and the swinging door to the kitchen. It was almost always playing. She loved "Stardust" and "Chattanooga Choo-Choo," but the most often played song was "Praise the Lord and Pass the Ammunition." A poster on the wall beside the jukebox pictured a sinking ship and a somber Uncle Sam with a finger to his lips and the legend: LOOSE LIPS SINK SHIPS. Grandmother told her it meant no one should talk about the troop convoys that went through on Highway 66 or where they were going, or talk about soldiers' letters that sometimes carried information that got past the censors. Grandmother said that's why they had to be so careful about the food, to make sure there was enough for Jimmy and all the other boys. And that's why they couldn't drive to Tulsa to see Mom. There wasn't enough gas. Grandmother said even a cupful of gas might make a difference one day whether some boy—like Jimmy—lived or died.

Two of the front tables needed clearing. But she made a circuit of the occupied places first.

Deputy Sheriff Carter flicked his cigar and ash dribbled onto his paunch, which started just under his chin and pouched against the edge of the table. He frowned at black and white squares on the newspaper page. He looked at Mr. Hudson across the table. "You know a word for mountain ridge? Five letters." He chewed on his pencil. "Oh, yeah," he murmured. He marked the letters, closed the paper, leaned back in the booth. "Heard they been grading a road out near the McLemore place."

Mr. Hudson clanked his spoon against the thick white coffee mug. "Got some more java, Gretchen?"

She nodded.

Mr. Hudson pursed his thin mouth. "Bud McLemore's son-in-law's a county commissioner, Euel. What do you expect?"

Gretchen hurried to the hot plates behind the counter, brought the steaming coffeepot, and refilled both men's mugs.

The deputy sheriff's face looked like an old ham, crusted and pink.

"Never no flies on Bud. Maybe my youngest girl'll get herself a county commissioner. 'Course, she spends most of her time at the USO in Tulsa. But she's makin' good money at the Douglas plant. Forty dollars a week." Then he frowned. "But it's sure givin' her big ideas."

Gretchen moved on to the next booth, refilled the cups for some army officers who had a map spread out on the table.

The younger officer looked just like Alan Ladd. "I've got it marked in a grid, sir. Here's the last five places they spotted the Spooklight."

The bigger man fingered his little black mustache. "Lieutenant, I want men out in the field every night. We're damn well going to get to the bottom of this business."

Gretchen took her time moving away. The Spooklight. Everybody in town knew the army had set up a special camp about six miles out of town just to look for the Spooklight, those balls of orange or white that rose from nowhere and flowed up and down hills, hung like fiery globes in the scrawny bois d'arc trees, sometimes ran right up on porches or over barns. Some people said the bouncing globes of light were a reflection from the headlights on Highway 66. Other folks scoffed, because the lights had been talked about for a hundred years, long before cars moved on the twisting road.

Gretchen put the coffee on the hot plate, picked up a damp cloth and a tray. She set to work on the table closest to the army officers.

". . . Sergeant Ferris swore this light was big as a locomotive and it came rolling and bouncing down the road, went right over the truck like seltzer water bouncing in a soda glass. Now, you can't tell me," the black mustache bristled, "that burning gas acts like that."

"No, sir." The lieutenant sounded just like Cornel Wilde saluting a general in that movie about the fall of Corregidor.

The kitchen door squeaked open. Her grandmother's red face, naturally ruddy skin flushed with heat from the stove, brightened and she smiled. But she didn't say a word. When Gretchen was little, she would have caroled, *"Komm her, mein Schatz."* Now she waved her floury hands.

Gretchen carried the dirty dishes into the kitchen. The last words she heard were like an Abbott and Costello radio show, a nonsensical mixture, ". . . soon as the war's over . . . set up search parties . . . I'm gonna see if I can patch those tires . . . good training for night . . ."

Four pies sat on the kitchen's center table, steam still rising from the latticed crusts. The smell of apples and cinnamon and a hint of nutmeg overlay the onions and liver and fried okra cooked for lunch.

"Oh, Grandmother." Gretchen's eyes shone. Apple pie was her favorite food in all the world. Then, without warning, she felt the hot prick of tears. Jimmy loved apple pie, too.

Grandmother's big blue eyes were suddenly soft. She was heavy and moved slowly, but her arms soon enveloped Gretchen. "No tears. Tomorrow ve send Jimmy a stollen rich with our own pecans. Now, let's take our pies to the counter. But first," she used a sharp knife, cut a generous wedge, scooped it out, and placed it on a plate, "I haf saved one piece—ein—for you."

The pie plates were still warm. Gretchen held the door for her grandmother. It was almost like a festive procession as they carried the pies to the counter.

The officers watched. Mr. Hudson's nose wrinkled in pleasure. Deputy Carter pointed at a pie plate. "Hey, Lotte, I'll sure take one of those." There was a chorus of calls.

Grandmother dished up the pieces, handing the plates to Gretchen, then stood at the end of the counter, sprigs of silver-streaked blond hair loose from her coronet braids, her blue eyes happy, her plump hands folded on her floury apron. Gretchen refilled all the coffee cups.

Grandmother was behind the cash register when Mr. Hudson paid his check. "Lotte, the deputy may have to put you in jail, you make any more pies like that."

Grandmother's face was suddenly still. She looked at him in bewilderment.

Mr. Hudson cackled. "You sure don't have enough sugar to make that many pies. You been dealing in the black market?"

Grandmother's hands shook as she held them up, as if to stop a careening horse. "Oh, nein, ne—no, no. Not black market. Never. I use honey, honey my cousin Ernst makes himself."

The officers were waiting with their checks. The younger blond man, the one who looked like Alan Ladd, smiled warmly. *"Sprechen Sie Deustch? Dies ist der beste Apfelkuchen den ich je gegessen habe."*

The deputy tossed down a quarter, a dime, and a nickel for macaroni and cheese, cole slaw, pie, and coffee. He glowered at Grandmother. "No Heinie talk needed around here. That right, Lotte?" He glared at the soldier. "How come you speak it so good?"

The blond officer was a much smaller man, but Gretchen loved the way he looked at the deputy as if he were a piece of banana peel. "Too bad you don't have a German *Grogbmutter* like she and I do." He nodded toward Gretchen. "We're lucky, you know," and he gave Grandmother a gentle smile. *"Danke schön."*

But Grandmother's shoulders were drawn tight. She made the change without another word, not looking at any of the men, and when they turned toward the front door, she scuttled to the kitchen.

Gretchen waited a moment, then darted after her.

Grandmother stood against the back wall, her apron to her face, her shoulders shaking.

"Don't cry, Grandmother." Now it was Gretchen who stood on tiptoe to hug the big woman.

Her grandmother wiped her face and said, her accent even more pronounced than usual, "Ve haf vork to do. Enough now."

As her grandmother stacked the dirty dishes in the sink, Gretchen took a clean recipe card. She searched through the file, then printed in large block letters:

LOTTE'S APPLE HONEY VICTORY PIE

6 tart apples
1 cup honey
2 tbs. flour
1 tsp. cinnamon
dash nutmeg
dash salt
pastry

She took the card and propped it by the cash register.

Back in the kitchen, Grandmother scrubbed the dishes in hot soapy water then hefted a teakettle to pour boiling water over them as they drained. Gretchen mopped the floor. Every so often, the bell jangled from the front and Gretchen hurried out to take an order.

The pie and all the food was gone before five. Grandmother turned the sign in the front window to CLOSED. Then she walked wearily to the counter and picked up the recipe Gretchen had scrawled.

"Let's leave it there, Grandmother." Gretchen was surprised at how stern she sounded.

Her grandmother almost put it down, then shook her head. "Ve don't vant to make the deputy mad, Gretchen."

Gretchen hated hearing the fear in Grandmother's voice. She wanted to insist that the recipe remain. She wanted to say that they hadn't done anything wrong and they shouldn't have to be afraid. But she didn't say anything else as her grandmother held the card tight to her chest and turned away.

"You go on home, Grandmother. I'll close up." Gretchen held up her hands as her grandmother started to protest. "You know I like to close up." She'd made a game of it months ago because she knew Grandmother was so tired by closing time that she almost couldn't walk the half-mile to the house, and there was still the garbage to haul down to the incinerator and the menus to stack and silverware to roll up in the clean gingham napkins and potatoes to scrub for tomorrow and the jam and jelly jars to be wiped with a hot rag.

Gretchen made three trips to the incinerator, hauling the trash in a wheelbarrow. She liked the creak of the wheel and the caw of the crows and even though it was so hot she felt like an egg on a sizzling griddle, it was fun to use a big kitchen match and set the garbage on fire. She had to stay until she could stir the ashes, be sure the fire was out. She tipped the wheelbarrow over and stood on it to reach up and catch a limb and climb the big cotton-wood. She climbed high enough to look out over the town, at the cafe and at

McGrory's gas station and at the flag hanging limp on the pole outside the post office.

If it hadn't been for the ugly way the deputy had acted to Grandmother, Gretchen probably would never have paid any attention to him. But he'd been mean, and she glowered at him through the shifting leaves of the cottonwood.

He didn't see her, of course. He was walking along the highway. A big truck zoomed over the hill. When the driver spotted the deputy's high-crowned black hat and khaki uniform, he abruptly slowed. But the deputy wasn't paying any attention, he was just strolling along, his hands in his pockets, almost underneath Gretchen's tree.

A hot day for a walk. Too hot a day for a walk. Gretchen wiped her sticky face against the collar of her blouse. She craned for a better look. Oh, the deputy was turning into the graveyard nestled on the side of the hill near the church. The graveyard was screened from most of the town by a stand of enormous evergreens, so only Gretchen and the crows could see past the mossy stone pillars and the metal arch.

Gretchen frowned and remembered the time when Mrs. Whittle caught Sammy Cooper out in the hall without a pass. She'd never forgotten the chagrin on Sammy's face when Mrs. Whittle said, "Samuel, the next time you plan to cut class, don't walk like you have the Hope diamond in your pocket and there's a policeman on every corner." Gretchen wasn't sure what the Hope diamond was, but every time any of the kids saw Sammy for the next year, they'd whistle and shout, "Got the Hope diamond, Sammy?"

The deputy stopped in a huge swath of shade from an evergreen. He peered around the graveyard. What did he expect to see? Nobody there could look at him.

Gretchen forgot how hot she was. She even forgot to be mad. She leaned forward and grabbed the closest limb, moved it so she could see better.

The deputy made a full circle of the graveyard, which was maybe half as big as a football field, no more than forty or fifty headstones. He passed by the stone angel at Grandpa Pfizer's grave and her dad's stone that had a weeping willow on it. That was the old part of the cemetery. A mossy stone, half fallen on one side, marked the grave of a Confederate soldier. Mrs. Peters took Gretchen's social studies class there last year and showed them how to do a rubbing of a stone even though the inscription was scarcely legible. Gretchen shivered when she saw the wobbly, indistinct gray letters: Hiram Kelly, age 19, wounded July 17, 1863 in the Battle of Honey Springs, died July 29, 1863. Beloved Son of Robert and Effie Kelly, Cherished Brother of Corinne Kelly. Some of the graves still had little American flags, placed there for the Fourth. A half-dozen big sprays marked the most recent grave.

Back by the pillars, the deputy made one more careful study of the church and the graveyard, then he pulled a folded sheet of paper from his pocket and knelt by the west pillar. He tugged at a stone about three inches from the ground.

Gretchen couldn't believe her eyes. She leaned so far forward her branch creaked.

The kneeling man's head jerked up.

Gretchen froze quieter than a tick on a dog.

The sun glistened on his face, giving it an unhealthy, coppery glow. The eyes that skittered over the headstones and probed the lengthening shadows were dark and dangerous.

A crow cawed. A heavy truck rumbled over the hill, down Main Street. The faraway wail of Cal Burke's saxophone sounded sad and lonely.

Gradually, the tension eased out of the deputy's shoulders. He turned and jammed the paper into the small dark square and poked the stone over the opening, like capping a jar of preserves. He lunged to his feet and strode out of the cemetery, relaxing to a casual saunter once past the church.

Gretchen waited until he climbed into his old black Ford and drove down the dusty road.

She swung down from the tree, thumped onto the wheelbarrow, and jumped to the ground. The bells in the steeple rang six times. She had to hurry. Grandmother would have a light supper ready, pork and beans and a salad with her homemade Thousand Island dressing and a big slice of watermelon.

Gretchen tried not to look like she had the Hope diamond in her pocket. Instead, she whistled as though calling a dog and clapped her hands. A truck roared past on its way north to Joplin. Still whistling, she ran to the stone posts. Once hidden from the road, she worked fast. The oblong slab of stone came right off in her hand. She pulled out the sheet of paper, unfolded it.

She'd had geography last spring with Mrs. Jacobs. She'd made an A. She liked maps, liked the way you could take anything, a mountain, a road, an ocean, and make it come alive on a piece of paper.

She figured this one at a glance. The straight line—though really the road curved and climbed and fell—was Highway 66. The little squiggle slanting off to the northeast from McGrory's station was the dusty road that led to an abandoned zinc mine, the Sister Sue. The X was a little off the road, just short of the mine entrance. There was a round clock face at the top of the sheet. The hands were set at midnight.

She stuffed the folded sheet in its dark space, replaced the stone. X marks the spot. Not a treasure map. That was kid stuff in stories by Robert Louis Stevenson. But nobody hid a note in a stone post unless they were up to something bad, something they didn't want anybody to know about. Tonight. Something secret was going to happen tonight. . . .

Gretchen pulled the sheet up to her chin even though the night oozed heat like the stoves at the cafe. She was dressed, a T-shirt and shorts, and her sneakers were on the floor. She waited until eleven, watching the slow crawl of the hands on her alarm clock and listening to the summer dance of the June bugs against her window screen. She unhooked the screen, sat on the sill, and dropped to the ground. She wished she could ride her bike, but somebody might be out on the road and see her and they'd sure tell Grandmother. Instead, she figured out the shortest route, cutting across the McClelland farm, careful to avoid the pasture where Old Amos glared out at the world with reddish eyes, and slipping in the shadows down Purdy Road.

The full moon hung low in the sky, its milky radiance creating a black and cream world, making it easy to see. She stayed in the shadows. The buzz of the cicadas was so loud she kept a close eye out for headlights coming over the hill or around the curve.

Once near the abandoned mine, she moved from shadow to shadow, smelling the sharp scent of the evergreens, feeling the slippery dried needles underfoot. A tremulous, wavering, plaintive shriek hurt her ears. Slowly, it subsided into a moan. Gretchen's heart raced. A sudden flap, and an owl launched into the air.

Gretchen looked uneasily around the clearing. The boarded-over mine shaft was a dark mound straight ahead. There was a cave-in years ago, and they weren't able to get to the miners in time. In the dark, the curved mound looked like a huge gravestone.

The road, rutted and overgrown, curved past the mine entrance and ended in front of a ramshackle storage building, perhaps half as large as a barn. A huge padlock hung from a rusty chain wound around the big splintery board that barred the double doors.

Nothing moved, though the night was alive with sound, frogs croaking, cicadas rasping.

Gretchen found a big sycamore on the hillside. She climbed high enough to see over the cleared area. She sat on a fat limb, her back to the trunk, her knees to her chin.

The cicada chorus was so loud she didn't hear the car. It appeared without warning, headlights off, lurching in the deep ruts, crushing an overgrowth of weeds as it stopped off the road to one side of the storage shed. The car door slammed. In the moonlight, the deputy's face was a pale mask. As she watched, that pale mask turned ever so slowly, all the way around the clearing.

Gretchen hunkered into a tight crouch. She felt prickles of cold, though it was so hot sweat beaded her face, slip down her arms and legs.

A cigarette lighter flared. The end of the deputy's cigar was a red spot. He leaned inside the car, dragging out something. Metal clanked as he placed the things on the front car fender. Suddenly he turned toward the rutted lane.

Gretchen heard the dull rumble, too, loud enough to drown out the cicadas.

Dust swirled in a thick cloud as the wheels of the army truck churned the soft ruts.

The sheriff was already moving. He propped a big flashlight on the car fender. By the time the driver turned and backed the truck with its rear end facing the shed, the sheriff was snipping the chain.

The driver of the truck wore a uniform. He jumped down and ran to help and the two men lifted up the big splintery board, tossed it aside. Each man grabbed a door. They grunted and strained and pulled and finally both doors were wide open. The soldier hurried to the back of the truck, let down the metal back.

Gretchen strained to catch glimpses of the soldier as he moved back and forth past the flashlight. Tall and skinny, he had a bright bald spot on the top of his head, short dark hair on the sides. His face was bony, with a beaked nose and a chin that sank into his neck. He had sergeant stripes on his sleeves. He was a lot smaller and skinnier than the deputy, but he was twice as fast. They both moved back and forth between the truck and the shed, carrying olive-green gasoline tins in each hand.

Once the sergeant barked, "Get a move on. I've got to get that truck back damn quick."

Even in the moonlight, the deputy's face looked dangerously red and he huffed for breath. He stopped occasionally to mop his face with an oversize handkerchief. The sergeant never paused, and he shot a sour look at the bigger man.

Gretchen tried to count the tins. She got confused, but was sure there were at least forty, maybe a few more.

When the last tin was inside the shed, the doors shoved shut, the chains wrapped around the board, the deputy rested against his car, his breathing as labored as a bulldogger struggling with a calf.

The sergeant planted himself square in front of the gasping deputy and held out his hand.

"Goddamn, man—" the deputy's wind whistled in his throat—"you gotta wait till I sell the stuff. I worked out a deal with a guy in Tulsa. Top price. A lot more than we could get around here. Besides, black-market gas out here might get traced right back to us."

"I want my money." The sergeant's reedy voice sounded edgy and mean.

"Look, fella." The deputy pushed away from the car, glowered down at the smaller man. "You'll get your goddamn money when I get mine."

The soldier didn't move an inch. "Okay. That's good. When do you get yours?"

The deputy didn't answer.

"When's the man coming? We'll meet him together." A hard laugh. "We can split the money right then and there."

The deputy wiped his face and neck with his handkerchief. "Sure. You can help us load. Thursday night. Same time."

"I'll be here." The sergeant moved fast to the truck, climbed into the front seat. After he revved the motor, he leaned out of the window. "I'll be here. And you damn sure better be."

• • •

Grandmother settled the big blue bowl in her lap, began to snap green beans.

Gretchen was so tired her eyes burned and her feet felt like lead. She swiped the paring knife around the potato. "Grandmother, what does it mean when people talk about selling gas on the black market?"

Grandmother's hand moved so fast, snap, snap, snap. "We don't have much of that around here. Everyone tries hard to do right. The gas has to be used by people like the farmers and Dr. Sherman so he can go to sick people, and the army. The black market is very wrong, Gretchen. Why, what if there wasn't enough gas for the Jeeps and tanks where Jimmy is?"

There wasn't much sound then but the snap of beans and the soft squish as the potato peelings fell into the sink.

Gretchen tossed the last potato into the big pan of cold water. She scooped up the potato peels. "Grandmother, who catches these people in the black market?"

Grandmother carried her bowl to the sink. "I don't know," she said uncertainly. "I guess in the cities the police. And here it would be the deputy. Or maybe the army."

Gretchen put the dirty dishes on the tray, swiped the cloth across the table.

Deputy Carter grunted, "Bring me some more coffee," but he didn't look up from his copy of the newspaper. He frowned as he printed words in the crossword puzzle.

Across the room, the officer who looked like Alan Ladd was by himself. He smiled at Gretchen. "Tell your grandmother this is the best food I've had since I was home."

Gretchen smiled shyly at him, then she blurted, "Are you still looking for the Spooklight?"

His eyebrows scooted up like snapped window shades. "How'd you know that?"

She polished the table, slid him an uncertain look. "I heard you yesterday," she said softly.

"Oh, sure. Well," he leaned forward conspiratorially, "my colonel thinks it's a great training tool to have the troops search for mystery lights. The first platoon to find them's going to get a free weekend pass."

Gretchen wasn't sure what a training tool was, or a free pass, but she focused on what mattered to her. "You mean the soldiers are still looking for the lights? They'll come where the lights are?"

"Fast as they can. Of course," he shrugged, "nobody knows when or where they're going to appear, so it's mostly a lot of hiking around in the dark and nothing happens."

Gretchen looked toward the deputy. He was frowning as he scratched out a word, wrote another one. She turned until her back was toward him. "They say that in July the lights dance around the old Sister Sue mine. That's what I heard the other day." Behind her, she heard the creak as the deputy slid out of the booth, clumped toward the cash register. "Excuse me," she said quickly and she turned away.

The sheriff paid forty-five cents total, thirty for the Meatless Tuesday vegetable plate, ten for raisin pie, a nickel for coffee.

When the front door closed behind him, Gretchen hurried to the table. As she cleared it, she carefully tucked the discarded newspaper under her arm.

"A cherry fausfade, please." She slid onto the hard metal stool. The soda fountain at Thompson's Drugs didn't offer comfortable stools like those at the Victory Cafe.

"Cherry phosphate," Millard Thompson corrected. He gave her the sweet smile that made his round face look like a cheerful pumpkin topped by tight coils of red hair. Millard was two years older than she and had lived across the road from her all her life. He played the tuba in the junior high band, had collected more tin cans than anybody in town, and knew which shrubs the butterflies liked. Once he led her on a long walk, scrambling through the rugged bois d'arc to a little valley covered with thousands of monarchs. And in the Thompson washroom, he had two shelves full of chemicals and sometimes he let her watch his experiments. He even had a Bunsen burner. And Millard's big brother Mike was in the 45th, now part of General Patton's Seventh Army. They hadn't heard from him since the landings in Sicily and there was a haunted look in Mrs. Thompson's eyes. Mr. Thompson had a big map at the back of the store and he moved red pins along the invasion route. Mike's unit was reported fighting for the Comiso airport.

Gretchen looked around the store, but it was quiet in midafternoon. Millard's mother was arranging perfumes and powders on a shelf behind the cash register. His dad was in the back of the store behind the pharmacy counter. "Millard," she kept her voice low, "do you know about the black market?"

He leaned his elbow on the counter. "See if I got enough cherry in. Yeah, sure, Gretchen. Dad says it's as bad as being a spy. He says people who sell on the black market make blood money. He says they don't deserve to have guys like Mike ready to die for them."

Gretchen loved cherry fausfades (okay, she knew it was phosphate but it had always sounded like fausfade to her) but she just held tight to the tall beaded sundae glass. "Okay, then listen, Millard . . ."

Gretchen struggled to stay awake. She waited a half-hour after Grandmother turned off her light, then slipped from her window. Millard was waiting by Big Angus's pasture.

As they hurried along Purdy Road, Millard asked, "You sure it was Deputy Carter? And he said it was for the black market?"

"Yes."

Millard didn't answer but she knew he was struggling with the truth that they couldn't go to the man who was supposed to catch bad guys. When they pulled the shed doors wide and he shone his flashlight over the dozens and dozens of five-gallon gasoline tins, he gave a low whistle. Being Millard, he picked up a tin, unscrewed the cap, smelled.

"Gas, all right." There was a definite change in Millard's voice when he spoke. He sounded more grownup and very serious. "We got to do something, Gretchen."

She knew that. That's why she'd come to him. "I know." She, too, sounded somber. "Listen, Millard, I got an idea. . . ."

He listened intently while she spoke, then he looked around the clearing, his round face intent, measuring. Then he grinned. "Sure. Sure we can. Dad's got a bunch of powdered magnesium out in the storeroom. They used to use it with the old-fashioned photography." He looked at her blank face. "For the flash, Gretchen. Here's what we'll do. . . ."

Gretchen could scarcely bear the relief that flooded through her when the young lieutenant stopped in for coffee and pie Wednesday afternoon. When she refilled his cup, she said quickly, "Will you look for the Spooklight tonight?"

The lieutenant sighed. "Every night. Don't know why the darned thing's disappeared just when we started looking for it."

"A friend of mine saw it last night. Near the Sister Sue mine." She gripped her cleaning cloth tightly. "If you'll look there tonight, I'm sure you'll find it."

It was cloudy Wednesday night. Gretchen and Millard moved quickly around the clearing, Gretchen clambering up in the trees, Millard handing her the pie tins she'd brought from the cafe. She scrambled to high branches, fastened the tins with duct tape.

She was panting by the time she finished. She tried to catch her breath as Millard unwrapped the chain to the big shed. The big chain clanked as he tossed it aside. Gretchen helped him tug the doors wide open. She stepped inside and carefully tucked the newspaper discarded by the sheriff between two tins.

Millard was a dark shadow behind her. "Do you think they'll come?"

"Yes. Oh, Millard, I believe they will. I do." There had been a sudden sharpness in the young officer's eyes. She'd had the feeling he really listened to her. Maybe she felt that way because she wanted it so badly, but there was a calmness in her heart. He would come. He would come.

Millard took his place high in the branches of an oak that grew close to the boarded-over mine shaft. Gretchen clutched the huge oversize flashlight and checked over in her mind which trees had the pie tins and how she could move in the shadows to reach them.

Suddenly Millard began to scramble down from the tree. "Gretchen, Gretchen, where are you?"

"Over here, Millard." She moved out into the clearing. "What's wrong?"

He was panting. "It's the army, but they're going down the wrong road. They're on the road to Hell Hollow. They won't come close enough to see us."

Gretchen could hear the noise now from the road on the other side of the hill.

"I'll go through the woods. I've got my stuff." And Millard disappeared in the night.

Gretchen almost followed. But if Millard decoyed them this way, she had to be ready to do her part.

Suddenly a light burst in the sky and it would be easily seen from Hell Hollow road. Nobody who knew beans would have thought it was the Spooklight but, by golly, it was an odd, unexplained flash in the night sky. Then came another flash and another.

Shouts erupted. "Look, look, there it is!"

"Quick. This way!"

"Over the hill!"

If Millard had been there, she would have hugged him. He'd taken lumps of the powdered magnesium, wrapped them in net (Gretchen found an old dress of her mom's and cut off the net petticoat), and added string wicks that he'd dipped, he told her earnestly, in a strong solution of potassium nitrate. Now he was lighting the wicks and using his slingshot to toss the soon-to-explode packets high in the air.

Gretchen heard Millard crashing back through the woods. He just had time to climb the oak when the soldiers swarmed into the clearing. Gretchen slithered from shadow to shadow, briefly shining the flash high on the tins. The reflected light quivered oddly high in the branches. She made her circuit, then slipped beneath a thick pine and lay on her stomach to watch.

Two more flares shone in the sky and then three in succession blazed right in front of the open shed doors.

The local *Gazette* used headlines as big as the Invasion of Sicily in its Friday edition:

ARMY UNIT FINDS BLACK MARKET GAS AT SISTER SUE MINE

Army authorities revealed Thursday afternoon that unexplained light flashing in the sky Wednesday night led a patrol to a cache of stolen gasoline . . .

It was the talk of the town. Five days later, when Deputy Sheriff Euel Carter was arrested, the local breakfast crowd was fascinated to hear from Mr. Hudson, who heard it from someone who heard it on the post, "You know how Euel always did them damfool crossword puzzles. Well," Mr. Hudson leaned across the table, "seems he left a newspaper right there in the storage shed and the puzzle was all filled out in his handwriting. Joe Bob Terrell from the *Gazette* recognized his handwriting, said he'd seen it a million times in arrest records. The newspaper had Euel's fingerprints all over it and they found his prints on the gas tins. They traced the tins to Camp Crowder and they checked the prints of everybody in the motor pool and found some from this sergeant, and his were on half the tins and on the boards that sealed up that shack by the Sister Sue. They got 'em dead to rights."

Gretchen poured more coffee and smiled. At lunch the nice officer— she'd known he would come that night—had left her a big tip. He'd looked at her, almost asked a question, then shook his head. She could go to Thompson's for a cherry fausfade in a little while and tell Millard everything she'd heard. It was too bad they couldn't tell everyone how clever Millard had been with the magnesium. But that was okay. What really mattered was the gas. Now maybe there'd be enough for Jimmy and Mike.

Carolyn Wheat

Show Me the Bones

CAROLYN WHEAT, much-traveled former Brooklyn defense attorney, received an Edgar nomination for her first novel, *Dead Man's Thoughts*, and has continued to win acclaim ever since. Wheat brings a quiet authority to her work, a sense that she has been there and back and thus feels no need to resort to melodrama or TV hokum. Her sensible, engaging voice does the job quite nicely, and does it every time. Here is an especially good Wheat story. This first appeared in *Diagnosis Dead*.

Show Me the Bones

Carolyn Wheat

H e doesn't look like a bloodhound," the little girl said. Her hair was dirty and so was her sharp little face and so were her bare feet.

What was the mother thinking, bare feet on this hard desert ground with spiky plants and lizards and scorpions and God knew what else? I had on my day hikers, the hightops, and two pair of socks under that. But then I intended to walk as far as the track would lead me, and the kid meant to stay in her mean little yard, among children's toys left out so long their bright colors had faded long ago because it hardly ever rained out here.

"He's not a bloodhound, honey," I said in a syrupy tone I barely recognized as my own. Why I invariably called all kids honey or sweetie or some other cotton-candy nickname I couldn't say. Except, I suppose, that they made me nervous with their direct little eyes and blunt questions. "He's a Bouvier, and his name is Polo."

"Can I pet him?" She edged her dirt-smudged hand with its bitten nails toward Polo's curly black head. Her thin wrists were scarred, I hoped from cacti and not abuse. The long red-tipped tendrils of ocotillo had sharp thorns; maybe she'd reached in to touch the flowers and torn her skin on the long needles.

"Do you think he'll find my sister?" The little girl's voice sounded squeezed through a thin tube, and she directed her gaze toward the ground instead of looking at me with her intense blue eyes.

God, I hope not, kid.

See, I never actually told the families what Polo was. They saw a dog, they figured "rescue." They figured tracking meant hunting for a living person on the move through the scrub. They didn't know Polo was a cadaver dog, trained to forget the living and find the dead.

I cleared my throat and said, "He's a good dog. He'll do his best, and so will I."

"Dogs always find lost people, don't they?" Now she gave me the full force of those blue eyes, gazing at me with a luminous innocence that pushed the breath out of my lungs. She looked both hopeful and scared to death, as if in some part of her eight-year-old brain she knew her sister wouldn't be found alive.

The ten-year-old had been missing five days now. Five long days and nights. The trackers worked all night; you didn't stop if you thought you might find a living child in need of medical care. But if you were looking for a body, you waited for first light.

There were four of us sheriff's department K-9 dog handlers gathered in the inky blue early morning. Devon had Kali, her black lab, on a long canvas leash. Kali roamed the perimeter, sniffing at each prickly pear, every cactus and bush, then looking back at Devon for confirmation that she was doing a good job. I always had the feeling the dogs were perpetually surprised to realize that their humans didn't actually smell the same things they did.

Scout, Jen's golden retriever, waved her feathery blond tail and sniffed the people instead of the bushes. Ruth's Daisy, the Doberman, wanted to do the same, but the child edged away as the Dobe headed toward her with a determined expression in her doggy brown eyes. Poor Daisy; she was as sweet as her name, but the Doberman reputation preceded her, and people often looked deathly afraid when all she wanted was to lick their faces.

We were waiting for one more team, and finally the metallic blue van with Nancy and Toby skidded into the dirt driveway. I even said to the kid, "Here comes a bloodhound," as if to reassure her that we were really taking her sister's disappearance seriously.

Blood drained from the child's face as Nancy slid open the door of her van and Toby bounded out. "A real bloodhound," she whispered.

"Do they smell the blood?" I had to strain to hear the words, then realized that in her ears, the word *bloodhound* carried sinister overtones.

But how to answer? How to say, well, no, it's not blood so much as the scent of a decaying corpse. Not exactly a reassuring reply.

Before I could formulate a suitable response, a deputy walked toward me and said, "We ready to get this show on the road?"

There were cops all over the place. The sheriff's vans and cars were parked farther along the dirt road, and they'd made a makeshift headquarters in the workshop at the rear of the little frame house. Radios crackled and guys milled around aimlessly while pretending to be incredibly busy. The real work was in the backcountry and everyone knew it. The cops who were still here were just waiting for news from the desert, news that would have them summoning an evac helicopter and a medic—or a crime scene team.

As the days and nights passed, the evac helicopter seemed less and less likely.

I didn't like being so close to the family of the missing child. I preferred law enforcement to keep itself separate from the grieving and the wailing, but out here in the middle of absolute backcountry nowhere, Ocotillo Wells, California—which called itself a town but was in reality a gas station, a hamburger joint, fourteen houses, and thirty mobile homes—there was nowhere to go that would insulate us from the little girl's devastating blue eyes.

Toby lived up to her expectations. She watched with undisguised fascination as the big brown animal loped along the hardpacked dirt, snout to the ground like a living vacuum cleaner, sniffing up every trace of scent. At one point, he stopped, threw back his head, and emitted his mournful howl.

The cops stopped talking. Jen and Ruth, who'd been gossiping in low tones, went silent, too, although they'd heard Toby's war cry a hundred times before. Something about that sound went right through a person, brought back tales of banshees and spirits of the dead crying from the grave.

The little girl burst into tears and ran toward the house. I wanted to stop her, to call out something that would reassure her, but I had no words. We were out here to find the body of her sister, and no sugar-coating was going to soften that blow.

It was time to get moving. Toby was ready, and that meant the rest of us were too. All the dogs were straining their leashes, eager to hit the trail and do the job they'd been trained for.

The sergeant broke us into smaller units. Each dog would accompany a sheriff's team heading in a different direction; we'd cover the backcountry near town first, hoping the child hadn't been abducted by a car and driven to El Centro.

Most of the other teams got into cars to be driven to a point of origin, but Polo and I would walk from the hamburger joint at the edge of town, right off Interstate 8. I would be with two deputies, one male, one female, both young and eager.

"First time you've worked with dogs?" I knew the answer by the way they eyed our animals, but I wanted to open conversation. They nodded in unison and introduced themselves as Don and Sarah.

When we reached the hamburger stand, which wasn't open for business but still emanated a strong odor of cooking grease, Polo bounced on his bear-like legs and jumped on me. "No, babe, not now," I said. "We're going to work, Polo." I leaned in close and spoke directly into his tiny black ears with a deep-voiced seriousness that Polo had been trained to recognize as meaning business.

"Find the bones, Polo. Find the bones." Polo leaped and gave a single bark to tell me he understood. I unhooked his leash and let him race into the brush.

Bones. Saying "find the bones" instead of "find the body" made it sound clean and bloodless. But the kid was gone only five days, and that meant whatever we found, it wouldn't be nice clean bleached bones like the skulls in a Georgia O'Keeffe painting. It would be messy and bloated and there would be flies. And the dogs would love it.

I liked this job, in a strange and horrible way. I liked being out in the wilderness and I liked giving Polo a job. Dogs were meant to work; they went a little crazy if all they were expected to do was entertain their humans. And I liked being of help to people, which finding bodies was when you thought about it. People needed to know the truth about their missing children or parents or whoever, and they needed the comfort of bodies recovered and buried according to their rituals.

Polo and I were trained for tracking the living as well as the dead, but somehow it was the cadaver searches we were assigned to the most. Toby, on the other hand, almost always worked living cases, but Nancy had been out of town when this child went missing, so she wasn't available for the early search teams, and Toby had to make do with bones instead of sniffing the kid's sweater.

See, living people all smell different, and you use an item with a person's individual scent on it in order to set the smell, get the dogs familiar with the exact scent they're tracking. But dead people all smell alike. So all you have to say is "find the bones" and the dogs will let you know when they find any dead human.

It was the finding-the-body part I didn't like very much, and the main reason for that was that the dogs loved it as much as I hated it. Polo loved it on a pure animal level, reveling in the smells and the grue, rolling in the human goop caused by a badly-decayed body, trying to eat the flesh and, in one memorable instance, carrying a decapitated head in his wide maw. I loved my big black bear of a dog, but it was hard to pet him for a little while after that, and if his tongue touched my flesh, I washed immediately.

But I was back on the trail the next week, with a Sunday morning training stint in between. The work had to be done, had to come before my distaste.

We walked a good five miles, mainly in silence on my part, although Don and Sarah talked in low tones. It was as if the kid, the little sister, walked with me and I didn't want to seem frivolous in the face of her loss.

Polo raced ahead, plunged into the brush, sniffed everything, and then ran back to me, urging us to move faster. At one point, he lingered over a cholla cactus wound around with jimsonweed; I stepped gingerly into the desert tangle and made my way toward him, only to find a very ripe jackrabbit corpse.

"Polo," I said, deliberately sharpening my voice, "those are not the bones. Find the bones, Polo. Show me the bones."

He was reluctant to leave his prize, but he really did know the difference between lunch and his job, so he trotted away, albeit not without a few fond looks back at the dead jack. The deputies gave one another surreptitious glances that said, boy are we wasting our time out here with this big ragmop of a dog. Wish we had the bloodhound.

Well, Polo and I would show them.

I hoped.

The morning sun popped up over the horizon with incredible swiftness, and the desert took on a new and colorful persona. Wildflowers bloomed in profusion, thanks to recent rains; cactus flowers were an improbable fuschia and there were poppies and desert lilies and yucca flowers standing straight as sentries over six feet tall.

The heat was growing by geometric proportions. I'd drunk half my water already and soaked my bandanna in it to keep the back of my neck cool.

The desert plants didn't care about the heat. They didn't care about anything, with their prickles and their leather skins, the gray-green not-quite-leaves that didn't even look plantlike. There were wildflowers smaller than your tiniest toenail and big yellow blooms on the barrel cacti and the long red-tipped ocotillo. Hawks circled overhead, and for a minute I wondered if we waited long enough, would we see turkey vultures and then we wouldn't even need Polo, we'd just follow the carrion birds to where the child's body lay.

We were going to find a body. I knew it. The hollow place in my stomach knew it. Five days out here; the kid wasn't alive. She couldn't be.

The sound of rapid, joyous barks from up ahead stopped my musing and had me running toward the ironwood tree. Polo bounded up to me and circled me, bumping against me to move me faster. Bouviers are herd dogs, but instead of nipping at the heels of their cows, they push the animals into compliance, as Polo was trying to do now to me and the deputies.

"He found her?" Don asked, his voice carrying a world of skepticism.

"That's what he's telling us," I replied, moving as quickly as I could in the oppressive heat.

"Show me the bones, Polo," I said, the little shudder of anticipation turning into a full-fledged tremble. "Show me the bones."

Polo skidded on the edge of the wash and headed down the steep incline. I leaned over and had a look. The body lay at the bottom of the arroyo, sprawled in a posture no living creature could have tolerated. Polo barked and pawed the ground, circling the body in a gruesome dance of triumph, crowing over his find and nuzzling the body with his snout.

It was a man. A Mexican, probably an illegal trying to make it into the U.S. His black hair was matted with blood. There were flies all over the place and a smell you didn't have to be canine to recognize.

I stood in stunned silence, then reacted like a handler, reaching into my vest pocket for the goody box. I made my way with slow carefulness down the slope and joined the deputies at the body. I opened my tupperware box and took out a dog treat.

"What are you doing?" Sarah's gray eyes were wide with disbelief. "You think this is a good time to feed your dog?"

"I'm not feeding him," I replied. I leaned as close to the stinking corpse as I could, and held the dog treat in my open hand. Polo bounced and snatched it, then did another circle dance of triumph. "Good dog," I said with forced brightness. "Good Polo. What a good dog. You found the bones, Polo."

I turned back to Sarah. "I'm rewarding him. He has to associate treats with the scent of bodies if he's going to be a good cadaver dog."

"But it's the wrong body."

"He doesn't know that."

I could hear the crackle of Don's radio; he was calling our find in to headquarters.

Polo jumped up on me. "Oh, you good dog. Oh, you perfect and beautiful beast," I crooned, resolutely keeping my eyes locked on his sweet black face instead of looking at the dead man. I didn't want to see more of what I'd already seen—the horrible movement of the body, which meant that insect life was taking over inside the rapidly decaying corpse.

I was trying to breathe as little as possible. Sarah reached into her vest pocket and pulled out a tiny jar of Vicks. She scooped some out and pushed it under her nose, then handed it to me. I took it with a nod of gratitude and filled my nostrils with the strong scent of menthol, hoping to block out the overpowering odor of human rot.

Don's orders were to remain with the body while Sarah and I made our way back to Ocotillo Wells. We'd make a circle, continuing to search as we headed west.

I had to pull Polo away by brute force; every instinct in his body told him to stay with the dead man, to examine him fully and to—God forbid, but he was a dog, and dogs will be dogs—eat some of him. This I didn't explain to Sarah, somehow becoming as protective of her as I'd felt toward the little girl back at the frame house.

I walked for a while without giving a new order, letting Polo adjust to the fact that he was now heading away from "the bones" instead of toward them.

I saw the child's guileless blue eyes before me. *Will you find my sister?*

"Sarah?" I stepped up my pace until I strode next to the deputy, who was moving with angry swiftness. "Any news from the base?"

"You mean was the kid at her grandmother's eating cookies and milk? Not hardly. They're sending a helicopter and two more dog teams. Anybody finds that kid, it won't be us. Thanks to that damn body in the wash."

I nodded. I'd known that had to be the case; if there'd been news, Don would have said so. But the little ghost girl walking next to me had to hear it for herself.

I didn't even know her name, yet she was as clearly part of the expedition as Polo and I. The missing girl was Melissa Sue. Ten years old. The child at the base was about eight, although I wasn't much of a kid person, so she could have been seven or nine.

Why didn't I know her name? Why hadn't I asked?

What the hell was I going to say to her if—when?— we found her sister.

I didn't have to say anything. That was the cops' job. But I knew that this time I would. This time I couldn't just load Polo into the van and head home for a much needed hot shower, leaving the body and the search behind me. Pretending to myself that this had been no more than a practice run, with Body in a Bottle instead of the real thing.

It was time to give Polo his new command. I bent down and spoke into his tiny ear. He reeked of creosote bush and cadaver. "Find the bones, Polo. Go find the bones for me, boy."

He gave his yelp of understanding and bounded into the brush. He was matted with cactus fishhooks and spine clusters and his paws looked as if they hurt from the hard ground, but he set off with an enthusiasm that put Sarah and me to shame. We were spent, demoralized by the body in the wash, and more than ready to pack it in—but for the need to bring the little girl home for her final rest.

We passed mesquite and pencil cactus, sun-wilted evening primrose and century plants, huge feathery palo verde trees at the edge of arroyos, prickly pears six feet tall with giant red balls ready to open into fleshy blooms.

Some people thought the desert was beautiful. I thought it was scary as hell, a dangerous place where only the strong survived, and I felt about as strong as a pillow.

How in God's name was a ten-year-old going to survive out here, even if she was born and brought up in Ocotillo Wells?

We were approaching the town. I could tell because I heard the Interstate's low hum and caught a glimpse of dust rising from the dirt road behind the hamburger joint. More sheriff's cars, I supposed, come to join in what the newspeople would call the massive manhunt. Or maybe the newsvans themselves, each local channel out to get a sound bite for the evening report.

Massive girlhunt.

Where would a little girl go around here? This wasn't like my Michigan girlhood where there were creeks and parks and trees to climb, secret places only your best pals knew about. There was simply no shade anywhere, no honest-to-God trees to shelter you and let you climb into green, leafy hideaways.

My face was bright hot red despite the slathers of sunscreen and my straw hat. I was out of water, having given most of mine to Polo. We'd been out here five hours, and already we were ready to pack it in.

And Melissa Sue had been missing five days.

There was no way she could have carried five days' worth of water, and despite the recent rains, there weren't enough streams with drinkable water for her to stay alive.

Polo looked discouraged, too. He still sniffed the mesquite and the cactus, rubbed against the desert mistletoe and poked a very cautious nose into the ocotillo, but he moved more slowly and his tongue hung from his mouth as his craving for water grew more intense.

We had to stop. Sarah looked more than ready to take a shade break, and I didn't think there was much point in continuing the hunt. By now the town was in view; I could see the red roof of the hamburger place that was the town's only landmark.

Polo raised his head and sniffed the air. He stood, only his head moving this way and that, clearly trying to capture an elusive scent.

"Can't he hurry up?" Sarah's voice was sharp with fatigue and disappointment.

"I think he's on scent," I replied. "He may have something."

"Oh, come on, we're practically back at base. Every inch of this place has been searched already. It's probably another jackrabbit."

I ignored her and said, "Show me the bones, Polo. Show me the bones."

He gave his yelp of understanding and moved in the direction the scent led him.

You know the expression, being led around by the nose?

That's precisely what Polo looks like when he's on an elusive scent. His nose sniffs the air and he follows it. That simple. The shiny black nose catches a tiny whiff and he moves his head this way and that to make sure he's following the strongest odor.

Scent flows like water. If we could see what dogs smell, we'd see eddies and streams, scents blown on the air like twigs on top of a stream.

He was moving slowly. I liked that; it meant he had something and was being as careful as he could be to track it to the source.

"Show me. Show me the bones."

"There aren't going to be any damn bones."

I didn't usually tell sheriff's deputies to shut the hell up, but this was going to be an exception.

Polo barked. A single, sharp bark, and then he took off running toward a palo verde tree in the distance. I followed at the swiftest pace I could muster, while Sarah brought up a sullen rear.

He circled. He twisted his big black body and wagged his stub of a tail. His ears flattened and he bounded ahead, kicking up dust with his big bear-like paws.

"Find the bones," I called, which was pretty stupid because he was doing just that, but I wanted him to know I understood and appreciated.

Next to the palo verde stood an abandoned well. Polo circled it, then pawed the ground next to it.

"Oh, my God," I cried, racing toward the stone structure. "The kid's in the well."

Polo barked and pawed, lowering his muzzle to the dirt and then pawing again. His unmistakable signal that he'd found the bones.

The child's body was at the bottom of the long stone tunnel. Alice caught in the rabbit hole, forever in Wonderland.

Sarah called it in on her radio, her voice swelling with triumph, naively pleased at being the one to find the body. In this, she resembled Polo, who did his victory dance, although he was disappointed at not being able to get really close to the corpse. I took out my goody box and went through the reward ritual while I pondered the best way to break the news to the little girl back at the frame house.

And then I saw the jack.

Not a jackrabbit, but a little metal jack, the kind you scoop up after you bounce a rubber ball. I didn't know kids still played with jacks, and there was nothing to indicate how long the jack had lain in the gray desert dust, but the truth stabbed me like a pencil cactus thorn.

The child hadn't been hoping the bloodhound would find her sister. She'd been deathly afraid the bloodhound would unearth the truth. She knew where her sister was, but she'd been afraid to tell her parents.

Two little girls in the desert, playing wherever they could, using the thin shade of the palo verde and the stone well as their special place.

Had the child died instantly from the fall, or had she lain inside calling for help?

And why hadn't the little sister told her parents? Was the household so abusive that she was more afraid of the punishment than she was of her sister dying? Or was she simply too young to understand the consequences of falling into the well?

I would probably never know. I would go back into town and let Sarah do her cop duty, let the wheels of law enforcement turn with excruciating slowness.

I would put Polo in the back of my van, drive home and give both of us a long, scented bath to wash away the sweat and the smells, and I would write up my report and move on to the next search, the next body.

But I didn't think I'd ever go out tracking again without the little sister at my side, her blue eyes wide, her face pinched with the fear that the dogs would reveal hidden truth she was too afraid to face.

"Good dog, Polo," I said again, but it was hard to praise him for finding out what I hadn't really wanted to know.

J. A. Jance

A Flash of Chrysanthemum

When JUDY JANCE was just beginning her career, she spent a lot of lonely hours driving up and down the West Coast promoting her books via bookstore signings and interviews. As most writers will tell you, this is far more draining than actually writing books. Well, her efforts certainly paid off. She is now a national best-seller, and her books just keep on earning more and more praise. Her work is fun to read; she's a natural storyteller who knows her turf as well as she knows the human heart. This story first appeared in *Murder on Route 66*.

A Flash of Chrysanthemum

J. A. Jance

The year goes out in a flash of chrysanthemum:
But we, who cell by cell and
Pang upon pang, are dragged to execution,
Live out the full dishonor of the clay.

I first heard those words in a college auditorium on a January night alive with orange blossoms and promise when C. Day-Lewis, the English Poet Laureate, came to the University of Arizona to read his work. *Baucis and Philemon*, one of the poems he read that night, was delivered to an audience made up primarily of English Major, poetry devotees.

Only nineteen at the time, it was hard for me to imagine what those words meant. Oh, maybe my hips and waist would thicken one day, making my figure match my fifty-year-old mother's, but in reality that possibility seemed remote. In fact, it wasn't until I hit fifty myself when the idea of aging gained an actual foothold in my consciousness.

At fifty-one and finding myself beset with nights of sleep-depriving hot flashes, it was far easier to imagine what might happen. I could see then how that single troublesome molar—the lower left-hand one that for years had shied away from everything cold—might one day do something so drastic as to simply fall out. Or else have to be pulled. Or that my chins—all several of them—would gradually subside into the suddenly excess folds of skin that now flowed down what was once a reasonably slender neck.

It even crossed my mind at times that fading into what I imagined to be the gentle haze of Alzheimer's-induced forgetfulness might be simpler, for me, than dealing with either the ongoing battles between my two feuding daughters or with the once-favored son who hasn't spoken to Ted and me since two years ago last Christmas.

Those ideas came on gradually, creeping up almost imperceptibly over a period of time. But what I never imagined, not in all my wildest dreams— nightmares, if you will—was the appalling reality of what was actually to be. Or what is. No, I didn't see that coming, not in a million years.

We talked about it, Ted and I, when the diagnosis first came in during those stunned but strangely intimate and innocent days when Lou Gehrig was still a baseball player whose life and death had nothing whatsoever to do with me. We started out by reading all the available books and literature on the subject and by trying to imagine what it would be like. No matter how many books we read though, we weren't really prepared. Nobody ever is.

In our naivete, we didn't nearly grasp the grimly inexorable way in which my limbs would be deprived of all usefulness; how they would gradually give up the ghost while still apparently attached to what passes for a living, breathing body. We reassured each other, saying that we understood and that it would be all right. We were in love and we would get through it together somehow. But now, as my ruined body lies virtually helpless on a rail-lined hospital bed or sits trapped as a strapped-in prisoner in this damnable chair, my mind still roams free.

In my imagination I am once again a carefree child, clambering over the dusty, ocotillo-punctuated hills of my Arizona desert youth, leaping off rough burgundy chunks of long dead lava, or wading in the murky depths of some slime-bottomed, polliwog-teeming pond. That's part of the irony of it all. The body perishes but the mind persists, as though the stillness of the one somehow drives the other further and further into frantic hyperactivity.

In the beginning I thought that having time on my hands would be an unheard-of luxury, that I would find solace in doing some long-delayed reading or maybe in listening to books on tape. But that whole idea was an outright lie, a cruel hoax. Time is now my enemy—there is far too much of it—and I no longer have any patience for other people's words. As for my own words, the laborious process of typing them out, one arduous letter at a time, using the computer and my one big toe, takes too long. Far too long.

As I said, Ted and I talked about it all in the beginning. Now I can't talk anymore, and he barely does. At the onset, we both thought we were being very straightforward. And honest. And brave. Ted promised me then that he would gather up a cache of pills—enough to do the job—and that he would put them in a safe place so I would have them "when the time comes." That's how we always put it back then. "When the time comes."

It sounds now as though we more or less expected a timer to go off somewhere in the vast universe announcing that I was ready for the next step. Like a school bell ringing in an almost empty corridor, or like the stove-top timer that used to announce, with an annoying, noisy buzz, that it was time to take the cookies or the loaves of bread or the pumpkin pies out of the oven. Come to think of it, there's not that much baking going on in our house these days. I don't believe I've heard that buzzer sound once during the last two years. I don't suppose I'll ever hear it again.

But getting back to Ted and me, between the two of us, we never actually spoke about death or dying. Those words were far too blatant. Too blunt. Too coarse. They were always there between us—assumed but unacknowledged—like the stifling but unspeakable odor of a first-date fart. Except Ted and I weren't on a first-date basis anymore, not by a long shot. We have three grown children between us and two grandkids. We've barely seen them—the grandchildren, I mean—and I sometimes wonder if they'll even remember me when they're grown. Probably not. Maybe that's just as well.

The problem is the time for decisive action came and went. The bell rang and we did nothing. Ted probably still has that deadly assortment of pills, squirreled away somewhere out of sight if not out of mind, but they're useless to me now—useless to both of us. I can no longer swallow. If he gave them to me now—if he mashed them up in a selfless act of love and somehow mixed them into the gray gruel that flows through my feeding tube, the authorities would have him up on murder charges so fast it would make his head swim.

At the time we were discussing the pills, back when we both still believed them to be our option of last resort, I guess we both thought they would be a blessing for me, an escape that would allow me to dodge the worst of what was coming. I know now, that isn't true, either. At this moment, the pills would help me and I would welcome them, but Ted's the one who really needs them. Not for him to take himself, of course, but for me. He needs to be set free of me and of everything that goes with me—of all the unrelenting labor and responsibility. And of the awful sores. But most of all, of the smells.

They say you can't smell yourself, but that's not true. I wake up sometimes in the middle of the night with my heart pounding in my chest and feeling as though I'm drowning. When I come to my senses and can finally breathe again, the first thing I notice is the odor. *What is it?* I wonder. *Is something rotten? What can it be?* Eventually I realize that what I'm smelling is me. I can't get away from that appalling stench, and neither can Ted. There's no perfume strong enough to disguise it or to cover it up, and there's no escape from it, either.

Did I mention before that I am writing this with my big toe? Poor, patient, loving Ted never said a word about how much it cost to rig this keyboard so I could use it with my one good foot, but it does take forever, tapping out one paltry letter at a time. In the good old days, I used to be a touch typist. Sometimes, in my dreams, my fingers still fly over the keyboard. The letters appear on the screen seemingly by magic, almost as fast as I can think them.

It's a wonderful dream when it happens. It reminds me of one I used to have when I was a child—a dream about running side by side with a guy named Jim Thorpe. He would smile down at me encouragingly and say, "Come on, kid. You can do it. We'll run fast enough to catch the wind."

Moving fingers. Moving legs. Catching the wind. They're all just dreams now. Figments of my imagination. Pieces of a long-lost if not forgotten past.

But where was I? Oh, I remember, Ted—poor Ted. Sometimes I feel more sorry for him than I do for me. Back in the old days, when sticky murder plots still leaked out through my fingers as easily as a slender thread of spun-glass Karo Syrup flows out of its crystal clear bottle, I could have told him how to do it. I probably could even have given him some pointers about how to get away with it. But Ted's beyond that now. I can no longer swallow, and he's too worn out with taking care of me to think about doing anything else.

I've been busy dying, and so has he. I don't think he even has enough strength left over to consider how life will be for him once all this is over; once I'm gone and he no longer has to spend every waking moment worrying about me—worrying and taking care.

I started writing this weeks ago, whenever Ted was out of the room and unable to see what I was doing. Now's the time to finish it.

It's our wedding anniversary today—our thirty-fifth. Yesterday, just as I asked, he brought me here to the same place we came years ago on our wedding night. We were both beginning teachers then, with matching first-year contracts in Bullhead City. It was semester break, and we had been on our way to the Grand Canyon. We had honeymoon reservations in Bright Angel Lodge, but we never made it there. A sudden late January blizzard closed roads all across northern Arizona and New Mexico. We spent both days of our two-day honeymoon stranded in a godforsaken place called Kingman.

I think we must have rented one of the last rooms left in town. We spent the whole time in an upstairs room in this same motel, although now there's a different name on the sign out front. Tonight we're in a downstairs, wheelchair-accessible room. On our wedding night, we had a glorious dinner in the dining room—prime rib and baked potatoes, followed by baked Alaska. We spent the rest of the evening in the bar dancing to a three-piece country combo.

It wasn't until we went upstairs to bed that we discovered how close our room was to the railroad tracks. Freight trains came rumbling past at least three times overnight and woke us up. Each time that happened we made love. It was wonderful.

Things are different now. The trains still run, but making love is out of the question. The motel is a little rundown. No band in the bar. I couldn't eat the food, of course, but Ted said it wasn't all that good anyway, certainly not as good as he remembered. After dinner, he asked me what I wanted to do. He offered to put me to bed and turn on the TV. He was being so nice about it—so good and patient and loving—that it took a while for me to pick the necessary fight. It's hell starting a fight when you have to squeeze the ugly words out through your body one impatient letter at a time.

GO AWAY, I told him. LEAVE ME ALONE. He read the words I'd written on the screen, but even then he was still willing to get me ready for bed before he went out. I told him, NO. JUST LEAVE. Finally he did.

He must be mad or hurt or maybe both, because he's been gone for at least two hours now. That's longer than he's ever left me alone before. And that's exactly what I've needed—time alone.

The wheelchair runs on commands from the same keyboard I'm typing this on. G is for GO and S for STOP. This is a handicapped room, so the door has a handle rather than a knob. After half an hour of terrible struggle, I've finally managed to pull it open.

The air outside is cold as I sit here drenched in sweat with the door wide open and with the wind whistling in. I know timing is everything. Last night I stayed awake all night and clocked the trains. The next one is due in twenty minutes. The track is just a little more than a block away. If I go too soon, someone might see me at the crossing and try to pull me out of the way. If I arrive too late, I'll miss it—miss my only chance. My last chance.

I've come as far as I want to down this miserable road. I don't want to travel any farther—not for me and, even more so, not for Ted.

It can't be too much longer now. I wish I could leave the computer here in the room and out of harm's way, but it's attached to the chair and so the machine has no choice. Whither I go, it must go too—sort of like Ruth and her mother-in-law.

It's cold now. Dreadfully cold. And the light blanket Ted draped over my legs when we were inside isn't nearly enough out here in the freezing night air.

Back when we were here before, the whole building shook each time a train came through town. That was what woke us up—the shaking. I'm shaking now. I don't know if it's because I'm cold or if it's because the train is finally coming. If it is the train, it's still so far up the track that I can't see the headlight. But it will have to come soon, looming up over me out of the darkness, turning night to day. And, like Philemon's chrysanthemum, changing my life—or what passes for it anyway—into something else entirely.

Thank you, Ted. Thank you for everything, and especially for the flash. I love . . .

Loren D. Estleman

The Man in the
White Hat

LOREN D. ESTLEMAN, like Bill Pronzini, has an affinity for both the Chandleresque mystery novel and the authentic novel of the West. If you want to read some of the best western fiction of the past few decades, try Estleman's *City of Widows, The Stranglers,* or *Gunman.* He is equally good at crime fiction. Amos Walker is his most famous creation, a hardworking working-class private eye from Motor City, but Estleman has launched a few other series as well, notably the supremely comic "Pepper" in the novel of the same name. This story first appeared in the May issue of *Ellery Queen's Mystery Magazine.*

The Man in the White Hat

Loren D. Estleman

A painting the size of a barn door greeted Valentino inside the entrance to the Red Montana and Dixie Day Museum on Ventura. In it, an implausibly young Montana sat astride a rearing white stallion—Tinderbox, of course—smiling broadly and waving his milk-colored Stetson. Across from it hung a more subdued study of Dixie Day, the cowboy hero's wife, younger still and pretty in tailored white buckskins, leading her mare Cocoa. The guard stationed between the paintings found the visitor's name on the guest list and directed him to the reception.

He found the guests shuffling around a floor with a tile mosaic of Montana and Day backed by Old Glory. Scooping a glass of champagne from a passing tray, he wandered along the walls, admiring the framed stills from the couple's many horse operas until someone signaled for attention.

Red Montana in person was not as tall as he appeared on film, and he had put on weight since retirement; his chins spilled over the knot of his silk necktie. His suit, with flared lapels and arrow pockets, was beautifully cut, although it probably hadn't cost much more than his head of silver hair, a tribute to the wigmaker's craft. His voice was reedy with age, but retained an echo of the hearty bray of a circus ringmaster.

"Howdy, friends and neighbors. I ain't tall on speechifyin', so I'll make this short and sweet. As of this moment, the Dixie Day Foundation has raised more than two million dollars for cancer research. Dixie ain't feeling up to joining us, but she asked me special to thank all you folks for opening up your hearts and pocketbooks."

Hands clapped, flashguns went off. The cowboy star issued a mock-stern order not to be bashful about "bellyin' up to the cook wagon," and then the assembly broke into small groups. Valentino joined a line waiting to shake Montana's hand. He found the old man's grip surprisingly firm.

"You're that detective feller."

Valentino clarified. "*Film* detective. Actually, I'm just an historian."

"Meet me in the curator's office in five minutes."

There were exhibition rooms off the corridor, but Valentino didn't look inside any of them. He'd heard Montana had had the original Tinderbox stuffed and mounted and was reluctant to find out that the story wasn't just an urban myth.

It was obvious the curator's office actually belonged to Montana. The walls were covered with autographed pictures of him shaking hands with various presidents, Ernest Hemingway, and Albert Einstein. Montana's famous silver-studded saddle perched on a stand behind a desk supporting a computer console and a fax machine. The old man was seated at the desk, signing his name to one of a stack of eight-by-ten glossies at his elbow. He placed it on the stack and thanked Valentino for coming.

"Thank you for the invitation." He'd wondered why he'd been on the list, since neither he nor the UCLA Film Preservation Department had contributed to the Dixie Day Foundation.

"They tell me you can sniff out a foot of silver-nitrate stock in a pile of horse manure."

"I hope I'll never have to," Valentino said. "But I've found portions of lost classic films in some unlikely places."

"I need someone with detective skills. I'd go to a pro, but I've been in the movie business sixty years. I only trust film people. I hear you can keep a secret."

"It's important if I'm going to stay ahead of Viacom and Ted Turner." He wondered where this was headed.

"I'm counting on that." Montana produced a key ring with a silver horse's head attached, unlocked a drawer, and drew out an eight-by-ten Manila envelope. "You're aware my wife is dying."

Valentino expressed sympathy. All Hollywood knew Dixie Day had inoperable cancer and that the couple had chosen to spend her last months raising money for cancer research. Her popularity as the Sweetheart of the Range was an asset to the cause.

"These were faxed to me here last week." Montana opened the envelope and handed him a sheaf of paper.

It was plain fax stock. The images that had been scanned onto the sheets were smudged and grainy, but Valentino recognized Dixie Day's face from her old movies. She appeared no older than twenty, naked in the arms of an unclothed anonymous male.

"Are you sure they're genuine?"

"I checked that out years ago, the first time I saw them. They're enlargements of frames from a stag film Dixie made before she broke in at RKO. I paid a hundred thousand cash for the negative, and what I was assured was every existing print, and burned them. I thought that was the end of it."

"You can never be sure how many prints were made. Do you think it's the same blackmailer?" He gave back the pictures.

"I have no idea. I put the cash in a paper sack in a locker at LAX, as I was instructed in the letter that came with the sample print. The next day the negative and prints came by special delivery. I never made direct contact with anyone. This time I haven't even received a demand. Just these." He jammed the sheaf back into the envelope, returned it to the drawer, and closed and locked it. "I want you to find out who sent them."

"I wouldn't know where to start."

"Talk to Sam O'Reilly. He's living at the Actors' Home."

"Your old sidekick? I thought he died."

"He pretty much did, as far as the studios were concerned: drank himself right out of paying work. He's always blamed me for not going to bat for him. Drunks are never responsible for the jackrabbit holes they step in. It'd be just like him to try and get back at me by ruining Dixie's reputation."

"Why me? You've offered to match every dollar the Foundation brings in. That means you can afford to hire a private agency and pay for its discretion."

"I told you, I only trust film people. And I've got incentive. Switch off that light, will you, son?"

Valentino flipped the switch next to the door, plunging the room into darkness. At the same moment, Montana pressed something under the desk. A white screen hummed down from the ceiling and a wall panel opened behind the desk, exposing a projector. Montana pressed something else and the projector came on with a whir.

For the next five minutes, the film detective was entranced by ancient black-and-white images of galloping horses and smoking six-guns, accompanied by a tinny soundtrack full of thundering music and hard-bitten frontier dialogue. When his host turned off the projector, it took him a moment to find the light switch.

"*Six-gun Sonata*," Valentino said, recovering. "The first feature to pair Red Montana and Dixie Day. I heard it was lost."

"I bought it from Republic cheap in nineteen forty and put it in a vault. Later I struck off a new master on safety stock and destroyed the original nitrate print. A collector offered me a quarter-million for it last year. I told him I didn't have it. What do I need with another quarter-million? Now I'm offering it to you, payable on delivery of the blackmailer's name."

"I'm really not that kind of detective."

Montana sat back, resting his hands on his paunch. "*Six-gun Sonata* means nothing to me. If you turn me down, I'll burn it."

"What makes that different from blackmail?"

"I didn't say I was better than this scum. Just richer."

Valentino thought. He was reeling from the double blow of finding, then perhaps losing, a cinematic treasure and learning that this champion of the Code of the West had much in common with the blackguards he'd pursued in feature after feature.

"I'll see O'Reilly," he said. "I can't promise anything."

"There's the difference." Montana took a cigar from the box on the desk and produced a lighter with a diamond horseshoe on it. "I can." The jet of flame signaled the end of the meeting.

"He said *that*?"

Sam "Slap" O'Reilly hadn't changed so much physically that the film detective couldn't recognize him from his comic bits in Red Montana movies. The whiskey welts on his long horsey features were new and his hair was thin, but brushed neatly. His room at the Motion Picture Actors' Home was as tidy as the man himself, seated in a deep armchair in loose tan slacks, slippers, and a white shirt buttoned to the neck. There was nothing present to mark his career in movies, only family photographs and a letter in crayon from a great-grandchild, tacked to a bulletin board.

"Montana's a liar," he went on. "It's true my drinking cut short my livelihood, but I never asked anyone to bail me out, least of all him. I haven't touched a drop in thirty years."

"What split you up, if not that?" Valentino asked.

"We never did like each other. Audiences liked me, and that was enough to keep me on contract. But I never really hated him until he stole Dixie from me."

"You and Dixie Day?"

He grinned, spurring memories of his old dimwit persona. "I was quite a man with the ladies off the set, guess you didn't know that. But it was a mistake to introduce Dixie to Montana. We were shooting a three-day oater on loan to RKO. He talked to the director and got her a bit, one line. The audience fell for her. Republic signed her and the next thing you know they're both billed above the title. They got married a year later."

"You must resent them both."

"Not Dixie. You can't blame a girl for taking advantage of a break, and anyway I don't think she felt anything for me. I did for her, though. Montana knew that, and he went after her the way he went after money and glory, and God help whoever got in his way."

"That was almost sixty years ago. A long time to be angry."

"I'm not angry. I was for a long time, but I got over it. If I'd married Dixie I'd have messed that up just like I messed it up with the woman I did marry." His face went slack. "Who'd you say you were with, again? My memory isn't so good these days."

"The Film Preservation Department at UCLA. I'm trying to track down a movie Dixie Day made before she met Red Montana." He'd cooked up the half-lie on the way there from the museum.

"I wouldn't know anything about it. I'd only been going out with her a couple of weeks when I brought her to the set. We met at a party. She came there with a cameraman. I'll remember his name in a minute." His mind wandered. "I hear Dixie's in a bad way."

"The doctors don't give her long to live."

"I'm sorry. She was a good old gal, too good for Montana. I hope that crumb doesn't stuff her like he did Tinderbox."

"The cameraman," Valentino prompted.

"Cameraman?" When the muscles in O'Reilly's features let go, he truly looked old. "Uh. Dick Hennessey. I remember his name on account of Hal Roach bounced him later. It was a big scandal at the time. Cops busted him for shooting stag films on the side."

The only promising-looking Richard Hennessey listed in Los Angeles County ran a production company in Pasadena. He answered his own telephone.

"My father was a cameraman," he told Valentino. "He passed away six years ago."

"I'm very sorry. I'm looking for a film he might have shot back in the thirties."

"For Hal Roach?"

"No, it was something on the side."

"Oh, you mean the porno stuff. Can't help you there. The judge had it all burned after Pop was convicted. He did a hundred and thirty-six hours of community service, a record then. Fatty Arbuckle didn't get that."

Valentino didn't bother pointing out Arbuckle was acquitted.

Hennessey's candor had surprised him. "That must be a painful memory."

"Not at all. Pop opened his own photo-supply store and did all right. His films were tame by today's standards. The A studios shoot steamier stuff all the time and get away with an R rating."

"You *saw* some of his stag films?"

"Better than that. I was his assistant. The only ten-year-old apprentice cinematographer in the business."

Hennessey Productions worked out of an ornate old Queen Anne house on San Diego Boulevard. The film detective tiptoed among the cables and equipment cluttering a large room on the ground floor and shook hands with a thickset man in shirtsleeves standing with a director half his age. Nearby a young couple sat up in bed, the woman smoking, the man having his makeup touched up by a technician. They were plainly naked under the sheet.

Hennessey was a ruddy-faced sixty-something, with gold chains around his neck and his hair dyed glossy black. "We're shooting a two-reeler for the Playboy Channel," he said. "I'm not doing anything Pop didn't do, but now it's respectable."

He and his visitor adjourned to a break room equipped with a refrigerator and microwave oven. They sat down at a laminated table.

"Valentino. Any relation?"

"My father says no. Let's talk about yours."

"Gladly. I owe everything to Pop. He helped me get set up in business and loaned me money to stay afloat through the last recession."

"You don't think it was irresponsible to expose you to his stag operation at such an early age?"

"I was a Hollywood brat. If you want to hear about exposing, talk to the producer who exposed himself to Shirley Temple in his office at Fox. At least my old man taught me a trade."

"Did that trade include Dixie Day?"

Hennessey showed no surprise. "Your eyes would pop out of your head if I told you the names of the future movie queens who took off their clothes for my father. I could make a fortune off cable if those films still existed."

"One of them does."

"It's true the cops missed one when they raided the studio. It was being developed in a custom lab at the time. I remember Pop saying something about it, but I don't know if Dixie Day was in it. It wasn't among his stuff when he died."

"You said he made you a loan before he died. May I ask how much it was?"

"A hundred thousand dollars."

Valentino dropped his gaze. He didn't want the glint to show. "That was generous."

"You could have knocked me over with a chorus boy. I never dreamed anyone could put aside that much selling Minoltas to tourists."

"Did he keep records?"

"He was anal about it. I've got three file cases in the basement. You can take a look if you'd like."

Valentino said, "I'd like."

The Montana-Day "ranch"—the Circle M—comprised fourteen acres in the Hollywood Hills, a tract that cost as much as a thousand-acre spread in Texas. The house was a rambling hacienda, 10,000 square feet of pink adobe with a red tile roof. The guard at the gate was got up like an old-time lawman, complete with Stetson and sheriff's star. He was expecting Valentino and waved him on through.

A stout Mexican woman in maid's livery led the visitor to a bright sunroom walled in with glass on three sides, where an old woman awaited him in a wheelchair. She spoke quietly to a younger woman in a nurse's uniform, who left the room on rubber heels.

"I met the original Valentino once, when I was seven years old," said the old woman. "You favor him."

"So I've been told. Thank you for seeing me, Miss Day. Or do you prefer Mrs. Montana?"

"Miss Day will do." The reply held a harsh edge. She had aged well, and skillful makeup disguised most of the ravages of her illness. The turban she wore to cover the baldness caused by radiation therapy was an exotic touch, but he could still see in her that well-scrubbed, all-American quality that had won the simple hearts of Depression audiences. The Wild West Show glitter she wore in public was conspicuously absent from her present costume of blouse, slacks, and open-toed shoes. "How is Dick Junior? All grown up and then some, I suppose. His father certainly kept him busy around the set."

Over the telephone, he'd told her he'd spoken with Richard Hennessey. "I was afraid you'd deny knowing either of them," he said.

"You can't make the past go away by pretending it didn't exist. Lord knows I would if I thought it would work."

"I spent two hours in Hennessey's basement going through his father's records. He wrote down everything, even the details of his blackmail."

"That alone proves he wasn't cut out for it. He was desperate to save his son from bankruptcy or he never would have considered it. He came to see me while Red was in L.A., supervising the construction of the museum. He brought a print of the film with him. He offered to show it to me in the screening room, but I said that wouldn't be necessary. I knew what was on it. You saw some of the frame enlargements. I had a good body, don't you think?"

"You were a beautiful woman." He didn't know what else to say.

"Poor Dick. Do you know what he was asking for the film? Ten thousand dollars. I told him he could get ten times that from Red. He said he preferred dealing with me. He was so nervous, and so ashamed. I think he'd have given it to me for nothing if it weren't for Junior's situation. He would have been that glad to be out of it."

"Why didn't you pay him?"

"I couldn't. I don't have any money. The museum, this ranch, all the bank accounts and investment portfolios are in Red's name. I haven't had control of a cent since the day we married. I have to ask him for money to visit the beauty parlor. My husband is a mean, stingy man, Mr. Valentino. And that's not even his worst quality."

Valentino said nothing. He felt he was on the verge of learning something he'd just as soon never know; but the hints Dick Hennessey, Sr. had dropped into his daily journal had started him in a direction he couldn't reverse.

"Red has a violent temper. All our friends think I suffer from migraines. That's what Red tells them when they visit and I'm upstairs waiting for my bruises to heal. In nineteen fifty he threw me down a flight of stairs and told the press I broke my leg when I fell while exercising Cocoa, my mare. I won't go into every incident. It galls him to pay the servants as much as he must to keep them from selling the real story to the tabloids."

"Why didn't you divorce him?"

"Weakness. Pride. Red Montana and Dixie Day is one of the great love stories of Hollywood. Who was I to blow apart the fairy tale? The old studio system made us slaves to our public images. By the time I finally stopped caring, it was too late. You get used to living in hell. That doesn't mean you stop hating the devil."

Valentino had begun to experience the same dizzy sensation he'd felt at the museum. "What are you trying to tell me?"

"I haven't many weeks left," she said. "I suppose it's the time for confessions."

"*You're* the blackmailer?"

"Only indirectly. I told Dick he could squeeze a hundred thousand out of Red easily. I even helped him work out the details. The only thing my husband has is the pure white image of Red Montana and Dixie Day. It's an icon. He's built his fortune on it; it's his ticket to immortality. I knew if Dick succeeded I'd never hear a word about it from Red. I was right.

"Dick offered to split the money with me," she went on. "I didn't want it, but I did ask him for one thing."

"A print of the stag film."

She smiled a Dixie smile, straight off the milk carton.

"You shouldn't sell yourself short as a detective. I'd planned to release it to an exhibitor when Red died, but fate forced my hand. In a way I was glad. Now I'd get to watch him suffer."

"You sent him the frame enlargements."

"A very old friend of mine made them in the film laboratory at Sony. I felt the need to torment Red. They'll drive him crazy until I'm gone. He'll think he's safe then. What he doesn't know is I've arranged for my friend to make additional prints and send them to every sleazy theater and cable station in Southern California. Let Red try to exploit *that* for his own glory the way he did my terminal cancer. The only thing I've had since our wedding that was truly mine."

She balled her fists on the arms of the wheelchair. Beneath the makeup her face was a naked skull. "Think of it. However long he outlives me, he'll bear the stigma of the has-been cowboy hero who married Jezebel. And when he's gone, the world will be only too relieved to forget us both."

Suddenly Valentino found that sun-filled room in the Hollywood Hills suffocating. He wanted to be anywhere else.

His hostess misinterpreted his discomfort. "I'm sorry, Mr. Valentino. Whatever my husband promised you, I assure you he won't honor it when he hears the truth. You'd be better off telling him you failed. Is there something I can do to make it up to you? I'd offer to autograph a picture, but I don't think it will be worth much for long."

Valentino thought of *Six-gun Sonata*, that monument to chivalry and innocence, as thin as the celluloid it was made of. He didn't think he could watch it, or any Montana-Day picture, without seeing a bloated egomaniac and his battered, bitter wife. He shook his head and left. He didn't breathe easily again until he'd descended into the smog and smut of Los Angeles.

Gary Phillips

'53 Buick

The Jook is one of the most startling novels of the past few years. You may think you know Los Angeles, but whatever your preconceptions, GARY PHILLIPS will quickly and forcefully change your mind. Phillips is a hands-on political man, a pro who helps other pros get elected and a wise observer of the sociopolitical scene on the West Coast. He's written a handful of other novels, all of them original and explosive. This story first appeared in *Murder on Route 66.*

'53 Buick

Gary Phillips

Barreling out of Amarillo, the sand-storm swooped in just as Dolphy Ornette steered the black and red 1953 Buick Roadmaster directly into its path. Route 66 lay flat and hard and open before him like a whore he knew back home in Boley, Oklahoma. Some Friday nights men would be stepping all over each other in the service porch off her rear bedroom waiting their turn.

He'd bought the car two years ago when he'd cashiered out of Korea with his corporal's wages. He'd fought a war just like his older brother had not more than a decade before. Of course, just as with that war, the down-town white men suddenly got a lot of "we" and "us" in their speeches, and told the colored boys it was their duty to go protect freedom. His brother didn't make it back from the war.

Back in '42 the enemy were krauts and nips. In '51 they were the god-damn gooks. White man always could come up with colorful names for everybody else except himself. Dinge, shine, jig, smoke, coon, even had dago, wop, mick, kike for those whites who talked their English with an accent or ate food that they definitely didn't serve down at the corner diner.

The NAACP also said negroes should fight, prove they were loyal Americans and that they could face 'em down with the best of them. So they soldiered up. Surely that would show the ofays back home, things would have to improve in housing and jobs once our boys got back. The black soldiers who returned with memories of lost lives and innocence and blood had the nerve to demand what was theirs from the big boss man. Naw boy, things is going back the ways they always was. Sure Truman integrated the troops in Korea, but that was war time. This was peace.

A steady hammering of sand rapped against his windshield. Earlier, before the break of dawn, he could tell what was coming as he stood gassing the Buick at the dilapidated station in McLean. The old Confederate who ran the place wasn't inclined to sell him gas, but business wasn't exactly knocking down his weather-beaten door, so a few colored dollars would do him.

The wind off the Panhandle drove the sand at the glass with a fine consistency that reminded him of the sound when his mama fried up cornmeal in a pan. But the car's road-devouring V-8 and the Twin-Turbine Dynaflow torque converter kept the machine steady and on course across the blacktop. He was glad he'd paid extra for the power steering, even though at the time he did think it was a mite sissified. The twelve-volt charging unit was doing its job. The dash lights didn't dim like his DeSoto's used to do.

He drove on and on with the sandstorm ranging around his car like the song of one of those sea mermaids luring you. Like you'd get so hot to be with her you wouldn't notice until it was too late as a giant squid popped the eyes out of your head as it squeezed your ribcage together.

Dolphy Ornette kept driving, periodically glancing at the broken yellow line dotting the center of the two-lane highway. The pelting sand sounded a lullaby of nature's indifference to humanity. He drove on because he needed to put distance between himself and where he'd left, and because he needed to get where he was going. Not that he thought they'd suspect him. No, the big boss man couldn't conceive of a black man being that clever. A couple of them might wonder what had put it in his head to quit. But he'd waited weeks after filching the doohickey to announce he was going back to Boley.

Anyway the generals and the chrome dome boys would be too busy trying to figure out how the dirty reds had stolen the gizmo. A blast of wind, like the swipe of a giant's backhand, caused the front end of his car to swerve viciously to the right. His hands tightened on the wheel, and he managed to keep the Roadmaster under control. Ornette slowed his speed to compensate for the turbulence. It wouldn't do to flip over now.

He should'a rotated the tires before he left, but he had other matters to deal with. Up ahead, an old Ford F-1 truck with rusted fenders weaved to and fro. The trailer attached to it shimmied like one of those plastic hula girls he'd seen in the rear window of hot rods.

Ornette slowed down, watching the taillights of the trailer blink through the sheet of brown blur swirling before him. It sounded as if a thousand snares in a room full of drums were being beat. The red lights before him swayed and jerked.

On he drove through the gale until it was no more, and all that remained was a night with pinholes for stars, and a silver crescent of a moon hanging like it was on a string. He pulled over somewhere the hell in New Mexico. Using the flashlight, he checked the windshield. The glass was pitted and several spiderweb cracks like children's pencil marks worked at the edges. But the metal molding seemed intact. He tapped the butt of the flashlight against the windshield in several places and it held.

He popped the hood to check the hoses and then cleaned away the grit on the radiator with a whisk broom he took from the glove compartment.

Looking toward a series of lights, Ornette figured he'd take a chance and see if he could get accommodations. He had a copy of the Negro Motorist Green Book in the glove box. It was the black traveler's guide to hospitable lodging, and to which lodging was to be avoided.

At the moment, Dolphy Ornette was too tired and too ornery to give a damn. As he drove closer he could see a neon sign of a cowgirl straddling a rocket with a saddle around its mid-section. Blinking yellow lightning bolts zigzagged out of the rear of the rocket. The motel rooms were done up like a series of movie rockets had landed tail first in the dirt. The place was called the Blast-Off Motor Lodge. Beneath the girl on the sign was a smaller sign announcing cocktails. If they rented him a room, they'd probably take his money for scotch, he wistfully concluded. He patted the trunk and walked inside.

Ivan Monk looked up from the sepia-hued postcard of the Blast-Off Motor Lodge to the elderly woman. They were sitting in her cramped kitchen, the door to the oven open and set at 350 degrees. Its stifling heat made the sitting and listening to the woman's story that much more difficult. Outside, the temperature was in the comfortable low seventies.

"Mr. Ornette liked to keep mementoes. Know where you been, and look forward to where you going, he was wont to say." She tapped the postcard with her delicate fingers.

"And you want me to find his Buick?" Monk repeated, to make sure he wasn't getting delirious from the heat.

She nodded. "1953, Roadmaster Riviera hardtop coupe, yes sir. It was like something out of Flash Gordon that car. What with that bright ol' shiny grill like giant's teeth and those portholes, four of 'em, lined along the side." She shook her head in appreciation. The black wig she had on slipped a little and she adjusted it in one deft motion.

"I remember it so vivid, that Tuesday he drove up in his beautiful car to the rooming house. Had us a wonderful three story over on Maple near Twenty-fourth. All that's Mexican now." She tucked in her bottom lip, willing herself not to go on about the old days.

"Those cars were classics," Monk agreed. "But Mrs. Scott, why do you want to find Ornette's Buick, and why now?" The heat was too much. His shirt felt like it was stapled to his skin.

"It was a gorgeous car, you said so yourself." She touched her head and looked over at the kettle on the stove. "Tea, Mr. Monk?"

Is the old girl part polar bear? "No thanks."

She got up in the quilted housecoat she had on and poured herself some tea. Standing at the stove she said, "Mr. Ornette kept that car in fine running condition. He heard anything wrong with the engine and he'd get it down to the mechanic lickity-split." She stirred and sipped. "There were a couple of mechanics he particularly liked going to. One of them had a shop over on

Avalon." She inclined her head. "Had some kind of royal name, you know? The Purple Prince, no that's the skinny child who runs around with the butt cut out of his jeans."

"Kings High Auto Repair," Monk supplied.

"Why yes, that was it. But he couldn't still be around, could he?"

"No, my father died some time ago."

She halted the cup at her cracked lips. "My goodness, that was your daddy's business?" She laughed heartily. "The Lord sure moves in his ways, doesn't he? It's providence then that I got to talking to your mother after church last Sunday, and she getting you to come here and see me about my need." She laughed some more.

Monk's father had won the stakes with a kings high full house poker hand to make the down payment on the garage. The rest he'd borrowed from a gambler he'd been in the Army with in Korea.

"Mrs. Scott, I'd still like to know why you want to find this car. Did Dolphy Ornette skip out on his rent years ago and now for some reason you want him to make good?" He had to find a way out of this silly business gracefully so as not to offend her or his mother.

"Child, Dolphy Ornette died in 1968."

"And he kept the Roadmaster all that time?"

"Yes he did. He wasn't living with us by then, but my sister, who knew some of his friends, used to see him around town in it. Oh yes," she said animatedly, "he kept that vehicle in good running condition."

"And what happened to the car after Mr. Ornette died?"

She raised her head toward the ceiling, the steam from the cup drifting past her. Momentarily, Monk had the impression her head existed detached from her body. "When we heard about his getting killed, my sister and—"

"Killed?" Monk exclaimed.

"Yes, didn't I tell you?" She sat down at the table with its worn Pionite topping again.

Details definitely weren't Mrs. Scott's thing. "How'd it happen? Don't tell me it was because somebody wanted his car."

"No, nothing like this carjacking foolishness we got today, no. When Dolphy got back from Denver he had more get up and go. We'd known him before the Korean action. My sister had gone around with him before. But when he came back to town, he seemed more focused I'd guess you'd say. Before he was just interested in fast cars and club women." She made a disapproving sound in her throat.

"But when he came back to Los Angeles in 1955, he was like a man afire. He got himself into community college while he waited tables over at the Ambassador Hotel on Wilshire. He soon had a delivery service operating for colored businesses in town and on up into Pasadena. He did all right," she said proudly.

"His death?"

"Shot in the face one night as he came out of his office on Western."

"The police find the killer?"

"No. Some said it was a jealous business rival. Others said it was white folks who had delivery services and couldn't abide a black man taking business away from them."

"And the car?"

"I was raising a family and working part-time at the phone company, Mr. Monk. I couldn't rightly say."

Was she ever going to explain why it was she wanted this car so much now? If there'd been rumors of money hidden in it, like Ornette didn't trust banks? Surely she didn't believe it would still be hidden in it after all this time. The Buick was probably long since recycled metal, and was part of a building in Tokyo by now.

Mrs. Scott, anticipating his next question, rummaged in the lidless cigar box she'd plucked the Blast-Off Motor Lodge postcard out of a few minutes ago.

"Here," she finally said, "this is a picture of the car. You can see Dolphy with his foot on the bumper, right over the license plate. My sister Lavinia took that shot right in front of our place on Maple."

"Come on, baby, snap that damn thing," Ornette growled. He pulled on the crown of his Flechet.

"Take your hat off, the shade from it's blocking your face."

"Maybe I don't want my face in the picture."

Lavinia Scott put a hand on a packed hip.

Ornette complied. He put one of his new two-tone Stacey Addams on the Buick's bumper. His foot directly over the black license plate and yellow numbers and letters. The first thing he'd done coming back was to re-register the car in California. It wouldn't do to get pulled over by the law for out-of-state-plates.

She wound the film in the Brownie camera, held the thing against her stomach and sighted his reflected image in the circle of glass. She snapped off two shots rapidly.

"Let's go now," he ordered. Ornette plopped his hat back on and got in behind the wheel of the Buick. Lavinia squirreled the little camera away in her purse and joined him on the passenger side.

"You been back a month now and you still haven't told me about your job in Denver."

"I told you I'm planning on going to school 'fore I get my ideas set up." He steered the car onto Maple and headed south toward Jefferson.

"See, that's what I'm talking about, Dolph, you all the time ducking the question." She studied her lips in her compact's mirror, applying a thin coat of lipstick. "You know perfectly well what I'm talking about. What was it like working at the PX? It had to be exciting what with everybody returning from the war."

He grinned, showing his gold side tooth. "Like any other slave a colored man can get, sugar honey. Punch that clock and hit that lick."

She gave him a playful slap on the arm. "You so bad."

"That's why you dig me."

She giggled. Then she leaned over and kissed him on the neck. He took a hand off the big steering wheel and rubbed her leg.

"Don't you go getting too frisky mister, I'm a churchgoing woman." But she didn't remove the hand.

"Don't I know it. Got your nosey sister askin' me when it is I'm going to get down to church every Saturday evening since I been back."

"She's concerned for your welfare," Lavinia Scott teased, touching his shoulder.

"Soon, if things go right, we ain't gonna have none of those worries. I mean money or our future." He piloted the Roadmaster west along Jefferson toward the Lovejoy Fish House.

"You been hinting around about something since you been back. What is it?"

Ornette beamed at her and chuckled. "Maybe I'll show you. You keep riding with me, sugar honey, you won't have to ask for no more. For nothin'."

She squinted at him, not convinced but intrigued nonetheless. She was about to speak when the car suddenly lurched to a stop. Behind them, a Mercury slammed on its brakes, its front end meeting the rear of the Buick.

"Goddammit, kid," he yelled.

A boy of about nine looked aghast into the windshield of the Buick. His ball had rolled back to his feet, but he was too frightened to move.

"Oh lord, I think he's going to cry." She unlatched the door.

Ornette had a hand to his face. "Goddammit, Goddammit."

Lavinia went to comfort the child.

Ornette also got out to talk to the Mercury's driver. He was a small, stout man in horn-rimmed glasses and a beret. Influenced, no doubt, by the fashion fad among be-bop jazz men. The man was looking down at where his bumper had gone over the Buick's and was now pressed against the trunk.

"Looks like we can get them apart. How 'bout you get your trunk open and let's use your tire iron for leverage."

"Ain't got no spare," Ornette said hurriedly. He gritted his teeth, staring at the trunk. "I'll get on it and push, you put your car in reverse."

"You might dent it."

Ornette just stared mutely at the trunk.

The man hunched his shoulders and got back in his car.

Ornette got on his trunk and planted his Stacey Addams on the Mercury's bumper. His weight sunk the Buick's rear enough that the bumpers came free with little effort.

"I'm prepared to call it square if you are," the small man said.

"Yeah." Ornette absently stuck out his hand, still glaring at the trunk.

The other man shook the limp hand, and got back into his car.

Lavinia had calmed the child down. Ornette dabbed at his forehead with the sleeve of his camel hair coat. He parked the Buick, taking care to lock the doors.

By the time he'd done that and walked to where Lavinia stood, the kid was on his way with his ball. The child waved at the nice lady.

"Happy?" He sounded nervous.

"Don't like to see anyone disappointed," she said.

He shifted his shoulders beneath his box coat. "That's what makes you so special."

She hooked her arm in his and together they entered the Lovejoy Fish House, right beneath the huge plaster and wood bass suspended over the entrance.

Monk carefully refolded the brittle newspaper clipping from the Eagle newspaper. A piece on the visit of young starlet Dorothy Dandridge to the Lovejoy Fish House in November of 1952 was accompanied by a photo of the establishment. Mrs. Scott had told him about the incident with the child when she'd chanced upon the clipping. She said too that not soon after that, Lavinia and Ornette had broken up. The sister would never say why.

Mrs. Scott had loaned him the box of small knickknacks, postcards, photos and clippings. Many of them seemed to have belonged to Ornette, or were possibly sent to Lavinia by him. But it was all she had, she'd told him in that Hades of a kitchen. And couldn't he for an old woman, a friend of his mother's, spend a few days looking for the Buick, please?

Listlessly, he sifted through the contents of the box that now sat on his desk. There was part of a Continental Trailways bus ticket, more photos, a couple of rings, some buttons, an old-fashioned skeleton key and another postcard. This one depicted a landscape shot in the Painted Desert in Arizona. It was blank on the back.

Monk threw the postcard back into the cigar box and shoved the thing aside. What a pain in the ass.

Delilah Carnes, the fine all-purpose admin assistant and researcher he shared with the rehab firm of Ross and Hendricks, entered the room. She wore a mid-thigh-length form-fitting black skirt and shocking blue silk blouse.

"Here's what I got from a check of the license plate number you gave me, Fearless Fosdick."

From the National Personnel Records Center in St. Louis, Monk had obtained Dolphy Ornette's service record which included his social security number. The SSN, the magic number to open up the doors to one's life in the not so private modern world.

"Let me guess, somebody filed a certificate of non-operation with the DMV sometime in the mid-eighties and that was all she wrote."

"Indeed," she said, sitting down and crossing well-defined legs on the couch. "Yet a callback I got from New Mexico showed the car was registered again in Gallup in 1988. Nothing after that."

"Registered to who?" Monk didn't hide his displeasure. "So now I'm supposed to go on my own dime to Gallup and prowl around junkyards for this car?"

Delilah laughed. "Your client said she'd pay you with three fresh-baked sweet potato pies. After all, she *is* on a fixed income, Ivan."

"All her money must go for her heating bill," he groused. "Who re-registered the car?"

Delilah checked her printout. "A Delfuensio DeZuniga. I called the number matching the address, but it's been disconnected. I've got half a white page of DeZunigas currently in Gallup."

Monk groaned. "How about any moving violations?"

"Yeah, I ran that too." She leafed through a couple of sheets, then settled on a page. "DeZuniga got a ticket for having a taillight out in 1989. Here in town."

She got up and handed him the sheet, pointing at the location of the infraction. Monk recognized the area as near Elysian Park where the LAPD's academy was, and where cholos and their rukas kicked it in the park. Bordering the park was the Harbor Freeway, the 110, as it became the Pasadena heading north.

"The 110 used to be part of Route 66," Monk noted aloud.

"And?" Delilah asked.

"Nothing, really. Ornette had driven Route 66 into L.A. though."

"The address listed for DeZuniga at the time of the infraction is the one in Gallup," she added, walking out of the office.

"Maybe he was in town visiting relatives," Monk called out. He was not going to drive or fly to New Mexico on this vehicular McGuffin of a favor. His phone bill was going to be on him though, as he knew he was going to have to run down as many DeZunigas as he could to satisfy Mrs. Scott that he'd done what he could. His mother, he told himself, was going to hear about this for years to come. He marched into the rotunda to retrieve the white and yellow pages, and got busy.

Later, tired of getting answering machines, nadas, and busy signals from DeZuniga households in Gallup, he was glad to take a break. He left his office and drove his midnight blue 1964 Galaxie with its refitted 352-cubic-inch V-8 east on Washington Boulevard leaving downtown Culver City. The carburetor had been running sluggish, but he hadn't had time to fool with the fuel mixture screws. At Cattaraugus he cut over to the Santa Monica Freeway and headed east. Driving in the fairly unobstructed early afternoon flow, he was happy to find the car's engine smoothed at a higher sustained speed.

Eventually Monk was on the 5 and took the exit in the City of Commerce. Following the directions, he wound up at the Southern California Buick Association headquarters a little before two in the afternoon. On time for the appointment he made. The headquarters was also the business address of Willy Serrano, a machine shop operator where they rebuilt car and truck engines.

A boss black and white 1955 Special Riviera hardtop with the sporty mag rims sat in the slot marked "owner." During the early to mid-fifties, the Special Buick was the car to have among true believers.

Monk chatted with Serrano in his parts- and paper-cluttered office in the rear of the machine shop. Through the door the muffled sounds of lathes turning and metal being ground could be heard.

"I looked back in our membership records there, Ivan." Serrano was a large, gregarious man who favored pointed cowboy boots, a Western-style shirt, and a buckle with his initial on it. A white Stetson with three "Xs" on the band rested on top of a file cabinet.

"Sure enough, there was a Jessie DeZuniga in the club in the early nineties. He didn't renew for ninety-four. I recall talking to him once or twice, I think. But I couldn't tell you why he didn't re-join."

A machinist stuck his head in, and said something in Spanish to Serrano. He answered in the same language and the door closed again.

Monk found out Jessie was in his early thirties and got the last known address for him. It was on Callumet in the Echo Park section, near Elysian Park. He thanked the man and drove back into Los Angeles. Nobody was home at the small frame house on Callumet.

He went over to Barrigan's restaurant on Sunset and had a late lunch, topped off with a Cadillac margarita, one made from the good tequila. Then he called his office from a pay phone. Delilah told him their back check on Ornette's social security number had turned up his employment record. She'd leave the report on his desk.

Afterward, he wandered along the shops on North Vermont, the happening avenue for this season. In the window of a clothing store called Red Ass Monkey, the female mannequin's larger-than-usual breasts strained her top. She was in a latex mini and thick-soled studded boots astride a stuffed wild boar. Around six, he went back to the house. A cherry 1971 Camaro with fat rear tires was now in the driveway.

"Sorry, my friend," Jessie DeZuniga said, taking another swig on his beer at the door. The younger man had been home ten minutes from work, and was in his undershirt and blue work khakis. "Somewhere around here I kept the paperwork, but yeah, I sold the Buick about four years ago. It was a sweet car, I'll tell you, homes. But you know I already got one honey," he indicated his rebuilt Camaro, "plus two kids, and the old lady always going on about how I'm putting more money and attention into my dad's car than her."

He took another pull, then tipped the can at Monk's Ford. "But I guess you know something about that."

Monk nodded agreeably. "My old lady is always yapping about that too, but these are classics, right? A man has to have a hobby." Monk was lying, his significant other, Judge Jill Kodama, liked his Galaxie.

"Yeah," DeZuniga commiserated. One of his children, a young girl who must have been a third grader, popped up. "Pops, when you gonna fix dinner?" She averted her eyes from Monk, who smiled at her.

"Wife works nights," DeZuniga explained.

"I'm going to let you handle your business, Jessie. Do you remember the name of the guy who bought it?"

"It was a woman, young, hip hop Chinese chick. Can't say what her name was now. She answered my ad in the Auto Trader, and made the best offer."

He'd already mentioned that his father had died. Monk asked as he stepped from the porch, "Do you know how your father acquired the Buick after Dolphy Ornette was shot?"

Jessie DeZuniga looked at Monk as if he'd grown a second head. "Don't you know? My father and Mr. Ornette knew each other from this Army base—I think it was in Alamogordo. Dad worked in a bar in town, and Mr. Ornette worked at the base, janitor or orderly, something like that. This wasn't the bar the Army people went to either. This was the one the townspeople went to."

"Ornette must have been the only black man in there."

"He got along." DeZuniga opened the door wider and gestured with the can. "Look at this."

On a tan-colored living-room wall hung several photos in what appeared to be handmade wooden frames. DeZuniga pointed at one. The shot captured men and women, Chicano, white and one black man who Monk presumed was Dolphy Ornette. All were sitting or standing at the bar.

"That's my father." He touched the can to a smiling bartender leaning on the bar, looking in the direction of the camera's lens. Ornette was a couple of stools down, raising his beer to the photographer. It was an afternoon because through the bar's windows Monk could make out the Buick and several other cars parked at an angle in front of the place. Beyond the cars in the distance were white gypsum mounds.

The backwards script painted on the front window was discernible too. Monk stared at it, trying to decipher the Spanish words.

"Flor Silvestre," DeZuniga added. "The Windflower Cantina. Anyway," DeZuniga continued, "the car was at our crib in Gallup months before my dad heard he got shot. Mr. Ornette had brought it there. At least that's what my dad had said. I wasn't even two when all this went on."

His daughter called him again and he told Monk he'd call if he found the papers. The PI returned to his office and Ornette's job history. The official record backed up what Mrs. Scott had related to him, that Ornette had worked in a PX supply depot in Denver. Yet there was that picture and what the younger DeZuniga had said. And Monk was no geographer—Denver might have white hills like New Mexico for all he knew.

At ten thirty that evening, he had an answer for the discrepancy.

"Who was that on the phone?" Jill Kodama asked, handing him a tumbler of Johnny Walker Black and ice. They were in the study of the house they shared in Silverlake. Her name on the mortgage. One day, Monk figured, he'd get used to calling it his home too. "One of your chippies, darling?" She turned on the TV.

"Information broker I use from time to time. His specialty is out-of-date locations. He confirms that the Flor Silvestre Cantina was in Alamogordo in the fifties, the time period Ornette told Lavinia Scott he was working in Colorado."

"What do you make of that?" she asked, interested.

Monk crossed his arms. "Maybe he left behind another girlfriend he didn't want Lavinia to know about. According to the sister—"

"The one that's going to pay you in pies."

"Uh-huh. She said her sister and Ornette broke up one afternoon after he'd returned from an errand in Pasadena. Whatever it was it set something off, and Lavinia came home swearing she'd never have anything to do with that crazy man again. Her exact words."

Kodama flipped through channels. "She, that is Lavinia, say what was so crazy?"

"No, Mrs. Scott says she'd never talked about it, even when the two would be out and would chance to see Ornette."

"What happened to the sister?" She settled on the History Channel.

"You know I never really asked her that? I assumed she died."

On the screen a mushroom cloud shot through with colonized oranges and reds blossomed on screen as an offscreen narrator droned on about America's love/hate relationship with nuclear power. This image dissolved to one of fifties downtown, fantastically backlit by a nuclear blast in the Nevada desert some 300 miles away, as the narrator continued.

"The stealth bomber flies out of White Sands now," Kodama said, eyeing the explosion. "But in the fifties and sixties, nuclear testing used to go on there."

Monk made an exasperated sound. "And Roswell's in New Mexico, Jill. You think Ornette was a space alien? Was the car his disguised flying saucer and Verna Scott needs to go home?"

"Okay, smart ass, then why does the old girl want the car? Sentimental reasons? Why did Ornette conceal where he worked? Why take Route 66 when the way to drive from Alamogordo to here is a different highway. Unless he was backtracking to throw somebody off his trail. And why is it the Buick hasn't shown up on any of your checking since Jessie DeZuniga sold it?"

"Whoever bought it never bothered to get it registered. The Buick's probably sitting in some garage now, the tires going to rot, the gas in the tank turning to gum. The proud possession of a weekend shade tree mechanic who keeps telling himself any Saturday now he's gonna get back out there and get this bad boy running.

"Anyway, why does he fill in the gaps for me with that bit about his father and Ornette knowing each other and Ornette leaving the car with his dad?"

"Don't be naive, baby," Kodama responded. "You've done that with the cops. Give them enough of the truth you figure they'll find out one way or the other, but also hold back. That way they believe you, and don't look twice in your direction.

"And," she went on, "why didn't the DMV check what you told me you did when you got back to the office this evening to produce a release certificate from Jessie DeZuniga?"

"It was a spot check going by the license plate. I don't have DeZuniga's social security number."

"He's the last known owner."

"You're much too suspicious for a judge."

"Press him for the paperwork. Maybe then you can avoid all the bugging your mother and Mrs. Scott are going to do if you leave it hanging."

Monk had to concede her logic.

Over the next several days he called DeZuniga several times and it was one excuse after the other as to what might have happened to those papers. But as much as he bugged the younger man, Mrs. Scott bothered him more. Repeatedly asking about any leads. On Friday, Monk broke down.

"I'm concentrating on a guy named DeZuniga, okay?" Monk rubbed his face as he held the receiver to his ear.

"Can you spell that, dear, my hearing's not so good."

He could just picture her standing in her hot kitchen in her quilted housecoat. He spelled the man's first and last name for her and assured her that he'd have something to report by the end of the weekend. He intended to have something by then one way or the other.

Monk had considered staking out DeZuniga in the evenings. But that would mean renting a regular car on his own dime or at the least borrowing his sister's Honda Civic as he'd done sometimes in the past. His '64 Ford was not what one would call a car that blended. Plus a black man sitting night after night in a car in a Latino neighborhood could not expect to not get noticed.

He hoped DeZuniga was being on the level when he said his wife worked nights, as it would ensure he couldn't move around too much until the weekend.

This turned out to be the case.

DeZuniga, the wife and kids drove out to a small frame house in Whittier early Saturday morning. He went inside and left his wife and kids waiting in her Camry. About fifteen minutes later, he was backing out of the driveway behind the wheel of the 1953 red and black Buick Riviera Roadmaster. It looked and sounded new. The family then drove back to Echo Park. Monk followed in his sister's Civic.

"Look man," he began, approaching a surprised DeZuniga in front of his house. "What you do with your car is your business. If you would just let this old lady, my client Mrs. Scott, see the car." Monk stopped a good few feet in front of DeZuniga so as not to be perceived as a threat. "I don't know why, but she's been—"

A Bell Cab pulled up in front of the house. The driver got out and opened the door to let Mrs. Verna Scott out. She paid him and he departed.

Mrs. Scott looked in awe at the Buick.

The children were bothering their mother for something and DeZuniga waved them inside.

"I didn't want to tell you I had it 'cause some others had been around asking about it around a year ago," Jessie DeZuniga said. "They offered me all kinds of money, but something about them." He frowned. "I told them I'd already sold the car. They said they'd been away but had made it back and needed to have the Buick."

DeZuniga looked at the car longingly. "My dad made me promise him to keep the car. Not to sell it, ever. Normally, I keep the Buick in my neighbor's garage down the street. But I moved it out to my cousin's that first night you were here."

"And my constant calling got you jumpy."

"Yeah. That time a year ago when these dudes showed up, the car just happened to be out at my cousin's pad."

"Where you went this morning?"

"Uh-huh. At that time he was redoing the upholstery. I knew they didn't believe I'd sold the car. I spotted them keeping watch on the house. But I out-waited them and finally they went away. Now, I was going to drive it to Moreno Valley, and leave it with my sister-in-law."

Monk was thinking about Ornette's unsolved murder.

And that he'd given the car to DeZuniga's father as if he'd anticipated someone would be coming after him. "What did these men look like?"

"X-Files type, you know. Creepy, pasty-faced white boys. Big overcoats, hands in pockets, lips didn't move and shit."

Monk was about to ask more questions but the gun in Mrs. Scott's hand got his and DeZuniga's attention. It wasn't much of a gun, but it could sting.

"Open the trunk, please," she asked forcefully.

Bemused, DeZuniga did so.

"My sister would lay awake nights telling me," Verna Scott didn't finish her sentence. Like a mouse to cheese, she went to the now-open trunk compartment. Monk and DeZuniga got in position to watch her.

"Ain't nothing back there but the spare and a tool box," DeZuniga offered.

The old girl was halfway in the trunk. "Dolphy showed it to her and it scared her. It was too much for her then. Years later," she grunted with effort, "she always regretted she didn't help him sell it."

"Sell what?" Monk moved forward to get a better look.

"But who would buy it?" she said to herself. He found out the thing was more trouble than it was worth. But by then, he couldn't turn it in either without going to jail forever. "Here it is, here's the latch."

Monk and DeZuniga moved forward to see what she was doing.

Suddenly a brilliant glow shot from the trunk and Mrs. Scott's wiggling form was swallowed by tendrils like beams of light.

"What the hell is that?" DeZuniga shouted, shielding his eyes. Sound seemed to be evaporating.

"Your dad never mentioned this?" Monk tried to move but it was as if some kind of heavy gravity was weighing him down. He and the other man sank to their knees.

"What the hell's going on?" The scintilla throbbed in his ears and he felt as if his heart was going to stop. Monk's world was a white hot essence where he couldn't tell up or down, back or front.

There was an even brighter flash, then birds could be heard chirping again in the morning air. Once the two men got their orientation back, they realized the Buick and Mrs. Scott were gone.

The men in uniform who arrived to question them just stood there peering at them doubtfully. Their story was that they'd been carjacked by an old lady with a pea shooter. Later, the plainclothes went over and over the story with them separately. They unswervingly kept to their version of what had happened. Each had agreed before DeZuniga had called the law not to mention the light thing. They didn't directly talk about it when they were finally let go seven hours later.

"Sorry about the Buick, that was a beautiful car, man." Monk shook DeZuniga's hand.

"Yeah. Think my dad and Mr. Ornette knew this would happen?"

Monk didn't have an answer. Didn't want to even consider one.

Route 66 stretched before them, the stars overhead like tiny pin pricks of light in an ebony-colored cloth. The moon was full and incandescent. Ornette Dolphy, his Flechet perched at an angle, sat at the wheel with Lavinia Scott beside him. In the back seat of the '53 Buick Roadmaster sat Verna Scott and Delfuensio DeZuniga. On the roadway some had called the mother, and others Camino de la muerte, the four drove on and on. Before them lay hope and knowledge and the road. But they didn't drive with haste, they went as if they had all the time in the world to get there.

James W. Hall

Crack

JAMES W. HALL is one of a sudden swarm of authors writing about South Florida. But where other authors end, he is just getting started, combining one-of-a-kind characters with plots that could exist only in the multicultural melting pot of the Florida panhandle. His novels include *Body Language, Red Sky at Night, Mean High Tide,* and *Rough Draft.* Every time you think he's exhausted his bag of tricks, he pulls out another surprise that leaves you breathless. An original in a field that is becoming crowded more rapidly each year, he's one author whose books always stand out. This story first appeared in *Murder and Obsession.*

Crack

James W. Hall

When I first saw the slit of light coming through the wall, I halted abruptly on the stairway, and instantly my heart began to thrash with a giddy blend of dread and craving.

At the time, I was living in Spain, a section named Puerto Viejo, or the Old Port, in the small village of Algorta just outside the industrial city of Bilbao. It was a filthy town, a dirty region, with a taste in the air of old pennies and a patina of grime dulling every bright surface. The sunlight strained through perpetual clouds that had the density and monotonous luster of lead. It was to have been my year of *flamenco y sol*, but instead I was picked to be the Fulbright fellow of a dour Jesuit university in Bilbao on the northern coast where the umbrellas were pocked by ceaseless acid rain and the customary dress was black—shawls, dresses, berets, raincoats, shirts, and trousers. It was as if the entire Basque nation was in perpetual mourning.

The night I first saw the light I was drunk. All afternoon I had been swilling Rioja on the balcony overlooking the harbor, celebrating the first sunny day in a month. It was October and despite the brightness and clarity of the light, my wife had been darkly unhappy all day, even unhappier than usual. At nine o'clock she was already in bed paging aimlessly through month-old magazines and sipping her sherry. I finished with the dishes and double-checked all the locks and began to stumble up the stairs of our two-hundred-fifty-year-old stone house that only a few weeks before our arrival in Spain had been subdivided into three apartments.

I was midway up the stairs to the second floor when I saw the slim line of the light shining through a chink in the new mortar. There was no debate, not even a millisecond of equivocation about the propriety of my actions. In most matters I considered myself a scrupulously moral man. I had always been one who could be trusted with other people's money or their most damning secrets. But like so many of my fellow Puritans I long ago had discovered that when it came to certain libidinous temptations I was all too easily swept off my safe moorings into the raging currents of erotic gluttony.

I immediately pressed my eye to the crack.

It took me a moment to get my bearings, to find the focus. And when I did, my knees softened and my breath deserted me. The view was beyond anything I might have hoped for. The small slit provided a full panorama of my neighbors' second story. At knee-high level I could see their master bathroom and a few feet to the left their kingsize brass bed.

That first night the young daughter was in the bathroom with the door swung open. If the lights had been off in their apartment or the bathroom door had been closed I might never have given the peephole another look. But that girl was standing before the full-length mirror and she was lifting her fifteen-year-old breasts that had already developed quite satisfactorily, lifting them both at once and reshaping them with her hands to meet some standard that only she could see. After a while she released them from her grip, then lifted them on her flat palms as though offering them to her image in the mirror. They were beautiful breasts, with small nipples that protruded nearly an inch from the aureole, and she handled them beautifully, in a fashion that was far more mature and knowing than one would expect from any ordinary fifteen-year-old.

I did not know her name. I still don't, though certainly she is the most important female who ever crossed my path. Far more crucial in my life's trajectory than my mother or either of my wives. Yet it seems appropriate that I should remain unaware of her name. That I should not personalize her in any way. That she should remain simply an abstraction—simply the girl who destroyed me.

In the vernacular of that year in Spain, she was known as a *niña pera*, or pear girl. One of hundreds of shapely and succulent creatures who cruised about the narrow, serpentine roads of Algorta and Bilbao on loud mopeds, their hair streaming in their wake. She was as juicy as any of them. More succulent than most, as I had already noticed from several brief encounters as we exited from adjacent doors onto the narrow alley-streets of the Old Port. On these two or three occasions, I remember fumbling through my Spanish greetings and taking a stab at small talk while she, with a patient but faintly disdainful smile, suffered my clumsy attempts at courtesy. Although she wore the white blouse and green plaid skirts of all the other Catholic schoolgirls, such prosaic dress failed to disguise her pearness. She was achingly succulent, blindingly juicy. At the time I was twice her age. Double the fool and half the man I believed I was.

That first night, after a long, hungering look, I pulled away from the crack of light and with equal measures of reluctance and urgency, I marched back down the stairs and went immediately to the kitchen and found the longest and flattest knife in the drawer and brought it back to the stairway, and with surgical precision I inserted the blade into the soft mortar and as my pulse throbbed, I painstakingly doubled the size of my peephole.

When I withdrew the blade and applied my eye again to the slit, I now could see my *niña pera* from her thick black waist-length hair to her bright pink toenails. While at the same time I calculated that if my neighbors ever detected the lighted slit from their side and dared to press an eye to the breach, they would be rewarded with nothing more than a static view of the two-hundred-fifty-year-old stones of my rented stairwell.

I knew little about my neighbors except that the father of my pear girl was a vice-consul for that South American country whose major role in international affairs seemed to be to supply America with her daily dose of granulated ecstasy.

He didn't look like a gangster. He was tall and elegant, with wavy black hair that touched his shoulders and an exquisitely precise beard. He might have been a maestro of a European symphony or a painter of romantic land-scapes. And his young wife could easily have been a slightly older sister to my succulent one. She was in her middle thirties and had the wide and graceful hips, the bold, uplifting breasts, the gypsy features and black unfathomable eyes that seemed to spring directly from the archetypal pool of my carnality. In the Jungian parlance of my age, the wife was my anima, while the daughter was the anima of my adolescent self. They were perfect echoes of the dark secret female who glowed like uranium in the bowels of my psyche.

That first night when the bedsprings squeaked behind me, and my wife padded across the bedroom floor for her final visit to the bathroom, I allowed myself one last draught of the amazing sight before me. The *niña* was now stooped forward and was holding a small hand mirror to her thicket of pubic hair, poking and searching with her free hand through the dense snarl as if she were seeking that tender part of herself she had discovered by touch but not yet by sight.

Trembling and breathless, I pressed my two hands flat against the stone wall and shoved myself away and with my heart in utter disarray, I carried my lechery up the stairs to bed.

The next day I set about learning my neighbors' schedule and altering mine accordingly. My wife had taken a job as an English teacher in a nearby *insti-tuto* and was occupied every afternoon and through the early evening. My duties at the university occupied me Monday, Wednesday, and Friday. I was expected to offer office hours before and after my classes on those days. However, I immediately began to curtail these sessions because I discovered that my *niña pera* returned from school around three o'clock, and on many days she showered and changed into casual clothes, leaving her school garb in a heap on the bathroom floor as she fled the apartment for an afternoon of boy-watching in the Algorta pubs.

To my department chairman's dismay, I began to absent myself from the university hallways immediately after my last class of the day, hurrying with my umbrella along the five blocks to the train station so I could be home by 2:55. In the silence of my apartment, hunched breathless at my hole, I watched her undress. I watched the steam rise from her shower, and I watched her towel herself dry. I watched her on the toilet and I watched her using the sanitary products she preferred. I watched her touch the flawless skin of her face with her fingertips, applying makeup or wiping it away. On many afternoons I watched her examine herself in the full-length mirror. Running her hands over that seamless flesh, trying out various seductive poses while an expression played on her face that was equal parts exultation and shame—that peculiar adolescent emotion I so vividly recalled.

These were the times when I would have touched myself were I going to do so. But these moments at the peephole, while they were intensely sexual, were not the least masturbatory. Instead, they had an almost spiritual component. As though I were worshiping at the shrine of hidden mysteries, allowed by divine privilege to see beyond the walls of my own paltry life. In exchange for this gift I was cursed to suffer a brand of reverential horniness I had not imagined possible. I lusted for a vision that was forever intangible, a girl I could not touch, nor smell, nor taste. A girl who was no more than a scattering of light across my retina.

Although I never managed to establish a definite pattern to her mother's schedule, I did my best to watch her as well. At odd unpredictable hours, she appeared in my viewfinder and I watched the elder *niña pera* bathe in a tub of bubbles, and even when her house was empty, I watched her chastely close the bathroom door whenever she performed her toilette. I watched her nap on the large brass bed. And three times that fall in the late afternoons, I watched her slide her hand inside her green silk robe and touch herself between the legs, hardly moving the hand at all, giving herself the subtlest of touches until she rocked her head back into the pillow and wept.

I kept my eye to the wall during the hours when I should have been preparing for my classes and grading my students' papers and writing up their weekly exams. Instead, I stationed myself at the peephole, propping myself up with pillows, finding the best alignment for nose and cheek against the rough cool rock. I breathed in the sweet grit of mortar, trained my good right eye on the bathroom door and the bed, scanning the floor for shadows, primed for any flick of movement, always dreadfully alert for the sound of my wife's key in the front door.

After careful study, I had memorized her homecoming ritual. Whenever she entered our apartment, it took her two steps to reach the foyer and put down her bag. She could then choose to turn right into the kitchen or take another step toward the stairway. If she chose the latter, almost instantly she would be able to witness me perched at the peephole, and my clandestine life would be exposed. In my leisure, I clocked a normal entry and found that on average I had almost a full twenty seconds from the moment her key turned the tumblers till she reached the bottom of the stairs, twenty seconds to toss the pillows back into the bedroom and absent myself from the hole.

I briefly toyed with the idea of revealing the peephole to her. But I knew her sense of the perverse was far short of my own. She was constitutionally gloomy, probably a clinical depressive. Certainly a passive-aggressive, who reveled in bitter non-response, bland effect, withdrawing into maddening hours of silence whenever I blundered across another invisible foul line she had drawn.

I watched the father too, the vice-consul. On many occasions I saw him strip off his underwear and climb into the shower, and I saw him dry himself and urinate and brush his teeth. Once I saw him reach down and retrieve a pair of discarded briefs and bring the crotch to his nose before deciding they were indeed fresh enough to wear again. He had the slender and muscular build of a long-distance runner. Even in its slackened state his penis was formidable.

On one particular Sunday morning, I watched with grim fascination as he worked his organ to an erection, all the while gazing at the reflection of his face. And a few moments later as the spasms of his pleasure shook him and he was bending forward to ejaculate into the sink, the *niña pera* appeared at the doorway of the bathroom. She paused briefly to watch the vice-consul's last strokes, then passed behind him and stepped into the shower with a nonchalance that I found more shocking than anything I had witnessed to that point.

Late in November, the chairman of my department called me into his office and asked me if I was happy in Spain, and I assured him that I most certainly was. He smiled uncomfortably and offered me a glass of scotch and as we sipped, he told me that the students had been complaining that I was not making myself sufficiently available to them. I feigned shock, but he simply shook his head and waved off my pretense. Not only had I taken to missing office hours, I had failed to return a single set of papers or tests. The students were directionless and confused and in a unified uproar. And because of their protests, much to his regret, the chairman was going to have to insist that I begin holding my regular office hours immediately. If I failed to comply, he would have no choice but to act in his students' best interest by calling the Fulbright offices in Madrid and having my visiting professorship withdrawn for the second semester. I would be shipped home in disgrace.

I assured him that I would not disappoint him again.

Two days later after my last class of the day as I walked back to my office, all I could think of was my *niña pera* stripping away her Catholic uniform and stepping into the shower, then stepping out again wet and naked and perfectly succulent. I turned from my office door and the five scowling students waiting there and hurried out of the building. I caught the train just in time and was home only seconds before she arrived.

And this was the day it happened.

Breathless from my jog from the train station, I clambered up the stairs and quickly assumed my position at the slit, but was startled to see that it was not my *niña pera* beyond the wall, but her father, the diplomat in his dark suit, home at that unaccustomed hour. He was pacing back and forth in front of the bathroom, where a much shorter and much less elegant man was holding the head of a teenage boy over the open toilet bowl. The young man had long stringy hair and was dressed in a black T-shirt and blue jeans. The thug who was gripping him by the ears above the bowl was also dressed in black, a bulky black sweatshirt with the sleeves torn away and dark jeans and a black Basque beret. His arms were as gnarled as oak limbs, and the boy he held was unable to manage even a squirm.

The vice-consul stopped his pacing and spat out a quick, indecent bit of Spanish. Even though the wall muffled most conversation, I heard and recognized the phrase. While my conversational skills were limited, I had mastered a dozen or so of the more useful and colorful Spanish curses. The vice-consul had chosen to brand the boy as a pig's bastard child. Furthermore, a pig covered in its own excrement.

Though my disappointment at missing my daily appointment with the *niña pera* deflated my spirits, witnessing such violence and drama was almost fair compensation. My assumption was that my neighbor was disciplining the young man for some botched assignment—the most natural guess being that he was a courier who transported certain highly valued pharmaceutical products that happened also to be the leading export of the vice-consul's country. The other possibility, of course, and one that gave me a particularly nasty thrill, was that the boy was guilty of some impropriety with the diplomat's daughter, my own *niña pera*, and now was suffering the dire consequences of his effrontery.

I watched as the vice-consul came close to the boy and bent to whisper something to him, then tipped his head up by the chin and gave some command to the thug. The squat man let go of the boy's right ear, and with a gesture so quick I only caught the end of it, he produced a knife and slashed the boy's right ear away from his head.

I reeled back from the slit in the wall and pressed my back against the banister and tried to force the air into my lungs.

At that moment I should have rushed downstairs, gotten on the phone, and called the militia to report the outrage beyond my wall. And I honestly considered doing so. For surely it would have been the moral, virtuous path. But I could not move. And as I considered my paralysis, the utter selfishness of my inaction filled me with acid self-contempt. I reviled myself even as I kept my place. I could not call for help because I did not dare to upset the delicate equipoise of my neighbors' lives. The thought of losing my *niña pera* to the judicial process, or even worse to extradition, left me lifeless on the stairway. Almost as terrifying was the possibility that if I called for the militia, a further investigation would expose the slit in the wall and I would be hauled out into the streets for a public thrashing.

For a very long while I did not move.

Finally, when I found the courage to bring my eye back to the crack in the wall, I saw that the thug had lifted the boy to a standing position before the toilet, and the vice-consul had unzipped him and was gripping the tip of his penis, holding it out above the bloody porcelain bowl, a long steak knife poised a few inches above the pale finger of flesh.

The vice-consul's arm quivered and began its downward slash.

"No!" I cried out, then louder, "No!"

My neighbor aborted his savage swipe and spun around. I watched him take a hesitant step my way, then another. His patent-leather shoes glowed in the eerie light beyond the wall. Then in an unerring path he marched directly to the wall where I was perched.

I pulled away, scooted backward up the stairs, and held my breath.

I waited.

I heard nothing but the distant siren wail of another supertanker coming into port.

I was just turning to tiptoe up to the bedroom when the blade appeared. It slid through the wall and glittered in the late-afternoon light, protruding a full five inches into my apartment. He slipped it back and forth as if he, too, were trying to widen the viewing hole, then drew it slowly out of sight. For a second I was in real danger of toppling forward down the flight of stairs, but I found a grip on the handrail and restrained myself on the precarious landing.

Though it was no longer visible, the knife blade continued to vibrate in my inner sight. I realized it was not a steak knife at all, but a very long fillet knife with a venomous tapered blade that shone with the brilliance of a surgical tool. I had seen similar knives many times along the Algorta docks, for this was the sort of cutlery that saw service gutting the abundant local cod.

And while I held my place on the stairs, the point of the knife shot through the wall again and remained there, very still, as eloquent and vile a threat as I had ever experienced. And a moment later in the vice-consul's apartment I heard a wet piercing noise followed by a heavy thunk, as if a sack of cement had been broken open with the point of a shovel.

A second later my wife's key turned in the front-door lock and she entered the apartment, shook her umbrella, and stripped off her rain gear and took her standard fifteen seconds to reach the bottom of the stairs. She gazed up and saw me frozen on the landing and the knife blade still shimmering through the wall of this house she had come to despise. For it was there in those four walls that I had fatally withdrawn from her as well as my students, where I had begun to match her obdurate silences with my own. In these last few months I had become so devoted to my *niña pera* that I had established a bond with this unknown juvenile beyond the wall that was more committed and passionate than any feelings I had ever shown my wife.

And when she saw the knife blade protruding from the wall, she knew all this and more. More than I could have told her if I had fallen to my knees and wallowed in confession. Everything was explained to her, my vast guilt, my repellent preoccupation, the death of our life together. Our eyes inter-locked, and whatever final molecules of adhesion still existed between us dis-solved in those silent seconds.

She turned and strode to the foyer. As I came quickly down the stairs, she picked up her raincoat and umbrella and opened the heavy door of our apartment and stepped out into the narrow alley-street of the Old Port. I hurried after her, calling out her name, pleading with her, but she shut the door behind her with brutal finality.

As I rushed to catch her, pushing open the door, I nearly collided with my succulent young neighbor coming home late from school. She graced me with a two-second smile and entered her door, and I stood on the stoop for a moment looking down the winding, rain-slicked street after my wife. Wretched and elated, I swung around and shut myself in once more with my utter depravity.

I mounted the stairs.

There was nothing in my heart, nothing in my head. Simply the raging current of blood that powered my flesh. I knelt at the wall and felt the mag-netic throb of an act committed a thousand times and rewarded almost as often, the Pavlovian allure, a need beyond need, a death-hungering wish to see, to know, to live among that nefarious family who resided only a knife blade away.

I pressed my eye to the hole and she was there, framed in the bathroom doorway wearing her white blouse, her green plaid skirt. Behind her I could see that the toilet bowl had been wiped clean of blood. My *niña pera's* hands hung uneasily at her sides and she was staring across the room at the wall we shared, her head canted to the side, her eyes focused on the exact spot where I pressed my face into the stone and drank her in. My pear girl, my succulent child, daughter of the devil.

And though I was certain that the glimmer of my eye was plainly visible to her and anyone else who stood on that side of the wall, I could not pull myself from the crack, for my *niña pera* had begun to lift her skirt, inch by excruciating inch, exposing those immaculate white thighs. And though there was no doubt she was performing under duress and on instructions from her father, I pressed my face still harder against the wall and drank deep of the vision before me.

Even when my succulent one cringed and averted her face, giving me a second or two of ample warning of what her father was about to do, I could not draw my eye away from the lush expanse of her thighs.

A half second later her body disappeared and a wondrous flash of dark-ness swelled inside me and exploded. I was launched into utter blankness, rid-ing swiftly out beyond the edges of the visible world, flying headlong into a bright galaxy of pain.

And yet, if I had not passed out on the stairway, bleeding profusely from my ruined eye, if somehow I had managed to stay conscious for only a few seconds more, I am absolutely certain that after I suffered the loss of sight in my right eye, I would have used the last strength I had to reposition myself on the stairway and resume my vigil with my left.

In the following months of recuperation and repair, I came to discover that a man can subsist with one eye as readily as with one hand or leg. For apparently nature anticipated that some of us would commit acts of such extreme folly and self-destructiveness that we would require such anatomical redundancy if we were to survive. And in her wisdom, she created us to be two halves co-joined. So that even with one eye, a man can still see, just as with only a single hand he may still reach out and beckon for his needs. And yes, even half-heartedly, he may once again know love.

Laurie R. King

Paleta Man

LAURIE R. KING's first novel, *A Grave Talent,* featured San Francisco police detective Kate Martinelli; her second, *The Beekeeper's Apprentice,* was as far from her first book as possible, teaming a teenage girl with none other than the great sleuth himself, Sherlock Holmes. Since then she has alternated series, both meeting with great acclaim. Whether she's exploring the underbelly of San Francisco or the slums of Victorian London, her voice and characterization are always right on the money. Her recent novels include *A Darker Place* and *Night Work*. In "*Paleta* Man," nominated for the 1999 Edgar award for short fiction, she takes a break from her series characters for this tale of an unlikely avenger who will do whatever he must to maintain the peace in his neighborhood. This story first appeared in *Irreconcilable Differences*.

Paleta Man

Laurie R. King

Ellos me llaman "paleta man."

They call me "*paleta* man," and I must remember now to use the English language of this country.

Paleta is ice cream, so I suppose in English you would call me the ice cream man. But in the town where I now live, the ice cream man drives an old white truck whose sides are covered with pictures of his products and signs saying WATCH FOR CHILDREN, and he plays a song on the scratchy loudspeaker of his truck, the same notes playing over and over so loud they can be heard for a mile, a noise that drives all the adults crazy until they come out of their houses and shake their fists and throw rocks and beer cans at his truck.

I do not drive a white truck with loud music. Trucks cost much money, even the old ones, and I am a poor man.

Pero yo soy contento; I am content being a *paleta* man. I own a small cart with three wheels and a handle to push it by, with thick insulated sides and a pair of harmonious bells that hang from the crossbar of the handle. The children listen for me, and when I turn the corner of their street and play my pair of bells, they run out with their coins in their hands to stand looking at the front of my cart where I have a line of pictures that show what the cart contains. The children make their decisions, and then they point or they tell me what they want and I reach in to pull out their *paletas* and close the top quickly to keep the cold in, and I take their money, give them their change if they have any coming, and I wish them a good day. They are polite children, most of them, as the children of poor people tend to be, and they thank me and they take the wrappers from their *paletas*, and I walk on, leaving them to their young pleasures of sweet ice. Here, now, I am a *paleta* man. I sell small measures of happiness in a way that allows me to be out in the open air, and gives me gentle exercise, and keeps me in contact with friendly children. Why would I not be content?

True, it is not much of a job for a man. Certainly it is a job beneath a man who has been to university, who was the headmaster of a village school, in the peaceful days before the soldiers came.

In a better time, another age, I would still be living in that village, writing mathematical problems on the chalkboard and telling the children about history and government and the rules of grammar. I would still have a wife and two sons to greet me when I came home in the afternoon and to sit around the table in the dinner hour and around the fire in the evenings, the boys and their father doing homework while the mother bends over her embroidery and mending. But the war began, and our village was very near to where the revolt first boiled up out of discontent and hunger and envy and the two ways of life that can never be reconciled, and before we thought to worry, there were rebels in the village, and then soldiers, and between the rope sandals of the one and the leather boots of the other, my quiet village was trampled to death.

I was away when the village died, off on a training course for my school, when suddenly the room I was sitting in began to buzz with rumor, and I left the seminar and hitchhiked in trucks and on motorscooters and ran in my city shoes until I reached my village to find smoke and uniformed men and people with television cameras and the tents of the Red Cross, filled with my groaning friends and neighbors.

My younger son looked like he was sleeping, lying peacefully against the big tree in our front garden while men armed with guns and cameras trotted past in the road outside the hedges and somewhere nearby a woman shrieked and shrieked. Lying sleeping against the tree where some soldier had caught him up and thrown him, breaking his head against the hard trunk.

My older son looked like he was dead. A bayonet or a machete had entered him four or five times, but he was still alive when I found him in the Red Cross tent. He had been found in the door of my schoolroom, and taken to the doctors, but he never woke, never heard my voice again before he died. It still comes to me, all these years later, how very strange it was, that one boy with such terrible wounds could live longer than another boy whose head showed so little damage.

My wife died too. I will say no more about her death, because when I do she haunts my dreams, and I am ready to forget. I cannot forget, of course, any more than my schoolteacher's hands can forget the feeling of killing two of the men responsible for the death of my village, once I had caught up with them. Blood is so very hot; it shocks the skin when it spills, and the hands never forget the sensation.

But now I am no longer a schoolmaster, no longer a father taking his revenge. I am a *paleta* man, content to walk up and down the streets of my route in the footsteps of all the men who once would have gone here, the milkmen and delivery boys, the knife sharpeners and brush sellers and itinerant window washers. Now there is only me and the boy who delivers the paper from his bicycle in the afternoons, and the postman, who is friendly but who wears an official uniform and has no time to listen to problems or to help. Everyone else drives here in a car or a truck, and is kept alone by the metal skin of his vehicle.

Except for me. For perhaps ten months of the year I am here nearly every day, up and down my route, through the neighborhood that lies between the busy shops of the main street and the open fields and big concrete buildings where the town's deliveries arrive and are shipped away, the buildings where men come to buy pipe and gravel and women in polished cars drive to the wholesale bakery and take away to their large homes many strange and delightful foods like fresh tortillas and spicy empanadas and brightly colored Mexican pastries.

I call it my neighborhood, my *barrio*, because I work there, but I do not actually live there. I live a few miles away in a small rusty trailer grown over by a single, enormous rosebush with flowers of palest yellow, very like the rosebush my young wife planted at our front door in my village in the hills. Near the trailer I have built an arbor to hold the vines of melon and grape and chayote squash, which makes a cool shady area I can enjoy on the rare hot days I do not go to town. The trailer and arbor are surrounded by my garden of nopal cactus and tomatillo plants and marigolds, of chiles and summer squashes and other vegetables, all of it set in a square of ground fenced off from a big field that is planted with strawberries or lettuce or cabbages in different years. It is a long, dusty walk along the busy highway pushing my *paleta* cart, but it is my home, and although I have no family and few friends come to visit me, I enjoy my garden and my chickens. In the winter, when people do not buy as much ice cream, I dig in the garden and repair the arbor and read the books that I borrow from the library, and in the summer evenings when I have finished selling *paletas* I sit under the arbor or in the doorway of my trailer surrounded by the smell of roses and watch the cars fly past.

Most of the people who live in the neighborhood where I work would not stay there if they had another choice. Trains rumble too close to the houses, the big delivery trucks sit for hours with their engines running and make the air smell, and wandering dogs are hit and killed by speeding teenagers in their crazy bright cars. Or they are hit and not killed, and that is worse.

It was just such a thing that got me started on the other side of my work as a *paleta* man, a dog that was struck and half crushed and lay in the street, suffering loudly but refusing to die.

I was two streets away when I heard the shriek of the tires and the loud gulping howl of the dog, and I knew at once what it was. The noise did not stop. All the time I walked with my cart down one street and up the next, ringing my bells loudly, the dog continued to howl. When I finally turned the corner past the sweet-smelling *panaderia* and I saw the faces of the mothers and the children where they stood in a knot around the crushed dog, I knew that it would be up to me to stop the noise that had twenty small children clutching their ears, tears pouring down their twisted faces into their mouths.

I knew the dog, of course. Any man who walks the streets must know which dogs have to be watched and which are trustworthy, and this old bitch was a sweet-tempered, toothless old animal with dry yellow fur. Her boy loved her, and sometimes bought an extra ice cream just for her.

She was lying where the speeding car had tumbled her, and I knew she was howling from terror, not from pain—that spinal cord could no longer be carrying any messages from any part of her behind the shoulders. But she could not get to her feet to run away, and her nose must have told her of her injuries even if her other senses did not.

When a living body is violated and the skin breached, what spills out is too real for the eyes to accept it. Blood is too red, the organs too alive; the mind turns away. However, when a person has done as many things in a long life as I have, the eye is given distance. My eyes saw mostly the horror of the children, whose mothers should have hurried them indoors and turned up the televisions in their houses loud enough to dominate all other sounds.

I opened the top of my *paleta* cart and took out two ice cream bars, and I went over to the dog. I squatted down in front of her, where she could see me, and put out my hand—carefully, because a mortally wounded animal is an unpredictable thing.

She knew me, her eyes told me that, and though she kept howling mightily, she watched me, too. I held up one of the ice creams and began to unwrap it, and when it was free of its paper I took it by its stick and laid it along her rigid, howling tongue. It took a minute for the sensation to travel to her brain, but then the terrible noise faltered, and went by fits and starts, until finally she gave a last yip and her mouth closed greedily on the cold, creamy bar.

She slobbered and chewed and gummed the stick dry, and when she remembered and began to yip again I unwrapped the other one and placed it in her mouth with my right hand while I stroked her head with my left, talking to her in a quiet voice. I let her finish the ice cream bar, and then I bent over her so the children would not see what I was doing and I gently put both hands on her neck and with a clean jerk I put her beyond the reach of her misery.

One of the mothers brought an ancient rag of a curtain, which we draped across the old dog's back end, leaving only her peaceful, ugly face with the ice cream still on the muzzle. I encouraged the children to pat the face of their peaceful old friend, and sold them some ice creams, and we all went back to our work. Eventually the city came and removed the dog's body, and that was the end of it.

But it was also the beginning.

The incident with the dog occurred when I had only been in the town for three years, and it was my second season behind the *paleta* cart, but after that day I was everyone's *tío*, their helpful uncle. The women refused to let their children buy from the noisy truck when it ventured into my territory, just drove him off with their stares and their closed purses. They found small jobs, and paid me for them when they could, and when I would permit it. I carried groceries back from the market on top of my sturdy little cart, with pregnant women leading small children by my side; with my cart too I transported chairs, mattresses, and baby beds from one house to another in the neighborhood. I even did those small jobs in a house that women have never been taught and landlords put off—repairing a spitting light switch, putting a strong new lock on a door after an angry boyfriend has broken down the old one, opening a window sealed shut by the paint of years.

Then there were the tasks for which I would not take money, the wandering children, the small boy who had locked himself inside a bathroom, the old woman nobody had seen all day, lying in her bed in sheets wet with urine, taken away in an ambulance and placed in a home that people mentioned in lowered voices. For these tasks I could not, as a man, accept payment. I asked only that they bought my *paletas,* even if they were sometimes a little soft and the selection was limited, and turn their backs on the man in the white truck.

I see that I have gone on and on with my story, and yet only now is the story of Señora Robinson beginning. But I do not apologize, because without knowing about the cart and the crushed dog and the little jobs old Tío Jaime the *paleta* man was sometimes called on to perform, my involvement in one woman's problems would surely seem insane, ungodly as well as illegal, and even the stuff of an old man's imagination.

But now you know that I am Tío, the *paleta* man, and I am a friend to the neighborhood.

Because I walk through my *barrio* and do not steer a noisy truck down its streets, I get to know the people very well, even those who do not have children. I know when the husband of one house has a job, because his children buy real ice creams instead of the cheap frozen water pops. I hear when the teenage son of one family gets arrested, and when a girl gets in trouble, and which of the children leave school to go to work in the shops and fields and which families will struggle to give their sons and daughters the full four years of high school they will need to get a real job and move beyond the neighborhood. These things and more I know, because I have eyes and I have ears and I am on the streets for people to talk to.

So I knew that the husband of Señora Robinson beat her up regularly, on the first and third Fridays of every month. He would receive his pay, he would cash it at the cashing service next door to the bar on Main Street, he would go into the bar, and some hours later he would go home drunk and hit her. The next day she would not come out of her house. Two or three days later, she would emerge to buy from me one of the ice cream cups I sell to be eaten with a small flat wooden spoon, as a little reward, I think, for surviving another around with her husband's fists, and as a tiny gesture of revenge, that his money should be spent on her luxury.

On those days I did not want to accept her money. I did, because I thought that if I refused to take it, she would not come out to buy this taste of sweetness for herself. I also decided that in this matter, this woman's small pride might be more important than my own.

She was a nice woman, was Señora Robinson, pretty in that pale way some Anglos have when their hair is too dark to be called blond and too light to be brown. She was a tiny woman, smaller even than my wife, whose head used to rest beneath my chin when I wrapped my arms around her and held her close. Señora Robinson's house was the cleanest place in a neighborhood of clean houses—which could not have been easy, since it stood at the end of the busy road with its back on a field, from both of which the dust rose in clouds at every wind. She had a nice garden, too, vegetables and flowers, and when she bought her little cup of chocolate ice cream and peeled off the top to eat it slowly, sometimes we would stand and pass a few words about her garden. Two or three times I brought her cuttings or seeds from my own garden, so that next to her front door there grew a small rose of palest yellow. I looked at it every time I went past her gate, greeting it as a friend.

Señora Robinson had no real neighbors. On one side of her house lay the yards of a plumbing supply business, on the other rose up the high, blank wall of a warehouse. Across the street was a printer's, and behind her back fence stretched the fields. It was a busy place during the day, but everything shut down in the evenings, so that after dusk the street was deserted, and people rarely went there. She had no neighbors, although everyone in the neighborhood knew who she was, and if there was no true feeling for her, there was some sympathy.

One day, three days after the first Friday in the month of May, I sold her a cup of chocolate ice cream. She had trouble holding the flat wooden spoon because one of her fingers was in a splint. I said nothing and went about my business, but a short time later I stood with my elbow on the fence of another woman who lived not far from the Robinson house, making conversation.

Señora Lopez was a retired cannery worker whose children had grown and whose fingers itched for grandchildren to care for. She had spent most of her life organizing people, from her husband to the union, and I knew well that nothing would give her greater pleasure than organizing Señora Robinson. I leaned against the fence watching three children revel in the sugary pleasures of their *paletas*.

"Do you know Señora Robinson?" I asked her. "In the house near the plumbing supply?"

"Sure. She's very stuck-up."

Actually, what she said was that Señora Robinson acted like she had a stick up a part of her body. I said, "It's not the stick up there that troubles her, it's the fist she gets in her face."

"She's not the only one in this neighborhood," said Señora Lopez. She sounded as if she was throwing the problem away, but in truth I knew that she was one of those that women in trouble turned to, and she could be as fierce as a tiger in how she helped them. We often act in ways that conceal our true feelings, especially when those feelings are strong.

"That is true," I said, trying to sound like I was apologizing for all the wrongdoing by all the men who ever lived. "But she is also very young, little more than a child, and without friends and family. It is too bad she cannot find some way of reaching out for friendship. Maybe she could take a cooking class down at the adult school, if her husband would let her. She was asking me the other day about how to make *chiles rellenos*. What do I know? Ah well, I must be going. My ice creams will melt in this sun."

As I left, I let my eyes rest on the row of young, healthy chile plants she had along the side of her house. *Chiles rellenos*, indeed.

That is how Señora Robinson made friends in her neighborhood, and how she learned that Tío the *paleta* man was a helpful sort of fellow, and finally how there were services in the community to help women like her, and things you could divorce a man for that didn't involve calling the police. Señora Lopez told me one day that Señora Robinson had asked her what was meant by "irreconcilable differences." Señora Lopez had to explain the phrase to me as well, but when I understood it, I agreed that it was good that in this country a divorce could be had for such a simple reason.

Over the next few weeks I thought she was going to make it. It seemed to me as if the yellow rose nodded at me in approval when one third Friday of the month went past and on the Saturday morning she was at work in her garden. Señora Lopez brought other women to see the small, pale Anglo woman. The smell of chiles and cumin sometimes overcame the dust smell of the plumbing supply yard next door, and Señora Robinson began to blossom like a neglected plant given water and sun. I told myself what a clever fellow I was, to set such a thing in motion. Why, why do we never learn?

In truth, though, it should have ended happily. In my village it might have, because the women were strong and in and out of each other's lives all the time, and had brothers and uncles to help them. In this country it is not always that way. It is especially not that way for the poor.

Perhaps if I had not interfered, if I had not arranged for Señora Lopez to take Señora Robinson under her wing, then nothing worse would have happened other than Señora Robinson's black eyes and careful walk. I did mean well, but I saw only one week later that I was wrong, and I saw where it would end.

The following Wednesday Señora Robinson lost his job, and that evening his wife came very near to losing her life. If one of Señora Lopez's friends had not been bringing a paper bag full of tomatillos to Señora Robinson, and heard what was happening inside the house, and run to call the police, the husband might have murdered her. Instead, he was jailed for two days until Señora Robinson came home from the hospital with plaster on her arm, and when she would not press charges, he moved back home.

Two months later it happened again.

Six weeks after that, again.

I was no longer content in that neighborhood. The inability of the police to stop a man from beating his wife to death preyed on my mind and gave me nightmares when I saw my own wife's end come on her. A thick layer of invisible smoke seemed to lie over the whole area, and the *paleta* cart became heavier and heavier to push toward it as the cool mornings of autumn came along.

Señora Lopez did not give up. She checked on her Anglo friend every day. She brought her food, took her to visit other women, made her get involved in some committee that was working to force the city to install stop signs and traffic bumps. She took her to the doctor to have the plaster removed from her arm, and to the clinic to have the stitches taken out, and to the emergency room to have her ribs X-rayed, and all the while she talked to Señora Robinson about her options. She could divorce him, she could get a job, she could hide in the women's shelter, she could get something called a restraining order. Señora Robinson listened to all the advice, and nodded, and did nothing. She stopped coming out of her house to buy a cup of ice cream from me, her house stopped smelling like cumin, and when I caught glimpses of her, she seemed to me even smaller, stopped over and thin as a broomstick.

When Señora Lopez explained to me about the restraining order, I only looked at her. Señor Robinson was a very big man. Until losing his job for showing up at work drunk, he had made his living moving heavy objects from trucks to warehouses and back again, and his shoulders were massive. I could not imagine a piece of paper restraining those shoulders. Señora Lopez saw the doubt in my eyes and shrugged. He did not want his wife to leave him; no one in the neighborhood wanted her to stay. The differences in the two points of view were as far apart as those of the government and the rebels in my village. And as likely to lead to bloodshed.

That shrug of Señora Lopez's stayed with me all that day and into the night. I sat long in the doorway of my trailer, the last roses drooping off the vine above my head, and I looked off into the soft darkness, and heard the cars and trucks go by. If a woman wants to kill herself, the shrug said, what can we do?

I did not think that Señora Robinson wished to kill herself. I thought that she was trying to become so small that her husband would not see her, to make herself so without presence as a person that she would be invisible to his eyes. In that way, she would be safe. A restraining order, her spine said to me, would only make him more angry. A flight to a shelter, her bent head whispered, would only rouse his possessive fury.

I thought she was right. That night beneath the dying roses, I decided that she was right to be afraid, that the police were helpless to do anything permanent and the court system of Señora Lopez would be unable to move fast enough to stand in Señora Robinson's way. It was, in truth, a task for a single man.

I could not do it without her permission, though. I decided that the next day, if I saw her, I would ask Señora Robinson if she wished to be free of her husband. I would consider it my service to the peace of the neighborhood.

I dreamed of my wife that night, standing with both our sons in the door of our small house in the village. She said nothing, but I thought she was pleased with me. In my dream, the rose around the door was in full bloom. It smelled like my wife's hair when we lay in each other's arms.

I had made my decision, to perform this service to the neighborhood, and for pretty, childlike Señora Robinson, and for the shades of my family. I did not have a lot of time, though, because soon the rains would begin and a *paleta* man sells nothing in the rain.

During my hours of walking the route and ringing my two harmonious bells, I thought carefully about how I would do this thing. I did not wish to spend the rest of my days in prison, nor did I wish to have Señora Robinson accused. The man had to disappear.

In a hardware store I bought a strong pulley, a package of sturdy rope, and a metal object in the shape of an *S* to hold the pulley. Rough burlap sacks are almost unknown in this country, but I found some strong cotton sacks used to make sandbags when the river floods, and took those.

Everything else I already had: rubber gloves I used when mixing chemicals to spray in the garden, a box of heavy garbage bags I found by the side of the road one year, a shovel, and of course my knife.

In the sunny mornings I dug along the back fence of the property and planted cuttings of the pale yellow rose. Late in the evenings I removed the roses and dug the holes deeper, filled the cotton bags with the soil, and then put them back into the hole before planting the roses again. One wet day I constructed a tripod to hold the pulley. And I waited.

I very nearly waited too long. A day or two later, the sun came back out, the children were again interested in cold treats, and the *paleta* man loaded his cart with ice creams on sticks and frozen juice bars and a few cups with chocolate ice cream that you eat with flat wooden spoons.

Señora Robinson had been taken to the hospital again. This time she would be in for days, even a week. Her husband had been arrested, and was out on bail.

I stood looking at the child who told me this news, my mind whirling, until the gentle touch of a hand on mine brought me back to the street.

"Are you okay, Tío?"

"Yes of course, Tomás. Oh—I'm sorry. Here is your juice bar. No, I was only wondering if I remembered to turn off the heat under my coffeepot. I think I did. How is your mama? Good, good. And what do you want today, Esmerelda?"

I am an old man on the outside, but still there are times when the young heart beats as strongly within me as ever it did, when the blood rises up in disgust or rage or sometimes even lust. It leaves me shaken and empty when it passes, feeling as old as I look, but this time I would not allow it to pass until I had used it. I would hold it close and nurture it, and I would be a young man again, for a time.

The sun went behind clouds in the afternoon, and by dinnertime a light rain was falling, which was good. I left my *paleta* cart hidden behind one of those large metal refuse bins they call Dumpsters, and I walked home in the dark by a back way, where people would only see a man in a dark raincoat, not the *paleta* man without his cart.

In my trailer, I turned on lights, cooked a dinner and forced myself to eat it, cleaned up and watched the television, and turned off the lights at ten o'clock, only a little earlier than the houses nearby were used to seeing. I then changed into my oldest clothes, put my knife and my rubber gloves in my pockets, resumed my cold, wet raincoat, and walked back to town.

I had thought I would try to kill Señora Robinson's husband in the bathtub, to make cleaning up easier, but I changed my mind when I saw how the rain was coming down ever harder. There would be no reason to dirty his wife's house with my boots and his blood.

I knocked on his door at a quarter after eleven. I had to pound, over the sound of the rain and to wake him from his drunkenness in front of the television. He came to the door, blinking and holding on to the jamb, and I had to tell him twice how sorry I was that I drove into the side of his truck.

He roared when he understood me, roared like a bear and shoved me aside so that I nearly fell. I followed him down the steps, and then I stepped off the pathway and stood in the middle of the patch of lawn, waiting for him. He finished looking for the damage on his precious truck and staggered back toward me, soaked and furious, shouting and waving his fists.

There had been no one to hear when this man hit his wife and made her cry out; the thing that protected him before would be his undoing now. I waited until he was standing in front of me, preparing to do to my face what he did to his wife's, and then I drew my knife from my pocket and I killed him.

The two soldiers I hunted down all those years ago had taught me much about killing. After the first, I learned that it is mostly when the knife comes out that blood is shed, and especially when it is removed before death. Señora Robinson's husband was dead before he fell to the lawn. I left the knife where it was while I turned off the house lights, closed the front door, and went to fetch my *paleta* cart from behind the Dumpster.

The cart is not large, and I am no longer a strong man, so I knew that I would have to transport him in two pieces. It was not pleasant, but that is what I did, placing his remains in the rain-slick garbage bags and running the garden hose for a long time in the place where I had worked. It took the entire package of bags, most of the night, and more energy than I thought I possessed, but I got all of him to my home before dawn. I left him in my garden shed along with the clothes I had worn, then scrubbed myself in all the hot water the trailer's small tank held, and finally fell into bed.

The next day the rain was less, but no one would expect the *paleta* man to be out. That too was a good thing, because the young strength of disgust and rage had left me by then, and I felt old and weak and more than a little sickened by what I had done. I lay in bed all that day. When darkness fell I rose and forced myself to eat, and then I set up my tripod and pulley, carefully took up the roses I had planted in the holes along the back fence and dug down into the soil beneath. The heavy sandbags filled with soil came up easily with the help of the tripod and pulley, and the first hole was quickly emptied. And filled again. Then the second one, with Señor Robinson's upper half.

They were both very deep holes. I dug them along the back fence line because I did not care to have the grapes and the melon vines that I eat from sinking their roots into that man, and to put him closer to the trailer would have given me bad dreams of his torso clawing its way across the ground to my steps. The back fence was much better.

The next day was clear and warm. I pulled a sheet of plastic from the pile of prunings I had been keeping dry, and I burned them, along with a few pieces of trash from the garden shed like soiled rubber gloves and some old clothing.

Then the *paleta* man loaded up his cart and went back to his neighborhood, to sell his *paletas* to the children who lived there.

All of that happened nearly two years ago. The police questioned many people about the strange disappearance of an unpopular man, but they made no arrests; after all, Señora Robinson was in the hospital when her husband went away. And who did she know who might have done away with her husband so efficiently? Her only friend was Señora Lopez, and troublemaker though that woman might be, the thought of Señora Lopez as part of a murder plot was impossible. No, Señora Robinson had no one who might have removed her husband for her; the man must have been involved in some bad affair, crossed some dangerous man while drunk. It was a mystery.

The other day I had two visitors, who drove into my yard about half an hour before sunset, when the shadows stretched long and the summer heat was beginning to cool from the air.

Señora Lopez had never said anything to me about the strange disappearance of Señora Robinson's husband. She did not say anything the other evening, either, when she and Señora Robinson, who was in truth a handsome woman, stood in my dusty yard admiring the garden. Señora Lopez studied the heavy leaves of the grapes on the arbor, the heavily loaded tomato and pepper bushes, and the great jungle the yellow rose has become over the front of the trailer.

The two ladies had spent the day making tamales, which is a dish a cook embarks on when she wants to share her kitchen with the world. They brought me a large plateful. I thanked them both, and we talked for a few minutes. They politely refused my offer of a cold drink, and then they left.

Just a friendly visit.

But before she got into her car, Señora Lopez looked long and hard at the glory of my back fence, where half a dozen cuttings now cover a hundred feet. She looked at it, and she looked at me, and she had a very small smile on her face as she drove away.

The pale yellow roses are, in truth, very beautiful.

Y soy contento.

And I am content.

Stuart M. Kaminsky

Snow

Another mystery writer who is adept at just about whatever historical period or genre he tries is STUART M. KAMINSKY. Inspector
Porfiry Rostnikov is an intelligent Moscow policeman forever dis-
trusted by his superiors and always being assigned "impossible" cases,
which he solves with aplomb. Private detective Toby Peters lives and
works in and around Hollywood of the 1940s, taking on cases for
stars like Judy Garland and the Marx Brothers. Rarely has an author
worked in two so dissimilar series with the same incredible skill. A
former president of Mystery Writers of America, he has also written plays, screenplays, and biographies of such noted celebrities as
Clint Eastwood and director John Huston. His short fiction has
appeared in anthologies such as *Guilty as Charged, The Mysterious
West,* and *Funny Bones.* This story first appeared in *First Cases,* Volume III.

Snow

Stuart M. Kaminsky

If there had been less blood, following the trail in the snow would have been quite difficult. For one thing, the sun was just beginning, slowly, lazily, to rise over Moscow. For another thing, the snow was still falling. Not as heavily as it had throughout the night but enough to quickly fill in footprints.

Porfiry Petrovich Rostnikov, though the temperature hovered in the 20s, was warm in the heavy wool coat of his uniform. And his cap? He perspired under it and would gladly have taken it off as he trudged forward if it were not for the watchful eye of the detective with whom he had been teamed on the call.

Rostnikov had been a policeman for less than a month. His training had been minimal and his apprenticeship to an indifferent veteran had been enough to make the young policeman briefly reconsider his choice of profession.

"This way," Rostnikov said over his shoulder.

Behind him Inspector Luminiov grunted and though Porfiry Petrovich did not turn his head, he could tell from the smell that the inspector had paused to light a cigarette.

The trail of blood went around a corner of the block of four-story concrete apartment buildings. Somewhere in the distance, Rostnikov heard the clang of a trolley.

Rostnikov wanted to run, to find the end of this stream of vermilion that rested atop the clean whiteness, but he could not. His leg would not permit it. Rostnikov talked to his leg, muttered to his leg, sometimes within himself, sometimes aloud.

"Leg," he said now. "A child has been taken, a baby. The child is in the hands of a man who has killed, a man who may well be mad."

Although his leg did not use words, the answer was clear to the burly young policeman with a broad face that could only be Russian.

"When that German tank came, you could have pulled me out of its path," said his leg.

"We've been through this," said Rostnikov dragging his reluctant, crippled leg behind him. "I was a boy soldier, a little boy in a large ragged uniform. I was trapped."

"That does me little good," said the leg.

"Then," said Rostnikov, "we must simply learn to live together, to cooperate."

"I have no desire to cooperate," his leg responded.

"Then," said Rostnikov, "I shall have to resign myself to making the best of things."

"What? What did you say?" asked Luminiov, moving to Rostnikov's side.

"Talking to myself," said Rostnikov. "That way."

He pointed across the street. There was no traffic. In this forgotten neighborhood of crumbling ill-built tenements, there were no cars but those belonging to the police and no State-paid old women with brooms to tirelessly clear the sidewalks and streets.

The trail of blood led across the street toward the doorway of a building that looked like all the buildings that faced and surrounded it. Four-foot-high drifts of snow sloped up the side of the building, covering all but the very tips of the barred ground floor windows.

Luminiov let out a sigh of boredom, took a deep drag of his cigarette, and looked at the dark doorway. Luminiov was a lean man of about forty with white hair who looked as if he were half-asleep. Rostnikov knew his superior had been drinking heavily the night before, possibly even into the early hours of the morning. Vodka left no smell, but Rostnikov knew well the signs. They were with him every day on the streets of Moscow. Dostoyevsky had written about those signs and the dazed dangers of vodka a century ago.

Luminiov wore a black overcoat. He unbuttoned it and removed his pistol from a holster that was badly in need of polishing.

"Follow the trail," said Luminiov. "I'll stay out here in case he tries to escape this way."

Rostnikov nodded. He had no choice. Had he been given the choice he would have left Luminiov outside in any case. If the man were in the building, he was probably carrying the child. Rostnikov had no doubt that the Inspector at his side would fire at man and child if there were even the slightest chance that the man might be carrying a weapon.

Porfiry Petrovich Rostnikov had no desire to die. He had a wife. She was pregnant with their first child. He had much to live for, but the murderer who had entered the building had taken a baby.

Rostnikov limped toward the entryway of the apartment building. As he moved, he looked up at the falling snow. Looking up saved his life. The block of concrete was coming straight at him. Rostnikov rolled to his right as the jagged missile crashed through the snow a few feet away.

"Are you all right?" Luminiov called with a vague interest rather than real concern.

"I am alive. I appear to be uninjured," said Rostnikov, rolling over awkwardly and looking up to be prepared for any other rocks amid the snow.

"Good," said Luminiov.

Through the thin flurry of white flakes, Rostnikov could see a figure at the edge of the roof.

"Go away!" shouted the man. He had something in his arms. It wasn't a block of concrete. It was a baby. The baby was crying.

Rostnikov looked at Luminiov, who was drawing his gun, and shouted up at the man on the roof.

"Step back. I'm coming up."

"No."

Rostnikov rose awkwardly.

Though the distance was not great, the weather was a problem. Luminiov's shot struck the edge of the roof with an echoing RRRING.

"Don't!" shouted Rostnikov both at Luminiov and the man on the roof.

The man hesitated and raised the infant over his head.

"He won't shoot again," Rostnikov shouted to the man on the roof.

Luminiov was aiming more carefully now. Rostnikov turned to his superior and said loud enough for the man on the roof to hear, "If you are responsible for that baby's death, I will kill you."

"You will kill me?" said Luminiov, turning his weapon on the young officer.

"Yes," said Rostnikov calmly.

He had seen babies die in the war, had witnessed the bodies of many, but the babies, the dead babies had wounded him more than any wounds inflicted on him by the Nazis.

Luminiov put his gun hand to his side and said with a shrug, "We'll talk about this later. We will talk. Be sure of that."

Rostnikov knew that Luminiov had few choices. If he shot Rostnikov, not only would he have to explain why he had done so, he would also have to cope with the madman on the roof.

"Go," said Luminiov.

"I'm coming up," called Rostnikov. "Have you got a blanket, sweater, something up there?"

"Blanket? No."

"The baby must be very cold. Take off your coat or something."

The man on the roof stepped back. His uniform now wet with snow, Porfiry Petrovich Rostnikov moved into the entryway, which smelled of the thousands of cigarettes smoked by the out-of-work residents who gathered each day with nothing to do but argue and complain.

The door was not locked. None of the doors to these concrete tributes to Stalin were ever locked. There was no point to a lock. Any nine-year-old could get through with a piece of wire and a laugh.

The inner lobby was dark, cold, unheated. Since every building was heated by the central gas system, usually buildings like this were too hot or too cold. This one on this day was too cold.

There was a concrete stairway with a rusting metal railing. He went to it and began moving slowly upward, coaxing his complaining left leg, promising it rest later.

The climb was slow though Rostnikov wanted to move quickly. He encountered no one coming down. It was still too early and the gunfire may well have convinced those few who had reason to arise early that they had better reason to stay locked in their apartments a bit longer.

Luminiov had taken the call only an hour earlier. Rostnikov had been the only uniformed officer available in the district station. Luminiov had simply pointed to him and said, "You," not even asking the young uniformed officer his name. Rostnikov had been waiting for his partner, his senior partner who was, once again, late for their shift.

Rostnikov had followed the Inspector. They had said little on the way to the scene.

Rostnikov knew Luminiov by sight. Luminiov was vaguely aware of the short, burly policeman only because the man had sad eyes and a crippled leg. Luminiov, had he been able to stir enough interest within himself, might have asked how a cripple could become a policeman. Had he asked, Rostnikov would have told him that he had drifted through jobs in a factory, as a trolley conductor until, at the age of thirty-three, he had decided to become a policeman. His war record had been enough to get him the job and, until now, a series of crimes no greater than rousting drunks. Most of his brief career as a policeman had involved following his partner, who made the rounds of blackmarketers who doled out bribe money which Rostnikov refused to take a share of. His refusal, rather than making his partner suspicious, had pleased the veteran, who did not have to share his take.

This moment, however, this very moment was the height of his brief career as a policeman. He did not think of that now. He would later, but not at this moment. He had glimpsed the baby on the roof and that sight now drove him. As he moved forward, he remembered the apartment where minutes ago they had discovered what remained of the dead woman.

There had been a tiny, single room large enough for a bed, a makeshift crib, a torn sofa, a wooden table with a piece of wood under one of the four legs to keep it from toppling over, and three unmatched chairs. There was a very small alcove which had been turned into a kitchen area. There was also the dead woman in the middle of the room.

She was very thin, and still wore a sweater she no longer needed to help ward off the cold. She no longer had a face.

The reason for her lost identity was a bloody block of wood near the door, a block of wood like so many in Moscow apartments, a block of wood to jam against the door to keep out intruders who ignored locks.

Luminiov had stepped back into the second floor hallway and caught an old woman peeking out of her door.

"You," he called sternly. "Out here. We are the police."

The old woman reluctantly came into the hallway and down to the small apartment where Rostnikov was examining but not touching the body.

"Where is the baby?" Rostnikov asked before Luminiov could ask a question.

"Is she, yes, she is dead," said the old woman.

"The baby," Rostnikov repeated gently. "The crib is still warm, damp. The baby has a fever. Where is the baby?"

Luminiov had leaned back against the wall, lit a cigarette, and watched with a hint of amusement. This was routine. The husband or boyfriend had done this. Cramped in a little hole. No job. Too cold to walk off anger. Perhaps drunk. The baby crying. Regimes had changed but in more than 500 years, Russians had not. The baby was probably dead somewhere nearby. No one would miss it. And if it lived who would take care of it?

The sun was definitely out now though it was visible only as a vague sullen glow through the still falling snow. Now, people began to slowly emerge from the apartment buildings, bundled, trudging, glancing at Luminiov, who knew that he was supposed to secure the scene, keep people away. A falling child or, worse, a falling stubborn young policeman with a bad leg could hit one of them.

Luminiov looked up and saw nothing at the edge of the building. He stepped back a dozen paces into the doorway of a boarded-up apartment building.

Rostnikov climbed the last narrow stairway to the door to the roof. If it was locked or barricaded, he would have to decide on whether he would go back or attempt to break through. A breakthrough might panic the bleeding man.

The door was not locked but the wind made it difficult to push open. When he did, he looked around for the man and baby. The snow was swirling harder atop the roof than on the street below, but it was not a terrible snowstorm.

Even without the trail of blood on the rooftop snow and the deep footprints, he would have quickly found the man who made no attempt to hide or respond. The baby, wrapped in a thin sheet, was cradled in the man's right arm. The left arm hung at the man's side. He wore a flannel shirt, which was not tucked in, and blood dripped from his dangling fingers.

The man himself was big, overweight, thin hair, about forty years old, and filled with panic.

"You shoot me and I throw him over the edge. I swear. And I'll jump too. If you don't care, shoot me. You know what? I don't care. What is there for me? I'll go to jail, execution. Better to die now."

Below, on the street, a young woman urged on by her friends approached the policeman smoking in the doorway of the boarded-up building. Her mission was to find out what was happening. Her sister lived in the building the policeman was looking at.

She started to speak but Luminiov waved her away and looked up at the roof across the street. Loud voices were coming from up there and if there was silence Luminiov could just make out what was being said.

"What's the baby's name?" asked Rostnikov, moving forward a step.

"Alexander," the man said, looking at the baby.

"He is yours?"

"I think so. Who knows? She was no beauty. I mean . . . but there are men. And I'm not much . . . What difference does it make now?"

"Can you hold Alexander up so I can see his face?" asked Rostnikov as he limped another step forward.

"Stop!" shouted the man.

Rostnikov stopped.

"You mind if I sit over there? On the vent?"

"You'll be cold. You'll have to sit in the snow," the man said.

Rostnikov shrugged.

"Better a wet bottom than an angry leg."

"Sit, but I'm getting weak," said the man. "I'm going to throw him over the edge and then follow him."

Rostnikov moved to the vent and sat. It was cold. He looked around. The snow was now coming down harder.

"We're in for three feet at least," said Rostnikov, rubbing his left leg with his gloved hands.

"Is someone coming behind you? Are you planning to trick me? If someone comes through that door—"

"No one but me is coming," said Rostnikov. "You're cold. The baby's not wrapped warmly enough. Will you accept my coat? You can tuck the baby under it."

"Alexander," said the man.

"Yes, Alexander," repeated Rostnikov. "And you are?"

"A dead man."

"Yes, but does the dead man have a name?"

"Ivan," he said. And then he laughed. "Millions of Ivans. One more will die. Millions of Alexanders. Dead people don't need coats. When we were alive we could have used your coat but . . . dead people don't . . ."

". . . need coats," Rostnikov said, shifting his wet behind.

"Yes."

"What do you know about plumbing, Ivan?" asked Rostnikov.

"Plumbing. Nothing. I am . . . was a painter."

"Apartments?"

"Yes."

Rostnikov nodded solemnly.

"Are you a good painter?"

"When I have enough time, good brushes, good paint but I haven't had work for . . . I don't know."

Ivan tried to lift his dangling arm to put around the baby. The arm resisted and then slowly moved as Ivan bit his lower lip. When he did get his injured arm around the baby, the thin sheet was covered instantly in blood.

"Plumbing," Rostnikov said.

"I don't care about plumbing," said Ivan, tears welling in his eyes.

"Intricate," said Rostnikov. "Intricate but logical if done right like the inside of a body. You know, veins, arteries, intestines."

"I'm not interested," said Ivan.

Something stirred to Rostnikov's left. A man in an overcoat wearing a cap and carrying something in his right hand stomped up the stairs from below and onto the roof. Ivan moved to the edge of the roof, stumbling, bleeding.

Rostnikov forced himself up and called, "No, he is not a policeman."

The baby began to whimper, too cold to really cry.

Ivan looked back at the bewildered man, who carried a shovel.

"What?" asked the man, looking at the policeman and the bleeding Ivan.

"Who are you?" Rostnikov asked.

"Who am I?"

"Yes, that is the question," said Rostnikov. "The prize for the correct answer may be the saving of a life, maybe two lives."

"I . . . I am Julian Korianovich. When it snows, I shovel the roof so it doesn't collapse the way it did in . . . I don't know, a year, two years after it was built."

"You get paid for this?" asked Rostnikov, turning his back to Ivan and the whimpering child.

Julian Korianovich looked at the baby and bleeding man. Julian Korianovich touched his full mustache with his gloved hand.

"Paid? Something, a little, not much. I have a room, my wife and I. We don't . . . What is happening?"

"Snow," said Rostnikov, looking up. "We are talking and watching the snow fall."

"Stop!" shouted Ivan.

Rostnikov turned to the man.

"Why did you kill her?"

"She . . . No room. She complained, complained, complained. She drove me mad. I didn't think. I just wanted her to unfold her arms and stop looking at me like that, stop playing with the buttons on that damned sweater."

"How did you get injured?"

Ivan looked down at his arm. His face had turned nearly white from the loss of blood.

"She shot me," he said. "She had a gun. I didn't know she had a gun. We could have sold it. Instead she shot me. I had just hit her once. She said she had decided to shoot me the next time I hit her. She shot me and then . . . Where did she get money to buy a gun?"

"Where is the gun?" asked Rostnikov.

"I don't know. In the room."

"No," said Rostnikov.

The baby continued to whimper.

"Then," said Ivan, trying to think, "it is in my pocket."

With that he attempted to move his injured arm to the pocket of his pants, but the arm would not obey. He could not shift the baby.

"It is in my pocket," he said. "If I could get it out, I would shoot myself. Maybe I would shoot you and the shoveler too. Why should you live if my baby and I are dead? You don't believe me, do you?"

"I believe you," said Rostnikov.

"I believe you too," said Julian the roof shoveler.

"Now, it is time," said Ivan sadly, looking down at the baby.

Rostnikov began moving toward the man and the whimpering infant, circling to the left. Ivan moved back.

"I'm enjoying our talk," Rostnikov said.

"I am too weak to talk," said Ivan. "Too weak. And there is nothing to talk about."

"Did you know that the American president was murdered?" asked Rostnikov, moving slowly forward.

"Kennyadi is dead? You lie."

"Why would I lie? Would you like to know how he died? Where? It was in Texas."

"A cowboy shot him," said Julian the shoveler.

"Don't run at me," said Ivan, who had backed up to the very edge of the roof.

"With this leg? I can do many things, but running is not one of them. The snow is stopping. It is time to end this. Hand me the baby."

"No," said Ivan, crying. He bent his head, kissed the child, and with what little remained of his strength he dropped the baby off the roof.

Julian screamed in sudden fury and ran at Ivan, shovel held high. Rostnikov stepped between the two men and put his arms around the screaming attacker. The man found himself lifted into the air.

"Stop," Rostnikov said gently. "I have work to do."

He dropped the man gently in the snow and Julian began to weep.

"I just came up to shovel the snow," he said.

Ivan was tottering on the edge of the roof. With his free hand he fumbled at the pocket where the gun was awkwardly tucked. Rostnikov tried to move forward quickly but he was unable to reach Ivan before he pulled out the weapon.

Instead of aiming it at his own head, the pale bleeding man pointed it weakly in the general direction of Porfiry Petrovich Rostnikov.

The shot crackled in the cool morning air.

Ivan let out a small sigh, crumpled, and tumbled backward off the roof. Rostnikov moved as quickly as he could to the place where Ivan had fallen. Below him, the dead Ivan lay sprawled, a snow angel, and Inspector Luminiov stood with his gun in his hand and a whimpering baby in his arms.

"The baby," cried a thoroughly confused Julian, tugging at his mustache. "The baby."

"The baby is alive," Rostnikov said, limping to the open door.

When he got to the street, Luminiov stood alone next to the body in the snow. People were watching from a distance, uncertain about what they had seen beyond a baby being thrown from a roof and a man being shot by the police.

Luminiov handed the child to Rostnikov and took off his coat to wrap the baby in.

"You are a man to be watched," Luminiov said, putting his weapon back in the now exposed holster.

"Watched?" asked Rostnikov, touching the baby's cheek. It was cool but not cold and the baby was crying. A good sign. Rostnikov wrapped Alexander in Inspector Luminiov's coat, removed the glove on his right hand, and put his small finger into the infant's mouth. The baby began to suck. Another good sign.

"You maneuvered him to the edge of the roof," said Luminiov, lighting a cigarette. "I heard. You maneuvered him over the deepest drift of snow. You kept him talking while he grew weaker so he couldn't throw the baby, only drop it. And when it was clear the snow was about to stop and the drift wouldn't get any deeper . . . Confirm my observation, Officer."

Rostnikov was looking at the baby.

"I am not that smart, Inspector."

"Oh, but you are. You are a man to watch, Officer—?"

"Rostnikov, Porfiry Petrovich Rostnikov."

"I've had someone call an ambulance," said Luminiov. "Let's get out of the cold. When they take the baby and the body, I'll let you buy me a drink."

"I would like to go to the hospital with Alexander," said Rostnikov.

"Alexander?"

"The baby."

"Yes, Alexander. Sentiment can ruin a promising career," said Luminiov with a smile.

Rostnikov said nothing. The snow had completely stopped. Moscow was covered in white. It was winter, the favorite season of Russians.

Eleanor Taylor Bland

The Canasta Club

ELEANOR TAYLOR BLAND created mystery fiction's first African-American female detective, Marti MacAlister, in her debut novel, *Dead Time*, and has never looked back. A cost accountant who lives in Waukegan, Illinois, she manages to write an average of a book a year despite keeping a full-time job. Hopefully, with the success she's been enjoying with her series, she'll be able to quit that job soon. Her short fiction has appeared in *Women on the Case*, edited by fellow Illinois author Sara Paretsky, and *The Night Awakens*, edited by Mary Higgins Clark. Recent novels include *Scream in Silence* and *Tell No Tales*. This story first appeared in *Murder on Route 66*.

The Canasta Club

Eleanor Taylor Bland

It began snowing as Detectives Marti MacAlister and Matthew "Vik" Jessenovik drove past Springfield, Illinois. Three and a half hours later they had traveled another seventy-two miles. Visibility was close to zero and Route 55 all but impassable by the time they reached their exit. Josephina Hanson, the woman they were going to see, had been told that her eighty-seven-year-old sister Agatha was dead; what she didn't know was that the cause of death was something other than old age and natural causes. Marti pulled into a Phillips 66 and tried to get something on the radio besides static while Vik filled the tank and got directions to the address they were looking for. Over the phone, a Miss Evangeline Roberts had explained that although it could be considered an old folks' home, since elderly ladies lived there, it certainly was not a nursing home.

"We are just getting along in years," she told Marti. "We are not senile or in any way incapacitated, unless you consider being hard of hearing or visually impaired or using a cane."

Vik had not been eager to come here, but because it looked like a homicide they had no choice. The toxicology reports that came late yesterday afternoon had identified poison, and Agatha Hanson had been dead for almost a month. The case was already cold.

The car door opened. Vik said something but it was muffled by the scarf that covered everything below his eyes. He knocked snow from his boots and brushed it off of his wool cap before he got in.

"We lucked up, MacAlister. And we lucked out. The place we're looking for is only a mile and half up that road." He pointed. "It shouldn't take us more than two hours to get there. The bad news is there's no way in hell we're going to make it back to Lincoln Prairie today. There's close to a foot of snow on the ground and another five to seven inches predicted. And guess what—the storm stayed south of Chicago. If we had waited a couple of days we wouldn't be stuck here."

"Did you remember to phone home?"

"My place, yours, and I left a message for the lieutenant. Everyone knows we made it here, so just stay on the road."

Marti hunched forward with her forehead inches from the windshield. The snow was coming down so fast that even with the wipers on high she had difficulty seeing anything. "I hope I can spot another car's headlights while I still have enough time to stop or get out of the way."

"Just worry about staying on the road," Vik advised. "Nobody but a fool would drive around in this."

"It only took half an hour," she said when she pulled into the driveway alongside a rambling two-story house with a wraparound porch. The force of the wind slammed the car door shut and pushed her against the front fender as soon as she got out. She fought against it, with Vik right behind her, grabbed the railing and hauled herself up the front steps.

"Oh, do come in," a stoop-shouldered woman said, opening the door before they could ring the bell. "I've been watching for you. I didn't think you would make it." The wind blew the door so hard it banged against the wall. The carpet was covered with snow before they made it inside. Vik slammed the door shut.

Vik and Marti introduced themselves and showed the woman their shields.

"I'm Evangeline Roberts; we spoke on the phone." Her breath smelled of peppermint. "I can't remember the last time we've had police officers here, not unless you count the time Claudette Colbert managed to get herself stuck in a drainage pipe. She's one of our cats."

The woman sounded more excited than concerned. She didn't reach Marti's shoulder. As Marti looked down at her blue-gray hair, teased and stiff with hair spray, she could see the scalp.

"Let me take your coats. I'd better take them to the kitchen and hang them up. They are covered with snow. And I'll have to have Elmer mop up in here before someone breaks their neck, or worse, a hip."

Vik took Marti's coat and kept his own. "Let me, ma'am."

As they followed her, she moved quickly and with far more agility than Marti expected. The kitchen wasn't as cozy as the porch had implied. The appliances were commercial and stainless steel. There were enough gadgets to stock a small store. There was just a hint of basil in the air and loaves of bread were rising on a countertop. Marti's stomach rumbled. They hadn't stopped to eat since lunch and it was well past dinner time.

"Have you eaten?" Miss Roberts asked.

"No, ma'am," Vik said.

"Well, the dining room is right over here and I'll fix you a little something right away. Josephina is playing canasta and there is no interrupting them once they cut the cards."

An elevator had been installed by the dining area. Everything was chintz and maple and meals were served at round tables seating four, with seasonal centerpieces of evergreen and holly.

"No need to rush, you won't be going back out tonight. We can put you up right here. This town is so small we don't have anything but that rinky-dink little motel, right off the highway. Route Sixty-six it used to be. They even had a TV show named for it with a song and all. Route Sixty-six it still is, as far as I'm concerned, even if they did make it much too wide and renamed it Route Fifty-five."

Marti asked for a telephone.

"The lines are down, dear, but not to worry. We've got an emergency generator if the lights go." She brought them steaming bowls of beef stew, homemade biscuits, and real butter, followed by hot coffee and apple pie.

"I told Josephina you were here. They are right in the middle of their canasta game and were more than a little annoyed by the interruption."

After they had eaten the last bit of pie crust, Miss Roberts led them to the rear of the house. From the hallway, Marti could see an older man mopping up near the front door. Elmer, she assumed. As she watched, he straightened up, put his hand to the small of his back, then continued mopping in a slow circular pattern. Marti wondered what his relationship was to the others. If he didn't live in, and wasn't the next door neighbor, he would be spending the night here too, just as she and Vik would.

"You'll have to wait," Miss Roberts advised. "They play most evenings from right after dinner until bedtime. Once they shuffle and cut the deck, they get madder than buzzards without a carcass if you bother them. Here we are."

Windows ran the length of the porch, which had been closed in and winterized. The windows were bare except for vertical blinds, which were open. A white curtain of icy snow made tapping sounds against the glass. Marti thought of the heating bills first, then the pleasure of looking out and watching the seasons change. A log burning in a fireplace added a homey touch, but Marti doubted that the fire gave off much heat.

Everyone was in pairs. Two ladies sat at the far end of the room, watching a television with the volume turned up. Two ladies were knitting. Two who looked enough alike to be related napped in rocking chairs with their feet on hassocks and fat cats curled up in their laps.

Four women sat at a table. The one with hands crippled with arthritis had arranged her cards in some kind of cardholder. Marti studied each in turn and wondered which was Josephina Hanson. She had seen the dead woman at the morgue, as well as in photographs. None of the card players resembled her. She didn't see anyone to pair with Miss Hanson.

"Jeez," Vik whispered, shielding his mouth with his hand. "Do you think there's anyone in here under ninety? I haven't seen this many old people since my great Uncle Otto died. They had to put him in a nursing home when he was ninety-seven because he kept falling out of his wheelchair."

"I don't think any of these ladies is that old," Marti whispered back. She looked at the two in the rocking chairs and changed her mind. "Maybe those two." She nodded toward them. A walker with wheels and shelves was parked by one of the rockers.

Vik rubbed his arms, then scratched them.

"Old age isn't contagious," Marti said, under her breath. "Cut that out."

"This place is giving me the creeps. There has to be someplace else we can stay."

Marti nodded in the direction of the windows. "Got any ideas as to how we'll get there?"

Vik muttered something in Polish.

There was plenty of seating available, but nothing that looked comfortable. The chairs and sofas had straight backs and hard seats that were high from the floor. Most had pillows or an extra cushion. Marti chose a chair close enough to the card table to eavesdrop. The women played like gamblers even though there was no money on the table: all business, no small talk, certainly not any gossip. What conversation there was was mostly about melds. Canasta didn't sound anything like poker or even bid whist. Bored, Marti watched as one of the old ladies by the television stood up and steadied herself with a cane. She thought of her grandmother and how difficult getting up and down had been for her and understood the reason for the chairs and sofas.

Everything had been adapted to meet the needs of the occupants: extra space between tables and chairs; a counter that ran the length of the windows, with books and magazines and needlework and yarn all within easy reach. There were no scatter rugs, no high or low shelves or storage areas. Sweaters hung on hooks and there was a stack of afghans. This was not anything like any nursing home she had ever been in. It was an old house; remodeling it must have been expensive.

A clock chimed the half hour. Marti glanced at her watch. It was after ten. Vik leaned over and said, "I told you old people don't go to bed early. See, they don't do enough to get tired."

The conversation at the table became louder. Chairs were pushed back. One woman detached herself from the group and walked over to them. Her movements were slow but she was not infirm.

"Miss Hanson?"

"Yes." She was short and plump with a round face and granny glasses. Her deceased sister had been much taller and three years older. There was no facial resemblance whatsoever. "Agatha has been dead for a month now, but if you had to come out in weather like this . . . What is it?"

"Is there someplace where we can talk?" Marti asked.

"Yes, right here." She pulled up a chair. "In just a few minutes."

"Here we are, ladies." Miss Roberts bustled in carrying a tray with glasses and a bottle of brandy. All of the women but two shared a nightcap. Marti and Vik declined but accepted mulled cider.

"So," Josephina Hanson said when they were alone, "what is it?"

Marti decided to be direct. "Someone poisoned your sister."

"Oh dear. But who? And how, I mean what?"

"When is the last time you saw her?"

"Oh, it's been ten years now. Not since Howie died. He was our brother."

"Had you spoken with her on the phone recently?"

"Not since June nineteenth, her birthday. We always call on birthdays and Christmas."

Marti supposed that at their age, and with this much distance between them, calls that infrequent might not be considered unusual. Neither woman had married. They had shared equally in their parents' estate. Agatha had lived alone in a small apartment. Frugal until the end, she had directed that there be no service, that her body be cremated and her ashes scattered on a bluff overlooking Lake Michigan. Josephina had inherited more from her sister than from her parents. It seemed as if they should have been closer.

"Do you have any idea of who her friends were?" The neighbors hadn't known of any.

"There was Opal, and Mary Sue, but both of them have been dead ten or twelve years now."

"Was there anyone else?"

"The mailman. She said he was a very pleasant young man and always reliable."

He was close to retirement and had worked that route for years. He found her body the day after she died. She remembered him in her will.

"Was there anyone else? A repairman? Someone trying to sell her something?"

"Agatha was not one to be taken in by strangers."

Agatha had not made any unusual withdrawals or any other bequests either. If someone had tried to swindle or otherwise pry money from her, apparently they had not been successful. If only she hadn't kept so much to herself.

As soon as Josephina Hanson excused herself to go to bed, Vik said, "That's another problem. How much can someone that old remember? And did you see how she leaned forward to listen to you and then talked too loud? Uncle Otto did that, too. He never wore a hearing aid though. One day he just couldn't hear anything at all."

"Vik, she did hear me."

"Right, but will she remember anything you said this time tomorrow? And it's been months since she talked with her sister. How do you expect her to remember any of that? We're talking about old people, Marti, real old people."

Marti leaned toward him and whispered, "What if she hired someone to kill off Agatha for her money?"

"Don't be ridiculous. At her age, how much money could she need? Living here is probably cheaper than her sister's living expenses were."

"I don't think so," Marti said. "This looks like an expensive arrangement. Greed, Vik. Think about it."

"I just did. There's got to be some other reason. You know how old people are. She trusted someone and kept money in the house. They stole from her and killed her when she found out. Or maybe she let them think they were going to get something when she died and they helped her on her way."

"How about the mailman?" Marti suggested.

"For ten thousand dollars?" He considered that. "We'll have to check him out. Did the sister's reaction surprise you?"

"Not if they've only spoken to each other three times a year for the past ten years. I'm wondering why. Something must have happened between them."

Although she would not admit it to Vik, the biggest problem she had questioning the elderly was not knowing how much of what they recalled was reliable. Then there was that ingrained habit of being respectful to her elders. She had also observed that death seldom surprised or frightened them, especially if they were old enough to have lost family members and friends.

"I can't read Josephina at all. There's something very matter-of-fact in her attitude. I don't know if it's acceptance, or indifference, or if she knows more about her sister's death than she's telling us." Tomorrow she would have to rule out two of those possibilities, even if she was disrespectful, even if Josephina did get upset.

Vik went to the window. "It's still snowing. It's drifted up to the windowsill. I bet we can't even see the car. If you tell anyone that we spent the night in an old folks' home, MacAlister, with eleven little old ladies and two cats . . ."

"Me?" If word of this got around the precinct they would both be the butt of everyone's jokes. "As far as I'm concerned, this place has vacant rooms and that makes it a motel."

"Just don't forget that. If anyone ever finds out I spent the night with a bunch of senile old women . . ."

"They are old, Jessenovik, but I don't see any indications of senility. There is a difference."

"Oh, yeah? Try telling that to an eighty-year-old man."

Miss Roberts showed Vik to a sofa in a small den. Marti got a guest room on the first floor that was a few feet bigger than a closet. "I'm afraid we've never had anyone sleep over, dear," Miss Roberts explained. "We do have the stray niece and nephew here and there. It isn't something we want to encourage." The nightgown the woman gave her was several sizes too small. Marti stretched out on the bed fully clothed and covered herself with the extra quilt. She didn't like being in a strange bed and the mattress on this one was lumpy. The bedding smelled of sachet and the springs creaked. She doubted that anyone who slept here would want to do it again.

Marti didn't think she would fall asleep. A loud scream followed by hysterical crying awakened her. She rushed into the hall just as Vik came out of the den. He let her go ahead of him.

"Elmer, my God, Elmer!" Miss Roberts sobbed. Fully dressed, she was standing in a doorway.

Marti got close enough to see Elmer lying in a small heap on the floor. The bedroom wasn't any bigger than the one she was in. There was no sign of a struggle.

"Miss Roberts . . ."

The woman turned. "He can't be dead," she said. "He just can't be dead, not Elmer. He's only seventy-three." Her shoulders shook as she sobbed. "He just can't be dead. Nobody in our family has ever died younger than eighty."

Marti stayed with Miss Roberts while Vik knelt beside Elmer and checked for some sign of life. She wished she had asked more questions last night and knew who Elmer was.

Vik looked up and shook his head. "Miss Roberts, we need to call for an ambulance and notify the police."

"The phone lines are still out."

"Then we have to leave him here until we can get help."

"But he . . . he's just lying there . . . he . . . shouldn't we . . ."

"No."

Vik came out of the room and closed the door. "Since everyone in the house seems to be up . . ."

Marti turned to see all of the women, still in their nightclothes, standing close enough to hear what was being said but too far away to see into the room.

"Why don't we all come this way," Marti urged.

"Yes, yes," Miss Roberts agreed. "Breakfast is just about ready. I was so busy making sure those orange yeast rolls didn't burn on the bottom that I didn't even notice how late it was. Elmer always was a late sleeper, never gets up until half past six."

"Perhaps if everyone had breakfast," Marti urged.

"Yes, of course, but poor Elmer. It must have been his heart."

"Did he have heart trouble?"

"No. There was nothing wrong with his health. His eyesight wasn't what it used to be, but I never could convince him to get glasses."

"Is he a relative, ma'am?" Marti asked.

"He's my brother. My baby brother." The tears started flowing again.

"Did he live here with you?"

"Ye-e-e-s." Her shoulders heaved as she nodded.

"At least he didn't suffer," Marti said. That tended to have a calming effect for some reason. Marti wasn't sure why; like Vik said, dead was dead.

"He was always such a good boy, and handy too. He could fix just about anything. I don't know what I'm going to do without him."

"He would want you to go on."

"I know."

"We need to secure this room, ma'am," Vik said. "Just temporarily. Is there a key?"

Miss Roberts took a ring of keys from her apron pocket. "This one."

Vik slipped the key off, locked the door and pocketed the key. "Are there any other keys to this room?"

"Just Elmer's." She dabbed at her eyes and Marti expected more tears. Instead, Miss Roberts squared her shoulders and went into the dining room. "Now my dears, if you'll just give me a few minutes, breakfast will be served forthwith."

The ladies seemed subdued but otherwise okay. If it weren't for the two empty places at the table where the ladies with the cats were sitting, everything probably would have been okay. Within minutes everyone was looking there, and soon tears began trickling down their creased and wrinkled faces.

Marti shook her head when Vik motioned toward the front of the house. She was out of everyone's line of vision and curious to hear what they might say.

"How will we ever manage?" one said.

"How will Evangeline manage?" asked another. "He's been her right hand since Marjorie died. If he hadn't agreed to move in . . ."

"She'll find someone," one of the cat owners said.

"But dear," said the woman sitting beside her, "who can we trust?"

That said, everyone was silent.

When the door to the kitchen opened and Miss Roberts wheeled in a two-tiered tray loaded with food, the ladies hardly noticed. Marti wanted to reach for a crisp piece of bacon, that and one of those yeast rolls.

While the ladies had breakfast, Vik checked outside.

"No change," he said. "If there were any footprints leading to the house the wind has taken care of them."

Miss Roberts brought in orange rolls and a carafe of coffee. "I tried to call Chief Harrolson. Why on earth can't they get the lines fixed? It's never taken this long. Elmer said we needed to get some kind of radio. I don't know why I didn't listen to him."

After she left, Vik reached for one of the rolls, changed his mind and rubbed his hands together. "There's over a foot and a half of snow out there and from the looks of it there hasn't been a plow within miles of here. There's no point in digging the car out and neither of us thought to bring snow shoes or skis. And, all of this stayed south of Chicago. This isn't our case, Marti. This isn't our jurisdiction."

"We're peace officers, Vik." She didn't like this any better than he did and for the same reasons. "We are the only peace officers around."

"I'd be willing to consider natural causes if it wasn't for Josephina's sister," Vik said.

"We'd better treat this one like a homicide, Jessenovik. Just in case."

"You know what that means."

"That the killer is right here in the house."

"And not a day under seventy-five unless there's someone younger hiding in the attic or the basement."

"I think that's pretty unlikely, but let's get permission to take a look."

Vik agreed.

Marti found Miss Roberts in the kitchen. "Is it okay if we take a look around?"

She seemed puzzled, but the oven timer distracted her and she agreed.

"You notice anything about this setup?" Vik asked after they checked the attic and the second floor.

Marti had, but she didn't say anything.

"We've got one room with twin beds, one room with a single bed and the other four bedrooms have a double bed, one with a commode beside it."

"Umm humm."

"And, everyone seems to be in pairs."

"Umm humm."

"The two with the cats look so much alike that they have to be related, and with her sister dead, Evangeline is alone. That accounts for the twin beds and the single bed."

"Umm humm."

"But these are old ladies, Marti. Really old ladies."

"Umm humm."

"I'll be damned."

Vik paced for a moment, stopped, then said, "You know what? I'm going to pretend I didn't notice any of that. And you are not going to repeat it to anyone."

Marti didn't answer. "Lovely old house," she said as they went downstairs.

There wasn't anyone hiding in the cellar either.

They looked in on Elmer again. "Jeez," Vik said. "He's still dead."

"We'd better hope it was natural causes," Marti said, "and not something he ate."

"Ordinarily, MacAlister, when more than one death comes this close to the same person I rule out coincidence, but in this case natural causes makes sense. If the coroner hadn't run those toxicology tests, we wouldn't have known what killed the sister. It's going to take that with Elmer too."

Marti walked around the perimeter of the room. "I think Miss Roberts's permission to look around included looking around in here. Her exact words were 'Do whatever you feel is necessary to make sure we're all safe.' "

"I'm sure of it," Vik agreed. "That certainly includes anything we can do that might prevent someone killing them." He pulled open a drawer.

Twenty minutes later they concluded that Elmer wore his socks until there were holes in the toes and the heels; he owned three rifles, including one that looked like it had seen action in the civil war; and he had probably never thrown away a piece of paper in his life.

"They're organized, though," Vik said. "Some are in alpha order, some numeric and others by type. He must have spent hours in here sorting them out. Beats the hell out of listening to women talk. He even has other people's pieces of paper. He must have filched them out of their wastebaskets. A paper fetish. That's a new one."

"Going through it will give the local force something to do while they're waiting for the toxicology reports."

"Poor man, I bet he was driven to this, living with so many old women."

"Scary, isn't it?" Marti said.

"What?"

"One of these sweet little old ladies could be a real killer."

"Maybe it's time we got to know them a little better, MacAlister. We've got to do something while we're waiting for an open telephone line or a plow."

"What I'd really like is some food that I was sure was safe to eat."

They waited until all the ladies went upstairs to get dressed, then went to the kitchen.

"Miss Roberts," Marti said, pretending surprise. "You cleaned up everything already. We thought you'd be much too upset to bother, and we haven't eaten anything yet."

"Oh, let me fix you something." She seemed to be getting over the shock of finding her brother dead. Maybe she was just keeping busy.

"Oh no," Marti said. "I'll do it myself, and clean up afterwards. Why don't you just sit and talk with us while I cook." She kept it simple, lots of eggs, plenty of bacon and a stack of toast. "We'll reimburse you, ma'am."

"Why I wouldn't hear of it. If you weren't here, with poor Elmer . . . and all . . ."

Miss Roberts hovered. Marti wasn't sure if it was because she never allowed anyone to cook in her kitchen, or if she was watching for an opportunity to slip a little something into the food. Did Miss Roberts have a reason to want her brother dead? If so, did she want Josephina's sister dead too?

"This is a lovely place you have here," Marti said. "What made you think of it? Has everyone always lived in this town?"

"It was a wonderful idea, wasn't it? We didn't want to end up alone. I'm the only one who was born here. Josephina and I met years ago at the Art Institute in Chicago. A couple of us have known each other since we took an extension course at the University in Bloomington. Then there were the cat shows. I used to raise and show Persians; when the last of them died, I didn't replace her."

"And now you're all here."

"This was my parents' home and my grandparents' before them. We've been together over fifteen years now."

Vik made a face, as if he'd just bitten into something sour.

"How do you manage financially?"

"None of us is poor. We could live on our own, at least for a while longer, but eventually we would end up in nursing homes and this is so much nicer. We have a woman who comes in and does most of the cooking, another who cleans. And, when the time comes, there's money put aside for nursing care. We can all just stay here until . . ." She put her hands to her face and cried. "Elmer was my baby brother. He was the only blood relative I had."

Marti put her arms about the old woman's shoulders and walked with her to the porch.

"Money," Vik said when she returned. "If Josephina hadn't seen her sister in years . . . we need to find out about her finances, too."

"And Elmer," Marti said.

"I don't know. He isn't our case anyway. If there is a case."

"These women aren't going to tell us anything, Vik, not unless they tell us accidentally. They are not going to do anything to jeopardize this arrangement." She thought about that. "If the deaths are related, even if they are not, that has to be the motive, something that would jeopardize their being here together."

"Right, MacAlister, and that could be damned near anything. They could all die without us ever finding out."

"Okay, okay. Let's start with what we know. Agatha died from an overdose of this stuff." She took out her notebook and read off the name of the poison. "It's tasteless, and lethal in a very small dose. The best place to find it is in antique shops. People collect the cans that it came in, sometimes there's residue inside."

"So, which one of these ladies do you think was a chemist or a pharmacist?" From the tone of his voice, Marti knew Vik was being sarcastic.

"They were born in the twentieth century. There is that possibility."

"Or it could be a relative or a friend. Then there is always the question of how the poison got from here to Lincoln Prairie. Maybe it was the one with the cane and she walked there, or took the bus. We're leaving Elmer's death up to the locals and focusing on what we came here for. Suspects, motives, and opportunity."

"We're batting zero on all three, Jessenovik, and with Elmer's death, I don't think these ladies are going to be inclined to talk with us about anything."

"Too bad we didn't have a reason to question them last night."

Marti tapped her pen against her notebook. "Antiques. Miss Roberts didn't mention anything about that."

"They've all got a bunch of old stuff in their rooms."

Marti didn't know enough about antiques to know what was valuable and what was not, but maybe that wasn't important. "The second bedroom on the right," she said.

"The one with the junky stuff?"

"Odd stuff, Vik. Things you might pick up on vacation. Nostalgia stuff. The old Log Cabin Syrup can made like a log cabin. That cracked Ovaltine cup. The kewpie doll, the Lionel train caboose, the Route 66 memorabilia."

"A cigarette roller," Vik said. "My father had one."

Everything had been arranged so decoratively about the room that she hadn't thought of it as junk at all. She would have to find out whose room it was without alerting the occupant. "There were a number of old containers. Let's see." She flipped through her notes and read off a description of the can the poison could have been packaged in.

"Oh sure, MacAlister. Didn't you notice? There was one of those right on the nightstand. Look, killing old Elmer is one thing, but Agatha lived a couple hundred miles away. Assuming that one of these ladies did do it, how did she get there?"

"I'll have to think about that," Marti admitted.

Lunch was served promptly at noon. Another check confirmed that the telephone was still out of order and not only had the street not been plowed, but it was snowing again, with another four to six inches predicted. Marti eavesdropped on the dayroom conversation, which consisted of canasta, a biography of Abigail Adams, and cat habits and behavior.

Vik looked at the tureens of soup and thick wedges of freshly baked bread and shook his head.

"You're getting paranoid, Jessenovik," Marti scolded, not that she intended to eat any of it either. Agatha's last meal had consisted of zucchini bread and preserves laced with poison.

"He has a trick stomach," she explained. "Do you mind if we just fix ourselves something?"

Miss Roberts was busy serving and just nodded.

The ladies did speak a bit loudly. With the dining room and kitchen doors open, Marti could hear most of what was said.

"Did you get the mail yet, dear?"

"What?"

"I ordered a new dish and place mat for Muffie over a week ago."

"Well, they won't come today."

"Why on earth not?"

"The blizzard, old girl. We've got snow out there."

"But why should that . . ."

"Did you see that jigsaw puzzle catalog that come in the other day? I'm ordering if anyone wants to send their order in with mine."

A lively discussion ensued on what was available in the current crop of catalogs as well as which companies misrepresented their products and who took the longest as well as the least time to ship. By the time Vik had approved lunch meat, cheese, and store-bought bread, the ladies had reached the catalog-order-from-hell stage of the conversation.

"I'm not making coffee," Marti said. "It's either what's in the pot or you can drink tap water."

Vik scowled, then relented and held out his cup.

"You'll have to decide for yourself about cream and sugar."

"Black," he said.

The discussion on catalog orders continued.

"Now you know what you have to look forward to, Jessenovik."

"I'm going fishing when I retire."

"I'm sure there's a catalog available with fishing lures if you can't make it to the hardware store in your wheelchair." She wished for the homemade bread as she bit into her sandwich. The cheese was a delicious hard cheddar.

"Delivery companies must love this place," Vik said. "With no deliveries in two days they must have a half a truckload of stuff to bring out here."

"Deliveries," Marti said. "They can pick up stuff too."

"So?"

"What if the poisoned preserves were shipped to Agatha?"

"I like that, MacAlister. I like that."

"Elmer," they both said at once.

Sandwiches and coffee in hand, they went to his room and began searching through all of his mail receipts.

"Here," Marti said, holding one up. "It's addressed to Agatha Hanson and it's dated the day before she died. It was shipped one-day service."

"The sister sent it."

"No, Jessica Perkins did."

"Which one is that?"

"I don't know, but this is as good a time as any to find out."

Jessica Perkins turned out to be a member of the canasta club, the one with severe arthritis. The scent of camphor wafted into the room as she came in. She was not Josephina's partner.

"Miss Perkins," Marti began. "What did you send to Agatha Hanson last month?"

"Why would I send her anything? I didn't even know her."

So much for being direct and catching her off guard.

"Could you explain why your name is on this receipt?"

Miss Perkins looked at it, then gazed calmly at Marti and said, "I have no idea."

Marti doubted that she could have filled out the mailing information. Elmer must have done that.

"Ma'am," Vik said. "Does it seem at all strange to you that Elmer Roberts had this in his possession and now he too is dead?"

"Why no, officer." She actually fluttered her eyelashes. "Perhaps Elmer mailed the package himself, and used my name."

As soon as Miss Perkins walked out of the room, Vik said, "Crafty old bird."

"What did I tell you about assuming senility, Jessenovik?"

Josephina Hanson was next. Marti had little hope of getting anything out of her either.

"Miss Hanson, we found this receipt among Elmer Roberts's belongings."

The woman's expression didn't change as she looked at it, but her hand trembled, unless she had tremors.

"Why are you asking me about this?"

"Did you send a package to your sister?"

"No."

"Do you know why anyone else would send her a package, express delivery, the day before she died of poisoning?"

"What kind of poison?" There was a catch in her voice.

"A poison that isn't sold over the counter anymore but is sold in containers that can be found in antique shops because they are considered collectibles."

"I see."

"Were you close to your sister, Miss Hanson?"

"We were adopted. We didn't have the same real parents. We weren't really sisters. Just legally."

Marti thought of the apartment Agatha had lived in, furnished with only the essentials. She wondered how long the woman's body would have gone undiscovered if the mailman hadn't been concerned enough to look in on her.

"Your sister didn't have any friends, Miss Hanson. She didn't have what you have. She was very much alone. Someone sent her a loaf of homemade bread and a jar of poisoned preserves. She thought it was a gift. She ate it and she died."

Tears ran down Josephina's cheeks. She dabbed at her eyes. "She didn't want any friends. She wanted to be alone. She was always like that."

"She was grateful enough for the gift to eat it."

"She was probably too cheap to buy it."

"Cheap enough to leave you quite a bit of money, Miss Hanson."

"I did not need Agatha's money."

"Didn't you, Josephina?" It was a guess, but Marti saw the woman's hand tighten around a wad of tissue.

"Is that why you sent the package to your sister?"

"I didn't," she whispered. "I couldn't hurt anyone."

Marti couldn't decide whether or not she was telling the truth.

"Who else knew you needed money?"

She shook her head.

"Someone knew. Who was it?"

There was no response. Josephina and Agatha didn't like each other. They weren't related by blood. Apparently Josephina felt little attachment or loyalty to her. But Agatha thought she was receiving a gift.

"Did you exchange birthday presents?"

"No."

"Christmas gifts?"

"No."

"Then Agatha must have been very pleased to receive a package. Even if someone else sent it, she would have believed it was your idea, your way of giving her something. Was that something that would have made her happy?"

"I don't know."

"Did you ever forget to call her?"

"Once or twice."

"What happened?"

"Nothing. I don't know."

"Would the gift have pleased her?"

"Maybe."

"Would it have pleased your parents?"

Josephina hesitated, wiped at tears again. "Very much."

"How would they feel if they knew you were responsible for her death?"

"But I didn't . . . I only told Jessica my money would run out in a few years. A few years, for God's sake, I could be dead in a few years. How did I know . . . I don't know . . . I don't know. I don't."

"You're upset, ma'am," Vik said. "Maybe you need to lie down."

"Yes," she agreed. He helped her from the room.

When they spoke with Jessica Perkins again, there was a defiant tilt to her chin.

"You knew that Josephina was having financial difficulties," Marti said.

"Nobody else here knows how to play canasta."

"Ma'am?"

"How would we play canasta without Josephina? We've played canasta for over twenty years. Just the four of us. How could we replace her?"

"Could you please tell me what happened, ma'am?"

"I couldn't write. Not the label, not anything. Elmer did it for me." She held up her hands. "I can barely eat with them."

"Why did you kill him, ma'am."

"Because he knew, damn it, because he knew. And he would have told you as soon as he found out why you were here."

"Canasta," Vik said, as Marti drove home. "Two people dead because of a card game. I suppose I've heard worse, but you'd think someone that old would know better. She's probably old enough to get away with it, too. They can just keep continuing the case until she checks out."

Marti turned on the windshield wipers. They were approaching the Chicago city limits and it was beginning to snow. This time the storm was expected to hit the city and points north.

Doug Allyn

Unchained Melody

DOUG ALLYN constantly surprises his readers with fresh approaches to traditional mystery ideas. He also has a good sense of how most middle-class folks live and what they want from life—especially those who hail from the Midwest, Allyn's home. His stories of Tallifer, the wandering minstrel, have appeared in *Ellery Queen's Mystery Magazine* and *Murder Most Medieval*. His story "The Dancing Bear," a Tallifer tale, won the Edgar award for short fiction for 1994. His other series character is veterinarian Dr. David Westbrook, whose exploits have recently been collected in the book *All Creatures Dark and Dangerous*. A smart but sensible stylist and purveyor of soft laughs as well as hard thrills, Allyn is always worth reading. This story first appeared in the January issue of *Ellery Queen's Mystery Magazine*.

Unchained Melody

Doug Allyn

Till death do us part," Shelley sighed. "What a hoot. Why don't they just say till one of you gets bored or gets hot for some brainless little twit with tighter buns."

"Sometimes marriages break up," Gwen Marchand said. "It's no disgrace." She was at her desk, her feet up, watching Shelley pace. The divorce hearing had gone smoothly, no scenes, no last-second motions. Piece of cake. Twenty minutes to flush fifteen years. It was Gwen's sixth divorce case of the week. It was Shelley's first. And the reality that her marriage was truly over was just beginning to sink in.

"I didn't cry," Shelley said, wonderingly. "I thought I might break down and bawl."

"Maybe you're not completely unhappy it's over," Gwen said, glancing at her watch. "We got you a handsome settlement if I do say so myself; you're still young, and you're a successful businesswoman."

"If I hadn't worked so hard at being successful I might still have a marriage. And I'm not young either. I'm thirty-six and feel fifty."

"And your ex is forty-two and trying to act twenty-two. Or eighteen. Look, Shel, I'm your friend and your attorney, in that order. I'm no shrink, but I've seen a lot of divorces. Stop blaming yourself. Nothing you did wrecked your marriage. Leonard hit forty and panicked, that's all. It happens. A lot. Men buy convertibles, cap their teeth, tint what hair they have left, and then dump their wives for younger women. This may sound cold, but the divorce really had very little to do with you. It was all about him."

"You're right. That does sound cold."

"Sorry, but I see this syndrome at least twice a week. It happens a lot. I'm just sorry it happened to you."

"Me, too."

"Yeah, well, maybe it's not such a bad thing, Shel. You've always been so damned serious, so eager to make good, to please your profs or your friends or your husband. I swear to God you only married Leonard to make your folks happy. Okay, you're a free woman now. Why don't you put that over-achiever's brain of yours to work on your own needs for a change? You've got your looks and a few bucks. Have some fun, honey. Be happy."

"Happy? Gwen, for the past fifteen years happiness has been closing a deal or getting promoted. I haven't the faintest idea what else it means anymore."

"Well, I hate to advise and run, but I've got a pretrial hearing at four." She hesitated in the doorway. "Tell me something, Shel. Were you always such a grind? I mean, was there ever a time when you had fun? When you were really happy?"

"I'm not sure," Shelley mused. "Maybe there was. Once."

Papa Henry, the cook at Motown Underground, serves the best barbecued ribs in the city of Detroit, bar none. The jukebox pumps out solid-gold Motown soul which keeps the place jumpin' but even so, Axton spotted Shelley as soon as she walked in.

She was dressed high-fashion casual: a Ralph Lauren denim jacket and jeans, tooled, Tony Lama boots. Mid-thirtyish, with frosted blond hair and anxious eyes. She spotted Ax too, no major feat since he had the only white face in the place. He was dressed in low fashion: leather jacket, jeans, and workboots, rumpled sandy hair and a face scarred in an accident a few years before. She strode directly to his booth.

"Mr. Axton? I'm Shelley Dawson. Sorry to interrupt your lunch. Gwen Marchand suggested I see you and said you'd probably be here if you weren't in your office."

Ax nodded. "It's my second home. Sit down, please. I'm just having coffee, would you like some?"

"Nothing, thanks." She glanced around uneasily, but not because of the surroundings, Ax thought.

"I've done a few jobs for Gwen," he offered. "Divorce investigations, mostly. I don't do that kind of work anymore."

"I already have a divorce, Mr. Axton. It was final yesterday, in fact, so I don't need any help in that department. Actually, I'm hoping you can find someone for me."

"Let me guess. Your ex-husband's new playmate?"

"Not at all, I've known her for years. She was his receptionist. I wish them luck. Well, maybe that's not quite true, but I don't wish them harm, at least. No, I want you to find a man I used to know. A boy, really, or at least he was when I knew him. His name is Chet Konerinski."

"Why do you want to find him?"

"Does that matter?"

"It does to me. If he owes you money, I find him one way. If he's wanted by the law, I have to use legal channels and keep the cops informed. And if he's done you dirt and you want his legs broken, I won't find him at all."

"It's nothing like that. He, um, he was my boyfriend. In high school."

"High school?" Ax echoed. "Where and when?"

"Clarkston, twenty years ago."

"Twenty years? First love, first kiss? Something like that?" Ax leaned back in the booth, eyeing her curiously. "You said your divorce was final yesterday. No offense, but maybe you should wait a few weeks to let things shake out, then decide if you still want to hire me."

"I've wasted too much time already, Mr. Axton. Fifteen years of my life. There's nothing sudden about this. I've given it a lot of thought over the past few months. Chet and I were together in high school. Young lovers. I went away to college, Chet went into the army. And we . . . grew apart. I was majoring in business administration and Chet was basically a construction worker. And so I married someone else. A mistake, as it turned out. In my heart, I think I knew it at the time. I just didn't have the courage to go after what I really wanted."

"And now you want to turn back the clock? Suppose he's married?"

"Then good for him and God bless. Look, this isn't quite the romantic gesture it may seem. I've analyzed my life and think I've identified the point where it derailed, a single bad decision. I married the wrong man. I'm fully aware that my emotional equilibrium might be . . . unsteady at the moment, which is why I want facts. I'm also aware that just because Leonard was the wrong man doesn't necessarily make Chet the right one. But I need to settle it for myself, one way or the other. Otherwise, I'll always wonder and I don't much care for uncertainty. Do you follow my logic?"

"Yes, ma'am, I think so. You know that song, 'Unchained Melody'? The Righteous Brothers?"

She nodded, puzzled.

"Every time I hear it I get a flash of Janey Gilliland, a girl I was totally hung up on in high school. Puppy love. I've been in love a few times since and I know the difference now. Still, whenever I hear that song, I think of her. 'Unchained Melody.' "

"Do I strike you as the puppy-love type, Mr. Axton?"

"No, ma'am. Far from it."

"Good. Because I'm not and never was. There was nothing puppy about what Chet and I had. It was the most intense experience of my life."

"Then why did you marry someone else?"

"Gwen says I was trying to please my parents. Perhaps she's right. Chet was off playing soldier and Leonard was a rising young attorney with a great future. It seemed like the . . . logical choice at the time. But I also may have been testing Chet's love. If he really cared, he would have come back and tried to carry me off or something. That's another question I'd like answered. Why didn't he? Do you think you can find him?"

"Possibly," Ax said with a shrug. "I can give it a try. Did Gwen tell you my rates?"

She nodded.

"Then I'll need as much information as you can give me: Konerinski's full name, date of birth, Social Security number if you know it, his father's name, any living relatives you can remember, anyplace he ever worked, that sort of thing."

"I assembled all the information I could remember about Chet earlier this morning," she said, fishing an envelope out of her purse, handing it to him. "Your retainer's in there as well."

He opened it, scanned the computer printout, glanced at the check, and smiled. "You're one very efficient lady."

"I know," she said. "That's always been my problem."

The Internet had changed everything. Ax seldom hit the streets to find people anymore. A resourceful, streetwise cyber-surfer, he frequently tracked down a subject in an hour or less, often much less. Sometimes he was almost embarrassed to charge a client for an hour's work when he nailed a skip trace on the first scan.

Not this time, though. Despite his not so common name, Chester Arthur Konerinski was a tough hunt. Ax began with a telephone directory scan beginning in Clarkston, gradually widening the search into nearby area codes. No hits. A dozen Konerinskis, but no Chet. Not even a C.

No cause for panic. Any of the listed Konerinskis might be a relative, but it was too soon to try phoning them. Checking the data Shelley provided, Ax backtracked and scored a hit on Konerinski's army discharge, which listed his military serial number, which was also his Social Security number. Using that number, he began scanning the big credit-reporting agencies.

Multiple hits. Credit records at Sears, J.C. Penney's, and a sporting-goods chain. The Sears record was from California, the other two were Chicago, but none was current. Konerinski apparently moved around. Shelley said he'd worked construction. Maybe he was still in that trade.

A check of union membership rolls scored a hit. He'd been a CIO member for three years, but was listed as lapsed years before. In fact, except for his credit records, which were damned sparse, this guy seemed to be all but invisible. That wouldn't be unusual if Konerinski was in the street life, a dope dealer say, or a hood, but that didn't square with the very proper Shelley Dawson's obsession with him.

On a hunch, Ax checked his service number against Social Security payments, and there it was. Chester Arthur Konerinski was on the disabled list. He'd been receiving a partial disability pension since he'd gotten a medical discharge from the army at age twenty-three.

That's why his work record was sparse. He was either too messed up to work or he'd been working jobs that weren't carried on the books to keep from screwing up his pension. The disability payments went to a post-office box, but a single call to a contact with the postal service yielded a home address and his unlisted phone number. Chester Arthur Konerinski lived in a rented home in Dearborn. Ax dialed the number.

"Hello?"

"Is a Mr. Chester Konerinski there, please?"

"Who is this?"

"Mr. Konerinski, I'm Harry Blaine with Continental Septic Tank service. We're running a special—" Click. The line went dead. Bingo. Gotcha.

The address was a brick bungalow in a blue-collar neighborhood: cookie-cutter houses with postage stamp yards, sagging carports, and gravel driveways. Ax guessed the rent would average four or five bills a month, tops, but at least Konerinski wasn't starving. He parked his Camaro on the street and walked to the front door. Noticed a curtain move as he approached. Someone watching?

He pressed the buzzer and the door opened a crack, secured by a chain bolt.

"Mr. Konerinski? My name's Axton. I'm a private investigator." He held up his license to the partially open door. "Could we talk a minute?"

"What's this about?"

"It's a little complicated. Did you know a girl in high school named Shelley Keyes? Her married name's Dawson?"

Konerinski hesitated a moment, then nodded. "Yeah, I remember Shel. What about it?"

"Well, she remembers you, too. She hired me to find you, in fact. Can we talk inside? It's a little chilly out here."

Again the hesitation. "Hang on a sec." Konerinski unfastened the chain bolt and opened the door. He was barefoot, clad in a T-shirt and jeans. Dark hair cropped almost military short. A hard body, lean and muscular, with a hawk nose and wary eyes. He didn't offer to shake hands, but it might not have been a discourtesy. His right hand was a stainless-steel prosthesis attached to a socket and a leather strap midway up his forearm.

"Nice place," Ax said, glancing around. Worn carpeting, cheap vinyl furniture, a TV with a Rent-to-Own sticker on it.

"It's just temporary. Why did Shel want to find me?"

"She said you two dated some in high school, is that right?"

"Actually we were . . . steadies. 'Steadies.' That's a word you don't hear much anymore. We were talkin' about getting married. When she went away to college, I enlisted in the army. She 'Dear Johned' me while I was in the base hospital at Fort Bragg."

"That's where you lost your arm?"

"Yeah. Nothin' heroic about it. We were building a barracks and some moron dropped a pallet of concrete blocks on me."

"Shelley didn't know?"

"Nah. When I got her letter I was hurtin' so bad it almost seemed like a blessing in a way. It was better she dumped me before she saw how I was. One less thing to deal with, you know? My mom wrote me when she got married. I wasn't happy about it but what the hell. I had other things to worry about, like learning to tie my shoes one-handed. Ever try it?"

"Once," Ax nodded. "I cracked up a bike, broke up my right arm pretty bad, got my face rearranged. Has Shelley got any beef with you? Any reason at all to wish you harm?"

"Harm me? Shel? No, why should she?"

"Just being careful. When I hire on to find somebody I like to be sure everything's on the level. Are you still sore about the 'Dear John'?"

"Get real, Axton, it was nearly twenty years ago. Look, what's the bottom line here? What does she want?"

"Just to see you again. Is that okay with you?"

Chet eyed him, reading his face. Then nodded slowly, showing the faintest trace of a smile. "Why not?"

Ax arranged a coffee date at a cafe in Greektown near the Renaissance Center, a place he chose himself. Neutral ground. Plus he could keep an eye on things from a bookshop across the street. He told himself he was taking extra care because Konerinski struck him as a bit of a hard case and Shelley Dawson was at a vulnerable time in her life.

But the truth was, he was curious too. He'd played a lot of roles in his professional life: bouncer, bodyguard, bill collector. But never Cupid.

Chet arrived half an hour early. Ax watched him pace the block slowly, trying to look casual. Finally Chet bought a newspaper at a kiosk on the corner and loitered, pretending to read while keeping an eye on the coffee shop, hoping to see without being seen.

Shelley arrived early, too, by ten minutes. Dressed to the nines, she hurried into the coffee shop, looked around, then took a booth in the window. Chet watched from behind his paper for a while, apparently reluctant to go in now that the moment had come. Ax thought he might leave without seeing her. He didn't.

Instead, he tossed the newspaper in a trash bin, squared his shoulders, and strode into the shop. Shelley rose, smiling, as he entered. And burst into tears when she saw his steel hand.

Ax watched awhile from the bookstore as they talked, gazing into each other's eyes across a tiny Formica table and twenty years. Catching up.

They looked so intense with each other that Ax began to feel like a damned window peeper. But also a little like the Lone Ranger. His work here was done. Time to saddle up and ride off into the sunset to seek out new damsels to rescue. Or maybe some collard-green gumbo and grits. As he walked out to his car he found himself whistling "Unchained Melody." And smiling.

"You should have told me," Shelley said, her voice still unsteady. "I'd have come to you in a heartbeat, you know that."

"I thought I did. Until I got your letter."

"Damn it, Chet, the first six months you were in the army I got exactly one letter, two postcards, and a three A.M. phone call when you were drunk as a skunk and feeling sorry for yourself. I thought you were having the time of your life and you'd forgotten all about me. When I wrote to tell you I was marrying Leonard I half hoped you'd come to my rescue and carry me off."

"Sorry. I wasn't doing much carrying at the time. Still can't, for that matter."

"But why didn't you at least tell me you'd been hurt?"

He shrugged, looking away. "I thought about writing to you but . . . Hell, I was afraid you might come because you felt sorry for me. Or worse, you might not come at all. Frankly, I was already coping with about all the pain I could handle."

"I'm so sorry. If I'd known . . . God. I messed up, didn't I?"

"It was probably for the best, Shel. Look at you, you're . . . elegant. A real lady. Maybe you're going through a rough patch now but your life likely turned out better than anything we would have had together. You were right about me. I was satisfied in the army until the accident, and I've just kinda drifted since."

"Maybe you needed a reason not to. Someone to give you direction. You, um, you never got married?"

"Nope," he conceded. "Never did. I'm not the marrying type. Lucky for you."

"I don't feel lucky, Chet." She leaned forward, her eyes seeking his. "I feel like I blew our chance back then. I thought I was being practical, doing the smart thing. But it was only the selfish thing. Can you forgive me?"

"Don't be a dope, Shel, there's nothing to forgive anymore. Never was, really. Look, we were teenyboppers with a bad case of hot pants for each other—"

"No, it was more than just sex and you know it. We were in love. Young love, maybe, but that's what it was."

"Okay, maybe it was. But we were only kids. I'm not a kid anymore, Shel, haven't been for a long time. If you think our breakup was a mistake, I'm sorry. I don't see it that way. It's history. *Qué será, será,* as the spicks say."

"You know I hate language like that," she said automatically.

"Actually, I'd forgotten," he said, rising. "There were a couple of things I'd forgotten about. Like how superior you could be. When you went away to college maybe it was no accident I headed the other direction, babe. You were brighter than I was and we both knew it. Ever wonder how I felt about that? Look, it was great to see you again, Shel. Maybe I needed some questions answered too, without even knowing it. Okay, they're settled, no hard feelings. But let's not do it again anytime soon, okay? I'll see you around."

"Chet, wait!" She grabbed his wrist, flinched at the touch of cold metal but held on. "Look at me. Can you honestly say you don't still have some feelings for me?"

He started to speak, then shook his head and gently disengaged her hand from his stainless-steel wrist. "Let it go, Shel. You did the right thing all those years ago, believe me. Take care of yourself."

He turned and stalked out of the cafe and didn't look back. Shelley crumpled, awash in a tidal wave of regrets: the divorce, the mistakes she'd made over the years, but especially, blowing her chance with Chet. All over again.

No. She hadn't. He'd walked away from her, that was all. The way she'd left him the last time. So they were even. But that didn't mean it was over. If she'd learned one lesson from the business world, it was never to take no for an answer.

She hurried out of the cafe and spotted him disappearing around the corner two blocks up. Throwing her pride to the wind, she sprinted after him, but as she rounded the corner she barreled into a businessman, sending them both sprawling to the sidewalk.

"Jesus, lady, what's the rush?" The man helped her up as passersby eyed them curiously. Past his shoulder she saw Chet climb into a Cadillac Seville at the far end of the block and pull away into the stream of traffic.

"Are you okay? You ought to be more careful."

"Wrong," Shelley said, taking a deep breath. "I've been too careful for too darned long already."

Papa Henry's was nearly empty, which suited Ax just fine. He ordered a slab of baby back ribs and a Killian's Red at the counter, then wandered to the jukebox in the corner and scanned the titles for "Unchained Melody." He was fumbling for some change when Papa edged up beside him at the box, three hundred pounds of muscle, gristle, and attitude jammed into a chef's outfit. Papa'd learned to cook in 3000 Cooper Street, Jackson prison, and still talked out of the side of his mouth in a prison-yard whisper, inaudible to eavesdroppers.

"Who you got pissed off at you, Ax?"

"Nobody special I know of. Why?"

"Two guys were in earlier askin' about you. Mexican gangbangers from Saginaw. Calera and Salazar. Know 'em?"

"Not that I recall."

"Better think harder. I know Cholo Salazar from the gray-bar motel.

Skinny dude, built like a snake and twice as mean. He was carryin' iron, kept gropin' it when he asked about you."

"What did he want to know?"

"The book. Who you are, what you're into, if you're mobbed up with anybody heavy."

"What'd you tell him?"

"That I serve ribs and greens here, but I might add a taco fricassee to the menu if he asked me any more dumb-ass questions. Said you were righteous and to take his act on the road."

"How'd he react?"

"No problem for me. Might be for you, though. Them boys are both pros. You sure you don't know 'em from somewhere?"

"Never heard of them," Ax said, genuinely baffled. "But it sounds like I'd best check 'em out. Do me a favor, Papa, change my rib order to a sandwich to go, will you? I'd better get back to the office."

Salazar was easy to find. Ax pulled up the Law Enforcement Information Network on his computer, punched in Salazar, nickname Cholo, and immediately got multiple hits. The guy's life would've made a dozen dandy gangsta-rap videos. Juvy convictions for grand theft auto and assault, three adult falls for armed robbery that added up to a dozen years hard time, including the stretch at Jackson he'd spent with Papa.

Calera offered more of a challenge because there were a half-dozen Caleras on the LEIN net. Ax quickly zeroed in on a Juan Orozco Calera convicted with Salazar of an '87 credit-union holdup in Midland.

Bad guys, no doubt about it. Serious hoods. He enlarged their mug shots on-screen and scanned them closely. Dead, cell-block eyes, pitted faces, mean/ugly enough to be brothers. Not pans you'd forget. Which was why Ax was damn sure he'd never set eyes on either of them before. So why were they looking for him?

Collecting debts from lowlifes occasionally got Axton crossways of gangsters, but he hadn't worked the Saginaw area for nearly a year. Most of his current cases were cut and dried, gambling debts or skip traces. Nothing to get hung about. The only new thing . . .

He punched Chester Arthur Konerinski into the LEIN. And there it was. Damn. Multiple hits, the guy had a major sheet. No wonder he hadn't found much of a work record for him. He'd taken extensive vacations from the job market for jail terms in Milan and Jackson. His most recent stretch coincided with Salazar's. And for the same crime, robbery while armed. They had to know each other.

Ax sagged back in his chair. Sweet Jesus. Shelley Dawson hired him to find her long-lost puppy love, and he'd hooked her up with a freakin' ex-con bank robber.

Maybe it wasn't too late. He flipped through his Rolodex and called Shelley's home phone. Got a recording. Left a "call me ASAP" message. Tried Gwen Marchand next; another recording. Terrific. Just terrific.

Shelley thought about showing up on Chet's doorstep wearing nothing at all. A fur coat, high heels, maybe a red ribbon at her throat. Gift-wrapped. The image made her laugh aloud. She owned a fur coat, but as for the rest, she'd always been more comfortable making love in the dark, even on her honeymoon. And after Leonard had put on weight, the darker the better.

It was taking all of her courage just to show up at Chet's home unannounced. He'd all but said he never wanted to see her again, but he was angry when he said it. Well, he had a right to be. She'd dumped him all those years ago and she'd flinched when she touched his steel wrist. He was probably afraid of being rejected again, that's all. He still cared for her. She was sure of it. Well, almost. Okay, maybe not sure at all.

Hell, who was she kidding? The only thing she was certain of was that if she didn't stop driving past the address listed in Axton's report, she'd lose heart altogether. She guided her station wagon to the curb, sat there a moment to get her breathing under control, then got out and marched up to the door of the shabby brick bungalow.

As Shelley reached for the doorbell, she hesitated. She could hear the murmur of voices inside. Did he have company? Another woman? This was crazy. Find a phone and call him first before you make a complete fool of yourself.

She turned to leave and bumped up against a skinny Latin with acne-scarred cheekbones and snake eyes.

"Go on in, lady." He yanked open the front door and thrust her into the living room. Four men kneeling around a coffee table jumped up startled as she stumbled in: Chet, a bullet-headed black, a hulking teen in a black Megadeth T-shirt, and a rat-faced Latin with a goatee.

"Found her outside," Salazar said, holding Shel's arm in an iron grip. "She drove past two, three times, casin' the house. Anybody know her?"

"She's nobody," Chet said. "An old girlfriend."

"The one who hired that dick to find you?" Salazar snapped. "You said you blew her off. So why's she here?"

"She ain't here about anything," Chet said. "I'll take care of it. Come on, Shel."

"She ain't goin' noplace, man, she's seen too much already," Salazar snapped, gesturing at the building diagram on the coffee table. "I ain't doin' no more time just because you can't keep your wanger zipped up."

"Please," Shelley said shakily, "I don't know what's going on, I—"

"Until maybe you see some reward money on TV and decide to rat us out," Salazar snarled. "You're stayin', bitch, and that's it."

"Chet, please," Shel pleaded. "I just want to go home."

Chet scanned the hard-eyed group around the table, but found no allies. "Sorry, Shel," he said, shaking his head. "I told you to give it up. You should've listened."

"Good, it's settled," Salazar said, "and since we got us a share and share alike deal goin' here, the only question is how you wanna put it out, lady. Easy or hard?"

"No, that's not the question," Ax said softly, sliding out of the darkened kitchen, a Browning nine-millimeter centered on Salazar's midsection. "The question is whether you'll still be breathin' in five seconds. Don't do anything sudden, Cholo, just let her go. If everybody stays cool, nobody has to bleed." Ax circled around Salazar and jammed the gun muzzle against his ribcage.

"This is how it's gonna go, guys. None of you are wanted right now or the heat would be kickin' in the door already. But they know who you are and that you're here, so whatever you're planning is pretty much blown, you know? I'd cut my losses and bag it if I were you, but you can decide that after the lady and I split."

"You're goin' nowhere!" Salazar snapped. "You can't take all of us."

"That won't matter to you, Cholo. You won't be around to see it. C'mon, don't be stupid. It's over. Let her go."

For a frozen moment, Ax thought Salazar might be crazy enough to try him. He wasn't. He shrugged and released Shel. She stumbled toward Axton, eyes streaming, confused.

"My car's out front," he said, keeping his tone conversational. "The silver Camaro. Go on, I'll be along in a minute."

Shel tottered out. "I'm leaving now," Ax said. "If anybody comes through that door after us I'll empty a clip into this place and leave you boys to explain that bank diagram on the table to the law."

"We know who you are, Axton," Salazar said. "And where you live."

"I'm not hard to find," Ax admitted, backing toward the door. "But there's no percentage in it, man. Be more trouble than it's worth. Besides, you got no real beef with me. Chet here's the one who whizzed in your punch bowl. Maybe you'll wanna talk to him about it after I'm outa here. Y'all take care now."

He backed out the open door without lowering his piece, and then he was gone. No one moved until they heard the car rumble off in the dark. Then Salazar started for the bedroom.

"Where are you going?" Chet asked uneasily.

"To pack," Cholo said. "Man's right, this deal's over. Or it will be after we settle up with you, chump."

In the car, Shelley listened numbly as Ax explained that Chet Konerinski'd spent the past fifteen years as a stickup artist or a prison yardbird. She was so quiet he thought she might be in shock, but when she spoke her voice was remarkably level.

"I feel like a total fool," she said, wiping her eyes with her wrist.

"You? Hell, Shelley, you weren't the one who screwed up, I was. You hired me to check out Konerinski. I blew it."

"I hired you to *find* him," she corrected. "And you did. And I would have been in a lot of trouble if you hadn't shown up when you did. Actually, it could have been even crazier than it was. I, um, I almost arrived on Chet's doorstep in a fur coat."

"A coat? I don't follow you."

"It doesn't matter. Maybe I'll tell you about it sometime."

"Look, the bottom line is, you'd never have gone there if I'd done my job right. The problem was, you seem like such a civilized type it never occurred to me to run Konerinski through the law-enforcement net. His work record was uneven, but I assumed that was because of his bad arm. This mess is on me, Shelley. It was totally my fault."

"Okay, fine. You blew it, Axton, and saving my neck doesn't alter the fact that you're an incompetent schmuck. There, is that better?"

"Not really." Ax smiled. "Are you all right?"

"I'm a little shaky. It happened so fast I didn't really have time to get scared. I'll probably be a basket case tomorrow, but . . . in a way it's almost funny."

"What is?"

"I've felt more alive in the past few days than I have for years. I'd forgotten how it feels to be young. To lead with my heart instead of my head. Even as bad as things turned out, I'm not sorry I tried. Does that sound crazy?"

"Completely."

"Really? Aren't you the guy who remembers a girl you dated in high school every time you hear a certain song? What was it?"

"Unchained Melody," he admitted.

"I rest my case, Mr. Tough-guy. I don't think you've outgrown all that 'love, true love' nonsense any more than I have."

"Maybe not. Not yet, anyway."

"But you think we will? Eventually?"

He glanced at her a moment, then slowly shook his head. "I hope not," he said.

Rob Kantner

Something Simple

ROB KANTNER has enjoyed one of those careers that moves
steadily forward, and his skills match his sales. He has turned Detroit
into a realm of his own. Though he is surrounded by Motor City
authors like Elmore Leonard and Loren D. Estleman, his low-key,
effective novels featuring private detective Ben Perkins, including
Concrete Hero, Back Door Man, and *Man in Detroit,* are carving a solid
niche for themselves. You'll see that the following story holds a
number of quiet surprises that will stay with you for a while. He gets
better with each new story. This story first appeared in the June issue
of *Alfred Hitchcock's Mystery Magazine.*

Something Simple

Rob Kantner

The first Monday of the New Year found us still digging out from the first big storm of the winter. Four days before, an Alberta Clipper had blown through the Great Lakes region, gifting us with twenty-one inches of snow. Behind that, an Arctic air mass depressed highs to twelve at best. All this fouled up the roads, loused up New Year's Eve, and kept me on the clock all weekend long.

Well, that's what they pay me the big bucks for. And besides, this being metro Detroit, we expect such events. We welcome them, even. They give us a chance to be as tough as we talk.

Relieved to be back indoors, I trudged into the cozy warmth of the Norwegian Wood maintenance office. My people were deployed on the day's chores around the complex, dealing with busted pipes, tenants' gripes, and snow and ice or a combination thereof. Time for a smoke. Time for some coffee. Time for—

"Good morning, Ben," Shyla said.

She sat in my chair behind the plain, gray steel desk, slumped down so low I hadn't noticed her. "Morning," I said, not bothering hiding my surprise as I unbuttoned my peacoat. "You working this week? I thought you were back at school."

"Classes start tomorrow," Shyla said, straightening. I noticed that she had poured herself some coffee, smoked two cigarettes already. She had also switched my desk radio from 'ABX over to one of those Ani DiFranco stations. That's our Shyla, I thought with a smile. "Got a minute?" she asked.

"Sure, kid." Grabbing a chair, I sat down facing her and dug a short cork-tipped cigar out of my shirt pocket. Shyla Ryan was slight but not short, five seven or so. Her blond hair was a close-cropped cap around a pretty face graced with high cheekbones and striking bright blue eyes. She wore a light brown jacket over a snug, longsleeved dark brown top. Her lipstick was the color of her top, making her look even paler than usual. Unlike many her age, she had pierced no parts, at least none I could see. She seemed restless and intense, which was typical of her, and worried, which was not. "What's up?" I asked.

"I need your help," she said.

"Sure," I answered. Flaring a wood match, I lighted my cigar. "What's the story?" I asked, thinking college problems, car problems, maybe boy problems. Here's the windup and now the pitch, a nice high slow one for old Ben to hit out of the park for her.

"My dad's disappeared," she said, fidgeting. "Can you find him for me?"

A few years before, I got asked that a lot. A few years before, the answer was easy. Now the question came rarely, and when it did, it threw up all kinds of red flags. Looking into Shyla's blue eyes, I realized how troubled she was. Damn, I thought. "I'd like to help," I said, exhaling smoke. "But that's really something for the police to deal with."

Her eyes flashed. "You sound like my mother," she said. "I already talked to the police, filed a report. They just shrugged at me." She leaned forward, slender hands knotted. "I'm sure something awful has happened to Daddy. You've got to help me."

Stalling, I asked, "Well, how long has it been since—"

"Thursday," she said. "He called me Thursday. Said things were getting fixed. He sounded really happy. But after that I heard nothing. Yesterday I went to his place. He hasn't been there. No one's seen him." Taking a cigarette out of her small purse, she put it to her lips, bending forward to accept my light. Nodding her thanks, she took a big hard hit and looked at me, exhaling. "I am so scared, Ben," she said quietly. "He never goes away without letting me know. Never."

" 'His' place," I said, waving out the wood kitchen match. "Your parents divorced?"

"Separated," she answered. "He moved out four months ago. My mother has been such a bitch to him." She took another drag. "So how about it?" she asked, brightening. "Will you help me?"

Hating myself now, I said, "Wish I could. But I don't do that kind of stuff any more. Been out of it for years."

"But you used to," she pressed. "I heard all about you. Marge has told me things, and Mrs. Janusevicius—"

"Be careful what you believe," I advised. "The stories get wilder in the retelling."

"I heard you were awesome," she said quietly.

I shook my head. "Work with the police, Shyla. This kind of thing, it's their job."

Now she was blinking, and I feared what was coming. "What they said, Marge, and Mrs. J, and the colonel and everybody—what they told me," she

said, voice shaking a bit, "is that you always came through for your friends."
She stared straight at me, blue eyes shiny. "Aren't I your friend, Ben?"

The cell phone whistled just as I was wheeling my Mustang out of the parking lot. Bracing the wheel with my knee, I jammed the shifter into third with one hand and pressed SND with the other. "Perkins."

"You called?" came Carole's voice.

"Morning, Your Honor," I said, and braced myself. "About tonight."

"Yes?"

"Instead of picking up Rookie at the courthouse, how's about if I swing by your place later, around suppertime."

"Works for me," she answered. "But doesn't that take you out of your way?"

"Most likely not. I've got some running around to do up that way today."

Pause. "But it's only nine A.M. now."

"I know," I said hastily. "So, is it—"

"Why don't you just pick her up at the daycare when you're ready? They're open until—"

"Be less pressure," I said, "if we do the handoff up at your house."

Long pause. "What are you up to, Ben?"

Damn. This is what happens, when they've known you for years and have clocked all your moves. I sighed. "I'm doing some checking up for a friend of mine."

"Now there's a phrase I haven't heard in awhile," she said. " 'Checking up.' " From her tone you'd think I'd uttered a most odious obscenity. "What sort of 'checking up,' Ben?"

"Shyla Ryan, woman I work with," I said. "College kid. Temps for Marge in the rental office during breaks. Her dad's dropped out of sight, she asked if I'd do some looking around. I told her I'd help out."

The tension was so tangible I could almost touch it. "God, this scares me," she whispered. "All those familiar terms. 'Dropped out of sight.' 'Looking around.' 'Help out.' "

"Nothing to be scared of," I said.

"It's something simple. Trust me."

"You promised to stay out of that work."

"It's not 'work.' I'm not getting paid."

"Don't fence with me!" she flared. "Back then you didn't get paid either, half the time. That didn't stop you from getting stabbed and beaten up and *shot*."

I shook my head. "Nobody's getting shot."

I heard her intake of breath, uncharacteristically shaky. "Is this Shyla person . . . *special* to you?"

Knowing what she was really asking, I replied patiently, "She's a kid. We work together. I know how you feel about this, but . . . I sat there and looked at her and listened to her. In my mind's eye she looked like Rookie twenty years down the line."

I heard her inhale. "How manipulative of you to drag Rachel into this."

"Happens to be the truth," I said mildly.

Another pause. "You won't forget to pick her up tonight," she said.

"I won't forget."

In the background I could hear a female voice. Carole murmured something. To me she said, briskly, "You did promise me, you know. And Rachel, too."

"I know. And I've been keeping it. And I know this nudges it."

"Just so we understand each other. No rough stuff. Promise?"

I took a deep breath. "Promise."

"All right." She sounded cheerier, if only a little. "At least you told me. That's an improvement."

"Yes," I replied. "It is."

Randy Ryan's apartment building was in Bloomfield Township, well north of the city, off Telegraph and Long Lake. It was a long low single story brick structure, capped with a massive layer of icy snow. The eaves were fringed with long, lethal-looking icicles stabbing downward. For Bloomfield, the place seemed low-rent and highly transient. Might as well have put "Divorced Dads Welcome" on their sign out front.

The parking lot sported a white 'Vette and a blue Crown Vic but no large black Ford Expedition with white fuzzy dice dangling from the mirror. I wedged my Mustang in a parking spot between the Vic and a mountainous pile of plowed snow.

Huddled in my peacoat, fists clenched in pockets for warmth, I crunched across the hard-packed white stuff toward the door of Apartment 3. Already I knew what I'd find. Second-hand mismatched furniture. Worn appliances. Neutral colors on the walls, the trim, in the carpet. TV and maybe a CD player. And few personal touches except—if Shyla's description of their relationship was any indication—a picture or two of her arm-in-arm with her dad, smiling at the camera.

Five minutes later I left, my expectations fully confirmed. Only there was just one picture, of Shyla alone, probably her high school graduation portrait a couple of years earlier. Her hair had been brown then and longer. She looked younger and more innocent, one to whom less had happened. Same blue eyes, though.

Of Ryan himself there was no recent sign. As Shyla had told me, the sinks were dry, the bed was neatly made, and what looked like several days' worth of mail scattered the foyer carpet. To the front storm door were stuck three yellow tried-to-deliver sticky notes, from UPS or OOPS or somebody like that. The earliest one was dated December thirtieth.

I'd knocked on the other seven doors. The two that answered claimed no knowledge of Randy Ryan, past or present. I reboarded the Mustang and, heat on high, headed south on Telegraph. Normally four lanes each way, Telegraph was down to two narrow lanes now. They were walled with high white drifts that were already turning gray-black from tailpipe crud. The traffic ran slow and sullen, the lights especially lengthy at Quarton and Maple.

Worst of all was the sprawling interchange where Telegraph intertwined with the Reuther and the Lodge freeways. There the cars, the SUV's, and the big rigs crept along in ten foot lurches. They noisily merged and disengaged like icy, metallic, salt-encrusted lovers, tailpipes sending up thick streams of inky exhaust like plumy cats' tails into the frigid midmorning air. I just lived through it, smoking a cigar, playing Buddy Guy's latest on the CD, tolerant, patient. Downright tranquil even. Surely in no hurry to meet Randy Ryan's estranged wife.

"Oh, you," she said, grimacing at me through the storm door. "Jennifer told me about you. Come on in, I guess."

Jennifer? I wondered. Then, as I stepped inside, it clicked. "Thanks for your time," I said. "I'm just wondering if—"

"I know why you're here," Virginia Ryan said, turning on me. Physically, she was quite different from Shyla, besides being older. Short and quite round, lipless and worn, she had short wavy dark hair and deep worry lines. Her eyes were as narrow and hard and colorless as shards of window glass. She wore dark stirrup pants and a light sleeveless shirt. Silver wedding rings twinkled as she gestured. This was, I sensed, a woman who liked to throw things, starting with words and moving on, as needed, to heftier items. "You're trying to find that sorry, sleazebag, soon-to-be-ex-husband of mine."

"No," came another voice as Shyla entered the room. "He's looking for Daddy. Hi, Ben," she added, giving me a small wave.

"Hey, kid."

The three of us stood, for a moment seemingly immobilized by tension. The living room of the small Redford Township ranch-house was a kaleidoscope of beige: dark, medium, and light. The furniture and decorations were rounded, puffy, and plush. The scent was potpourri and sweetish, with the hint of recently baked bread and remote tobacco smoke. "Can we sit down?" I asked.

"Well," the mother said, "I'm going to. You do what you want." She went to the sofa and sat on its edge, facing me, and hovered over the coffee table. On it was scattered piles of what looked like mail. "As to Randy, I'll tell you the same thing I've told Jennifer." She ripped open an envelope, using considerably more force than needed. "He's taken that money he stole and run off with that hillbilly slut girlfriend of his."

Shyla, who stood in the archway to the dining room, scowled. "That's so unfair. You don't know anything about a girlfriend—"

"I have all the evidence I need," her mother cut in flatly, unfolding an ad.

"And the money thing, too," Shyla charged on, "you don't *know* that. You're just connecting dots. It's what you always do. You sit around and stew about things and—"

"For God's sake!" Virginia snapped, slamming the ad down. "The police were here, Jennifer! Your father's *boss* has filed a *complaint!*"

"Did you ever get his side of it?" Shyla asked hotly. She was hugging herself, and her blue eyes were a tad glassy. "Of course not. Because you *want* to believe—"

"Whoa!" I interjected, making the T with both hands. "Hold the phone. Steady on, as we say." The women looked at me, expressions eerily identical in their annoyance. "One thing at a time, if we could."

"Who asked you?" Virginia retorted, head cocked at an angry angle.

"I did," Shyla said.

"None of this is any of your business, *Jennifer!*"

"I'm involved in it, too, you know," Shyla replied stubbornly.

"Please," I said, holding up both hands. "Let me get the information I need, and I'll scoot."

Virginia ripped open another envelope and huffed a sigh. "Whatever."

"Okay." I picked through the scraps of facts in my head, framing questions. Or trying to. It had been a long, long time. Surely this was easier years ago. "You mentioned a girlfriend and evidence. What can you tell me about that?"

Virginia gave Shyla a cold smile and a glance. "I found a greeting card she sent him. A sexy greeting card. Left nothing to the imagination."

"Because you went through his briefcase!" Shyla put in. "You always do that, Virginia. Snoop through people's private things."

"He's my husband," her mother answered. "He's not allowed to have secrets from me." Shyla, rolling her eyes, hugged herself tighter and looked away. "So I checked our phone bills, line by line," Virginia went on, opening another envelope. "There were lots of long distance calls to Georgia. Which makes sense because that's where Plant Two is and Randy calls there a lot. But I found a lot of other Georgia calls, to just one particular number. Place called MO-tee-yay. That's how I found out about *her.*"

"I don't buy it," Shyla said airily.

I looked at the mother. "Can you give me the woman's name and number? I'll need to touch base with her."

Virginia shrugged. "You want to waste your time, that's your business."

I looked at her again, seemingly engrossed in a bill of some kind. More there than met the eye. I was pretty sure Shyla was blind to it. To see what I saw, you have to have lived a lot of years, taken a lot of shots. "Now, on this embezzlement thing—"

"*Alleged* embezzlement," Shyla corrected.

"Yes, thank you." Virginia was ignoring me, but I talked to her anyway. "You said a cop came out here? What jurisdiction?"

"Farmington Hills, I think," Virginia said, setting the bill aside. "That's where the main plant is." She picked up a catalogue-sized envelope and shredded the end open. "I don't remember the officer's name." She extracted some papers. "It was *so* embarrassing," she whispered, "that bastard putting me through this."

Then, staring at the papers in her hands, she froze. "Oh," she said, more to herself than to us, "for God's sake." Squinting at the papers, she whispered, "He sold it. The son of a bitch *sold* it."

"What?" Shyla asked guardedly.

Virginia looked at her daughter. "The farm!" she answered. "He sold the farm!" Looking at the paper again, she read: "Please consider this formal acknowledgment of the sale of the property located at blah blah blah." In grim silence she skimmed further. " 'Two hundred twenty—two hundred twenty-three thousand dollars, less our standard commission of.' " With a toss she skittered the paper onto the coffee table top and looked up at Shyla with weary anger. "This is your father," she said, tone deceptively mild. "He cheated on me, he stole from his company, and now he's stolen from *us*."

"I don't believe it," Shyla said.

"That was our estate," Virginia murmured. "I'm entitled to half of it as part of the settlement. Now he's run off with it."

"It was in his family," Shyla put in. "It was Daddy's before you married him. You aren't entitled to a dime of it."

"Oh, so you're a lawyer now!" Virginia sneered. "Grow *up*, little girl. *This* is him," she charged on, waving the letter. "*This* is your father. *This* is what he's about. He's a liar and a cheat and a crook. He betrayed me, and you just wait, he'll betray you, too!"

Raising her head, Shyla replied, "He's the best daddy a girl could ever want."

Though there's no such thing as good timing in a situation like this, to me it seemed like high time to leave. I rose. "I'd better get going," I told Virginia. "Could I trouble you for the info on that woman down in Georgia?"

After a moment's frozen silence, Virginia got wearily to her feet. "I suppose," she grumped. "Why are you even wasting your time with this? Can't you see what's going on here? Don't you have better things to do?"

Feeling Shyla's eyes on me, I shrugged. "Said I'd help out."

"I suggest," Virginia Ryan said, "that you just let it go."

With a glance at Shyla, who was watching me tensely, I said easily, "Thing about me is, once I get started, I don't quit. Not unless the client waves me off." Some things have changed, I thought. But not that. I looked at Shyla. "Do I keep going?"

"Yes!" Shyla said, fists thrusting upward, beaming at me.

•   •   •

By now the traffic had eased up some. Even so, the massive drifts of snow made Telegraph slow as I motored north. To get to Farmington Hills I needed the Reuther freeway west, and it was once again stop-and-go through the metastatic clover leaves of Reuther/Lodge/Northwestern/Telegraph. Turning off Buddy Guy, I used the opportunity to mash out Doreen Mason's 706 area-code number on the cell phone.

"Hah. This is Doh-reen," recited the high, breathy, voice on tape some seven hundred miles south. "Ah cain't tawk now, but if you leave your name, an' your number, Ah'll—" Hitting END, I tossed the cell phone on the bucket seat and returned my full attention to my driving. I could have left a message, but some creaky old detective instinct told me not to. Better to try again later and catch her off-guard.

At the Farmington Hills police station I was kept waiting for a long time in the dim, stuffy, noisy visitor area. How well I remembered this waiting-around jazz from way back when. Detective work, I recalled, was long stretches of boredom interrupted by extended periods of waiting. Interspersed, at the oddest times, with quick bursts of pure terror, which for me, back then, had been a diseased form of fun. Like the times I almost got garroted, and thonked in the head with a ball bat, and shot in the butt.

But that was then, back in those bad old days of seemingly endless Republican presidents. I'm too old for that now, I told myself. Besides, I swore an oath to Carole and Rachel, the women in my life. No rough stuff. Dragging myself away from the memories, I killed time scoping out the other visitors who drifted in and out of the cop house. Their grumpy demeanor was typical of involuntary visitors. I amused myself trying to determine which were perpetrators, which were perpetratees. And which were both (attorneys, natch) and which were that most dubious and threatened of species, the innocent bystander.

"Mr. Perkins?"

I glanced over at the plain steel door by the counter and nodded. The man, a short, well-built specimen in dark pants and a tieless white shirt, strolled toward me. No smile, I noticed as I rose. No greeting. No offer of a handshake. Just, "You're here about Randy Ryan?"

"Yes. Appreciate your seeing me, Detective—"

"Shanahan. So where is he?" the cop asked abruptly, hooking hands in his pants pockets.

That caught me off-guard. I studied the lawman briefly. He had very curly dark hair cut quite short, a squarish, flat, cop face with just the faintest of age lines, gray eyes of Navy steel. He was younger than me, which was no surprise, there being, I've noticed, more of those each day.

"That's what I'd like to know," I answered.

He blinked. "What's your interest?"

"His daughter asked me to find him," I replied. The cop said nothing. Remembering that to be a rather effective investigative technique, I made a mental note. "Talk to him lately?"

"Not since Thursday," Shanahan answered. "He was supposed to turn himself in. Never showed."

"So you're charging him?"

"Embezzlement. His employer swore out a complaint."

"How's it look?"

"Dead-bang, man. Couple hundred grand. A slam-dunk." Shanahan seemed to relax just slightly. "Buzz is, he's a bright guy, but no matter how hard I look, I don't see anything all that clever about how he worked it. Dumb stealing from dumber." *Typical*, he could have said but did not have to.

Poor Shyla, I thought. "So you talked to him Thursday?"

"Yeah, he called in. Surprised hell out of me," Shanahan added, looking anything but surprised. "I guess he sensed we were set to scoop him. Said he'd come in voluntarily." He shook his head. "Just a diversionary tactic. I waited till eight, got caught in the snowstorm, missed my kid's hockey game. No sign of Ryan, then or since. From that I am forced to infer that he has skipped."

Which of course made Virginia Ryan's theory look better and better. I thought for a moment. "So I take it you've posted surveillance teams at the airports and train stations and bus stations and—"

"Yeah, right," Shanahan said, with just the faintest smile. "We've put the word out. He'll turn up. He'll bust a red light or get ratted out by a friend or—hey," he said, squinting at me, "maybe you'll even find him. You're some kind of detective, I take it?"

"Used to be."

"Not any more?"

"Nope," I replied, smiling. "Went legit."

Next stop was Ryan's employer's place on Northwestern. Instead of heading there right away, I fired up the Mustang motor to get some heat into the frigid car, and hit SND on the cell phone to redial Doreen Mason's number. While listening to it ring, I looked idly at the phone bill Virginia Ryan had given me. Fully half the entries were highlighted in bright yellow and were virtually identical—to the 706 number in a Georgia town called Motier, which Ryan had pronounced MO-tee-yay but was actually, I suspected, pronounced Mo-TEER.

"Ah don't wont inny!" came a loud female voice in my ear.

"Ms. Mason?" I asked.

"Will you *leave* me alone," she charged on, accent a foot thick. "I don't buy things on the phone, and I never will, and—"

"I'm not a salesman," I said. "I'm calling about Randy."

Her pause was just a tad too long. "Who?"

"Randy Ryan," I said, and took the plunge, no doubt a bit too precipitously. "Is he there?"

Cell phone static hissed in my ear for a moment. "I don't know who you're talking about," she said. "Who are you?"

"Name's Perkins," I said. "I'm calling from Michigan. I'm looking for Randy." An inspiration came, and I went with it. "His daughter asked me to find him."

"Yeah?" Doreen asked, tone challenging. "His daughter, huh." Pausing she asked abruptly, "What's her name?"

"Shyla."

"No. Her real name," she prodded cagily.

"Jennifer. And her mother's Virginia. And he works for Brighton-Leopold." Or worked, I thought but did not say. "I know the whole deal," I said quietly. "I got your number from Virginia." Doreen did not reply. I sensed she was not all that quick on the uptake. "What made you think I was a salesman?" I asked.

"Caller I.D. said 'anonymous,' " she answered. "That usually means telemarketer." Static hissed again for a moment, and when Doreen spoke again, she sounded tired. "Randy's not here. I don't know where he is."

Of course she could have been lying. I did not need to hark back to my investigating days to recall that people frequently lie, even when they don't have to. But I decided to go with it for now. "Are you still . . . involved with him?"

"No. He broke it off."

"When?"

"Last week he called."

"When last week?"

"I don't know. Wednesday, Thursday, what does it matter? He called and said it was over, done with. Said he was going away for a long time. Said it was the best for all concerned." With each phrase I heard the emotion welling up in her. Now she paused, and when she spoke again, she sounded steadier, and quite dull. "I told him it was all right. I told him whatever he wanted, whatever was best for him." She sighed. "I've always heard about 'if you love something, let it go.' What they don't talk about is how much it hurts."

I let a silence grow, thinking about what she had said. "So you don't know where he is."

"No, sir."

Keeping my voice easy I said, "Don't know if I buy that, Doreen. I mean, he's flown the coop and took a pot of money with him, and you were his sweetie—"

"Oh, don't get me wrong," she cut in, tone pointed. "If he'd asked me, I'd be with him this instant. He's the sweetest, kindest man. But I knew, somehow I knew all along, it would never end up that way. And I was right."

I believed her.

"If she'd ever been nice to him," Doreen murmured. "That's all the man ever needed was a little kindness. And love. And acceptance. That's all. If she'd ever given him that, he'd never have looked at me twice. I ain't no prize."

"Not to pick a fight with you but you seem like a very nice person to me."

That brought a hint of warmth, a touch of playfulness to her tone. "Aw, what do you know from all the way up there? Listen . . . when you find him?"

"Yes?"

"Tell him I'm praying for him."

Brighton-Leopold Corp. was one of those downsized, streamlined, New Age companies with no receptionist. The foyer of the large flat anonymous building was in fact empty except for a row of plastic visitor chairs and a table scattered with magazines and literature. A vacant desk bore a phone and a sign saying "Please call the extension of the person you are seeing, and have a seat."

With the sign was a helpful list of about fifty names and extensions. Randy Ryan's name was on it. But there were no titles or positions or helpful hints like, "This guy is Randy's boss." Then I noticed several names in a clump: LEOPOLD N., LEOPOLD P., LEOPOLD T. There being no Brighton listed, I did the next best thing and called the first Leopold.

"Yes?"

"Mr. Leopold?"

"He's in a meeting."

"It's very urgent. It's about Randy Ryan."

"Oh. Surely. Please hold." From the quickening in the young man's voice, I inferred that the mention of Ryan had struck a nerve. I waited. Almost at once the gray steel door buzzed and opened, and a short, roundish man bustled through. As I hung up the phone, the man wheezed, "Where's Randy?"

I stood and said, "Wish I knew, sir. I'm Ben Perkins. You're Mr. Leopold?"

"Neal." His black hair was a bushy black mop around a fleshy face anchored with thick glasses. He wore dark pants and a nondescript dress shirt unbuttoned at collar and cuffs. He had the look of a teddy-bearish absent-minded professor, but his eyes were steady and careful as he stuck a pawlike hand out for me to shake. "Have you seen him?"

"No, sir. His daughter asked me to—"

"He'd better move fast," Leopold said. "If you're in touch with him, tell him I can't keep the wolves at bay much longer."

"Wolves?"

"My partners." He looked wounded and anxious, hope fading in his eyes. "When Randy called and said he'd make good, I told my partners, look, he does this and we drop the charges, make it all go away." He sighed. "It's been, what? Four days now? And now you say he's missing?" He stared at me. "I just can't stand up for him for much longer. My partners—"

"I understand," I said, which was not strictly true—it hardly ever is—but saying so usually quiets people down. "So he called you and offered to—"

"Every nickel," Leopold assented, bushy head bobbing. "That's what he said. 'Every nickel' he'd pay back."

"When did he call you?"

Squinting, Leopold counted back. "Thursday." Hm. Seemed to me that day had been mentioned before. Could this be a Clue? Or simply what my friend Raeanne calls a "co-inky-dink"?

Leopold charged on. "He pays the money back, it's all forgiven, see? He keeps his job, it'll all be like it was before. That's what I promised him."

"Seems right generous of you."

Leopold made an it's-nothing gesture with shoulders, hands, a brief bow of his head. "He's like part of the family. We all make mistakes, we all do dumb things. Nothing is stranger than what actually happens. Life goes on—"

"Neal?" came a voice from the door. A mere slip of a young man, shaved nearly bald and wearing white over tan, seemed to slither in. He extended an envelope to his boss and whispered, "Excuse me. Thought you should see this right away."

Leopold took the opened envelope in his big hairy hands and shook out a what looked like a business card. There was also an elongated piece of yellow paper. The owner's eyes squinted at the latter, then widened behind the thick lenses. He positively beamed, holding the larger item up like a diploma. "He did it!" Leopold crowed.

It was a check. From where I stood, I could not make out the details. The young man said, softly and sibilantly acerbic, "What makes you think it's any good?"

Leopold flipped the check around and read. "Pay to the order of Brighton-Leopold Corp. four hundred ten thousand dollars. Signed, Randy Ryan." The man was positively glowing; I thought he might do a jig right there. "Of course it's good," he said to the younger man. "He said he'd come through, and he did. End of discussion." Turning to me, Leopold seized my hand. With a slight bow, he pumped it hard, as if I'd had anything to do with anything. "Thank you. Thank you so much."

"Well, sir, I—"

"And when you find Randy," Leopold commanded, letting go and pointing at me like the I WANT YOU poster, "you tell him it's time to come home now."

But he was still missing. Which, in light of what had just happened, made no sense.

But then little in this work ever does. *This* part I remembered all too well.

I sat in the icebox Mustang, running the engine to warm it up. Flurries fell on the flat snow-covered plain, adding insult to icy injury. Just past the parking lot, beyond a mountain of freshly plowed snow, trucks crept along 10 Mile Road. Why? I asked myself. Why do I still live in Michigan? More to the point, why am I out here in the bitter snowy cold, twisted around a mental axle trying to figure out this Randy Ryan mess? Where I should be is back in my warm, pleasant, Norwegian Wood maintenance office. In full control of my own little world. Listening to 'ABX and drinking coffee and smoking cigars.

But . . . I had promised.

So get on with it, stupid.

Now. The central theory had been that Randy Ryan had absconded with a pile of embezzled money, perhaps into the arms of his girlfriend in Georgia. That theory was now inoperative. So where was he?

At times like this, when your Big Theory goes poof, the only thing to do is start over with what you know for sure. In sequence. Think orderly for once, I told myself. When did Shyla last hear from her dad? Thursday, she had said this morning, I was sure of it.

On Randy's apartment door, the oldest UPS delivery sticky note was dated . . . December thirtieth, which was . . . Thursday. So he had not been back there since.

Then there was Doreen Mason. I was pretty sure she had told me it was Thursday when Randy called her to break off their affair. What about Shanahan, the detective? He'd said that Randy had promised to turn himself in on Thursday. And when Randy called Neal Leopold to tell him he was making things right, that had been last Thursday, right? Correct.

Thursday, Thursday, Thursday. All these things in one day this was not just a "co-inky-dink." Back there in Leopold's office I had heard a tinny little ringing in my ear—that long-dormant detective instinct saying, this is something important, pay attention, idiot.

And every one of the contacts he had made had been by phone. The logical question was, from where had he called? How could I find out?

Ah yes.

Clenching the smoldering cigar in my teeth, I picked up the cell phone and mashed SND. Ringing, then *click*, and the taped answering spiel started. I overrode with "Doreen, pick up, please? It's Ben again."

Click. "Well he*llo* there," she purred. "I was hoping you'd call back."

Nice as it is to be come on to, I had no time for flirting, or interest in it, either. "Well, I need a bit more information if you don't mind. About Randy."

"Uh-huh," she replied, resigned.

"When was it he called you? To, uh—"

"To dump me?" she supplied, tone patient. "Um. Let's see. Thursday, that's right. I know because I went to a New Year's Eve-Eve party, and—"

"This is important. Where did he call you from?"

"I don't know. He didn't say."

"Doreen, please," I said patiently. "You have Caller I.D., right?"

"That's right!" She seemed surprised to hear this. "It's in the kitchen, that's why I didn't see it when he called."

"Can you check it for me now and tell me where he called from?" I asked.

"Okay." Fumbling noises and then she said, "Hope it's still in here. I get a lot of calls, it might have . . . let's seeeeee . . ." Long pause, silence. "Well, this must be it," she said. "It's the only one I don't recognize from Thursday."

"Read it to me," I said, groping paper and pen out of my glovebox.

"*Redemp Eee See*," she said slowly and then recited a phone number in the 248 area code. "What the heck is that? And where the heck is 248?"

Redemption Episcopal Church is on Quarton Road in Bloomfield Township, several blocks east of Telegraph. I got there during lunch hour but luckily found the lone office worker eating a sandwich at her desk. I hadn't gotten half my question out of my mouth when she started shaking her head. "You'll need to see Father Dave about that," she said, not unkindly.

"Is he here?"

"He should be free." She put down her sandwich. "Come along."

I followed her down a narrow hallway to the end office. It was all glass on one wall, bookshelves on the others. Its occupant rose to greet me as we entered. He was evidently a person of the cloth. But you would not have known it from his dark Dockers pants and open-necked pale blue polo shirt. He also looked way too young to be a priest. "Dave Collins," he said, shaking hands with a very firm grip and a very direct look in the eye. "How can I help you?"

"Ben Perkins," I said as the office worker stepped out, clicking the door shut behind her. "I'm here about one of your, uh . . . congregation people."

"A parishioner?" Collins asked, eyebrow arched. "Please, have a seat."

Okay, I was nervous, as I always am around people with a direct line to God. I sat on a sofa under the light of a floor lamp. Had it not been on, we'd have both been in deep shadows. The light from outside had dimmed considerably in the darkening sky. Looked like another storm, I thought.

"Yes, a parishioner," I said as Collins sat down in his desk chair, facing me. "Randy Ryan."

"Mm," the reverend said, expression placid, not at all wary.

Not knowing how much to tell him, I stuck with the essentials. "He's missing. Hasn't been seen since Thursday."

"Oh no."

"Unless, of course, you've heard from him."

"No, I have not."

"But you saw him that day, right?"

Collins considered that. "What is your interest, if I may ask?"

"His daughter asked me to find him."

"You're a detective?"

"Not hardly. Just a friend, helping a friend out."

"I see."

He said nothing. Neither did I until it occurred to me that he had ducked my question. "You saw Randy last Thursday, right? I know he was here, he made a phone call from here." And maybe more than one, I realized.

"Thursday, Thursday," Collins murmured. "Yes, of course. The day of the big storm."

"Whatever." I felt that incomparable rush that you get when you're on to something. "What was he here about?"

The priest tipped his head back a bit, watching me, expression kind, perhaps even a bit amused. "You know I can't talk about things like that, Ben," he answered. "And besides, it's not really what you need to know."

I wanted to retort, Look, you be the preacher and I'll be the detective, okay? But that would have been impertinent. I did my best to smile back. "Then what is it I really need to know, Father?"

"Where he was headed when he left here. And I can tell you that." He smiled. "Home."

Another fond hope blown to bits. I mean, after seeing Neal Leopold I thought I had figured out what Randy's deal was. I hoped, upon meeting Father Dave, that he would confirm it. Instead he felt obliged to play coy and sent me ricocheting back into the icy outdoors on yet another wild goose chase. "Home," my Aunt Lizzie's butt. No way did Randy go home last Thursday after seeing the padre. He had not been back there. I was sure of it.

Even so, I wheeled north toward Randy's Long Lake apartment. Might as well check it out again. Nothing else to do. I felt fatigue in my legs and back, a numbing of the spirit, the sour taste of having been laughed at. This was such a joke. I never liked going over the same unfruitful ground a second and third time. It always meant that I'd missed something. Had been less than brilliant. Had been, as Raeanne likes to say, "a mere mortal."

Feeling sour, I smoked a cigar. I went over Randy's chronology again, probing for soft spots. Propelled the Mustang north in the thick Telegraph Road traffic, piloting along between the high walls of plowed blizzard snow. Did the litany, each time ending up with "home." Which made no sense.

Unless.

What if home did not mean Randy's apartment? What if home meant Redford Township, where he'd lived with Virginia and Shyla?

Well now. This was more interesting. And it made all kinds of sense, given the other things Randy had done that day. But if he had gone there, Virginia would have mentioned it. Wouldn't she?

But she had not. Why not?

Perhaps because . . . because something really ugly had happened?

Availing myself of a median crossover, I switched sides to southbound Telegraph and motored along, Redford-bound. I made fairly good time despite the old snow, new snow, and traffic. I thought about Virginia's flinty eyes, the set of the scowl on her face, the tone of utter contempt and loathing in her voice as she spoke of her errant husband. The sense I had had that this was a woman who threw things with grim purpose and deadly aim. I remembered how she had tried repeatedly to wave me off the case. Oh, my imagination did all kinds of things as the big Mustang wheels ate up several snow-packed miles. I pictured Virginia aiming a pistol. Randy going down. Blood splattering a beige wall. His body wrapped in plastic, entombed under a snow-covered pile of boards behind the garage . . .

Of course the scenario was dumb and obvious, but most real-life murders are just that. I played around with different elements as Tel-Twelve Mall approached. This was always one of the worst traffic choke-points in all of metro Detroit, and today was no exception. As the traffic lurched along in its stop-and-go fashion, I wound back the tape in my mind and replayed how it might have gone down. Randy leaving the church, inspired, fervent, anxious to get to her. Motoring south on Telegraph, just as I was doing. Except that this had been Thursday afternoon when the blizzard hit, the big Alberta Clipper, right? So he was in a hurry, trying to get there before everything shut down. He had come flying along here and—

And just as I was doing now, Randy had approached the interlocking cloverleaves where Telegraph met Reuther Freeway/Lodge Freeway/Northwestern Highway.

But Thursday there had not been snowpack on the macadam and lines of crawling cars and walls of plowed snow on both sides and flurries flying in the air. Thursday had been, as Father Dave had said, "the day of the storm." The Alberta Clipper had struck right about the time Randy barreled south on Telegraph. There had been a howling wind and snow pouring down like porridge. The pavement had slickened up, and there'd been nothing on the sides of the road to stop him from—

And that's when it came to me.

Leaning forward, gripping the deep-dish Mustang wheel, I stared through the windshield. I thought about angles and distances and timing, the vastness of the cloverleaf. The great expanses of open land with its slopes and gullies and blind spots. I thought about Virginia Ryan again, too, but this time there was no gun in her hand, as I knew in my heart there had never been.

Hitting the brakes, I halted the Mustang in the left-hand lane, right in the middle of the cloverleaf. Traffic continued to pass on my right. I mashed the four-way lights, shut off the engine, and got out.

Instantly the wind tried to bite me through. I turned up the collar of my peacoat and buttoned it tight and jammed the cell phone in my back pocket. The wall of snow rose eight feet or more, a slanting slope of grayish white interspersed with big black icy chunks. Bracing myself, I began to climb up the wall of icy snow, virtually on all fours, freezing my hands as I clambered up, shoes slipping, fingers freezing as I fought for purchase.

I was halfway up when a male voice hollered from down below. "Hey, moron!"

Looking down, I saw a big beefy guy leaning through the window of his white Olds Intrigue. "What're you doing parking there, ya idiot? Jamming up all the traffic here!"

"Got business," I called back. "Possess your soul in patience. Jackass," I added, just for his information.

"You move that damn car," he bawled, "or I'll rearrange your face for ya!"

I hesitated. From inside came that dark chuckling feeling I remembered so well, the feeling of *all-righty-then, let's party*. And I thought about going back down there and dragging him through the window and using him for a pogo stick or something.

But "no rough stuff," Carole had said.

And I had promised.

And all the man wanted was a clear ride home.

So I grinned and waved. "Back in a minute," I called and, with final scrambling effort, propelled myself over the summit of the snowdrift and down the other side.

Stretched out before me was a rising snowy plain, truly tundra as far as I could see, unmarked by anything, manmade or otherwise. I was calf-deep in the icy white stuff, but down here it was loose and wet, biting like frozen fingers through the soles and sides of my utterly inappropriate shoes. My enthusiasm for my brainstorm began to wane. I mean, there was no evidence here, none that I could see. Unless you looked a certain way at the surface of the snow. Was there an unnatural unevenness there? Kind of like faint ruts, way way down? Hard to tell, especially in the gray light with flurries angling down. We'd gotten, after all, twenty-one inches of snow on Thursday. Plenty enough to cover his tracks if he'd come skidding through here early enough.

But where would he have ended up?

The slope rose and then crested. From here I could not see what was beyond it. Quelling one more urge to turn around and get back into the nice warm Mustang, I tromped uphill through the knee-deep snow. It packed its way up under my pants cuffs and down into my shoes, causing my feet and lower legs to dampen and then numb. Hugging myself, I forced myself ahead, eyes on the prize, the crest of the slope. Beyond was a whole lot more white nothing. But this was a downslope, with several intermediate mounds, leading to what looked like a gully and another hill beyond. Amazing that this vast open area could exist here in the heart of a cloverleaf. Invisible to anyone passing by, especially with those walls of plowed snow alongside the roads.

Following the path of least resistance, I marched down the slope, aiming for the halfway point between two of the intermediate mounds. My legs were now numb from the knees down. The wind had picked up and was waging a serious attack on my coat. I hunched as I tromped along, hands fisted in the coat pockets. My chin was buried in the collar, mouth muttering monotonous oaths on the general theme of *the things I do, the things I do*. The snow fell thicker and dusk did, too. I did not realize how bad my vision was getting until I was barely twenty feet from the thing.

It was the first manmade object I'd encountered. It was a large, slanted rectangle, white, of course, being covered with snow except for just a black tip up high, the right angle of what appeared to be a rear fender.

My breath caught in my throat. Incipient hypothermia forgotten, I spread my arms and ran, high-stepping. The vehicle was nose-down, thrust like a blunt spear into what had to have been a sharp depression in the ground. Of course I could not tell that for sure, given the drifts of snow. As I drew nearer, I could see the whitish faint outlines of a rear wheel and a roofline. The ghostly silhouette of an urban assault vehicle, perhaps of the Ford Expedition variety.

Panting, I thrashed to a stop at the vehicle and brushed at the window. Peering in, I squinted long and hard. As my vision adjusted to the deeper dimness, I could just barely make out the interior white fuzzy dice hanging crazily from the sideways rearview mirror and, on the passenger side, the faint, crumpled outline of a body.

"So, it's true then," Shyla murmured, eyes downcast. "He did do all those things Virginia said."

" 'Fraid so," I replied.

We stood in a hallway of the emergency room at Metro Detroit General. Around us bustled orderlies and nurses and people pushing gurneys bearing bodies, not all of them animate. The closed door in front of us said EXAM ROOM 2. NO ADMITTANCE. I was finally starting to thaw out and was leaving little puddles of melted snow on the linoleum floor around me.

Shyla shivered in her coat and hugged herself, half turned from me. "But why?" she asked softly.

I shrugged. "He's just a man. People do bad things sometimes. It's what happens." I could relate. I thought, but did not say, that Randy Ryan had shown all the signs of a man who had gotten just so sick of himself. I could relate to that, too.

"What's important," I added, "is he was turning things around, trying to make things right."

The young woman's pale face crumpled, and she tottered to me, engulfing herself in a big hug. "It's just so unfair!" she murmured into my neck through sobs. "Now he won't get the chance to finish the job."

I patted her back. "Don't be too sure of that, kid. Doc says he's got a fighting chance of—"

"Is this the room?" came a voice from behind me. We turned to see Virginia Ryan approaching, hatless, wearing a dark winter coat, short dark hair askew, lipless face pale, eyes icy as the outside. "Where is he?"

"What are you doing here, Virginia?" Shyla asked, disengaging from me.

"Your detective friend called me," the mom said. "Which is only right, since I'm still your father's wife, Jennifer. Surprised?"

Shyla's eyebrows arched. "Not that Ben called you," she said. "Surprised you'd care enough to show."

Virginia stepped closer to us and glanced at the door.

"How is he?"

"He's in a coma," I answered. "Way dehydrated. Core temp is low. But in a way the freezing cold actually helped him. Retarded the bleeding from his crash injuries."

"Will he live?" Virginia asked evenly.

"They won't say for sure, naturally," I answered. "Even if he does, he might lose some—"

The exam room door opened, and a nurse looked out at us. "Ms. Ryan?" Both women stepped forward. "Only one at a time," the nurse commanded.

Shyla shot her mom a look. "Can I go first, Mother?" she asked.

"Very well, Shyla."

The daughter went inside and closed the door. For long moments the mother and I just stood there. I could not help wondering if they were giving up on him in there, if I had been too late, with all my banging around and rookie mistakes. What Virginia was thinking was anyone's guess. Presently she asked with the usual abruptness, "Well, are you going to tell me?"

"Tell you what, ma'am?"

"What he was doing up there. How he got in this fix."

"Well, before the crash, he'd been to see his priest."

"Confessing all?" Virginia asked, trying to sound hard and cynical and not quite succeeding.

"Don't know about that," I answered easily. "I do know about some of the other things he did while he was with Father Dave. If you're ready to hear."

She stared at me. "Well?"

I looked at her. Ready or not, I thought, here it comes. "Well, from Father Dave's office he called his lady friend in Georgia and told her it was over. He called his boss to tell him he'd be making restitution for the money he stole. He called Detective Shanahan to tell him he was turning himself in. He called Shyla to tell her everything was getting fixed." Virginia's expression did not change. I thought my words were just bouncing off her, bouncing off the armor of her preconceived notions. "I know these things for a fact."

"And then," she said, "he took off from there, headed for the airport. He was blowing town. He did all that stuff to throw everyone off the scent—"

"That's one way to connect the dots," I cut in. "But there's another way."

She was looking at me intently now. "Yes?"

"Number one, if he were headed for the airport, he'd have turned west. Instead, he kept going south. You know where he was bound for, Virginia. You know it in your heart."

"Where?" she asked, voice small.

"To your house. To see you. My guess is, to beg for your forgiveness."

Just then came Shyla's voice from inside the exam room: "*Yes!*"

Virginia blinked. Her throat worked. She cupped her mouth with a hand that trembled. I reached for the doorknob and opened the door. With a last glance at me, Virginia dashed through, and the door eased shut again.

Suddenly alone, I stared at the closed door. Reached out for the knob again, hesitated, let my hand drop. Under these circumstances the last thing they needed was me hanging around. I had never felt so suddenly useless. For a moment the unfairness of it blazed in my mind. Over already? Where was the applause, the admiration, the atta-boys? Where were the simple thank-yous, for heaven's sake?

But this too I remembered from the old days. The better the job you've done for a client, the less you exist for them when the job is over. Once they're out of the woods, clients make haste to forget how desperate they were for your help. It's just human nature.

But that was okay, I thought as I headed for the exit. I had, after all, promises to keep and better things to do. Such as go home and change out of my wet clothes and then pick up the girl of my dreams from her daycare.

Edward D. Hoch

The Circle of Ink

When you write about ED HOCH, the temptation is to dwell on his prolific writing career. Although he is probably the most prolific short story writer in the history of mystery, with a story in every issue of *Ellery Queen's Mystery Magazine* for more than twenty years, what is often overlooked about him is the sheer quality of his work. Whether he's working on a locked-room setup featuring his police detective Captain Leopold, or going rustic with one of his more laid-back series characters, or even getting tough (his collection of hard-boiled stories will be published soon), he is always totally in charge of his material. And what wonderful material it is. Read the following and see if you don't agree. This story first appeared in the September/October issue of *Ellery Queen's Mystery Magazine*.

The Circle of Ink

Edward D. Hoch

It had been decades since Ellery Queen lectured on Applied Criminology at a university, and the changes that time had wrought were immediately obvious, even to his nonacademic eye. Classroom dress had become so casual, for students and instructors alike, that he dared not venture into those august halls in anything like the English tweeds he'd worn a generation earlier. Yet the tools of learning that his audience of undergraduates possessed were anything but casual. There were tape recorders and laptop computers ready to capture every word and impression he might scatter across the vast lecture hall.

On this Tuesday in early May the subject was "The Detective Story," part of a seminar on modern writing in which he'd agreed to participate. The task, urged on him by Associate Professor Virgil Meadler, was not all that onerous, consisting of a single hour's lecture followed by a question period. Ellery was amused to note that even in a college classroom someone still asked him where writers got their ideas, and he mentioned it to Professor Meadler while they chatted at the conclusion of the session.

"I know," Meadler said. "They all want to be writers and they think there's some secret formula to it." He was a tall, handsome man in his early thirties, wearing rimless glasses that blended well with his angular face. When he'd first called Ellery to invite him to the seminar he admitted to having read only one Queen novel. "But my mother is a great fan of yours," he'd quickly added.

"Well," Ellery told him now, "I think the session went well. A few of them even had books for me to sign afterward."

"It went splendidly! I only wish all of our guest lecturers were as good as you."

As he parted from Meadler in the lecture hall, he was aware of a tall, attractive young woman heading down the aisle in his direction. One more book to sign, he guessed, and greeted her with a pleasant smile.

"Mr. Queen?" she asked, producing a tape recorder from her voluminous purse. "I'm Pia Straton, co-anchor of Channel Three News."

"And you want to ask me where I get my ideas," Ellery murmured.

She tossed her curly brown hair as if rejecting the idea. "I want to ask you if you're here at the university to help your father investigate the murder of Professor Androvney."

He was taken off guard by her question. "What's that?"

"You are the son of Inspector Richard Queen, are you not?"

"I haven't spoken to Dad all week. We lead separate lives. I don't know anything about a murder."

She seemed about to pursue it, but a young man carrying a television camera on his shoulder had appeared in the lecture-hall doorway. "Pia, it looks like they're leaving!"

"I'm coming!" She snapped off the tape recorder and bolted up the aisle without even a goodbye. Ellery stared after her until she disappeared from view, then strode up the aisle himself.

On his way out to the parking lot he came upon Professor Meadler deep in conversation with an older, white-haired man. They broke off their talk as he approached, and Meadler held out his arm. "Ellery, I want you to meet our Dean of Arts and Letters, Professor Charles Cracken, our foremost authority on Dante. Charles, this is Ellery Queen. I was just telling you what a fine lecture he gave."

The man shook hands with Ellery. "Ah, yes, Mr. Queen. I have enjoyed your books."

"Thank you."

Virgil Meadler smiled. "He needs something to read besides that old fourteenth-century literature he teaches." It seemed like a continuation of some friendly ribbing from the past.

"I hope my books help you to relax," Ellery said. His eyes had gone to the other side of the parking lot where he could see a group of students surrounding some police cars and a windowless white van he recognized as the morgue wagon. "A reporter was just asking me if I knew anything about a murder. Have you had some trouble here?"

Dean Cracken's face turned serious. "One of our associate professors was found shot to death in his office. We're trying not to comment about it until we know the facts. Unfortunately, someone tipped off the news people."

"I've found it's very difficult to keep murder quiet."

"We don't know the circumstances," Meadler told him. "Professor Androvney was a troubled man with many problems. He may have shot himself."

Professor Cracken shook his head sadly. "The man had great potential. I was hoping one day he would replace me as dean."

Ellery caught sight of his father getting into one of the unmarked cars. He decided he'd have to call him that evening.

"Dad, how've you been?"

Richard Queen's voice was raspy, as if he might be getting a spring cold. "Can't complain, Ellery. Doing well for an old man. I heard you were at the university today."

"I saw you at a distance. What's this about some professor being shot?"

"That's the least of it," he replied with a sigh. "Can you come over tonight?"

"Sure, I'll be there right after dinner."

"Come now. You know how Jesse loves to feed you."

Jesse Sherwood had been a brisk and buxom nurse approaching fifty when Richard Queen took a bride for the second time in his life. Ellery was both surprised and delighted by the event, especially when he observed his father's renewed vigor and joy of living. There was no more talk of full retirement from the NYPD, though he had worked out an arrangement allowing more time for them to travel.

Ellery arrived at his father's place on the stroke of six and was surprised to find them both in front of the television set watching the Channel Three Nightly News. He recognized Pia Straton's curly brown hair on the screen immediately. "Channel Three News has learned through reliable sources in the police department that the murder of Professor Androvney in his office at the university today may be linked to four other shooting deaths on the Upper West Side during the past few weeks. Police refuse to speculate that this is the work of a serial killer, but Ellery Queen, the noted author and amateur detective, was observed on the campus this afternoon."

"Is this true?" Ellery asked. "There've been four previous killings?"

Inspector Queen looked grim. "We were hoping to keep it quiet until there was some sort of lead. You remember what happened with the Cat stranglings some years back. The whole town went wild."

"There'll be no keeping it a secret now, not with the media on it. Show me what you've got, Dad."

He pulled over the fancy leather briefcase Ellery had given him for his sixtieth birthday and removed a stack of files. "These are my own copies," he explained. "The originals are in the office. I knew this damned briefcase would come in handy for something." The briefcase had led to a lot of kidding from Sergeant Velie and others, and Inspector Queen stopped carrying it. Ellery had reluctantly agreed that he'd never been the briefcase type.

"There are four cases?" Ellery asked, staring at the folders on the coffee table. Jesse had gone off to the kitchen.

"Four before today, Ellery. Take a look."

The first one chronologically was Mavis O'Toole, a call girl with a lengthy arrest record. The police figured she'd been gunned down by her pimp or some rival. It had happened nearly a month ago, on Tuesday, April sixth, two days after Easter. Eight days later a middle-class butcher named Frank Otter had been killed as he emerged from a Broadway steak house.

"Ellery studied the morgue shot of the corpulent man. "He liked to eat."

"That he did," the old man agreed.

"How do you know it was the same killer?"

"Two things. The same gun, a twenty-two-caliber target pistol, was used in both killings. Since no one heard a shot outside the steak house, it's probably equipped with a silencer. No shots were heard in the other killings either."

"The markings on the bullets match?"

Inspector Queen nodded. "I know what you're going to say, Ellery. A twenty-two target pistol with a silencer is a favorite weapon for a mob hit. But Frank Otter had no mob connections we can find."

"Mistaken identity?"

"That's always a possibility."

"What about the other two?"

His father opened the next folder. "Sidney James, a landlord known locally as the Miser of Morningside Heights. He was shot while jogging in Morningside Park. That was two weeks ago today. Then, last Friday, a second woman was killed. Laura Autumn, president of the Autumn Agency, a small marketing firm. She was shot as she was entering her apartment building on Cathedral Parkway, around the corner from St. John the Divine. She had a bag of groceries from the Morningside Shopping Mall nearby. Until we got a match on the bullets we thought she'd been shot by one of several employees she'd fired last week after an angry outburst in the office."

"Dad, you said two things proved these were the work of one killer. What's the other thing, besides the gun?"

"There was a small red circle on the back of each victim's left hand. It was done in ink, probably by a rubber stamp."

Then Jesse was calling them for dinner.

In the morning the killings were front-page news, and Ellery found them the lead story on the television news as well. There were even photographs of the three male and two female victims. The stories revealed that they'd all been shot with the same gun, but made no mention of the ink circle on the back of their hands. One of the tabloids had provided a map of the Upper West Side with each crime scene marked with a convenient X. It showed that the killings formed a rough circle with the university at the center.

Perhaps that was all the killer intended. Perhaps the murders would stop now.

But Ellery wasn't betting on it. Just before noon he took the subway up to Morningside Heights.

The neighborhood had always been an area in transition, for as long as Ellery could remember. Old brick apartment houses from the twenties and earlier now served as off-campus housing for undergraduates, and an abandoned armory had been turned into the Morningside Shopping Mall. As he was approaching this solid-looking structure, a familiar figure came hurrying out, past the food vendors that surrounded the entrance. He realized it was Virgil Meadler, his host at the university the previous day. The professor, carrying no obvious purchases, headed in the opposite direction and Ellery decided to take a look at Manhattan's version of a shopping mall.

His first impression was of a welter of signs proclaiming everything from *Flowers and Plants for Your Terrace Gardens* to *Supplies for the Student and Home Office*. There was even one that read *Your Parking Free Next-Door if You Make a Purchase!* The mammoth armory had been converted into a warren of small- and medium-sized shops serving just about any need. A fortune-teller announced her trade with a neatly lettered sign: *Madame Beatrice—Reader Advisor—No Appointment Necessary*. A bald man in a turtleneck sweater was just leaving as Ellery strolled by. Further along he found a sporting-goods store that sold .22-caliber target pistols. He looked them over for several minutes and inquired about buying one but was told he needed a permit to purchase a handgun in New York state, even for target practice. He'd known that, of course, but he was just testing the market. "I got to obey the laws," the clerk told him. "Too bad these goons selling guns on every street corner don't have to."

On his way back to the entrance, Ellery saw a tall, slender woman standing in the open doorway of the fortune-teller's shop, by a beaded curtain. She had long gray hair and was probably close to sixty. He noticed her watching him and strolled over. "Would you like a free reading?" she asked, extending a deck of cards.

Ellery smiled. "I thought fortune-tellers used crystal balls."

"I have one if you'd prefer," she answered. "Made of the finest Waterford."

He knew she was playing with him then and he followed her inside. "Aren't fortune-tellers unusual in Manhattan these days?" he said.

"There are hundreds of us if you know where to look. I've been doing it for over thirty years. Check the phone book sometime." She'd seated herself behind a small, plain table and placed the cards there. Behind her, a dark velvet drape hid the wall of the shop, and a few pillows were scattered on the floor.

"I suppose I don't get out as much as I should," Ellery murmured. "What do you want me to do, pick a card and you'll tell me its meaning."

Madame Beatrice smiled wisely. "Oh, I'm certain you know the meaning of all the cards, Mr. Queen. You wrote a mystery novel about it once."

He was momentarily at a loss for words. This woman had not only recognized him but remembered a novel he'd written decades earlier. He recovered enough to ask, "Is my face that well known in these parts, or are you a mind reader as well as a fortune-teller?"

She pulled aside the velvet drape to reveal bookshelves lined with modern novels, predominantly mysteries. He recognized at least a dozen of his titles among them. "On slow days I do lots of reading," she admitted. "You've always been one of my favorites, and your photo is on the jackets. I have to hide them from my clients, though. They would expect me to be reading something far more esoteric."

"You'd make a fine detective," Ellery told her. "You probably encounter all classes of people."

"I do indeed," Madame Beatrice told him. She seemed to hesitate and then went on. "My last client, not ten minutes ago, is a violent man awaiting sentencing for assaulting a taxi driver. He wondered if the cards could indicate the length of his prison stay."

Ellery remembered the bald man in the turtleneck. "I imagined your customers to be young girls wondering when they'd marry."

The fortune-teller snorted. "More likely young girls wondering if they are with child, although those have fallen off with the popularity of home pregnancy tests."

He nodded, a smile playing about his lips. "Much more accurate than a deck of cards." He started to leave. "It was a pleasure meeting you, Madame Beatrice."

"Will you sign one of your books before you go?"

"Certainly." He took out a pen. "Whichever one you'd like."

"I suppose it should be the one about the cards," she decided, taking down *The Four of Hearts*.

As he left the converted armory and started across the street he became aware of a cluster of police cars, not unlike those he'd seen at the university the previous day. They were by the entrance to a ramp garage next to the armory. "Ellery!" a familiar voice called out, and he saw his father waving to him.

He hurried over to join the old man. "What is it, Dad? Not another—"

"Dead man in a car, shot in the head. We may have another one. I'm on my way up now to take a look." His face was grim. "Come along."

Inspector Queen moved up the ramp to the second level with remarkable speed for a man his age, and Ellery had to hurry to keep pace. Sergeant Velie and an assistant medical examiner were already on the scene, along with police technicians and the garage manager. The body was slumped over the steering wheel of a blue compact car, and a bullet wound in the left temple was obvious.

"Looks like a twenty-two caliber again," Velie said, with a nod toward Ellery.

"The circle on his hand?" Inspector Queen asked.

"It's there."

The assistant medical examiner moved out of the way, and Ellery got his first look at the body. He recognized the bald man in the turtleneck, Madame Beatrice's last customer. "I just saw this man in the mall!"

"His driver's license says his name is Warren Cashmere. The dashboard computer came up with an arrest record for a few assaults."

"I didn't know his name, Dad, but I just saw him next-door, coming out of the fortune-teller's."

"How long ago was that?"

"Maybe forty, forty-five minutes."

The medical examiner looked up and nodded. "Sounds about right. He hasn't been dead long."

"Woman parked next to him reported the body," Sergeant Velie said. "The driver's window was open. Someone walked up to the car and shot him."

"Not someone he feared," Ellery observed, "or he wouldn't have rolled down the window. People don't usually park their cars with the windows open." He leaned over for a closer look and saw the little red circle stamped on the back of the victim's left hand.

"What does that damned circle mean?" his father asked.

"Some sort of organization? There's an old Edgar Wallace novel called *The Crimson Circle*—"

But the garage manager, a stout black man named Martin King, had a more prosaic explanation. "The mall customers can get stamped like that when they buy something. I give 'em free parking."

Inspector Queen was unhappy. Too many things were happening too fast. "That Channel Three woman, Pia Straton, has been on my neck," he grumbled.

"Mine too," Ellery agreed. The body had been removed and they were leaving the ramp garage. "You'll want to have Velie question the mall's fortune-teller, Madame Beatrice. She told me the victim was awaiting sentencing for assaulting a taxi driver. He came in to find out how long he'd be locked up."

The inspector grunted. "He won't have to worry about that now." As they parted he said, "Let's set up a meeting at my office tomorrow morning. Meantime I'll try to find out how many of the victims had a connection with the Morningside Shopping Mall."

"I can help on that, Dad," Ellery volunteered. "I'll talk to Professor Androvney's friends at the university."

"Good."

Ellery found Virgil Meadler in his little office on the second floor of the Arts and Letters building, staring out the partly opened window at some sort of demonstration on the quadrangle. "What is it?" Ellery asked. "Graduation fever?"

"Nothing so ordinary. For its last event of the academic year, the student council invited Uncle Sam Tusker to speak here Friday afternoon."

Ellery remembered reading something about it in the papers months ago. Uncle Sam Tusker, a former government employee, had been charged with treason the previous year for selling certain classified information to unnamed Middle Eastern countries. A man of benevolent appearance with white hair and an Uncle Sam goatee, he'd pleaded he was merely trying to fulfill the somewhat ambiguous instructions he'd received. A jury believed him, and he was acquitted of the treason charge, causing an uproar in the press. Now he was speaking at college campuses, ostensibly to pay off his legal expenses. Protesters believed he was spreading an anti-American message.

"Not a very pleasant ending to a week that's already seen a campus murder," Ellery observed.

"What can we do?" Meadler asked with a shrug. "The university has always been a forum for dissent, and after all, the man was acquitted by a jury." He shuffled some papers on his desk. "Now what brings you here, Ellery? I have to tell you my students are still talking about your entertaining lecture yesterday. They learned a great deal from it."

"I'm glad of that. Actually, there's been another murder."

"Another since yesterday?"

"Afraid so. This morning, in the parking garage adjoining the Morningside Shopping Mall. I'm helping my father with the investigation and I wanted to ask you a bit more about Professor Androvney. Did he have any enemies on campus?"

"Not really. There are always some disgruntled students around. He was a heretic of a sort, always going against prevailing opinion on just about any subject. That irritated some of the students. But then, I suppose you can find one or two such people among the faculty on any campus."

"Did he spend much time at the Morningside Shopping Mall?"

Virgil Meadler snorted. "Androvney hated the place! He'd never go near it. He thought the old armory should have been converted into an arts center."

"That's odd," Ellery said. His father was leaning now toward a theory that the ink circle on the victims' hands was not left by the killer but was merely a sign the victims had recently shopped at Morningside.

"Have you been to the mall?" the professor asked.

Ellery smiled. "Just this morning. I had a nice chat with your mother."

"My—" The surprise was evident on his face.

"Madame Beatrice is your mother, isn't she?"

"She told you?"

"She didn't have to. I saw you coming out of the mall earlier today, without any packages. You'd told me your mother was a fan of my books, and when I met Madame Beatrice she showed me her Queen collection. You were there visiting her this morning, weren't you?"

He seemed annoyed at Ellery's discovery. "I'm certainly not ashamed of what my mother does. She raised me as a single parent and saw to it that I had every scholarship opportunity. I owe all this to her," he said with a wave of his arm. "She comes to see me occasionally and I stop by to see her. But I don't want a situation where my students start pestering her to predict what marks I'll give them. She runs her own operation, and I'm the first to admit she's something of a con artist. Her little table has a hidden drawer so she can vanish or produce cards pretty much on demand. She gives customers the readings she thinks they want. Nothing wrong with that, I suppose, but it's best that we lead separate lives as much as possible."

"I understand perfectly. She's a most pleasant woman. She's become involved in this only because the latest victim visited her for a reading just before he was killed." Ellery filled him in on the details. "There seems to be a connection between the mall and some of the victims." He didn't elaborate about the inked circles found on their hands.

"Is there any common link between these people?" Meadler asked.

"None that we've found. We have a call girl, a butcher, a landlord, a marketing executive, a literature professor, and now a petty criminal. Nothing in common except they all lived or worked in this general area."

"I suppose victims of serial killers don't usually have much in common, unless the crimes are sexual in nature."

Ellery leaned back in his chair. "The term *serial killer* is popular these days, but it shouldn't be confused with series killers, ones who kill a certain number of people with a goal in mind. A serial killer usually keeps on until he's caught. A series killer will stop after achieving his goal."

"I don't see where there's much difference. They're both insane."

"But in the case of a series killer the insanity has been twisted into a pattern the killer can see. If you find the pattern, you find the killer."

"You sound as if you've had experience with this."

"A little," Ellery admitted. "One time—"

There was a knock on the door and Dean Cracken poked his head in. "Sorry, Virgil. I was next door in my office and I didn't know you were occupied."

Ellery stood up. "I was just leaving."

"No, no, sit down! As a matter of fact, I wanted to speak with you too, Mr. Queen. My wife just phoned from home to say there's been another killing. She saw it on the news." He'd come all the way into the office and set his bulging briefcase on the floor. It reminded Ellery of the one he'd given his father as a Christmas gift. "Is that true?"

"I'm afraid so," Ellery acknowledged. He quickly described the killing at the mall, leaving out mention of Madame Beatrice.

"Will this thing never end?" Dean Cracken asked.

"Mr. Queen thinks it'll end if we can discover the pattern behind it," Meadler told him.

"Pattern?"

"I don't believe the killings are random," Ellery said. "There's a pattern, and the killer wants us to find it. Otherwise, why use a weapon that can be so easily identified? Most series killers use a knife or some form of strangulation. They rarely commit a string of killings using the same handgun."

"Do you think it's someone on campus?"

"On campus or at the mall or in the neighborhood. That's all I can say with some certainty."

The dean shook his head sadly and then turned to Professor Meadler. "Virgil, my other problem is that I traditionally introduce the student council's final speaker of the year. It's going to be very difficult for me to say anything good about Uncle Sam Tusker. I was wondering if you had any suggestions."

The demonstration out on the quadrangle had grown noisy again, as if to punctuate the dean's request. Meadler closed the window and said, only half humorously, "Tell them he's your favorite traitor and let it go at that."

"You're no help. Can you imagine the gall of the man, billing himself as Uncle Sam when he was just acquitted of treason! I've been here thirty-five years and this is the first traitor we've ever invited to speak at the university. And I have to write up some remarks welcoming him!"

"Keep your briefcase handy in case the demonstrators start throwing eggs. It makes an effective shield."

"Don't worry, I will. My wife calls it my security blanket. Someday I'll even look inside it. I think I still have lecture notes in there from last semester."

"If you're really worried," Ellery suggested, "you could have the audience pass through a metal detector on the way in."

"I hope we haven't come to that," Dean Cracken answered sourly.

After he'd left, Ellery asked, "Does he always carry the briefcase?"

"Usually he forgets it and leaves it in the lecture hall or his office. One of the students has to retrieve it for him."

"He must be nearing retirement age."

Meadler nodded. "Two more years. Androvney was in line to head up Arts and Letters until he got himself killed. Now I don't know who'll get it."

"Start campaigning," Ellery said with a wink.

Pia Straton was waiting for him at his apartment downtown. "Mr. Queen," she called out, running up to him.

He glanced around. "Where's your camera today?"

"It's just me. I want to talk about these killings, off the record."

Ellery hesitated only a moment. "All right, come on up. But it's strictly off the record."

He led her to the fifth floor and unlocked the door to his apartment overlooking the East River. "What a view!" she exclaimed. "You can see all the way down to the Brooklyn Bridge."

"It lifts my spirits," he admitted. "I suppose you're here because of the latest killing." They sat down opposite each other.

"That's number six, right? And the first time there've been two in two days."

"Correct."

"What does it mean?"

"Off the record? We may be heading toward a climax, if only we can work out the pattern in time to avoid it."

"Pattern? Then you don't think these are random killings?"

"No, there's a pattern. It just starts in the wrong place."

He could see the anticipation in her eyes. "Can you make that a bit clearer to me, Mr. Queen? Ellery?"

"I'm afraid not. What I've got is only the beginning of an idea, and I may be entirely wrong."

"Is there any way I can help?"

He thought about that. "Do you know this man Uncle Sam Tusker?"

"I interviewed him once after his acquittal."

"He's speaking at the university Friday afternoon. I'd like to meet with him before his speech."

She nodded. "I could arrange that. But how can Tusker be connected with the killings?"

"I didn't say he was," Ellery told her. "You'll just have to trust me."

At ten o'clock the following morning he was in his father's familiar office at One Police Plaza. Sergeant Velie was there too, along with two other detectives assigned to the case. "We have forty men and women in all working on it," Inspector Queen said, "and I have authorization to double that if need be. We need to crack this thing, Ellery. Do you have anything for us?"

"Some vague ideas, nothing I can put into words yet."

Against one wall of the office was a large blackboard on which had been placed photographs of the six victims. Each was numbered, beginning with the call girl, Mavis O'Toole. "We've definitely placed her at the shopping mall," the old man said. "She was well known in the neighborhood. The next two, Frank Otter and Sidney James, also shopped there."

Ellery nodded. "And Laura Autumn. She was carrying a bag from the mall when she was shot. But we've got problems with number five. I understand Professor Androvney hated the place and wouldn't go near it."

"Do we know how long this circle of ink lasts after it's stamped on the customers' hands?" the inspector asked.

"It wears off in a day," Velie answered, "sooner with one or two vigorous washings."

There was a phone call from the medical examiner's office and Velie took it. He listened for a moment and then passed the phone to Ellery's dad. "You'd better take this. It's important."

Richard Queen swore only on rare occasions, but this was one of them. He hung up and said, to no one in particular, "There's another one."

"Just this morning, Dad?"

The old man shook his head. "Friday, April second. Four days before Mavis O'Toole. I guess that shoots our theories all to hell."

"How do they know—?"

"The victim was a Korean convenience-store owner named Kim Hwan, up on Amsterdam Avenue. He was shot once in the chest that evening and robbery appeared to be the motive, although nothing was taken. Someone in the lab just remembered the murder weapon was a twenty-two and compared the bullet to the ones in our recent killings. It matched."

"The red circle, Dad?" Ellery asked anxiously.

"There was no red circle. Nobody noticed one and nothing shows on the morgue photos."

They all stared silently at the blackboard.

Finally, Ellery got up and went to the board. He erased the numbers by each photograph and wrote in *1. Kim Hwan.* Then he numbered the others in their proper order. "So we have seven victims instead of six."

"What does it mean, Ellery?"

"Do we have any record of Kim Hwan's funeral?"

"Funeral? How can that possibly matter?"

"It might, Dad." He turned to Sergeant Velie. "We need details of the funeral service."

"You got it, Ellery." He went off to check the records.

"You're on the trail of something," his father said. "I know that pensive expression."

"It's so wild I hate to put it into words, at least not quite yet."

The inspector sent the other two detectives off to bolster their patrols of the Morningside Heights neighborhood. When they were alone, he asked, "Will there be more killings?"

"Not if we can stop them. Not if I can beat the killer to his eighth victim."

Sergeant Velie returned, looking smug. "That was easy. His widow says he was a Buddhist back in the old country, but he never practiced it here. There was no religious service, and the body was cremated."

"Does that answer your question, Ellery?"

Suddenly it clicked into place, not everything, but an important part. "Come on, Dad! Velie, where's your car? We have to get up to that shopping mall before there's another killing."

"Who—?"

"A fortune-teller named Madame Beatrice. Come on!"

Ellery phoned the woman and warned her to be on her guard.

"We're on the way up there," he said.

Velie used his siren all the way up Broadway, while Ellery's father called for additional support. They reached the mall seconds before two squad cars, and Ellery was already on the pavement, leading the way. Shoppers gawked and cleared a path for them. Ellery had Madame Beatrice's shop in sight when they heard the single shot. Velie and the inspector had their guns drawn as they burst through the beaded curtain. Madame Beatrice was on the floor behind her little table, bleeding from a wound in her side.

"That way," she gasped, pointing toward a fire exit in the rear of the shop. "He went that way."

Ellery and Velie were through the door in an instant, down an enclosed corridor that led to an outside fire door. The panic bar had a spot of blood on it, which Ellery pointed out to the sergeant as they went through. Then they were outside, next to the ramp garage, and the door had swung shut behind them.

"We'll have to go back around and in the front," Ellery said. "Get your men to search the garage."

"What are we looking for?"

"Anyone suspicious. He'll still have the gun on him. And probably traces of blood. He hasn't finished yet."

Ellery ran around to the front of the mall, where police were holding back a panicked crowd. "What is it?" Pia Straton yelled, rushing forward with her cameraman.

"You're always on the scene, aren't you?"

"It's my job. What happened?"

"Another shooting. You'll get details later." Then he pushed his way through to the fortune-teller's shop.

His father and one of the officers were on their knees beside the woman while the officer tried to stanch the flow of blood from her side. "Ambulance is on the way," the old man told him. "She's trying to talk."

Ellery knelt beside her. "It's Ellery Queen, Madame Beatrice."

"I know. I'm not dead yet."

"You're going to be all right. Do you know who shot you?"

"He pulled down a ski mask as he entered. I saw the gun and ducked as he fired. he came at me again and I tried to fight him off. He should have my blood on him."

"Don't worry, we'll get him." The ambulance crew arrived and Ellery had time for only one more question. "Did he try to put a circle on the back of your hand, maybe with a rubber stamp?"

"I don't know. God, this hurts! Give me something for the pain."

Ellery and his father stood up, turning her over to the ambulance attendants. Inspector Queen spoke in a low voice. "The bullet went through her dress and the fleshy part of her side, then out again. We're trying to find where it hit."

Madame Beatrice had been reading when the killer entered, and the drapes in front of her bookcase were partly open. It was Velie who found the bullet, embedded in the spine of *The Innocence of Father Brown*. The lab people took it, along with the smear of blood from the fire-exit door.

"What do they say about her?" Ellery asked his father.

"She'll pull through, despite the loss of blood."

"Have someone phone the university and tell Professor Virgil Meadler about it, Dad."

"Why him?"

"She's his mother."

Friday was one of those warm May mornings in New York when dark clouds move across the sky threatening momentary downpours. Ellery purposely avoided reading the papers as he hurried through breakfast. That afternoon Uncle Sam Tusker would be speaking at the university, and Pia Straton had promised him a meeting before that. She'd called earlier to confirm their appointment and promised to pick him up at his building.

He paused only to call his father at Headquarters. "Dad, what's the news this morning?"

"Madame Beatrice, or Beatrice Meadler to use her proper name, is coming along fine. Her son's been up to see her. She may be released from the hospital tomorrow or Sunday. The lab boys verified that it was her blood on the fire-exit door all right, and they also verified that the bullet came from the same gun that killed seven people so far. It's madness, Ellery. The man's going to keep on killing until he's stopped."

"The end is in sight, Dad."

"What's that supposed to mean?"

Instead of answering, Ellery asked, "Do you have a guard on Madame Beatrice?"

"Of course."

"She should be safe, but the person we're dealing with isn't completely rational."

"You can say that again! Where will you be if I need you?"

"At the university, for Uncle Sam Tusker's speech."

"That traitor!"

"Exactly, Dad. Here's what we have to do. Can Velie be at the university in twenty minutes . . . ?"

Pia Straton was waiting for him downstairs in the Channel 3 van. He got in and she cut over to Broadway, following the route he'd taken to the mall the previous day. "I hope you realize I'm doing you a big favor with this Uncle Sam business, Ellery, and I expect a big favor in return."

"What would that be?"

"I want an exclusive when you crack the case."

He smiled. "If I crack it, Pia, I promise you'll be there."

Though it was not yet one, a crowd was already forming for the afternoon's talk. "Classes are about over," Pia explained as she found a parking space. "Next week is graduation." She hustled Ellery through a side door of the university theater and up the stairs to a private lounge where Virgil

Meadler and a few others were waiting with the acquitted traitor. Ellery was relieved to see Sergeant Velie among them.

Uncle Sam Tusker was true to his press reports. A slender man in his sixties with white hair and a goatee, he did indeed resemble the traditional image of Uncle Sam. Ellery found it a bit disheartening that such a man might be preaching treason against his country. They shook hands as Pia introduced them, and Uncle Sam said, "I've heard a great deal about you, Mr. Queen. Something of an amateur detective, aren't you?"

"At times, when I'm not writing," Ellery admitted. "That's why I asked Pia to bring me here."

Uncle Sam smiled. "You can't be investigating me!"

Ellery glanced around the room and lowered his voice a bit. "My investigation has nothing to do with your politics, or with the charges brought against you. I have to tell you an attempt may be made to kill you today."

The smile became a laugh. "You know how many times my life's been threatened? I take that in stride. I'll tell you something, Mr. Queen. If you're alive you have to rile the passions of the people. I want them to rise up against the government or against myself, it doesn't matter which. The sound of shooting is better than the sound of silence."

"—the sound of—"

The door swung open and Dean Charles Cracken strode in, carrying his bulging briefcase.

Ellery knew. He knew it all now. It was madness, but he'd found the real pattern at last.

Virgil Meadler was introducing Tusker to the dean. "This is our Dean of Arts and Letters, Professor Charles Cracken. He'll make the opening remarks."

Dean Cracken was unbuckling his briefcase. "Perhaps you'd like to see what I'm going to say about you, Mr. Tusker."

Now, Ellery said: Stop him, Velie! But the words were frozen in his throat.

"—what I'm going to say about you, Mr. Tusker."

Stop him, Velie!

"Stop him, Velie! There's a gun in his briefcase!"

Dean Cracken looked up, startled, as Velie lunged at him, knocking the briefcase from his hands. It fell to the floor, spewing its contents, and there among them was the .22-caliber target pistol with its silenced barrel.

It was later that afternoon, after the excitement had passed, when Ellery, Inspector Queen, Sergeant Velie, and Pia Straton arrived at Madame Beatrice's hospital room. "How are you today?" Ellery asked.

"Can't complain," the fortune-teller told him. She was propped up in the hospital bed with two pillows behind her. "What's all this about?"

"We arrested the man who shot you. He was taken into custody this afternoon at the university."

"Anyone I know?"

"Dean Cracken," Ellery told her.

"Dean—"

"It seems he killed seven people over the past several weeks. You would have been eighth and Uncle Sam Tusker would have been ninth. That was the pattern."

"I guess you'd better explain it," she said, looking from Ellery to Inspector Queen.

"It's madness, of course, but series murders always are. Only a madman would kill nine people so they would fit into the nine circles of Dante's Hell."

Pia Straton, who'd been a silent observer until now, gave a little gasp and turned on her tape recorder. She'd wanted to bring a camera too, but Ellery had ruled that out. Inspector Queen said, "You'd better explain your reasoning, Ellery."

"Gladly. I learned the first time I ever met Dean Cracken that he was the university's foremost authority on Dante. He taught Dante, he knew Dante and *The Divine Comedy* better than anyone else. I became aware early on that the victims of these killings seemed to all have some character flaw—a call girl, an overweight butcher, a miserly landlord, a wrathful woman who fired her employees, a professor said to be a heretic, and a violent man facing a prison sentence for assaulting a taxi driver. They were almost the seven deadly sins, but not quite."

"But the nine circles of Dante's Hell, Ellery?" the old man asked. "I still need convincing."

"So did I, but it came with your discovery of an earlier killing, the true first in the series. A Korean shopkeeper, born a Buddhist but practicing no religion when he died. He was bound for Dante's first circle. Translations of *The Divine Comedy* vary, but generally it goes more or less like this. In the first circle is limbo, for the virtuous heathens. The second circle is reserved for the lustful and lascivious, the third for the gluttons, the fourth for the miserly, the fifth for the wrathful, the sixth for the heretics, the seventh for the violent."

"Which brings you to me," Madame Beatrice said.

Ellery nodded. "The eighth circle, reserved for liars, fortune-tellers, thieves, and others. As soon as I knew the pattern, I guessed you'd be the next victim."

"And Uncle Sam Tusker?" Velie asked.

"The ninth circle, the very bottom of Dante's Hell, is reserved for traitors."

Even Pia Straton seemed spellbound by the enormity of it. "Has Dean Cracken confessed?"

"Not yet," Inspector Queen replied. "But we tested the gun in his briefcase this afternoon. It fired all seven of the fatal shots, and the bullet that wounded Madame Beatrice."

"Thank God it's over," the fortune-teller said with a sigh.

"Can I call this in to the station?" Pia Straton asked, anxious to catch the five o'clock local news.

"You can if you want," Ellery said. "But you may prefer to wait a few moments. You see, after all my clever reasoning, connecting Dean Cracken to these killings because he was the Dante expert, I overlooked two things. The first was the circle of red ink on the back of the victims' hands. It was missing from Kim Hwan's hand, but appeared on all the others until Madame Beatrice, where we interrupted the crime during its commission. What it told me was that the circle was a mere happenstance, not part of the original plan at all. Victims two through five had the circle simply because they'd received free parking at the shopping mall's ramp garage. When the killer realized this, it became a perfect way to tie Professor Androvney's killing in with the others, even though he never went to the mall."

His father's voice was solemn. "It still could be Cracken. What's the second thing you overlooked?"

"A fat man, a heathen, a miser, a fortune-teller, a traitor, might all be known in the community. But how would Cracken have known that Warren Cashmere was awaiting sentence for an act of violence? The pattern had to be completed today, remember, with the killing of Uncle Sam Tusker. How could he have known of Cashmere's crime and just where he'd be on Wednesday?"

"He might have known the man, read about it in the papers."

"No, Dad, it's not likely. There was something else too, something that revealed the truth to me yesterday. I played along today, knowing Tusker wouldn't be killed, just to see how far it would go."

Pia's finger was on the tape recorder button. "What are you saying?"

"That Dean Charles Cracken is innocent. He killed no one. The killer is lying here before us. Isn't that right, Madame Beatrice?"

Her eyes shifted to each of their faces in turn. "Why, that's impossible," she said after a moment's hesitation. "I'm the only one who *couldn't* have killed them. You're forgetting, Ellery, that you saw Warren Cashmere leaving my shop. And you were with me at the time he was killed."

"As I discovered yesterday, the back of your shop leads to a fire door that exits right next to the ramp garage where he was shot. You'd already stamped his hand with the circle when he paid you for reading his fortune, so you knew he was parked in the garage. You propped open the fire door, went into the garage, and shot him with your silenced target pistol, while I was looking at pistols in the mall's sporting-goods store. It would have taken you less than five minutes. When you saw me walking by, seconds after your return, you recognized me from my book-jacket photos and enticed me in for a perfect alibi. Perhaps you'd persuaded your son to invite me to the university in the first place. You wanted me to follow your false trail to Cracken."

"But I was shot myself, by that gun in the dean's briefcase."

"That was the one mistake you made, and I almost didn't catch it. As my dad and Velie and I entered the mall yesterday and hurried toward your shop, we all heard a single shot as the supposed killer fired and hit you in the side. It was Uncle Sam today, in one of his crazed statements, who told me the sound of shooting is better than the sound of silence. But it wasn't true with you. We heard the shot when we shouldn't have, because all the crimes were committed with a silenced pistol! You couldn't shoot yourself with the real murder weapon because it was already hidden among the papers in the dean's bulging briefcase. You couldn't plant it there later because you knew you'd be in the hospital. As the gun dealer told me, it's easy to buy a weapon on any street corner up here, but it's not so easy if you need a silencer. Sometime late Wednesday or early Thursday you got into the dean's office and hid the real murder weapon in his briefcase. If anyone saw you, it would have been explained as a visit to see your son Virgil in the next office. You'd previously fired a shot from the real gun into the spine of one of your books, where we'd recover it. Yesterday you pricked your finger and left a drop of your blood on that exit door, then took a second twenty-two-caliber target pistol, fired it through your dress and a roll of flesh in your side, and screamed for help. The second gun went into a secret drawer in your desk that your son mentioned to me, and the bullet that wounded you probably went into a pillow. I'd called to say we were on the way, so you fired the shot when you heard the approaching siren."

His father was shaking his head. "I can see it, Ellery, but I still can't believe it."

"Then think about this. Why would the killer wear a ski mask when he intended to kill his victim? The mask could only serve as evidence against him. Also, why were so many of the victims customers of the mall? Why did the killer use a gun, easily linked to the killings if found, rather than a knife or other weapon? And why did the killer add Professor Androvney to the list even though he didn't frequent the mall?"

"Why, Ellery?"

"She lied about the ski mask, of course, and many of the victims after the first one were her own customers. She used the gun for two reasons: so she could stay safely out of reach of her stronger victims, and so the killings could be linked through the matching bullets. As for Androvney, he had to be killed because he was in line to be Dean of Arts and Letters, a position she wanted for her son."

Madame Beatrice started to rise from her bed. "You're a devil, damn you!"

"With Androvney dead and Dean Cracken arrested, if not convicted, in the killings, her son Virgil became a likely candidate for the position."

"She did it all for her son?"

"I think only half for her son. Cracken had been at the university for thirty-five years, remember, and she'd been telling fortunes about that long. I think Cracken was her lover all those years ago, and the father Virgil Meadler never knew he had."

"Now that's guesswork, Ellery."

"Is it, Dad? Cracken was a Dante expert, perhaps obsessed with the subject. Wouldn't he be naturally attracted to a young woman named Beatrice, the name Dante gave to his own ideal of womanhood in *The Divine Comedy*? And if their union brought forth a son, wouldn't Beatrice have named him Virgil, after the Roman poet who guided Dante through the circles of Hell?"

She was staring at them now with eyes that seemed suddenly blank. "You mean I did it all for nothing? All this planning, all these killings? For nothing?"

"Does Dean Cracken know Meadler is his son?" Ellery asked quietly.

"I never told him, but he may have suspected. He was so obsessed with Dante that I wanted it to be like this. None of the people I killed were worthwhile anyway. They all deserve their places in Dante's Hell. I deserve it too." And then she was silent.

Ellery turned to Pia Straton. "You can phone in your story now," he said.

On the way out of the hospital he came upon Virgil Meadler on his way in. "Ellery," the professor asked, "how's my mother today?"

Carol Gorman

The Death Cat of
Hester Street

CAROL GORMAN has won numerous awards for her young adult
and juvenile novels. *The Washington Post* recently noted that Gorman's latest novel, *Dork in Disguise,* is "a wonderfully accurate novel."
Over the past few years, she's also begun selling stories to the adult
markets, as here. *Publishers Weekly* called this historical mystery "truly
entertaining," while *Mystery News* said, "Gorman's characters come
to life (on nineteenth-century) Hester Street." This story first
appeared in *Cat Crimes Through Time.*

The Death Cat of Hester Street

Carol Gorman

Fifty times I'm telling you, Herman Epstein can make you happy!" Rose Bochlowitz said. "He's a good man, Lena. He's also a butcher, of course, so every day you'll never go hungry. Did you see the way he looked at you?"

"Oh, Mama," Lena said, pushing away a stray wisp of dark hair that had escaped the knot on her head, "let's not talk about it again. It's too hot."

Lena and Rose Bochlowitz, carrying their sacks sewn from coarse cloth, made their way along crowded Hester Street, weaving around pushcarts and wagons. All around them, a clamor of voices called out in Yiddish, German, English, and Russian as peddlers and buyers haggled over the price of potatoes, pumpernickel and suspenders. The air was still and rank. Above them, residents of the tenement apartments sat on fire escapes, sipping water or cheap beer and waited for a cooling breeze that never came.

"Five cents everyone pays the butcher to cut off the chicken's head, but Herman Epstein won't take it from you!" Rose said, stepping around a pile of horse manure in the street. "He looks at you with such affection, *Lenale*. It's good I happened to meet you there to see such a thing."

Rose and Lena plodded on, their cotton skirts swirling around their legs. Sweat wetted their underarms and stained their shirtwaists.

Lena blotted her forehead with a handkerchief. She was not only hot, but tired. She had spent ten hours on her feet at Gibson's dress shop with only one twenty-minute break for lunch. As the manager, she watched over the cash girls and salesgirls and worked as hard as they did. At least it was the dull season. During the fall and winter, she worked a twelve-hour day before returning after supper to do the bookwork until midnight or later. But then she didn't have to deal with this heat. It was a heat that could suffocate, that could drain a person's energy and strength in less than an hour.

The shadows were lengthening along the street as people headed home to apartments to fix their evening meals.

"One thing more I will say, and then I will say it no more," Rose said. Lena rolled her eyes upward, and Rose waggled her finger at her daughter. "Better you should marry Herman Epstein now and eat, than wait for God knows who and starve."

"Mama, this is America," Lena said. "Women in America marry for love."

Rose ignored her. "Esther Rossman is getting married, and she's twenty-two years old. In one year, maybe she'll have a baby! Twenty-six you are— may you live to be a hundred—and you have no man, no nothing. Maybe you'd like Nathan Samuelson. I saw him and his mother, the fortune lady, this morning on Hester Street. Such a nice young man! I told him about you and how well you're doing at Gibson's—"

"Mama, I'll find my own man. Lots of men come into the shop."

"To buy something for their wives or lady friends," Rose said. "No man walks into a dress shop who isn't taken."

"Well, I won't marry a man I don't love. If I don't find the right man, I won't get married."

Rose looked horrified. "*Bays di tsung!* Of course, you'll get married. God forbid such a thought should enter your head!"

A white cat, its fur darkened and matted with filth, suddenly appeared at their feet, streaked over Lena's shoe, scrambled across the street and disappeared behind an ash can left for the dumping cart.

"*Gottenyu!*" Rose screamed, grabbing Lena's arm protectively. "Turn your face, Lena! Don't look at the cat! Come with me, come, come." She dragged Lena into a shoe-repair shop where she collapsed against the wall, her breath coming in ragged gasps.

"What is it?" Lena asked, her eyes wide in horror. "Mama, you look as if you've seen a ghost. It's just a cat."

"It touched you, Lena? Tell me—"

"It ran over my shoe—"

Rose gasped and clasped her hands together. "The fortune lady, Mrs. Samuelson. We must see her!"

"Whatever are you talking about?"

"A terrible thing, that cat," Rose said. "It's the Death Cat."

Lena frowned. "The Death Cat?"

Rose was still breathing heavily. "It showed up, the cat did, the day Mrs. Solomon got the first signs of consumption."

"Oh, Mama, that was just a coincidence."

"A coincidence she tells me!" Rose said, exasperated. "I haven't said everything there is to tell. Now listen. Mr. Levi fell down the stairs and broke his neck. That terrible thing was there, too."

"Mama—"

"And what about poor Mrs. Gitelson? Walking she was, minding her own business, and the Death Cat jumped out, and she fell right down on the street and died! Someone should kill the evil thing and bury its body in a place far away."

"Mama," Lena said, "there's no such thing as a Death Cat. It probably eats its weight in rats every day." She smiled. "We shouldn't kill it; we should invite it into the apartment."

Rose grabbed Lena's arms. "Don't get near the cat again. Promise me, Lena, promise me."

Lena sighed. "I won't go near the cat, Mama."

"Now we talk to the fortune lady," Rose said.

"Why? Mama, I have to go home and pluck this chicken."

"Chickens can wait. The fortune lady will tell us what we need to know."

"Mama, if you're playing matchmaker again—"

"Who said anything about her son Nathan?"

"You did. Not two minutes ago. Besides, we don't have the money to pay for a fortune."

"Five cents. So I won't get the scissors sharpened this week. I can sew shirts with dull scissors. My daughter's life is more important. Come."

The fortune lady lived on the fifth floor of a brick tenement house on Orchard Street. Odors from clogged toilets, left unattended by the landlord, and garbage smells from the air shaft, hung in the still air and mixed with the aromas of dinners cooking.

The women climbed flight after flight of dark, creaky steps. The temperature rose the higher they climbed, and at every landing, Rose stopped to catch her breath.

"Mama, this is crazy," Lena said at the fifth floor. "Just because a cat—"

"A terrible thing, that cat," Rose said again, leaning heavily against the clammy wall.

"Have you asked Mrs. Samuelson for a fortune before this?"

"Once I came with Ruth Frank," Rose said. "She told the truth: that Ruth's daughter would marry in a year, and she did!"

"Oh, Mama."

"Well, so maybe it was two and a half years." Rose shrugged. "But she got married! That's the important thing." She pointed down the hall. "Over there."

A handwritten sign outside the back right apartment said Fortunes Told.

"Here," Rose said and rapped on the door.

After a moment, the door was yanked open. A small, stooped woman stood in the doorway. Her dark hair was threaded with gray, braided and pinned in a circle on her head.

"Mrs. Bochlowitz, twice in one day I see you," she said in Yiddish.

Rose answered her, in Yiddish, "Mrs. Samuelson, a fortune is what we want for my daughter, Lena."

The woman motioned them to come in and led them through her small kitchen and into her parlor. The room was very dark and hot. Lena moved quickly to the window, hoping for a breath of air. She was disappointed. Five stories below was a narrow concrete courtyard, surrounded with tall, brick buildings that blocked the sun and any breeze that might be stirring outside.

Turning from the window, Lena gazed around the dimly lit room for the first time. It was nearly empty; the wooden floor had been swept clean. The walls were bare except for a clock that ticked softly on the far wall. The only furniture was the tiny wooden table and two chairs standing next to her at the window. Two plain pieces of thin cotton, stretching across the window, served as a curtain.

"Come," Mrs. Samuelson said. "Sit."

She took a chair and sat at the table. That left only one remaining chair, and Rose gestured for Lena to take it.

"Mrs. Samuelson," Lena said in Yiddish as she sat, "my mother thinks—"

"Five cents," the woman said in English, tapping the table. Then reverting to Yiddish, "Put it here."

Lena felt resentment toward her mother for insisting on this fortune that they couldn't afford. She frowned at Rose and pulled the nickel out of her knotted handkerchief. She laid it on the table.

"Where's the crystal ball?" Lena murmured in English, and the woman looked up at her sharply.

"I must go into a trance now," she said, and closed her eyes.

"Mrs. Samuelson—" Rose said anxiously.

The woman opened her eyes. "So how can I go into a trance if you talk to me, eh?"

"I have to know," Rose said, drawing closer. "Is my daughter in danger? The Death Cat touched her just now."

"The Death Cat?"

"A terrible thing, that cat," Rose said, worry lines deepening in her forehead. "It appears and people die."

The woman peered closely at Lena. "And you touched this thing, this Death Cat?"

"A white cat ran over my foot," Lena said, waving a hand impatiently. "I don't believe in such things. My mother is a little super—"

"A white cat?" Mrs. Samuelson said. Her voice became soft and she stared out the window. "Like a ghost."

"Mrs. Samuelson, I really don't think—"

"Silence," Mrs. Samuelson said, closing her eyes once more. "I'm going into a trance."

She began to hum in low tones and rock back and forth. Lena glanced at her mother, who bent over the fortune lady, her eyes wide with fear.

Lena sighed heavily. It had been a long day, and she still had to pluck and dress that chicken.

Mrs. Samuelson let out a groan. She stopped rocking and, with her eyes still closed, said, "It is night. A warm night. I see a shop—"

"Yes, yes!" Rose cried. "Gibson's! I told you about it this morning. Lena works there."

"The dress shop—" Mrs. Samuelson said, nodding. "Someone is moving in darkness."

"Outside the shop?" Rose whispered.

"No, I see inside. Someone is—yes, someone has broken in and is robbing—"

A look of horror crossed the woman's face. "No, no! Terrible! I can't watch! It's awful, terrible, terrible."

Her eyes flew open and she leaped to her feet. "Go!" she cried. "Now. Both of you. You must leave my house."

"But what did you see?" Rose cried, her face ashen. "A thing so terrible you can't watch? But my daughter! What will happen to my Lena?"

Lena watched with a mixture of horror and fascination. Whatever it was that Mrs. Samuelson imagined she saw, it was enough to frighten the woman terribly and send a chill up her own back.

The apartment door opened, and a young man walked in.

"Hello," he said and smiled. "Mrs. Bochlowitz, is it?" He looked at Lena then and opened his mouth to speak, but then he saw the horrified look on his mother's face. "What's going on?"

"Go!" Mrs. Samuelson said again to Lena and her mother. "And never come back here!"

"Mother!" the young man said. "What's wrong?"

"It's all right," Lena said, holding up her hand. "We're going, Mrs. Samuelson."

She walked Rose across the parlor floor, out the kitchen door and into the hall.

Lena bustled Rose down the five flights of steps and out into the busy street.

"Lena, I'm so frightened!" Rose cried. "A terrible thing is waiting to happen. You heard Mrs. Samuelson."

"No, Mama," Lena said. "It was just in her imagination."

"But the Death Cat always comes before a terrible thing!" Tears welled in Rose's eyes and she clutched Lena's arms.

"*Lenale,* you can't go back to the dress shop! Especially at night."

Lena steered Rose toward their apartment on Broome Street and began walking, her arm around her mother.

"Of course I'm going back. I can only get the bookwork done after the shop has closed. There's no time during the day."

"Some terrible person is going to rob it!"

"Mrs. Samuelson doesn't know anything," Lena said.

"The police," Rose said. "We must tell the police."

"What? I thought you didn't trust the police."

"What's not to trust? My daughter is in trouble."

"I'm not in trouble!" Lena said. "And what are you going to tell them,

Mama? That we saw a white cat and a fortune lady went into a trance and saw a burglary? How can I tell them that?"

"You speak," Rose said. "You have a mouth. They'll listen."

"They won't listen," Lena said. "They'd think we're two crazy ladies."

Rose turned abruptly and headed across the street.

"Mama, where are you going?"

"To the police," Rose said, walking straight ahead. "So they think I'm crazy. I'll protect my daughter."

"Not now, please," Lena said wearily, hurrying to catch up. "It's hot and I'm tired, and I have to pluck this chicken."

"Always with the chicken!" Rose said, continuing on her way. "I worry about my daughter's life, and she talks to me about chickens! Come. We'll talk to the police. Later we pluck the chicken."

Detective Gabriel Goldman, leaning back in his desk chair, listened to Rose's story. No expression crossed his face. Occasionally, he glanced at Lena, but his face didn't give a clue as to what he was thinking.

He was a handsome man, Lena observed. But he was laughing at them behind that mask of his, she was sure of it. She felt the heat rise in her cheeks.

"So, of course, we came to the police," Rose concluded. "You will make sure Gibson's is not robbed by that horrible man, and my daughter will be safe." She nodded once, sat back in her chair and folded her arms across her lap, a gesture that put a physical "period" at the end of her story.

The room at the police station was crowded with desks and people. For a moment, Goldman said nothing, and Lena was suddenly aware of how noisy the room was.

Goldman stared thoughtfully at Rose. Then he shifted in his chair.

"Uh, Mrs. uh—" he glanced at the paper on his desk, "—Mrs. Bochlowitz, I appreciate your concern for your daughter."

Here it comes, Lena thought. He thinks Mama's crazy.

"But you understand that I can't put officers around a shop simply because of a dream—"

"What dream?" Rose said. "A *trance* it was! Mrs. Samuelson goes into a trance. Don't ask me how she does it, she just does it. And she sees things. She saw something terrible."

"And the Death Cat brought this on."

Lena, her face flaming, rose from her chair. "Come on, Mama, I told you he wouldn't believe you."

Goldman leaned forward in his chair and caught Lena's arm. "Now, I didn't say I didn't believe it."

Lena stopped and stared at him. "You believe Mama?"

"Well—no," he said, "but I didn't say it. Up until now, that is."

Lena shook her arm free. "Come on, Mama." She gently pulled Rose to her feet. "I won't have him laughing at us."

"Miss Bochlowitz," Goldman said seriously, "that's the last thing in the world I would do to you."

Lena glanced at him to see if he were making sport of them, but his face was boyishly earnest.

"Thank you for listening, Mr. Goldman. But I think we've taken up enough of your time."

"Lena, he has to help us," Rose said. "You can't go back to Gibson's. Something terrible will happen!"

"Miss Bochlowitz—"

"Come on, Mama." Lena pulled her mother across the crowded room and outside.

"But what will we do, Lena?" Rose cried. "There's danger at the shop!"

"That's nonsense. I don't believe a word of it."

"You can't go back, Lena."

"I'm sorry, Mama, but I can't quit my job. Positions are too hard to find. It took me eight years to work up from cash girl to manager. Do you have any idea how many girls would give everything they have to get out of the factories or give up their pushcarts? I'm one of the lucky ones, Mama."

"No job is worth the danger that waits for you, Lena. So you don't believe the fortune lady. You must believe the Death Cat!"

The argument continued through the evening as they plucked and dressed the chicken, browned the onions on top of the coal stove for *paprikasch* and during the cleanup after their meal.

"I'm going to go back to the shop now," Lena said, drying her hands on an old, worn towel. "I must catch up on the bookwork, and I don't want to hear a word about it."

"No, Lena!"

"It's too hot in the bedroom," Lena said. "Why don't you sleep on the fire escape tonight? Maybe there will be a breeze. I'll join you after I get home."

"So how can I sleep if my daughter is getting herself killed?"

"I'll be back before you know it."

"It's too dangerous. Please, Lena."

Lena washed her face at the kitchen sink, used the toilet outside the apartment in the hall and returned to the parlor where her mother paced.

"I'll wait until you're settled on the fire escape," Lena said.

"Please don't go, *Lenale*."

"Mama, I have no choice. I've always gone back to do the bookwork at night. I won't stop now because of some silly—"

"Who knows how the fortune lady sees things?"

Lena sighed heavily. She helped her mother into her night shift. Rose washed up at the kitchen sink, all the while fretting aloud about the Death Cat. Then she left to use the toilet.

After the kitchen door closed behind her mother, Lena moved quickly into the bedroom and dropped to her knees. She reached under the bed, heard a scurrying and snatched her hand back. A rat.

She hurried to the kitchen and lit a candle. Grabbing a broom in the corner, she tiptoed back into the bedroom and shoved the broom under the bed. The broom was the weapon they always used for killing rats in the apartment. Now, though, Lena only wanted the rat out of the way so it wouldn't bite her.

She tipped the candle carefully to see under the bed and grabbed a ball bat that she'd used as a girl to play One O'Cat. The rat scurried to a dark, far corner. "I'll get you later," Lena whispered.

She leaned the bat against the wall next to the doorway leading to the kitchen.

Rose returned, and Lena helped her mother out the parlor window and onto the metal fire escape, still warm from the heat of the day. She handed Rose a blanket and pillow.

"Good-night, Mama," Lena said. "And don't worry."

"Don't worry she says. My daughter is going to be robbed or killed, and I'm supposed to be happy." Her face etched with anxiety, Rose reached out to take Lena's hand. "May God go with you, *Lenale*."

Lena reached into the dark bedroom and grabbed the bat just before leaving the apartment. She descended the two flights of stairs and pushed open the heavy wooden door to the outside. At the corner, she turned south onto Orchard where the peddlers were packing up their wares. Some were already heading down the street toward the pushcart barn, talking and complaining about the heat. Overhead, residents sat or lay on the fire escapes, quietly waiting for sleep to come.

Lena walked a block and turned right onto Grand. The shop fronts were dark, but overhead the new electric streetlights were casting a buttery glow over the neighborhood. Lena tucked the bat under her arm and reached into her purse for the shop key.

She didn't exactly believe the fortune lady's vision. Her mother believed in a lot of superstitions, and Lena usually laughed about them. But once in a while, her mother would predict something, and weirdly enough, it would come true. At least often enough to make her cautious. Lena felt a little silly carrying the bat with her, but it was somehow reassuring to feel the weight and density of the hard wood under her fingers.

Lena unlocked the shop, tiptoed inside and locked the door behind her. She stood in the gloom and waited for her eyes to adjust to the darkness.

Gradually, inky forms took shape, standing like cemetery statues around the room. Mannequins dressed in Gibson's finery posed in shadowy groups of twos and threes. Dresses hung from hangers on wire racks. Tables featuring Lena's artistic displays of scarves and jewelry squatted around the room looking like so many hunched monsters in the darkness.

The quiet was unnerving.

Still, hot air hung heavily around Lena. She wiped sweat from her chin and forehead, then walked quickly over the wooden floor to a small window at the front and lifted it a few inches. A faint breeze wafted inside. Lena squatted next to the window and let a whisper of air cool her face. She took a few deep breaths, then returned to the back of the shop where the cash table stood.

Like most of the shops along Grand, Gibson's was still using gas lanterns inside. Lena rested the bat on the table, picked up the leather-bound book that contained the shop's financial figures, and reached up to turn on the lights. She had put a quarter into the meter on the wall just yesterday, so all she had to do was turn the switch.

The front shop door rattled softly. Lena froze and listened. The sound came again, and she grabbed the bat and crouched behind the cash table. She rose slightly and squinted over the cash register into the darkness. On the other side of the glassed-in shop door, was the figure of a man hunched over in the gloom. A small sound of breaking glass pierced the quiet, and in moments, the door swung open, and the man was inside.

Lena gripped her bat tightly and kept low. Surely the burglar's first stop would be the cash register; he was already heading in her direction.

Lena scrambled quietly to the end of the cash table and rounded the far side just as the intruder reached it.

The register drawer opened with a loud *jang!* that rang through the silent shop. Lena peeked over the cash table and watched as the robber stuffed money from the drawer into a bag. Maybe he would take what he wanted and leave. Maybe if she were very quiet and kept low, he wouldn't see her. After he was gone, she would be safe.

When the register was empty, he slammed the drawer shut and moved to the table where Lena had carefully arranged a display of jewelry and accessories. In a crouch, she moved behind a mannequin, putting a little more distance between herself and the robber.

With one broad stroke of his arm, he swept all of it—the necklaces, bracelets, rings and hair clips—off the table and into his bag.

That's when something changed inside Lena. He was so greedy, so callous about these treasures that customers saved for and bought with their hard-earned pay from the sweatshops or their factory jobs. How dare he steal from Gibson's where she and her girls worked so hard! Would Mr. Gibson fire a few of the girls to make up for the loss? Would the rest of them have to work that much harder to make up for fewer shop girls to wait on the customers?

Rage boiled inside of Lena. She would *not* wait quietly and let this horrible person walk off with Gibson's money and merchandise.

She brought her bat, and she would use it. But she would have to be closer to the robber.

Her heart hammering her ribs, she moved once more, this time around the mannequin, toward the shadowy figure that was now stuffing shirtwaists from a rack into his bag.

Lena gripped her bat and moved closer—and stepped on her skirt. She tripped and fell forward into the mannequin which toppled onto the floor, sending a hat flying and spreading its dress in disarray.

In a moment, the man was on Lena, grabbing her from behind. She was so frightened, she forgot for a moment that she still held the bat at her side. By the time she remembered, it was too late to raise it. "And who is *this*?" he said, yanking her to her feet and spinning her around. The streetlight shone behind him, and his face was in deep shadow. The beer on his breath was nearly overpowering. "Well, well, were you waiting for me, eh? We could have some fun tonight."

And that's when it happened.

A small form scrambled out of the darkness and ran between the robber's legs. The man's toe caught on the creature, and he lost his balance, falling to the side, letting go of Lena.

"*Rrreowwwww!*"

Lena had just enough time to raise her bat and bring it down on the back of the intruder's shoulders and head.

The man slumped to the floor and lay there without moving.

Lena stared at him, clutching the bat to her chest.

"Miss Bochlowitz! Are you there?" The voice came from outside the shop. The door burst open, and a man entered. "Miss Bochlowitz, it's Detective Goldman. Are you all right?"

He walked around a display, and saw Lena with her bat and the dark form of the man stretched out on the floor. He scratched his head. "I'd say you're doing all right for yourself, Miss Bochlowitz. I thought I'd walk past the shop on my way home, and I saw the broken glass—"

Goldman turned the man over. Lena leaned down and peered into his face. She gasped. "It's the fortune lady's son!"

"But to bring that terrible thing *home,* Lena!" Rose said. She stood over the kitchen counter where she was chopping onions for chicken soup.

The white cat crouched over a dish on the floor and greedily ate the chicken livers Lena had given it.

"Mama, the cat saved my life, climbing through the window that way! That's a big accomplishment for such a small creature."

"I don't like it, this cat being here. It's a feeling in my stomach. And my stomach never lies."

"I think she'll bring us *good* luck, Mama," Lena said. "She's already killed a rat."

Rose's eyes opened wide. "This mangy Death Cat is a *she*?"

"I think I'll call her Miss Pluck. She certainly has a lot of it."

"And dirt. This cat has a lot of dirt."

A rap sounded at the door. Lena crossed the tiny kitchen in three steps and opened the door.

"Mrs. Samuelson!" Lena stepped back. "Please come in," she said in Yiddish.

"Mrs. Samuelson?" Rose wiped her hands on a rag.

The fortune lady took a couple of timid steps into the kitchen.

"I'm sorry to disturb you," the woman said. She looked at the floor. "My son—I'm sorry."

"It wasn't your fault," Lena said. "There's no need for you to apologize."

"Yes, I must." The woman began to tremble, and Lena pulled out a chair for her. She sat. "You see, in my trance I saw the robber."

"Yes, you saw him in the shop."

"But I saw his face. My son's face. It was terrible. I saw blood dripping from his ears. I saw him, and I knew he would rob the shop." A long moment passed. "I was frightened for him, and I told you nothing."

"You were protecting your son," Lena said.

"A hundred times that night I told him not to go out."

"Children never do what you tell them," Rose said. Lena looked up at her, and she shrugged. "So all right, *some* children never do what you tell them."

Lena put a hand on Mrs. Samuelson's shoulder. "It turned out fine, Mrs. Samuelson. How is your son?"

"He'll be all right," the woman said. "He must go to jail first." She stood. "I'm going to visit him now." She looked down at the floor and gasped. "The ghost cat—"

"The Death Cat," Rose corrected her. "My daughter has invited it to stay with us."

The woman's eyes widened.

"It's a good cat," Lena said. "Thank you for stopping to see us, Mrs. Samuelson."

The fortune lady said good-bye and disappeared out the kitchen door.

"She saw her son's face," Rose said. "You see, the fortune lady knows these things!"

"Yes, Mama."

Rose looked down at the cat who was sauntering into the parlor. "The cat is full of dirt, Lena. My clean house—"

"Mr. Goldman is going to help me give it a bath tonight."

Rose gasped. "The policeman? He's coming here?"

Lena's cheeks reddened. "Yes. He says he wants to see me again. We'll bathe the kitty and then go for a walk."

"This is a romantic evening, washing a flea-bitten cat?"

Lena beamed. "It's a start."

Rose sighed. "What's with young women in America, eh? They marry for love; they clobber robbers over the head; they wash filthy cats for a little romance." She glanced up at Lena. "They aren't interested in butchers."

"You're right, Mama," Lena said, smiling.

Rose shrugged. "So my daughter loves a policeman—"

"I don't love him, Mama! We just met!"

"So my daughter just met a policeman. If that's what she wants—"

"Mama," Lena said, covering her mother's hand with her own. "Maybe I'll fall in love; maybe I won't. But I'm happy."

"So my daughter's happy. The policeman can't support her as the butcher can, so maybe they'll starve. We have a Death Cat living with us, eating chickens at sixteen cents a pound. So, maybe we save money, eh? Instead of paying the butcher five cents to cut off a chicken's head, we can bring home the live chicken and let the Death Cat kill it. As long as my daughter is happy."

"Oh, Mama!" Lena laughed.

Rose shrugged and smiled. "As long as my daughter is happy."

Peter Crowther

Dark Times

Though **PETER CROWTHER** works primarily in fantasy and horror, he enjoys stretching his wings with the occasional very good mystery story. His short stories featuring private detective Koko Tate are paradigms of the hard-boiled mystery story. Since the early 1990s, Crowther has sold some seventy short stories and poems to a wide variety of magazines and anthologies on both sides of the Atlantic. He has also recently added two chapbooks, *Forest Plains* and *Fugue on a G-String*, and a single-author collection, *The Longest Single Note,* to his credits. He lives in Harrogate, England, with his wife and two sons. In "Dark Times" Peter skillfully combines elements of mystery and horror into an engaging story that could have been written only by him. This story first appeared in *Subterranean Gallery*.

Dark Times

Peter Crowther

R alph?"
"Yeah, it's Ralph." Ralph Wilson nodded and switched the phone receiver into his left hand so that he could kill the sound of *The Jerry Springer Show* on the TV remote with his right, the one that wasn't warped out of shape with the arthritis. "Who's that?"

"Phil." The voice sounded distant, surrounded by static. "Phil Casimeer?"

Ralph held onto the sigh and turned away from the TV and the spectacle of a man wearing earphones trying to stop two grown women fighting only to end up on the receiving end himself. "You at home?"

"Yes."

"You sound funny." He turned to face the TV screen. "Don't tell me you've bought a 'hand-free'?" The idea of Phil Casimeer buying anything that was even vaguely technological seemed ridiculous. The scene on the TV changed from the man with the headphones—who was now standing up and waving his arms for the women to get back—to a shot of the audience who were all on their feet apparently shouting and clapping. Then another cut, this time to Springer himself, looking sincere and holding his mic like it was an oversized popsicle. Thankfully the little mute sign was showing on the screen in the top left corner. The last thing Ralph needed right now was one of Jerry Springer's half-baked philosophies.

"I need you to come over, Ralph," Phil Casimeer croaked.

Now the sigh came. Another of Casimeer's wacky schemes. First the rearranging of all the furniture—"feng shui," Phil had called it, or something like that—so as to get the best vibes possible for the house. Who the hell ever heard of a house having "vibes"? Then some much-needed help positioning a series of huge standing stones in a line down the backyard that led down onto the old creek. Near broke Ralph in two and he had all on stopping

Steph from getting right on the phone and giving Phil Casimeer a piece of her mind.

"Okay. When? I have to go to the store first thing, for Steph, but—"

"I need you to come over now, Ralph." This time the croak had turned into a chesty wheeze, like a voice through water.

Ralph turned away from the screen again. Casimeer definitely sounded strange. "Are you sick, Phil? Do you want me to call—"

"I'm not sick," the voice said, its tone and volume sinking and rising. "Leastwise, it's nothing that can be cured from the drugstore."

"You *are* sick. Listen—"

"No, you listen. I'm covering my mouth, that's why I probably sound strange."

"You're covering your mouth?" Ralph switched hands again. "Why you doing that, Phil?" For a second, listening to his own voice, Ralph was reminded of the old Bob Newhart sketch about Walter Raleigh introducing tobacco to civilization. *And then you do* what, *Walt? You set* fire *to it?*

"No time to explain. Come now, Ralph. I'm begging you."

Ralph glanced at the wall clock: 10:40.

"I know it's late," Casimeer whispered, "but I really do mean it. You're the only one I can turn to."

"Won't tomorrow do? Tell me tomorrow will do, Phil."

"Tomorrow won't do, Ralph. Tomorrow will be too late. It has to be now. Tonight."

Another sigh. It was a good thing that Stephanie was staying with her sister over in Bridgeport. At least Ralph wouldn't have to put up with her complaining that he should tell the old coot where to get off.

The thing was, Ralph was almost as old as Phil, both of them having bid a fond but tearful farewell to big seven-oh some years back, and he hadn't the heart to rain on an old friend's parade. But the years had done something strange to Phil—particularly the long years since cancer took his beloved Nancy while she was still in the bloom of life and reaching eagerly for 60 and the prospect of more time with Phil when he retired from the Savings and Loan company down at Kittery.

The long lonely years that followed Nancy's death had made Phil Casimeer introverted and thoughtful, forever locked away in regular consignments of old books he got sent through the mail . . . books with weird names—sometimes in Latin—and by authors whose names Ralph couldn't even pronounce. There was no way any of these guys ever appeared in the bestseller lists—Ralph had checked once in the Waldenbooks down at the mall where a cheery girl with a huge overbite he just couldn't take his eyes off had looked at him vaguely when he read the names he had hastily scribbled on the back of an envelope once over at Phil's house while Phil was using the john.

But friendship was friendship and you never knew when the time might come that *he'd* need some help—or just a little companionship (they were none of them getting any younger), which is why Ralph reckoned Phil Casimeer kept on getting him over to his house on these flaky projects.

"Okay," he said. "Do I need to bring anything? Tools, that kind of stuff?"

There was a pause. Ralph guessed Phil was shaking his head. "Just bring your glasses."

"My *glasses?* I *always* wear my glasses, Phil, you know that. How'm I supposed to drive over to you if I don't wear—"

"Your *reading* glasses. Bring your reading glasses."

"Okay," Ralph said, making to hang up. Christ, now Phil wanted someone to read to him.

"Oh, and Ralph?"

"Yeah?"

"Bring some light. Lots of light."

"Light?"

"Yes, flashlights. And bring your Zippo, maybe some matchbooks . . . maybe even some candles? That kind of thing. And get here as fast as you can. I'll leave you a note."

"A note? Why a note? You going some—"

But the line was dead.

Ralph stared at the TV screen for a couple of minutes without removing the mute. Then he dug some candles out of the cupboard under the kitchen sink—Steph always kept a few tied up in green garden twine, in case the power went out—and he brought the big flashlight out of the garage. He hadn't smoked for almost 20 years but the old tin where he used to keep a pack of Marlboros still provided a home for the Zippo Steph had bought him way back when he was still a youngster. He lifted the tin to his nose and breathed in the warm and intoxicating smell of tobacco, then closed the tin and dropped the lighter into his pants pocket.

The final thing he almost forgot: his reading glasses. They were lying open on top of an Elmore Leonard paperback beside the easy chair. As he folded them up and slipped them into his shirt pocket, Ralph had an urge just to plop down in the chair and pick up the book. But the urge passed, like all urges pass, given time.

Minutes later—after killing the mute and filling the house with sound again—he was in the old Fairlane that was now more rust than paint and heading down to the old mill road and out toward Phil's house.

The road was empty and quiet, just the way it always was. Nobody used it any more, hadn't done since the Interstate was extended to take the main traffic away from Bridgeport. Now there was only the occasional farm machinery or kids on bikes, and the road was more than ever showing the signs of wear. No, not signs of wear . . . because there was nothing wearing on it: these were signs of neglect. Like all folks heading for the eighty-mark, Ralph knew all about those signs.

The moon was full and the cloud cover high, with the wind blowing the clouds across the moon and sending rippled shadows scudding like waves across the corn at either side of the road. Ralph watched them breaking against the old fence at the bottom of the steep bank to the left and then building up again on the other side, like they were appearing from beneath the road, rolling away from him into the distance.

He pulled up on the gravel of Phil Casimeer's front sweep at a little before 11, suddenly hoping that Stephanie didn't get it into her head to call him goodnight. She'd wonder where the hell he was. But it was too late to worry about that now.

With the flashlight tucked under his left arm and the candles in his jacket pocket, Ralph scrunched up to Phil's front door and beat it with his hand, calling out, "This is the police, Casimeer. We know you're in there so come out with your hands up."

There was no response.

He waited a minute or two, looking up at the moon and watching his breath cloud out in front of him, then he knocked again. "Phil? It's Ralph."

Still no response.

It was about now, in the cheesy horror movies that Ralph liked to watch (much to Steph's despair) on the SciFi channel, that a dog howled somewhere in the distance. But the night stayed quiet. Ominously quiet.

Maybe it's too quiet, a soft but insistent voice whispered in the back of Ralph's head.

Ralph stepped back from the door and looked at the upstairs rooms.

As if on cue, a cloud freed itself from the moon's pull and, in the brief instant before another took its place, moonlight splashed across the front of the house washing over the window briefly before rolling off to the side and tumbling to the ground where it scurried over to the rickety fence and the long grass that led down to the old creek way down through the woods.

Just for a second or two, Ralph fancied he'd seen someone at one of the upstairs windows and he'd been about to wave but then, when the cloud covered the moon again, he saw that the window was empty and dark.

Come to think of it, the whole house was dark. But then hadn't Phil asked him to bring candles and a flashlight? Sure, that's what was wrong: a power outage.

He turned to the window to his left—the living room window, as he recalled—and, sweeping the flashlight over it, Ralph thought he had seen, just for a moment, a darkness loom up against the glass and then fall back when the beam hit it. Why was Phil making out he wasn't home when he'd asked him to come all the way over? Didn't make sense.

But what had he said about the note? That didn't make a whole lot of sense either.

You know what? the secret voice whispered in the back of Ralph's head. *Maybe you'll go in there and find the old fart hanging from one of the upstairs beams like an early Christmas decoration. Maybe that's what he meant about the note.*

Ralph wanted to tell the voice that Phil Casimeer was not an old fart but he knew it wasn't worth the effort. They were all old farts on *this* bus. The trouble was Ralph didn't know where this bus was going.

He felt the tell-tale rumble from his guts that signified he needed to go sit on the john for a half-hour and read a magazine. But he couldn't do that. He couldn't go and leave Phil.

He reached for the door handle and turned it. The door wasn't locked.

It drifted open with just the hint of a squeak, gathering momentum at a certain point until it banged against the stop behind it.

Ralph stayed where he was and played the flashlight beam down the dark hall, over the carpet and the old bureau stuffed full of papers, until it came to rest on the kitchen door. The door was closed.

He moved the beam back down the other side of the hall, across the door to the living room on the left—also closed—and then over to the staircase. Nothing. Nothing unusual but nothing usual either.

He lifted the flashlight so that the beam traveled up the stairs, sliding stealthily up the wall away from the banister, as though the light felt just like Ralph . . . needing to set against something solid, keeping a watch upwards at all times in case . . .

Ralph frowned. In case what? What was he expecting, for crissakes?

How about in case one of those decomposing ghoul-things from the old comic books leans over the top rail dropping pieces of moldy flesh on any surprise visitors? the secret voice said, a smile playing on the words.

The beam had reached that point on the staircase where the stairs curved around to the left up to the landing.

"Phil? You up there? It's Ralph."

Silence.

Then, when the beam was right at the top of the first flight, Ralph saw the vaguest flicker of movement caught in the glare. He squinted, jiggling the flashlight side to side and straining to make out what it was, but still didn't move across the threshold.

Then he saw it. It was smoke: not a lot—in fact, it appeared to be just one wafting trail of thick dark vapor—but it was smoke. What else could it be?

"Jesus Christ," Ralph muttered. He rushed into the house and started up the stairs, keeping the beam trained ahead of him.

Halfway up, he slowed down, heart beating in his chest. And then he stopped. The smoke didn't seem like any smoke he had ever seen before—or, at least, it wasn't behaving like any smoke he had seen before.

The single tendril of this particular smoke was snaking toward the shuddering light-splash on the wall at the head of the first flight as though it were alive, creeping along to the edge of the splash like it was testing it . . . a smoke-child dipping its toe into the ocean of light before making the Big Dash Out Into The Waves Of Shimmering Brightness.

Keeping his eyes on it—and leaning on the banister to keep his hand still and the flashlight beam steady—Ralph shouted up to the floor above. "Phil? I'm here on the stairs—you okay?"

The smoke reached the light, seemed to touch the periphery of the splash of brightness, and then pulled back, curling up on itself like a plant frond that had touched a flame. Looking down, Ralph saw another one snaking along the carpet on the top of the first riser moving to the left, moving stealthily like a rear guard making a pincer operation, moving around behind the enemy's flank while one of its number kept the enemy occupied elsewhere.

"Phil, this is the damnedest—"

He watched the same thing happen with this second shoot. It touched the circle of light and pulled back, curling around and settling down on the top stair.

"Phil, if you can hear me, shout. If you can't speak, then just . . . just thump the floor, or make a noise or something."

The second tendril was moving toward Ralph, slithering along the carpet and edging its way over the edge of the top stair down toward the next.

"Phil, there's smoke out here."

Think again, buddy boy, the secret voice said. *If that's smoke, then I'm the King of Siam.*

Ralph trained the flashlight down onto the smoke and watched it shrivel up on itself and pull back, first onto the top stair and then back up the few stairs to the left, out of sight.

"Well, whatever it is, it doesn't like the light," Ralph muttered.

He shone the beam back on the facing wall and was dismayed to see that there were more tendrils now: they had sneaked out while the beam was elsewhere and were slithering across the empty wall like clinging vines. Some were even extending themselves, moving completely away from the wall and through the open air, moving . . .

Toward *him*.

Ralph took a couple of steps back down the stairs, keeping the beam splayed in front of him. Then he thought of Phil. He was up there—somewhere—and Ralph couldn't just go off and leave him. After all, old farts had to stick together. And whatever it was—the smoke stuff—it didn't like the light.

"Okay," Ralph announced, an edge to his voice. "I'm coming up."

Holding the flashlight in his good right hand, Ralph started up the stairs, waving at the smoke with his left. When his hand touched it—and it did *touch* it—Ralph thought for a second that he could actually feel the smoke. He watched it bend around his hand, pulled with the momentum of his arm like a ribbon, following the sweep but not breaking. He jerked his hand back and shone the flashlight beam on it. There was nothing to see.

But he wasn't about to swing his hand at the stuff again. It had felt . . . felt *wrong*, somehow.

He was at the turn now. Six more steps lay between him and the landing. He held onto the banister, shining the flashlight onto the smoke and shaking his head in wonder as he watched it pull away from the light.

The remaining steps he took carefully, pausing on each one, until he stood on the landing.

All of the upstairs doors were open except one.

As far as Ralph could recall, that was Phil's bedroom. The one he used to share with Nancy when she was still alive.

"Phil?"

The call was half-hearted now. Ralph no longer expected to get an answer. Which might have been fine if this were daylight and he'd just called around to chew the fat for a while but half-expecting Phil to be out taking one of his constitutional walks. But it wasn't daylight—in fact, there wasn't any light at all—and Ralph knew damned well that Phil was in here somewhere. And he knew Phil should be able to hear his calls. He may be an old fart but he wasn't a deaf old fart.

Then he saw the paper.

At first, it was just a splash of whiteness on the carpet, caught in the flashlight's beam. But then he saw what it was: two or maybe three sheets of paper half-sticking out from beneath the closed door.

And there was something else protruding from beneath that door.

The smoke was pulsing out in a thick slice, curling up into the air and snaking every which way like a lace curtain, its fronds interweaving and separating.

Ralph shone the light at the smoke and smiled as it pulled back in on itself. He half fancied he could hear muted sighs of pain, which was ridiculous: who ever heard of smoke that felt pain?

He shuffled along the landing until he was in front of the door and reached down for the papers. As he expected, there was writing on them. He pulled his reading glasses from his shirt pocket and changed them with his regular pair. Then he looked at the writing. The first words were:

Ralph: careful when you open the door.

Ralph continued to read.

This isn't easy. I haven't much time. I'm keeping it in here with me but it'll get out. Keeping the door closed will slow it down. It doesn't like the light but it can absorb it. Use the candles.

Ralph frowned. The words were getting harder to read. He swept the flashlight around him and saw that the smoke had been taking advantage of his preoccupation with the note. It was all around him now, brushing his face like a spiderweb. He held the beam on it, watching the stuff frizzle back away from him. But the beam seemed dimmer than it had been.

Ralph turned it on himself and stared into the bulb. It was growing fainter, even though he knew he'd changed the batteries only last week.

It doesn't like the light but it can absorb it, the small voice in Ralph's head whispered, repeating Phil's words from the note. *Use the candles.*

Ralph pulled one of the candles from his jacket pocket and held the Zippo to it. The flame against the waxed wick crackled and then took. He looked around on the floor for something to stand the candle in and saw a pile of books. He halved the pile and set the candle between the two smaller piles, feeling a little more comfortable as he watched it flicker.

Turning back to the papers, Ralph read:

It's black magic. Ralph. Real black magic. I was trying to get to talk to Nancy. Trying everything. I went one step too far. It's just blackness. And I've

He turned to the next page.

set it free. I've released a blackness into the world and I can't stop it. What you have to do is find something in the book that says how to send it back. I tried to find something but I couldn't see. It was coming out of my eyes, my nose, my mouth—it was coming out of everywhere, Ralph. God knows but I'm sorry.

Ralph looked up at the closed door. "Phil? Can you hear me?"

He leaned toward the door, resting his head against the wood. Was that movement he could hear? A kind of frantic rustling?

He looked back at the paper, turned to the next sheet.

You have to stop the blackness. It'll take all the light everywhere and make everything just darkness. But more than that, there are things inside it that want to get out. I haven't seen them but I've heard them. I can't write more hope this makes some kind of sense don't forget to be careful when you open the door—use the boo

The writing ended. Phil Casimeer's usually careful hand had turned, in the space of just three pages, into an uneven scrawl which eventually came to an end in the middle of a word.

Ralph glanced down at the candle. Two strands of smoke had curled themselves around the base and were already snaking their way to the flickering wick. He shone the flashlight on the door and saw—in a beam that was definitely weakening—

It's being absorbed, the secret voice confided quietly.

—the smoke still swirling out from the narrow gap beneath the wood. He took a deep breath, ignoring the growing need to empty his bowels, and reached forward for the door handle. He turned it, slowly, and pushed the door open.

The room beyond looked like it was on fire although flames were nowhere to be seen. The black smoke was everywhere, but here near the door it was patchy, swirling and somehow incomplete.

At the rear of the room it was solid. More than that, it seemed to be moving.

All of the smoke—even this smoke—was doing smoky movements . . . movements which could be argued were merely reactions to air currents. But the solid thick denseness of the smoke banked up at the back of the room— through which Ralph could see absolutely no trace of anything familiar— was another story. This smoke was moving in an altogether different way: it was moving the way a sack moves when there's something in there.

. . . there are things inside it, Phil's letter had said, *that want to get out.*

Ralph looked down and saw a smoke-shrouded shape on the floor to his left. This was where the smoke was coming from, buffeting out in thick clouds that swirled immediately around themselves as though excited to be free. Ralph shone the weakening flashlight beam at the shape and, just for an instant, saw a bare foot twitching before a thick gasp of smoke pushed from beneath the trouser cuff above the ankle and spiraled up into the air.

"Phil?"

He didn't really expect an answer. He was just pleased to hear a voice . . . even though it was his own.

Waving the smoke out of the way, Ralph knelt down beside his friend.

Phil Casimeer's eyes were still open but they were not seeing anything. Thin tendrils of blackness were twirling out of the sockets around the eyes themselves to meet up with similar emissions from Phil's nostrils and his open mouth. The entire body was shaking as though on a continuous electrical charge, causing the smoke trails to shudder as they came out into the air.

Ralph reached out a hand and felt the old man's wrist for a pulse. There wasn't one. He was pleased, in a way. He could not have borne the realization that his friend was still somehow alive. He looked down the full length of the quivering body and saw black ribbons wafting into the air from his friend's open fly and from beneath each trouser cuff. He could guess which orifices they were using.

Even seventy-four years' experience had not prepared Ralph Wilson for what was happening at Phil Casimeer's house. Ralph didn't think *any* amount of experience could prepare someone for this.

He looked around in desperation, wondering what he should do now.

The wall of smoke at the rear of the bedroom was making tearing noises, the bulges on its surface growing more pronounced.

He glanced back at the door and saw the candle he had left out on the landing flickering, close to being extinguished by the smoke halo that had surrounded the flame, dancing and swirling.

Ralph sat down next to Phil Casimeer and shone the flashlight.

Everywhere was Nancy, he now saw.

Laid out on the floor behind the door were various items of women's clothing—Ralph didn't doubt they were Nancy's, hoarded by her husband that she may wear them once more.

Propped up by the skirting board alongside the clothes were photographs: some featured Phil—albeit a Phil Casimeer of varying ages—and one or two (Ralph saw with a twinge of sadness more profound than any he had felt before) even featured Ralph himself. But every single one featured Nancy Casimeer, always smiling, always loving.

So this had been Phil's plan all along: to bring his wife back, somehow. To defy the very laws of nature by employing some fabled dark forces.

Very dark, indeed, the secret voice trilled with amusement. *Just look around you . . . yes, very dark indeed.*

To wrest her back from the grave.

Then he saw, amidst the clothes and the photographs—and even a hairbrush that clearly still contained long strands of hair that Phil would have given his right arm for even thirty years ago—was a book.

But this was no mere page-turner purchased from the mall or rescued from the twirling metal racks in the airport. This book was the granddaddy of all books everywhere and anytime . . . the book that Mickey Mouse used to animate the brooms and mops, the towering tome into which the birth of the entire galaxy was recorded even as it was happening, a book whose cloth covers were fashioned out of cosmic debris and star matter, whose vellum pages were stained from the blood of gods and the breath of night. And this was the book from which Phil Casimeer had called forth darkness to the Earth.

The book which

use the book

Ralph Wilson must somehow employ to send it back.

Ignoring the gathering smoke and the rending noises from the black wall at the rear of the room—whose boundary was inching its way closer to the door onto the landing—Ralph scurried awkwardly across to the clothes and the photographs. And to the book, which lay open in a fashion that was as menacing as it was inviting.

He propped the flashlight against a framed photograph of Phil and Nancy on a beach—the pair of them smiling at some long-forgotten passerby whose services they had begged to record the moment for posterity—and twisted the book around.

The text was small and, even with his reading glasses, difficult to decipher. The thick margin at either side of the page contained scribbled notes in a variety of hands. Previous owners, Ralph thought—and, just for a second, he wondered what had become of them.

None of it meant anything to him.

He flicked the pages, first backward and then forward searching for some clue . . . some helpful key or advice for the casual browser. But there was nothing, or at least nothing that seemed to make any sense.

The sound of movement from behind him sent Ralph pitching headlong into the neatly arrayed clothes, and he braced himself for something taking hold of him from behind. When nothing happened, he turned around, his face still resting against one of Nancy Casimeer's sweaters, and saw, through the thickening darkness now barely relieved by the flashlight, Phil's body being pulled into the wall-bank which had now reached over his friend's feet.

The entire process took little more than a few seconds, and then the body was gone.

use the book

"How?" Ralph shouted at the black wall, its protuberances thrusting out like the sun's promontories before settling once more into the maelstrom of encroaching darkness. "*How* do I use the book?"

Ralph tried to convince himself that the sounds coming from behind the black screen did not remind him of animals eating.

He pulled himself to his knees and stared once more at the open pages. What did Phil have in mind? He must have had a plan.

Ralph replayed the phone conversation—suddenly unable to believe that it had taken place little more than an hour ago—in an effort to get a clue. But the clue, when it came, did not come from Phil Casimeer: it came from Bob Newhart.

And then you do what, *Walt? You set* fire *to it?*

And then the flashlight went out.

The sudden plunge into darkness both froze Ralph and propelled him into action.

He reached into his pocket and removed the Zippo that Stephanie had bought him. Trying not to fumble—and desperately trying not to imagine the slowly advancing wall of darkness and the things that lay behind it (and which even now might be escaping from, now that all trace of light had disappeared from the room)—he slipped off the base and, reaching out blindly so that he knew the exact location of the book, inserted his thumbnail into the screw that allowed gas to be inserted.

Hey, that thing has been in your dope tin for more than five Presidential terms, amigo, the secret voice whispered. *Why not just pull down your pants, stick your head between your legs and kiss your ass adios. You feel like a sleep, don'tcha? All old farts gotta get their rest, and you got a long one coming up . . . you and the rest of humanity.*

"Come on, loosen!" Ralph shouted, pleased once more to hear his voice.

Something brushed against his face and, though only for a second, Ralph relaxed his sphincter. The warm wetness in the seat of his pants felt good.

He waved his arm aggressively and shouted, "Get away!"

Whatever it was moved off, twisting itself into the darkness that surrounded it.

Suddenly, the moon shone through the bedroom window, bathing the entire room in light even though more than half of the window's area had been taken over by the black wall. But now Ralph saw, just before another cloud obscured the room, one of the protuberances in the side of the black bank had stretched itself fully out. It had looked like one of the hand contortions his father used to make shadow-beak shapes against the nightlight to scare the impossibly young Ralph Wilson. And it had seemed to be searching the room, looking for something, suddenly pulling back in the sudden brightness.

Now what could it be looking for? the secret voice in Ralph's head mused.

Ralph turned his back to the wall, paradoxically comforted by the return to darkness, and concentrated on the Zippo's screw. It came free just as he realized that if the hand-beak thing had been pulling back when the moon shone into the room then it was probably out again now that it was dark. Or maybe it would wait a while . . . hold off until the black bank completely obscured the window . . . or maybe yet again it was right behind him—right now!—snaking up to his neck, opening those beaky jaws . . .

He turned the screw frantically with his thumbnail, not daring to look around.

Something across the room fell over with a clunk.

The screw from the Zippo fell to the floor with a tiny clatter.

Ralph reached out for the book and upturned the Zippo over it, reassured by the smell of lighter fluid.

Something was scraping behind him, moving across the floor.

Another clunk.

Ralph leaned down over the book, hardly daring to breathe, and felt the pages. They felt wet. He dabbed a finger in the wetness and brought it up to his nose. Yes!

He held the Zippo against the wetness and flicked the flint-wheel.

There was a tiny spark on the second flick but then nothing.

He gave up after about a dozen attempts and reached into his jacket pocket for the matchbook.

A sound that was a cross between the dinosaurs in the *Jurassic Park* movies and the volcano in *Dante's Peak* rent the room and shook the glass in the windows.

Ralph figured that the hand-beak thing was now fully out. He had been feeling the swirling fronds of smoke against his face and in his hair for some time now and he guessed that the black wall pretty much now filled the entire room. He tried to pull himself into a ball, tucking his knees up under his chest and wincing at the sharp arthritic pain, and pulled one of the matches free from the book.

He felt again for the wet patch, found it, and struck the match.

It lit first time.

He dropped it on the wet patch.

The match went out.

Another clatter from behind him prefaced another glass-shaking roar.

The second match would not light and Ralph tossed it to the side of the book, and pulled another one free.

The door banged—either it banged open or it banged shut: it hardly seemed to matter.

Ralph struck the third match and it lit. He cupped it in his hand and leaned down to the book's pages, sniffing for the smell of lighter fluid. When he found it, he lowered the match carefully and stroked the wet patch. It lit.

Then it burst into flames, the sound of it like music to Ralph's ears.

He felt something cold on his neck, like a breeze from an open window, and he rolled to the side, knocking over some of the carefully set-out framed photographs. Whatever it had been swung over where he had been crouched, touched the rising flames from the book, and pulled back.

Ralph had barely seen it, his hand up in front of his face as a means of protection.

The book was crackling, burning brighter than any simple few drops of lighter fluid had any right to burn, but Ralph wasn't complaining. The pages lifted one by one into the growing blaze, curling over and igniting so that another might take its place.

Moonlight flooded the room.

Ralph blinked and then blinked again.

The room was empty.

The darkness was gone.

Ralph pulled himself into a sitting position and waited, watching the pages burn.

Eventually, the carpet alongside the book was burning.

Ralph got to his feet and staggered out onto the landing. There had been no sign of Phil Casimeer amidst the wreckage of his friend's bedroom.

Minutes later, as he slumped back into the old Fairlane, wincing at the squashing feeling between his legs, Ralph looked back at the house. The glow in the bedroom would take a while before it caught fully he didn't think there was any chance of it going out.

At least that made him feel good.

The clock in the car registered 12:40.

It would probably be too late to call Stephanie at her sister's when he got home. But Ralph didn't think that mattered. Better late than never. And that was something that Ralph just didn't want to think about.

Peter Tremayne

Those That Trespass

When he's not writing, Peter Berresford Ellis teaches law in London, England. Under his pseudonym, PETER TREMAYNE, he writes mysteries involving Sister Fidelma, whose appearances are sought by readers around the world. He conceived the idea of Sister Fidelma, a strong-willed seventh-century Celtic lawyer, to demonstrate for his students that women could be legal advocates under the Irish system of law, little knowing what impact his novel would have on the historical mystery subgenre. Sister Fidelma has since appeared in eight novels, the most recent being *The Spider's Web,* and many short stories, which have been collected in the book *Hemlock at Vespers and Other Sister Fidelma Mysteries.* He has also written, under his own name, more than twenty-five books on history, biography, and Irish and Celtic mythology. A native of Coventry, England, he has written a column for the *Irish Democrat* since 1987. This story first appeared in Volume II of *Chronicles of Crime.*

Those That Trespass

Peter Tremayne

The matter is clear to me. I cannot understand why the Abbot should be bothered to send you here."

Father Febal was irritable and clearly displeased at the presence of the advocate in his small church, especially an advocate in the person of the attractive, red-haired religieuse who sat before him in the stuffy vestry. In contrast to her relaxed, almost gentle attitude, he exuded an attitude of restlessness and suspicion. He was a short, swarthy man with pale, almost cadaverous features; the stubble of his beard, though shaven, was blue on his chin and cheeks and his hair was dark like the color of a raven's wing. His eyes were deep-set but dark and penetrating. When he expressed his irritability his whole body showed his aggravation.

"Perhaps it is because the matter is as unclear to the Abbot as it appears clear to you," Sister Fidelma replied in an innocent tone. She was unperturbed by the aggressive attitude of the priest.

Father Febal frowned; his narrowed eyes scanned her face rapidly, seeking out some hidden message in her features. However, Fidelma's face remained a mask of unaffected candor. He compressed his lips sourly.

"Then you can return to the Abbot and report to him that he has no need for concern."

Fidelma smiled gently. There was a hint of a shrug in the position of her shoulders.

"The Abbot takes his position as father of his flock very seriously. He would want to know more details of this tragedy before he could be assured that he need not concern himself in the matter. As the matter is so clear to you, perhaps you will explain it to me?"

Father Febal gazed at the religieuse, hearing for the first time the note of cold determination in her soft tones.

He was aware that Sister Fidelma was not merely a religieuse but a qualified advocate of the Brehon law courts of the five kingdoms. Furthermore, he knew that she was the young sister of King Colgú of Cashel himself, otherwise he might have been more brusque in his responses to the young woman. He hesitated a moment or two and then shrugged indifferently.

"The facts are simple. My assistant, Father Ibor, a young and indolent man, went missing the day before yesterday. I had known for some time that there had been something troubling him, something distracting him from his priestly duties. I tried to talk to him about it but he refused to be guided by me. I came to the church that morning and found that the golden crucifix from our altar and the silver chalice, with which we dispense the communion wine, were both missing. Once I found that Father Ibor had also vanished from our small community here, it needed no great legal mind to connect the two events. He had obviously stolen the sacred objects and fled."

Sister Fidelma inclined her head slowly. "Having come to this conclusion, what did you do then?"

"I immediately organized a search. Our little church here is attended by Brother Finnlug and Brother Adag. I called upon them to help me. Before entering the order, Finnlug was master huntsman to the Lord of Maine, an excellent tracker and huntsman. We picked up the trail of Ibor and followed it to the woods nearby. We were only a short distance into the woods when we came across his body. He was hanging from the branch of a tree with the cord of his habit as a noose."

Sister Fidelma was thoughtful. "And how did you interpret this sight?" she asked quietly.

Father Febal was puzzled. "How should I interpret this sight?" he demanded.

Fidelma's expression did not change.

"You tell me that you believed that Father Ibor had stolen the crucifix and chalice from the church and run off."

"That is so."

"Then you say that you came across him hanging on a tree."

"True again."

"Having stolen these value items and run off, why would he hang himself? There seems some other illogic in this action."

Father Febal did not even attempt to suppress a sneer.

"It should be as obvious to you as it was to me."

"I would like to hear what you thought." Fidelma did not rise to his derisive tone.

Father Febal smiled thinly.

"Why, Father Ibor was overcome with remorse. Knowing that we would track him down, realizing how heinous his crime against the Church was, he gave up to despair and pronounced his own punishment. He therefore hanged himself. In fact, so great was his fear that we would find him still alive, he even stabbed himself as he was suffocating in the noose, the knife entering his heart."

"He must have bled a lot from such a wound. Was there much blood on the ground?"

"Not as I recall." There was distaste in the priest's voice, as if he felt the religieuse was unduly occupied with gory detail. "Anyway, the knife lay on the ground below the body where it had fallen from his hand."

Fidelma did not say anything for a long while. She remained gazing thoughtfully at the priest. Father Febal glared back defiantly, but it was he who dropped his eyes first.

"Was Father Ibor such a weak young man?" Fidelma mused softly.

"Of course. What else but weakness would have caused him to act in this manner?" demanded the priest.

"So, you recovered both the crucifix and chalice from his person, then?"

A frown crossed Father Febal's features as he hesitated a moment. He made a curiously negative gesture with one hand.

Fidelma's eyes widened and she bent forward.

"You mean that you did not recover the missing items?" she pressed sharply.

"No," admitted the priest.

"Then this matter is not at all clear," she observed grimly. "Surely, you cannot expect the Abbot to rest easy in his mind when these items have not been recovered? How can you be so sure that it was Father Ibor who stole them?"

Fidelma waited for an explanation but none was forthcoming.

"Perhaps you had better tell me how you deem this matter is clear then?" Her voice was acerbic. "If I am to explain this clarity to the Abbot, I must also be clear in my own mind. If Father Ibor felt that his apprehension was inevitable and he felt constrained to inflict the punishment of death on himself when he realized the nearness of your approach, what did he do with the items he had apparently stolen?"

"There is one logical answer," muttered Father Febal without conviction.

"Which is?"

"Having hanged himself, some wandering thief happened by and took the items with him before we arrived."

"And there is evidence of that occurrence?"

The priest shook his head reluctantly.

"So that is just your supposition?" Now there was just a hint of derision in Fidelma's voice.

"What other explanation is there?" demanded Father Febal in annoyance.

Fidelma cast a scornful glance at him.

"Would you have me report this to the Abbot? That a valuable crucifix and a chalice have been stolen from one of his churches and a priest has been found hanged but there is no need to worry?"

Father Febal's features grew tight.

"I am satisfied that Father Ibor stole the items and took his own life in a fit of remorse. I am satisfied that someone then stole the items after Ibor committed suicide."

"But I am not," replied Fidelma bitingly. "Send Brother Finnlug to me."

Father Febal had risen automatically in response to the commanding tone in her voice. Now he hesitated at the vestry door.

"I am not used . . ." he began harshly.

"I am not used to being kept waiting." Fidelma's tone was icy as she cut in, turning her head away from him in dismissal. Father Febal blinked and then banged the door shut behind him in anger.

Brother Finnlug was a wiry-looking individual; his sinewy body, tanned by sun and wind, proclaimed him to be more a man used to being out in all sorts of weather than sheltering in the cloisters of some abbey. Fidelma greeted him as he entered the vestry.

"I am Fidelma of . . ."

Brother Finnlug interrupted her with a quick, friendly grin. "I know well who you are, lady," he replied. "I saw you and your brother, Colgú the King, many times hunting in the company of my Lord of Maine."

"Then you know that I am also an advocate of the courts and that you are duty bound to tell me the truth?"

"I know that much. You are here to inquire about the tragic death of Father Ibor." Brother Finnlug was straightforward and friendly in contrast to his superior.

"Why do you call it a tragic death?"

"Is not all death tragic?"

"Did you know Father Ibor well?"

The former huntsman shook his head. "I knew little of him. He was a young man, newly ordained and very unsure of himself. He was only here about a month."

"But Father Febal has been here for some years?"

"Father Febal has been a priest here for seven years. I came here a year ago and Brother Adag has been here a little more than that."

"I presume that the members of your little community were on good terms with one another?"

Brother Finnlug frowned slightly and did not reply.

"I mean, I presume that there was no animosity between the four of you?" explained Fidelma.

Finnlug's features wrinkled in an expression which Fidelma was not able to interpret.

"To be truthful, Father Febal liked to emphasize his seniority over us. I believe he entered the Church from some noble family and does not forget it."

"Was that attitude resented?"

"Not by me. I was in service to the Lord of Maine. I am used to being given orders and to obeying them. I know my place."

Was there a slight note of bitterness there? Fidelma wondered.

"If I recall rightly, the Lord of Maine was a generous man and those in his service were well looked after. It must have been a wrench for you to leave such an employer to enter religious life?"

Brother Finnlug grimaced.

"Spiritual rewards are often richer than temporal ones. But, as I say, I have been used to service. The same may be said for Brother Adag, who was once a servant to another lord. But he is somewhat of a simpleton." The monk touched his forehead. "They say such people are blessed of God."

"Did Father Ibor get on well with Father Febal?"

"Ah, that I can't say. He was a quiet young man. Kept himself to himself. I do not think he liked Father Febal. I have seen resentment in his eyes."

"Why would he be resentful? Father Febal was the senior of your community. Father Ibor should have recognized his authority without question."

The monk shrugged.

"All I can say is that he was hostile to Father Febal's authority."

"Why do you think he stole the items from the church?" Fidelma asked the question sharply.

Brother Finnlug's expression did not alter. He simply spread his arms.

"Who can say what motivates a person to such actions? Who can know the deep secrets of men's hearts?"

"That is what I am here to discover," Fidelma replied dryly. "Surely, you must have an idea? Even to hazard a guess?"

"What does Father Febal say?"

"Does it matter what he says?"

"I would have thought that he was closer to Father Ibor than either Brother Adag or myself."

"Closer? Yet you said there was hostility between them."

"I did not mean close in the manner of friends. But they were priests together. Of similar social backgrounds, unlike Adag and I. As brothers of this community, our task was more like servants in this church rather than the equals of Fathers Febal and Ibor."

"I see." Fidelma frowned thoughtfully. "I am sure the Abbot will be distressed to learn that this is the way your community is governed. We are all servants of God and all one under His Supreme Power."

"That is not exactly the Faith which Father Febal espouses." There was clearly bitterness in his voice.

"So you do not know why Ibor might have stolen the items?"

"They were items of great value. They would never be poor on the proceeds of that wealth."

"They?"

"I mean, whoever stole the items."

"You have a doubt that Father Ibor stole them, then?"

"You are sharp, Sister. Alas, I do not have the precise way with words that you do."

"Why do you think Father Ibor hanged himself having fled with these valuable items?"

"To avoid capture?"

"Your reply is in the form of a question. You mean that you are not sure of this fact either?"

Brother Finnlug shrugged. "It is difficult for me to say. I cannot understand why a priest should take his life in any event. Surely no priest would commit such a sin?"

"Would you say that you cannot be sure that Father Ibor took his life?"

Brother Finnlug was startled. "Did I say that?"

"You implied it. Tell me, in your own words, what happened during the last two days. Had there been any tension between Ibor and Febal or any one else?"

Finnlug set his jaw firmly and stared at her for a moment.

"I did hear Father Ibor arguing the night before he disappeared."

Fidelma leaned forward encouragingly.

"Arguing? With Father Febal?"

Brother Finnlug shook his head.

"I cannot be sure. I passed his cell and heard his voice raised. The other voice was quiet and muffled. It was as if Father Ibor had lost his temper but the person he was arguing with was in control."

"You have no idea who this other person was?"

"None."

"And you heard nothing of the substance of the argument?"

"I caught only a few words here and there."

"And what were these words?"

"Nothing that makes sense. Ibor said: 'It is the only way.' Then he paused, and after the other person said something, he replied: 'No, no, no. If it has to end, I shall not be the one to end it.' That was all I heard."

Fidelma was quiet as she considered the matter.

"Did you interpret anything from these words, especially in the light of what subsequently happened?"

Brother Finnlug shook his head.

The door of the vestry suddenly opened and Father Febal stood on the threshold; his features wore a peculiar look of satisfaction. He was clearly a man who had heard some news which pleased him.

"We have found the thief who took the crucifix and chalice from Father Ibor," he announced.

Brother Finnlug rose swiftly to his feet. His eyes flickered from Father Febal to Sister Fidelma. Fidelma saw something in his eyes and could not quite interpret the expression. Was it fear?

"Bring the thief forth," she instructed calmly, remaining seated.

Father Febal shook his head. "That would be impossible."

"Impossible?" asked Fidelma with a dangerous note to her voice.

"The thief is dead."

"You'd best explain," Fidelma invited. "In detail. Does this thief have a name?"

Father Febal nodded. "Téite was her name."

There was a deep intake of breath from Brother Finnlug.

"I take it that you knew her, Brother Finnlug?" Fidelma turned her head inquiringly.

"We all did," replied Father Febal shortly.

"Who was she?"

"A young girl who lived not far from our community in the forest. She was a seamstress. She sewed garments for our community. She also laundered clothes for us."

"Where was she found and how was she identified as the thief?"

"Her cabin is within a short distance of where we found Father Ibor," explained the priest. "I understand from Brother Adag that she had picked up some garments from the community, and when she did not return with them this morning, as she had arranged, Brother Adag went to her cabin and found her . . ."

Fidelma raised a hand to silence him.

"Let Brother Adag come forth and tell me his story in his own words. It is proper that I hear this matter at first hand. You and Brother Finnlug may wait outside."

Father Febal looked uncomfortable.

"I think that you had better be warned, Sister."

"Warned?" Fidelma's head came up quickly to stare at the priest.

"Brother Adag is slightly simple in nature. In many ways his mind has not matured into adulthood. His role in our community is to do simple manual tasks. He . . . how shall I explain it? . . . has a child's mind."

"It might be refreshing to speak with one who has remained a child and not developed the contrived attitudes of an adult." Fidelma smiled thinly. "Bring him hither."

Brother Adag was a handsome youth, but clearly one who was used to taking orders rather than thinking for himself. His eyes were rounded and seemed to hold an expression of permanent innocence; of inoffensive naiveté. His hands were calloused and showed that he was also a man used to manual work.

"You found the body of the woman, Téite, in her cabin, so I am told?"

The young man drew his brows together as if giving earnest consideration to the question before answering.

"Yes, Sister. When she did not arrive here at midday, with some garments which she had collected the day before and promised to deliver, Father Febal sent me to fetch them. I went to her cabin and she was lying stretched on the floor. There was blood on her clothing. She had been stabbed several times."

"Ah? So Father Febal sent you to her cabin?"

The youth nodded slowly.

"How old was this woman, Téite? Did you know her?"

"Everyone knew her, Sister, and she was eighteen years and three months of age."

"You are very exact." Fidelma smiled at his meticulous diction, as if he considered each word almost before he uttered it.

"Téite told me her age and, as you ask me for it, I told you." It was a simple statement of fact.

"Was she pretty?"

The youth blushed a little. He dropped his eyes.

"Very pretty, Sister."

"You liked her?" pressed Fidelma.

The young man seemed agitated. "No. No, I didn't," he protested. His face was now crimson.

"Why ever not?"

"It is the Father's rule."

"Father Febal's rule?"

Brother Adag hung his head and did not reply.

"Rule or not, you still liked her. You may tell me."

"She was kind to me. She did not make fun like the others."

"So, what persuaded you that she had stolen the crucifix and chalice from Father Ibor?"

The young brother turned an ingenuous look upon her. "Why, the chalice was lying by the side of her body in the cabin."

Fidelma hid her surprise.

"The chalice only?" She swallowed hard. "Why would someone enter her cottage, kill her and leave such a valuable item by the body?"

Brother Adag clearly did not understand the point she was making. He said nothing.

"What did you do after you found the body?" she continued after a pause.

"Why, I came to tell Father Febal."

"And left the chalice there?"

Brother Adag sniffed disparagingly.

"I am not stupid. No, I brought it with me. Father Febal has been searching for it these last two days. I brought it back to Father Febal for safekeeping. I even searched for the crucifix but could not find it there."

"That is all, Adag. Send Father Febal in to me," Fidelma instructed the youth.

The priest entered a moment later and sat down before Fidelma without waiting to be asked.

"A sad tale," he muttered. "But at least the matter should be cleared up to your satisfaction now. You may return to give your report to the Abbot."

"How well did you know this woman, Téite?" asked Fidelma, without commenting.

Father Febal raised his eyebrows a moment and then sighed.

"I have known her since she was a small girl. I went to administer the last rites when her mother died. Téite had barely reached the age of choice then. However, she had a talent with a needle and therefore was able to make a good living. She has lived within the forest these last four years to my knowledge and often repaired or made garments for our community."

"Did Father Ibor know her?"

Febal hesitated and then gave an odd dismissive gesture with his hand.

"He was a young man. Young men are often attracted to young women."

Fidelma glanced at the priest curiously.

"So Father Ibor was attracted to the girl?" she asked with emphasis.

"He was in her company more than I found to be usual. I had occasion to reprimand him."

"Reprimand him? That sounds serious."

"I felt that he was neglecting his duties to be with the girl."

"Are you telling me that there was a relationship between Father Ibor and this girl?"

"I am not one to judge such a matter. I know only that they were frequently in one another's company during the past few weeks, almost since the time he arrived at our little community. I felt that he was ignoring his obligation to his community. That is all."

"Did he resent your admonition?"

"I really have no idea whether he resented my telling him or not. That was not my concern. My concern was to bring him to an awareness of what was expected of him in this community."

"You did not have an argument about it?"

"An argument? I am . . . I *was* his superior, and when I told him of my concern that should have been an end to the matter."

"Clearly it was not an end to it," observed Fidelma.

Father Febal gave her an angry look. "I do not know what you mean."

"The events that have unfolded since you told Father Ibor that he was spending too much time with Téite have demonstrated that it was not an end to the matter," Fidelma pointed out coldly. "Or do you have some other interpretation of these events?"

Father Febal hesitated. "You are right. You are implying that the two of them were in the plot to steal the artifacts from the church and, having done so, Father Ibor was overcome with remorse and killed himself . . ." The priest's eyes suddenly widened. "Having killed the girl first," he added.

Fidelma reflectively stroked the side of her nose with a forefinger.

"It is an explanation," she conceded. "But it is not one that I particularly favor."

"Why not?" demanded the priest.

"The hypothesis would be that the young priest was so enamored of the girl that they decided to run away, stealing the valuable objects as a means of securing themselves from want and poverty. We would also have to conclude that, having reached as far as the girl's cabin, the young priest is overcome with remorse. He quarrels with the girl and stabs her to death. Then, leaving the precious chalice by her body, yet curiously hiding the crucifix, he wanders into the forest and, after traveling some distance, he decides he is so distressed that he hangs himself. Furthermore, while hanging, suffocating to death, he is able to take out a knife and stab himself through the heart."

"What is wrong with that surmise?"

Fidelma smiled thinly. "Let us have Brother Adag back here again. You may stay, Father Febal."

The ingenuous young monk stood looking from Fidelma to Father Febal with unstudied innocence.

"I am told that it was you who saw Téite when she came to the community yesterday?"

The boy was thoughtful.

"Yes. It is my task to gather the clothes that need washing or mending and prepare a bundle for Téite."

"And this you did yesterday morning?"

"Yes."

"Téite collected them? These were garments for sewing?"

"And two habits for washing. Father Febal and Brother Finnlug had given me . . . They had been torn and one bloodied in the search for Father Ibor."

"Let me be sure of this," interrupted Fidelma. "Téite collected them yesterday morning?"

Brother Adag looked across at Father Febal, dropped his eyes, and shifted his weight from one foot to another.

"Yes, yesterday morning."

"You are sure that she collected them after the search had been made for Father Ibor then?"

"Yes; Father Ibor was found on the day before."

"Think carefully," snapped Father Febal irritated. "Think again."

The young monk flushed and shrugged helplessly.

Father Febal sniffed in annoyance.

"There you are, Sister, you see that little credit may be placed on this simpleton's memory. The clothes must have been taken before we found Father Ibor."

The young monk whirled around. For a moment Fidelma thought that he was going to attack Father Febal for both hands came up, balled into clenched fists. But he kept them tight against his chest, in a defensive attitude. His face was red and there was anger in his eye.

"Simple I may be but at least I cared for Téite." There was a sob in his voice.

Father Febal took an involuntary step backward.

"Who did not care for Téite?" Fidelma prompted gently. "Father Ibor?"

"Of course he did not care. But she cared for him. She loved him. Not like . . ."

The youth was suddenly silent.

"I would take no notice of this boy's foolishness, Sister," Father Febal interposed blandly. "We all know what happened."

"Do we? Since we are talking of people being attracted to this young girl, was Brother Finnlug attracted to her?"

"Finnlug?" Brother Adag grimaced dismissively. "He has no time for women."

Father Febal looked pained. "Brother Finnlug has several faults. Women were certainly not one of them."

"Faults?" pressed Fidelma with interest. "What faults does he have then?"

"Alas, if only he had the gift of spirituality we would be compensated. He is of use to us only in his ability to hunt and gather food for our table. He is not suited for this religious life. Now, I think we have spoken enough. Let us call a halt to this unhappy affair before things are said that may be regretted."

"We will end it only when we discover the truth of the matter," replied Fidelma firmly. "Truth is never to be regretted." She turned to the youth. "I know you liked the girl Téite. Yet now she is dead and has been murdered. Father Febal's rule does not apply now. You owe it to your feelings for her to tell us the truth."

The boy stuck out his chin. "I am telling the truth."

"Of course you are. You say that Father Ibor did not like Téite?"

"He did not love her as I did."

"And how did Téite feel to Ibor?"

"She was blinded by Father Ibor's cleverness. She thought that she loved him. I overheard them. He told her to stop . . . stop pestering, that was his word . . . stop pestering him. She thought that she loved him just as Father Febal thought that he loved her."

The priest rose angrily. "What are you saying, boy?" he thundered. "You are crazy!"

"You cannot deny that you told her that you loved her," Brother Adag replied, not intimidated by the priest's anger. "I overheard you arguing with her on the day before Father Ibor died."

Father Febal's eyes narrowed.

"Ah, now you are not so stupid that you forget times and places and events. The boy cannot be trusted, Sister. I would discount his evidence."

"I loved Téite and can be trusted!" cried Brother Adag.

"I did not love her . . ." Father Febal insisted. "I do not love anyone."

"A priest should love all his flock," smiled Fidelma in gentle rebuke.

"I refer to the licentious love of women. I merely looked after Téite when her mother died. Without me she would not have survived."

"But you felt, perhaps, that she owed you something?"

Father Febal scowled at her.

"We are not here to speak of Téite but the crime of Father Ibor."

"Crime? No, I think that we are here to speak of a crime committed against him rather than by him."

Father Febal paled. "What do you mean?"

"Téite was murdered. But she was not murdered by Father Ibor. Nor was she responsible for stealing the crucifix nor chalice, which was found so conveniently by her body."

"How have you worked this out?"

"Send for Brother Finnlug. Then we may all discuss the resolution of this matter."

They sat in the small vestry facing her: Father Febal, Brother Finnlug, and Brother Adag. Their faces all wore expressions of curiosity.

"I grant that people behave curiously," began Fidelma. "Even at the best of times their behavior can be strange, but I doubt that they would behave in the manner that is presented to me."

She smiled, turning to each of them in turn.

"What is your solution to this matter?" sneered the priest.

"Certainly it would not be one where the murder victim appears alive and well after the murderer has hanged himself."

Father Febal blinked. "Adag must be mistaken."

"No. Father Ibor and the artifacts vanished the day before yesterday. You immediately raised the alarm. Brother Finnlug tracked Ibor through the forest and you found him hanging from a tree. Isn't that right?"

"Quite right."

"Had he killed Téite, as is now being suggested, before he hanged himself, she could not have come to the community yesterday noon to pick up the garments that needed sewing."

"Why do you discount the fact that Adag might be confused about the day?"

"Because he gave Téite two habits that had been torn and bloodied in the search for Father Ibor, those worn by you and Finnlung when you found him hanging on the tree. Doubtless they will be found in her cabin to prove the point." Fidelma paused. "Am I to presume that no one thought to tell the girl that Ibor had just been discovered having hanged himself? She did think she was in love with him?"

"I did not see the girl," Father Febal replied quickly. "Brother Adag did."

"And Brother Adag admits that he loved Téite," added Brother Finnlug cynically.

The young man raised his head defiantly.

"I do not deny it. But she didn't return my love, she loved Father Ibor who rejected her."

"And that made you angry?" asked Fidelma.

"Yes. Very angry!" replied Brother Adag vehemently.

Brother Finnlug turned to gaze at his companion in suspicion. "Angry enough to kill them both?" he whispered.

"No," Fidelma replied before Brother Adag could put in his denial. "Ibor and Téite were not killed in anger, but in cold blood. Weren't they, Brother Finnlug?"

Brother Finnlug turned sharply to her, his eyes suddenly dead. "Why would I know that, Sister Fidelma?"

"Because you killed them both," she said quietly.

"That's nonsense! Why would I do that?" exploded the monk, after a moment's shocked silence.

"Because when you stole the crucifix and chalice from the church, you were discovered by Father Ibor. You had to kill him. You stabbed him in the heart and then took the body to the forest where you concocted a suicide by hanging. Then you realized the knife wound could not be hidden and so you left the knife lying by his body. As if anyone, hanging by a cord from a tree, would be able to take out a knife and stab themselves in the heart. How, incidentally, was the poor man able to climb to the branch to hang himself? No one has reported to me any means whereby he could have climbed up. Think of the effort involved. The body was placed there by someone else."

She gazed at Father Febal who was deep in thought. He shook his head, denying he could offer an explanation.

Fidelma returned her gaze to Brother Finnlug. "You concocted an elaborate plan to deceive everyone as to what had truly happened."

There was a tension in the vestry now.

"You are insane," muttered Brother Finnlug.

Fidelma smiled gently.

"You were huntsman to the Lord of Maine. We have already discussed what a generous man he was to those in his service. None went in want, not even when the harvest was bad. When I asked you what reason you had to leave such a gainful employer, you said it was because of your spiritual convictions. Do you maintain that? That you rejected the temporal life for the spiritual life?"

Father Febal was gazing at Brother Finnlug in bemusement. The monk was silent.

"You also revealed to me, unwittingly perhaps, your resentment at the structure of this community. It it was a spiritual life you wanted, this was surely not it, was it?"

Father Febal intervened softly. "The truth was that Finnlug was dismissed by the Lord of Maine for stealing and we took him in here."

"What does that prove?" demanded Finnlug.

"I am not trying to prove anything. I will tell you what you did. You had initially hoped to get away with the robbery. The motive was simple, as you told me; the sale of those precious artifacts would make you rich for life. That would appease your resentment that others had power and riches but you did not. As I have said, Ibor discovered you and you stabbed him and took his body to the forest. When you returned, you realized that you had his blood on your clothing.

"The theft was now discovered and Father Febal sought your help. The blood was not noticed. Maybe you put on a cloak to disguise it. You, naturally, led him to Father Ibor's body. Everything was going as you planned. Father Ibor had been blamed for the theft. Now Father Febal was led to believe that Ibor must have killed himself in a fit of remorse. Even the fact that Ibor had been stabbed was explained. The fact that there was little blood on the ground did not cause any questions. You could pretend that the bloodstains were received in the search for Ibor. Perhaps you, Finnlug, came up with the idea that the missing crucifix and chalice had been taken by some robber.

"The following day Téite, unaware, came to collect the sewing and washing. Adag had gathered the washing as usual, including your habit, the bloodstained one. You had not meant the girl to have it. You hurried to her cottage to make sure she did not suspect. Perhaps you had made your plan even before you went there? You killed her and placed the chalice by her side. After all, the crucifix was such as would still give you wealth and property. It was known that Téite and Ibor had some relationship. Everyone would think the worst. All you had to do was return and bide your time until you could leave the community without arousing suspicion."

Brother Finnlug's face was white.

"You can't prove it," he whispered without conviction.

"Do I need to? Shall we go to search for the crucifix? Will you tell us where it is . . . or shall I tell you?" She stood up decisively as if to leave the room.

Brother Finnlug groaned, raising his hands to his head.

"All right, all right. It is true. You know it is still hidden in my cell. It was my chance to escape . . . to have some wealth, a good life."

Father Febal walked slowly with Fidelma to the gate of the complex of buildings which formed the community.

"How did you know where Brother Finnlug had hidden the crucifix?" he asked.

Sister Fidelma glanced at the grave-looking priest and suddenly allowed a swift mischievous grin to flit across her features.

"I didn't," she confessed.

Father Febal frowned. "How did you know then . . . ? Know it was Finnlug and what he had done?" he demanded.

"It was only an instinct. Certainly it was a deduction based on the facts, such as they were. But had Brother Finnlug demanded that I prove my accusation, I do not think I would have been able to under the strictures of the proceedings of a court of law. Sometimes, in this business of obtaining proof, more depends on what the guilty person thinks you know and believes that you can prove than what you are actually able to prove. Had Brother Finnlug not confessed, I might not have been able to clear up this business at all."

Father Febal was still staring at her aghast as she raised her hand in farewell and began to stride along the road in the direction of Cashel.

Phil Lovesey

Blitzed

PHIL LOVESEY is a second-generation crime writer, being the son of award-winning Peter Lovesey. A former advertising copywriter, he is the author of three novels: *Ploughing Potter's Field, Death Duties,* and *When the Ashes Burn*. He has also published a number of short stories and is a regular contributor to *Ellery Queen's Mystery Magazine*. This story first appeared in the June issue of that magazine.

Blitzed

Phil Lovesey

"I wish to confess to murdering my husband."

The harassed Desk Sergeant nodded sagely at the old woman. It was always the bloody same. The cranks and crazies seemed to deliberately wait for his shift to have their fun. He sighed heavily. "Very good, Mrs. . . ."

"Parker. Muriel Parker." The accent was home counties, the slightly powdered face bright, alert.

"And can you tell us the name of your G.P., love?" Standard procedure, he'd most likely discover the poor old dear had absconded from the local twilight home for the bewildered.

"I fail to see the relevance," Muriel replied. "I'm here to confess to a major crime, and I demand to be treated with some civility." Her eyes held his defiantly. "Now run along and fetch DCI Jessop. Quickly. I haven't got all day!"

The Desk Sergeant wearily picked up the phone, turning slightly from the neatly dressed woman and whispering, "Sorry to bother you, Guv. A gentle mental's just bowled up asking for you. . . . No, old girl, she is, spouting something about murdering her old man. . . . OK. . . . I'll tell her." He replaced the phone. "DCI Jessop's on his way down, Madam."

A tight-lipped smile betrayed the irritation. "I do have ears, Sergeant, and I find your manner most discourteous."

He blushed before taking down Muriel's details.

Five minutes later, DCI Jessop entered reception. Late fifties, portly, balding, well on the way to his second ulcer. "Mrs. Parker?"

She beamed and offered her hand, scrutinizing every line on his puffy face. "You don't look well," she said. "Not like the newspaper photograph at all."

"Mrs. Parker, I don't mean to be rude but the Sergeant told me . . ."

"I've come to confess to murder," she confirmed, chin jutting proudly.

Jessop shot the grinning Sergeant a filthy look. "Do you want to come with me, love? Have a cup of tea, yeah?"

"Very kind, thank you."

He led Muriel toward a side door, stopping to collect a piece of note-paper from the winking Sergeant. He read it and sighed, throwing his eyes to the nicotine-stained ceiling. Gilbert and Sullivan had it bang to rights, his bloody lot certainly wasn't a happy one.

They entered a small interview room stinking of cigarettes and disinfectant. Muriel sat down, eyes twinkling, face as bright as a button, the total antithesis of her world-beaten companion.

"Just like those dreadful little rooms in The Bill," she said excitedly. "And can I say, Inspector, what a pleasure it is to meet you at last."

Jessop rubbed his brow, attempting to massage away the near-permanent frown. Jesus, was it only ten in the morning? He placed the Sergeant's note gently on the scarred desk between them. "Mrs. Parker," he said slowly, trying to muster some empathy for the deluded old bat. "While you were waiting for me, Sergeant Stebbins . . ."

"I beg your pardon?"

"Stebbins," Jessop explained, raising his voice unnecessarily. "The Desk Sergeant."

"Frightful man," Muriel replied. "Very rude."

"Quite," Jessop agreed, anxious to move on. "Well he rang your house and spoke to your husband."

Muriel stared blankly back.

Jessop read from Stebbins' notes. "According to Mr. Parker, he's very much alive and wonders if you could pick up a bag of greengages while you're in town."

The old woman blushed a little. "Well, I couldn't possibly tell Albert the truth, could I? Shock'd most likely kill him."

"So you accept, Mrs. Parker, that you didn't actually murder your husband?"

"Albert?" She looked as confused as Jessop. "I never said I did. Did I?"

"But you told the Sergeant . . ."

"That I murdered my husband, yes."

"But he's alive, Mrs. Parker!"

She blinked twice, then smiled. "For goodness' sake!" she laughed. "You think I'd kill dear Albert!" The tiniest of chuckles escaped. "Oh dear me, Inspector!"

Jessop was ten seconds from the end of his tether. He rose to his tired feet. "Don't forget the fruit, Mrs. Parker," he said through gritted teeth.

But Muriel wasn't to be budged. "My first husband," she calmly announced. "I murdered Clive Upton, my first husband."

Jessop slumped back into the chair. What the hell, it was a slow crime day, the villains were still sleeping off the night before, he was out of the office and away from the paperwork. May as well listen to the old girl for a few minutes. "Clive Upton?" he repeated, trying to sound interested.

"Bastard, he was!" Muriel spat, surprising Jessop with the intensity. "Lazy, idle, two-timing; good-for-nothing little shi—"

"Mrs. Parker, please." Jessop suppressed a smile. He'd never heard such a sweet looking old lady swear before. "When exactly did you . . . ?"

"Kill the swine?"

Jessop nodded.

"Twenty-first October, nineteen forty-one. About midnight."

Jessop wished he hadn't given up smoking. Now would have been the perfect moment to reach for a B&H, light up, draw deeply on the brown poison and slowly drift a thousand mental miles from this ludicrous woman and the stifling room. Any minute now, he thought to himself, Jessop will barge in with details of the nuthouse she belongs in, and it's "Bye-bye Mrs. P." Entertaining while it lasted, anyway. "But it's nineteen ninety-seven, Mrs. Parker."

"So it's about time I told you the truth, Detective Chief Inspector Jessop."

He leaned forward conspiratorially. Playtime was over. "If I were you," he whispered. "I'd let sleeping dogs lie. If you've got away with it until now, then—"

"Inspector Jessop!" Muriel interrupted sharply. "I have no intention of any such thing. It's taken me a long time to find you and—"

"Me?"

"You, Inspector."

He leaned back, scrutinizing her carefully. Smartly dressed, neatly presented, honest face. Against all his instincts, he gave her one more chance. "I'm listening," he said gruffly. "Why me?"

She dismissed the question with one wave of her fragile hand. "It was during the Blitz," she said brightly. "I'd been married to Clive for six years. Childhood sweethearts, you know the thing."

Jessop wondered if he could be bothered with the inevitable history lesson.

"Clive failed all the service medicals because he was deaf in one ear. Looking back, I suspect he made the whole thing out to be a damned slight worse than it was. He wasn't the type to fall for his country."

"Sensible chap," Jessop replied, wondering if he'd feign deafness if he was married to the acid-tongued woman.

"Coward, more like," she hissed, eyes narrowing at the memory. "He became an Air Raid Patrol warden, walking the streets at night, checking the neighborhood for chinks."

"The Chinese?"

"Light," she snapped. "It was the blackout. Any escaping light would have given away our position to the Luftwaffe. So he was out most nights, while I was stuck inside on my own."

"Can't have been easy." Jessop observed the beginnings of a tear welling in Mrs. Parker's right eye.

"Then," she sighed. "The gossip started. Whispered words as I queued for rations. Young women, widowed by the war, missing their menfolk, giggling to each other, sniggering at what a wonderful job Clive had done in their bedrooms."

"I'm sorry," Jessop replied.

"It got worse, got so I could barely leave the house for the ridicule. A local girl was pregnant. It had to be Clive. One night, I followed him. Discreetly, at a distance, through the darkened streets. My heart raced with excitement and dread. I just had to know the truth for myself."

Muriel's voice cracked a little. "He went into a local girl's house. Let himself in, for Christ's sake! Didn't come out for an hour at least. I stood in the street and cried, really cried. Then, the sirens screamed. Thousands of feet above my head, the Germans began bombing the town."

Jessop found himself unintentionally absorbed, hanging on Muriel's every word, watching as she hung her frail head in shame. For many moments she sat perfectly still in the claustrophobic silence, Jessop still wondering why she'd chosen him to be sole witness to her confession.

At last she cleared her throat, looked up and continued. "There was so much rubble around, Inspector. The whole ghastly thing was so hideously easy." The watery eyes pleaded for forgiveness.

Jessop kept silent, heeding the memory of his own mother, who'd often weep quietly over long distant memories of the war. How she'd sit him down as if to divulge some ancient secret, then simply mist over with the pain of it all. And in truth, Jessop admitted, there was no way he could ever understand her terror. How could anyone born since the war? Foreign planes in their thousands dropping bombs on our homes? It just seemed too inconceivable.

Muriel blew her nose. "Of course Clive was shocked to see me standing there. The street was in chaos. Two houses had been hit. I knew I didn't have long before the emergency services arrived. I hit him in the face with a brick. Then again. Then again. He fell down, unconscious." Muriel's pained face appealed for understanding. "I dragged him toward the smoldering building, covered his body with rubble, then left. Running as fast as I could."

"Mrs. Parker," said Jessop gently. "Whatever happened, happened such a long time ago. You were upset, being bombed, I mean. . . ."

"I murdered my husband, Inspector."

"Was there a postmortem?"

She nodded. "They put it down to the blast. Four died in the house, and he was found where I left him, buried in the rubble outside. He died a hero. Should have been in a shelter, you see. They thought he was racing to help."

He smiled. "So he fell for his country after all?"

She returned it. "The curious thing, Inspector, is that they never found his hat."

Jessop felt the hairs on the back of his neck begin to rise. Hat? Tin hat? ARP hat? Good God, surely not . . . ? He watched as Mrs. Parker reached into her handbag and brought out an article clipped from the local newspaper.

"You, in your office, I believe?"

Jessop stared back at his own black and white image, beaming from the page, encouraging everyone to join Neighborhood Watch. He nodded.

Muriel touched his sleeve. He didn't pull back. "I knew it had to be you," she said softly. Her slender finger traced the photo, pointing to a black tin hat mounted on the back wall of Jessop's office. The letters ARP were still clearly visible. "Did your mother ever tell you the truth?"

Jessop shook his head. Could this really be happening? Would the trail end right here, after all these years? "She willed it to me after she died," he replied, a lump building at the back of his throat. "I'd often catch her cleaning it. It was one of her most treasured . . ." He trailed off, bewildered.

Muriel filled in the gaps. "After Clive died, the pregnant girl moved away and had a little boy, but never married. I moved too, but still kept in contact with some of my true friends. They told me the woman was happy, the child grew into a fine young man and joined the police. His name was Jessop, Neal Jessop."

Emotion began to flood through the shaking inspector.

Muriel stood, preparing to leave. "I saw the article quite by chance. It had to be you. The same smile, you see."

Jessop hid his face in his hands. "Clive Upton was my father?"

"And I murdered him. I'm truly sorry for that. Your father may have made a lousy husband, Inspector, but he also made a wonderful son. I thought you deserved to know that."

"But why tell me now?"

She pulled his hands from his head. "So there's no need to look anymore."

The door opened. Stebbins breezed in, stooping to whisper in his Guvnor's ear. "Not a thing on her. Clean as a whistle."

Jessop pulled himself together. "Thank you, Sergeant." He turned to Muriel. "And thank you, Mrs. Parker."

She smiled. "The least I could do after all this time."

Stebbins' confusion was obvious. "Shall I see Mrs. Parker out?" he offered.

"Before you do," Jessop replied. "Take her up to my office. There's an old tin hat on the wall that belongs to her. Will you make sure she gets it?"

Muriel shook Jessop warmly by the hand.

"After all," he smiled. "I don't think I need it anymore. And you'll be needing something to carry those greengages home in, won't you?"

Jeffery Deaver

For Services Rendered

HBO made a very good original movie from JEFFERY DEAVER's *A Maiden's Grave,* which became one more sign that Deaver's new authority as a writer is a given in mystery fiction. He's a best-seller who writes thoughtful, powerful novels in a serious but always entertaining way. There are some critics who believe that his short fiction is even better. He writes in virtually every mystery subgenre in his shorter pieces and imbues each one with his own special take on contemporary life. This story first appeared in the November issue of *Ellery Queen's Mystery Magazine.*

For Services Rendered

Jeffery Deaver

At first I thought it was me . . . but now I know for sure: My husband's trying to drive me crazy."

Dr. Harry Bernstein nodded and, after a moment's pause, dutifully noted his patient's words on the steno pad resting on his lap.

"I don't mean he's *irritating* me, driving me crazy that way—I mean he's making me question my sanity. And he's doing it on purpose."

Patsy Randolph, facing away from Harry on his leather couch, turned to look at her psychiatrist. Even though he kept his Park Avenue office quite dark during his sessions, he could see that there were tears in her eyes.

"You're very upset," he said in a kind tone.

"Sure, I'm upset," she said. "And I'm scared."

This woman, in her late forties, had been his patient for two months. She'd been close to tears several times during their sessions but had never actually cried. Tears are important barometers of emotional weather. Some patients go for years without crying in front of their doctors, and when the eyes begin to water, any competent therapist sits up and takes notice.

Harry studied Patsy closely as she turned away again and picked at a button on the cushion beside her thigh.

"Go on," he encouraged. "Tell me about it."

She snagged a Kleenex from the box beside the couch, dabbed at her eyes. But she did so carefully; as always, she wore impeccable makeup.

"Please," Harry said in a soft voice.

"It's happened a couple of times now," she began reluctantly. "Last night was the worst. I was lying in bed and I heard this voice. I couldn't really hear it clearly at first. Then it said . . ."

She hesitated. "It said it was my father's ghost."

Motifs in therapy didn't get any better than this, and Harry paid close attention.

"You weren't dreaming?"

"No, I was awake. I couldn't sleep and I'd gotten up for a glass of water. Then I started walking around the apartment. Just pacing. I felt frantic. I lay back in bed. And the voice—I mean, *Pete's* voice—said that it was my father's ghost."

"What did he say?"

"He just rambled on and on. Telling me about all kinds of things from my past. Incidents from when I was a girl. I'm not sure. It was hard to hear."

"And these were things your husband knew?"

"Not all of them." Her voice cracked. "But he could've found them out. Looking through my letters and my yearbooks."

"You're sure he was the one talking?"

"The voice sounded sort of like Peter's. Anyway, who else would it be?" She laughed, her voice nearly a cackle. "I mean, it could hardly be my father's ghost, now, could it?"

"Maybe he was just talking in his sleep."

She didn't respond for a minute. "See, that's the thing . . . He wasn't in bed. He was in the den, playing some video game."

Harry continued to take his notes.

"And you heard him from the den?"

"He must have been at the door . . . Oh, Doctor, it sounds ridiculous. I know it does. But I think he was kneeling at the door—it's right next to the bedroom—and was whispering."

"Did you go into the den? Ask him about it?"

"I walked to the door real fast, but by the time I opened it he was back at the desk." She looked at her hands and found she'd shredded the Kleenex. She glanced at Harry to see if he'd noticed the compulsive behavior, which of course he had, and then stuffed the tissue into the pocket of her expensive beige slacks.

"And then?"

"I asked him if he'd heard anything, any voices. And he looked at me like I was nuts and went back to his game."

"And that night you didn't hear anymore voices?"

"No."

Harry studied his patient. She'd been a pretty girl in her youth, Harry supposed, because she was a pretty woman now. Her face was sleek and she had the slightly upturned nose of a Connecticut socialite who debates long and hard about having rhinoplasty but never does. He recalled that Patsy'd told him her weight was never a problem; she'd hire a personal trainer whenever she gained five pounds. She'd said—with irritation masking secret pride—that men often tried to pick her up in bars and coffee shops.

He asked, "You say this's happened before? Hearing the voice?"

Another hesitation. "Maybe two or three times. All within the past couple of weeks."

"But why would Harry want to drive you crazy?"

Patsy, who'd come to Harry presenting with the classic symptoms of a routine midlife crisis, hadn't discussed her husband much yet. Harry knew he was good-looking, a few years younger than Patsy, not particularly ambitious. They'd been married for three years—second marriages for both of them—and they didn't seem to have many interests in common. But of course, that was just Patsy's version. The "facts" that are revealed in a therapist's office can be very fishy. Harry Bernstein worked very hard to be a human lie detector and his impression of the marriage was that there was much unspoken conflict between husband and wife.

Patsy considered his question. "I don't know. I was talking to Sally . . ." Harry remembered her mentioning Sally, her best friend. She was another Upper East Side matron—one of the ladies who lunch—and was married to the president of one of the biggest banks in New York. "She said that maybe Peter's jealous of me. I mean, look at us—I'm the one with the social life, I have the friends, I have the money . . ." He noticed a manic edge to her voice. She did, too, and controlled it. "I just don't *know* why he's doing it. But he is."

"Have you talked to him about this?"

"I tried. But naturally he denies everything." She shook her head and tears welled in her eyes again. "And then . . . the birds."

"Birds?"

Another Kleenex was snagged, used, and shredded. She didn't hide the evidence this time. "I have this collection of ceramic birds. Made by Boehm. Do you know about the company?"

"No."

"They're very expensive. They're German. Beautifully made. They were my parents'. When our father died, Steve and I split the inheritance, but he got most of the personal family heirlooms. That really hurt me. But I did get the birds."

Harry knew that her mother had died ten years ago and her father about three years ago. The man had been very stern and had favored Patsy's older brother, Stephen. He was patronizing to her all her life.

"I have four of them. There used to be five, but when I was twelve I broke one. I ran inside—I was very excited about something and I wanted to tell my father about it—and I bumped into the table and knocked one off. It broke. My father spanked me with a willow switch and sent me to bed without dinner."

Ah, an Important Event. Harry made a note but didn't pursue the incident any further at the moment.

"And?"

"The morning after I heard my father's ghost for the first time . . ." Her voice grew harsh. "I mean, the morning after *Peter* started whispering to me . . . I found one of the birds broken. It was lying on the living room floor. I asked Peter why he'd done it—he knows how important they were to me—and he denied it. He said I must have been sleepwalking and did it myself. But I know I didn't. Peter had to've been the one." She'd slipped into her raw, irrational voice again.

Harry glanced at the clock. He hated the legacy of the psychoanalysts: the perfectly timed fifty-minute hour. There was so much more he wanted to delve into. But patients needed consistency and, according to the old school, discipline. He said, "I'm sorry but I see our time's up."

Dutifully, Patsy rose. Harry observed how disheveled she looked. Yes, her makeup had been very carefully applied, but the buttons on her blouse weren't done properly. Either she'd dressed in a hurry or hadn't paid attention. One of the straps on her expensive tan shoes wasn't hooked.

She rose. "Thank you, Doctor. . . . It's good just to be able to tell someone about this."

"We'll get everything worked out. I'll see you next week."

After Patsy had left the office, Harry Bernstein sat down at his desk. He spun slowly in his chair, gazing at his books—the *DSM-IV, The Psychopathology of Everyday Life*, the APA *Handbook of Neuroses*, volumes by Freud, Adler, Jung, Karen Horney, hundreds of others. Then out the window again, watching the late afternoon sunlight fall on the cars and taxis speeding north on Park Avenue.

A bird flew past.

He thought about the shattered ceramic sparrow from Patsy's childhood: What a significant session this had been.

Not only for his patient. But for him too.

Patsy Randolph—who had, until today, been just another mildly discontented middle-aged patient—represented a watershed event for Dr. Harold David Bernstein. He was in a position to change her life completely.

And in doing so, he could redeem his own.

Harry laughed out loud, spun again in the chair, like a child on a playground. Once, twice, three times.

A figure appeared in the doorway. "Doctor?" Miriam, his secretary, cocked her head, which was covered with fussy white hair. "Are you all right?"

"I'm fine. Why're you asking?"

"Well, it's just . . . I don't think I've heard you laugh for a long time. I don't think I've *ever* heard you laugh in your office."

Which was another reason to laugh. And he did.

She frowned, concern in her eyes.

Harry stopped smiling. He looked at her gravely. "Listen, I want you to take the rest of the day off."

She looked mystified. "But . . . it's quitting time, Doctor. I was going to—"

"Joke," he explained. "It was a joke. See you tomorrow."

Miriam eyed him cautiously, unable, it seemed, to shake the quizzical expression from her face. "You're sure you're all right?"

"I'm fine. Good night."

"Night, Doctor."

A moment later he heard the front door to the office click shut.

He spun around in his chair once more, reflecting: Patsy Randolph . . . I can save you and you can save me.

And Harry Bernstein was a man badly in need of saving.

Because he hated what he did for a living.

Not the business of helping patients with their mental and emotional problems—oh, he was a natural-born therapist. None better. What he hated was practicing Upper East Side psychiatry out of a stuffy office. It had been the last thing he'd ever wanted to do. But in his second year of Columbia Medical School, the tall, handsome student met the tall, beautiful assistant development director of the Museum of Modern Art. Harry and Linda were married before he started his internship. He moved out of his fifth-floor walkup near Harlem and into her townhouse on East Eighty-First. Within weeks she'd begun changing his life. Linda was a woman who had high aspirations for her man (very similar to Patsy, in whose offhand comment several weeks ago about her husband's lack of ambition Harry had seen reams of anger). Linda wanted money, she wanted to be on the regulars list to benefits at the Met, she wanted to be pampered at four-star restaurants in Eze and Monaco and Paris.

A studious, easygoing man from a modest suburb of New York, Harry knew that by listening to Linda he was headed in the wrong direction. But he was in love with her so he *did* listen. They bought a co-op in a high-rise on Madison Avenue and he hung up his shingle (well, a heavy brass plaque) outside this three-thousand-dollar-a-month office on Park and Seventy-Eighth Street.

At first Harry had worried about the astronomical bills they were amassing. But soon the money was flowing in. He had no trouble getting business; there's no lack of neuroses among the rich, and the insured, on the isle of Manhattan. He was also very good at what he did. His patients came and they liked him and so they returned weekly.

"Nobody understands me, sure we've got money but money isn't everything and the other day my housekeeper looks at me like I'm from outer space and it's not my fault and I get so angry when my mother wants to go shopping on my one day off and I think Samuel's seeing someone and I think my son's gay and I just cannot lose these fifteen pounds . . ."

Their troubles may have been plebeian, even laughably minor at times, but his oath, as well as his character, wouldn't let Harry minimize them. He worked hard to help his patients.

And all the while he neglected what he really wanted to do. Which was to treat severe mental cases. People who were paranoid schizophrenics, people with bipolar depression and borderline personalities—people who led sorrowful lives and couldn't hide from that sorrow with the money that Harry's patients had.

From time to time he volunteered at various clinics—particularly a small one in Brooklyn that treated homeless men and women—but with his Park Avenue caseload and his wife's regimen of social obligations there was no way he could devote much time to the practice. He'd wrestled with the thought of just chucking his practice and working at the clinic full-time. Of course, if he'd done that, his income would have dropped by ninety percent. He and Linda had had two children a couple of years after they'd gotten married—two sweet daughters whom Harry loved very much—and their needs, very expensive needs, private school sorts of needs, took priority over his personal contentment. Besides, as idealistic as he was in many ways, Harry knew that Linda would have left him in a flash if he'd quit his practice and started working full-time in Brooklyn.

But the irony was that even after Linda *did* leave him—for someone she'd met at one of the society benefits that Harry couldn't bear to attend— he hadn't been able to spend any more time at the clinic than he had when he'd been married. The debts Linda had run up while they were married were excruciating. His older daughter was in an expensive college, and his younger was on her way to Vassar next year.

Yet, out of the dozens of patients who whined about minor dissatisfactions, here came Patsy Randolph, a truly desperate patient . . . a woman telling him about ghosts, about her husband trying to drive her insane, a woman clearly on the brink.

A patient, at last, who would give Harry a chance to redeem his life.

That night he didn't bother with dinner. He came home and went straight into his den, where sat stacked in high piles a year's worth of professional journals that he'd never bothered to read since they dealt with serious psychiatric issues and didn't much affect the patients in his practice.

He kicked his shoes off and began sifting through them, taking notes. He found Internet sites devoted to psychotic behavior and he spent hours on-line, downloading articles that could help him with Patsy's situation.

Harry was rereading an obscure article in the *Journal of Psychoses*, which he'd been thrilled to find—it was the key to dealing with her case—when he sat up, hearing a shrill whistle. He'd been so preoccupied that he'd forgotten he'd put on the tea kettle for coffee. . . . But then he glanced out the window and realized that it wasn't the kettle at all. The sound was from a bird sitting on a branch nearby, singing. The hour was well past dawn.

At her next session Patsy looked worse than she had the week before. Her clothes weren't pressed. Her hair was matted and hadn't been shampooed for days, it seemed. Her white blouse was streaked with dirt and the collar was torn. Her skirt was rumpled, too, and there were runs in her stockings. Only her makeup was carefully done.

"Hello, Doctor," she said in a soft voice. She sounded timid.

"Hi, Patsy, come on in. . . . No, not the couch today. Sit across from me."

She hesitated. "Why?"

"I think we'll postpone our usual work and deal with this crisis. About the voices. I'd like to see you face-to-face."

"Crisis." She repeated the word warily as she sat in the comfortable arm-chair across from his desk. She crossed her arms, looked out the window—these were all body-language messages that Harry recognized well. They meant she was nervous and defensive.

"Now, what's been happening since I saw you last?" he asked.

She told him. There'd been more voices—her husband kept pretending to be the ghost of her father, whispering terrible things to her. What, Harry asked, had the ghost said? She answered: What a bad daughter she'd been, what a terrible wife she was now, what a shallow friend. Why didn't she just kill herself and quit bringing pain to everyone's life?

Harry jotted a note. "It was your father's voice?"

"Not my *father*," she said, her voice cracking with anger. "It was my *hus-band*, pretending to be my father. I told you that."

"Where was Peter when you heard him?"

She studied a bookshelf. "He wasn't exactly home."

"He wasn't?"

"No. He went out for cigarettes. But I figured out how he did it. He must've rigged up some kind of a speaker and tape recorder. Or maybe one of those walkie-talkie things." Her voice faded. "Peter's also a good mimic. You know, doing impersonations. So he could do *all* the voices."

"*All* of them?"

She cleared her throat. "There were more ghosts this time." Her voice rising again, manically. "My grandfather. My mother. Others. I don't even know who." Patsy stared at him for a moment, then looked down. She clicked her purse latch compulsively, then looked inside, took out her compact and lipstick. She stared at the makeup then put it away. Her hands were shaking.

Harry waited a long moment then asked, "Patsy . . . I want to ask you something."

"You can ask me anything, Doctor."

"Just assume—for the sake of argument—that Peter wasn't pretending to be the ghosts. Where else could they be coming from?"

She snapped, "You don't believe a word of this, do you?"

The most difficult part of being a therapist is making sure your patients know you're on their side while pursuing the truth. He said evenly, "It's cer-tainly possible what you're saying. But I think you should consider that there's another possibility."

"Which is?"

"That you did hear something—maybe your husband on the phone, maybe the TV, maybe the radio, but whatever it was had nothing to do with your father's ghost. You projected your own thoughts onto what you heard."

"You're saying it's all in my head."

"I'm saying that maybe the words themselves are originating in your subconscious. What do you think about that?"

She considered this for a moment. "I don't know. . . . It could be. I suppose that makes some sense."

Harry smiled. "That's good, Patsy. That's a good first step, admitting that."

She seemed pleased, a student who'd been given a gold star by a teacher.

Then the psychiatrist grew serious. "Now, one thing—when the voices talk about hurting yourself . . . you're not going to listen to them, are you?"

"No, I won't." She offered a brave smile. "Of course not."

"Good." He glanced at the clock. "I see our time's just about up, Patsy. I want you to do something. I want you to keep a diary of what the voices say to you."

"A diary? All right."

"Write down everything they say and in a month or so we'll go through it together."

She rose. Turned to him. "Maybe I should just ask one of the ghosts to come along to a session. . . . But then you'd have to charge me double, wouldn't you?"

He laughed. "See you next week."

At three o'clock the next morning, Harry was wakened by a phone call.

"Dr. Bernstein?"

"Yes?"

"I'm Officer Kavanaugh, with the police department."

Sitting up, trying to shake off his drowsiness, he thought immediately of Herb, a patient at the clinic in Brooklyn. The poor man, a mild schizophrenic who was completely harmless, was forever getting beat up because of his gruff, threatening manner.

But that wasn't the reason for the call.

"You're Mrs. Patricia Randolph's psychiatrist. Is that correct?" the officer continued.

His heart thudded hard. "Yes, I am. Is she all right?"

"We've had a call . . . We found her in the street outside her apartment. No one's hurt, but she's a bit hysterical."

"I'll be right there."

When he arrived at the Randolphs' apartment building, ten blocks away, Harry found Patsy and her husband in the front lobby. A uniformed policeman stood next to them.

Harry knew that the Randolphs were wealthy, but the building was much nicer than he'd expected. It was one of the luxurious high-rises that

Donald Trump had built in the eighties. There were penthouse triplexes selling for twenty million, Harry had read in the *Times*.

"Doctor," Patsy cried when she saw Harry. She ran to him. Harry was
careful about physical contact with his patients. He knew all about transference and countertransference—the perfectly normal attraction between
patients and their therapists—but contact had to be handled carefully. Harry
took Patsy by the shoulders so that she couldn't hug him and led her back to
the lobby couch.

"Mr. Randolph?" Harry asked, turning to him.

"That's right."

"I'm Harry Bernstein."

The men shook hands. Peter Randolph was very much what Harry was
expecting. He was a trim, athletic man of about forty. Handsome. His eyes
were angry and bewildered. He reminded Harry of a patient he'd treated
briefly—a man whose sole complaint was that he was having trouble main-
taining a life with a wife and two mistresses. Peter wore a burgundy silk
bathrobe and supple leather slippers.

"Would you mind if I spoke to Patsy alone?" Harry asked him.

"No. I'll be upstairs if you need me." He said this to both Harry and the
police officer.

Harry glanced at the cop, too, who also stepped away and let the doctor
talk to his patient.

"What happened?" Harry asked Patsy.

"The bird," she said, choking back tears.

"One of the ceramic birds?"

"Yes," she whispered. "He broke it."

Harry studied her carefully. She was in bad shape tonight. Hair stringy,
robe filthy, fingernails unclean. As in her session the other day, only her
makeup was normal.

"Tell me about what happened."

"I was asleep and then I heard this voice say, 'Run! You have to get out.
They're almost here. They're going to hurt you.' And I jumped out of bed
and ran into the living room and there—there was the Boehm bird. It was
broken. The robin. It was shattered and scattered all over the floor. I started
screaming—because I knew they were after me." Her voice rose. "The
ghosts . . . They . . . I mean, Peter was after me. I just threw on my robe and
ran."

"And what did Peter do?"

"He ran after me."

"But he didn't hurt you?"

She hesitated. "No." She looked around the cold, marble lobby with
paranoid eyes. "Well, what he did was, he called the police . . . But don't you
see? Peter didn't have any choice. He *had* to call the police. Isn't that what
somebody would normally do if their wife ran out of the apartment screaming? He had to shift suspicion away from him." Her voice faded.

Harry looked for signs of overmedication or drinking. He could see none. She looked around the lobby once more.

"Are you feeling better now?"

She nodded. "I'm sorry," she said. "Making you come all the way over here tonight."

"That's what I'm here for. . . . Tell me: You don't hear any voices now, do you?"

"No."

"And the bird? Could it have been an accident?"

She thought about this for a moment. "Well, Peter *was* asleep . . . Maybe I was looking at it earlier and left it on the edge of the table." She sounded perfectly reasonable. "Maybe the housekeeper did it."

The policeman looked at his watch and then ambled over. He asked, "Can I talk to you, Doctor?"

They stepped into a corner of the lobby.

"I'm thinking I oughta take her downtown," the cop said in a Queens drawl. "She was pretty outta control before. But it's your call. You think she's E.D.?"

Emotionally disturbed. That was the trigger diagnosis for involuntary commitment. If he said yes, Patsy would be taken off and hospitalized.

This was the critical moment. Harry debated.

I can help you and you can help me. . . .

He said to the cop, "Give me a minute."

He returned to Patsy, sat down next to her. "We have a problem. The police want to take you away. And if you claim that Peter's trying to drive you crazy or hurt you, the fact is, the judge just isn't going to believe you. And they're going to put you into custody."

"Me? *I'm* not doing anything! It's the voices! It's them . . . I mean, it's Peter."

"But they're not going to believe you. That's just the way it is. Now, you can go back upstairs and carry on with your life or they can take you downtown to the city hospital. And you don't want that. Believe me. Can you stay in control?"

She lowered her head to her hands. Finally she said, "Yes, Doctor, I can."

"Good. . . . Patsy, I want to ask you something else. I want to see your husband alone. Can I call him, have him come in?"

"Why?" she asked, her face dark with suspicion.

"Because I'm your doctor and I want to get to the bottom of what's bothering you."

She glanced at the cop. Gave him a dark look. Then she said to Harry, "Sure."

"Good."

After Patsy'd disappeared into the elevator car the cop said, "I don't know, Doctor. She seems like a nut case to me. Things like this . . . they can get real ugly. I've seen it a million times."

"She's got some problems, but she's not dangerous."

"You're willing to take that chance?"

After a moment he said, "Yes, I'm willing to take that chance."

"How was she last night, after I left?" Harry asked Peter Randolph the next morning. The two men sat in Harry's office.

"She seemed all right. Calmer." Peter sipped the coffee that Miriam had brought him. "What exactly is going on with her?"

"I'm sorry," Harry said, "I can't discuss the specifics of your wife's condition with you. Confidentiality."

Peter's eyes flared angrily for a moment. "Then why did you ask me here?"

"Because I need you to help me treat her. You do want her to get better, don't you?"

"Of course I do. I love her very much." He sat forward in the chair. "But I don't understand what's going on. She was fine until a couple of months ago—when she started seeing *you*, if you have to know the truth. Then things started to go bad."

"When people see therapists they sometimes confront things that they never had to deal with. I think that's Patsy's situation. She's getting close to some important issues. And that can be very disorienting."

"She claims I'm pretending to be a ghost," Peter said sarcastically. "That seems a little worse than just disoriented."

"She's in a downward spiral. I can pull her out of it . . . but it'll be hard. And I'll need your help."

Peter shrugged. "What can I do?"

Harry explained, "First of all, you can be honest with me."

"Of course."

"For some reason she's come to associate you with her father. She has a lot of resentment toward him, and she's projecting that on you. Do you know why she's mad at you?"

There was silence for a moment.

"Go on, tell me. Anything you say here is confidential—between you and me."

"She might have this stupid idea that I've cheated on her."

"Have you?"

"Where the hell do you get off, asking a question like that?"

Harry said reasonably, "I'm just trying to get to the truth."

Randolph calmed down. "No, I haven't cheated on her. She's paranoid."

"And you haven't said or done anything that might trouble her or affect her sense of reality."

"No," Peter said.

"How much is she worth?" Harry asked bluntly.

Peter blinked. "You mean, her portfolio?"

"Net worth."

"I don't know exactly. About eleven million."

Harry nodded. "And the money's all hers, isn't it?"

A frown crossed Peter Randolph's face. "What're you asking?"

"I'm asking, if Patsy were to go insane or to kill herself, would you get her money?"

"Go to hell!" Randolph shouted, standing up quickly. For a moment Harry thought the man was going to hit him. But he pulled his wallet from his hip pocket and took out a card. Tossed it onto Harry's desk. "That's our lawyer. Call him and ask him about the prenuptial agreement. If Patricia's declared insane, or if she were to die, the money goes into a trust. I don't get a penny."

Harry pushed the card back. "That won't be necessary. . . . I'm sorry if I hurt your feelings," Harry said. "My patient's care comes before everything else."

Randolph adjusted his cuffs and buttoned his jacket. "Accepted."

"So you're not whispering to her, pretending to be her father. You're not breaking those birds of hers."

"Of course not."

Harry nodded and looked over Peter Randolph carefully. A prerequisite for being a therapist is the ability to judge character quickly. He now sized up this man and came to a decision. "I want to try something radical with Patsy and I want you to help me."

"Radical? You mean, commit her?"

"No, that'd be the worst thing for her. When patients are going through times like this you can't coddle them. You have to be tough. And force *them* to be tough."

"Meaning?"

"Don't be antagonistic, but force her to stay involved in life. She's going to want to withdraw—to be pampered. But don't spoil her. If she says she's too upset to go shopping or go out to dinner, don't let her get away with it. Insist that she does what she's supposed to do."

"You're sure that's best?"

Sure? Harry asked himself. No, he wasn't the least bit sure. But he'd made his decision. He had to push Patsy hard. He told Peter, "We don't have any choice."

But as the man left the office Harry happened to recall an expression one of his medical school professors used frequently. He said you have to attack disease head-on. "You have to kill or cure."

Harry hadn't thought of that expression in years. He wished he hadn't today.

The next day Patsy walked into his office without an appointment.

In Brooklyn, at the clinic, this was standard procedure and nobody thought anything of it. But in a Park Avenue shrink's office, impromptu sessions were taboo. Still, Harry could see from her face that she was very upset and he didn't make an issue of her unexpected appearance.

She collapsed on the couch and hugged herself closely as he rose and closed the door.

"Patsy, what's the matter?" he asked.

He noticed that her clothes were more disheveled than he'd ever seen. They were stained and torn. Hair bedraggled. Fingernails dirty.

"Everything was going so well," she sobbed, "then I was sitting in the den and I heard my father's ghost again. He said, 'They're almost here. You don't have much time left. . . . ' And I asked, 'What do you mean?' And he said, 'Look in the living room.' And I did, and there was another one of my birds! It was shattered!" She opened her purse and showed Harry the broken pieces of ceramic. "Now there's only one left! I'm going to die when it breaks. I know I am. Peter's going to break it tonight! And then he'll kill me."

"He's not going to kill you, Patsy," Harry said calmly, patiently ignoring her hysteria.

"I think I should go to the hospital for a while, Doctor."

Harry got up and sat on the couch next to her. He took her hand. "No."

"What?"

"It would be a mistake," Harry said.

"Why?" she cried.

"Because you can't hide from these issues. You have to confront them."

"I'd feel safer in a hospital. Nobody'd try to kill me in the hospital."

"Nobody's going to kill you, Patsy. You have to believe me."

"No! Peter—"

"But Peter's never tried to hurt you, has he?"

A pause. "No."

"Okay, here's what I want you to do. Listen to me. Are you listening?"

"Yes."

"You know that whether Peter was pretending to say those words to you or you were imagining them, *they weren't real.* Repeat that."

"I . . ."

"Repeat it!"

"They weren't real."

"Now say, 'There was no ghost. My father's dead.' "

"There was no ghost. My father's dead."

"Good!" Harry laughed out loud. "Again."

She repeated this mantra several times, calming each time she did. Finally, a faint smile crossed her lips.

Harry squeezed her hand.

Then she frowned. "But the bird . . ." She opened her purse and took out a dozen pieces of shattered ceramic.

"Whatever happened to the bird doesn't matter. It's only a piece of porcelain."

"But . . ." She looked down at the broken shards.

Harry leaned forward. "Listen to me, Patsy. Listen carefully." Passionately, Harry Bernstein said, "I want you to go home, take that last bird, and smash the hell out of it."

"You want me to . . ."

"Take a hammer and crush it."

She started to protest but then she smiled. "Can I do that?"

"You bet you can. Just give yourself permission to. Go home, have a nice glass of wine, find a hammer, and smash it." He reached under his desk and picked up the wastebasket. He held it out for her. "They're just pieces of china, Patsy."

After a moment she tossed the pieces of the statue into the container.

"Good, Patsy." And—thinking, *To hell with transference*—the doctor gave his patient a huge hug.

An hour later Patsy Randolph returned home and found Peter sitting in front of the television.

"You're late," Peter said. "Where've you been?"

"Out shopping. I got a bottle of wine."

"We're supposed to go to Jack and Louise's tonight. Don't tell me you forgot."

"I don't feel like it," she said. "I don't feel well. I—"

"No. We're going. You're not getting out of it." He spoke in that abrupt tone he'd been using recently.

"Well, can I at least take care of a few things first?"

"Sure. But I don't want to be late."

Patsy walked into the kitchen, opened the bottle, and poured a large glass of the expensive merlot. Just like Dr. Bernstein had told her. She sipped it. She felt good. Very good. "Where's the hammer?" she called.

"Hammer? What do you need the hammer for?"

"I have to fix something."

"I think it's in the drawer beside the refrigerator."

She found it. Carried it into the living room.

Peter glanced at it, then back to the TV. "What do you have to fix?"

"You," she answered and brought the heavy tool down on the top of his head with all her strength.

It took another dozen blows to kill him, and when she'd finished she stood back and gazed at the remarkable patterns the blood made on the carpet and couch. Then she went into the bedroom and took her diary from the bedside table—the one Dr. Bernstein had suggested she keep. Back in the living room, Patsy sat down beside her husband's corpse and in her diary she wrote a rambling passage about how, at last, she'd gotten the ghosts to stop speaking to her. She was finally at peace. She didn't add as much as she wanted to; it was very time-consuming to write using your finger for a pen and blood for ink.

When Patsy'd finished, she picked up the hammer and smashed the Boehm ceramic owl into dust. Then she began screaming as loudly as she could, "The ghosts are dead, the ghosts are dead, the ghosts are dead!"

Long before she was hoarse the police and medics arrived. When they took her away she was wearing a straitjacket.

A week later Harry Bernstein sat in the prison hospital waiting room. He knew he was a sight—he hadn't shaved in several days and was wearing wrinkled clothes—which, in fact, he'd slept in last night. But he didn't care. He stared at the filthy floor.

"You all right?" This question came from a tall, thin man with a perfect beard. He wore a gorgeous suit and Armani-framed glasses. He was Patsy's lead defense lawyer.

"I never thought she'd do it," Harry said to him. "I *knew* there was risk. I *knew* something was wrong. But I thought I had everything under control."

The lawyer looked at him sympathetically. "I heard you've been having some trouble, too. Your patients . . ."

Harry laughed bitterly. "Are quitting in droves. Well, wouldn't you? Hell, Park Avenue shrinks are a dime a dozen. Why should they risk seeing me? I might get them killed or committed."

The jailor opened the door. "Dr. Bernstein, you can see the prisoner now."

He stood slowly, supporting himself on the door frame.

The lawyer looked him over and said, "You and I can meet in the next couple of days to decide how to handle the case. The insanity defense is tough in New York, but with you on board I can make it work. We'll keep her out of jail. . . . Say, Doctor, you going to be okay?"

Harry gave a shallow nod.

The lawyer said kindly, "I can arrange for a little cash for you. A couple thousand—for an expert-witness fee."

"Thanks," Harry said. But he instantly forgot about the money. His mind was already on his patient.

The room was as bleak as he'd expected.

Face white, eyes shrunken, Patsy lay in bed, looking out the window. She glanced at Harry, didn't seem to recognize him.

"How are you feeling?" he asked.

"Who are you?" She frowned.

He didn't answer her question either. "You're not looking too bad, Patsy."

"I think I know you. Yes, you're . . . Wait, are you a ghost?"

"No, I'm not a ghost." Harry set his attaché case on the table. Her eyes slipped to the case as he opened it.

"I can't stay long, Patsy. I'm closing my practice. There's a lot to take care of. But I wanted to bring you a few things."

"Things?" she asked, sounding like a child. "For me? Like Christmas. Like my birthday."

"Uh-hum." Harry rummaged in the case. "Here's the first thing." He took out a photocopy. "It's an article in the *Journal of Psychoses*. I found it the night after the session when you first told me about the ghosts. You should read it."

"I can't read," she said. "I don't know how." She gave a crazy laugh. "I'm afraid of the food here. I think there are spies around. They're going to put things in the food. Disgusting things. And poison. Or broken glass." Another cackle.

Harry set the article on the bed next to her. He walked to the window. No trees here. No birds. Just gray, downtown Manhattan.

He said, glancing back at her, "It's all about ghosts. The article."

Her eyes narrowed and then fear consumed her face.

"Ghosts," she whispered. "Are there ghosts here?"

Harry laughed hard. "See, Patsy, ghosts were the first clue. After you mentioned them in that session—claiming that your husband was driving you crazy—I thought something didn't sound quite right. So I went home and started to research your case."

She gazed at him silently.

"That article's about the importance of diagnosis in mental-health cases. See, sometimes it works to somebody's advantage to *appear* to be mentally unstable—so they can avoid responsibility. Say, soldiers who don't want to fight. People faking insurance claims. People who've committed crimes." He turned back. "Or who're *about* to commit a crime."

"I'm afraid of ghosts," Patsy said, her voice rising. "I'm afraid of ghosts. I don't want any ghosts here! I'm afraid of—"

Harry continued like a lecturing professor. "And ghosts are one of the classic hallucinations that sane people use to try to convince other people that they're insane."

She stopped speaking.

"Fascinating article," Harry continued, nodding toward it. "See, ghosts and spirits *seem* like the products of delusional minds. But, in fact, they're complex metaphysical concepts that someone who's really insane wouldn't understand at all. No, true psychotics believe that the actual *person* is there speaking to them. They think that Napoleon or Hitler or Marilyn Monroe is really in the room with them. You wouldn't have claimed to've heard your father's *ghost*. You would actually have heard *him*."

Harry enjoyed the utterly shocked expression on his patient's face. He said, "Then, a few weeks ago, you admitted that maybe the voices were in your head. A true psychotic would never admit that. They'd swear they were completely sane." He paced slowly. "There were some other things, too. You must've read somewhere that sloppy physical appearance is a sign of mental illness. Your clothes were torn and dirty, you'd forgotten to do straps . . . but your makeup was always perfect—even on the night the police called me over to your apartment. In genuine mental-health cases, makeup is the first thing to go. Patients just smear their faces with it. Has to do with issues of masking their identity, if you're interested.

"Oh, and remember, you asked if a ghost could come to one of our sessions? That was very funny. But the psychiatric literature defines humor as ironic juxtaposition of concepts based on common experience. Of course, that's contrary to the mental processes of psychotics."

"What the hell does that mean?" Patsy spat out.

"That crazy people don't make jokes," he summarized. "That cinched it for me that you were sane as could be." Harry looked through the attaché case once more. "Item number two." He looked up, smiling. "After I read that article and decided you were faking your diagnosis—and listening to what your subconscious was telling me about your marriage—I figured you were using me for some reason having to do with your husband. So I hired a private eye."

"Jesus Christ, you did what?"

"Here's his report." He dropped the folder on the bed. "It says, basically, that your husband *was* having an affair and was forging checks on your main investment account. You knew about his mistress and the money and you'd talked to a lawyer about divorcing him. But Peter knew that you were having an affair too—with your friend Sally's husband. Peter used that to blackmail you into not divorcing him."

Patsy stared at him, frozen.

He nodded at the report. "Oh, you may as well look at it. Pretending you can't read? Doesn't fly. Reading has nothing to do with psychotic behavior; it's a developmental and IQ issue."

She opened the report, read through it, then tossed it aside disgustedly. "Son of a bitch."

Harry said, "You wanted to kill Peter and you wanted me to establish that you were insane—for your defense. You'd go into a private hospital. There'd be a mandatory rehearing in a year and, bang, you'd pass the tests and be released."

She shook her head. "But you knew my goal was to kill Peter? And you let me do it! Hell, you *encouraged* me to do it."

"And when I saw Peter I encouraged *him* to antagonize you. . . . It was time to move things along. I was getting tired of our sessions." Then Harry's face darkened with genuine regret. "I never thought you'd actually kill. I thought you'd *try*—maybe hit him a few times with the hammer. Then you'd get off on the insanity defense and he'd run for the hills—and agree to the divorce—because he didn't want to be married to a crazy woman. But I got it wrong. What can I say? Psychiatry's an inexact science."

"But why didn't you go to the police?"

"Ah, that has to do with the third thing I brought for you."

I can help you and you can help me. . . .

He lifted an envelope out of his briefcase. He handed it to her.

"What is this?"

"My bill."

She opened it. Took out the sheet of paper.

At the top was written: *For Services Rendered*. And below that: *$10 million*.

"Are you crazy?" Patsy gasped.

Harry had to laugh at her choice of words. "Peter was nice enough to tell me exactly what you were worth. I'm leaving you a million . . . which you'll probably need to pay that slick lawyer of yours. He looks expensive. Now, I'll need cash or a certified check before I testify at your trial. Otherwise I'll have to share with the court my honest diagnosis about your condition."

"You're blackmailing me!"

"I guess I am."

"Why?"

"Because with this money I can afford to do some good. And help people who really need helping." He nodded at the bill. "I'd write that check pretty soon—they have the death penalty in New York now. Oh, and by the way, I'd lose that bit about the food being poisoned. Around here, if you make a stink about meals, they'll just put you on a tube." He picked up his attaché case.

"Wait," she begged. "Don't leave! Let's talk about this!"

"Sorry." Harry nodded at a wall clock. "I see our time is up."

Minette Walters

The Tinder Box

It's always fun to watch a writer come up with a fresh, new treatment of old story patterns and conventions. MINETTE WALTERS has done just that by combining the traditional English mystery with psychological suspense. Her books have won numerous awards in the less than ten years that she has been writing. Her first book, *The Icehouse,* was published in 1992. *The Sculptress* (1993) is an especially fine example of her craft and art. Her first four books, *The Icehouse, The Sculptress, The Scold's Bridle,* and *The Dark Room,* were made into movies for the BBC. This story first appeared in the December issue of *Ellery Queen's Mystery Magazine.*

The Tinder Box

Minette Walters

1

***The Daily Telegraph—Wednesday, 24th June, 1998

SOWERBRIDGE MAN ARRESTED

Patrick O'Riordan 35, an unemployed Irish laborer, was charged last night with the double murder of his neighbors Lavinia Fanshaw, 93, and her live-in nurse, Dorothy Jenkins, 67. The murders have angered the small community of Sowerbridge where O'Riordan and his parents have lived for fifteen years. The elderly victims were brutally battered to death after Dorothy Jenkins interrupted a robbery on Saturday night. "Whoever killed them is a monster," said a neighbor. "Lavinia was a frail old lady with Alzheimer's who never hurt a soul." Police warned residents to remain calm after a crowd gathered outside the O'Riordan home when news of the arrest became public. "Vigilante behavior will not be tolerated," said a spokesman. O'Riordan denies the charges.

11:30 P.M.—Monday, 8th March, 1999

Even at half past eleven at night, the lead news story on local radio was still the opening day of Patrick O'Riordan's trial. Siobhan Lavenham, exhausted after a fourteen-hour stint at work, listened to it in the darkness of her car while she negotiated the narrow country lanes back to Sowerbridge village.

". . . O'Riordan smiled as the prosecution case unfolded . . . harrowing details of how ninety-three-year-old Lavinia Fanshaw and her live-in nurse were brutally bludgeoned to death before Mrs. Fanshaw's rings were ripped from her fingers . . . scratch marks and bruises on the defendant's face, probably caused by a fight with one of the women . . . a crime of greed triggered by O'Riordan's known resentment of Mrs.

*Fanshaw's wealth . . . unable to account for his whereabouts at the time of the mur-
ders . . . items of jewelry recovered from the O'Riordan family home which the thirty-
five-year-old Irishman still shares with his elderly parents . . ."*

With a sinking heart, Siobhan punched the Off button and concentrated on her driving. *"The Irishman . . ."* Was that a deliberate attempt to
inflame racist division, she wondered, or just careless shorthand? God, how
she loathed journalists! Confident of a guilty verdict, they had descended on
Sowerbridge like a plague of locusts the previous week in order to prepare
their background features in advance. They had found dirt in abundance, of
course. Sowerbridge had fallen over itself to feed them with hate stories
against the whole O'Riordan family.

She thought back to the day of Patrick's arrest, when Bridey had begged
her not to abandon them. "You're one of us, Siobhan. Irish through and
through, never mind you're married to an Englishman. You know my
Patrick. He wouldn't hurt a fly. Is it likely he'd beat Mrs. Fanshaw to death
when he's never raised a hand against his own father? Liam was a devil when
he still had the use of his arm. Many's the time he thrashed Patrick with a
stick when the drunken rages were on him, but never once did Patrick take
the stick to him."

It was a frightening thing to be reminded of the bonds that tied people
together, Siobhan had thought as she looked out of Bridey's window toward
the silent, angry crowd that was gathering in the road. Was being Irish
enough of a reason to side with a man suspected of slaughtering a frail
bedridden old woman and the woman who looked after her?

"Patrick admits he stole from Lavinia," Siobhan had pointed out.

Tears rolled down Bridey's furrowed cheeks. "But not her rings," she said.
"Just cheap trinkets that he was too ignorant to recognize as worthless paste."

"It was still theft."

"Mother of God, do you think I don't know that?" She held out her
hands beseechingly. "A thief he may be, Siobhan, but never a murderer."

And Siobhan had believed her because she wanted to. For all his sins, she
had never thought of Patrick as an aggressive or malicious man—too relaxed
by half, many would say—and he could always make her and her children
laugh with his stories about Ireland, particularly ones involving leprechauns
and pots of gold hidden at the ends of rainbows. The thought of him taking
a hammer to anyone was anathema to her.

And yet . . . ?

In the darkness of the car she recalled the interview she'd had the
previous month with a detective inspector at Hampshire Constabulary
Headquarters who seemed perplexed that a well-to-do young woman
should have sought him out to complain about police indifference to the
plight of the O'Riordans. She wondered now why she hadn't gone to him
sooner.

Had she really been so unwilling to learn the truth . . . ?

The detective shook his head. "I don't understand what you're talking about, Mrs. Lavenham."

Siobhan gave an angry sigh. "Oh, for goodness sake! The hate campaign that's being waged against them. The graffiti on their walls, the constant telephone calls threatening them with arson, the fact that Bridey's too frightened to go out for fear of being attacked. There's a war going on in Sowerbridge which is getting worse the closer we come to Patrick's trial, but as far as you're concerned, it doesn't exist. Why aren't you investigating it? Why don't you respond to Bridey's telephone calls?"

He consulted a piece of paper on his desk. "Mrs. O'Riordan's made fifty-three emergency calls in the eight months since Patrick was remanded for the murders," he said, "only thirty of which were considered serious enough to send a police car to investigate. In every case, the attending officers filed reports saying Bridey was wasting police time." He gave an apologetic shrug. "I realize it's not what you want to hear, but we'd be within our rights if we decided to prosecute her. Wasting police time is a serious offense."

Siobhan thought of the tiny, wheelchair-bound woman whose terror was so real she trembled constantly. "They're after killing us, Siobhan," she would say over and over again. "I hear them creeping about the garden in the middle of the night and I think to myself, there's nothing me or Liam can do if this is the night they decide to break in. To be sure, it's only God who's keeping us safe."

"But who *are* they, Bridey?"

"It's the bully boys whipped up to hate us by Mrs. Haversley and Mr. Jardine," wept the woman. "Who else would it be?"

Siobhan brushed her long dark hair from her forehead and frowned at the detective inspector. "Bridey's old, she's disabled, and she's completely terrified. The phone never stops ringing. Mostly it's long silences, other times it's voices threatening to kill her. Liam's only answer to it all is to get paralytically drunk every night so he doesn't have to face up to what's going on." She shook her head impatiently. "Cynthia Haversley and Jeremy Jardine, who seem to control everything that happens in Sowerbridge, have effectively given carte blanche to the local youths to make life hell for them. Every sound, every shadow has Bridey on the edge of her seat. She needs protection, and I don't understand why you're not giving it to her."

"They were offered a safe house, Mrs. Lavenham, and they refused it."

"Because Liam's afraid of what will happen to Kilkenny Cottage if he leaves it empty," she protested. "The place will be trashed in half a minute flat. . . . You know that as well as I do."

He gave another shrug, this time more indifferent than apologetic. "I'm sorry," he said, "but there's nothing we can do. If any of these attacks actually happened . . . well, we'd have something concrete to investigate. They can't even name any of these so-called vigilantes . . . just claim they're yobs from neighboring villages."

"So what are you saying?" she asked bitterly. "That they have to be dead before you take the threats against them seriously?"

"Of course not," he said, "but we do need to be persuaded the threats are real. As things stand, they seem to be all in her mind."

"Are you accusing Bridey of lying?"

He smiled slightly. "She's never been averse to embroidering the truth when it suits her purpose, Mrs. Lavenham."

Siobhan shook her head. "How can you say that? Have you ever spoken to her? Do you even *know* her? To you, she's just the mother of a thief and a murderer."

"That's neither fair nor true." He looked infinitely weary, like a defendant in a trial who has answered the same accusation in the same way a hundred times before. "I've known Bridey for years. It's part and parcel of being a policeman. When you question a man as often as I've questioned Liam, you get to know his wife pretty well by default." He leaned forward, resting his elbows on his knees and clasping his hands loosely in front of him. "And sadly, the one sure thing I know about Bridey is that you can't believe a word she says. It may not be her fault, but it *is* a fact. She's never had the courage to speak out honestly because her drunken brute of a husband beats her within an inch of her life if she even dares to think about it."

Siobhan found his directness shocking. "You're talking about things that happened a long time ago," she said. "Liam hasn't struck anyone since he lost the use of his right arm."

"Do you know how that happened?"

"In a car crash."

"Did Bridey tell you that?"

"Yes."

"Not so," he countered bluntly. "When Patrick was twenty, he tied Liam's arm to a tabletop and used a hammer to smash his wrist to a pulp. He was so wrought up that when his mother tried to stop him, he shoved her through a window and broke her pelvis so badly she's never been able to walk again. That's why she's in a wheelchair and why Liam has a useless right arm. Patrick got off lightly by pleading provocation because of Liam's past brutality toward him, and spent less than two years in prison for it."

Siobhan shook her head. "I don't believe you."

"It's true." He rubbed a tired hand around his face. "Trust me, Mrs. Lavenham."

"I can't," she said flatly. "You've never lived in Sowerbridge, Inspector. There's not a soul in that village who doesn't have it in for the O'Riordans and a juicy tidbit like that would have been repeated a thousand times. Trust *me*."

"No one knows about it." The man held her gaze for a moment, then dropped his eyes. "It was fifteen years ago and it happened in London. I was a

raw recruit with the Met, and Liam was on our ten-most-wanted list. He was
a scrap-metal merchant, and up to his neck in villainy, until Patrick scuppered
him for good. He sold up when the lad went to prison and moved himself and
Bridey down here to start a new life. When Patrick joined them after his
release, the story of the car crash had already been accepted."

She shook her head again. "Patrick came over from Ireland after being
wounded by a terrorist bomb. That's why he smiles all the time. The nerves in
his cheek were severed by a piece of flying glass." She sighed. "It's another
kind of disability. People take against him because they think he's laughing at
them."

"No, ma'am, it was a revenge attack in prison for stealing from his cell
mate. His face was slashed with a razor. As far as I know, he's never set foot in
Ireland."

She didn't answer. Instead she ran her hand rhythmically over her skirt
while she tried to collect her thoughts. *Oh, Bridey, Bridey, Bridey . . . Have you
been lying to me . . . ?*

The inspector watched her with compassion. "Nothing happens in a
vacuum, Mrs. Lavenham."

"Meaning what, exactly?"

"Meaning that Patrick murdered Mrs. Fanshaw"—he paused—"and
both Liam and Bridey know he did. You can argue that the physical abuse he
suffered at the hands of his father as a child provoked an anger in him that he
couldn't control—it's a defense that worked after the attack on Liam—but it
won't cut much ice with a jury when the victims were two defenseless old
ladies. That's why Bridey's jumping at shadows. She knows that she effectively
signed Mrs. Fanshaw's death warrant when she chose to keep quiet about
how dangerous Patrick was, and she's terrified of it becoming public." He
paused. "Which it certainly will during the trial."

Was he right, Siobhan wondered? Were Bridey's fears rooted in guilt?
"That doesn't absolve the police of responsibility for their safety," she
pointed out.

"No," he agreed, "except we don't believe their safety's in question.
Frankly, all the evidence so far points to Liam himself being the instigator of
the hate campaign. The graffiti is always done at night in car spray paint, at
least a hundred cans of which are stored in Liam's shed. There are never any
witnesses to it, and by the time Bridey calls us the perpetrators are long gone.
We've no idea if the phone rings as constantly as they claim, but on every
occasion that a threat has been made, Bridey admits she was alone in the cottage. We think Liam is making the calls himself."

She shook her head in bewilderment. "Why would he do that?"

"To prejudice the trial?" he suggested. "He has a different mind-set to
you and me, ma'am, and he's quite capable of trashing Kilkenny Cottage
himself if he thinks it will win Patrick some sympathy with a jury."

Did she believe him? Was Liam that clever? "You said you were always
questioning him. Why? What had he done?"

"Any scam involving cars. Theft. Forging M.O.T. certificates. Odometer fixing. You name it, Liam was involved in it. The scrap-metal business was just a front for a car-laundering operation."

"You're talking about when he was in London?"

"Yes."

She pondered for a moment. "Did he go to prison for it?"

"Once or twice. Most of the time he managed to avoid conviction. He had money in those days—a lot of money—and could pay top briefs to get him off. He shipped some of the cars down here, presumably with the intention of starting the same game again, but he was a broken man after Patrick smashed his arm. I'm told he gave up grafting for himself and took to living off disability benefits instead. There's no way anyone was going to employ him. He's too unreliable to hold down a job. Just like his son."

"I see," said Siobhan slowly.

He waited for her to go on, and when she didn't he said: "Leopards don't change their spots, Mrs. Lavenham. I wish I could say they did, but I've been a policeman too long to believe anything so naive."

She surprised him by laughing. "Leopards?" she echoed. "And there was me thinking we were talking about dogs."

"I don't follow."

"Give a dog a bad name and hang him. Did the police *ever* intend to let them wipe the slate clean and start again, Inspector?"

He smiled slightly. "We did . . . for fifteen years. . . . Then Patrick murdered Mrs. Fanshaw."

"Are you sure?"

"Oh, yes," he said. "He used the same hammer on her that he used on his father."

Siobhan remembered the sense of shock that had swept through the village the previous June when the two bodies were discovered by the local milkman after his curiosity had been piqued by the fact that the front door had been standing ajar at 5:30 on a Sunday morning. Thereafter, only the police and Lavinia's grandson had seen inside the house, but the rumor machine described a scene of carnage, with Lavinia's brains splattered across the walls of her bedroom and her nurse lying in a pool of blood in the kitchen. It was inconceivable that anyone in Sowerbridge could have done such a thing, and it was assumed the Manor House had been targeted by an outside gang for whatever valuables the old woman might possess.

It was never very clear why police suspicion had centered so rapidly on Patrick O'Riordan. Gossip said his fingerprints were all over the house and his toolbox was found in the kitchen, but Siobhan had always believed the police had received a tipoff. Whatever the reason, the matter appeared to be settled when a search warrant unearthed Lavinia's jewelry under his floorboards and Patrick was formally charged with the murders.

Predictably, shock had turned to fury but, with Patrick already in custody, it was Liam and Bridey who took the full brunt of Sowerbridge's wrath.

Their presence in the village had never been a particularly welcome one—indeed, it was a mystery how "rough trade like them" could have afforded to buy a cottage in rural Hampshire, or why they had wanted to—but it became deeply unwelcome after the murders. Had it been possible to banish them behind a physical pale, the village would most certainly have done so; as it was, the old couple were left to exist in a social limbo where backs were turned and no one spoke to them.

In such a climate, Siobhan wondered, could Liam really have been stupid enough to ratchet up the hatred against them by daubing anti-Irish slogans across his front wall?

"If Patrick *is* the murderer, then why didn't you find Lavinia's diamond rings in Kilkenny Cottage?" she asked the inspector. "Why did you only find pieces of fake jewelry?"

"Who told you that? Bridey?"

"Yes."

He looked at her with a kind of compassion. "Then I'm afraid she was lying, Mrs. Lavenham. The diamond rings were in Kilkenny Cottage along with everything else."

2

11:45 P.M.—Monday, 8th March, 1999

Siobhan was aware of the orange glow in the night sky ahead of her for some time before her tired brain began to question what it meant. Arc lights? A party? Fire, she thought in alarm as she approached the outskirts of Sowerbridge and saw sparks shooting into the air like a giant Roman candle. She slowed her Range Rover to a crawl as she approached the bend by the church, knowing it must be the O'Riordans' house, tempted to put the car into reverse and drive away, as if denial could alter what was happening. But she could see the flames licking up the front of Kilkenny Cottage by that time and knew it was too late for anything so simplistic. A police car was blocking the narrow road ahead, and with a sense of foreboding she obeyed the torch that signaled her to draw up on the grass verge beyond the church gate.

She lowered her window as the policeman came over, and felt the warmth from the fire fan her face like a Saharan wind. "Do you live in Sowerbridge, madam?" he asked. He was dressed in shirtsleeves, perspiration glistening on his forehead, and Siobhan was amazed that one small house two hundred yards away could generate so much heat on a cool March night.

"Yes." She gestured in the direction of the blaze. "At Fording Farm. It's another half-mile beyond the crossroads."

He shone his torch into her eyes for a moment—his curiosity whetted by her soft Dublin accent, she guessed—before lowering the beam to a map. "You'll waste a lot less time if you go back the way you came and make a detour," he advised her.

"I can't. Our driveway leads off the crossroads by Kilkenny Cottage and there's no other access to it." She touched a finger to the map. "There. Whichever way I go, I still need to come back to the crossroads."

Headlights swept across her rearview mirror as another car rounded the bend. "Wait there a moment, please." He moved away to signal toward the verge, leaving Siobhan to gaze through her windscreen at the scene of chaos ahead.

There seemed to be a lot of people milling around, but her night sight had been damaged by the brilliance of the flames; and the water glistening on the tarmac made it difficult to distinguish what was real from what was reflection. The rusted hulks of the old cars that littered the O'Riordans' property stood out in bold silhouettes against the light, and Siobhan thought that Cynthia Haversley had been right when she said they weren't just an eyesore but a fire hazard as well. Cynthia had talked dramatically about the dangers of petrol, but if there was any petrol left in the corroded tanks, it remained sluggishly inert. The real hazard was the time and effort it must have taken to maneuver the two fire engines close enough to weave the hoses through so many obstacles, and Siobhan wondered if the house had ever stood a chance of being saved.

She began to fret about her two small boys and their nanny, Rosheen, who were alone at the farmhouse, and drummed her fingers impatiently on the steering wheel. "What should I do?" she asked the policeman when he returned after persuading the other driver to make a detour. "I need to get home."

He looked at the map again. "There's a footpath running behind the church and the vicarage. If you're prepared to walk home, I suggest you park your car in the churchyard and take the footpath. I'll radio through to ask one of the constables on the other side of the crossroads to escort you into your driveway. Failing that, I'm afraid you'll have to stay here until the road's clear, and that could take several hours."

"I'll walk." She reached for the gear stick, then let her hand drop. "No one's been hurt, have they?"

"No. The occupants are away."

Siobhan nodded. Under the watchful eyes of half of Sowerbridge village, Liam and Bridey had set off that morning in their ancient Ford Estate, to the malignant sound of whistles and hisses. "The O'Riordans are staying in Winchester until the trial's over."

"So we've been told," said the policeman.

Siobhan watched him take a notebook from his breast pocket. "Then presumably you were expecting something like this? I mean, everyone knew the house would be empty."

He flicked to an empty page. "I'll need your name, madam."

"Siobhan Lavenham."

"And your registration number, please, Ms. Lavenham."

She gave it to him. "You didn't answer my question," she said unemphatically.

He raised his eyes to look at her but it was impossible to read their expression. "What question's that?"

She thought she detected a smile on his face and bridled immediately. "You don't find it at all suspicious that the house burns down the minute Liam's back is turned?"

He frowned. "You've lost me, Ms. Lavenham."

"It's *Mrs.* Lavenham," she said irritably, "and you know perfectly well what I'm talking about. Liam's been receiving arson threats ever since Patrick was arrested, but the police couldn't have been less interested." Her irritation got the better of her. "It's their son who's on trial, for God's sake, not them, though you'd never believe it for all the care the English police have shown them." She crunched the car into gear and drove the few yards to the churchyard entrance where she parked in the lee of the wall and closed the window. She was preparing to open the door when it was opened from the outside.

"What are you trying to say?" demanded the policeman as she climbed out.

"What am I trying to say?" She let her accent slip into broad brogue. "Will you listen to the man? And there was me thinking my English was as good as his."

She was as tall as the constable, with striking good looks, and color rose in his cheeks. "I didn't mean it that way, Mrs. Lavenham. I meant, are you saying it was arson?"

"Of course it was arson," she countered, securing her mane of brown hair with a band at the back of her neck and raising her coat collar against the wind which two hundred yards away was feeding the inferno. "Are you saying it wasn't?"

"Can you prove it?"

"I thought that was your job."

He opened his notebook again, looking more like an earnest student than an officer of the law. "Do you know who might have been responsible?"

She reached inside the car for her handbag. "Probably the same people who wrote 'IRISH TRASH' across their front wall," she said, slamming the door and locking it. "Or maybe it's the ones who broke into the house two weeks ago during the night and smashed Bridey's Madonna and Child before urinating all over the pieces on the carpet. Who knows?" She gave him credit for looking disturbed at what she was saying. "Look, forget it," she said wearily. "It's late and I'm tired, and I want to get home to my children. Can you make that radio call so I don't get held up at the other end?"

"I'll do it from the car." He started to turn away, then changed his mind. "I'll be reporting what you've told me, Mrs. Lavenham, including your suggestion that the police have been negligent in their duty."

She smiled slightly. "Is that a threat or a promise, Officer?"

"It's a promise."

"Then I hope you have better luck than I've had. I might have been speaking in Gaelic for all the notice your colleagues took of my warnings." She set off for the footpath.

"You're supposed to put complaints in writing," he called after her.

"Oh, but I did," she assured him over her shoulder. "I may be Irish, but I'm not illiterate."

"I didn't mean—"

But the rest of his apology was lost on her as she rounded the corner of the church and vanished from sight.

Thursday, 18th February, 1999

It had been several days before Siobhan found the courage to confront Bridey with what the detective inspector had told her. It made her feel like a thief even to think about it. Secrets were such fragile things. Little parts of oneself that couldn't be exposed without inviting changed perceptions toward the whole. But distrust was corroding her sympathy and she needed reassurance that Bridey at least believed in Patrick's innocence.

She followed the old woman's wheelchair into the sitting room and perched on the edge of the grubby sofa that Liam always lounged upon in his oil-stained boiler suit after spending hours poking around under his unsightly wrecks. It was a mystery to Siobhan what he did under them, as none of them appeared to be drivable, and she wondered sometimes if he simply used them as a canopy under which to sleep his days away. He complained often enough that his withered right hand, which he kept tucked out of sight inside his pockets to avoid upsetting people, had deprived him of any chance of a livelihood, but the truth was, he was a lazy man who was only ever seen to rouse himself when his wife left a trailing leg as she transferred from her chair to the passenger seat of their old Ford.

"There's nothing wrong with his left hand," Cynthia Haversley would snort indignantly as she watched the regular little pantomime outside Kilkenny Cottage, "but you'd think he'd lost the use of both hands the way he carries on about his disabilities."

Privately, and with some amusement, Siobhan guessed the demonstrations were put on entirely for the benefit of the Honorable Mrs. Haversley, who made no bones about her irritation at the level of state welfare which the O'Riordans enjoyed. It was axiomatic, after all, that any woman who had enough strength in her arms to heave herself upstairs on her bottom, as Bridey did every night, could lift her own leg into a car. . . .

The Kilkenny Cottage sitting room—Bridey called it her "parlor"—was full of religious artifacts: a shrine to the Madonna and Child on the mantelpiece, a foot-high wooden cross on one wall, a print of William Holman Hunt's "The Light of the World" on another, a rosary hanging from a hook.

In Siobhan, for whom religion was more of a trial than a comfort, the room invariably induced a sort of spiritual claustrophobia which made her long to get out and breathe fresh air again.

In ordinary circumstances, the paths of the O'Riordans, descendants of a roaming tinker family, and Siobhan Lavenham (née Kerry), daughter of an Irish landowner, would never have crossed. Indeed, when she and her husband, Ian, first visited Fording Farm and fell in love with it, Siobhan had pointed out the eyesore of Kilkenny Cottage with a shudder and had predicted accurately the kind of people who were living there. Irish Gypsies, she said.

"Will that make life difficult for you?" Ian had asked.

"Only if people assume we're related," she answered with a laugh, never assuming for one moment that anyone would. . . .

Bridey's habitually cowed expression reminded Siobhan of an ill-treated dog, and she put the detective inspector's accusations reluctantly, asking Bridey if she had lied about the car crash and about Patrick never striking his father. The woman wept, washing her hands in her lap as if, like Lady Macbeth, she could cleanse herself of sin.

"If I did, Siobhan, it was only to have you think well of us. You're a lovely young lady with a kind heart, but you'd not have let Patrick play with your children if you'd known what he did to his father, and you'd not have taken Rosheen into your house if you'd known her uncle Liam was a thief."

"You should have trusted me, Bridey. If I didn't ask Rosheen to leave when Patrick was arrested for murder, why would I have refused to employ her just because Liam spent time in prison?"

"Because your husband would have persuaded you against her," said Bridey truthfully. "He's never been happy about Rosheen being related to us, never mind she grew up in Ireland and hardly knew us till you said she could come here to work for you."

There was no point denying it. Ian tolerated Rosheen O'Riordan for Siobhan's sake, and because his little boys loved her, but in an ideal world he would have preferred a nanny from a more conventional background. Rosheen's relaxed attitude to child rearing, based on her own upbringing in a three-bedroom cottage in the hills of Donegal where the children had slept four to a bed and play was adventurous, carefree, and fun, was so different from the strict supervision of his own childhood that he constantly worried about it. "They'll grow up wild," he would say. "She's not disciplining them enough." And Siobhan would look at her happy, lively, affectionate sons and wonder why the English were so fond of repression.

"He worries about his children, Bridey, more so since Patrick's arrest. We get telephone calls too, you know. Everyone knows Rosheen's his cousin."

She remembered the first such call she had taken. She had answered it in the kitchen while Rosheen was making supper for the children, and she had been shocked by the torrent of anti-Irish abuse that had poured down the line. She raised stricken eyes to Rosheen's and saw by the girl's frightened expression that it wasn't the first such call that had been made. After that, she had had an answerphone installed, and forebade Rosheen from lifting the receiver unless she was sure of the caller's identity.

Bridey's sad gaze lifted toward the Madonna on the mantelpiece. "I pray for you every day, Siobhan, just as I pray for my Patrick. God knows, I never wished this trouble on a sweet lady like you. And for why? Is it a sin to be Irish?"

Siobhan sighed to herself, hating Bridey's dreary insistence on calling her a "lady." She did not doubt Bridey's faith, nor that she prayed every day, but she doubted God's ability to undo Lavinia Fanshaw's murder eight months after the event.

And if Patrick was guilty of it, and Bridey knew he was guilty . . .

"The issue isn't about being Irish," she said bluntly, "it's about whether or not Patrick's a murderer. I'd much rather you were honest with me, Bridey. At the moment, I don't trust any of you, and that includes Rosheen. Does she know about his past? Has she been lying to me, too?" She paused, waiting for an answer, but Bridey just shook her head. "I'm not going to blame you for your son's behavior," she said more gently, "but you can't expect me to go on pleading his cause if he's guilty."

"Indeed, and I wouldn't ask you to," said the old woman with dignity. "And you can rest your mind about Rosheen. We kept the truth to ourselves fifteen years ago. Liam wouldn't have his son blamed for something that wasn't his fault. 'We'll call it a car accident,' he said, 'and may God strike me dead if I ever raise my hand in anger again.'" She grasped the rims of her chair wheels and slowly rotated them through half a turn. "I'll tell you honestly, though I'm a cripple and though I've been married to Liam for nearly forty years, it's only in these last fifteen that I've been able to sleep peacefully in my bed. Oh yes, Liam was a bad man, and oh yes, my Patrick lost his temper once and struck out at him, but I swear by the Mother of God that this family changed for the better the day my poor son wept for what he'd done and rang the police himself. Will you believe me, Siobhan? Will you trust an old woman when she tells you her Patrick could no more have murdered Mrs. Fanshaw than I can get out of this wheelchair and walk. To be sure, he took some jewelry from her—and to be sure, he was wrong to do it—but he was only trying to get back what had been cheated out of him."

"Except there's no proof he was cheated out of anything. The police say there's very little evidence that any odd jobs had been done in the manor. They mentioned that one or two cracks in the plaster had been filled, but not enough to indicate a contract worth three hundred pounds."

"He was up there for two weeks," said Bridey in despair. "Twelve hours a day every day."

"Then why is there nothing to show for it?"

"I don't know," said the old woman with difficulty. "All I can tell you is that he came home every night with stories about what he'd been doing.

One day it was getting the heating system to work, the next re-laying the floor tiles in the kitchen where they'd come loose. It was Miss Jenkins who was telling him what needed doing, and she was thrilled to have all the little irritations sorted out once and for all."

Siobhan recalled the detective inspector's words. *"There's no one left to agree or disagree,"* he had said. *"Mrs. Fanshaw's grandson denies knowing anything about it, although he admits there might have been a private arrangement between Patrick and the nurse. She's known to have been on friendly terms with him. . . ."*

"The police are saying Patrick only invented the contract in order to explain why his fingerprints were all over the manor house."

"That's not true."

"Are you sure? Wasn't it the first idea that came into his head when the police produced the search warrant? They questioned him for two days, Bridey, and the only explanation he gave for his fingerprints and his toolbox being in the manor was that Lavinia's nurse had asked him to sort out the dripping taps in the kitchen and bathroom. Why didn't he mention a contract earlier? Why did he wait until they found the jewelry under his floorboards before saying he was owed money?"

Teardrops watered the washing hands. "Because he's been in prison and doesn't trust the police . . . because he didn't kill Mrs. Fanshaw . . . because he was more worried about being charged with the theft of her jewelry than he was about being charged with murder. Do you think he'd have invented a contract that didn't exist? My boy isn't stupid, Siobhan. He doesn't tell stories that he can't back up. Not when he's had two whole days to think about them."

Siobhan shook her head. "Except he couldn't back it up. You're the only person, other than Patrick, who claims to know anything about it, and your word means nothing because you're his mother."

"But don't you see?" the woman pleaded. "That's why you can be sure Patrick's telling the truth. If he'd believed for one moment it would all be denied, he'd have given some other reason for why he took the jewelry. Do you hear what I'm saying? He's a good liar, Siobhan—for his sins, he always has been—and he'd not have invented a poor, weak story like the one he's been saddled with."

3

Tuesday, 23rd June, 1998

It was a rambling defense that Patrick finally produced when it dawned on him that the police were serious about charging him with the murders. Siobhan heard both Bridey's and the inspector's versions of it, and she wasn't surprised that the police found it difficult to swallow. It depended almost entirely on the words and actions of the murdered nurse.

Patrick claimed Dorothy Jenkins had come to Kilkenny Cottage and asked him if he was willing to do some odd jobs at the Manor House for a cash sum of three hundred pounds. "I've finally persuaded her miserable skin-flint of a grandson that I'll walk out one day and not come back if he doesn't do something about my working conditions, so he's agreed to pay up," she had said triumphantly. "Are you interested, Patrick? It's a bit of moonlighting . . . no VAT . . . no Inland Revenue . . . just a couple of weeks' work for money in hand. But for goodness sake don't go talking about it," she had warned him, "or you can be sure Cynthia Haversley will notify social services that you're working and you'll lose your unemployment benefit. You know what an interfering busybody she is."

"I needed convincing she wasn't pulling a fast one," Patrick told the police. "I've been warned off in the past by that bastard grandson of Mrs. F's and the whole thing seemed bloody unlikely to me. So she takes me along to see him, and he's nice as pie, shakes me by the hand and says it's a kosher contract. We'll let bygones be bygones, he says. I worked like a dog for two weeks and, yes, of course I went into Mrs. Fanshaw's bedroom. I popped in every morning because she and I were mates. I would say 'hi,' and she would giggle and say 'hi' back. And yes, I touched almost everything in the house—most of the time I was moving furniture around for Miss Jenkins. 'It's so boring when you get too old to change things,' she'd say to me. 'Let's see how that table looks in here.' Then she'd clap her hands and say: 'Isn't this exciting?' I thought she was almost as barmy as the old lady, but I wasn't going to argue with her. I mean, three hundred quid is three hundred quid, and if that's what was wanted I was happy to do the business."

On the second Saturday—"the day I was supposed to be paid . . . shit . . . I should have known it was a scam . . ."—Mrs. Fanshaw's grandson was in the Manor House hall waiting for him when he arrived.

"I thought the bastard had come to give me my wages, but instead he accuses me of nicking a necklace. I called him a bloody liar, so he took a swing at me and landed one on my jaw. Next thing I know, I'm out the front door, facedown on the gravel. Yeah, of course that's how I got the scratches. I've never hit a woman in my life, and I certainly didn't get into a fight with either of the old biddies at the manor."

There was a two-hour hiatus during which he claimed to have driven around in a fury wondering how "to get the bastard to pay what he owed." He toyed with the idea of going to the police—"I was pretty sure Miss Jenkins would back me up, she was that mad with him, but I didn't reckon you lot could do anything, not without social services getting to hear about it, and then I'd be worse off than I was before . . ."—But in the end he opted for more direct action and sneaked back to Sowerbridge Manor through the gate at the bottom of the garden.

"I knew Miss Jenkins would see me right if she could. And she did. 'Take this, Patrick,' she said, handing me some of Mrs. F's jewelry, 'and if there's any comeback I'll say it was my idea.' I tell you," he finished aggressively, "I'm gutted she and Mrs. F are dead. At least they treated me like a friend, which is more than can be said of the rest of Sowerbridge."

He was asked why he hadn't mentioned any of this before. "Because I'm not a fool," he said. "Word has it Mrs. F was killed for her jewelry. Do you think I'm going to admit having some of it under my floorboards when she was battered to death a few hours later?"

Thursday, 18th February, 1999

Siobhan pondered in silence for a minute or two. "Weak or not, Bridey, it's the one he has to go to trial with, and at the moment no one believes it. It would be different if he could prove any of it."

"How?"

"I don't know." She shook her head. "Did he show the jewelry to anyone *before* Lavinia was killed?"

A sly expression crept into the woman's eyes as if a new idea had suddenly occurred to her. "Only to me and Rosheen," she said, "but, as you know, Siobhan, not a word we say is believed."

"Did either of you mention it to anyone else?"

"Why would we? When all's said and done, he took the things without permission, never mind it was Miss Jenkins who gave them to him."

"Well, it's a pity Rosheen didn't tell me about it. It would make a world of difference if I could say I knew on the Saturday afternoon that Patrick already had Lavinia's necklace in his possession."

Bridey looked away toward her Madonna, crossing herself as she did so, and Siobhan knew she was lying. "She thinks the world of you, Siobhan. She'd not embarrass you by making you a party to her cousin's troubles. In any case, you'd not have been interested. Was your mind not taken up with cooking that day? Was that not the Saturday you were entertaining Mr. and Mrs. Haversley to dinner to pay off all the dinners you've had from them but never wanted?"

There were no secrets in a village, thought Siobhan, and if Bridey knew how much Ian and she detested the grinding tedium of Sowerbridge social life, which revolved around the all-too-regular "dinner party," presumably the rest of Sowerbridge did as well. "Are we really that obvious, Bridey?"

"To the Irish, maybe, but not to the English," said the old woman with a crooked smile. "The English see what they want to see. If you don't believe me, Siobhan, look at the way they've condemned my poor Patrick as a murdering thief before he's even been tried."

Siobhan had questioned Rosheen about the jewelry afterward and, like Bridey, the girl had wrung her hands in distress. But Rosheen's distress had everything to do with her aunt expecting her to perjure herself and nothing at all to do with the facts. "Oh, Siobhan," she had wailed, "does she expect me to stand up in court and tell lies? Because it'll not do Patrick any good when they find me out. Surely it's better to say nothing than to keep inventing stories that no one believes?"

11:55 P.M.—Monday, 8th March, 1999

It was cold on the footpath because the wall of The Old Vicarage was reflecting the heat back toward Kilkenny Cottage, but the sound of the burning house was deafening. The pine rafters and ceiling joists popped and exploded like intermittent rifle fire while the flames kept up a hungry roar. As Siobhan emerged onto the road leading up from the junction, she found herself in a crowd of her neighbors, who seemed to be watching the blaze in a spirit of revelry—almost, she thought in amazement, as if it were a spectacular fireworks display put on for their enjoyment. People raised their arms and pointed whenever a new rafter caught alight, and "oohs" and "aahs" burst out of their mouths like a cheer. Any moment now, she thought cynically, and they'd bring out an effigy of that other infamous Catholic, Guy Fawkes, who was ritually burned every year for trying to blow up the Houses of Parliament.

She started to work her way through the crowd but was stopped by Nora Bentley, the elderly doctor's wife, who caught her arm and drew her close. The Bentleys were far and away Siobhan's favorites among her neighbors, being the only ones with enough tolerance to stand against the continuous barrage of anti-O'Riordan hatred that poured from the mouths of almost everyone else. Although as Ian often pointed out, they could afford to be tolerant. "Be fair, Siobhan. Lavinia wasn't related to them. They might feel differently if she'd been *their* granny."

"We've been worried about you, my dear," said Nora. "What with all this going on, we didn't know whether you were trapped inside the farm or outside."

Siobhan gave her a quick hug. "Outside. I stayed late at work to sort out some contracts, and I've had to abandon the car at the church."

"Well, I'm afraid your drive's completely blocked with fire engines. If it's any consolation, we're all in the same boat, although Jeremy Jardine and the Haversleys have the added worry of sparks carrying on the wind and setting light to their houses." She chuckled suddenly. "You have to laugh. Cynthia bullied the firemen into taking preventative measures by hosing down the front of Malvern House, and now she's tearing strips off poor old Peter because he left their bedroom window open. The whole room's completely saturated."

Siobhan grinned. "Good," she said unsympathetically. "It's time Cynthia had some of her own medicine."

Nora wagged an admonishing finger at her. "Don't be too hard on her, my dear. For all her sins, Cynthia can be very kind when she wants to be. It's a pity you've never seen that side of her."

"I'm not sure I'd want to," said Siobhan cynically. "At a guess, she only shows it when she's offering charity. Where are they, anyway?"

"I've no idea. I expect Peter's making up the spare-room beds and Cynthia's at the front somewhere behaving like the chief constable. You know how bossy she is."

"Yes," agreed Siobhan, who had been on the receiving end of Cynthia's hectoring tongue more often than she cared to remember. Indeed, if she had any regrets about moving to Sowerbridge, they were all centered around the overbearing personality of the Honorable Mrs. Haversley.

By one of those legal quirks of which the English are so fond, the owners of Malvern House had title to the first hundred feet of Fording Farm's driveway while the owners of the farm had right of way in perpetuity across it. This had led to a state of war existing between the two households, although it was a war that had been going on long before the Lavenhams' insignificant tenure of eighteen months. Ian maintained that Cynthia's insistence on her rights stemmed from the fact that the Haversleys were, and always had been, the poor relations of the Fanshaws at the Manor House. ("You get slowly more impoverished if you inherit through the distaff side," he said, "and Peter's family has never been able to lay claim to the manor. It's made Cynthia bitter.") Nevertheless, had he and Siobhan paid heed to their solicitor's warnings, they might have questioned why such a beautiful place had had five different owners in under ten years. Instead, they had accepted the previous owners' assurances that everything in the garden was lovely—*You'll like Cynthia Haversley. She's a charming woman.*—and put the rapid turnover down to coincidence.

Something that sounded like a grenade detonating exploded in the heart of the fire and Nora Bentley jumped. She tapped her heart with a fluttery hand. "Goodness me, it's just like the war," she said in a rush. "So exciting." She tempered this surprising statement by adding that she felt sorry for the O'Riordans, but her sympathy came a poor second to her desire for sensation.

"Are Liam and Bridey here?" asked Siobhan, looking around.

"I don't think so, dear. To be honest, I wonder if they even know what's happening. They were very secretive about where they were staying in Winchester; unless the police know where they are, well"—she shrugged—"who could have told them?"

"Rosheen knows."

Nora gave an absentminded smile. "Yes, but she's with your boys at the farm."

"We are on the phone, Nora."

"I know, dear, but it's all been so sudden. One minute, nothing; the next, mayhem. As a matter of fact, I did suggest we call Rosheen, but Cynthia said there was no point. 'Let Liam and Bridey have a good night's sleep,' she said. What can they do that the fire brigade hasn't already done? Why bother them unnecessarily?"

"I'll bear that in mind when Cynthia's house goes up in flames," said Siobhan dryly, glancing at her watch and telling herself to get a move on. Curiosity held her back. "When did it start?"

"No one knows," said Nora. "Sam and I smelled burning about an hour and a half ago and came to investigate, but by that time the flames were already at the downstairs windows." She waved an arm at The Old Vicarage. "We knocked up Jeremy and got him to call the fire brigade, but the whole thing was out of control long before they arrived."

Siobhan's eyes followed the waving arm. "Why didn't Jeremy call them earlier? Surely he'd have smelled burning before you did? He lives right opposite." Her glance traveled on to the Bentleys' house, Rose Cottage, which stood behind The Old Vicarage, a good hundred yards distant from Kilkenny Cottage.

Nora looked anxious, as if she, too, found Jeremy Jardine's inertia suspicious. "He says he didn't, says he was in his cellar. He was horrified when he saw what was going on."

Siobhan took that last sentence with a pinch of salt. Jeremy Jardine was a wine shipper who had used his Fanshaw family connection some years before to buy The Old Vicarage off the church commissioners for its extensive cellars. But the beautiful brick house looked out over the O'Riordans' unsightly wrecking ground, and he was one of their most strident critics. No one knew how much he'd paid for it, although rumor suggested it had been sold off at a fifth of its value. Certainly questions had been asked at the time about why a substantial Victorian rectory had never been advertised for sale on the open market, although, as usual in Sowerbridge, answers were difficult to come by when they involved the Fanshaw family.

Prior to the murders, Siobhan had been irritated enough by Jeremy's unremitting criticism of the O'Riordans to ask him why he'd bought The Old Vicarage, knowing what the view was going to be. "It's not as though you didn't know about Liam's cars," she told him. "Nora Bentley says you'd been living with Lavinia at the manor for two years before the purchase." He'd muttered darkly about good investments turning sour when promises of action failed to materialize and she had interpreted this as meaning he'd paid a pittance to acquire the property from the church on the mistaken understanding that one of his district councillor buddies could force the O'Riordans to clean up their frontage.

Ian had laughed when she told him about the conversation. "Why on earth doesn't he just offer to pay for the cleanup himself? Liam's never going to pay to have those blasted wrecks removed, but he'd be pleased as punch if someone else did."

"Perhaps he can't afford it. Nora says the Fanshaws aren't half as well off as everyone believes, and Jeremy's business is no great shakes. I know he talks grandly about how he supplies all the top families with quality wine, but that case he sold us was rubbish."

"It wouldn't cost much, not if a scrap-metal merchant did it."

Siobhan had wagged a finger at him. "You know what your problem is, husband of mine? You're too sensible to live in Sowerbridge. Also, you're ignoring the fact that there's an issue of principle at stake. If Jeremy pays for the cleanup then the O'Riordans will have won. Worse still, they will be seen to have won because *their* house will also rise in value the minute the wrecks go."

He shook his head. "Just promise me you won't start taking sides, Shiv. You're no keener on the O'Riordans than anyone else, and there's no law that says the Irish have to stick together. Life's too short to get involved in their ridiculous feuds."

"I promise," she had said, and at the time she had meant it.

But that was before Patrick had been charged with murder. . . .

There was no doubt in the minds of most of Sowerbridge's inhabitants that Patrick O'Riordan saw Lavinia Fanshaw as an easy target. In November, two years previously, he had relieved the confused old woman of a Chippendale chair worth five hundred pounds after claiming a European directive required all hedgerows to be clipped to a uniform standard. He had stripped her laurels to within four feet of the ground in return for the antique, and had sold the foliage on to a crony who made festive Christmas wreaths.

Nor had he shown any remorse. "It was a bit of business," he said in the pub afterward, grinning happily as he swilled his beer, "and she was pleased as punch about it. She told me she's always hated that chair." He was a small, wiry man with a shock of dark hair and penetrating blue eyes which stared unwaveringly at the person he was talking to—like a fighting dog whose intention was to intimidate. "In any case, I did this village a favor. The manor looks a damn sight better since I sorted the frontage."

The fact that most people agreed with him was neither here nor there. The combination of Lavinia's senility and extraordinary longevity meant Sowerbridge Manor was rapidly falling into disrepair, but this did not entitle anyone, least of all an O'Riordan, to take advantage of her. What about Kilkenny Cottage's frontage? people protested. Liam's cars were a great deal worse than Lavinia's overgrown hedge. There was even suspicion that her live-in nurse had connived in the fraud, because she was known to be extremely critical of the deteriorating conditions in which she was expected to work.

"I can't be watching Mrs. Fanshaw twenty-four hours a day," Dorothy Jenkins had said firmly, "and if she makes an arrangement behind my back, then there's nothing I can do about it. It's her grandson you should be talking to. He's the one with power of attorney over her affairs, but he's never going to sell this place before she's dead because he's too mean to put her in a nursing home. She could live forever the way she's going, and nursing homes cost far more than I do. He pays me peanuts because he says I'm getting free board and lodging, but there's no heating, the roof leaks, and the whole place is a death trap of rotten floorboards. He's only waiting for the poor old thing to die so that he can sell the land to a property developer and live in clover for the rest of his life."

Monday, 8th March, 1999

The crowd seemed to be growing bigger and more boisterous by the minute, but as Siobhan recognized few of the faces, she realized word of the fire must have spread to surrounding villages. She couldn't understand why the police were letting thrill-seekers through until she heard one man say that he'd parked on the Southampton Road and cut across a field to bypass the police block. There was much jostling for position; the smell of beer on the breath of one man who pushed past her was overpowering. He barged against her and she jabbed him angrily in the ribs with a sharp elbow before taking Nora's arm and shepherding her across the road.

"Someone's going to be hurt in a minute," she said. "They've obviously come straight from the pub." She maneuvered through a knot of people beside the wall of Malvern House, and ahead of her she saw Nora's husband, Dr. Sam Bentley, talking with Peter and Cynthia Haversley. "There's Sam. I'll leave you with him and then be on my way. I'm worried about Rosheen and the boys." She nodded briefly to the Haversleys, raised a hand in greeting to Sam Bentley, then prepared to push on.

"You won't get through," said Cynthia forcefully, planting her corseted body between Siobhan and the crossroads. "They've barricaded the entire junction and no one's allowed past." Her face had turned crimson from the heat, and Siobhan wondered if she had any idea how unattractive she looked. The combination of dyed blond hair atop a glistening beetroot complexion was reminiscent of sherry trifle, and Siobhan wished she had a camera to record the fact. Siobhan knew her to be in her late sixties because Nora had let slip once that she and Cynthia shared a birthday, but Cynthia herself preferred to draw a discreet veil over her age. Privately (and rather grudgingly) Siobhan admitted she had a case, because her plumpness gave her skin a smooth, firm quality which made her look considerably younger than her years, though it didn't make her any more likable.

Siobhan had asked Ian once if he thought her antipathy to Cynthia was an "Irish thing." The idea had amused him. "On what basis? Because the Honorable Mrs. Haversley symbolizes colonial authority?"

"Something like that."

"Don't be absurd, Shiv. She's a fat snob with a power complex who loves throwing her weight around. No one likes her. *I* certainly don't. She probably wouldn't be so bad if her wet husband had ever stood up to her, but poor old Peter's as cowed as everyone else. You should learn to ignore her. In the great scheme of things, she's about as relevant as birdshit on your windscreen."

"I *hate* birdshit on my windscreen."

"I know," he had said with a grin, "but you don't assume pigeons single your car out because you're Irish, do you?"

She made an effort now to summon a pleasant smile as she answered Cynthia. "Oh, I'm sure they'll make an exception of me. Ian's in Italy this week, which means Rosheen and the boys are on their own. I think I'll be allowed through in the circumstances."

"If you aren't," said Dr. Bentley, "Peter and I can give you a leg-up over the wall and you can cut through Malvern House garden."

"Thank you." She studied his face for a moment. "Does anyone know how the fire started, Sam?"

"We think Liam must have left a cigarette burning."

Siobhan pulled a wry face. "Then it must have been the slowest-burning cigarette in history," she said. "They were gone by nine o'clock this morning."

He looked as worried as his wife had done earlier. "It's only a guess."

"Oh, come on! If it was a smoldering cigarette you'd have seen flames at the windows by lunchtime." She turned her attention back to Cynthia. "I'm surprised that Sam and Nora smelled burning before you did," she said with deliberate lightness. "You and Peter are so much closer than they are."

"We probably would have done if we'd been here," said Cynthia, "but we went to supper with friends in Salisbury. We didn't get home until after Jeremy called the fire brigade." She stared Siobhan down, daring her to dispute the statement.

"Matter of fact," said Peter, "we only just scraped in before the police arrived with barricades. Otherwise they'd have made us leave the car at the church."

Siobhan wondered if the friends had invited the Haversleys or if the Haversleys had invited themselves. She guessed the latter. None of the O'Riordans' neighbors would have wanted to save Kilkenny Cottage, and unlike Jeremy, she thought sarcastically, the Haversleys had no cellar to skulk in. "I really must go," she said then. "Poor Rosheen will be worried sick." But if she expected sympathy for Liam and Bridey's niece, she didn't get it.

"If she were *that* worried, she'd have come down here," declared Cynthia. "With or without your boys. I don't know why you employ her. She's one of the laziest and most deceitful creatures I've ever met. Frankly, I wouldn't have her for love or money."

Siobhan smiled slightly. It was like listening to a cracked record, she thought. The day the Honorable Mrs. Haversley resisted an opportunity to snipe at an O'Riordan would be a red-letter day in Siobhan's book. "I suspect the feeling's mutual, Cynthia. Threat of death might persuade her to work for you, but not love or money."

Cynthia's retort, a pithy one if her annoyed expression was anything to go by, was swallowed by the sound of Kilkenny Cottage collapsing inward upon itself as the beams supporting the roof finally gave way. There was a shout of approval from the crowd behind them, and while everyone else's attention was temporarily distracted, Siobhan watched Peter Haversley give his wife a surreptitious pat on the back.

4

Saturday, 30th January, 1999

Siobhan had stubbornly kept an open mind about Patrick's guilt, although as she was honest enough to admit to Ian, it was more for Rosheen and Bridey's sake than because she seriously believed there was room for reasonable doubt. She couldn't forget the fear she had seen in Rosheen's eyes one day when she came home early to find Jeremy Jardine at the front door of the farm. "What are you doing here?" she had demanded of him angrily, appalled by the ashen color in her nanny's cheeks.

There was a telling silence before Rosheen stumbled into words.

"He says we're murdering Mrs. Fanshaw all over again by taking Patrick's side," said the girl in a shaken voice. "I said it was wrong to condemn him before the evidence is heard—you told me everyone would believe Patrick was innocent until the trial—but Mr. Jardine just keeps shouting at me."

Jeremy had laughed. "I'm doing the rounds with my new wine list," he said, jerking his thumb toward his car. "But I'm damned if I'll stay quiet while an Irish murderer's cousin quotes English law at me."

Siobhan had controlled her temper because her two sons were watching from the kitchen window. "Go inside now," she told Rosheen, "but if Mr. Jardine comes here again when Ian and I are at work, I want you to phone the police immediately." She waited while the girl retreated with relief into the depths of the house. "I mean it, Jeremy," she said coldly. "However strongly you may feel about all of this, I'll have you prosecuted if you try that trick again. It's not as though Rosheen has any evidence that can help Patrick, so you're simply wasting your time."

He shrugged. "You're a fool, Siobhan. Patrick's guilty as sin. You know it. Everyone knows it. Just don't come crying to me later when the jury proves us right and you find yourself tarred with the same brush as the O'Riordans."

"I already have been," she said curtly. "If you and the Haversleys had your way, I'd have been lynched by now, but, God knows, I'd give my right arm to see Patrick get off, if only to watch the three of you wearing sackcloth and ashes for the rest of your lives."

Ian had listened to her account of the conversation with a worried frown on his face. "It won't help Patrick if he does get off," he warned. "No one's going to believe he didn't do it. Reasonable doubt sounds all very well in court, but it won't count for anything in Sowerbridge. He'll never be able to come back."

"I know."

"Then don't get too openly involved," he advised. "We'll be living here for the foreseeable future, and I really don't want the boys growing up in an atmosphere of hostility. Support Bridey and Rosheen by all means"—he gave her a wry smile—"but do me a favor, Shiv, and hold that Irish temper of yours in check. I'm not convinced Patrick is worth going to war over, particularly not with our close neighbors."

It was good advice, but difficult to follow. There was too much overt prejudice against the Irish in general for Siobhan to stay quiet indefinitely. War finally broke out at one of Cynthia and Peter Haversley's tedious dinner parties at Malvern House, which were impossible to avoid without telling so many lies that it was easier to attend the wretched things. "She watches the driveway from her window," sighed Siobhan when Ian asked why they couldn't just say they had another engagement that night. "She keeps tabs on everything we do. She knows when we're in and when we're out. It's like living in a prison."

"I don't know why she keeps inviting us," he said.

Siobhan found his genuine ignorance of Cynthia's motives amusing. "It's her favorite sport," she said matter-of-factly. "Bearbaiting . . . with me as the bear."

Ian sighed. "Then let's tell her the truth, say we'd rather stay in and watch television."

"Good idea. There's the phone. *You* tell her."

He smiled unhappily. "It'll make her even more impossible."

"Of course it will."

"Perhaps we should just grit our teeth and go?"

"Why not? It's what we usually do."

The evening had been a particularly dire one, with Cynthia and Jeremy holding the platform as usual, Peter getting quietly drunk, and the Bentleys making only occasional remarks. A silence had developed around the table and Siobhan, who had been firmly biting her tongue since they arrived, consulted her watch under cover of her napkin and wondered if nine forty-five was too early to announce departure.

"I suppose what troubles me the most," said Jeremy suddenly, "is that if I'd pushed to have the O'Riordans evicted years ago, poor old Lavinia would still be alive." He was a similar age to the Lavenhams and handsome in a florid sort of way—*Too much sampling of his own wares,* Siobhan always thought—and loved to style himself as Hampshire's most eligible bachelor. Many was the time Siobhan had wanted to ask why, if he was so eligible, he remained unattached, but she didn't bother because she thought she knew the answer. He couldn't find a woman stupid enough to agree with his own valuation of himself.

"You can't evict people from their own homes," Sam Bentley pointed out mildly. "On that basis, we could all be evicted any time our neighbors took against us."

"Oh, you know what I mean," Jeremy answered, looking pointedly at Siobhan as if to remind her that she was tarred with the O'Riordans' brush. "There must be something I could have done—had them prosecuted for environmental pollution, perhaps?"

"We should never have allowed them to come here in the first place," declared Cynthia. "It's iniquitous that the rest of us have no say over what sort of people will be living on our doorsteps. If the Parish Council was allowed to vet prospective newcomers, the problem would never have arisen."

Siobhan raised her head and smiled in amused disbelief at the other woman's arrogant assumption that the Parish Council was in her pocket. "What a good idea!" she said brightly, ignoring Ian's warning look across the table. "It would also give prospective newcomers a chance to vet the people already living here. It means house prices would drop like a stone, of course, but at least neither side could say afterward that they went into it with their eyes closed."

The pity was that Cynthia was too stupid to understand irony. "You're quite wrong, my dear," she said with a condescending smile. "The house prices would go *up*. They always do when an area becomes exclusive."

"Only when there are enough purchasers who want the kind of exclusivity you're offering them, Cynthia. It's basic economics." Siobhan propped her elbows on the table and leaned forward, stung into pricking the fat woman's self-righteous bubble once and for all, even if she did recognize that her real target was Jeremy Jardine. "And for what it's worth, there won't be any competition to live in Sowerbridge when word gets out that, *however* much money you have, there's no point in applying unless you share the Fanshaw mafia's belief that Hitler was right."

Nora Bentley gave a small gasp and made damping gestures with her hands.

Jeremy was less restrained. "Well, my God!" he burst out aggressively. "That's bloody rich coming from an Irishwoman. Where was Ireland in the war? Sitting on the sidelines, rooting for Germany, that's where. And you have the damn nerve to sit in judgment on us! All you Irish are despicable. You flood over here like a plague of sewer rats looking for handouts, then you criticize us when we point out that we don't think you're worth the trouble you're causing us."

It was like a simmering saucepan boiling over. In the end, all that had been achieved by restraint was to allow resentment to fester. On both sides.

"I suggest you withdraw those remarks, Jeremy," said Ian coldly, rousing himself in defense of his wife. "You might be entitled to insult Siobhan like that if your business paid as much tax and employed as many people as hers does, but as that's never going to happen I think you should apologize."

"No way. Not unless she apologizes to Cynthia first."

Once roused, Ian's temper was even more volatile than his wife's. "She's got nothing to apologize for," he snapped. "Everything she said was true. Neither you nor Cynthia has any more right than anyone else to dictate what goes on in this village, yet you do it anyway. And with very little justification. At least the rest of us bought our houses fair and square on the open market, which is more than can be said of you or Peter. He inherited his, and you got yours cheap via the old-boy network. I just hope you're prepared for the consequences when something goes wrong. You can't incite hatred and then pretend you're not responsible for it."

"Now, now, now!" said Sam with fussy concern. "This sort of talk isn't healthy."

"Sam's right," said Nora. "What's said can never be unsaid."

Ian shrugged. "Then tell this village to keep its collective mouth shut about the Irish in general and the O'Riordans in particular. Or doesn't the rule apply to them? Perhaps it's only the well-to-do English like the Haversleys and Jeremy who can't be criticized?"

Peter Haversley gave an unexpected snigger. "Well-to-do?" he muttered tipsily. "Who's well-to-do? We're all in hock up to our blasted eyeballs while we wait for the manor to be sold."

"Be quiet, Peter," said his wife.

But he refused to be silenced. "That's the trouble with murder. Everything gets do damned messy. You're not allowed to sell what's rightfully yours because probate goes into limbo." His bleary eyes looked across the table at Jeremy. "It's your fault, you sanctimonious little toad. Power of bloody attorney, my arse. You're too damn greedy for your own good. Always were . . . always will be. I kept telling you to put the old bloodsucker into a home but would you listen? Don't worry, you kept saying, she'll be dead soon . . ."

00:23 A.M.—Tuesday, 9th March, 1999

The hall lights were on in the farmhouse when Siobhan finally reached it, but there was no sign of Rosheen. This surprised her until she checked the time and saw that it was well after midnight. She went into the kitchen and squatted down to stroke Patch, the O'Riordans' amiable mongrel, who lifted his head from the hearth in front of the Aga and wagged his stumpy tail before giving an enormous yawn and returning to his slumbers. Siobhan had agreed to look after him while the O'Riordans were away and he seemed entirely at home in his new surroundings. She peered out of the kitchen window toward the fire, but there was nothing to see except the dark line of trees bordering the property, and it occurred to her then that Rosheen probably had no idea her uncle's house had gone up in flames.

She tiptoed upstairs to check on her two young sons who, like Patch, woke briefly to wrap their arms around her neck and acknowledge her kisses before closing their eyes again. She paused outside Rosheen's room for a moment, hoping to hear the sound of the girl's television, but there was only silence and she retreated downstairs again, relieved to be spared explanations tonight. Rosheen had been frightened enough by the anti-Irish slogans daubed across the front of Kilkenny Cottage; God only knew how she would react to hearing it had been destroyed.

Rosheen's employment with them had happened more by accident than design when Siobhan's previous nanny—a young woman given to melodrama—had announced after two weeks in rural Hampshire that she'd rather "die" than spend another night away from the lights of London. In desperation, Siobhan had taken up Bridey's shy suggestion to fly Rosheen over from Ireland on a month's trial—"*She's Liam's brother's daughter and she's a wonder with children. She's been looking after her brothers and her cousins since she was knee-high to a grasshopper, and they all think the world of her.*"—and Siobhan had been surprised by how quickly and naturally the girl had fitted into the household.

Ian had reservations—"*She's too young . . . she's too scatterbrained . . . I'm not sure I want to be quite so cozy with the O'Riordans."*—but he had come to respect her in the wake of Patrick's arrest when, despite the hostility in the village, she had refused to abandon either Siobhan or Bridey. "Mind you, I wouldn't bet on family loyalty being what's keeping her here."

"What else is there?"

"Sex with Kevin Wyllie. She goes weak at the knees every time she sees him, never mind he's probably intimately acquainted with the thugs who're terrorizing Liam and Bridey."

"You can't blame him for that. He's lived here all his life. I should imagine most of Sowerbridge could name names if they wanted to. At least he's had the guts to stand by Rosheen."

"He's an illiterate oaf with an IQ of ten," growled Ian. "Rosheen's not stupid, so what the hell do they find to talk about?"

Siobhan giggled. "I don't think his conversation is what interests her."

Recognizing that she was too hyped-up to sleep, she poured herself a glass of wine and played the messages on the answerphone. There were a couple of business calls followed by one from Ian. *"Hi, it's me. Things are progressing well on the Ravenelli front. All being well, hand-printed Italian silk should be on offer through Lavenham Interiors by August. Good news, eh? I can think of at least two projects that will benefit from the designs they've been showing me. You'll love them, Shiv. Aquamarine swirls with every shade of terra cotta you can imagine."* Pause for a yawn. *"I'm missing you and the boys like crazy. Give me a ring if you get back before eleven, otherwise I'll speak to you tomorrow. I should be home on Friday."* He finished with a slobbery kiss which made her laugh.

The last message was from Liam O'Riordan and had obviously been intercepted by Rosheen. *"Hello? Are you there, Rosheen? It's . . ."* said Liam's voice before it was cut off by the receiver being lifted. Out of curiosity, Siobhan pressed one-four-seven-one to find out when Liam had phoned, and she listened in perplexity as the computerized voice at the other end gave the time of the last call as "twenty thirty-six hours," and the number from which it was made as "eight-two-seven-five-three-eight." She knew the sequence off by heart but flicked through the telephone index anyway to make certain. *Liam & Bridey O'Riordan, Kilkenny Cottage, Sowerbridge, Tel: 827538.*

For the second time that night her first instinct was to rush toward denial. It was a mistake, she told herself. . . . Liam couldn't possibly have been phoning from Kilkenny Cottage at eight-thirty . . . The O'Riordans were under police protection in Winchester for the duration of Patrick's trial. . . . Kilkenny Cottage was empty when the fire started. . . .

But, oh dear God! Supposing it wasn't?

"Rosheen!" she shouted, running up the stairs again and hammering on the nanny's door. "Rosheen! It's Siobhan. Wake up! Was Liam in the cottage?" She thrust open the door and switched on the light, only to look around the room in dismay because no one was there.

Siobhan had raised the question of Lavinia Fanshaw's heirs with the detective inspector. "You can't ignore the fact that both Peter Haversley and Jeremy Jardine had a far stronger motive than Patrick could ever have had," she pointed out. "They both stood to inherit from her will, and neither of them made any bones about wanting her dead. Lavinia's husband had one sister, now dead, who produced a single child, Peter, who has *no* children. And Lavinia's only child, a daughter, also dead, produced Jeremy, who's never married."

He was amused by the extent of her research. "We didn't ignore it, Mrs. Lavenham. It was the first thing we looked at, but you know better than anyone that they couldn't have done it because you and your husband supplied their alibis."

"Only from eight o'clock on Saturday night until two o'clock on Sunday morning," protested Siobhan. "And not out of choice either. Have you any idea what it's like living in a village like Sowerbridge, Inspector? Dinner parties are considered intrinsically superior to staying in of a Friday or Saturday night and watching telly, never mind the same boring people get invited every time and the same boring conversations take place. It's a status thing." She gave a sarcastic shrug. "Personally, I'd rather watch a good Arnie or Sly movie any day than have to appear interested in someone else's mortgage or pension plan, but then—*hell*—I'm Irish and everyone knows the Irish are common as muck."

"You'll have status enough when Patrick comes to trial," said the inspector with amusement. "You'll be the one providing the alibis."

"I wouldn't be able to if we'd managed to get rid of Jeremy and the Haversleys any sooner. Believe me, it wasn't Ian and I who kept them there— we did everything we could to make them go—they just refused to take the hints. Sam and Nora Bentley went at a reasonable time, but we couldn't get the rest of them to budge. Are you *sure* Lavinia was killed between eleven and midnight? Don't you find it suspicious that it's *my* evidence that's excluded Peter and Jeremy from the case? Everyone knows I'm the only person in Sowerbridge who'd rather give Patrick O'Riordan an alibi if I possibly could."

"What difference does that make?"

"It means I'm a reluctant witness, and therefore gives my evidence in Peter and Jeremy's favor more weight."

The inspector shook his head. "I think you're making too much of your position in all of this, Mrs. Lavenham. If Mr. Haversley and Mr. Jardine had conspired to murder Mrs. Fanshaw, wouldn't they have taken themselves to— say, Ireland—for the weekend? That would have given them a much stronger alibi than spending six hours in the home of a hostile witness. In any case," he went on apologetically, "we are sure about the time of the murders. These days, pathologists' timings are extremely precise, particularly when the bodies are found as quickly as these ones were."

Siobhan wasn't ready to give up so easily. "But you must see how odd it is that it happened the night Ian and I gave a dinner party. We *hate* dinner parties. Most of our entertaining is done around barbecues in the summer when friends come to stay. It's always casual and always spur-of-the-moment and I can't believe it was coincidence that Lavinia was murdered on the one night in the whole damn year for which we'd sent out invitations"—her mouth twisted—"*six weeks in advance. . . .*"

He eyed her thoughtfully. "If you can tell me how they did it, I might agree with you."

"Before they came to our house or after they left it," she suggested. "The pathologist's timings are wrong."

He pulled a piece of paper from a pile on his desk and turned it toward her. "That's an itemized British Telecom list of every call made from Sower-bridge Manor during the week leading up to the murders." He touched the last number. "This one was made by Dorothy Jenkins to a friend of hers in London and was timed at ten-thirty P.M. on the night she died. The duration time was just over three minutes. We've spoken to the friend and she described Miss Jenkins as at 'the end of her tether.' Apparently Mrs. Fanshaw was a difficult patient to nurse—Alzheimer's sufferers usually are—and Miss Jenkins had phoned this woman—also a nurse—to tell her that she felt like 'smothering the old bitch where she lay.' It had happened several times before, but this time Miss Jenkins was in tears and rang off abruptly when her friend said she had someone with her and couldn't talk for long." He paused for a moment. "The friend was worried enough to phone back after her visitor had gone," he went on, "and she estimates the time of that call at about a quarter past midnight. The line was engaged so she couldn't get through, and she admits to being relieved because she thought it meant Miss Jenkins had found someone else to confide in."

Siobhan frowned. "Well, at least it proves she was alive after midnight, doesn't it?"

The inspector shook his head. "I'm afraid not. The phone in the kitchen had been knocked off its rest—we think Miss Jenkins may have been trying to dial nine-nine-nine when she was attacked"—he tapped his finger on the piece of paper—"which means that, with or without the pathologist's timings, she must have been killed between that last itemized call at ten-thirty and her friend's return call at fifteen minutes past midnight, when the phone was already off the hook."

5

00:32 A.M.—Tuesday, 9th March, 1999

Even as Siobhan lifted the receiver to call the police and report Rosheen missing, she was having second thoughts. They hadn't taken a blind bit of notice in the past, she thought bitterly, so why should it be different today? She could even predict how the conversation would go simply because she had been there so many times before.

Clam down, Mrs. Lavenham. . . . It was undoubtedly a hoax. . . . Let's see now. . . . Didn't someone phone you not so long ago pretending to be Bridey in the throes of a heart attack . . . ? We rushed an ambulance to her only to find her alive and well and watching television. . . . You and your nanny are Irish. . . . Someone thought it would be entertaining to get a rise out of you by creeping into Kilkenny Cottage and making a call. . . . Everyone knows the O'Riordans are notoriously careless about locking their back door. . . . Sadly we can't legislate for practical jokes. . . . Your nanny . . . ? She'll be watching the fire along with everyone else. . . .

With a sigh of frustration, she replaced the receiver and listened to the message again. *"Hello? Are you there, Rosheen? It's . . ."*

She had been so sure it was Liam the first time she heard it, but now she was less certain. The Irish accent was the easiest accent in the world to ape, and Liam's was so broad any fool could do it. For want of someone more sensible to talk to, she telephoned Ian in his hotel bedroom in Rome. "It's me," she said, "and I've only just got back. I'm sorry to wake you but they've burned Kilkenny Cottage and Rosheen's missing. Do you think I should phone the police?"

"Hang on," he said sleepily. "Run that one by me again. Who's they?"

"I don't know," she said in frustration. "Someone—anyone—Peter Haversley patted Cynthia on the back when the roof caved in. If I knew where the O'Riordans were I'd phone them, but Rosheen's the only one who knows the number—and she's not here. I'd go back to the fire if I had a car—the village is swarming with policemen—but I've had to leave mine at the church and yours is at Heathrow—and the children will never be able to walk all the way down the drive, not at this time of night."

He gave a long yawn. "You're going much too fast. I've only just woken up. What's this about Kilkenny Cottage burning down?"

She explained it slowly.

"So where's Rosheen?" He sounded more alert now. "And what the hell was she doing leaving the boys?"

"I don't know." She told him about the telephone call from Kilkenny Cottage. "If it was Liam, Rosheen may have gone up there to see him, and now I'm worried they were in the house when the fire started. Everyone thinks it was empty because we watched them go this morning." She described the scene for him as Liam helped Bridey into their Ford Estate then drove unsmilingly past the group of similarly unsmiling neighbors who had gathered at the crossroads to see them off. "It was awful," she said. "I went down to collect Patch, and bloody Cynthia started hissing at them so the rest joined in. I really hate them, Ian."

He didn't answer immediately. "Look," he said then, "the fire brigade don't just take people's words for this kind of thing. They'll have checked to make sure there was no one in the house as soon as they got there. And if

Liam and Bridey *did* come back, their car would have been parked at the front and someone would have noticed it. Okay, I agree the village is full of bigots, but they're not murderers, Shiv, and they wouldn't keep quiet if they thought the O'Riordans were burning to death. Come on, think about it. You know I'm right."

"What about Rosheen?"

"Yes, well," he said dryly, "it wouldn't be the first time, would it? Did you check the barn? I expect she's out there getting laid by Kevin Wyllie."

"She's only done it once."

"She's used the barn once," he corrected her, "but it's anyone's guess how often she's been laid by Kevin. I'll bet you a pound to a penny they're tucked up together somewhere and she'll come wandering in with a smile on her face when you least expect it. I hope you tear strips off her for it, too. She's no damn business to leave the boys on their own."

She let it ride, unwilling to be drawn into another argument about Rosheen's morals. Ian worked on the principle that what the eye didn't see the heart didn't grieve over, and refused to recognize the hypocrisy of his position, while Siobhan's view was that Kevin was merely the bit of "rough" that was keeping Rosheen amused while she looked for something better. *God knew every woman did it . . . the road to respectability was far from straight. . . .* In any case, she agreed with his final sentiment. Even if it were Liam who phoned from the cottage, Rosheen's first responsibility was to James and Oliver. "So what should I do? Just wait for her to come back?"

"I don't see you have much choice. She's over twenty-one so the police won't do anything tonight."

"Okay."

He knew her too well. "You don't sound convinced."

She wasn't, but then she was more relaxed about the way Rosheen conducted herself then he was. The fact that they'd come home early one night and caught her in the barn with her knickers down had offended Ian deeply, even though Rosheen had been monitoring the boys all the time via a two-way transmitter that she'd taken with her. Ian had wanted to sack her on the spot, but Siobhan had persuaded him out of it after extracting a promise from Rosheen that the affair would be confined to her spare time in future. Afterward, and because she was a great deal less puritanical than her English husband, Siobhan had buried her face in her pillow to stifle her laughter. Her view was that Rosheen had shown typical Irish tact by having sex outside in the barn rather than under the Lavenhams' roof. As she pointed out to Ian: *"We'd never have known Kevin was there if she'd smuggled him into her room and told him to perform quietly."*

"It's just that I'm tired," she lied, knowing she could never describe her sense of foreboding down the telephone to someone over a thousand miles away. Empty houses gave her the shivers at the best of times—a throwback to the rambling, echoing mansion of her childhood, which her overactive imagination had peopled with giants and specters. . . . "Look, go back to sleep and

I'll ring you tomorrow. It'll have sorted itself out by then. Just make sure you come home on Friday," she ended severely, "or I'll file for divorce immediately. I didn't marry you to be deserted for the Ravenelli brothers."

"I will," he promised.

Siobhan listened to the click as he hung up at the other end, then replaced her own receiver before opening the front door and looking toward the dark shape of the barn. She searched for a chink of light between the double doors but knew she was wasting her time even while she was doing it. Rosheen had been so terrified by Ian's threat to tell her parents in Ireland what she'd been up to that her sessions with Kevin were now confined to somewhere a great deal more private than Fording Farm's barn.

With a sigh she retreated to the kitchen and settled on a cushion in front of the Aga with Patch's head lying across her lap and the bottle of wine beside her. It was another ten minutes before she noticed that the key to Kilkenny Cottage, which should have been hanging from a hook on the dresser, was no longer there.

Wednesday, 10th February, 1999

"But why are you so sure it was Patrick?" Siobhan had asked the inspector then. "Why not a total stranger? I mean, anyone could have taken the hammer from his toolbox if he'd left it in the kitchen the way he says he did."

"Because there were no signs of a break-in. Whoever killed them either had a key to the front door or was let in by Dorothy Jenkins. And that means it must have been someone she knew."

"Maybe she hadn't locked up," said Siobhan, clutching at straws. "Maybe they came in through the back door."

"Have you ever tried to open the back door to the manor, Mrs. Lavenham?"

"No."

"Apart from the fact that the bolts were rusted into their sockets, it's so warped and swollen with damp you have to put a shoulder to it to force it ajar, and it screams like a banshee every time you do it. If a stranger had come in through the back door at eleven o'clock at night, he wouldn't have caught Miss Jenkins in the kitchen. She'd have taken to her heels the minute she heard the banshee-wailing and would have used one of the phones upstairs to call the police."

"You can't know that," argued Siobhan. "Sowerbridge is the sleepiest place on earth. Why would she assume it was an intruder? She probably thought it was Jeremy paying a late-night visit to his grandmother."

"We don't think so." He picked up a pen and turned it between his fingers. "As far as we can establish, that door was never used. Certainly none of the neighbors report going in that way. The milkman said Miss Jenkins kept it bolted because on the one occasion when she tried to open it, it became so wedged that she had to ask him to force it shut again."

She sighed, admitting defeat. "Patrick's always been so sweet to me and my children. I just can't believe he's a murderer."

He smiled at her naivete. "The two are not mutually exclusive, Mrs. Lavenham. I expect Jack the Ripper's neighbor said the same about him."

01:00 A.M.— Tuesday, 9th March, 1999

People began to shiver as the smoldering remains were dowsed by the fire hoses and the pungent smell of wet ashes stung their nostrils. In the aftermath of excitement, a sense of shame crept among the inhabitants of Sowerbridge—*schadenfreude* was surely alien to their natures?—and bit by bit the crowd began to disperse. Only the Haversleys, the Bentleys, and Jeremy Jardine lingered at the crossroads, held by a mutual fascination for the scene of devastation that would greet them every time they emerged from their houses.

"We won't be able to open our windows for weeks," said Nora Bentley, wrinkling her nose. "The smell will be suffocating."

"It'll be worse when the wind gets up and deposits soot all over the place," complained Peter Haversley, brushing ash from his coat.

His wife clicked her tongue impatiently. "We'll just have to put up with it," she said. "It's hardly the end of the world."

Sam Bentley surprised her with a sudden bark of laughter. "Well spoken, Cynthia, considering you'll be bearing the brunt of it. The prevailing winds are southwesterly, which means most of the muck will collect in Malvern House. Still"—he paused to glance from her to Peter—"you sow a wind and you reap a whirlwind, eh?"

There was a short silence.

"Have you noticed how Liam's wrecks have survived intact?" asked Nora then, with assumed brightness. "Is it a judgment, do you think?"

"Don't be ridiculous," said Jeremy.

Sam gave another brief chortle. "Is it ridiculous? You complained enough when there were only the cars to worry about. Now you've got a burned-out cottage to worry about as well. I can't believe the O'Riordans were insured, so it'll be years before anything is done. If you're lucky, a developer will buy the land and build an estate of little boxes on your doorstep. If you're unlucky, Liam will put up a corrugated-iron shack and live in that. And do you know, Jeremy, I hope he does. Personal revenge is so much sweeter than anything the law can offer."

"What's that supposed to mean?"

"You'd have been wiser to call the fire brigade earlier," said the old doctor bluntly. "Nero may have fiddled while Rome burned, but it didn't do his reputation any good."

Another silence.

"What are you implying?" demanded Cynthia aggressively. "That Jeremy could somehow have prevented the fire?"

Jeremy Jardine folded his arms. "I'll sue you for slander if you *are*, Sam."

"It won't be just me. Half the village is wondering why Nora and I smelled burning before you did, and why Cynthia and Peter took themselves off to Salisbury on a Monday evening for the first time in living memory."

"Coincidence," grunted Peter Haversley. "Pure coincidence."

"Well, I pray for all your sakes you're telling the truth," murmured Sam, wiping a weary hand across his ash-grimed face, "because the police aren't the only ones who'll be asking questions. The Lavenhams certainly won't stay quiet."

"I hope you're not suggesting that one of us set fire to that beastly little place," said Cynthia crossly. "Honestly, Sam, I wonder about you sometimes."

He shook his head sadly, wishing he could dislike her as comprehensively as Siobhan Lavenham did. "No, Cynthia, I'm suggesting you knew it was going to happen, and even incited the local youths to do it. You can argue that you wanted revenge for Lavinia and Dorothy's deaths, but aiding and abetting any crime is a prosecutable offense and"—he sighed—"you'll get no sympathy from me if you go to prison for it."

Behind them, in the hall of Malvern House, the telephone began to ring. . . .

Wednesday, 10th February, 1999

Siobhan had put an opened envelope on the desk in front of the detective inspector. "Even if Patrick is the murderer and even if Bridey knows he is, it doesn't excuse this kind of thing," she said. "I can't prove it came from Cynthia Haversley, but I'm a hundred percent certain it did. She's busting a gut to make life so unpleasant for Liam and Bridey that they'll leave of their own accord."

The inspector frowned as he removed a folded piece of paper and read the letters pasted onto it.

HAnGInG IS TOo GOoD foR THE LikEs of YOU. BUrN in h e l l

"Who was it sent to?" he asked.

"Bridey."

"Why did she give it to you and not to the police?"

"Because she knew I was coming here today and asked me to bring it with me. It was posted through her letterbox sometime the night before last."

("They'll take more notice of you than they ever take of me," the old woman had said, pressing the envelope urgently into Siobhan's hands. "Make them understand we're in danger before it's too late.")

He turned the envelope over. "Why do you think it came from Mrs. Haversley?"

Feminine intuition, thought Siobhan wryly. "Because the letters that make up 'hell' have been cut from a *Daily Telegraph* banner imprint. It's the only broadsheet newspaper that has an 'h,' an 'e,' and two 'l's in its title, and Cynthia takes the *Telegraph* every day."

"Along with how many other people in Sowerbridge?"

She smiled slightly. "Quite a few, but no one else has Cynthia Haversley's poisonous frame of mind. She loves stirring. The more she can work people up, the happier she is. It gives her a sense of importance to have everyone dancing to her tune."

"You don't like her." It was a statement rather than a question.

"No."

"Neither do I," admitted the inspector, "but it doesn't make her guilty, Mrs. Lavenham. Liam and/or Bridey could have acquired a *Telegraph* just as easily and sent this letter to themselves."

"That's what Bridey told me you'd say."

"Because it's the truth?" he suggested mildly. "Mrs. Haversley's a fat, clumsy woman with fingers like sausages, and if she'd been wearing gloves the whole exercise would have been impossible. This"—he touched the letter—"is too neat. There's not a letter out of place."

"Peter then."

"Peter Haversley's an alcoholic. His hands shake."

"Jeremy Jardine?"

"I doubt it. Poison-pen letters are usually written by women. I'm sorry, Mrs. Lavenham, but I can guarantee the only fingerprints I will find on this— other than yours and mine, of course—are Bridey O'Riordan's. Not because the person who did it wore gloves, but because Bridey did it herself."

01:10 A.M.—Tuesday, 9th March, 1999

Dr. Bentley clicked his tongue in concern as he glanced past Cynthia to her husband. Peter was walking unsteadily toward them after answering the telephone, his face leeched of color in the lights of the fire engines. "You should be in bed, man. We should all be in bed. We're too old for this sort of excitement."

Peter Haversley ignored him. "That was Siobhan," he said jerkily. "She wants me to tell the police that Rosheen is missing. She said Liam called the farm from Kilkenny Cottage at eight-thirty this evening, and she's worried he and Rosheen were in there when the fire started."

"They can't have been," said Jeremy.

"How do you know?"

"We watched Liam and Bridey leave for Winchester this morning."

"What if Liam came back to protect his house? What if he phoned Rosheen and asked her to join him?"

"Oh, for God's sake, Peter!" snapped Cynthia. "It's just Siobhan trying to make trouble again. You know what she's like."

"I don't think so. She sounded very distressed." He looked around for a policeman. "I'd better report it."

But his wife gripped his arm to hold him back. "No," she said viciously. "Let Siobhan do her own dirty work. If she wants to employ a slut to look after her children then it's her responsibility to keep tabs on her, not ours."

There was a moment of stillness while Peter searched her face in appalled recognition that he was looking at a stranger, then he drew back his hand and slapped her across the face. "Whatever depths you may have sunk me to," he said, "I am *not* a murderer. . . ."

★★★LATE NEWS—The Daily Telegraph—Tuesday, 9th March, A.M.

IRISH FAMILY BURNED OUT BY VIGILANTES

The family home of Patrick O'Riordan, currently on trial for the murder of Lavinia Fanshaw and Dorothy Jenkins, was burned to the ground last night in what police suspect was a deliberate act of arson. Concern has been expressed over the whereabouts of O'Riordan's elderly parents, and some reports suggest bodies were recovered from the gutted kitchen. Police are refusing to confirm or deny the rumors. Suspicion has fallen on local vigilante groups who have been conducting a "hate" campaign against the O'Riordan family. In face of criticism, Hampshire police have restated their policy of zero tolerance toward anyone who decides to take the law into his own hands. "We will not hesitate to prosecute," said a spokesman. "Vigilantes should understand that arson is a very serious offense."

6

Tuesday, 9th March, 1999

When Siobhan heard a car pull into the driveway at 6:00 A.M she prayed briefly, but with little hope, that someone had found Rosheen and brought her home. Hollow-eyed from lack of sleep, she opened her front door and stared at the two policemen on her doorstep. They looked like ghosts in the gray dawn light. Harbingers of doom, she thought, reading their troubled expressions. She recognized one of them as the detective inspector and the other as the young constable who had flagged her down the previous night. "You'd better come in," she said, pulling the door wide.

"Thank you."

She led the way into the kitchen and dropped onto the cushion in front of the Aga again, cradling Patch in her arms. "This is Bridey's dog," she told them, stroking his muzzle. "She adores him. *He* adores her. The trouble is he's a hopeless guard dog. He's like Bridey"—tears of exhaustion sprang into her eyes—"not overly bright—not overly brave—but as kind as kind can be."

The two policemen stood awkwardly in front of her, unsure where to sit or what to say.

"You look terrible," she said unevenly, "so I presume you've come to tell me Rosheen is dead."

"We don't know yet, Mrs. Lavenham," said the inspector, turning a chair to face her and lowering himself onto it. He gestured to the young constable to do the same. "We found a body in the kitchen area, but it'll be some time before—" He paused, unsure how to continue.

"I'm afraid it was so badly burned it was unrecognizable. We're waiting on the pathologist's report to give us an idea of the age and"—he paused again—"sex."

"Oh, God!" she said dully. "Then it must be Rosheen."

"Why don't you think it's Bridey or Liam?"

"Because . . ." she broke off with a worried frown, "I assumed the phone call was a hoax to frighten Rosheen. Oh, my God! Aren't they in Winchester?"

He looked troubled. "They were escorted to a safe house at the end of yesterday's proceedings but it appears they left again shortly afterward. There was no one to monitor them, you see. They had a direct line through to the local police station and we sent out regular patrols during the night. We were worried about trouble coming from outside, not that they might decide to return to Kilkenny Cottage without telling us." He rubbed a hand around his jaw. "There are recent tire marks up at the manor. We think Liam may have parked his Ford there in order to push Bridey across the lawn and through the gate onto the footpath beside Kilkenny Cottage."

She shook her head in bewilderment. "Then why didn't you find three bodies?"

"Because the Estate isn't there now, Mrs. Lavenham, and whoever died in Kilkenny Cottage probably died at the hands of Liam O'Riordan."

Wednesday, 10th February, 1999

She had stood up at the end of her interview with the inspector. "Do you know what I hate most about the English?" she told him.

He shook his head.

"It never occurs to you, you might be wrong." She placed her palm on the poison-pen letter on his desk. "But you're wrong about this. Bridey cares about my opinion—she cares about *me*—not just as a fellow Irishwoman but as the employer of her niece. She'd never do anything to jeopardize Rosheen's position in our house, because Rosheen and I are her only lifeline in Sowerbridge. We shop for her, we do our best to protect her, and we welcome her to the farm when things get difficult. Under no circumstances *whatsoever* would Bridey use me to pass on falsified evidence, because she'd be too afraid I'd wash my hands of her and then persuade Rosheen to do the same."

"It may be true, Mrs. Lavenham, but it's not an argument you could ever use in court."

"I'm not interested in legal argument, inspector, I'm only interested in persuading you that there is a terror campaign being waged against the O'Riordans in Sowerbridge and that their lives are in danger." She watched him shake his head. "You haven't listened to a word I've said, have you? You just think I'm taking Bridey's side because I'm Irish."

"Aren't you?"

"No." She straightened with a sigh. "Moral support is alien to Irish culture, Inspector. We only really enjoy fighting with each other. I thought every Englishman knew *that*. . . ."

Tuesday, 9th March, 1999

The news that Patrick O'Riordan's trial had been adjourned while police investigated the disappearance of his parents and his cousin was broadcast across the networks at noon, but Siobhan switched off the radio before the names could register with her two young sons.

They had sat wide-eyed all morning watching a procession of policemen traipse to and from Rosheen's bedroom in search of anything that might give them a lead to where she had gone. Most poignantly, as far as Siobhan was concerned, they had carefully removed the girl's hairbrush, some used tissues from her wastepaper basket, and a small pile of dirty washing in order to provide the pathologist with comparative DNA samples.

She had explained to the boys that Rosheen hadn't been in the house when she got back the previous night, and because she was worried about it she had asked the police to help find her.

"She went to Auntie Bridey's," said six-year-old James.

"How do you know, darling?"

"Because Uncle Liam phoned and said Auntie Bridey wasn't feeling very well."

"Did Rosheen tell you that?"

He nodded. "She said she wouldn't be long but that I had to go to sleep. So I did."

She dropped a kiss on the top of his head. "Good boy."

He and Oliver were drawing pictures at the kitchen table, and James suddenly dragged his pencil to and fro across the page to obliterate what he'd been doing. "Is it because Uncle Patrick killed that lady?" he asked her.

Siobhan searched his face for a moment. *The rules had been very clear. . . . Whatever else you do, Rosheen, please do not tell the children what Patrick has been accused of. . . .* "I didn't know you knew about that," she said lightly.

"Everyone knows," he told her solemnly. "Uncle Patrick's a monster and ought to be strung up."

"Goodness!" she exclaimed, forcing a smile to her lips. "Who said that?"

"Kevin."

Anger tightened like knots in her chest. *Ian had laid it on the line following the incident in the barn . . . You may see Kevin in your spare time, Rosheen, but not when you're in charge of the children. . . .* "Kevin Wyllie? Rosheen's friend?" She squatted down beside him, smoothing a lock of hair from his forehead. "Does he come here a lot?"

"Rosheen said we weren't to tell."

"I don't think she meant you mustn't tell me, darling."

James wrapped his thin little arms around her neck and pressed his cheek against hers. "I think she did, Mummy. She said Kevin would rip her head off if we told you and Daddy anything."

Later—Tuesday, 9th March, 1999

"I can't believe I let this happen," she told the inspector, pacing up and down her drawing room in a frenzy of movement. "I should have listened to Ian. He said Kevin was no good the minute he saw him."

"Calm down, Mrs. Lavenham," he said quietly. "I imagine your children can hear every word you're saying."

"But why didn't Rosheen tell me Kevin was threatening her? God knows, she should have known she could trust me. I've bent over backward to help her and her family."

"Perhaps that's the problem," he suggested. "Perhaps she was worried about laying any more burdens on your shoulders."

"But she was responsible for my *children*, for God's sake! I can't believe she'd keep quiet while some low-grade neanderthal was terrorizing her."

The inspector watched her for a moment, wondering how much to tell her. "Kevin Wyllie is also missing," he said abruptly. "We're collecting DNA samples from his bedroom because we think the body at Kilkenny Cottage is his."

Siobhan stared at him in bewilderment. "I don't understand."

He gave a hollow laugh. "The one thing the pathologist *can* be certain about, Mrs. Lavenham, is that the body was upright when it died."

"I still don't understand."

He looked ill, she thought, as he ran his tongue across dry lips. "We're working on the theory that Liam, Bridey, and Rosheen appointed themselves judge, jury, and hangman before setting fire to Kilkenny Cottage in order to destroy the evidence."

★★★The Daily Telegraph—Wednesday, 10th March, A.M.

COUPLE ARRESTED

Two people, believed to be the parents of Patrick O'Riordan, whose trial at Winchester Crown Court was adjourned two days ago, were arrested on suspicion of murder in Liverpool yesterday as they attempted to board a ferry to Ireland. There is still no clue to the whereabouts of their niece Rosheen, whose family lives in County Donegal. Hampshire police have admitted that the Irish guardee have been assisting them in their search for the missing family. Suspicion remains that the body found in Kilkenny Cottage was that of Sowerbridge resident Kevin Wyllie, 28, although police refuse to confirm or deny the story.

Thursday, 11th March, 1999—4:00 A.M.

Siobhan had lain awake for hours, listening to the clock on the beside table tick away the seconds. She heard Ian come in at two o'clock and tiptoe into the spare room, but she didn't call out to tell him she was awake. There would be time enough to say sorry tomorrow. Sorry for dragging him home early . . . sorry for saying Lavenham Interiors could go down the drain for all she cared . . . sorry for getting everything so wrong . . . sorry for blaming the English for the sins of the Irish. . . .

Grief squeezed her heart every time she thought about Rosheen. But it was a complicated grief that carried shame and guilt in equal proportions, because she couldn't rid herself of responsibility for what the girl had done. "I thought she was keen on Kevin," she told the inspector that afternoon. "Ian never understood the attraction, but I did."

"Why?" he asked with a hint of cynicism. "Because it was a suitable match? Because Kevin was the same class as she was?"

"It wasn't a question of class," she protested.

"Wasn't it? In some ways you're more of a snob than the English, Mrs. Lavenham. You forced Rosheen to acknowledge her relationship with Liam and Bridey because *you* acknowledged them," he told her brutally, "but it really ought to have occurred to you that a bright girl like her would have higher ambitions than to be known as the niece of Irish Gypsies."

"Then why bother with Kevin at all? Wasn't he just as bad?"

The inspector shrugged. "What choice did she have? How many unattached men are there in Sowerbridge? And you had to believe she was with someone, Mrs. Lavenham, otherwise you'd have started asking awkward questions. Still"—he paused—"I doubt the poor lad had any idea just how much she loathed him."

"No one did," said Siobhan sadly. "Everyone thought she was besotted with him after the incident in the barn."

"She was playing a long game," he said slowly, "and she was very good at it. You never doubted she was fond of her aunt and uncle."

"I believed what she told me."

He smiled slightly. "And you were determined that everyone else should believe it as well."

Siobhan looked at him with stricken eyes. "Oh God! Does that make it my fault?"

"No," he murmured. "Mine. I didn't take you seriously when you said the Irish only really enjoy fighting each other."

Thursday, 11th March, 1999—3:00 P.M.

Cynthia Haversley opened her front door a crack. "Oh, it's you," she said with surprising warmth. "I thought it was another of those beastly journalists."

Well, well! How quickly times change, thought Siobhan ruefully as she stepped inside. Not so long ago Cynthia had been inviting those same "beastly" journalists into Malvern House for cups of tea while she regaled them with stories about the O'Riordans' iniquities. She nodded to Peter, who was standing in the doorway to the drawing room. "How are you both?"

It was three days since she had seen them, and she was surprised by how much they had aged. Peter, in particular, looked haggard and gray, and she assumed he must have been hitting the bottle harder than usual. He made a rocking motion with his hand. "Not too good. Rather ashamed about the way we've all been behaving, if I'm honest."

Cynthia opened her mouth to say something, but clearly thought better of it. "Where are the boys?" she asked instead.

"Nora's looking after them for me."

"You should have brought them with you. I wouldn't have minded."

Siobhan shook her head. "I didn't want them to hear what I'm going to say to you, Cynthia."

The woman bridled immediately. "You can't blame—"

"Enough!" snapped Peter, cutting her short and stepping to one side. "Come into the drawing room, Siobhan. How's Ian bearing up? We saw he'd come home."

She walked across to the window from where she could see the remains of Kilkenny Cottage. "Tired," she answered. "He didn't get back till early this morning and he had to leave again at the crack of dawn for the office. We've got three contracts on the go and they're all going pear-shaped because neither of us has been there."

"It can't be easy for you."

"No," she said slowly, "it's not. Ian was supposed to stay in Italy till Friday, but as things are . . ." She paused. "Neither of us can be in two places at once, unfortunately." She turned to look at them. "And I can't leave the children."

"I'm sorry," said Peter.

She gave a small laugh. "There's no need to be. I do rather like them, you know, so it's no hardship having to stay at home. I just wish it hadn't had to happen this way." She folded her arms and studied Cynthia curiously. "James told me an interesting story yesterday," she said. "I assume it's true, because he's a truthful child, but I thought I'd check it with you anyway. In view of everything that's happened, I'm hesitant to accept anyone's word on anything. Did you go down to the farm one day and find James and Oliver alone?"

"I saw Rosheen leave," she said, "but I knew no one was there to look after them because I'd been—well—watching the drive that morning." She puffed out her chest in self-defense. "I told you she was deceitful and lazy but you wouldn't listen to me."

"Because you never told me why," said Siobhan mildly.

"I assumed you knew and that it didn't bother you. Ian made no secret of how angry he was when you came home one night and found her with Kevin in the barn, but you just said he was overreacting." She considered the wisdom of straight-speaking, decided it was necessary, and took a deep breath. "If I'm honest, Siobhan you even seemed to find it rather amusing. I never understood why. Personally, I'd have sacked her on the spot and looked for someone more respectable."

Siobhan shook her head. "I thought it was a one-off. I didn't realize she'd been making a habit of it."

"She was too interested in sex not to, my dear. I've never seen anyone so shameless. More often than not, she'd leave your boys with Bridey if it meant she could have a couple of hours with Kevin Wyllie. Many's the time I watched her sneak into Kilkenny Cottage only to sauce out again five minutes later without them. And then she'd drive off in your Range Rover, bold as brass, with that unpleasant young man beside her. I did wonder if you knew what your car was being used for."

"You should have told me."

Cynthia shook her head. "You wouldn't have listened."

"In fact, Cynthia tried several times to broach the subject," said Peter gently, "but on each occasion you shot her down in flames and all but accused her of being an anti-Irish bigot."

"I never had much choice," murmured Siobhan without hostility. "Could you not have divorced Rosheen from Liam, Bridey, and Patrick, Cynthia? Why did every conversation about my nanny have to begin with a diatribe against her relatives?"

There was a short, uncomfortable silence.

Siobhan sighed. "What I really don't understand is why you should have thought I was the kind of mother who wouldn't care if her children were being neglected?"

Cynthia looked embarrassed. "I didn't, not really. I just thought you were—well, rather more relaxed than most."

"Because I'm Irish and not English?"

Peter tut-tutted in concern. "It wasn't like that," he said. "Hang it all, Siobhan, we didn't know what Rosheen's instructions were. To be honest, we thought you were encouraging her to make use of Bridey in order to give the poor old thing a sense of purpose. We didn't applaud your strategy—as a matter of fact, it seemed like a mad idea to us—"He broke off with a guilty expression. "As Cynthia kept saying, there's no way she'd have left two boisterous children in the care of a disabled woman and a drunken man, but we thought you were trying to demonstrate solidarity with them. If I trust O'Riordans with my children, then so should the rest of you . . . that sort of thing."

Siobhan turned back to the window and the blackened heap that had been Kilkenny Cottage. *For want of a nail the shoe was lost . . . for want of a shoe the horse was lost . . . for want of mutual understanding lives were lost. . . .* "Couldn't you have told me about the time you went to the farm and found James and Oliver on their own?" she murmured, her breath misting the glass.

"I did," said Cynthia.

"When?"

"The day after I found them. I stopped you and Ian at the end of the drive as you were setting off for work and told you your children were too young to be left alone. I must say I thought your attitude was extraordinarily casual but—well"—she shrugged—"I'd rather come to expect that."

Siobhan remembered the incident well. Cynthia had stood in the drive, barring their way, and had then thrust her indignant red face through Ian's open window and lectured them on the foolishness of employing a girl with loose morals. "We both assumed you were talking about the night she took Kevin into the barn. Ian said afterward that he wished he'd never mentioned it, because you were using it as a stick to beat us."

Cynthia frowned. "Didn't James and Oliver tell you about it? I sat with them for nearly two hours, in all conscience, and gave Rosheen a piece of my mind when she finally came back."

"They were too frightened. Kevin beat them about the head because they'd opened the door to you and said if I ever asked them if Mrs. Haversley had come to the house they were to say no."

Cynthia lowered herself carefully onto a chair. "I had no idea," she said in an appalled tone of voice. "No wonder you took it so calmly."

"Mm." Siobhan glanced from the seated woman to her husband. "We seem to have got our wires crossed all along the line, and I feel very badly about it now. I keep thinking that if I hadn't been so quick to condemn you all, *no one* would have died."

Peter shook his head. "We all feel the same way. Even Sam and Nora Bentley. They're saying that if they'd backed your judgment of Liam and Bridey instead of sitting on the fence—" He broke off on a sigh. "I can't understand why we allowed it to get so out of hand. We're not unkind people. A little misguided . . . rather too easily prejudiced perhaps . . . but not *unkind.*"

Siobhan thought of Jeremy Jardine. Was Peter including Lavinia's grandson in this general absolution, she wondered.

7

09:00 A.M.—Friday, 12th March, 1999

"Can I get you a cup of tea, Bridey?" asked the inspector as he came into the interview room.

The old woman's eyes twinkled mischievously. "I'd rather have a Guinness."

He laughed as he pulled out a chair. "You and Liam both. He says it's the first time he's been on the wagon since his last stretch in prison nearly twenty years ago." He studied her for a moment. "Any regrets?"

"Only the one," she said. "That we didn't kill Mr. Jardine as well."

"No regrets about killing Rosheen?"

"Why would I have?" she asked him. "I'd crush a snake as easily. She taunted us with how clever she'd been to kill two harmless old ladies and then have my poor Patrick take the blame. And all for the sake of marrying a rich man. I should have recognized her as the devil the first day I saw her."

"How did you kill her?"

"She was a foolish girl. She thought that because I'm in a wheelchair she had nothing to fear from me, when, of course, every bit of strength I have is in my arms. It was Liam she was afraid of, but she should have remembered that Liam hasn't been able to hurt a fly these fifteen years." She smiled as she released the arm of her wheelchair and held it up. The two metal prongs that located it in the chair's framework protruded from each end. "I can only shift myself to a bed or a chair when this is removed, and it's been lifted out that many times the ends are like razors. Perhaps I'd not have brought it down on her wicked head if she hadn't laughed and called us illiterate Irish bastards. Then again, perhaps I would. To be sure, I was angry enough."

"Why weren't you angry with Kevin?" he asked curiously. "He says he was only there that night because he'd been paid to set fire to your house. Why didn't you kill him, too? He's making no bones about the fact that he and his friends have been terrorizing you for months."

"Do you think we didn't know that? Why would we go back to Kilkenny Cottage in secret if it wasn't to catch him and his friends red-handed and make you coppers sit up and take notice of the fearful things they've been doing to us these many months? As Liam said, fight fire with fire. Mind, that's not to say we wanted to kill them—give them a shock, maybe."

"But only Kevin turned up?"

She nodded. "Poor greedy creature that he is. Would he share good money with his friends when a single match would do the business? He came creeping in with his petrol can and I've never seen a lad so frightened as when Liam slipped the noose about his throat and called to me to switch on the light. We'd strung it from the beams and the lad was caught like a fly on a web. Did we tell you he wet himself?"

"No."

"Well, he did. Pissed all over the floor in terror."

"He's got an inch-wide rope burn round his neck, Bridey. Liam must have pulled the noose pretty tight for that, so perhaps Kevin thought you were going to hang him?"

"Liam hasn't the strength to pull anything tight," she said matter-of-factly, slotting the chair arm back into its frame. "Not these fifteen years."

"So you keep saying," murmured the inspector.

"I expect Kevin will tell you he slipped and did it himself. He was that frightened he could hardly keep his feet, but at least it meant we knew he was telling the truth. He could have named anybody . . . Mrs. Haversley . . . Mr. Jardine . . . but instead he told us it was our niece who had promised him a hundred quid if he'd burn Kilkenny Cottage down and get us out of her hair for good."

"Did he also say she had been orchestrating the campaign against you?"

"Oh, yes," she murmured, staring past him as her mind replayed the scene in her head. " 'She calls you thieving Irish trash,' he said, 'and hates you for your cheap, common ways and your poverty. She wants rid of you from Sowerbridge because people will never treat her right until you're gone.' " She smiled slightly. "So I told him I didn't blame her, that it can't have been easy having her cousin arrested for murder and her aunt and uncle treated like lepers"— she paused to stare at her hands—"and he said Patrick's arrest had nothing to do with it."

"Did he explain what he meant?"

"That she hated us from the first day she met us." She shook her head. "Though, to be sure, I don't know what we did to make her think so badly of us."

"You lied to your family, Bridey. We've spoken to her brother. According to him, her mother filled her head with stories about how rich you and Liam were and how you'd sold your business in London to retire to a beautiful cottage in a beautiful part of England. I think the reality must have been a terrible disappointment to her. According to her brother, she came over from Ireland with dreams of meeting a wealthy man and marrying him."

"She was wicked through and through, Inspector, and I'll not take any of her fault on me. I was honest with her from the beginning. We are as you see us, I said, because God saw fit to punish us for Liam and Patrick's wrongdoing, but you'll never be embarrassed by it, because no one knows. We may not be as rich as you hoped, but we're loving, and there'll always be a home for you here if the job doesn't work out with Mrs. Lavenham."

"Now Mrs. Lavenham's blaming herself, Bridey. She says if she'd spent less time at the office and more time with Rosheen and the children, no one would have died."

Distress creased Bridey's forehead. "It's always the same when people abandon their religion. Without God in their lives, they quickly lose sight of the devil. Yet for you and me, Inspector, the devil exists in the hearts of the wicked. Mrs. Lavenham needs reminding that it was Rosheen who betrayed this family . . . and only Rosheen."

"Because you gave her the means when you told her about Patrick's conviction."

The old woman's mouth thinned into a narrow line. "And she used it against him. Can you believe that I never once questioned why those poor old ladies were killed with Patrick's hammer? Would you not think—knowing my boy was innocent—that I'd have put two and two together and said, there's no such thing as coincidence?"

"She was clever," said the inspector. "She made everyone believe she was only interested in Kevin Wyllie, and Kevin Wyllie had no reason on earth to murder Mrs. Fanshaw."

"I have it in my heart to feel sorry for the poor lad now," said Bridey with a small laugh, "never mind he terrorized us for months. Rosheen showed her colors soon enough when she came down after Liam's phone call to find Kevin trussed up like a chicken on the floor. That's when I saw the cunning in her eyes and realized for the first time what a schemer she was. She tried to pretend Kevin was lying, but when she saw we didn't believe her, she snatched the petrol can from the table. 'I'll make you burn in hell, you stupid, incompetent bastard,' she told him. 'You've served your purpose, made everyone think I was interested in you when you're so far beneath me I wouldn't have wasted a second glance on you if I hadn't had to.' Then she came toward me, unscrewing the lid of the petrol can as she did so and slopping it over my skirt. Bold as brass she was with her lighter in her hand, telling Liam she'd set fire to me if he tried to stop her phoning her fancy man to come and help her." Her eyes hardened at the memory. "She couldn't keep quiet, of course. Perhaps people can't when they believe in their own cleverness. She told us how gullible we were . . . what excitement she'd had battering two old ladies to death . . . how besotted Mr. Jardine was with her . . . how easy it had been to cast suspicion on a moron like Patrick. . . . And when Mr. Jardine never answered because he was hiding in his cellar, she turned on me in a fury and thrust the lighter against my skirt, saying she'd burn us all anyway. Kevin will get the blame, she said, even though he'll be dead. Half the village knows he's been sent down here to do the business."

"And that's when you hit her?"

Bridey nodded. "I certainly wasn't going to wait for the flame to ignite."

"And Kevin witnessed all this?"

"He did indeed, and will say so at my trial if you decide to prosecute me."

The inspector smiled slightly. "So who set the house on fire, Bridey?"

"To be sure, it was Rosheen who did it. The petrol spilled all over the floor as she fell and the flint struck as her hand hit the quarry tiles." A flicker of amusement crossed her old face as she looked at him. "Ask young Kevin if you don't believe me."

"I already have. He agrees with you. The only trouble is, he breaks out in a muck sweat every time the question's put to him."

"And why wouldn't he? It was a terrible experience for all of us."

"So why didn't you go up in flames, Bridey? You said your skirt was saturated with petrol."

"Ah, well, do you not think that was God's doing?" She crossed herself. "Of course, it may have had something to do with the fact that Kevin had managed to free himself and was able to push me to the door while Liam smothered the flames with his coat, but for myself I count it a miracle."

"You're lying through your teeth, Bridey. We think Liam started the fire on purpose in order to hide something."

The old woman gave a cackle of laughter. "Now why would you think that, Inspector? What could two poor cripples have done that they didn't want the police to know about?" Her eyes narrowed. "Never mind a witch had tried to rob them of their only son?"

02:00 P.M.—Friday, 12th March, 1999

"Did you find out?" Siobhan asked the inspector.

He shrugged. "We think Kevin had to watch a ritual burning and is too terrified to admit to it because he's the one who took the petrol there in the first place." He watched a look of disbelief cross Siobhan's face. "Bridey called her a witch," he reminded her.

Siobhan shook her head. "And you think that's the evidence Liam wanted to destroy?"

"Yes."

She gave an unexpected laugh. "You must think the Irish are very backward, Inspector. Didn't ritual burnings go out with the Middle Ages?" She paused, unable to control her amusement. "Are you going to charge them with it? The press will love it if you do. I can just imagine the headlines when the case comes to trial."

"No," he said, watching her. "Kevin's sticking to the story Liam and Bridey taught him, and the pathologist's suggestion that Rosheen was upright when she died looks too damn flakey to take into court. At the moment, we're accepting a plea of self-defense and accidental arson." He paused. "Unless you know differently, Mrs. Lavenham."

Her expression was unreadable. "All I know," she told him, "is that Bridey could no more have burned her niece as a witch than she could get out of her wheelchair and walk. But don't go by what I say, Inspector. I've been wrong about everything else."

"Mm. Well, you're right. Their defense against murder rests entirely on their disabilities."

Siobhan seemed to lose interest and fell into a thoughtful silence which the inspector was loath to break. "Was it Rosheen who told you Patrick had stolen Lavinia's jewelry?" she demanded abruptly.

"Why do you ask?"

"Because I've never understood why you suddenly concentrated all your efforts on him."

"We found his fingerprints at the manor."

"Along with mine and most of Sowerbridge's."

"But yours aren't on file, Mrs. Lavenham, and you don't have a criminal record."

"Neither should Patrick, Inspector, not if it's fifteen years since he committed a crime. The English have a strong sense of justice, and that means his slate would have been wiped clean after seven years. Someone"—she studied him curiously—"must have pointed the finger at him. I've never been able to work out who it was, but perhaps it was you? Did you base your whole case against him on privileged knowledge that you acquired fifteen years ago in London? If so, you're a shit."

He was irritated enough to defend himself. "He boasted to Rosheen about how he'd got the better of a senile old woman and showed her Mrs. Fanshaw's jewelry to prove it. She said he was full of himself, talked about how both old women were so ga-ga they'd given him the run of the house in return for doing some small maintenance jobs. She didn't say Patrick had murdered them—she was too clever for that—but when we questioned Patrick and he denied ever being in the manor house or knowing anything about any stolen jewelry, we decided to search Kilkenny Cottage and came up trumps."

"Which is what Rosheen wanted."

"We know that now, Mrs. Lavenham, and if Patrick had been straight with us from the beginning, it might have been different then. But unfortunately, he wasn't. His difficulty was he had the old lady's rings in his possession as well as the costume jewelry that Miss Jenkins gave him. He knew perfectly well he'd been palmed off with worthless glass, so he hopped upstairs when Miss Jenkins's back was turned and helped himself to something more valuable. He claims Mrs. Fanshaw was asleep so he just slipped the rings off her fingers and tiptoed out again."

"Did Bridey and Rosheen know he'd taken the rings?"

"Yes, but he told them they were glass replicas which had been in the box with the rest of the bits and pieces. Rosheen knew differently, of course—she and Jardine understood Patrick's psychology well enough to know he'd steal something valuable the minute his earnings were denied—but Bridey believed him."

She nodded. "Has Jeremy admitted his part in it?"

"Not yet," murmured the inspector dryly, "but he will. He's a man without scruples. He recognized a fellow traveler in Rosheen, seduced her with promises of marriage, then persuaded her to kill his grandmother and her nurse so that he could inherit. Rosheen didn't need an alibi—she was never even questioned about where she was that night because you all assumed she was with Kevin."

"On the principle that shagging Kevin was the only thing that interested her," agreed Siobhan. "She *was* clever, you know. No one suspected for a minute that she was having an affair with Jeremy. Cynthia Haversley thought she was a common little tart. Ian thought Kevin was taking advantage of her. *I* thought she was having a good time."

"She was. She had her future mapped out as Lady of the Manor once Patrick was convicted and Jardine inherited the damn place. Apparently, her one ambition in life was to lord it over Liam and Bridey. If you're interested, Mrs. Haversley is surprisingly sympathetic toward her." He lifted a cynical eyebrow. "She says she recognizes how easy it must have been for a degenerate like Jardine to manipulate an unsophisticated country girl when he had no trouble persuading *sophisticated*"—he drew quote marks in the air—"types like her and Mr. Haversley to believe whatever he told them."

Siobhan smiled. "I'm growing quite fond of her in a funny sort of way. It's like fighting your way through a blackened baked potato. The outside's revolting but the inside's delicious and rather soft." Her eyes strayed toward the window, searching for some distant horizon. "The odd thing is, Nora Bentley told me on Monday that it was a pity I'd never seen the kind side of Cynthia . . . and I had the bloody nerve to say I didn't want to. God, how I wish—" She broke off abruptly, unwilling to reveal too much of the anguish that still churned inside her. "Why did Liam and Bridey take Kevin with them?" she asked next.

"According to him, they all panicked. *He* was scared he'd get the blame for burning the house down with Rosheen in it if he stayed behind, and *they* were scared the police would think they'd done it on purpose to prejudice Patrick's trial. He claims he left them when they got to Liverpool because he has a friend up there he hadn't seen for ages."

"And according to you?"

"We don't think he had any choice. We think Liam dragged him by the noose around his neck and only released him when they were sure he'd stick by the story they'd concocted."

"Why were Liam and Bridey going to Ireland?"

"According to them, or according to us?"

"According to them."

"Because they were frightened . . . because they knew it would take time for the truth to come out . . . because they had nowhere else to go . . . because everything they owned had been destroyed . . . because Ireland was home. . . ."

"And according to you?"

"They guessed Kevin would start to talk as soon as he got over his fright, so they decided to run."

She gave a low laugh. "You can't have it both ways, Inspector. If they released him because they were sure he'd stick by the story, then they didn't need to run. And if they knew they could never be sure of him—as they most certainly should have done if they'd performed a ritual murder—he would have died with Rosheen."

"Then what are they trying to hide?"

She was amazed he couldn't see it. "Probably nothing," she hedged. "You're just in the habit of never believing anything they say."

He gave a stubborn shake of his head. "No, there *is* something. I've known them too long not to know when they're lying."

He would go on until he found out, she thought. He was that kind of man. And when he did, his suspicion about Rosheen's death would immediately raise its ugly head again. Unless . . . "The trouble with the O'Riordans," she said, "is that they can never see the wood for the trees. Patrick's just spent nine months on remand because he was more afraid of being charged with what he *had* done . . . theft . . . than what he *hadn't* done . . . murder. I suspect Liam and Bridey are doing the same—desperately trying to hide the crime they have committed, without realizing they're digging an even bigger hole for themselves on the one they haven't."

"Go on."

Siobhan's eyes twinkled as mischievously as Bridey's had done. "Off the record?" she asked him. "I won't say another word otherwise."

"Can they be charged with it?"

"Oh, yes, but I doubt it'll trouble your conscience much if you don't report it."

He was too curious not to give her the go-ahead. "Off the record," he agreed.

"All right, I think it goes something like this. Liam and Bridey have been living off the English taxpayer for fifteen years. They get disability benefits for his paralyzed arm, disability benefits for her broken pelvis, and Patrick gets a care allowance for looking after both of them. They get mobility allowances, heating allowances, and rate rebates." She tipped her forefinger at him. "But Kevin's built like a gorilla and prides himself on his physique, and Rosheen was as tall as I am. So how did a couple of elderly cripples manage to overpower both of them?"

"You tell me."

"At a guess, Liam wielded his useless arm to hold them in a bear hug while Bridey leaped up out of her chair to tie them up. Bridey would call it a miracle cure. Social services would call it deliberate fraud. It depends how easily you think English doctors can be fooled by professional malingerers."

He was visibly shocked. "Are you saying Patrick never disabled either of them?"

Her rich laughter pealed around the room. "He must have done at the time. You can't fake a shattered wrist and a broken pelvis, but I'm guessing Liam and Bridey probably prolonged their own agony in order to milk sympathy and money out of the system." She canted her head to one side. "Don't you find it interesting that they decided to move away from the doctors who'd been treating them in London to hide themselves in the wilds of Hampshire where the only person competent to sign their benefit forms is—er—medically speaking—well, past his sell-by date? You've met Sam Bentley. Do you seriously think it would ever occur to him to question whether two people who'd been registered disabled by a leading London hospital were ripping off the English taxpayer?"

"Jesus!" He shook his head. "But why did they need to burn the house down? What would we have found that was so incriminating? Apart from Rosheen's body, of course."

"Sets of fingerprints from Liam's right hand all over the doorknobs?" Siobhan suggested. "The marks of Bridey's shoes on the kitchen floor? However Rosheen died—whether in self-defense or not—they couldn't afford to report it because you'd have sealed off Kilkenny Cottage immediately while you tried to work out what happened."

The inspector looked interested. "And it wouldn't have taken us long to realize that neither of them is as disabled as they claim to be."

"No."

"And we'd have arrested them immediately on suspicion of murder."

She nodded. "Just as you did Patrick."

He acknowledged the point with a grudging smile. "Do you know all this for a fact, Mrs. Lavenham?"

"No," she replied. "Just guessing. And I'm certainly not going to repeat it in court. It's irrelevant anyway. The evidence went up in flames."

"Not if I get a doctor to certify they're as agile as I am."

"That doesn't prove they were agile before the fire," she pointed out. "Bridey will find a specialist to quote psychosomatic paralysis at you, and Sam Bentley's never going to admit to being fooled by a couple of malingerers." She chuckled. "Neither will Cynthia Haversley, if it comes to that. She's been watching them out of her window for years, and she's never suspected a thing. In any case, Bridey's a great believer in miracles, and she's already told you it was God who rescued them from the inferno."

"She must think I'm an absolute idiot."

"Not you personally. Just your . . . er . . . kind."

He frowned ominously. "What's that supposed to mean?"

Siobhan studied him with amusement. "The Irish have been getting the better of the English for centuries, Inspector." She watched his eyes narrow in instinctive denial. "And if the English weren't so blinded by their own self-importance," she finished mischievously, "they might have noticed."

Jerry Sykes

Symptoms of Loss

JERRY SYKES has established himself at the forefront of a new generation of British writers with a stream of memorable stories. His stories have appeared in *Ellery Queen's Mystery Magazine, Cemetery Dance,* and *Hardboiled* as well as other publications in America, Britain, Italy, and Japan. He won the Crime Writers' Association's Gold Dagger for best short story in 1998 and was also short-listed for the award in 1999. His work often examines the hope and heartache of the inner-city's working class, and this story is no exception. This story was first published in *Crimewave,* June 1999.

Symptoms of Loss

Jerry Sykes

W hen I was a kid it seemed like every radio in the country was tuned to the same station.

Walking home from school on a hot summer afternoon I would catch the loose fragments of a song as they drifted through a stream of open windows and listen as they would roll into another three-minute twist of sound and emotion. It was as if each radio was a tiny speaker connected to an invisible jukebox loaded with all the hits from down the years, the music that had become as much a part of the atmosphere as the air we breathed.

Like most people I remember many of the songs from my childhood, although very few hold any special significance. It is only later, in adolescence, that we begin to attach certain records to defining moments in our lives, the heartfelt playlist invariably displaying symptoms of loss. As a child music is very much in the background, a soundtrack to our eddying emotions.

The radio in our house sat in the kitchen and the abiding image of my childhood is one of my mother, hands plunged deep into suds and staring out across the rumpled back garden, providing whispered harmonies.

She had been a professional singer back in the early sixties, nothing fancy, just one of a stable of backing singers contracted to one of the major record labels, but she had sung on a number of top thirty hits. Photographs of her at the time show that she had mastered the look, all solid hair and panda eyes, but she was destined never to make it out of the chorus.

My mother first met Greg Price, a skinny kid with dreams of stardom who would practice his Elvis swivel in the mirror until his legs ached, in September 1961 when they shared backing vocal duties on a Christmas record for some starch-hipped crooner. By the time the single hit number five the week before Christmas, my mother was pregnant and they were living together in a cold and damp fourth-floor bedsit in Hornsey. They were married on the first Saturday of the New Year.

In May 1962 my father was killed in a hit-and-run accident as he walked home from a late night recording session. His body was found slumped against a lamppost early the following morning by a man out walking his dog, the dog walking in lazy circles around my father and barking in his face.

My mother never remarried, although she was only seventeen when I was born in July that year. I remember a number of boyfriends, but none of them seemed to be around for more than a couple of months. Not that she was lonely; she had a wide circle of friends and my Aunt Celia would often come and stay with us for long periods of time, usually following a break-up with her most recent husband (four at the last count).

My mother loved the sweet soul music of Philadelphia and Motown, Curtis Mayfield and The Isleys, and I would often lie awake at night listening to her singing along with the radio in her tobacco-deep voice. I would imagine her standing in a pool of warm moonlight, hips moving in rhythm with the music, and my heart would trip with joy.

A few days before she died, I sat at her bedside and listened as she told me she had asked the minister to play a song at her funeral and he had agreed. She would not tell me the name of the song and in the days immediately following her death I hid from grief in trying to figure out what it might be. She had a black sense of humor and I soon narrowed it down to a shortlist of three: the first two on the list—Harold Melvin's *If You Don't Know Me By Now* and The Chi-Lites' *Have You Seen Her*—were a bit too obvious and in the end I settled on Marvin Gaye's *Abraham, Martin and John* with its poignant and telling refrain . . . "only the good die young."

But nothing could have prepared me for that moment when the minister hit the play button and the cool morning air was filled with the hiss of the small tape recorder giving way to a galloping drumbeat that roared across the small church like a parade of wild horses.

It took me a while to place the song but after a moment I recognized it as The Tornados' *Telstar*, an instrumental from the early sixties that was a hit on both sides of the Atlantic. There is no doubt that my mother would have known the song, but as to why she had chosen it to be played at her funeral . . .

I glanced around to check the faces of the other mourners. At my mother's request it was a small crowd, mainly friends she had known for a long time, people I had grown up with, crossing paths every couple of years. I saw no trace of recognition as the tape poured out the remains of the song. Most of the faces seemed to stare straight ahead, heads gently tilted back to stop the tears from falling, mouths tight in concentration.

Except for my Aunt Celia.

She held her face up to the ceiling and I saw a knowing smile grace her lips, crinkling the corners of her eyes. I stared at her, willing her to look over, and after a moment or so I was rewarded as her eyes flickered in my direction. Her smile seemed to jump out at me and I found myself smiling back at her.

It had been four years since I had last seen Celia, since my mother had moved out to Kent, and I had only spoken to her briefly before the service, but as I turned to face the front again the years slipped away and I caught a glimpse of myself in gray flannel shorts and knotted hair, always knotted hair.

Telstar returned to the rumbling of the turntable (my mother had made the tape herself, not even the minister had been allowed a preview) and the minister pushed the stop button on the tape recorder. After the service I thanked him for his kind words and for carrying out my mother's last wish and invited him back to the house for a drink.

A couple of days later I drove into London to visit my mother's solicitor.

It was a cold March day and the gray sky was filled with rolling clouds as I drove through the City and up into Islington. I left the car in Sainsbury's car park and walked through to Upper Street where the office was located over a remainder bookstore.

The stairwell smelled of paint from the DIY store next door and as I reached the first floor landing I felt a little light-headed and my vision briefly rippled in and out of focus. I pushed the door to the outer office open and entered a small reception area. A heavyset woman of around forty lifted herself from behind an old wooden desk and smiled, running her hands over her hips.

"Mr. Price, so sorry to hear about your mother. A lovely woman. You must forgive me for not coming to the funeral but we only heard the news yesterday when Mr. Rhodes got back from holiday." She came around the desk with both arms extended and for a moment I thought she was going to hug me.

"That's okay, it was only a small affair," I said, holding up my hands in a calming gesture to keep her at arms' length. "I'm sorry, Mrs. . . . ?" I pursed my lips, slowly shook my head.

"James," she said, stopping so close to me I could smell her perfume, or maybe the paint fumes had penetrated this room as well. "Audrey James. I knew your mother quite well, although of course we didn't see each other much since she moved out to Kent."

"No, she seemed to lose touch with a lot of her friends."

"Anyway," she continued, "Mr. Rhodes is expecting you; you can go straight through." She gestured to a door to the rear of her desk. "Can I get you anything?"

I nodded, still feeling the effects of the paint fumes. "Just a glass of water, thanks."

"A glass of water," she repeated, committing it to memory, and headed through the outer door.

I knocked on Rhodes' door and walked into his office.

He was standing at the window looking down at the traffic on Upper Street but turned as he heard me enter the room. He was a tall man, over six-six, and uncomfortable in his frame. To compensate he had developed a stoop, his head hanging low as if his neck stuck out horizontally instead of vertically from his torso. A navy pinstripe suit hung from bony shoulders and his long fingers looked like fleshy links of chain protruding from the cuffs.

"Ah, Jeff, how are you doing? Bearing up okay?"

I shrugged. "Fine, I suppose. As good as can be expected."

"Good, good." He spread his arm out in front of him. "Take a seat, make yourself comfortable."

I lowered myself into the dark green leather sofa set to the side of his desk.

Rhodes placed his hands above his hips and arched his back before settling behind the dark mahogany desk. He began riffling through some papers, slipping them back into blue folders. "If you'll just bear with me. . . . How's Nancy?"

"Fine."

"Kids?"

"They're okay. A bit young to understand, you know, although I do feel I should try and explain . . . heaven and hell and all that."

"Heaven and hell, yes, good," he mumbled, distracted. "Ah, here it is." He pulled a file from the stack at the side of his desk, read the label. "Er, no, not that one. Sorry . . ."

Rhodes continued to look through the files.

My mind drifted back to the day of the funeral. "Presumably you've looked over my mother's file since . . . since her death," I said. He peered up at me through twisted eyebrows, nodded imperceptibly. "I don't suppose you came across anything about *Telstar*—you know, the record from the sixties?"

Rhodes leaned back in his chair, a grin spreading across his face. His huge hands grasped the edge of the desk. "She told you?" he said.

I shook my head, puzzled. "It was played at the funeral, she asked the minister . . ."

He frowned, the lines in his forehead forming a deep V. "So she didn't tell you?"

I didn't understand and raised my hands in submission, shook my head again. "Tell me what? She told me she'd asked the minister to play a song at the funeral, a tape she'd made. *Telstar*. I never heard her mention it before."

Rhodes hunched over his desk, threaded his long fingers together. He looked like a vulture sitting on a rock. "In her will your mother left you just short of a million pounds in performing royalties from the recording of *Telstar*."

I looked at him blankly, trying to get a hold on the information he had just imparted. I searched for a betrayal of the words in his eyes but all I could see was true pleasure at the delivery of the surprise.

"Performing royalties? I don't understand. My mother, ah, *performed* on *Telstar*? She was a singer, a backing singer. *Telstar*'s an instrumental."

"Well as far as I am led to believe—and all that I have to go on is a letter from your mother—it was in fact your *father* who performed on the recording. And therefore, quite naturally, upon his death the royalties transferred to your mother, his wife."

Although we had never been poor, my mother and I had never had the sort of lifestyle that a million pounds could bring. "So where has the money been all this time?"

"A trust fund was set up in your name. To be realized upon your mother's death."

"And you didn't know anything . . ."

Rhodes cut me off with a shake of his head. "The first I knew of this was when I opened the letter yesterday morning."

"Did she mention anything else about my father?"

"No, nothing. She never talked about your father."

We sat in silence for a few minutes, absorbing the news. Rhodes eventually began detailing the remainder of the will but I had wandered into the shadows and alleys of my childhood and his words broke apart and disappeared before reaching my ears.

I knew very little about my father and had often wondered about him, but every time I thought about asking my mother I would be overcome with a terrible guilt, as if the very act of asking about him was to admit to my mother that her love was not enough. I had not even seen a photograph and over the years my image of him had developed into one featuring a blond Elvis pompadour dripping over a handsome face twisted and scarred by the elusive bittersweet taste of success.

The revelations about *Telstar* brought the image a little more into focus and with it a new determination to find out more about him.

Just north of Holloway Road station I pulled over behind a dark green VW van and climbed out of the car. I waited for a break in the traffic and then ran across the busy road. I stood on the edge of the pavement to avoid the crowds of people shuffling through the morning and took in the building before me.

The ground floor now formed part of a bicycle shop that sported a huge yellow sign running the length of three storefronts. Rows of bikes from kids' to professionals' were lined up outside the shop and neon-glow shirts filled the windows.

The circular blue plaque fixed to the wall between the windows on the first floor read:

JOE MEEK

RECORD PRODUCER

"THE TELSTAR MAN"

1929–1967
PIONEER OF SOUND
RECORDING TECHNOLOGY
LIVED, WORKED AND
DIED HERE

There are maybe a couple of hundred similar plaques scattered through-out London, each commemorating the life and work of people who have lived in the capital and located on the buildings most famously associated with them. Because of a twenty-year-dead rule the majority were for people of whom I had never heard or had little interest. I had seen the plaque in Holloway Road on many occasions and it didn't tell me anything about Meek that I didn't already know.

An independant record producer before the term was invented (he had often been dubbed the British Phil Spector), he had created a number of hits in the late fifties and early sixties before the worldwide success of The Torna-dos' *Telstar* (named after the first communications satellite) in 1962 had made him a household name. A promiscuous homosexual, the more famous he became, the more terrified he became of being involved in a scandal that would jeopardize his career. The terror had eventually led to his suicide in 1967, ironically the year in which homosexuality had ceased to be illegal.

I ran back across the street and pointed the car in the direction of the Central Library.

A huge Victorian slab of weathered stone, the inside of the library looked more like a video rental store but I managed to locate a couple of books that touched on Meek and *Telstar*.

I could find no mention of my father although I did come across a list-ing of the musicians that had played on *Telstar*—guitar, bass, keyboards, drums—so unless my father was working under a pseudonym then some-thing strange was happening. And while it was true that many singers at the time had their names changed to conjure up images of hot and rugged mas-culinity, the same could not be said for the backing musicians. That was cer-tainly the case with *Telstar*.

As for Meek himself, there were a couple of interesting facts concerning his extra-curricular activities. In 1963 he was arrested and charged with importuning in a public place, an event that served only to fuel his paranoia and lay him open to threats of blackmail. Even more interesting was the fact that prior to his suicide, Meek had shot and killed his landlady in a tormented rage over the possibility of being questioned by the police over the murder of a teenage boy. There was no suggestion that Meek himself had been involved in the murder in any way, but this time the fear had obviously been enough to push him over the edge.

Perhaps the most telling item of all, and certainly from my perspective, was that in the early sixties musicians (including those in successful groups) were simply hired hands and as such were paid a flat Musicians' Union rate for any recording sessions they played on, regardless of the outcome, demo or record, hit or no hit. The record company or, as in Meek's case, the independant producer, would retain all the rights to and subsequent royalties from the performances.

I left the library and wandered up to Highbury Fields where I sat on a bench and watched two men in suits kicking a football around, their red faces bubbling with perspiration. I thought about the million pounds and tried to retrace its route back to my father, but whichever way I turned it was an immediate dead end.

On the way home I drove through Camden Town and stopped in at Tower Records. As I expected, there was nothing under Meek or The Tornados but there was a whole pile of sixties compilations, mainly from '63 and The Beatles onward, and I managed to find one that contained *Telstar*.

As I listened to the track over and over I began to hear a kind of wailing sound hiding behind the drums as the song faded into darkness. The sound was not quite human but it was the closest thing to a vocal on the record and I wondered if it was in fact the sound of my father's million-pound performance. And then again, maybe it was just the sound of the silent scream of frustration in my head.

The following day the girls began asking questions about their grandmother. Since she had fallen ill and moved down to Kent a few years earlier they had spent a lot of time in each others' company and now, a week after her death, the girls were beginning to sense that something was wrong. Nancy could see I was still a little shaky and offered to break the news to them for me. I gratefully accepted and left her to it.

I drove over to my mother's house with the intention of sorting through her belongings. We had put the house on the market and the place needed to be cleared. Most of the stuff would be going straight to the charity shop but I wanted to sort through everything first to see if there was anything personal that I wanted to hold on to.

My mother had moved from a cramped two-bedroom flat into a spacious three-bedroom house and as she had never been a hoarder, her belongings rattled around the cold house.

I spent a couple of hours moving all the items intended for charity into the front room; all personal items I stacked into a cardboard box on the kitchen table to be taken home and sorted through later. As I worked I had a feeling that I was being watched, as if someone was looking over my shoulder, a sense of being temporarily haunted.

I left the bedroom until last believing that that would be the place where I was most likely to come across anything concerning my father. But my mother had never been one for sentiment and the only thing of interest I found was an old shoebox containing twenty mint copies of *Landing Lights*, the first record she had sung on, a stack of ten-by-eight promotional photos turning brown and curling at the edges, and a reel of tape from an old reel-to-reel tape recorder. I put the shoebox in the cardboard box on the kitchen table and then carried the box out to the car.

Celia Drake emerged from the patio doors carrying two cold cans of beer. She handed one to me and pulled the tab on the other, pouring the beer into a long glass before settling on the wooden bench and tucking her feet up under her thighs.

She offered me a cigarette and when I shook my head, she lit one for herself, tossing the match into a glass ashtray on the table between us. Her green eyes were violently alive in the sunlight.

I popped the tab on the beer and took a long swallow.

"You never met my father, did you?"

Celia shook her head. "No, that was before my time. I didn't meet Meg until, oh, sixty-four, I think. Sixty-four, sixty-five, sometime around then."

"My mum ever talk about him?"

A frown creased her face. "Not really. Maybe in the abstract, as if he was an interesting place she'd once visited or something." She fixed me with a stare. "Why, you keen to find out about him now?"

"Yeah, well, I always felt a little awkward before, you know. But I thought that now Mum's dead . . ." I shrugged. "Besides, I always got the feeling she was making it up as she went along when she spoke about him."

She lifted her face to the sun and smiled. "I know what you mean."

My mother would often make up stories about my father, romanticizing him, bedeviling him, weaving him into tales that I myself had read in the Sunday papers or seen on TV.

Celia pulled on the cigarette and blew a streamer of blue smoke into the air over her head. She looked at me with a directness I had never seen before and said, "You're going to find out sooner or later so you might as well hear it from me. Your mother and father were never married."

For some reason this did not shock me as much as I thought it would. Or Celia. She saw the lack of response in my eyes and said, "You don't seem surprised."

"No. I guess I never really thought of my mum as having been married. I mean, it was all over before I was born, and . . . well, I've never even seen a wedding photo or anything like that."

"Your father was just a kid who only ever wanted one thing in his life. To be a pop star. So what's he gonna do when he finds out your mum got herself knocked up? Put on a suit and go out and get himself a regular job? Besides, the way I understand it Meg was not the only one to fall for his charms."

"But she still used his name."

Celia shrugged her shoulders. "It was 1962. They were still locking up single mothers in mental hospitals back then, you know."

I took a sip of beer and looked out across the lawn; purple and yellow crocuses poked through the faded grass. I had not mentioned my inheritance to Celia; I wanted to piece together the story of my father without any prompts or false leads.

"You remember how he died?"

"Sure, he was hit by a car when he came out of The Rainbow one night. He'd been to see Billy Fury or one of those other guys he always wanted to be and stepped right out in front of a car. I heard he was a little drunk."

"Did anyone see it happen? Anyone with him?"

Celia shook her head. "I don't know. Meg never really talked about it."

"Would he have made it, do you think?"

"As a singer? Well, she always said he had a good voice and I think he did have some sort of deal with Joe Meek lined up when he had the accident. You know, the *Telstar* guy."

I nodded, a loose smile of recognition playing on my lips.

She pointed at me with her glass. "Bill Jackson, that's who you want to talk to. Shared a flat with Greg around about the time he was killed." She leaned forward and added, "Knew your mum, too. She had an affair with him right after you were born. Didn't last long but they were pretty close and stayed friends afterward."

"So he's still alive?"

"Had a card from him just last Christmas. He lives down your way on the coast somewhere near Deal." She gently tapped me on the arm. "I'll go get the address for you," she said and lowered her feet to the ground and walked into the house.

The thought of my mother being in love filled me with an unbearable feeling of sadness and when I moved to hug Celia before I left I felt a tear squeeze from my eye and my heart swell with warmth and pride at my mother's selfless devotion. I knew that she had had boyfriends, but how could my young heart have known if she had truly been in love and had put that love aside to care for me.

Deal was one of those old seaside towns that had died with the advent of cheap package holidays in the mid-sixties; it seemed appropriate that a musician whose career had been all but over when The Beatles were still in Hamburg should have chosen to retire there. As I drove through the outskirts of the town I tried to imagine what the place must have been like in its heyday, but none of the images that flickered in my head had any connection to the sad gray buildings and sad gray people that slumped along the side of the road.

I drove along the seafront past the pier. A number of people braved the cold wind blowing off the sea and a cafe at the end appeared to be open, but the whole place had the feeling of having been abandoned: a commuter town where everyone had forgotten to go back home again.

I headed out toward Kingsdown and as I moved into the countryside color began to bleed back into the landscape. I found the village without much trouble and, after stopping to ask directions in the village store, followed a narrow lane down to the coast road. Between the road and the sea a dozen or so wooden chalets kept watch across the channel.

I left the car on the road and walked up the narrow pathway to the sky blue chalet in the center of the row and knocked on the door. The chalets appeared to consist of a single room and I wondered how safe they would be in a storm; only fifty feet of pebbled beach separated them from the sea. The pastel paintwork only added to the sense of fragility.

Jackson was home and after I introduced myself he ushered me through the front door. I scanned the room: partitions in the two far corners isolated what I took to be a bedroom and a bathroom; a kitchen crept into the living area from the wall directly to my right. A battered acoustic guitar was the only sign of his past.

Jackson was a wiry man with his hair brushed back in a threadbare DA, drainpipe jeans, and a fisherman's smock. His eyes still held a boyish light and I wondered what had brought him to his isolated corner of the country. He made a pot of coffee and settled into an old armchair below the rear window. I pulled out a chair from the small dining table and sat facing him.

I started to ask him about my father but he held up his hand and stopped me. A dark sadness befell his eyes and he took a deep breath. "Joe Meek didn't used to write songs; he used to hear the completed record in his head and then try and capture that sound on tape. His flat, his studio, was always full of musicians: there'd be the rhythm section in the living room, guitar and vocals in the bedroom, keyboard in the loo, strings out in the hall and the brass section lined up down the staircase. Joe would be in the kitchen with his equipment pulling it all together. And if he didn't hear the sound he wanted, well, he'd try something else. I once saw him stamping on the bathroom floor to get just the right drum sound he wanted. He wasn't afraid to take risks and try something new. It was that same 'out-thereness' that pushed him to take risks in his private life and leave him open to predators.

"Your father wanted to be a star. He thought Billy Fury was the greatest singer he had ever seen, *Halfway to Paradise* the greatest song he had ever heard. He was like that, Greg, everything was big, he had no time for anything less. Fury was greater than Elvis, greater than Buddy Holly, and Greg Price was going to be bigger than all of them.

"He had some kind of deal with Meek to record a couple of songs with The Tornados—Greg liked the idea that they'd originally been Fury's band, as if he'd stolen them from him or something. But then Meek changed his mind. He had the idea for *Telstar* and wanted the band to become some sort of keyboards-led Shadows; the Shadows were incredibly popular at the time and Meek wanted a piece of the action. Greg was furious. He tried to black-mail Meek about his homosexuality, but Meek was already being leaned on by a bunch of goons and when they got to hear about it . . ." He drew a finger theatrically across his throat.

I stared at the man, incredulous. "Are you saying my father was murdered?"

"Well, it's more of a gut feeling, I don't have any proof."

I nodded for him to go on. I could feel my heart beat against my ribcage and my face felt numb. Suddenly a man who had been killed before I was born was the most real person in my life.

His shoulders had slumped and he stared out of the window. A watery redness had seeped into his eyes. "I remember him telling me that he'd been threatened by a couple of thugs one night, guys he'd seen hanging around the cafe near Meek's flat. I just thought it was another one of his stories, even after he was killed. There was nothing to suggest that the accident had been anything *but* an accident.

"But then a year or so later, when I'd been seeing Meg for a couple of months, Meek's assistant Johnny Wood asked me why I was still working, why didn't I just get hitched to your mum and retire. When I asked him what he meant, he said something about Greg having been sacrificed for her benefit."

" 'Sacrificed for her benefit.' You know what he meant by that?"

Jackson shook his head.

"Did you ask my mother what he may have meant?"

He shook his head again. "She wouldn't talk about it."

"Did my father play on *Telstar*? Is that what this guy Wood meant, do you think?"

Jackson looked at me with a puzzled expression on his face. "Your father was killed before *Telstar* was recorded," he said.

"Yes, of course," I said, the words drifting away from me.

My head was beginning to feel a little foggy and I suggested we take a walk along the beach and for a couple of hours he chatted about the early days of the British pop scene. Time had dulled his memory and there was only real feeling in his voice when he spoke of his old friends.

I could smell salt on the air and the rhythm of the surf breaking on the pebble beach had a calming and refreshing effect on me. I felt at ease for the first time since my mother's death.

As we walked back along the pathway and stopped in front of his chalet, Jackson said, "Greg was a ruthless man and a great user of people. He used your mother, dumped her the minute he heard she was pregnant. But he didn't deserve to die." He looked out across the flat gray expanse of the sea, his face heavy with a sadness that had been buried for a long time. "He was a good friend to me."

I drove home with the feeling that at last my father was becoming a real person, with flesh and blood and hopes and ambitions and a mean streak as wide as it was long.

I was still no clearer to finding the truth about *Telstar*, but Jackson had told me that Johnny Wood still lived at the flat in Holloway Road.

The following morning I stood outside the bike shop looking up at the windows on either side of the blue plaque. It was almost eleven and the blinds were still drawn. I rang the bell and waited.

The features on Wood's large face were bunched close together and large patches of tired skin reflected the dull light emanating from the naked bulb hanging from the ceiling of the hallway. Strands of brittle gray hair covered his scalp.

He closed his eyes and nodded as I introduced myself, as if he had been expecting me. He turned and I followed him up the stairs.

I refused the offer of a drink and sat on the edge of the sofa and waited for him to speak.

"I first met your father back in January '61," he began, a new energy in his eyes. "He was just a kid—nineteen, twenty—and like every other kid who came around he wanted to be a star. Joe used to let some of 'em hang around, helping out, running errands, that sort of thing. Good-looking kids, Joe always had good-looking kids hanging around, especially if they didn't mind staying over." He raised his eyebrows and looked at me knowingly. "Greg could sing a little, he even played on a couple of records, I think. He was never gonna be a star, but he kept on pestering Joe to let him make a record.

"One morning, right out of the blue, Joe tells me he's gonna let Greg do *Walk Her Home* with The Tornados backing him. I think Greg must've stayed over the night before . . ." Wood paused to light a cigarette and let the full meaning of his words sink in; I let his words hang in the air. "Told me to call in the guys, we were gonna do it that afternoon. Anyhow, a couple of hours later, Joe changed his mind, told me to scrap it."

"Greg was furious. He came around late that night smashed out of his head. It was around ten and I was in the kitchen recording some overdubs with Joe, who was in the living room. The two of them got into this huge argument, a fight—I could hear it all through the speakers in the kitchen—and Joe hit him over the head with a guitar. I heard this awful scream and ran into the living room, but Greg was already dead, just lying there with his head in this pool of blood. Joe was standing over him with the guitar still in his hand. Next thing I knew Meg was in the room—she'd been staying with Mrs. Harvey downstairs since Greg had walked out on her—pushing everyone around. She sent me out to the kitchen and told me to sit tight and I just sat there shaking, I was shaking so much I could hardly light a cigarette.

"When I turned up the next morning Joe was sitting in the living room just staring at the spot where Greg had fallen. He'd been up all night and his eyes were sunk deep in his face. He told me that they'd bundled Greg into the boot of his car and gone and dumped him in the road up behind The Rainbow someplace. Made it look like an accident." He pulled on the cigarette. "And then your mother asked me for a copy of the tape."

"The tape?" I said.

"Yeah, the tape. I'd left the machine running and got the whole thing down on tape."

I remembered the tape I had found in my mother's house. "You still have a copy?"

He shook his head, no.

It now seemed pointless asking whether or not my father had played on *Telstar*, the royalties had obviously been the payoff. "You know what happened after that?"

"Joe never mentioned it again. I think he went to the funeral, though."

"And you have no doubt that she was blackmailing him?"

"Joe was always getting blackmailed, he said it was the curse of the famous queer. I think he just dealt with it the same way he did any other threat—he paid up and hoped that she wouldn't come back for more."

A pained expression of satisfaction came over Wood's face and I had the feeling that he had been waiting in the flat for nearly forty years to tell me the story.

Over the next few days I tried desperately to hold on to the image I had of my mother. But it seemed that the more I learned about my father, the closer I came to knowing him, the further she slipped away, drifted into an alien darkness; the rasping angel of my childhood had become a dark and vengeful siren.

I had no intention of going to the police and I had no problem in reconciling myself to the money. Theoretically, it belonged to my father and whatever reservations I may have harbored about it being blood money soon dissolved when I told myself that because my mother had taken herself out of the loop (by creating the trust fund) it was a legitimate inheritance.

My acceptance of the money was also the acceptance of my father the star and his posthumous number one.

The beautiful irony of this did not strike me until a couple of months later. Nancy and I had stolen an early summer break from the kids and were enjoying a weekend in Brighton. Browsing among the junk shops in the Lanes on the Sunday morning, I came across an old tape recorder and I immediately thought of the reel of tape that I had found in my mother's house. After my meeting with Johnny Wood I had tried to forget about the tape but a primal curiosity got the better of me and I put down two crisp five pound notes on the glass counter and walked out of the shop with the tape recorder under my arm.

As soon as I got home I dug the shoebox containing the reel of tape out of the attic and set up the equipment. The tape had faded over the years and there was a persistent hiss but it was still possible to make out what was happening.

I listened with calm detachment as the sound of two men arguing broke into violence, cries of pain riding a backbeat of flesh being struck. And then there it was, the final heart-wrenching scream of my father as the killing blow of the guitar connected with his head.

But it was the realization that the cry was exactly the same cry that rode the fadeout of *Telstar* that brought the cold smile to my lips.

Antony Mann

Taking Care
of Frank

ANTONY MANN is an Australian writer living in England with his wife, Judy, and young son, Zachary. His short fiction has appeared in a wide range of British magazines and journals. For two years he wrote sports humor for the national broadsheet *The Guardian*. His voice is witty and acerbic, and there is always a surprise or two in store in his stories. This story first appeared in the June issue of *Crimewave*.

Taking Care of Frank

Antony Mann

Frank Hewitt was no ordinary celebrity. For one thing, he had talent. For another, he had that indefinable quality which meant it didn't matter that he didn't have *a lot of* talent. He was a star. The camera loved him just as he loved it, so that the public, who always wanted so badly to love what the camera saw, could love him too, and feel as though he loved them back. Not only that, he had a rare cross-media appeal. His voice was average and comforting enough that his interpretations of show tunes and middle-of-the-road classics would always be big sellers, but down the years he had also appeared in a number of very successful second-rate films. He was charming, and lovable, yet with an intriguingly sordid past. He did beer adverts, too.

The only trouble with Frank Hewitt was that he was still alive, and had been for some time. It was a growing disappointment to a lot of people who mattered in the entertainment industry. Somehow, despite his hard-boozing, chain-smoking, orgiastic journey through the world of showbiz, he had managed to avoid cancer, heart failure or a stroke and arrive at the age of seventy-three looking determined to make it to eighty and beyond.

His agent (and mine), Harry Schmeltzmann, spelled it out for me on the phone.

"The trouble is," Harry was saying, "I've got the people from CBC on my back about the tribute show. Then there's the biopics. Two telemovies and a feature. *The Hewitt Story, Frank Hewitt: The Story,* and *The Story of Frankie Hewitt.* It's a contractual thing. They can't go into full production until Frank actually kicks it. There are the exposés, too. Six unofficial biographies and two docufiction character assassinations for TV. Plus the arthouse revivals and video releases of his old movies. Not to mention the tapes and CDs of the recent Vegas shows, and the boxed sets and compilations. And guess what? There's an interactive CD-ROM lined up. Archive material and some stupid computer game and a Frank Hewitt quiz. That's without factoring in the hundred or so 'Frankie Hewitt Was a Fucking Genius' articles that the broadsheets and glossies can't run until he croaks. You know what it's about. All this crap is going to sell better when Hewitt is dead."

"But Hewitt is already old," I said. "Can't it wait until natural causes?"

"Wait? Why should it wait? A lot of people have put a lot of money into Frank's career down the years. They didn't know he was going to live this long, otherwise they might not have invested so much in the first place. Don't you think they deserve a decent return now, while *they* can enjoy it? Don't forget, Bendick, you'll be on a percentage of gross yield after Hewitt's death. If you knock him off."

"That percentage is microscopic, Harry, and you know it."

"The *percentage* might be minuscule, but the total yield adds up to quite a slice, Stan. And I'm on a percentage of *you*. So don't let me think any more that you're discouraging me from finding you gainful employment."

Not only that, but Harry must have been getting his own very special kickback from somewhere to be happy to sacrifice his ten percent of the fortune that Frank Hewitt pulled in every year.

"Hewitt's big, Harry," I said. "Very big. Won't there be more heat than usual from outside?"

"Possibly. But the dirt stays inside the industry, no matter who, no matter what. It has to. You know that. Stop looking for excuses."

"But I *like* Frank Hewitt," I said. "My dad liked Frank Hewitt. My grandfather *raved* about him."

"Jesus, Bendick, *everyone* likes Frank Hewitt, that's the point. Everybody *loves* him. Why do you think he's so huge? But the industry needs a boost. There hasn't been an elder statesman or Grand Dame of the entertainment world drop out of the firmament for some time now. Look, take it or leave it. I worked hard to get you this gig. I can always offer it to Grebb or Zabowski. . . ."

"No, no," I said, with some reluctance. "I'll do it. Better that he gets it from a fan, eh?"

"That's the spirit, Bendick," said Schmeltzmann. "And make it look like murder. We'll get bigger press that way."

Leo Zabowski rang an hour later. I knew his ugly voice at once.

"Bendick? It's Zabowski."

"I know who it is," I said.

"So you got the Frank Hewitt job."

"How did you find out?"

"Bad news travels fast, I guess." Zabowski didn't sound jealous at all, which was all wrong for him. "You know you only got it because Schmeltzmann is your agent *and* Frank Hewitt's, don't you?"

"Perhaps so, Zabowski, but ask yourself this: *why* is Schmeltzmann one of the biggest agents in Hollywood? Because he wouldn't touch second-raters like you with a barge-pole."

Zabowski laughed. It was one of my least favorite noises.

"Are you okay, Zabowski? You sound like you're choking on your own phlegm."

"That's hilarious, Bendick. Just remember. You might have worked with the big stars for the last few years, but your time is coming to an end. This business is crying out for some new blood."

"Keep dreaming, Zabowski. The world always needs dreamers, like Frank Hewitt sings."

"Yeah, well, anyway," said Zabowski flatly, his vitriol expended.

We waited then the both of us for the other to hang up. Eventually he got bored and softly put down the phone.

Hewitt's mansion, Cedar Grove, was out in The Hills beyond The Valley. Someone—possibly Hewitt—had cut some of the cedars down a long time ago to make way for the nine-hole golf course and the tennis courts. The two-story white house, too big for your average family but perfect for a living Hollywood legend, sat snugly against a backdrop of evergreens.

Hewitt's fourth wife Clarissa met me at the front door. I had seen her photo in the gossip sheets. She was slim and blond, perhaps naturally. Her face was set into a careless, superior expression that reflected wealth and the boredom that went with it, but she had kept her teenage looks, possibly because she was not long in her twenties.

"Stan Bendick?"

"That's right."

"Do you have your own gun or would you like to borrow one?" She walked me through into the tiled reception hall and to the base of a wide staircase that curved up and around. We were surrounded by *objects d'art*: Monets, Epsteins, Picassos and what have you, all waiting patiently to be fought over by Clarissa and the rival ex-wives and the eight or ten children from the previous marriages.

I patted my shoulder holster through my jacket. "As it happens, I brought my own."

"Fine. Frank should be upstairs. Third door on the left. Could you make it quick? I've got a hair appointment in forty-five minutes."

"I think your hair looks fine the way it is," I said.

She smiled sourly. "Well, thanks anyway, but what would you know?" She headed off to be rude to somebody else, but stopped in the doorway which led through to the rest of the ground floor. "Remember, third door on the left. Not second. *Third*."

"I can count to three," I replied.

"Congratulations."

•   •   •

The door was unlocked. Frank was in.

He sat facing away from me, dozing in a high-backed brown leather chair in front of wide clean windows that overlooked The Valley and the winding bitumen road that led from there to here. The room was clearly Frank Hewitt's space: the soothing blue carpet was plush, the dark relief wallpaper almost three-dimensional. Frames displayed movie posters behind polished glass, and antiquated gold and platinum records. There were video tapes, photo albums and hardbacks on shelves next to the TV and VCR. Opposite the windows, beside a connecting door that was shut, sat a telephone on a small three-legged table.

Even the back of his head looked famous. I might have shot him then and there, but this was the man whose songs my grandfather had slow-danced to while courting my grandmother, whose movies my dad had sat in the back row to watch as a kid. It had been my honor to permanently retire a lot of stars in the last few years, but never one as big as Frank Hewitt. I wanted to see his face. My shoes made no sound on the thick pile.

He sat in the chair in a lemon yellow terry toweling dressing gown and tartan slippers, the back of his skull at an angle against the headrest. His breathing was light. He had never been a handsome man and now, in his old age, his midriff was paunched and his around face wrinkled and worn. Yet even in repose he was larger than life. It's a pet theory of mine that people in the public eye are imbued with a residue of the abnormally great amount of attention that is paid them, a concentration of a kind of psychic energy if you like. This residual force is then radiated back to the public by the celebrity. It's a constant, unconscious process. It explains why, when you meet someone famous in the flesh, they always seem to be exaggerated in some way, operating in a different reality. It explains why we call them stars. I began to wish I'd brought a camera.

But there was no future in coming over all starstruck. It would only make things harder. I had to take care of Frank before he woke. I had drawn my revolver and was picking my spot when he opened his eyes and looked at me. He hadn't been asleep at all.

"Er, hello Mr. Hewitt," I said, lowering the gun sights.

"Call me Frank."

"Frank."

"Stan Bendick, isn't it?"

"Ah, that's right."

"I've heard about you, Bendick."

"You have?" Frank Hewitt had heard of *me*? I was flattered.

"We all have. You and your kind. Just because we're stars doesn't mean we're stupid. We know what goes on. We know where you live, what you look like. Whom you've murdered."

"Wow," I said. "That's great, Mr. Hewitt . . . I mean, Frank . . . I mean . . ."

"Did you meet Clarissa?"

"Who?"

"Clarissa. My wife."

"Yes, I did, she's a lovely young woman, Frank. You must be very much in love with her. . . ."

"She's a bitch, even worse than the others. Don't tell her, but I've cut her out of the will. Sure, she'll contest it, maybe even win, but I like the idea of her loathsome face twisting with selfishness and anger when she hears that she doesn't get a penny." He laughed, then pointed a stubby finger at me. "Let me tell you something about fame. It's only ever an accident, and it always ends in tears. I've had four loveless marriages, I've got nine children who either hate or fear me. All the money I've earned hasn't given me an ounce of joy or contentment. Any happiness I've had—and there hasn't been much— has come from the things that I could have had anyway, *without* being a star."

I hefted the gun in my hand.

"Maybe you could look at it this way. You'll be making a lot of *other* people happy when you die."

"You mean the rich moguls?" he said bitterly. "The studio and TV bosses and the soulless parasites who buzz around them like flies on shit? The people who pollute this filthy industry more and more with every passing year?"

"Yes, them, of course, but what I meant was the ordinary people in the street, the people who look up to you without knowing what really goes on behind the scenes. Your fans will love you a lot more when you're dead."

He raised an eyebrow, "You think so?"

"Of course. Just look at Elvis. John Lennon. Look at Princess Di. After *she* croaked, there were millions of people who suddenly realized how much they loved her who didn't know more than the first thing about her!"

"That's a good point, Bendick. Not good enough to make me think that I *deserve* to die, but a good point nonetheless."

"Thanks, Mr. Hewitt . . . Frank. . . ."

I could hear the chutter-chutter of a helicopter in the distance, rising up out of The Valley. All else was still. I raised the gun again.

"Before you do that, you might want to take a look at the news on television," said Frank.

"If it's all the same with you, I'll buy a newspaper on the way back to town."

"It's for your sake, not mine," he shrugged. He reached down and picked up the remote from the floor, then swiveled in his chair. He pressed 'on' and flicked through the channels until he found Cable News. A generic modern-style female cue-card reader with small eyes was halfway through reciting some lies about the economy, when either a mosquito got stuck in her ear or she was fed a line by the producer. She jiggled her earpiece and mustered a concerned frown, then stared into the camera.

"This just in," she said. "We're getting unconfirmed reports that singer and movie star Frank Hewitt is dead. Repeating, reports are coming in that

Frank Hewitt has been shot." Then, ruining my morning, a recent photo of me flashed up on a screen behind her. The newsreader continued, "Police are hunting for escaped lunatic Stan Bendick, who is wanted in connection with the shooting. Police are warning the public that Bendick is likely to be armed and dangerous, and a lunatic, and to only approach him if they can get away a clear shot with no risk to themselves. Cable News will be running a five-day Frank Hewitt retrospective, including concerts, interviews with family, friends, acquaintances and people who never knew him, and panels of experts discussing every nuance of his incredible career, as well as phone-ins, competitions and whatever else we can think of. But now let's cross to Ned Denverson in our Mobile Aerial Unit, which just happens to be in the general vicinity of Frank Hewitt's mansion in The Hills, Cedar Grove . . . can you hear me, Ned?"

"I can hear you," came Ned's voice. On screen now was an aerial view of the nine-hole golf course and the big white house. "We're approaching Cedar Grove right at this moment, Elise. All looks peaceful. Hard to imagine that only minutes ago, crazed gunman Stan Bendick allegedly shot Frank Hewitt five times in the head and left him lying in a pool of his own blood. We'll see if we can get a look at the room where we suspect Hewitt was mercilessly slain."

It was getting weird. I looked out the windows. The helicopter that I had heard was closer now. I could see it banking in toward the house. I looked at the gun in my hand. I looked at Frank. Had I *really* killed him? It didn't appear so, but then, hadn't they said so on TV?

"How did you know . . . ?"

"I heard the news crew setting up in the next room a couple of hours ago," said Frank. "Clarissa must have let them in. Just because I'm a star doesn't make me deaf."

"There's a news crew in the *next room*?"

"You've been stitched up, Bendick. You and me both."

He was right. As he used the remote to switch off the television, the connecting door opened and Leo Zabowski walked in holding a gun. The news crew followed behind. It was a location unit comprising a female presenter, a soundman and a handheld camera operator. There was a production assistant, too, a young man with a clipboard, and a pencil stuck behind an ear.

Zabowski was looking particularly repulsive today, I thought. Beads of sweat ran down his large bald head, adding their little bit to the stains on his shirt collar. His trousers were too baggy and, frankly, he could have done with cleaning his shoes. He was nervy and still overweight, although I'd heard he'd been trying to lose a few kilos.

"Zabowski, you're a disgrace," I said.

The presenter was a plasticky-looking brunette in her late twenties. I vaguely recognized her from the box. She glanced at Frank Hewitt sitting impassive in his leather swivel chair, then turned questioningly to Zabowski.

"He's not dead," she said.

"I'm sorry, Ms. Paxton," he said meekly. But with me, Zabowski was in a snarly mood. "You see, Bendick? You see? I was right! You can't do your job properly anymore! Why isn't Hewitt dead, eh? Tell me that!"

"We . . . er . . . got to chatting," I said.

"Chatting? *Chatting?* Well come on, Bendick! Shoot him!" Zabowski gestured wildly at the window behind. "The news 'copter is almost here! It's a live feed! Do you want them to see that Hewitt is still alive? It'll ruin the broadcast!"

As far as moments in my life go, it was an odd one. I knew I'd been set up by Harry Schmeltzmann to take the fall, and also that Leo Zabowski was there to gun me down after I'd immortalized Frank Hewitt. But Zabowski could have simply shot me while he had the chance, and then finished off Frank afterward. He made no move to. I noticed his body language. His stance indicated that he felt completely at ease. He saw no threat at all. And why should he? It was him standing next to the news crew, not me. He was on the side of the networks, caught in the illusion that the players in the world of TV and film are governed by a different set of rules from ordinary folk. I'm not saying that I didn't feel the temptation to go along with the plot, to play the part that had been written for me and slot unquestioning into prime time. I even felt the gun twitch in my hand and begin to slide across to where Frank Hewitt sat. Then I had a better idea. I shot Zabowski in the head.

The report was loud, but not surprising. It was a glancing blow that took a chunk of bone out of the top right-hand side of his skull. It all but knocked poor dumb Zabowski off his feet. With perplexed curiosity, he poked at the wound with a finger, marveling at the blood that ran down his hand, the sudden absence of cranium which over the years he had come to take for granted.

"Bendick?" he said, "what have you done?"

"Looks like I shot you, Zabowski."

"Fucking idiot! Don't you know that you've wrecked the program?"

"Sorry," I said. I meant it. I shot him again. This time he went down. Not even Zabowski's head was thick enough to sustain two bullets.

Now there was news, and the news crew jolted into motion reflexively. The dark-haired presenter, Ms. Paxton, took control with great efficiency, I thought. She whispered something in the ear of the production assistant, who nodded, then got on the phone. She stepped over Zabowski, strode to the windows and drew the curtains moments before the helicopter made its first pass. She instructed the crew, "Dick? Hal? Let's have one shot of the body and the gun, another of Bendick with *his* gun, then Frank in the chair. Then we'll start setting up sight and sound for interviews with both of them."

Dick and Hal set to work as ordered. Ms. Paxton sized me up.

"We'll do it this way," she said. "Turns out you're not escaped wacko Stan Bendick after all. You're actually unassuming Frank Hewitt fan Stan Bendick, who happened to be here at Cedar Grove getting Frank to sign some teddy bears for a charity auction. Lucky you carry a gun, otherwise you wouldn't have been able to thwart crazed gunman Leo Zabowski, recent escapee from the loony bin, who had broken into the house to kill Frank Hewitt and thus deprive the world of one of its greatest stars." She nodded to where the young production assistant was still talking animately into the telephone. "Mick's sorting it out now. We'll be running the correction on Cable in a few minutes." She smiled at me, almost like she meant it. "You're a hero, Bendick. How do you feel?"

"Not bad, considering."

She turned to Frank.

"Mr. Hewitt? I expect we'll generate enough news and spinoffery from this incident to keep you viable. How do *you* feel?"

"I feel like I need a new agent," he said.

He wasn't the only one.

The door opened. Clarissa walked in.

"I heard the shots," she said. "Did everything go all right?" She saw Frank. "Oh. Frank. You're alive. Thank God."

"And maybe a new wife," said Frank.

"Mr. Hewitt? . . . Frank?" I said. "There was something I was meaning to ask you before, but I never got the chance."

"What's that, Bendick?"

"Can I have your autograph?"

Edward Bryant

Styx and Bones

Back in the 1970s, when science fiction was undergoing some radical shifts in direction, a number of young writers came along and quickly established themselves as important new voices. ED BRYANT was one of those writers. What has been overlooked in all the tumult is how good he is at writing urban horror, a subgenre that walks a fine line between hard crime fiction and traditional horror. Since then, happily, he's been recognized as a true master in science fiction, horror, and hardboiled crime fiction as well. A long-awaited collection of his stories is due to appear soon. This story first appeared in the anthology *999,* edited by Al Sarrantonio.

Styx and Bones

Edward Bryant

He dreamed he woke up dead. Dead. Crushed. Every nerve pulled excruciatingly away from each muscle and each shattered bone. Awake and dead.

That was the confusion. The contradiction didn't occur to him until later. Much later. Now was only the pain.

Christ, he thought. *What's wrong?* It hurt so very much, and the least of the agony was a wasp drilling through his inner ear. He tried to reach to block the sound, but that motion only cranked the pain to a level that nauseated him. He couldn't raise his arms anyway.

Not a wasp. *No . . .* The noise was the telephone on the bedside table. He grabbed for it instinctively—*tried* to grab, could not. *What was wrong with his arms?* He bucked against the mattress, the tan print comforter sliding away from his lower body. Legs slipped off the mattress, feet slapping against the carpet and the slick mess of spilled magazines.

He smelled something heavy and terrible.

The sheet stuck to him as his body, levered upright, lurched against the bed table. His left arm swung around loosely, hand smacking the phone. It felt like incandescent steel wire flaring up molten inside his shoulder. He screamed.

The telephone tumbled to the floor as the handset swung around the base of the banker's lamp. The receiver jiggled up and down as if the coiled cord were the hemp rope dangling someone newly executed.

If he could have gotten his breath he might have cried. He heard the modulated wasp buzzing coming from the telephone earpiece. The tone was familiar and angry. He knew who it was. It didn't matter.

He needed help and so he sank to his knees attempting to align his face with the receiver.

"—the fuck are you doing, jerkweed?" the tinny voice was saying. "Too early for you? I told you last night I was coming over today to pick up my stuff."

His voice caught on a sob. "I need help," he gasped out. *"Please."*

Silence. Then the tenor of her voice changed. Curiosity and alarm replaced the fury with the suddenness of a carousel projector clicking ahead to the next slide. "Danny? What's wrong?"

"I don't know," he said. "I can't move."

"You're paralyzed?"

"No, no. My arms. *They* don't work. And it hurts," he said. "It hurts like a son of a bitch."

"Is this a goddamn trick?" she said. "Are you telling me the truth?"

"Yes," he said, voice catching on a sob he couldn't help. "Louisa, I swear to God something's really, really wrong."

"I'm on my way," she said.

"You got your key?" Danny said. "I can't unlock the door."

"I've got the key," Louisa answered. "I was gonna sharpen it like a razor and cut your balls off." Her voice sounded perfectly controlled. "I'm leaving now, baby. Hang on."

Danny heard the click as she set down her phone. He listened as the computerized phone company warning came, then the ear-rasping alert tone, finally silence on the line. Even if he used his teeth, there was no way he could hang up his phone.

He tried to sit up straight on the edge of the bed, wishing he were any-where else, *anyone* else.

What's happened to me? he thought. Was he whining? Of course he was whining. It hurt too damned much to be brave.

In the twenty minutes it took for Louisa to drive over, he managed to stagger downstairs to the kitchen. It was a cold, cold January morning and something had obviously happened to the heat. A few wisps of warmth emanated from the register just inside the kitchen. He stood there quietly, aching, attempting to soak up what furnace air he could.

He heard the front door open and close.

"Danny?" she called.

"In the kitchen."

He listened to the steps approach. He wanted to shut his eyes. Louisa poked her head through the kitchen doorway and surveyed him, eyes wide, head to feet. "Danny, sweetie, you are a mess." Her voice sounded sincere but amazed. She wrinkled her nose.

He knew how he appeared, standing naked save for his soiled briefs, back against the register, hands dangling in front of him with the thumbs locked together, liquid excrement drying in thin rivulets down his legs to the floor. Louisa shook her head. She involuntarily reached out toward him. As soon as her fingertips touched his arm, he cried out. She jerked back. "It hurts that much?" He nodded, jaws clenched. "You called a doctor?" He shook his head. "No," she said, "I guess you really couldn't." Louisa looked up at him from her five-feet-even vantage, chocolate eyes serious beneath the pixie-cut raven bangs. "First thing, maybe get you cleaned up a little?"

He nodded. "It's gotta help. Then call Dr. King."

"Call Dr. King now," she said. "Bath'll wait."

"Phone's upstairs," he said. "I couldn't hang it up."

"I'll take care of everything," Louisa said soothingly. "Don't you worry."

She followed him up the stairs. The cats were nowhere to be seen. He didn't blame them.

In the bedroom she unwound the receiver cord from around the lamp, then stood contemplating the bed. "We gotta get that cleaned up quick. Doctor'll wait. No one'll be able to live in this house with that stink."

"My briefs and the sheets," he said. "Just seal 'em in a plastic garbage bag and set them out in the trash. The comforter's expensive—maybe you can throw it over the picnic table in the backyard and let it dry. Then put it in another bag and I'll have it dry-cleaned."

She nodded and gingerly rolled the down comforter into a loose cylinder. "Bags in the kitchen?"

"In the broom closet."

In a few minutes Louisa was back with black mylar bags into which she matter-of-factly stuffed the soiled sheets. "Those too." She pointed at his briefs.

"They aren't much," he protested. "But it's cold up here."

"They're gross," she said evenly. "After you're clean you can wear a nice warm robe."

He tried to put his thumbs beneath the waistband. He couldn't. "What about Dr. King?"

She grabbed the waistband and skinned the briefs down his legs. "I changed my mind again. The doc can wait. You need some attention first."

There were two bathrooms in the house, both on the second floor. Only one had a tub and shower. Danny stepped into the tub and braced himself as she twisted the water knob. Nothing happened. "No pressure," she said. "No water at all."

"I should have let the faucets drip last night," he said. "I'll bet the pipes are frozen."

"Downstairs too?"

He started to shrug. Stopped. "It may be okay down there."

"I'll check. You stay here." In a minute she yelled from the foot of the stairs, "Water's running down here. I'll be up in a second." Actually it took quite a few seconds, but she started her own solo bucket brigade of saucepans full of steaming tap water.

He yelled as the first half gallon of what felt like scalding water cascaded down his back.

"Don't be a baby," she said. "You're just cold. I've checked the temperature. It'll be all right." Louisa poured another panful, then wet a washrag and
began to scrub him down. After the first few shocks, he had to admit the
water felt good. With his hands locked thumb to thumb in front of him, he
stared down at the brown eddy swirling in the drain. He felt more water,
more scrubbing. Eventually the draining water ran clear.

"Okay, step out of there." She toweled him down, attempting to be gentle when the cotton plush dragged across his shoulders. When he was reasonably dry, Louisa draped the blue terry cloth robe around his shoulders and
belted it at the waist. "Now lie down. We'll call the doctor."

The soiled sheets were no longer on the bed, but the mattress was still
wet and stained. It looked as though Louisa had given it a good scrubbing.
She spread a bath towel across the area, then fluffed out a cheap quilt from the
linen rack. "Okay, lie down." She efficiently flipped open an old wool blanket
and drew it up to his waist. "Comfy?"

"I guess," he said. "Comfy as I'm gonna get." He knew he didn't really
feel comfortable. But then who knew when his life was going to improve?
Lie down while he could. He did so, gingerly flopping back against the
mound of pillows Louisa had stacked.

Only after he'd painfully settled himself, he groaned.

"What's the matter?" said Louisa.

"I gotta pee."

"I'll help you up," she said.

"I'm not sure I can make it. My back and shoulders feel like they're
going to come apart if I move."

"Hmm," said Louisa. "You got a chamber pot?"

"No."

"Hold on," she said, turning and exiting the bedroom.

"Where are you going?"

Her voice floated back from the stairwell. "The kitchen."

Danny concentrated on using the muscles on the nether side of his
bladder. Suddenly he couldn't think of anything in the world he wanted
more than to relieve himself.

Louisa returned with an empty plastic two-liter Diet Coke bottle and a
pair of shears. His eyes widened. "What're the scissors for?"

She clicked them mischievously. "In case I have to whittle you down so
you'll fit the neck of this bottle."

"Ha ha," he said. "How about just trimming the neck?"

"Don't think you'll fit?"

"Even today," he said, "it looks like too tight a squeeze."

With a single scissors jab, she punched a hole at the base of the bottle
neck, then snipped a generous hole. "Big enough?"

"As long as I don't sneeze. Looks sharp." He spread his legs a little farther
apart as she placed the bottle between his thighs. Louisa deftly inserted his
flaccid penis into the hole. It occurred to him that the last time she'd touched

him there, she hadn't been nearly so clinical. But today he felt absolutely no excitement.

Just relief.

When he was done, she took the bottle away to the bathroom, then brought it back emptied and rinsed.

"So far, so good," she said.

"Will you call Dr. King?" Danny said. He knew the GP's office number by heart. Louisa held the receiver to his ear and he heard the clinic's receptionist answer. The woman tried to put him on hold; he argued eloquently. In less than a minute, the doctor was on the line.

Danny explained what had happened after his waking this morning from a sound sleep. Dr. King asked whether anyone was with him. "My friend Louisa." He glanced at her. "I think she'll drive me." She nodded vigorously. "Okay," he said. "One o'clock it is." She hung up the phone.

"Want some food?" she said.

He shook his head. "Coffee'd be good." The phone rang. "Weezie," he said. "Would you get that?"

She picked up the receiver. "Danny Royal's home," she said perkily. Then her expression darkened. "I don't think this is a good time for you to talk to him." Danny formed the word *who* with his lips. She shook her head. "He's not feeling very well right now." Pause. "No, call back another time. Or maybe not at all." Set the phone back in its cradle.

"Should I ask?" Danny said.

"Your *good friend* Iffie," Louisa said. Ice rimed her words. "She said she dreamed you were in trouble."

Danny stared back at her. "Hey, Ifetayo really is my friend. You know that. And she's Yoruba, by way of a family sidetrack to Port au Prince. She dreams, it's worth listening to."

"Let's get something straight," said Louisa angrily. "Friday night, I walked in and found *your friend* in your bed. With you, asshole."

"You should have called ahead," said Danny.

"Lame," she replied. "I think you were playing us off against each other for God knows how long."

"Ifetayo was really uncomfortable with this," he said placatingly. "Like I told you, she bowed out of the whole thing. I think she was pretty angry."

"Just like me?" Louisa's voice dripped venom briefly. "I meant it when I told you I was going to come by today to pick up my stuff—the cards, the sweaters, everything I ever gave you, every bit of myself."

His voice stayed calm. "So why didn't you?"

"Don't be an idiot. When I called you, and when I came over and saw you . . . You're a mess, Danny. You're in trouble. I think you're really sick. I want to take care of you." She set one cool hand gently on his forehead. "I love you. God knows why, but I do." Her voice ran down like a clock spring unwinding and she stopped.

"Did she say anything else?" Danny said. "Ifetayo?"

"You jerk," said Louisa. He felt her fingers tighten on his head, the nails beginning to dig into the skin. She took a deep breath. "She said you'd regret everything that's happened."

"A threat?" he said.

She shrugged. "How do I know? She's not my kind of people."

They stared at each other until Danny finally lowered his eyes. "I don't know how many times I can say it, Weezie. I'm sorry. I'm really sorry."

"You can say it lots," she answered. "Maybe eventually I'll believe it." After a time she said, "Danny, you really are a double-dyed prick bastard."

He tried to lighten things. He said, "Sticks and stones will break my bones, sweetie. Words won't hurt me."

"You ever hear about the river?" she said. "I'm guessing you have."

He looked bewildered. "What river?"

"The river Styx, dummy. Like the group. You know it was the river of hate? *Burning* hate? It circled hell nine times. That's a *lot* of anger, Danny."

He shook his head. "You've been reading up on all this?"

"I read more than you give me credit for, baby. I'm not just a stupid little costume girl." Then the anger left her voice again. She bent down and kissed him gently on the lips. "I'll make some coffee now." Louisa turned toward the door, then said over her shoulder, "I really will take care of you. You know that, don't you?"

She didn't wait for an answer.

Alone now, he lay there on the bed and tried to figure out what had happened. No, he thought, Louisa was by no means a stupid costume girl. True, he had never been knocked out by her intellect, but he'd realized a long time before that she was hardly unintelligent. It's just that he'd been doing his own thinking with definitely the wrong head when he'd met Louisa on the Papa Legba shoot. He'd been directing the musical video script he'd written for the distasteful speed metal group; she'd been paid by their manager some incredible pittance to keep their mutant Caribbean neo-Goth costumes stitched together. Also she was taking care of the quintet's hair and makeup.

Danny thought she was cute. And she responded. At the time, he didn't think it was wise to tell her about his on-again, off-again affair with Ifetayo. On that day, at that moment, it was off again, but he'd known the climate could change at any time. And it had.

So for the next two months he had tried with increasing desperation to balance the two women in his life, until the horrific Friday night when Louisa's unexpected visit had caught Danny in a highly compromising situation with Ifetayo. It had been like mixing oil and gasoline—and Danny's very presence, it seemed, was the match.

Screaming, crying, threatening, and the silence that was always more heartbreaking. The two women had left his house at different times, in different directions, and he'd guessed it unlikely that he would see either one again.

Until Sunday morning. Today.

Louisa entered the bedroom with a tray. She smiled. "Cream and sugar, sweetie, just like you always want it."

Did she know that about him? he thought. Well, obviously she did. "Thank you," he said.

She extended the cup of scalding coffee toward him—he held his breath—and she didn't spill a drop.

Dr. King was a brusque blond woman in her fifties who acknowledged Louisa's presence with a handshake and then proceeded to poke and prod Danny's body, hmm-ing and aah-ing when he winced at her fingers probing his arms and shoulders.

"We'll do a blood workup," she finally said. "But I suspect the verdict will be myositis."

"So what *is* that?" said Danny.

"Essentially a severe inflammation of the muscle tissue," she said, brow furrowing. "Sometimes virally triggered. It can be painful. You should recover."

"*Should* recover?" he said, realizing his voice was rising a little. "I've only got another week."

The doctor looked at him, expression puzzled. "You're not going to *die* from this, Daniel."

"No," he said. "What I mean is, my Guild health insurance expires in another week."

"Can't you renew it?"

"Not without a work contract," he said. "I had some hopes for a job, but I'm not gonna be able to work with my arms like this."

Louisa cleared her throat. Both Danny and Dr. King swiveled their heads to stare at her. "I can take dictation," she said. "I can help out."

"On the medical side of this," said Dr. King to Danny, "I could hospitalize you." She grimaced. "For a week. I don't think the myositis will be gone by then."

"I can take care of you at home," said Louisa. "You saw what I accomplished just this morning. I can keep you fed and clean, and medicated, if it comes to that."

Silence pooled in the examination room. Finally Dr. King shrugged. "I've got no problem with home care."

Danny opened his mouth to speak.

"Great!" said Louisa forcefully. "It's settled."

That afternoon, Danny and Louisa worked out some coping mechanisms. Much as he hated the indignity, she brushed his teeth, being exquisitely careful not to lacerate his gums. Then she worked out a system to skootch behind the pillows on the bed, and, lacing her fingers together into a double fist, to push against the small of his back so that he could more easily sit upright and get to his feet. At Danny's suggestion, she brought the cordless phone up from the office. He told her to fasten it securely to an eighteen-inch length of wooden lath with masking tape. He learned to dial it at arm's length, then to hold it to his head using the lath extension. As for the two-liter bottle with the widened hole, *nothing* improved on that.

When Danny got tired, Louisa left him to go shop for groceries. He slipped into an exhausted sleep. And dreamed.

Outlined by the moonlight shining through the east window. Ifetayo stood at the foot of his bed. His eyes flickered open and he admired the woman's supple musculature. There had been a time when he'd verbally compared her to a great jungle cat. That was just after he had hired her to work on a contract basis for him as an Internet researcher. She had laughed and asked him if he thought the image was at all racist. He wasn't sure, so kept that image to himself from then on.

"Hi, gorgeous," he said, mouth dry. "I'd get up—"

"—but you can't," she finished. "I know that very well." She brushed her long dark hair back from the one eye it had covered. "I wanted to see you before . . ." She hesitated.

"Before what?" Danny didn't like the sound of that.

"Before whatever may happen happens," Ifetayo finished.

"Don't give me any alt.philosophy," Danny said. "What's happening to me?"

Her generous lips curved in a smile half hidden by the darkness. "I don't like you much, lover."

Danny discovered he could barely force words from his own lips. "You mean you hate me?"

She seemed to ignore the question. "You'll get a gift," she said. Ifetayo sighed, sounding more sad than angry. Then she showed her teeth when she spoke. "You deserve anything you get."

"Iffie—" he said, unaccountably panicked.

The look was hard to read. "When you lie down with bitches—" she started to say.

And vanished. The moonlight evaporated. The bedroom flooded with austere late-afternoon sun. Danny blinked and drew in a ragged breath.

Louisa stood in the doorway. "Miss me?" she said.

Danny was never able to remember what he had for supper that night. He did recall that Louisa had fed him like a child, one bite at a time via fork or spoon. Going to sleep was akin to passing out.

In the morning, the phone rang and Louisa answered. It was Dr. King. Louisa handed the lath-handled portable over to Danny.

"I've got some test results back," said the doctor. "As I suspected, your

CPK is elevated, which supports the myositis scenario. But I'm wondering if perhaps the inflammation is secondary."

"What do you mean?"

"I happened to run into my favorite bone man this morning. He reminded me that secondary myositis can be the immune system's natural reaction to bone fragments in the tissue after a fracture."

"I'm not sure I understand."

"Can your friend—uh, Louisa?—bring you in this afternoon? I'm scheduling you for an MRI."

"What are you looking for?" said Danny.

Dr. King's reply was terse. "Fractures."

"He'll be there," said Louisa on the other phone.

The bone specialist at the hospital came across as a bit dubious about the need for the MRI scan. He asked Danny if the patient were *sure* he had simply awakened in pain. There was no trauma? he asked.

"I didn't even fall out of bed," Danny answered.

Maybe, the bone man suggested with a smile, one of Danny's old flames had sneaked in during the night with a ballpeen hammer and got in a few good licks before making her escape.

Danny was not amused.

He glanced at Louisa, who silently formed an interrogative word with her lips.

Ifetayo?

Danny shook his head. Iffie was quite angry with him, feeling he had betrayed her. But she wasn't malevolent. Was she? He didn't think so. He wished he could be more sure.

The MRI experience was painless but exhausting. The orderlies slid him off the gurney onto a ramp that in turn slipped into a claustrophobic tube that reminded Danny of a *Star Trek* prop. They gave him headphones and a choice of audio channels. He chose '80s pop.

Once he was crammed inside the tube, the music switched on and it was hard-core country. Then the magnetic scan sequences started and a sound like bones being ground in the teeth of a T-rex drowned out Jimmie Rodgers and Ernest Tubb.

Nearly an hour later, Danny was more than ready when the operators wheeled his ramp out of the bright white tube.

"The radiologist will look at all this," said the bone man. "We'll call you."

When they arrived back at Danny's house, they found a small parcel wrapped in brown butcher paper, tied with red yarn, waiting on the doorstep. There was no tag.

Inside, Louisa opened it for him. They both stared at the tiny black stone effigy. It gleamed with oil, exuding a sharp fragrance that opened Danny's sinuses instantly.

"The hell?" he said. He hesitated. "Voodoo?"

"Ifetayo," said Louisa flatly. She did not elaborate. "You want me to toss it?"

He shook his head. "Destroying it could be a trap. Just put it in a safe place."

"I won't let her do anything to you," Louisa said. "I love you." She kissed him, gently trailing the fingers of her right hand down the side of his face to the level of his mouth. She touched his lips. "You're tired. You ought to go back to bed."

"I'm ready," he said.

Ifetayo again appeared to him in his dream, though it was an experience akin to watching a blurry TV channel under siege from lightning strikes and rising static. Standing at the foot of his bed, she wore a multicolored long tribal dress. Danny realized he had never seen her clad in anything but conventional Western clothing.

". . . my name . . ." he heard her say, ". . . meaning." She looked frustrated, then appeared to attempt to repeat herself. ". . . Yoruba. It means 'love brings happiness.' " Some sort of cosmic interference blurred the sound. Ifetayo looked distressed. ". . . can mean so many things . . ." Her hand wove sinuously in the air between them. Danny glimpsed what might have been a cocoon of some sort, gleaming with an inner light.

Then Iffie blinked out of existence as if another hand had thrown a power switch.

Danny recalled no more of his dreams that night.

First thing in the morning, the radiologist called. Yes, Danny's bones did betray breaks. His right shoulder owned up to two long fractures just below the ball joint; his left shoulder, at least one. The bone doctor came on the line and expressed some wonderment.

"It's possible—" he said, and then interrupted himself. "You're sure there was no trauma you can recall?" There wasn't. "It's possible," he continued, "that you suffered convulsions in your sleep. Muscles can do that, you know. It's uncommon, but they can fracture some major bones."

Danny considered that, thought about his own body betraying him in so hideous a way. "But why?" he said.

"Hard to say at this point. A sharp drop in blood glucose level, perhaps. Maybe a reaction triggered by sleep apnea. There could be a neurological basis." He was silent for a few moments. "I'll talk with Dr. King. We may start some series of diagnostics."

Danny kept his own silence for a while before breaking it. "But soon," he said. "The tests should be as soon as possible." He didn't have the energy to explain himself.

The bone man agreed and rang off.

Louisa noted his evident distress and gently seated herself on the mattress beside him. "Don't worry, sweetie. No matter what happens with the doctors, I'll take care of you. I'll see that nothing else happens."

"Gonna shoot Ifetayo if it turns out she's put the juju on me?" he said, half serious.

"Yes," she answered, sounding completely serious. "She can't hurt you."

"Relax," he said, trying to affect some healthy bravado. "It isn't your job to be my bodyguard."

"But I love you," said Louisa. "I love you so very much." She hesitated. "Don't you love me too?"

It was his turn to hesitate. "I like you a lot," he said. "I'm really grateful for everything you're doing."

"But you don't love me?"

He heard an edge in her voice. "I probably will," he said. "Give me some time."

She did not sound placated. "Don't wait too long, Danny." She got up and walked across the hall to the smaller bathroom. The door closed behind her. Danny thought he could hear her crying. But when she finally came back out, her face was dry and she was smiling.

"We're going out to eat," she said. "To celebrate."

"Celebrate what?" he said. "I'm not exactly in a good space for going out."

"Celebrating our love," Louisa said. "And don't you worry about a thing." With that, she put clean socks and running shoes on his feet. Dressed in boxer shorts, he allowed her carefully to maneuver his arms through the sleeves of his long trench coat.

"Anybody checks, they'll think I'm a pervert on the way to a schoolyard," he said.

"Trust me." She led him down to the car and drove him to a very dark restaurant where they could sit in relative seclusion to the side of the dining room. With her help, he ordered soups and puddings and coffee. The dishes lined up like little soldiers, each with a thick straw extending up toward his mouth.

He didn't expect to like the experience. Getting out cheered him, he discovered.

The glow started to dissipate once they returned home. The caller ID indicated that Ifetayo had called. "Don't phone her back," Louisa said.

"This is my house," Danny said. My rules, he *almost* said. When he gingerly dialed Iffie's number, he got a "this number is not presently in service," intercept. "I should drive over," he said. "It might be important."

"No," Louisa said. "You can't do that."

"Will you drive me over?"

"No."

He heard the anger in her voice, and backed off. "Maybe tomorrow."

"No," she said. "Never."

They talked little more before he decided to go to sleep.

Ifetayo did not come to him in his dreams.

Danny awoke hearing—and feeling—the bones of his toes snapping. The little toes twitched, convulsed, broke like twigs being trampled underfoot. Then the next in line, as the pain grew, right up to and including the big toes. Both of them.

Crack!

He screamed at the dream.

It was not a dream.

The small bones in the arch of his right foot began to vibrate, then to bend under internal pressure. He remembered tugging the wishbone at childhood Thanksgivings and Christmases. The pain was intense. But it was multiplied by the ripping, crunching *sounds*, noises of destruction that arrowed right to his gut. He doubled up on the bed and tried to reach his feet, to massage them the way he used to soothe charley horses. It did no good—he couldn't make his arms work.

All those tiny bones destroyed themselves as he cried out.

Then Louisa was there with warm towels to wipe his sweaty face and to lay wet wraps across the savage pain in his feet. "There now," she said. "It will be okay. We'll manage the pain."

"Why?" he said, mind blurry with the tortured electricity from his feet and shoulders. "Why why why why . . ." He stopped when he was out of breath. It didn't take long.

"She won't hurt you again," Louisa said.

The meaning came through to him finally. "Who? Ifetayo?"

"Of course." Louisa continued mopping his forehead. "Now try to rest. Just breathe through the pain. You won't be able to walk for a while. But don't worry. I'll take care of everything. I love you."

A thought came to him. "Weezie, that *thing* Iffie left on the porch yesterday. The one you put in a safe place? I think you better destroy it."

"I already did, lover," she said reassuringly.

"Good." He shook his head. Words swam in his head and it was hard to articulate them in his throat. "I never believed in black magic."

"You don't have to," Louisa said. "It works anyway."

He began to sink away from consciousness, trying to elude the pain from which he'd begun to think there truly was no escaping. Louisa said something he couldn't quite make out. "What?"

"The river Styx is deep and wide," she said. "So much hate flows there." Then it was as though she'd switched channels. "The cats are out of hiding. I fed them. They like me."

"What do you . . ." He didn't find out *what* she meant. Blessed unconsciousness arrived first.

•   •   •

When he awoke again, Danny could barely move at all. Louisa sat beside the bed with a cup of hot coffee brewed and ready. She carefully helped him sip it.

"I'm afraid your legs aren't doing so well," she said.

"They hurt like my shoulders," he whimpered.

"You'll be staying at home for a while," she said sympathetically. "I'll make sure you're all right."

"We don't have to drive over to see Ifetayo," Danny said.

"Damn straight," she replied. "Wouldn't do much good anyway."

"What do you mean?"

She didn't answer. "That woman hated you," Louisa said. "The effigy I destroyed? The one she left? That was to make you impotent. I guess she figured it was poetic justice." Louisa sighed. "But she had no *right*."

Danny tried to raise his head to look at her. His fingers crawled along the top of the blanket like crippled spiders.

She glanced down. "Careful," she said. "Any more mischief and things could happen to all ten of those, even the thumbs." Then she grinned sunnily. "But I told you, I can take dictation. You'll do fine."

"What the hell are you talking about?" he mumbled. His vision suddenly irised in on something new crowning the bureau behind her. It was his picture in an antique metal frame. Something else leaned against the frame. It looked like a Ken doll wrapped tightly in monofilament—so much stranded bondage it could have been cocooned for the winter. Those tight bonds looked as though they were pulling the doll's limbs out of true, contorting them into unnatural positions. The arms, legs, hands, there the bonds stretched the thickest and tightest.

The meaning started percolating through his bleary, pain-shot mind. Weezie *loved* him.

As though reading his mind, she said, "Danny, I'll love you forever. I couldn't let *her* injure you. There was no way. I'll take care of you always. Count on it."

This was a delirium he knew he would not wake from.

It was hard now to hold on to anything secure. But he knew something beyond all else as he stared up at her serene smile.

Love will always triumph over hate.

Always.

Carol Anne Davis

Not Long Now

CAROL ANNE DAVIS's psychosexual novels include *Shrouded* (a realistic depiction of an increasingly murderous mortician) and *Safe as Houses,* about the crimes of a sadistic sociopath. *Shrouded* was hailed as the "debut of the year" by three reviewers while *Safe as Houses* has been described as "searing, potent, unsettling" and "unputdownable." The novels are set in her native Scotland, though she currently lives in England. Her frequently updated Web site can be found at www.tellitlikeitis.demon.co.uk. This story was first published in *QWF Magazine.*

Not Long Now

Carol Anne Davis

Sometimes you're still alive when they take both your kidneys out. That's one of the things they don't mention on the Organ Donor Card. You only find out if you become a medic or when . . .

But when I first met Barclay I knew nothing of such things. I only knew that my body worked and that men liked looking at it. As I ordered a vegetable pastry in the Medina my T-shirted breasts were the subject of a dozen male stares.

"I recognize that accent," an English voice said. I turned around to see a typically British stocky male frame and the most unusual brown eyes I have ever stared into. The kind of eyes that makes a woman who's been traveling light want to put on some heavy-duty makeup and blow-dry her hair. But the Tunisian marketplace didn't lend itself to mirrors or washrooms so I settled for pulling my stomach muscles in and my shoulders back. I wondered if he liked fair-cropped women with overdeveloped calf muscles and a slightly underdeveloped sense of direction. I tried to look and sound as if I didn't care.

After five minutes of swapping details on how we came to be in Sousse, Barclay looked at his heavy gold watch. "I have to work now."

"Oh, of course." I made my lips keep smiling to hide what I saw as a forthcoming rejection. His was the first English voice I'd heard since separating from my friend.

"But it would be nice to talk further," he continued, briefly touching my bare right arm.

I opted for a noncommittal nod but inside the people-who-need-people part of me had started singing. I wasn't spineless but it was hard work traveling, eating and sightseeing on my own. I'd seen gentle blue villages, coppery horses and sand-colored camels on my coach-bound journey and translated each sight into words which I longed to share.

Barclay was already seated at our table when I arrived at the restaurant. He stood up until I sat down. He looked even better than I remembered. "You seem to know your way around," I said lightly as he spoke fluent Arabic to the shy young serving boy.

He brushed imaginary dust from his lightweight suit. "Well, I've lived here for five years. I'm practically a native now."

"What made you emigrate?" I loved the bright sunlight and the beaches here but like most long haul tourists I was increasingly homesick.

"Well, I came out to run a fitness center franchise—and soon worked my way up to owning three of them. The living was easy so I stayed." I looked down at our smoked salmon starters as they arrived but the slight prickling of my face made me aware that he was still gazing at my small nose and a mouth that was slightly too wide to be considered beautiful. "So what brings *you* this far from home all by yourself?" he continued curiously.

I cut into the rasher-long strips of pink flesh. "Well, a colleague and I were made redundant at the exact same time."

"From where?"

"From the hill-walking company where we were guiders. You know, we'd take groups of six or eight away for a few days."

"A healthy break?"

"Until people tired of healthy holidays. Then we each got a couple of thousand pounds redundancy money so we thought we'd see the world."

It hadn't really been that simple, of course. I'd lived through quite a few sleepless nights, been turned down for several new jobs. I'd thought about becoming self-employed then realized that I wasn't quite sure if I wanted to continue in the hill-walking business. When Laurel had suggested this low-budget trip it had given me an excuse to put my life plan on hold.

Now I watched as Barclay finger-combed his impressively heavy black hair and I longed for a groin-tingling moment to do likewise. "And you chose Tunisia's tourist trap?"

I grinned at his teasing. "No, Sousse wasn't part of the plan until we met up with this Canadian group," I admitted, looking at his gold watch and knowing that he'd never traveled cheaply. "Laurel got off with one of the guys and . . ." I stretched my mouth ruefully wide.

"And three's a crowd?"

I looked back at him guiltily. "They were forever caressing and kissing and . . . well, it was awkward." I started to eat the parsley garnish, trying not to remember the moaning lust from their corner of the hut each night. "In the end they decided to do the nomadic bit and camel-trek across the Sahara for a fortnight. I waved them off then caught the next bus to Sousse on my own."

"And you plan to stay here for the rest of the year?"

"God, no." I'd only been here a week and had already spent too much of my budget on a pricy hotel that was extra-safe for solo women. "I reckon I'll stay till the end of the month then take a plane home."

"You're expected?" Barclay's eyebrows moved down and slightly closer together at the prospect of my leaving.

I wasn't, but just nodded and said, "By my friends."

"Perhaps they will spare you for a few more days." He leaned back in his chair as the Head Waiter approached with Dover sole and huge wooden bowls of the local salad. *They can spare me forever,* I thought wistfully, *if I get to live like this.*

I was twenty-eight. He was forty. We were old enough to . . . But at midnight he simply walked to the restaurant telephone and called me a cab.

"Can I meet you for lunch tomorrow?" he asked. I agreed to that and to meeting the next night. We ate out twice more then went to the subtitled cinema, me feeling exotic because I was the only woman there.

And still he didn't make a move. He seemed tentative, even shy. It just made me keener. I dreamed of him stripping and licking and entering me every night. By then I knew that I wouldn't return to England while Barclay was here and old-fashionedly courting me. I'd never felt so cherished in my life. I put my small hand on his knee as we watched the big screen, but he lifted it by the wrist and kissed each finger. Then he put it back on my lap murmuring, "Let's get to know each other fully first."

I was second to hit the beach on our fifth date. He was sitting patiently in the shade beside a little straw picnic hamper. We walked for miles till we came to an inlet that we had all to ourselves. "Eat, drink," Barclay said as we flopped on the sand. His voice quavered and he looked strangely moved.

I watched as he opened the basket and withdrew brie-and-apple-filled croissants and a prechilled silver flask. Soon the warmth and the food and juice made me feel tranquil. Tranquillity slipped into sleepiness and I closed my eyes . . .

I next opened them and stared at unfamiliar walls and unfamiliar shuttered small round windows. The metal bed I was lying in was also coolly alien to me. "Barclay?" I tried to call but my throat felt sore and my voice was diluted with disorientated fear.

After a few moments he arrived with some imported magazines which he put solicitously on my bedside cabinet. "I'm so glad you're back with us," he said, kissing the crown of my presumably-tousled head.

I blinked. "What happened? One minute I was talking to you, the next . . ."

"You passed out. It was more than a faint. I had to bring you here to the hospital. It's private, so you're in good hands," he said.

"I took out insurance . . ." I muttered, looking more closely at the en suite facilities of my large white room. This place screamed exclusive and expensive.

"No problem. I'll take care of everything," Barclay said.

And he did—oh God, how he did. A sweetly smiling Tunisian nurse came in and drew a vial of my blood. She murmured Arabic replies to my English queries. Later she gave me a chalky drink and I slept again. When I came to I felt as if I'd been unconscious for many vulnerable hours. My mouth was coated with bacteria and there was an unfamiliar film over my teeth.

Later Barclay entered the room with a big bunch of bananas and some bottled water. He looked so robust that I felt shrinkingly inferior and hid most of my head under the sheets. "What's wrong with me?" I muttered plaintively, still wanting him to see me at my best yet knowing my sleep-lined face made this impossible. "I feel so weak."

"They're not sure yet. They've been doing a few tests," my new boyfriend said.

For a moment his gaze flickered away from mine as if he had something to hide, and I wondered . . . But then I chided myself for doubting his hospitality. People did get sick abroad. It was a fact. I'd even seen people get ill back in Britain when we took them hill-walking. Their bodies were subjected to different temperatures, different levels of endurance and altitude, different food.

"How much longer d'you think I'll have to stay in isolation here?" I continued from my blanket hideaway, realizing that I'd yet to hear or see another patient.

"Not long now," Barclay said. The nurse came in and he got up to leave, murmuring something to her that my basic grasp of Tunisian couldn't follow. I noticed that he didn't kiss me goodbye or say when he'd see me next. *This time,* I thought, *I'll refuse the drink the nurse offers in case it contains a sedative.* Then I saw the syringe.

I watched her fingers apologetically encircle my arm, felt the particular sharp pain that only a needle can elicit. I looked at her and asked, "Why?" She kept her lids downcast and I saw that her lower lip was trembling. It was the last flesh I saw until . . .

Until sensation swam back to me again. There was a radiating anguish in my belly and to one side of my spine. I tried to open my eyes but the muscles of my eyelids couldn't follow my brain's wild signals. "Second clamp," an unfamiliar British voice said. It was followed by a scraping sound of metal on metal or something equally mechanical, then my suffering intensified. I tried to open my lips to scream but they were as heavy as twin trapdoors. I realized then that whatever anesthetic I'd been injected with had left me paralyzed.

People talk about straining to hear a sound—and I listened so hard that I felt as if my inner ears were turning outward. "*Behi,*" ("Good") I heard Barclay say. "*Shukran,*" ("Thank you") the shy nurse whispered. Then "Almost there," the British voice I'd heard a moment earlier said.

The torture intensified. I fought with the pain, fought against the pain. My brain begged for oblivion from the hellish intestinal acid. And suddenly my lids pushed open and I could see.

"Oh Christ," said the stranger who was dressed in an operative mask and gown as were the nurse and Barclay. "She's coming round."

"I . . . I gave her the smallest amount of anesthetic," Barclay stammered from his stance to the left of my abdomen. I glanced at his hands and saw them inside the river of red that had once been my belly. "I didn't want to risk anesthetic complications. It's best that she doesn't die on us until . . ."

"So shall I give her some more?" the stranger slurred.

"No, we're close enough," Barclay said. I stared in numb disbelief at the nurse and she stared back at me in open-mouthed and close-fisted horror. "I'm sorry," he said to me simply—and took the breathing tube out of my windpipe in one slow sure pull.

Over and out. I tried to suck in air but my throat and chest muscles were still paralyzed by the anesthetic so I couldn't breathe unaided. Hot mists of uncertain color sluiced through the inside of my head. I looked at all three and they looked back like robbers guilt-frozen on a security camera. Then Barclay returned to his surgical task.

Seconds later I surged way above my prostrate head, way above the helpless cut-open carnage of my lower body. The rush was instant, like an open balloon with the air escaping out. It was pure sensation, estranged from thought or chosen action. Then reason returned as I stabilized in the right-hand ceiling corner of the operating room.

And in a second I understood it all, as if I'd watched a film of the entire story. Understood that Barclay's twenty-year-old twin sons needed a kidney each if they were to survive. I saw their daily visits to the dialysis machine, the glucose it pumped around their listless bodies. Observed their hotly swelling joints and pain-filled eyes. For a moment I felt Barclay's pain too, the mental and emotional anguish of seeing his beloved progeny dying. But then I remembered my own loss and felt only rage.

How dare he sacrifice my life for that of his boys, for anyone? How could he deprive me of sixty more potentially eventful years? I'd seen some-one to love—but all he'd seen was a healthy young kidney donor. I'd seen a man with a spirit and a soul and he'd seen a woman with all her vital organs obligingly intact.

No wonder he hadn't made a sexual move—he hadn't wanted to risk impregnating me with another of his children. The tests he'd done after drugging me must have confirmed that I had kidney compatibility with his existing ones. I saw back, back, back to his wife, bringing forth his twins then bleeding to death within an hour of childbirth. I saw the boys' more recent kidney failure and their father's search for a donor he could ensnare.

I was the fifth girl to be ensnared—I watched a psychic replay of the first, second, third, and fourth potential victims. All had taken ill while dating him. All had been brought here and tested incompatible and had recovered with impressive speed. I was the first one whose chemistry had been exactly right for the twin boys and I was fit and fresh.

A fresh new kidney is a wonderful thing. They can chill and preserve it for up to twelve hours if the donor dies in a no-way-back road accident. But it's even better if they can take it from someone who is still breathing but technically dead. That way the surgeon gets to cut out a living organ for though the brain is seemingly lifeless the circulation's still helpfully alive. The medics take what they want from the unconscious patient—then they turn off the respiratory machine and he or she fully dies.

I wasn't brain-dead, of course—and now that I'm here in the alternative mode I never will be. All that I am now consists of endless and increasingly focused thought. No lust or irritation remain and I'm free of the doubts and fears which formerly shadowed me, but I'm left with a cognizant need for revenge. That need is seared into my spirit the way that an important exam date was in my former lifetime. I thought that retaliation was a human trait but now I'm nonhuman it certainly hasn't gone away.

Vengeance has been my spur for the six weeks since Barclay pulled the windpipe from my throat. I can see and hear everything that I did before. Hell, I watched them bury my body so deep that even the worms will never find it. And sometimes I walk, invisible, past the dinner table as Barclay talks to his healing sons. They assume that a donor died either naturally or in an accident, and are so grateful that in my former life I would have found their thankfulness quite touching. And they've already made great strides toward recovery.

I don't know if I'll recover the situation when I've done what I have to do, when I've avenged my cold destruction. All I know is that at the moment I'm in a disembodied No Persons Land. I won't call it No Man's or No Woman's Land for I'm in a form beyond gender. But I feel a sense of unbelonging like never before.

Jesus doesn't appear to want me for a sunbeam—at least he hasn't produced any beckoning bright tunnels. No dead relatives have come to take me to a better land. I just walk—well, sort of float—around the streets of Sousse or anywhere else I can think of. I need no clothes, food, shelter and no rest. I also have no one to talk to about my meticulous slow slaughter and no one can hear . . .

But more and more often I'm causing people to see. I think they see the things they least want to. Leastways, I've managed to make a certain scalpel move just a fraction of an inch when it's being handled by the surgical-assistance nurse. She's screamed each time and dropped the blade. I've felt her trembling. I know that she was blackmailed into helping Barclay out after hours, that she normally does a responsible nursing job.

I hear her pray for my soul in every section of the Mosque and she prays again at the hospital when she tends her own sick daughter. And I can see into her dreams and know that she's had enough.

So has the other British doctor who helped—I watch from a corner of his room as he searches through five years of ruined veins to find a fresh site for his daily heroin injection. Again, he's in his own private hell.

But some people deserve to suffer much, much more. Last week I transmogrified into a plasmatic shadow which darkened Barclay's sunlit operating room. He staggered back from the trolley and dropped the case notes he was carrying. My focus flagged and I disappeared from his view. Still I stayed around to watch and saw him rushing out to buy the local brandy, *boukha*. He's usually teetotal. He used to be a principled man.

I floated invisibly in front of him as he hurried back clutching his bottle of swirling liquid succor. His mouth twitched at the right-hand corner and he was white as milk beneath his year-round tan. The tan is real but his name isn't Barclay of course and he doesn't run a fitness franchise. And now that he's removed the black wig and tinted lenses he wore in public I can see that he has weak blue eyes and slightly thinning blond hair.

And a very thick hide. Yesterday I thought so hard about him stealing away my life that all three of the lightbulbs in his hospital study exploded. Today I made his pens burst and for the first time in years this private practice surgeon couldn't sign his patient's insurance claims.

He's still in denial, of course, still hoping that these actions are not those of a wronged and earth-roaming demon. "Are you all right, Dad?" ask his sons and I hear him say, "Just overwork, boys, just stress."

I hope that tomorrow will be the most stressful day of all. If not, I've lots of time. I'm in no hurry. Tomorrow's good though because he's driving to an understaffed friend's clinic, a drive along the narrow road that hugs the cliff. I'll float toward his windscreen with my torn open belly and he'll shriek and throw himself backward, as humans do when they're overwhelmingly afraid. He'll be a man confronting something that is nonhuman or subhuman, a man who'll hopefully lose control of the wheel as his eyes fix on my organless cavities . . .

If he dies I reckon he'll go to some unpleasant place, a kind of time out for sociopaths which involves a lot of retuning. And if he lives I'll summon up all my anger to appear before him again.

The ideal, of course, is for him to be pronounced brain-dead but alive in the breathing sense. I can cause that to happen by interfering with his scan so that his brain activity appears entirely absent. I'll make the dials say exactly what I want them to say. It's the thing I do best now that I am whatever I am—I steal energy. Sun and other people's stress and electricity all fuel my focused rage. So I'll make Barclay look like a hopeless human vegetable and the CPR team will sadly shake their heads.

But the urologists will nod and it'll be donor cards on the table time. They'll go soberly to his waiting and weeping twins. "We've got his request here but we still need your permission to remove his kidneys. If you could sign . . . ?"

"Oh yes," the boys will say, glad of some good coming out of this infernal badness, "Dad was so pleased when a card-carrying donor helped us."

And then it will be my turn to help. And I'll squeeze shut the tube that lets the anesthetic in so that Barclay wakes up midoperation. And I'll smile like a demon lover as his terrified eyes gaze into mine. Then I'll hold his lids shut so that no one else knows he is fully conscious. "Not long now," I'll whisper as the scalpel moves toward his fully sentient bare left side.

Mat Coward

The Shortest
Distance

MAT COWARD is a British writer better known in his native country than over here. The stories he sends across the water should change all that. He brings a special sardonic touch to his crime fiction, a touch that can sometimes sting with fury and other times touch with unexpected sentiment. Like many of the British authors writing today, his beat is the city and all of the various characters and stories found there, and he brings them alive as few others do. Other fiction by him appears in *A Treasury of Cat Mysteries* and *Once Upon a Crime*. "The Shortest Distance" first appeared in *Shots*, winter issue. His first novel was *Up and Down*.

The Shortest Distance

Mat Coward

Ugly people rule the world. All that frustrated sexual energy has to go somewhere.

My new client, Noel Bell, was certainly ugly, and he definitely ruled the world. His large, pink head had the in-and-out contours of a classic baking potato. The hairdo he favored was a flesh Mohican—hair down either side, a ridge of scalp in the middle. The world he ruled was called NoBell Developments.

"Leslie Queen," said Bell. "Androgynous sort of name, isn't it?"

People who rule worlds often like to waste the time of people who don't, with purposeless, mildly insulting banter. I knew that, so I said nothing.

Or rather, nothing is what I should have said. What I actually said, after enduring twenty minutes of his chitchat, was: "Mr. Bell, I'm seventy-three years old. I wonder which is going to happen first? My funeral, or you getting to the point."

Bell laughed. "That's funny," he said. "I like a guy who speaks his mind." Then he stopped laughing, and his face rearranged itself into a frown. "No, wait a minute, correction—I don't like a guy who speaks his mind. I was thinking of my brother. He's the one who likes a guy who speaks his mind. I'm the one who demands total subservience at all times. Is that understood, Mr. Queen?"

I didn't desperately need the money. My police pension paid my rent, kept me in whiskey and aspirin. Fact was, I could retire any time I felt like dying.

I didn't need the money, but I needed the work.

"Look, Mr. Bell, you think you have a problem and you think you need a private investigator to solve it for you and you think I'm the one you need. I've no idea about the first two, but you're right about the last one. So tell me what you want me to do, and we can move on to the part where I quote you twice my usual fee, you accept it without demur, and I go away cursing myself for not quoting treble."

He reached into a desk drawer, and brought out a red plastic document folder. "Take that away with you. Read my problem, solve it, and then present me with an invoice for treble your usual fee."

"Treble?"

"Treble."

I picked up the folder, and went away cursing myself for not quoting quadruple.

The folder contained what such folders in such circumstances always contain: a sad story about a spoiled child and a puzzled father.

Castor Bell, nineteen-year-old millionaire's son, worked in a pub in Willesden popularly known as The Morgue. Old-fashioned sort of place, the kind they used to call spit and sawdust. I didn't see any actual sawdust, which was a pity: it could've helped soak up the spit.

I'd never met Castor's mother, but I could see straightaway that he must take after her, in looks at least, because he wasn't ugly. Which, according to my theory, meant he'd never rule the world. But then, if your father's a millionaire, who cares?

I folded myself onto a bar stool, took off my hat, ordered a light and bitter, and lit a cigarette. Castor drew half a pint of flat bitter into a dirty glass and put it on the counter in front of me, next to a warm bottle of light ale.

"You do sandwiches?" I said.

He shook his head. "Sorry."

"Thank God for that." That won me a smile, but not much of one. About as much of a smile as it was worth, I suppose. The beer tasted worse than it looked, and smelled worse than either, so I decided to hell with the subtle approach. I cut to the chaser. "Give me a Scotch, will you, Mr. Bell?"

He didn't react to my naming him, didn't react at all, which was how I knew he'd noticed. "Any particular Scotch?"

"Whichever one comes in a clean glass."

He gave one of those small, upper-class laughs, the sort that sound like a cat starting to cough up a hairball and then losing interest halfway through. "We don't stock that brand," he said, serving me a Bell's from an optic. "But don't worry. Alcohol kills germs."

I said nothing. I was too busy figuring a way of getting the whiskey inside me without my lips touching the glass.

"So. You work for my father."

"Today, I do." I swallowed my disinfectant like a brave boy. "You going to tell your father I've been drinking on his time?"

Castor pushed off from the counter, and went to serve a middle-aged man at the other end of the bar who was drinking draft Guinness and wearing a suit and tie. The suit and tie told me he was the poorest man in the pub: he'd sold or lost all his clothes except those he'd be buried in. From the state of the suit, he'd already been buried in it once or twice.

"I'm not going to tell my father anything," said Castor, while he waited for the Guinness to settle. "Because I'm not going to speak to him." He used a palette knife to decapitate the pint, topped up the glass, and left it to settle again. That touched me—here was a kid taking the time to do a job properly, even when it was a crap job in a lousy place.

"He just wants to know if you're all right," I lied.

"Yeah! Like giving a shit about me is his specialist subject. Forget it, Mr. . . ."

"Queen," I said, and showed him one of my business cards. I didn't give him the card, because I hadn't got many left. My printer died last Christmas.

"You really a private investigator?" He studied my gray hair and my cheeks that met in the middle and I knew what was coming next. "No offense, man, but aren't you a little, you know, elderly, for that line of work?"

"Would you rather I drove a bus?"

Castor was really staring at me now. "You an ex-cop?"

"Very," I said.

"You believe in justice?"

"I'm in favor of it. I don't know if I believe in it."

He rubbed at his short, streaked hair, with long, soft fingers. "Jesus, what a weird planet. You ever get that feeling?"

"No," I said. "But then, I was born here."

"My shift ends in an hour. Could you wait around? I want to show you something."

It was two things. A building and a beautiful girl. Castor was in love with them both.

"Isn't it stunning?" he said. "Rossland House. Built as a private residence, two hundred years ago. Since then it's been a hospital, a school for paupers, a private house again, and now it's empty. Seriously neglected. But isn't it fantastic, Mr. Queen?"

"It's fine," I said. In a general way, I approve of buildings. They keep the rain out.

The beautiful girl, a tall, poised redhead, had been introduced as Vanessa. No last name was offered, and I didn't ask for one because Vanessa's eyes said she'd prefer it that way. It seemed a small price to pay for having such a creature hold one's gaze.

"Castor's father plans to knock it down," she said. "Can you believe that?"

"Just barely."

"To build a video superstore," said Castor. "Isn't that an incredible waste?"

"I'm with you there, son," I agreed. "Who needs to rent films, when you can see them on TV for free?"

Castor shook his head. "That's not what I meant—"

"Mr. Queen knows that, babe." Vanessa laid a hand on his arm, and just for a moment I hated him. "He's teasing. Aren't you, Mr. Queen?"

"It's not a joke!" said Castor. "And a lot of local people agree with us, they want to turn this into a community center. Don't you see? We can't just sit back while he reduces a wonderful, rare old building like this to rubble!"

"Well," I said, "rubble is his business. It's how he made his fortune—a fortune that'll be yours one day. He hasn't dispossessed you yet."

The boy turned away, obviously struggling with an impulse to hit me. I didn't wait around to see if he won.

I went home and changed my shirt, then spent the rest of the afternoon running errands for an old person, the old person being me and the errands including a urologist's appointment. It was late evening by the time I again unlocked the door to my two-room flat.

I stood there for a moment, trying to remember whether I'd left the light on when I went out. Maybe I had: my memory isn't what it used to be. Nor are my teeth, though my hat hasn't changed much.

I was still standing there, in doubt, when a man came out of my bedroom, carrying a small, black gun in a large, red hand. He was a big man, but not so big he couldn't get through the door. He was also ugly, but he didn't look like someone who'd ever ruled any world larger than a three-man prison cell.

"You're Queen," he said, covering me with the gun while he locked the front door.

"I already know that," I said. "So if that's all you came to tell me, I'm afraid you had a wasted journey."

He blinked several times, as he tried to work out what I was talking about. It occurred to me that this might take a while, and I wished I'd thought to bring along a puzzle-book.

"I get it," he said at last. "A smart-aleck."

"And for that you're going to kill me?" I said, sounding tougher than I felt. Or feeling tougher than I sounded. One of the two.

"Nobody said I should kill you, Granddad, just give you a message."

"I hope you've got it written down, Mastermind. Otherwise, it'd be quicker to kill me. And kinder, too."

He hit me with his empty hand. It hurt, but not like the urologist.

"Forget about the Bell kid," he said. "Drop the case." And then he left, before I could ask him how come his lips moved when he was thinking, but not when he was talking.

It had been a long day. My old CID sergeant used to say, when he was dying of cancer, "Better another long day than that final long night." He had a point, I suppose, if points are your thing.

I poured a drink, drank it, swilled out the glass, got undressed and got into bed, huddling against the cold of the sheets, ready for another long night. Not the long night, just a long night, but a long one, nonetheless, in a long, rarely broken series of long ones.

Either the whiskey or my clean conscience did the trick, though, for as soon as my head touched the pillow, a dark, swirling tunnel opened up before me, and I found myself falling, falling, falling, into a great void of utter blackness.

I don't know if I snore or not. I didn't used to, but these days, who's to say? I know I don't dream anymore, haven't done for years. I think that's because everything there is to see I've already seen with my eyes open.

The hammering on my door probably hadn't been going on for more than an hour by the time it woke me, and it probably wasn't any louder than a slow avalanche landing on a thin roof.

I managed to get the door open before it fell in, and my dressing-gown on before I fell out. Two victories in one morning, and I hadn't even had my first cigarette.

Two police officers fell through the doorway. The one that was plain-clothed, middle-aged, short and female looked at my dressing-gown, spent a few moments disliking it, then looked up at my face and shook her head, sadly.

"You're Queen," she said.

"I already know that—" I began, but she was too busy to catch the rest of my act.

"DI Murray." She flashed a card, and signaled to her young PC, who headed for the bedroom to begin silently dismantling the detritus of my life.

"If I ask if you've got a warrant, will you hold it against me?"

No reaction.

"I used to be in the job myself," I said, "if that makes any difference."

She looked at me with slightly more contempt than I deserved. Not a lot more, but enough to hurt. "Makes a difference to your pension," she said. "Makes sod-all difference to me."

"Want to tell me what you're looking for?"

"The blunt instrument," she said, her back to me as she searched my bookcase for blunt instruments.

"What blunt instrument?"

"The blunt instrument you used to kill Mr. Wise."

"Who's Mr. Wise?"

"The man you killed."

I'd heard better patter on Talent Nite at the Three Feathers. I put a hand on DI Murray's shoulder, and said "Look, will you just tell me—oof!"

She swung a sharp elbow into my groin and I suddenly decided to sit down on the floor and wheeze. It's not exactly yoga, but it's good for focusing the mind.

"This Mr. Wise," I said, as soon as I was able. "Where was he found? And if you say 'Where you left him,' I'm going to report you to the Commissioner for wearing red shoes with a blue skirt."

She didn't smile. I don't just mean there and then—my guess is she didn't smile ever. "Back of this building. In among the dustbins."

"He still there? May I peek?"

She scratched her ear, thinking about it. "Why not," she said eventually. "With any luck you'll get his blood on your shoes and I can nick you for that."

We left the boy scout hunting for porno under my bed, and walked down to the backyard. As advertised, a large corpse lay partially hidden by a wheeled bin. Mr. Wise, aka the thug from last night.

"You know him?" She watched my face for a reaction. Call me conceited, but I like to think she watched in vain. "He's known to us. Desmond Wise. Odd-job yobbo for a gang-connected demolition firm called Coots. Mean anything to you?"

I didn't answer. At that stage I wasn't sure which bits I was going to end up lying about. "He's been cleaned up," I said, pointing to some bloody smears on his bomber jacket.

"The killer took his cash and cards, is what we assume. Then wiped the jacket for prints."

I leaned forward and sniffed. Something was prickling my nostrils— something other than blood and garbage, and the everyday stink of the city. Which, come to think of it, is blood and garbage.

"What?" said Murray. "You half man, half bloodhound?"

"I smell beer."

"So? He was a man. All men smell of beer."

"Yeah," I said. But he hadn't smelled of beer when he'd left me. Besides, the smell of beer wasn't on him. It was on his jacket. "Tell me, Inspector, now that we've become so close. Why'd you knock on my door this morning? Apart from a kinky thing you have about seeing old men in their pajamas."

"Anonymous phone call. Gave us the meat." She nodded at the late Mr. Wise. "Gave us you for a garnish."

"But you didn't like the phone call much, which is why you didn't bother with a warrant."

She made no comment to that. I'd have fainted with shock if she had.

"So I'm free to go? Assuming your toy-boy hasn't found too many gore-encrusted candlesticks in my sock drawer."

She shrugged. I walked. I was almost out of sight before she called after me. "If you're thinking of going abroad, do me a favor."

"Yes?"

"Make it somewhere that has the death penalty."

• • •

I found my coat and hat amid the rubble of my rooms, and used the drive to my client's house on Hampstead Heath to sort things out in my aching head.

At the end of my first day on a new case, I get home, not to a roaring fire, but to a dim thug named Wise who warns me off the aforesaid case, acting on behalf of person or persons unknown. He leaves my flat, is somehow persuaded by further person or persons unknown to add a visit to the communal dustbins to his tour itinerary, where he's introduced to a blunt instrument or instruments unknown. Wise cracks, or at least his skull does, and someone (presumably the second person unknown; see above) dials three nines and drops my name in a CID duty officer's ear.

All pretty simple, really, as puzzles go. I'd figured out who by the first traffic lights. Why kept me busy until I reached the clean streets of Hampstead.

Mr. Bell, once I'd been admitted to his presence, spent five minutes telling me how he never saw anyone without an appointment, and then another five making sure I understand the gist of the first five. When it was my turn to speak, I kept it brief. We both had busy schedules that day.

"I met your son yesterday. I also met his girlfriend. This morning I met a copper called Murray, and last night I met a Coots enforcer named Wise. My hectic social life would be the envy of many a retired person."

I had his attention. "This chap Wise. What did he want?"

"Who cares? He's dead."

"I see." From Bell's face, he clearly thought I'd killed Wise. I let him think it.

"So if you want to know what he was up to, you'll have to ask Mr. Coots himself. You do have his phone number, don't you?"

"Seems I have no secrets left, Mr. Queen. Yes, Coots and I do have an . . . ongoing business relationship."

"The sinful art of merger, right? No, don't bother not answering, I'm really not interested. I'll take my check now, and see myself out."

He laughed, as hard as he could manage. Sounded like an asthmatic lizard. "Why would I pay you, Queen? I hired you to stop my son sabotaging my plans for Rossland House. In the event, all you seem to have achieved is a—a—"

I filled in the blank. "A gang war, Mr. Bell? As a result of which, I'd guess, you and Coots won't be developing Rossland House. So your son won't have anything to sabotage. So I've done my job." I stood up. "So I'll take my check."

He looked pale and shaken, serving beer at the far end of the bar. She looked pale and composed, sipping gin and tonic at the near end. They both looked young and rich. I looked old and poor, but I am blessed with a ruddy complexion.

"Does Castor know your surname?" I asked, keeping my voice quiet and my face loud.

She didn't hesitate. If she was truly as hard as she thought she was, it was a miracle her arse didn't break the bar stool. "Not my real one, no."

Castor had spotted me, and hurried over, his lips trembling, his death-white face sweating.

Vanessa Coots hopped her hips up onto the bar and kissed him on the nose. "Gotta go, babe. Mr. Q's giving me a lift to the tube. Phone you, OK?"

In the car she asked the final question first, which showed a certain chutzpah, if nothing else. "Are you going to turn us in?"

"No," I said.

She exhaled loudly, like a seal dying of a puncture wound. "Thanks, Mr. Q. You're a sweetie."

"And you're a lying, scheming, ruthless murderer. But you are a quick worker, I'll give you that. How did you find my address?"

"Castor followed you on his bike," she said, neither boasting nor apologizing, "while I phoned that sucker Wise, told him I had orders from Dad. Did he remember his message long enough to deliver it? Durrr, lay off de kid, mister. Honestly, that man was a joke!"

"Yeah. A regular scream." Rich, beautiful and cold. What a combination. "So I get the word from Wise, he exits my building, you pssst! at him from a shady corner, he shambles over, and Castor caves his head in."

"I do my own caving-in, thank you very much. I'm very strong, you know. I work out. I could crush your ribcage with these thighs." She hitched her skirt an inch. It was a long inch, and taking my eyes off it wasn't the easiest thing I ever did.

"I get the blame for putting out Wise's bright lights, the Bells and the Cootses go to war, the merger's off—"

"And Castor's lovely building is saved for the nation." She beamed at me, sitting on her fingers like a clever little girl.

"The building, yeah. That's Castor's motive. As for you—well, the fact that if it all works out you get rid of your father, his top people, and his main rival all at once, that's just coincidence. Pity you had to wipe the blood off that leather jacket with one of Castor's bar towels. Pity my sense of smell isn't as geriatric as my knees."

She giggled. "It was either a smelly old bar towel, or a three hundred quid silk scarf. Still, doesn't matter, does it, Mr. Q? Because you look on me as the daughter you never had, so you're going to let me get away with it."

"Believe me, Vanessa, if I could send you down without dropping Castor in it, you'd be wiping fingerprint ink off your fingers right now."

She looked puzzled. "Castor? What's that sorry little boy to you? You're not gay, I can tell you're not."

I didn't bother trying to explain—to her or to myself. "Let's just say there aren't enough barmen left in London who know how to serve a pint of stout."

She shrugged. She couldn't care less. About me, or pints of stout, or sorry little Castor.

"There are three conditions, Vanessa. You get Castor out of the country—today. As soon as he's safe, you tell him who you really are. After that it's up to him."

"Yah, can do," she said. After a moment she added, "And the third condition?"

Had I said three? I could only think of two. "Right. Third—you pay for transforming Rossland House into a community center, out of your sweet little allowance. Got it?"

"Deal. You're not making an heroic effort to prevent a gang war, then?"

"The more of your kind that kill each other, the more champagne I'll drink."

I pulled in by the tube station, kept the engine running. Vanessa ran her tongue lightly across her lips. "Is this the bit where you crush me to your manly chest and kiss me like I've never been kissed before?"

"It might be, but luckily for all concerned I have the wrong teeth in today."

"Your teeth look fine to me. I mean, they look false, sure, but they don't look as if they'd fall out or anything."

I gave her a smile. Nothing special, just an old one I didn't use any more. "If your teeth don't fall out it doesn't count as kissing, Ms. Coots. Not in my book."

She pouted fake disappointment. "Oh I get it. You're one of those tough guy detectives who thinks girls are a nuisance."

"Not to me they're not," I sighed. "Not in years."

I started to lean across her to open the door on her side, the way tough guys do, but then I thought better of that—I don't have such long arms. I let her open the damn door herself.

Then I went home, drank a significant amount of whiskey, and failed to sleep, safe in the knowledge that tomorrow would be another long day. Or else it wouldn't.

Marthayn Pelegrimas and Robert J. Randisi

I Love
Everything About You

As "Christine Matthews," MARTHAYN PELEGRIMAS has had stories published in *Deadly Allies, Lethal Ladies, Vengeance Is Hers, Ellery
Queen's Mystery Magazine, Love Kills,* and other anthologies. Under
her real name, she has published more than forty short stories in the
horror field, and had a story in *American Pulp* that has been optioned
for film. She was also the coeditor of *Lethal Ladies II* and the audio
anthology *Hear the Fear* and a contributor to *Writing the P.I. Novel.*

A long-time practitioner of the private eye novel, ROBERT J.
RANDISI has lately turned his talents to the police procedural, with
the same excellent results. His novels about Detective Joe Keough
have been garnering him the best reviews of his career. *Alone with
the Dead* (1995) and *In the Shadow of the Arch* (1998) were followed
by *Blood on the Arch*. His stand-alone procedural novel *The Sixth
Phase* is currently in paperback.

Together Robert J. Randisi and "Christine Matthews" have written *Murder Is the Deal of the Day* (St. Martin's Press, 1999), the first novel in the Gil and Claire Hunt series. *The Masks of Auntie Laveau* will appear from St. Martin's in 2001. They have also published short fiction together, including their powerful story in the anthology *Irreconcilable Differences*. Their story here first appeared in *Till Death Do Us Part*.

I Love Everything About You

Marthayn Pelegrimas and Robert J. Randisi

One

He sprays milk all over my clean table as he slurps down his Count Chocula. When he comes home from work he plops down in the recliner that takes up a large chunk of the corner of our small living room. Then he leans back, lets out a burp, and swings his big feet over the footrest, taking up even more space. When he's nervous, or just relaxing, he bites at his nails, makes this grinding, crunching noise. If I complain, or ask him to do that disgusting chewing in the bathroom, he tells me he's just trimming down the cuticle. Besides, if it bothers me, "Just leave the room."

We talked for years about going to Hawaii, our tenth anniversary was the target date. But the airlines went on strike that year, just around the time we were supposed to make all our reservations. When I cried, he shrugged, offered no alternative plans. Not one! I spent that anniversary evening reading a book; he slept in his recliner.

I know couples have to adjust, overlook the small stuff. And Lord knows I try being fair. Whenever I make him angry by pointing out some irritating habit, I quickly ask, "What do I do that drives you crazy? Tell me; I can take it." Then I look him square in the eyes, offer up my ego for him to kick around. What could be more fair?

He always takes a minute to think. Drags out my waiting. And then he says, "Nothing. I love everything about you."

How's a person supposed to fight against that?

It took me another ten years to understand how he thinks. To understand that his definition of love is the complete and total opposite of mine. I've learned a lot of life's lessons from him throughout the years. But two very important ones stand out in my mind. I've learned that the opposite of love isn't hate. It's indifference. Quiet, hard, cold indifference. And I've learned that major credit-card companies issue plastic to anyone—anyone—as long as they have a steady job; a few bucks in the bank, and haven't murdered a world leader.

It's his attitude toward money that infuriates me more than his attitude toward me. After he carried me over the threshold, into our first apartment, I remember looking up at him with such hope; God, I was so excited. I asked, "What do we do now? How do we begin our new life?"

"First off," he said seriously, "you get a job." And then he opened the desk drawer and brought out a handful of bills that he'd accumulated while he was supposed to be saving. Saving for our new life. His first time away from home had given him more than a taste of freedom, it had given him every credit card offered by any company. I counted twenty-three.

And so I worked and he worked. But while I saved, he spent. When there was no headway being made by all my efforts, I gave in and joined him. It's like living with an alcoholic who only wants his wife to sit down and have one drink with him. Keep him company and then he's okay.

"I'm not stopping you from buying anything you want! Here!" He throws the credit cards at me. "Go shopping. I haven't denied you anything. Ever. Have I?"

And I storm out of the apartment and drive to the mall. I buy things I don't need. By the time I get home, he apologizes. Then we have the "money talk," which ends with him cutting up a credit card—usually one that's maxed out and we can't use anyway—as proof of his resolve to work with me instead of against.

We begin again. I refrain from charging, stash part of our paychecks in the bank, and he fills out applications for new credit cards—just so we have money for an emergency—or a new stereo system. You can guess which one came first.

So the other night I'm sitting in the kitchen, listening to him snore in the other room. I realize we've been married for almost twenty-five years. Our silver anniversary is seven months from tomorrow. I told him I still wanted to go to Hawaii and he shrugged. Seems he's lost interest. Okay, we can go someplace else. I kissed his neck and tried leading him to the bedroom. He told me that making love to me was just too much damn trouble. When tears came to my eyes he acted as though he didn't notice. I hope he was acting.

When I stood back, took an honest look at him, I wondered why I tried so hard for so damn long. He's thirty pounds overweight, dull, and not interested in anything about me.

And that honest look made me feel better. I saw that none of this is my fault. Not our money problems, not his laziness, not even my nagging. So why should his death be my fault either?

Two

I tell her, "I love everything about you." But it's a lie.

Oh, it might have been true once, probably during our first three years together. I was twenty, she was nineteen when we married, and the first three years were kind of fun. I mean, we were still kids, right? Wasn't the idea in life to have fun? But we struggled, too, both working while I tried to write, to sell. I never went to college, you see. Got out of high school at sixteen, started working jobs during the day and writing at night. When we met she knew I wanted to write for a living, and when we married I told her, "We'll sink or swim on my writing." She wanted me to go to college, and so did my parents, but I thought she'd understand, even if they didn't. I guess I was looking for someone who would understand, even then.

When we were married three years, she asked, "Are you ready to stop this nonsense and go back to school to learn a profession?"

So much for understanding.

The first infidelity happened when we were married five years. Well, I found out when we were married six years. See, I thought I was so smart that night because I "felt" that something was wrong. I badgered her until she admitted she was having an affair and then—feeling so smart, right?—I asked, "How long has this been going on?" She replied, "A year." Boy, did that burst my bubble.

Well, our son was almost a year old at that point, and I stayed, even after the humiliation of her allowing her "lover" and his wife to become our "friends." Even after she told me she was waiting for him to make his decision about leaving his wife. Basically, I left *my* life in *his* hands, but I plead that I was young, and *stupid*. I took refuge in other things—my work, my kids, food—oh yeah, I gained weight, so what?

So I stayed to let it happen again, fourteen years later, with years in between of dissatisfaction, and neglect, even though we had another baby, another son; even though we shared the trauma of a miscarriage in between the two boys; even though I started to write for a living—did she read any of it? No! I immersed myself in my work, which she ignored except when the checks came in. (One day I came home from a meeting with a publisher and proudly announced that I had sold another book. I was selling a lot of them, then. Her reply was, "Jesus Christ, do I have to kiss your feet every time you sell a book?")

There were psychiatrists in those years, and Prozac—"You know," she said to me one day, "I'm almost happy"—and then we're married twenty years and I find out she's doing it again. Seeing somebody. Cheating. And who's not to say that she didn't do it all those years in between the three that I discovered?

So here I sit, considering my options. Leave? Stay and try to work it out? Why? After she tells me how cold I am, and how I think my shit doesn't stink, and how conceited and selfish I am. Here we sit, crumbling beneath the weight of infidelity—again. And consumer debt—again—brought on by years of spending I did to try and make her happy, not the least of which was a thirty-thousand-dollar Cadillac.

How dare she be angry! What has she got to be angry about? Who was unfaithful? Who pushed us to this? Who ignored my work until I had to go outside the house to talk about it? To share it with someone.

I feel the anger. Now. Finally. After more than twenty years of it, I feel the anger, and what jury would convict me—

I stop when I realize what I'm thinking. But I'd only have to face a jury if I was caught, and then what jury would convict me, once they heard about the adultery?

The lying.

The apathy.

Such bitterness has etched itself on her face—and what has she got to be so bitter about anyway? Who's done all the jumping through hoops?

I think it again, and I smile.

No jury would convict me.

Three

He looks good in that suit. I remember the day we bought it. I had to drag him into the store, kicking and fussing like he was a five-year-old, for God's sake. There was a black pinstriped one I liked, but he wouldn't even look at it. He insisted on dark blue. Then he carried on some more when I asked him to try it on. When he finally came out to stand in front of the three-way mirror, he looked so handsome. The saleswoman even stopped and commented on how that particular shade of blue complemented his eyes. He could wear his clothes so well—not like some men who look rumpled in even the most expensive silks or tweeds. After the hems of his slacks had been pinned up, he started complaining that he would never have much reason to wear the vest and wanted to return the whole thing to the rack and just buy a sport coat. But I convinced him that vests were always in style, and after an hour of coaxing, he grudgingly laid out two hundred dollars for the navy-blue three-piece suit. Remembering his anger that day and the way he froze me out at home later makes the situation almost funny . . . if it weren't so deadly serious.

I had never noticed the Thomas Schiller Mortuary before. Like most funeral homes, it is discreet, set back from the street, separated from adjacent businesses by a wide driveway and lots of bushes and trees. It blends in with the neighborhood; its sign is even made of the same wood as the house, painted the same beige as the siding. And when Patrick died so suddenly like that, I didn't have a clue where to begin. He was the first member of my family to die, well other than a great-grandparent or great-great-aunt, you know, an elderly person who had lived a very full life. He was certainly the first person I was totally responsible for, when it came to making all the arrangements, that is.

Mr. Schiller took me into his private office and after all the paperwork was finished up, we went into a display room filled with all sorts of caskets, in all price ranges. Patrick always shouted the loudest whenever I complained that we had made no provisions for our retirement or for the kids' college. "Let them make it on their own the way we have. I never got any help from anyone, why should they?" So not one ounce of guilt settled in when I refused to even consider the highly polished rosewood casket, or the hand-embroidered lining inside model number 103. The plainest and most inexpensive would have to do. There was no reconsidering.

"Flowers?" Mr. Schiller asked. "Would you like large arrangements on either side of your dearly departed?"

"No," I replied. "Just three roses in a vase with a card inscribed 'Beloved Father and Husband.' "

"And music. Did he have a favorite hymn?"

"No."

"What about the burial? Did you and your husband preplan anything? Is there a family plot somewhere?"

"No."

"Then I assume you'll be wanting to purchase two—side by side. It will save you any further distress and it's one more detail your children won't have to deal with later."

"No," I said. "Just one."

The announcement of Patrick's death brought mourners from the last few places he'd worked. Relatives I hadn't seen since Christmas two years ago, or Cousin Allan's graduation. Friends who read his obituary in the paper came to express their surprise, their disbelief at his untimely passing.

"Forty-five!" my mother-in-law kept repeating as if it were her mantra. "Forty-five. Too young. My baby was only forty-five!"

My mother kept saying how natural Patrick looked. "It's as if he's stretched out in his recliner at home. He looks too good to be . . . dead." And then she'd hug me and cry.

The kids were my only concern, but once they got over the shock, they fell back into the me-zone. You know, the place that swallows up selfish, self-centered people between the ages of one and twenty-five. Or any unmarried male of any age. They worried how the death of their father would affect their finishing college. I never told them that with the money from Patrick's life insurance policy we could afford for them both to attend private schools.

After the hundredth recounting of Patrick's accident, I decided to seek out a quiet place. Too many people, too many flowers were all closing in on me. As I passed through the doorway, I ran my fingers across the brass plate that announced my husband was laid out in chapel number four.

A long corridor led me to a small room next to the visitors' lounge. Mr. Coffee was gurgling in the corner. An old, overstuffed chair, covered in a forest-green velvet, looked too inviting to pass up. I sank into the cushions and closed my eyes. I was feeling calmer than I had in days, almost relaxed.

"Mrs. Albright?" A stranger stood in the doorway.

"Yes." I sat a little straighter as he walked into the room. He carried himself nicely.

"I don't mean to disturb you but I was told we have a mutual friend."

"We do? Who?"

When he said the name Dolan I looked away.

Four

Funeral homes depress me.

For a while, after my parents moved to Florida, I became the family's designated funeral attendee. When Aunt Sadie died, I went. When Uncle Tony passed away, there I was. When Cousin Joey kicked off, who went? So I've been to a lot of funerals, and a lot of funeral homes. The Thomas Schiller Mortuary was no different from the others. First, the quiet descended on you like a blanket. Then the smell, that clean smell they try to pump into the air so you can't smell the dead. Sterile end tables and lamps and chairs arranged throughout the lobby, and then in the "chapels" wooden or metal chairs in rows and rows, even though they are rarely all filled. Who has that many people who care, anyway?

My wife only drew about half a room, which is actually pretty good for somebody who died so bitter. Then again, she did always save the bitterness and venom for me. Some days she'd be pelting me with it and then the phone would ring. She'd pick it up and sweetness would come out of her mouth for whoever it was. But as soon as she hung it up, she was back at me without missing a beat, like a battering ram. That woman could hold a grudge, too, for days, weeks . . . sometimes longer, like our whole married life. Toward the end I got all the blame, I, she screamed, made her waste her life. This was a woman who never took responsibility for anything. Well, there she was now, in her casket, the bitterness lines smoothed out by experts, and I was willing to take full blame this time.

After all, I did kill her.

Kind of . . .

You know there are people you can get to do it for you. And there are people who know people who can do it for you. If there's only six degrees of separation between us and everyone else, that means hit men, too, doesn't it?

I was surprised that I only had to go through three degrees to find Dolan, but then, because I write mysteries, I do have some police connections.

Dolan's an odd hit man in that he likes to attend the funerals of the people he kills. So I wasn't surprised at all to see him among the bereaved. He offered his sympathies to Helen's mother and father, then to her sister and brother, and finally came to me. We walked off to the side so he could offer them in private.

"You did a good job," I said.

"You didn't want her marked," he answered, with a shrug, "and you wanted an accident. You got one."

"It was worth the price," I said. "You leaving now?"

"No. I have another client in the building."

"Oh? Where?"

"Right next door. Number four. Well, I have to go." He extended his hand and we shook. To anyone watching, it would look perfectly innocent.

After he left, curiosity took me to the doorway of chapel four. I watched as he extended his sympathies to the family there, and then to the wife. The little nameplate on the wall next to the door said PATRICK ALBRIGHT. Dolan and Mrs. Albright walked off to the side so he could offer her his sympathies in private. I could almost read their lips as they had a conversation much like the one he and I had had moments before.

Of course, I was watching her lips more than I was his. Her lips, her legs, she was a blond who looked great in black. And I didn't have any problems with ogling her, because I knew that although she was a "widow," she wasn't all that bereaved.

After all, she knew Dolan, didn't she?

I waited for Dolan to leave the building, finish visiting all his "clients." I couldn't stop thinking about the widow Albright, so I stayed at the doorway of Helen's chapel and watched. I figured sooner or later she was going to need a break. I knew what she was going through, trying to look forlorn and sad, all the while wanting to cheer. I was drawn to her because we had something very extraordinary in common and I knew by looking at her, even from across the room, that she'd never shower me with unwarranted venom.

Finally, she left the chapel and made a right, walked down the hall toward the lounge. I could hear the Mr. Coffee gurgling even as I approached the door. I stopped and looked inside. She had taken a seat without bothering with the coffee.

I knew it was silly, and chancy, but I couldn't stop myself. I walked over to where she was sitting and said, "Mrs. Albright?"

She looked up at me, her eyes wide with surprise, and I felt as if those eyes were looking right into me, right into my heart and my soul . . .

"I don't mean to disturb you but I was told we have a mutual friend."

"We do?" she asked, with just the slightest of frowns. "Who?"

Lloyd Biggle, Jr.

The Case of
the Headless Witness

LLOYD BIGGLE, JR.'s background is primarily science fiction, but, like so many master authors, when he turns his hand to the traditional historical mystery, one would have guessed he'd been writing them all his life. Recently he has made his home in the mystery field, producing well-regarded Sherlock Holmes pastiches—*The Quallsford Inheritance* and *The Glendower Conspiracy*. He has also begun his own contemporary mystery series featuring detective J. Pletcher and Reena Lambert, whose cases have gotten stranger and stranger as the series has progressed. In "The Case of the Headless Witness" he returns to Victorian England to solve a baffling mystery. It first appeared in the November issue of *Alfred Hitchcock's Mystery Magazine*.

The Case of
the Headless Witness

Lloyd Biggle, Jr.

It was a Sunday morning in June 1901, and I had reported to my employer, Lady Sara Varnly, for my daily instructions. It was a frustrating time for all of us. Lady Sara's immense network of informers had been turning up so little of interest that we'd begun to wonder whether London's criminals had unanimously conspired to take their holidays early. We were hopeful that Saturday night's reports would provide at least one crime worth contemplating, but thus far their ingenuity had not risen above the level of petty sordidness. As we talked, I chanced to glance out the window at normally nondescript and peaceful Connaught Mews.

Lady Sara noticed my astonished expression and was at my side instantly. Coming to a stop before her door was the most elaborate carriage that humble mews had seen in months. A splendidly matched pair of white horses stomped impatiently while overly tall, uniformed footmen diligently assisted the passengers to dismount. First came Chief Inspector Robert Mewer, Lady Sara's official contact at Scotland Yard, followed by Sir Edward Henry, who had been brought from India to introduce his system of fingerprinting and who, only a month before, had assumed the position of assistant commissioner and head of the Criminal Investigation Department, the C.I.D. Then came Sir Edward Bradford, commissioner of the Metropolitan Police, already a legend in his lifetime—when his arm was mangled by a tiger on a hunt in India, he had it amputated without an anesthetic—and, bringing up the rear and lord of all he surveyed—it obviously was his carriage—was the Home Secretary himself, Mr. C. T. Ritchie, looking, as he always did, as though he wished he were elsewhere.

"The Bank of England has been robbed!" Lady Sara exclaimed.

It did seem that nothing less serious would have brought so much police authority to Lady Sara's door.

Probably it was Inspector Mewer who ignored the bell pull and administered a knock that jarred the building.

"Sit down," Lady Sara said to me. "We haven't finished our discussion." I probably raised my eyebrows. "The last time I called on the Home Secretary he kept me waiting twenty minutes," Lady Sara said. "In deference to his age I'll make him wait only ten."

Charles Tupper, one of her footmen—Rick Allward was the other, and both of them were highly capable investigators—appeared a moment later to inform Lady Sara that she had visitors. He reeled off their names with a blankly innocent expression.

"Do they seem impetuous?" Lady Sara asked.

"Very. Rick invited them to sit down, but all four of them are pacing the floor."

"They need to be taught patience. Please tell them I will see them as soon as possible."

She made them wait the full ten minutes. Then we descended to her study, where we found them still pacing. Lady Sara quickly got them seated at the large oaken conference table in the center of the room.

It was the Home Secretary's first visit to Lady Sara's headquarters, and he looked about him distastefully. Like her living quarters upstairs, her study was sparsely furnished. There was no clutter, and everything there had a place and a use. The walls were lined with books on every conceivable subject because every aspect of human knowledge has some bearing on crime and criminals.

His gaze finally came to rest on a strangely fashioned object that lay in the center of the table. It was an enormous, and immensely complicated, cribbage board that had been invented by Lady Sara's father, the Earl of Ranisford. It was, in fact, the world's largest cribbage board, and the earl had designed it for a six-handed game of cribbage that he'd invented. Now it was used by Lady Sara to record her progress in solving crimes. The board's six tracks could accommodate six investigations simultaneously. Unfortunately, none of the tracks was in use.

It was a strange gathering. Lady Sara was her youthful and beautiful self despite her forty-plus years and the simplicity of her gown and coiffure, but the four men looked as though they had dressed for church the previous evening and spent the night in their clothing. Not only were they burdened by the cares of office or profession, but they had been suddenly aged by some new crisis. Only a matter of critical importance would have moved them to call unannounced, so Lady Sara wasted no time on formalities. "It might save time if my employees heard the problem directly from you," she said. "Have you any objections to that?"

They had none, so she quickly introduced us, "Colin Quick, my secretary; Charles Tupper and Rick Allward, investigators." She always gave us whatever titles seemed appropriate. We took our places at the table, and there was a long moment of silence. Then three of the callers turned to Chief

Inspector Mewer, who, when he saw that he was nominated, opened his notebook, cleared his throat, and began.

The chief inspector knew how to formulate a police report, but he had no notion at all of how to come to a point quickly. "Shortly after two o'clock this morning, Constable Padraic Cahill was walking his usual beat on Cheapside. He had come from Newgate Street, and at the intersection with St. Martin's-le-Grand, he met Constable John Snell, as was customary. The time, as noted by Constable Snell, was one fifty-seven. It had been a quiet night, and neither man had observed anything of special interest. Snell had reached the end of his beat; he turned back toward Aldersgate Street. Cahill proceeded along Cheapside, and Snell neither saw nor heard anything further of him.

"Our next witness is Constable Edward Price, whose beat runs along King Street and Queen Street. He customarily met Constable Cahill at the Cheapside intersection. The time was two thirty when he reached it. There was no sign of Cahill. Price walked a short distance down Cheapside toward Newgate Street, looking for him and listening. It was possible, of course, that Cahill had made an arrest and marched the culprit away or that he had responded to a distant constable's whistle that Price had been too far away to hear. Price neither saw nor heard anything unusual, so, properly, he continued his own patrol along Queen Street.

"At the end of his beat Price met his sergeant, Sergeant Charles Gossard, who was making his own rounds and checking up on his constables. Price had nothing to report except the failure of Constable Cahill to meet him. By that time it was after three o'clock. Gossard went to Cheapside immediately to look for Cahill. The street was quiet and all but deserted. The sergeant found two vagrants asleep in a doorway near Bow Lane and awakened them; neither had seen a constable, and neither had any idea how long he had been there. If Constable Cahill had passed them, he would have packed them off. The sergeant sent for assistance and organized a proper search—not only along Cheapside but also along the side streets where Cahill might have turned off—Bread Street, Cow Lane, Wood Street, Gutter Lane, Foster Lane, and their various offshoots. He found no trace whatsoever of Constable Cahill. No constable on patrol in the area had heard a police whistle.

"It was almost six o'clock by then, and information came from an entirely unexpected quarter, Chelsea. A hansom driver, one Chad Orling, saw something exceedingly strange as he approached the intersection of Fulham Road and Sewell Walk. 'Looked like some bloke standing in a 'ole,' he said. He pulled on the reins to guide the horse around it, but at that moment the horse went crazy. It reared repeatedly, and it was all he could do to get it under control again. At the same moment one Emmett Flynn, driving a four-wheeler and approaching from the opposite direction, had an identical problem with *his* horse. The ruckus made by the two rearing horses attracted the attention of Constable Jed Lowson, patrolling some distance away, and he came at a run to investigate. The object that alarmed the horses proved to be a human head held upright in a small frame of wood. And the head was that of Constable Padraic Cahill."

"How was the head severed?" Lady Sara asked.

"The division surgeon thinks it was done with an axe—wielded by an experienced person, since the head was severed with only a couple of strokes."

"Unlike some of the executions history describes," Lady Sara observed dryly. "I assume he was dead when he was beheaded. Were there any indications on the head of what killed him?"

"There were no signs of a head injury, if that's what you mean. The surgeon thinks he may have been strangled."

"His body will tell us—if we find it. His body is the missing witness in this case." Then she added, "Cheapside is a main thoroughfare. Didn't passersby observe anything out of the ordinary?"

"The normal heavy traffic bound for the docks or the markets doesn't occur on Sunday morning. Traffic would have been light, but certainly there should have been *some* traffic. We haven't found anyone who saw anything, and no one has come forward with information. It is still early for that kind of investigation, of course. We may have to appeal to the public for assistance."

"Was Constable Cahill married?" Lady Sara asked.

"He was," Chief Superintendent Mewer said. "With four young children. His wife took it hard, as is to be expected. She is in hospital, and neighbors are looking after the children." He added, "From all I am able to find out, Constable Cahill was a very steady, reliable man."

"The most tragic aspects of any crime," Lady Sara murmured, "are in its ramifications. A crime is like a whirlpool. Not only are the criminals and their victims engulfed, but a widening circle of innocent dependents and bystanders are sucked in as well."

The four men gazed solemnly at her. The Home Secretary said sententiously, "We can't have this, you know. A police constable abducted and decapitated. It won't do at all. We are throwing every resource available to us into the investigation, and we—the entire force—would appreciate it if you would help us."

"We know you have extensive resources of your own," Sir Edward Bradford said. "We also know you have sources of information the police can't touch."

Lady Sara turned to Rick and Charles. "Start at once. Charles to Cheapside, Rick to Chelsea. Gather all the assistance you can find, and listen for a buzz."

Both of them hurried away.

The Home Secretary was regarding her with puzzlement. "A buzz?"

"A rumor," Lady Sara said curtly. "Idle talk of any kind. Unfortunately, many citizens lose both their voices and their memories when they think the police are listening, but the street people who will be helping Rick and Charles may be able to pick up something. Now then."

She leaned back and thought for a moment. "The Metropolitan Inner Circle Underground doesn't run after midnight. The murderers had time to walk from Cheapside to Chelsea if they didn't dawdle, but more likely they walked a short distance and then hailed a cab. They could have followed a devious route with a series of cabs. You must interview every cab driver in Greater London who was on duty at the time and ask about a passenger with a large hatbox or suitcase."

"You are assuming they killed Cahill somewhere near Cheapside and transported only the head to Chelsea," Sir Edward Bradford said. "We don't know that."

"Of course not, but it is the simpler solution. A man's head can be carried about much less conspicuously than his whole body. If the murderers were wise, they disposed of the body at once. Cheapside is not all that distant from the river. Wherever the decapitation was done, there are three main questions we have to deal with: why Constable Cahill, why did he have to die, and why Chelsea? Despite the fact that he was both steady and reliable, it is always possible that some personal crisis overtook him while he was walking his beat. You will have to go into his private life thoroughly."

"We have already started," Chief Inspector Mewer said.

"Then I will leave that investigation to you, and I will concentrate on my three questions: why Cahill, why did he have to die, and why Chelsea?" She got to her feet. "I will report whenever I have anything to report. For now, all of us have work to do. Good morning, gentlemen."

Normally she would have offered refreshments of some kind and let them talk as long as they liked. On this morning she was in a hurry to start her own investigation.

The men thanked her and filed out. She said to me, "First, we must have a careful look at both locations. That may suggest something to us."

The word "cheap" originally meant "good value," and in medieval times Cheapside was London's original market, a fact reflected in the names of nearby streets: Bread, Milk, Wood, Poultry, Cow, Cornhill, Ironmonger. Gold-smith's Hall is nearby, as is Threadneedle Street. Almost until the nineteenth century Cheapside was the bustling center of London's economy; then it gradually lost out to the more stylish new establishments in the West End.

It was still a bustling market street on weekdays, crammed on either side with buildings of four to six stories whose ground and often upper floors were occupied by shops and business concerns. It seemed that every possible need could be satisfied there. It perfectly illustrated Dr. Samuel Johnson's remark, "There is in London all that life can afford."

On Sunday morning the bustle was missing. There were a few stragglers from an overly liquefied Saturday night. There also were well-dressed people on their way to an early service at St. Mary-le-Bow, one of the beautiful churches designed by Christopher Wren.

We descended from Lady Sara's carriage at the intersection with St. Martin's-le-Grand. It seemed appropriate that this search for murderers of a police constable should begin at the statue of Sir Robert Peel, who—as Home Secretary in the 1820's—reorganized the London police force.

As we walked slowly along Cheapside, I thought of Constable Cahill walking his dimly lit beat, and I kept asking myself what sort of criminal activity he could have happened onto that resulted in his death. There was nothing fancy about the Cheapside shops and businesses, but they perfectly summarized life in London in the year 1901. There was an establishment that offered baths, a barbershop, a news agent, a book dealer who seemed to deal mostly in secondhand books, a tobacconist, a grocer, a furrier, a millinery shop, a clothier, a chemist, a jeweler, a stationer, a butcher, a baker, a toy shop, a confectioner, a dealer in wines and spirits, a draper, a tailor, an office of Keith, Prowse, and Company, ticket agents—everything that life could afford was indeed available there. You could buy new shoes or a cobbler would repair the ones you were wearing while you waited. You could get yourself fitted with a truss or have glasses made, outfit your office or your flat, visit your bank, buy artificial teeth. You could sample special blends of tea or coffee. You could select provisions for your Sunday dinner or dine at any of a variety of restaurants. You could buy a new umbrella or have an old one recovered. You could buy new clothing or used clothing or have what you were wearing made more presentable.

But of course you could not do any of those things at two o'clock on Sunday morning. The crowds of business and professional men, the shopkeepers, clerks, customers, and passersby were gone, but the stage set and all its props remained, and somewhere in the dimly lighted streets and darkened buildings Constable Cahill had seen something that led to his death.

Lady Sara paused to look into a vacant shop. The window, below a large TO LET sign, was plastered with advertisements. The interior seemed to be empty.

"The constable could have discovered vagrants who had broken into vacant premises in search of a place to sleep," I suggested.

Lady Sara glanced sharply at me. "A vagrant would be unlikely to murder a police constable—and risk getting himself hanged—just to avoid a few days in jail, which would be nothing to him. And why would a vagrant decapitate his victim and spirit the head away to Chelsea? Why not dispose of the head the same way the body was disposed of—which seems to have been efficiently done, since an intense police search has turned up nothing."

"Even a vagrant could get violently angry over what he considered unjust treatment," I protested.

"The same could be said of a burglar who would face a long prison term. We are bound to look first for something much more significant—a crime of overwhelming importance for which discovery by a constable meant disaster to a promising enterprise and so gravely threatened those taking part that the constable had to die. Keep asking yourself what Constable Cahill could have seen."

We had reached Foster Lane, and Lady Sara turned into it. Near Cheapside there was the same clutter of business establishments. She stood there for a moment, scrutinizing establishments on both sides of the street.

Often I can follow Lady Sara's unspoken reasoning easily—up to a point—but her conclusions always leave me far behind. As Chief Inspector Mewer had pointed out, the procession of wagons to the markets and the docks, which goes on all night before every weekday, wouldn't have occurred early Sunday morning, but there should have been *some* traffic even if widely scattered. If a criminal wanted to avoid witnesses, he would keep to the side streets. Therefore it was entirely possible that after meeting Constable Snell, Cahill noticed something down a side street and went to investigate.

But what and where? The buildings along Foster Lane faced each other across the narrow street like rows of hieroglyphics waiting for someone to read them. I could only scrutinize them helplessly—if they had witnessed a horrible event early that morning, they weren't revealing it to me. It was difficult to say what Lady Sara saw. She often kept her observations to herself until the time came to arrange them into a case.

The constable could have seen something inside a shop, tried the door, found it open, gone in to investigate—and met his doom somewhere in the rear where a passerby wouldn't notice.

"Would Cahill have blown his whistle if he found signs of a break-in?" I asked.

"Perhaps if it were a flagrant break-in and the shop contained something extremely valuable. It depends on the circumstances and what he saw."

He wouldn't have blown his whistle for an unlocked door, I thought. He would have investigated, thinking it had been left unlocked by mistake— and he could have been murdered by a dishonest employee he found inside the store. But why would that employee chop off his head and take it to Chelsea?

We continued to walk along Cheapside and venture into side streets. Lady Sara seemed to be giving her closest scrutiny to jewelry stores, where merchandise of extremely high value could be carried off in a burglar's pockets, and to pubs, dealers in wines and spirits, and similar shops where a heavy volume of late Saturday business sometimes resulted in a large amount of moneys being left in the till by an incautious proprietor. A burglar about to make the haul of his professional career might be expected to react violently if disturbed by a police constable.

Having followed Lady Sara's unspoken chain of logic that far, I again found myself face-to-face with two of her questions: why cut off the constable's head, and why take it to Chelsea?

At the corner of Cow Lane was an establishment whose sign read GEO. MELLOR, JOB PRINTER, ADVERTISING POSTERS OUR SPECIALTY. The window was crowded with splendid multicolored posters displaying the printer's art. There also were rather ordinary examples of letterheads, billheads, imprinted envelopes, and calling cards.

We turned into Cow Lane. The shop behind the printshop seemed to be used for storage: pasteboard boxes were stacked along the walls and on top of a large table that stood in the center of the room. The window was framed by heavy drapes that opened to either side, and the heavy curtain on the door was raised. No doubt these had been left behind by the shop's former occupant. Lady Sara paused to contemplate this arrangement.

A helpful passerby told us, "That's part of the printshop. The entrance is in front. Closed today, of course." We thanked him.

"Nothing there worth stealing," I observed.

"Unless you are a printer," was Lady Sara's comment.

We walked a short distance along Cow Lane and then returned to Cheapside. At the corner of Wood Street were four venerable two-story buildings that had been built in 1687, shortly after the Great Fire of 1666 had destroyed most of the buildings in this area. Behind the end house was a plane tree, as remarkable a survivor as the buildings. Lady Sara gave much scrutiny and thought to the yard behind the building where the tree was growing. We explored Wood Street briefly and continued this process all the way to King and Queen streets, though Constable Cahill had not reached them. Then we turned back and followed the same procedure on the opposite side of Cheapside with Bow Lane and Bread Street.

At New Change we met Charles Tupper, who looked weary and discouraged. His helpers had turned up nothing at all. "Awkward day to investigate anyone but a clergyman," he said. "I was wondering if Cahill could have noticed a burglary in process and tried to arrest the perpetrators. Since it's Sunday, evidence of it won't be discovered until the shop opens tomorrow."

"It *is* an awkward day," Lady Sara agreed. "On the other hand, I am certain the police will have checked entrances and windows of every establishment in Cheapside and all of the connecting streets for signs of forcible entry."

Charles shrugged eloquently. None of that was of any help to him. "Where *are* the police?" he asked. "I haven't seen a constable or a detective since I arrived here."

"They worked here most of the night," Lady Sara said. "They have already investigated everything they could think of and gone to Chelsea. Probably they have finished with Chelsea also. If they had developed any leads at all, they wouldn't have asked for my help. Keep listening. When the taverns and public houses open, you may have better luck. Come, Colin."

She signaled to Old John Quick, her waiting coachman and my foster father, and a moment later we were on our way to Chelsea.

We rattled through streets that were all but deserted at that time of Sunday morning except for churchgoers, past St. Paul's, Ludgate Hill, Fleet Street, the

Strand, the Mall, Constitution Hill, Hyde Park Corner, Knightsbridge, and the Brompton Road. Finally we reached Fulham Road. Along the way, I kept wondering about the murderers. Had they hurriedly walked all this distance carrying Constable Cahill's head in a box or case of some kind, or had they taken a circuitous route with the help of a series of cabs? At the intersection of Fulham Road and Sewell Walk we found Rick Allward waiting not for us but for one of his informers.

"I have a buzz!" he said happily.

Lady Sara invited him to get into the carriage and tell us about it.

"It isn't a very loud buzz," he began apologetically, "but a buzz nevertheless. And it didn't happen Saturday night but Friday night. To be exact, shortly after midnight on Friday. A woman who resides in Sewell Walk got up to look after a crying baby, and she heard some kind of altercation in the street. She looked out and saw three people, two men and a woman." He paused. "One of the men was swinging a large sword."

There was a lengthy silence while both Rick and I waited for Lady Sara's reaction. "Chief Inspector Mewer said the constable's head was severed with two strokes of an axe," she said finally. "Would a sword have served the same purpose? Perhaps so if it were heavy enough and sharp enough.

"You are moving our equation back in time. Rather, you are adding to it. Now it reads: Shortly after midnight on Friday a man was swinging a sword in Sewell Walk. Early Sunday morning a police constable disappeared from Cheapside. Later Sunday morning his head was found in Chelsea at the intersection of Sewell Walk and Fulham Road. Is that how you construct it?"

Rick nodded. "The sword may've had nothing to do with it, but its being swung in Sewell Walk seems almost too much of a coincidence. It shouldn't be difficult to trace the prior history of the sword. I'm waiting for word about that now."

"It might tell us how the sword happened to come into the possession of the man who was swinging it on Friday night—but not whether he was also swinging it early Sunday morning if indeed he was."

"It ought to tell us who he is or show us a way to find out," Rick said. "Then we can ask him where and when he swung it and why."

"That would be an excellent step toward resolving the equation," Lady Sara said. "Please continue. Colin and I will have a look at Sewell Walk."

We drove all the way to Onslow Gardens and then walked back toward Fulham Road. Sewell Walk was a street of large detached residences, many of which offered rooms to let. Since it was Chelsea, these were called artists' studios. Each house had a small garden in front, and flowers were blooming lavishly. It was as ordinary a London street as one could imagine, but when I considered that it was a street in Chelsea, London's Bohemia, even the sword became commonplace.

As we approached Fulham Road, we found several houses being used for commercial purposes. Lady Sara nudged me. "Look! A link with Cheapside!"

The lower level of one house, reached by an areaway, had windows that extended just above ground level. A sign read JAMES ARLOTT JOB PRINTING.

I said indifferently, "Why not? There are printers scattered all over London."

"Job printers aren't all that common. They have to attract business from a considerable area because it takes a huge number of orders for calling cards and posters to meet the printer's overhead and give him a decent living. A sword being swung in Sewell Walk the night before Constable Cahill's severed head was found there is a coincidence. Now we have a second coincidence. Constable Cahill disappeared near a printshop in Cheapside, and his head was found near a printshop in Chelsea. How many coincidences are required before we start taking them seriously? Two? Three? A dozen?"

"I would want a trifle more evidence before I tried to make something of that one," I said.

"We are collecting the evidence now. The two printers certainly are a fact to make note of."

At the Fulham Road corner Rick was talking with a tall young woman in an ankle-length gown of bright red with a black shawl. She wore a rose in her long black hair, and there was a definite air of the gypsy about her.

"I don't know her name," the woman said. "I don't know the street number either, but it's in Sewell Walk. I could show you."

Rick explained to us, "This is Myra. She attended a party on Friday night; at the party some people whose names she doesn't know borrowed a sword from the hostess. No doubt it was they who were swinging a sword in the street."

"Excellent!" Lady Sara said. "Could you show us where the party took place?"

"Glad to." Myra strode quickly back the way we had come, along Sewell Walk, and the three of us followed. Near Onslow Gardens she turned in at a house that looked very much like all the others. As she led us up the path, she remarked over her shoulder, "Everyone calls her Queenie. I don't know her last name. She has a party every Friday night."

She knocked vigorously on the door. Some moments passed before a piping lilt of song could be heard in the passageway beyond. The door opened.

The strangest woman I had ever seen stood there. Her hair was waist-long. She wore a bright green coat and a bright yellow skirt, and tassels in every conceivable color were sewn to the coat. They dangled when she walked, and the effect was something like that of a longhaired yak except that she was small in stature with a figure that was slender, almost elfin.

"These people want to know about your sword," Myra told her. She didn't bother with introductions. Apparently no one in Bohemia ever bothered with introductions. Everyone knew everyone, but no one knew who anyone was.

Myra said, "I have to run," and hurried away with our thanks floating after her.

Queenie looked at the three of us doubtfully. "Please come in," she said.

The house was as queer as she was. The interior looked like an Oriental bazaar, with brazen lamps, candlesticks, bells, gongs, unidentifiable objects arranged everywhere. Lady Sara performed introductions, introducing herself first, and Queenie's eyes opened wide when she heard "Lady." Although every kind of person could be found in London's Bohemia, genuine ladies were evidently rare.

Queenie—we never learned her surname—got us seated and asked, "What was it you wanted to know?"

"Three people were seen in Sewell Walk shortly after midnight on Friday; one of them was swinging a sword. We are curious about the sword. Where did it come from?"

"The sword was mine," Queenie said. "It came from here." She pointed to a place on the wall. "It's been hanging there for years. Ben—he's an artist, I don't remember his last name—needed it for a picture he's painting, so I lent it to him."

"Who were the other two people?" Lady Sara asked.

"His wife Doll, she's a sculptress, and a young fellow—I think he's a writer, a poet or something. He's new—came for the first time on Friday. I didn't catch his name."

"Did it occur to you that a sword could be a dangerous weapon?" Lady Sara asked.

Queenie tilted back her head and laughed with a tinkling gurgle. "Not that sword. It's a stage prop. It's *huge*, taller than a man, looks like something a crusader might have carried. And it looks real, of course—that's the idea with a stage sword. But it's light and easy to wield, which a stage sword should be. It's actually flimsy."

"Then you don't think it could cause an injury?"

"I think the sword would bend before it hurt anyone."

"I suppose there was plenty to drink at your party," Lady Sara observed. She was trying to account for the midnight antics with the sword in the middle of Sewell Walk.

"Except for Quinn—he's an actor, always drinks whiskey—no one had anything but opal hush. We get our exhilaration from talk and singing."

I spoke for the first time. "Opal—hush? What's opal hush?"

"You've never tried opal hush?" she exclaimed. Her expression clearly indicated that I had led an unfortunately sheltered life. "You must try it now. Opal hush for all three of you?" She hurried away without waiting for an answer.

She returned with four wineglasses, a bottle of red claret, and a syphon. She filled the glasses three-quarters full with the claret and squirted lemonade into each, and a beautiful, iridescent, opal-like foam rose above the top of each glass. "Opal hush!" she chortled delightedly, passing the glasses around.

Lady Sara made small talk with her about her work—she also was a sculptress—while we sipped our opal hushes. I had to agree that one such drink was unlikely to intoxicate anyone to the point of sword swinging.

When we finished, Lady Sara thanked her, and we got to our feet. "I would like to see the sword," she said. "Could you give me the artist's address?"

Queenie frowned. "They moved recently. I have no idea where they are."

"Or the writer's address?"

Queenie shook her head. Bohemia was indeed a strange world. It was restricted to Chelsea, a relatively small area, and not only did no one know who anyone was, but it also seemed that no one knew where anyone lived.

"He arrived with Quinn," Queenie said after some thought. "The actor. Quinn might know. I can give you his address."

She did. With that, we thanked her again and left.

"We probably have as much as we need about the sword," Lady Sara said, "but we might as well take a look at it."

She sent Rick to find as many witnesses as he could to the Friday night sword swinging. He was to join us at the pub on the corner of Fulham Road and Sewell Walk after it opened. Lady Sara and I called on the actor.

Quinn had rooms in Priory Walk. He was in. He was a handsome, middle-aged man with a diminutive mustache, and he gave the impression of modest affluence—meaning he hadn't been out of work long. He was delighted to have visitors. He began acting immediately, playing the royal host, and Lady Sara's question about the young writer completely disrupted his performance.

"No idea who he is or where he lives," he said. "Met him at Kyushu Fujimura's place—Kyushu's a painter." He added, quite unnecessarily, "Japanese fellow. He might know. I can give you his address."

The painter was out. Directed by his landlady, we found him down by the Thames, painting. He did know the young writer's name—Raul Mowling—and his address in Fulham Road.

Mowling lived above a greengrocer. He was a Bohemian beginner—he had cut adrift from his former life to become a novelist or a poet or whatever, and it was only too obvious that he was counting his pennies and wondering how long it would be before he started earning something. His room was furnished with packing cases—even his bed consisted of three packing cases set end to end—and except for books obviously purchased second- or fourth- or eighth-hand, there was little else to be seen.

Our interest in the sword was quickly described. Someone had swung it in Sewell Walk on Friday night, and we wanted to see it.

"That was me swinging it," Mowling said. "I carried it for Ben. It looked atrociously heavy, but it wasn't."

Why swing it? He shrugged. When one had a sword in one's hands, there was a great temptation to swing it, especially after an exhilarating evening. Did he know where Ben lived? Oddly enough, he did. He was a stranger here himself, so he had the people he met write down their addresses for him.

A short time later we interrupted Ben at his work. He had a commission to do a mural—actually, a large painting—for an art-loving innkeeper somewhere in the country whose establishment was called St. George and the Dragon. The painting was to be large enough to cover an upper wall of the inn's public room, and it would depict the climactic moment of St. George's epic battle with the dragon. Ben had a model—a tall, gawky youth—posed in medieval armor. Like the sword, the armor was probably a stage prop. The model stood poised with sword uplifted, ready to deliver a deadly *coup de grâce* to the dragon, which as yet existed only as a sketch on the long canvas.

Our visit was brief. With the artist's wife Doll hovering anxiously in the background, Lady Sara examined the sword. I swung it once myself—carefully, since I was indoors—and we thanked Ben for his courtesy and left.

"What next?" I asked.

"The printshop," Lady Sara said.

By that time it was after one o'clock, and the public house on the corner of Sewell Walk and Fulham was open. Rick was waiting for us.

"My agents have found seven more people who witnessed the sword swinging," he said. "Three saw it in Sewell Walk and four in Fulham Road."

"That's what I needed to know," Lady Sara said. "It was done in poorly lighted streets just after midnight, but in Chelsea that constitutes a public event. At least half of Chelsea's population is still awake and active at that time. Probably everyone in Chelsea knew about the sword swinging by Saturday noon."

While we sipped our ale, Lady Sara slipped easily into conversation with the landlord. "I noticed you have a printer next door," she remarked. "There don't seem to be many of them around."

"Old Jim has been here for years," the landlord said. "Could have retired long ago, but he loves his work. Does excellent work, too. None better."

"I suppose over the years he has had a lot of apprentices," Lady Sara said.

"More than I could count," the landlord said. "Some good, some bad. Some spent time and money here when they should have been working. Some I never saw."

"There's a job printer in Cheapside. I was wondering whether he could be one of Old Jim's apprentices."

"Could be his nephew," the landlord said. "George—I don't remember his last name. He settled over that way when he got his master's papers."

"Did he get on well with his uncle?"

"Like a son to him. Comes to visit all the time. Was here just this past week—Friday night it was—and the two of them came in for their ale and talked until closing."

We finished our own ale and left. "We have our case," Lady Sara announced.

I said doubtfully, "Why Constable Cahill, why did he have to die, and why Chelsea?"

"All of that. The question is, what's to be done about it? Because we don't have a scrap of evidence." She thought for a moment. "The murder of a police constable is considered a serious matter on every level, and a judge should be lenient with his warrants. But we need at least one witness who is willing to commit perjury. Say a vagrant who awakened shortly after two in the morning in a convenient doorway and saw where Constable Cahill went. Could you find one for me?"

"I'll find you a dozen," Rick promised.

"One will suffice. If it turns out that I'm wrong, the vagrant can decide maybe he had a nightmare. Vagrants aren't considered very reliable witnesses anyway, so no one will think too much of it. Join Charles in Cheapside, and the two of you look for the most convincing lying witness you can find. Bring him to Connaught Mews. Colin and I will return there now and get hold of Chief Inspector Mewer. This will require some planning."

It required a ridiculous amount of planning before we arrived at the Cheapside printshop in a roundabout way at two o'clock Monday morning. The drapes in the window and door of the rear shop were tightly drawn. Chief Inspector Mewer's men had already taken up positions surrounding the building. The chief inspector himself kicked in the door to the Cow Lane storage room, and he and a picked squad of his men rushed inside—to catch a gang of counterfeiters in the act. They frantically tried to conceal the press in its hiding place under the floor, but sheets of counterfeit notes had been hung up to dry, and there were stacks of trimmed ten pound notes in several locations. There was, in fact, so much evidence scattered about that the counterfeiters would have needed half an hour's notice to dispose of it all.

They put up a fight regardless. There were five of them, all large and muscular, and the police almost had more than they could handle. The ensuing battle wrecked the table and smashed boxes of paper stock on all sides before the counterfeiters were subdued.

Lady Sara and I watched from the doorway. When it was finally over, she observed, "Constable Cahill—one man against that crew—never had a chance. Shall we go home?"

Later—it was all of five A.M.—the same distinguished visitors who had called Sunday morning waited on Lady Sara. This time they wanted to know how she had done it. The case was clinched by then. Constable Cahill's body had been found buried in the cellar under the shop on Cheapside. As Lady Sara had predicted, it would be an important witness against the murderers.

"From the beginning it was obvious that only Constable Cahill's discovery of a crime of considerable importance could have justified his murder and beheading," she said. "Discovery had to mean disaster to a promising venture and grave consequences to those taking part. Cheapside has few shops in which an ordinary burglary would meet those qualifications, but the printshop interested me. The crime of counterfeiting satisfied all of the requirements, and the fact that the printer's storage room was equipped with heavy drapes and a door shade intrigued me. I wondered what happened there that required such lavish means of concealment."

"The Bank of England bloke said their queer was the best he'd seen in the past forty years," Chief Inspector Mewer remarked.

"The counterfeiters knew how good it was. They were energetically printing notes as fast as they could and knew they were on the threshold of considerable wealth. Another week and their agents would have been passing the notes all over the country—and England might have faced economic disaster. That was the situation Constable Cahill walked into. What actually happened is clear enough. The counterfeiters were careless with the drapes or the door shade. Cahill, glancing down Cow Street, noticed a gleam of light where none should have been. He walked in that direction, looked through the gap in the drapes, and to his amazement saw a major counterfeiting operation taking place right before his eyes. It probably took him some time to collect his thoughts and try to decide what to do.

"If he tried to collar that mob on his own, he didn't last long," the chief inspector growled. He was wearing a battered face himself, a souvenir of the fracas in the shop.

"Give him credit for knowing better than that. He was probably trying to decide whether to blow his whistle for help—and give the culprits time to dispose of evidence and use whatever means of escape were available to them—or go for help, knowing that they and the evidence could have disappeared by the time he returned. But the gang had a lookout posted or noticed him from inside the shop. Members came up behind him, rushed him inside, and finished him off in short order.

"Then they sat down to consider their predicament. They knew headquarters would soon know the approximate place the constable had reached on his beat before he disappeared. They didn't want police continuously snooping in their neighborhood looking for clues, so they decided to transfer that attention to some remote location. George Mellor had been visiting his uncle in Chelsea on Friday night, and he'd seen the artists and writer in Sewell Walk with an enormous sword. Certainly others had seen them also. So Mellor had the brilliant idea of cutting off Cahill's head and leaving it at Fulham Road and Sewell Walk, an intersection any number of witnesses would be able to tell the police the sword swingers had passed on their way home. The police were bound to wonder what the connection was between the severed head and the sword, and they would waste considerable time trying to trace sword and swinger. Their attention might be permanently diverted from Cheapside.

"It might have worked, after a fashion, if Mellor hadn't forgotten one critically important fact. His uncle, also a printer, was located near the Chelsea intersection. In the end Mellor's diversion pointed directly back at Cheapside—and himself."

"Bunch of no-account scoundrels," Chief Inspector Mewer growled.

"I don't agree," Lady Sara said. "They were a decided cut above run-of-the-mill criminals. They were clever enough to recognize their predicament and creative enough to find an original way out of it. In doing so, they provided us with several hours of diversion on an otherwise uneventful Sunday. I feel I owe them something—I might even go to see them hanged. Now let's consider what can be done for Constable Cahill's widow and children."

Carole Nelson Douglas

The Mummy Case

It's difficult to know for which genre CAROLE NELSON DOUGLAS is most revered—her science fantasy, her historical mysteries, or her sardonic novels and stories about Midnight Louie, the sleekest cat in crime fiction. Douglas is one of those rare writers who can keep her readership no matter what she writes—proof that good work will be rewarded no matter what its breed. Her books have already begun to show up on best-seller lists, and it has become a certainty that Carole Douglas's readership will expand with each new book that is released. "The Mummy Case" first appeared in *Cat Crimes Through Time*.

The Mummy Case:
A Midnight Louie
Past Life Adventure

Carole Nelson Douglas

O ut of my way, Worthless One!" With these welcoming words, Irinefer the Scribe's sandal scuffs a cloud of desert dust into my delicate nostrils.

I sneeze, elude the kick that follows the scuff, and duck into the nearest doorway.

I may be Worthless, but I would think one of the Sacred Breed would get a little more respect in this Necropolis.

But when a Pharaoh dies, two things are certain: the eternal embellishment of his royal tomb will finally end, and the endless plotting by grave robbers to sack his tomb will begin.

Here on the shores of the river Nile, "eternal" and "endless" are pretty flexible concepts. I am lucky that we of the Sacred Breed are accounted to possess nine lives. Frankly, with such a heritage, there is little need for us to partake in stripping down to our remaining *Kas* and crossing the River of Death with our human master.

Even a Pharaoh is only accorded one *Ka,* or material soul. You would think these one-*Ka* wonders would not be so hasty to rip we of the Sacred-Breed-of-Nine-*Kas* from our earthly hides before our appointed times. But those unfortunate enough to have attended Nomenophis I, who decreed that his household servitors should be present in his tomb in more than pictorial fashion, had no choice. So came the ceremonial gutting, the claustrophobic swathing in a length of linen as long, narrow, and winding as the river Nile, and even the household car ends up with its empty hide preserved in its original shape and its innards in a jar more suitable for a potent attar of lotus. So much for being a Sacred Breed.

Yet some, especially the humans under discussion, consider Egypt the height of civilized society in these times and climes.

Perhaps I am a bit jaded. I have recently lost my own mother to the prevailing customs.

Our recently designed family cartouche bears the Eye of Horus, a symbol of theft and restitution. In one of those gory tales religion the world over seems to favor, the Egyptian god Horus's eye was stolen by his jealous brother Seth, but was restored by order of a court of gods. Perhaps this is where the "eye for an eye" adage I have heard in my travels came from. Or perhaps this is where the expression, also heard in my travels, "gypped" came from.

Since my mother and I were apparent imports to this land, being as black as a ceremonial wig rather than the usual burnt-cinnabar shade of both the people and felines who inhabit the Nile valley, we occupied an unusual place here.

The Egyptians called us by unpronounceable syllables we ignored whenever possible, but my moniker translates to "Heart of Night."

I suppose the title is a comment on our family's ebony good looks. My mother was known as Eye of Night, since it was her job to keep a vigilant watch on the persons and events surrounding Pharaoh, and to warn him of any untoward acts, such as attempted assassination.

It was obviously in her personal interest to keep our Pharaoh alive as long as possible.

Unfortunately, he died of indigestion, an internal affair my mother could have done nothing to prevent.

So passed his servants, including my esteemed maternal parent, in a paroxysm of the embalming arts that left the linen supply of Thebes in a severe shortage.

Not being a member of the Pharaoh's household, I escaped the general weeping and winding to live to mourn my mother's passing.

Unfortunately, I have lost not only a mother, but also my sole connection to the palace, where once I had visiting privileges as the offspring of a member of Pharaoh's bodyguard.

This has meant I must make my way in the City of Cats near the Necropolis. This is not the fabled Bubastis where Bastet Herself, mother of all cats, reigns, but a feline colony that forages in the shadow of the Pyramids, catching vermin unhoused by the constant construction and begging food from the artisans and slaves always laboring on the massive tombs, which give the term "work in progress" an entirely new dimension.

Since I am suspected of being a foreigner, and am now also an orphan bereft of parental protection, life after mother's death has not been easy.

The resident feline in the rooms beyond my doorway shelter swats me on the posterior.

"Out of my house, familyless foreigner. Positionless beggar!"

Like ill-tempered master, like servant, I think. I ebb before a paw gloved in sphinx-colored fur, a lean Abyssinian with a revolting kinship to the metalwork feline statues scattered about the royal city. Even the commonest felines here, being considered Sacred, think that they are to the linen and bronze born.

I slink away, contemplating another tasty repast of locusts and cactus-cider.

If only I could demonstrate that I possess some of my mother's peerless hunting instincts, I could win a place in the palace and sleep on an ebony-and-ivory inlaid chair with a zebra-hide pillow.

I would look very good against zebra-hide.

A hiss erupts from behind the mud-daub wall of another house.

I arch my back, preparing for defense.

But this sound is a *psst* for attention rather than the usual *ssst!* of hostility.

An aged Abyssinian who wears a palace collar is escorted by a pair of husky Necropolis cats, commoners, but uncommonly large.

"Heart of Night, I wish a word," says the old one.

"You are Ampheris, Counter of the Royal Vermin."

As an "outside" cat, Ampheris was not considered part of the royal household and thus escaped the recent bagging, binding, and burying.

"True. A pity that your revered mother has passed to the Underworld. She was a peerless hunter. Have you any talent along that line?"

I edge into the shade they occupy as if they owned it.

Ampheris nods at his bodyguard. They push a shallow bowl of sour goat's milk toward me. I lap delicately inside the scummy outer ring and consider. This is a serious matter if I am being offered drink. My whiskers twitch more at the scent of opportunity than at that of rancid milk.

We all crouch on our haunches.

"What is up?" I ask.

One bodyguard growls, as if I had made a jest.

The old man answers. I doubt his henchmen can talk. "It is what is up . . . and walking . . . that is the question. Son of She Who Sat Beside Pharaoh's Sandal." The royal groundskeeper is so old that his whiskers never stop trembling.

"Something walks here, in the Valley of the Kings? Or in the palace within the city?"

"Here," Ampheris hisses, his whiskers quivering anew. "Have you not heard?"

"I am not exactly *persona grata* in this Necropolis."

"I see why you are held apart. Perhaps it is the foreign words you employ, such as this *'persona grata.'* What language is that? Manx? Mesopotamian?"

"No, nothing edible. Something I picked up on my travels among the uncivilized tribes in the lands across from where the Nile empties into the sea."

"There is nothing solid beyond where the river Nile empties into the sea. But there is something . . . semisolid . . . here on the Necropolis under the shadow of the Pyramids."

I keep mum; that is the best way to learn things in the Eye of Horus game. My mama told me that much.

"I have seen it," one bodyguard growls, sounding ashamed. "In all my seven lives I have never seen anything so terrifying. A mummy that walks."

I nod to gain time. How can a mummy walk? The first thing the embalmers do is wrap every limb up tighter than the Pharaoh's treasure. Even a dead mummy cannot crawl. And they are all decidedly dead. I tell these Sacred ninnies so.

The old guy nods. "Yet this apparition has been seen by others of our kind here. It walks . . . upright. It . . . gleams linen-white in the moonlight."

"Has anyone attempted to question this restless mummy?"

One bodyguard catches my ruff tight in nail-studded paws. "Listen, stranger, you would not be so glib if you encountered this abomination. You would draw back and slink away and count yourself lucky to do so."

I shrug off his big mitts. "Maybe I would. And maybe I would not. Especially if there were something in it for me."

Their six amber eyes exchange glances before returning to confront my green ones.

"Should you banish this restless spirit," Ampheris says slowly, "the Sacred Breed of the Necropolis would deign to accept your unworthy presence. We would allow you to live and hunt among us."

"As if I would want to! No, I seek a more fitting reward. My mother's old position at the palace."

"Impossible! That is awarded at the discretion of Pharaoh."

"Perhaps you could trot indoors and put in a good word for me with Nomenophis II."

"For what?" snorts one of the bodyguard.

Ampheris nods and trembles. "Put this unnatural mummy to rest and we will see."

"It might be Nomenophis I, has anyone considered that? He is the most recently dead human of note."

Ampheris wrinkles his already creased forehead fur into a semblance of sand dunes. "But the mummy that has been glimpsed is not human."

"Of course it is not human if it is mummified, yet walking. It may be a demon, or a god. One never knows."

"Idiot foreigner!" scoffs a bodyguard. "This mummy is of our own breed."

"You mean that a mummified *cat* stalks the Necropolis?"

"Exactly," Ampheris says. "I fear that Pharaoh would not be sufficiently grateful for your laying such a thing to rest, as it is not his royal sire. The most reward you can hope for is a better toleration of your presence among the Sacred Breed."

I shrug. Any improvement in my status is a step up, and I come from a long line of high-steppers.

• • •

By the time the Sun God's boat is sinking slowly in the West, I have accosted and interrogated most of the individuals whose names were given to me.

It has not been easy. I have had sand kicked in my face and tail, and have been spit at and hit. I have even had to resort to pinning my witnesses against a wall until they burp up their stories like so many hair-balls.

My last victim . . . I mean, witness, is Kemfer the jeweler's companion. He is a wiry but cowering sort who wishes only to be off the streets before night falls and "it walks" again.

"How tall?" I ask.

"T-two tail-lengths. Let me go, please. My master is calling me home for supper."

I do indeed hear a human repeating "mau, mau," the Egyptian word for cat. "You say it walks upright on two legs, like a human? Then why do you think it is a cat?"

"The upright ears, you imbecile! Oh, sorry, I did not mean to call Your Honorableness names. Please let me go. It darkens."

"But you saw it by night?"

"Yes, and I will go forth by night no more."

"Are you sure you did not see the ears of Anubis?"

Now the creature trembles like old Ampheris. "The jackal-headed embalming god? Say not so, for then we are all doomed!"

"Well, I could use the company," I reply sourly. At least this sorry specimen of the Sacred Breed has a home to go to by night.

I relax my grip. The creature whines and kicks up a dust devil of sand as he streaks away.

I shake my head, only partly to dislodge the stray grains from my ears. My dear departed mama, foreign-born or not, was worth twenty of these craven Necropolis cats.

I see my only option is to hunt this apparition myself. And since pale funereal wrappings are its hallmark, I shall have to do so by night. At least it will not see me first.

I head down the mean streets that twist and turn past houses warmed by window-squares of lamplight toward the deserted valley where only the dead keep each other company.

I do not believe in risen spirits, mummified or not, but I have heard ample testimony that something unnatural prowls the Valley of the Kings.

I call upon the protection of Bastet as I move alone toward the artificial mountain range of tombs glowing softly gold in the last rays of the departing Sun God.

The hot sands are already cooling beneath my pads and night's sudden cloak blends into my despised dark fur. I am unseen but not sightless, silent but not mute, uncertain but not fearful.

Once human habitation has been left behind, only sand and stone stretch around me. I pause to listen to the skitter of the night, the scratch of verminous claws, the sinister hiss of scales slithering over sand, the distant call of a jackal.

I hear a sudden scramble behind a broken pyramid stone left to mark its own grave in the desert. This may be some nocturnal drama of stalk and kill, dueling beetles, anything normal to the night, but I hasten over, leap atop the cut stone and peer beyond.

My keen night vision sees sands swirling up, a mouse in their midst, eyes gleaming red, and a stiff, plunging, ghostly white figure lurching after it.

The hair lifts along my spine and tail.

For this creature indeed walks upright on two legs, yet its head has a distinctly catlike profile. Were it more than two tail-lengths tall, I would take it for the mummified form of Bastet herself, She of the Human Female Body and the Feline Head.

But all statues I have seen of Bastet cast her in a gigantic mold, three human-heights high. Even if the sculptors exaggerate in the way of men personifying gods, Bastet must be at least of human height.

Whatever this monster's composition or identity, I must challenge it, or fail.

I dive into the fray below, my arrival freeing the desert mouse to retreat into a crack in the stone block.

I am left facing a furious monster, a growling, spinning, spitting dervish of aggravated linen. Furnereal wrappings whip around the figure like human hair. I snag one with a claw and begin pulling. Perhaps the apparition is disembodied beneath the wrappings. Perhaps I will free a trapped spirit. . . .

I am hit by a dust-spout of linen and knocked onto my back. The weight crushes me to the desert floor until my spine is cradled by sand. My claws keep churning, snagging in linen and pulling, cutting, until loosened wrappings fall over my face, smothering me.

I fight the toils of the funereal art, digging my own grave deep into the sand, providing my own shredded cerements. My strength ebbs, and the monster atop me has grown no less heavy with the loss of its linens.

Yet it tires too. I finally open my grit-caked eyes to discover we have both ground ourselves into a sand-trap, our contending bodies frozen from further motion by the sand our fight has kicked up.

I feel matted fur sprouting like grass between the rows of savaged linen. Only the creature's face remains shrouded. Faint, eerie and still-angry moans emit from it.

I heave upright, dislodging drifts of sand over my face. After moments of furious kicking, I am upright and my exhausted opponent is encased in sand from neck to foot. Talk about a mummy case.

It now is high time to solve the mystery of the resurrected mummy. I start pawing delicately at the facial wrappings, loose but still intact.

I am beginning to suspect exactly *what* the mummy is.

A few dreadfully crumpled whiskers spring out from the unwinding linen. Then a spray of sand from a choked mouth. Finally I unveil an eye, which reflects gold in the moonlight, and I now know *who* it is.

The eye is green.

"Mummy!"

A hiss and spit are my only reward.

I unwind further, at last revealing the sadly abused fur and face of my supposedly former mother, Eye of Night.

"But you are three days dead!"

"Close," she agrees, struggling upright.

Her once-sleek black fur is mottled into curls by the linen's long press. Her poor tail has been bound to her body like a broken limb. Her mouth is dry with sand.

She pants. "And three days starved. See what you can get me."

I turn to the crack.

Later, after a desert buffet of fare far below the palace menu, my mother sits licking her lackluster fur in the moonlight, and tells me her story in a voice hoarse and shaking with anger.

"First," she says, "I have been prevented from joining my master in the afterlife. I will not sit beside his royal sandal on guard for eternity. Whoever has done this shall pay."

"Still, I am glad to see you alive."

"I will not be able to enjoy my additional life unless I find the person who has done this."

"Then the one behind your resurrection was human?"

"In word and deed. I was taken to the embalmer, where I was . . . hit upon the head. I naturally assumed the blow would be fatal to my earthly body and that I would awake in the underworld in the court of Pharaoh, in my rightful place of Pharaoh's Footstool."

I nod.

"But when I awoke, I was . . . alone. Wrapped in linen, it is true, but with my insides intact. I was neither here nor there, but in some blasphemous in-between state, that I knew immediately. But though I could see that, I could not see past these blinding bindings that you have removed." She paws the piled linen strips.

"Why? Why was I not permitted the ritual death and resurrection in the underworld? Was this some way to harm my master after death? It is a great puzzle."

"The great puzzle is that you are still alive, honored parent. You were abandoned in bindings in the waste between the Valley of the Kings and the Necropolis. You should have died of hunger, heat, or thirst, or been easy prey for some jackal. Yet you fought to free yourself from the bindings, and your struggles were seen by the Necropolis cats, who feared you as a demon."

"I was hungry. Hungry! As if I were alive. I could barely move at first, but finally my writhings loosened the linen and I could flail along like a fish spit out of the Nile to the shore."

"No doubt you bewailed your lot."

"I screamed to high heaven."

"No wonder they took you for a monster." I stand up and begin to dig in the sand.

"Excuse me, lad, but I do not think now is the time for a bathroom break, not when we face a conspiracy of great umbrage and import to all of Egypt. Pharaoh must not be cheated of his attendants in the afterlife. It is sacrilege."

"Perhaps," I say, still kicking sand, "but I think it is also something else far more common to this world than the next."

She sees that I have contrived to bury her wrappings under a mound of sand.

"You conceal the evidence of this outrage?"

"You must take on a new identity. You are not known in the Necropolis except by name and position. I can introduce you as my aunt from . . . Sumeria."

She rises weakly to her feet and stamps one. "Can you not understand, Heart of Night? My duty to Pharaoh is not over, so long as whoever has separated us for eternity lives."

"Oh, I see that perfectly well, Auntie . . . Jezabel. That is why we must keep you dead and buried until we can expose the criminal."

"How?" she wails in a fit of maternal exasperation.

"First," I say, "we must discover what and why. Only then will come 'who.'"

My mama is no shrinking lotus, but even she pauses when she realizes what our next step must be.

"You wish us to disturb the dead? To break into the tomb and desecrate the royal resting place?"

I have led her into the base of the Necropolis for a long drink from the potter's jar where he keeps water to moisten his wheel. Not a soul, human or feline, has stirred. Ordinarily the Sacred Breed overruns the Necropolis night and day, but the mummy sightings have driven them indoors.

"It is necessary. There is something I must see for myself in Pharaoh's tomb."

"I suppose," she says glumly, trying vainly to uncurl her whiskers by wetting them in the jar, "that is the place that I was meant to be."

"Exactly. Taking me there only fulfills your disrupted destiny. Besides, I know little of tomb construction, and I imagine you must have heard the plans discussed in the palace."

"Endlessly," she says tartly, rising off her haunches. "Then let us be off. I need to stretch my limbs."

I follow her lead, not caring to mention that her tail bends crookedly to the left. My mama has much in common with Bastet, in that she can be a benign godlike force and also one Hatshepsut of a demon-raiser when riled. Especially when raised from the dead.

The walk is long and the moon has only sailed halfway through the sky-bowl when we pause in the awesome shadow of the pyramid. This man-made mountain, smooth as sandalwood and as precisely pointed as an arrowhead made for a behemoth, seems like a monument worthy of its mighty occupant, Death.

My mama has finished lamenting her impious fate, though, and is all business.

"There are secret ways into every pyramid. Stones that balance upon the weight of a hair to spring open. Sniff for air."

So I come to scraping my nose raw along stone seams so narrow the advertised hair could hardly slip into them.

Suddenly my mama stretches up her front feet. Just as suddenly they plunge forward back to the level, taking her with them. I find the stone has swung open wide enough to admit a mouse. Apparently my food-starved mama fell right through. I must grunt and groan my way past, much compressing my innards. Maybe hers were removed after all. . . .

"Hush!" she warns from within.

I sense a draft of air and we soon are following it up a long stone-paved ramp.

"I have seen the plans," she hisses in the dark. "No one expects a cat, no matter how sacred, to understand the science of humans. But living in the palace taught me the value of learning the humans' labyrinthine ways."

Whatever, I just hope she can lead us out of this maze.

Then I see the light. My mama is a haloed silhouette ahead of me. She stops.

"This is wrong, Heart of Night. No one should be in the pyramid now."

"Not even some artisan finishing up a frieze?"

"No one."

Mama pads grimly forward, and I follow.

The passage opens into another, then finally into a large chamber lit by the flicker of an oil lamp. I brush by my mother to reconnoiter. She may know her pyramids, but I know the perfidy of humans from my time in the Necropolis.

But no humans are present, just the flickering lamp scenting the air with a rancid odor. Or, rather, the only humans present are a painted parade upon the walls. Several Eyes of Horus gaze down on me, as well as a number of insect- and animal-headed gods. I do not spot the Divine Bastet.

I do spot the massive stone sarcophagus that occupies the center of the room.

Mama jumps atop this with an impressive leap for one in her recent condition.

"It is untampered with," she reports with satisfaction. "In fact, from up here, I see no signs of disruption."

"There must be something. Why else the lamp?"

I take advantage of its erratic illumination to study the paintings. The figures, so stiff in their ceremonial headdresses, seem to move in the uncertain light. I see Nomenophis ministered to by serving girls. Offering something to wing-armed Isis. I see sacrificial geese and bulls. I see the noble cat in several representations, all sitting, all in formal profile, like the people. Like the people, the cats are all a burnt-sand color, ruddy-brown.

All except one.

The painting depicts Nomenophis in his throne room. Officials and gods gather 'round. At his feet crouches, not sits, a single cat. She is black.

"Look, Mama! You are in one of the paintings!"

"Hush, boy. Of course I am. As I should be here in my mummified form, with a canopic jar of my vitals nearby. Instead I am robbed. Robbed of my immortality. The painting is a lie! I am no longer Pharaoh's Footstool! . . ."

Her voice has risen to echo off the stone walls.

"Hush," I tell her in a reversal of roles. "Whoever has lit this lamp may still be within hearing."

I leap up beside her and survey the room in all its glory. I know Nomenophis inhabits a richly painted and inlaid mummy case beneath this stone sarcophagus. I know that beneath that his linen-wrapped mummy wears jeweled gold headpiece and collar.

But the tomb itself has not been breached.

I look around, until my eyes rest upon something that should not be here, but is.

My mother ceases her mourning long enough to notice and follow my fixed gaze.

"My mummy! It is here."

Indeed, a wrapped white figure of a cat sits upon a costly throne (quite appropriate placement for one of the Sacred Breed).

"Who has usurped my place?" my mama demands, assuming the very same combative crouch in which she is depicted so handsomely on the tomb wall.

"I am not sure that anyone has."

"And what does that mean?"

I am too busy casting my particular Eye of Horus, representing theft and restitution, about the premises. I spy a pile of linen windings near the oil lamp on the floor. The inspiration of Bastet floods my brain.

"I apologize for urging you to, er, shut up earlier, Mama. I think you should resume your caterwauling, but first . . ."

In a few minutes my mama's finest notes are bouncing off the sober faces of Isis, Osiris, Selkis, and Neith on all four walls.

I join her and quite an impressive chorus we concoct in the silence of a deserted tomb.

I soon hear running sandals slapping stones down the long, dark corridor leading toward us. I also hear the sweet sound of curses.

A moment later two kilt-swathed men burst into the lamplight.

That is when Mama and I proceed to dance atop Nomenophis's sarcophagus.

We are not particularly good dancers, but manage to totter on our hind feet and bat our flailing front feet enough to provide an artistic flurry among the mummy-wrappings that drape our assorted limbs.

"The fury of Bastet," howls one man, falling to his knees and pressing his forehead to the cold stone.

"We have offended the goddess!" screeches the other, doing likewise. "I told you we should not tamper with the mummy of the Sacred One."

At this, two of the Sacred Ones leap off the sarcophagus on to the temptingly revealed naked backs of the prostrate worshipers of Bastet.

Claws dig deep and often. The wretches' howls mingle with our own. They rise to evade our rear harrying, and find their faces being inscribed with the sacred sign of Bastet: four long parallel tracks repeated to infinity.

Soon we are alone in the tomb, listening to the eerie echoes of tormented escapees.

I leap off the royal masonry to meet the mummy who has replaced my mama.

"Heart of Night," she calls after me. "You have seen the Revenge of Bastet. Touch not the cat."

"I do not touch the cat . . .

". . . I level it." With one paw-blow I knock the mummy over and begin unraveling the wrappings. I am getting good at this.

While my mama howls her horror (receiving fresh echoes down the corridor with every bleat), I turn the mummy into shredded wheat.

Lo, this mummy's innards have been left inside too, only they gleam hard and gold in the lamplight.

"Those are the royal artifacts of Pharaoh," my mama says from her perch, stunned.

I nod. "That is why you were shuffled into some spare wrappings and thrown into the desert to die. Your false image here hid the items the servants filched during the funeral. Even as Pharaoh in all his richness was lowered into his sarcophagus, those vermin were wrapping priceless trinkets into a feline-shaped treasure chest. No wonder they fled just now as if the breath of Bastet were smoking their heels behind them."

"But they escaped."

"Marked by the tracks of Bastet? People will comment on their condition, and in their current state they will not have the wits to conceal anything. Also, the stone is askew that opens the secret passage we used. Someone will soon notice. We must guard the mummy treasure until the authorities arrive."

"But that may take hours, even days."

"Shall I go out and hunt food first, or you?"

. . .

So it is written that when Pharaoh's guard came to his father's tomb two days later, after the thieves had been found and confessed, a fierce black cat was found crouched over the spilled booty from the mummified cat wrappings.

The mummy of the former Pharaoh's cat, the valiant Eye of Night, was missing and presumed to have been assumed into the underworld by Bastet Herself, whose Terrible Tracks still marked the backs and faces of the would-be thieves.

And so it is now inscribed on the tomb walls of Nomenophis II, who will in his own day go into that underworld that all Egyptians long for, that the position of Pharaoh's Footstool is once again occupied, by Heart of Night, son of Eye of Night, who will live in human memory for two thousand years . . . or possibly more, so long as Bastet and the Sacred Breed are revered to the ends of the earth.

The Eye of Horus, representing theft and restitution, never sleeps. Evildoers, read Heart of Night's cartouche and weep.

Marcia Muller

Recycle

When MARCIA MULLER won the Lifetime Achievement Award from the Private Eye Writers of America, she was being rewarded for two different achievements—first, there were the novels and stories themselves, exemplary modern stories of detection and drama involving many tough, ethical themes; and second, the fact that her Sharon McCone books were really the first ever to give readers a serious female character who functions in the real world of private investigators. She's still giving us some of the best modern crime novels available. "Recycle" first appeared in *Mary Higgins Clark Mystery Magazine,* summer issue.

Recycle

Marcia Muller

On their fortieth birthday, most women want a little romance, right? Be taken out to dinner, given a present, maybe some flowers. Not McCone, though. She's one of a kind. On her fortieth, she wanted me to go with her to the dump.

Sure, I know we're supposed to call it a refuse-disposal site, but politically correct doesn't always cut it with me. A dump's a dump, and the proof of that's in the smell.

The dump we're talking about was in Sonoma County, some forty-five miles north of the Golden Gate, out in the middle of a lot of farmland near the town of Los Alegres. A long blacktop road led uphill from the highway; at the top, earthmovers worked on the edge of the landfill, and seagulls perched on a mountain of recycled yard waste.

"Nasty little scavengers flew twenty miles inland to feast at this fancy establishment," I commented.

McCone gave me a look that said she wasn't impressed with the gulls' navigational talents and then slammed on the brakes inches short of the bumper of a van crammed with plastic garbage bags—the last in a line of vehicles that were stopped at the gate waiting to pay the entrance fee.

"I know, Ripinsky, I know," she muttered, even though I hadn't said anything. "Eyes front." Then she steered her MG around the van and took a side road toward the recycling sheds—a row of board shacks surrounded by busted furniture and rusted appliances, where a hand-lettered sign advertised:

RECYCLED MERCHANDISE!
LOW PRICES!
HOUSEWARES, BOOKS, CLOTHING AND MORE!

Books? The morning was looking better. Maybe while she took care of her business, I'd lay hand to an old western for my collection.

We'd come north from San Francisco on a lead one of McCone's operatives had turned up, to hunt for a man calling himself Nick Galway. Not his real name; she had good reason to believe he was really the well-known sculptor Glenn Farrell. Ten years ago, Farrell had disappeared from his farm in Vermont, leaving behind his wife and child and taking with him the gold for three pieces of sculpture commissioned by a wealthy client who invested in precious metals and wanted some of his holdings put to esthetic use. Recently a friend of the client had spotted Farrell in Northern California, and the client hired McCone to find him and either take back the gold or turn Farrell over to the authorities.

It was odds-even that Galway/Farrell still had the gold. At least, if you took into account the condition of the caretaker's cottage he rented on a small ranch west of Los Alegres, where we'd stopped earlier. It was sagging and in bad repair, overgrown by ivy and surrounded by weeds and a collection of junk—not the sort of place anybody with the wherewithal to live the good life would've chosen.

When nobody came to the door we drove up to the main house, and McCone spoke with the white-haired landlady, Mrs. Mallory, who identified Glenn Farrell's photo as that of her tenant. She said he was probably scavenging at the dump as he did most mornings.

Now as we got out of McCone's MG, a dark-haired woman with a weather-beaten face and a grimy T-shirt came from the first of the sheds, carrying something that looked like part of a plane's prop. She saw us, did an about-face and tossed the thing into a refuse barrel. Then she asked, "Help you?"

McCone said, "I'm looking for Nick Galway. His landlady told me he'd probably be here."

She gave us an odd look, as if she couldn't imagine anybody wanting Galway. "Haven't seen him today. You a friend of his?"

"A friend of a friend asked me to look him up."

"Why? The lunatic owe him money or something?"

"Lunatic?"

"Well, what else would you call a guy who spends half his life scrounging for stuff?"

"What kind of stuff?"

"Anything. Everything. So long's it's free or dirt-cheap."

"What does he do with it?"

"Claims he's a sculptor. Says he used to be famous under another name. Made expensive art for rich folks, but now his art's in his junk. Weird way of putting it, huh?"

"Well, artists . . ."

"Yeah, artists. Comes around nearly every day, yaps at me the whole time. Nonsense about runnin' away from crass commercialism and middle-class values. I mostly don't listen."

"Well, if he comes in today, will you give me a call?" The woman nodded, and McCone wrote her cell-phone number on a scrap of paper, wrapped a twenty around it. "But don't tell him somebody's looking for him—okay?"

The dump lady grinned at the twenty. "He comes in, you'll hear from me."

In case Galway had turned up at home, McCone decided to check the ranch again, but nobody answered her knocks at the door of the cottage. She was just trying the knob and finding the door unlocked when an old sedan pulled up next to where I was sitting in the MG, and I recognized Mrs. Mallory, the landlady. She leaned out her window and asked me. "You didn't find Nick at the dump?"

"No, ma'am." I glanced at McCone. She'd turned away from the door, had her hands clasped innocently behind her. "The woman who runs the recycle shop says he hasn't been there today."

"Strange." She shut off her engine and got out of the car, spry and slim in her work shirt, jeans and mud-splattered boots—the kind of tough old bird that a lifetime of ranching breeds. She reminded me of my dead mother.

Shaking her key ring, she isolated a key and called to McCone, "We better check inside. Nick never stays away this long unless he's at the dump or—"

"The door's not locked," McCone said, and stepped inside.

I got out of the MG and followed at a distance. The case was McCone's, and I knew from long and sometimes hellacious experience to maintain a hands-off attitude.

The cottage was pretty dingy inside: matted pea-green shag carpet, scarred paneling, furniture that belonged at the dump—and had probably come from there. Mrs. Mallory went through the place calling out for Galway, while McCone followed close on her heels and I cooled mine in the front room. They came back, Mrs. Mallory shaking her head. "Not here. Worries me."

McCone asked, "Can you think of anyplace else he might've gone?"

"Did you check his studio?"

"I didn't know he had one. Where is it?"

"The barn. It's not used anymore, so I let him have it."

"So he's still sculpting?"

"Well, I wouldn't call it that. Don't know what I would call it. Maybe putting together atrocities. Huge, horrible things that're a mishmash of what he drags home from the dump. Let's see if he's there."

I wouldn't've let that barn stand two minutes on my ranch in Mono County. Of course, one good windstorm and it probably wouldn't be standing here much longer. The door was open, hanging crooked on weak hinges, and a rust-spotted pickup was nosed inside.

"Galway's?" McCone asked Mrs. Mallory.

The landlady nodded and called out to him. There was no answer.

Quiet there. Only the rustle of a eucalyptus windbreak and flies buzzing under the eaves. And a feeling of wrongness. I felt the hair on my neck bristle, looked at McCone and saw she was getting the same warning signs. Together we moved through the doorway and stopped by the truck.

The clotted shadow was broken by shafts of light from holes in the high roof. They filtered down on a couple of eight-foot towers shaped like oil derricks, made of metal, wood, glass and plastic. Their components were all different pieces of junk: beer cans, chair legs, bottles, parts of a baby stroller, an automobile bumper, fence rails, barbed wire, a window pane, a refrigerator drawer.

"My God," McCone said. She didn't mean it reverently.

My eyes had adjusted to the gloom now, and I saw other towers that were toppled and broken, lying on their sides and canted across one another as if an earthquake had hit the oil field. The one at the top of the heap was crowned by the blades from a small windmill.

"Stay here," McCone said to Mrs. Mallory. Then she started moving through the wreckage.

I followed, because I'd spotted what she had: a pair of blue-jeaned legs sticking out from under the bottommost tower. Blue-jeaned legs, and feet in shabby cowboy boots. McCone squatted down and shoved at the debris while I lifted. Together we cleared enough room so we could see the man's face.

Glenn Farrell, a.k.a. Nick Galway.

His neck was bent at an unnatural angle, the back of his head caved in and bloody.

McCone felt for a pulse, shook her head and pulled her hand away quickly. "He's cold," she said.

I heard a noise behind us, swiveled, and looked up at Mrs. Mallory. Her eyes moved from the body to us, shocked but unflinching. Yeah, a tough old bird like Ma.

"How did this happen?" she said.

I shook my head and stood up. Like he'd told the dump lady, Farrell's art was junk—or *in* his junk—and now his lifeblood mingled with it.

I glanced at McCone, who had stood up too. Her expression was as unflinching as Mrs. Mallory's, but I knew what was going on behind those steady dark eyes. She's seen a lot of death, my woman, but she's never grown indifferent to it, any more than I have. By all rights we should both be pretty callous: In her years as an investigator, she's had more than her share of nasty experiences, and my own past still gives me nightmares. But inside, we've got that essential spark of humanity—which was why we drew closer together now as we stared around at the wreckage.

Broken lamp globes. A vacuum-cleaner bag and part of a rusted wheel-barrow. Curved chromium chair arms. A 1973 Colorado license plate. Mason jars, shattered.

Broken mirror—bad luck proved. Chipped head of a grinning garden gnome and some paperback romance novels with holes drilled through them. A toaster's innards. Moth-eaten stuffed deer head. A busted axe. The top of a windmill with one blade missing. . . .

Behind us Mrs. Mallory asked again, "How did this happen?"

Hands-off attitude be damned! "I know how," I said. "Let's call nine-one-one."

It was an accident! An accident!" Mary Delmar, the dump lady, told the sheriff's deputy. "I snuck over there late last night to get his gold, and the crazy bastard must've seen my flashlight, because he came runnin' out to the barn and attacked me. I was defending myself when those towers started fallin' on us. I'm lucky I didn't end up like Nick!"

The deputy, whose name was Evans, rolled his eyes at McCone and me.

"Why the hell couldn't he just've stayed in bed?" Delmar added. "I'd already found the windmill blade. Why'd he have to come out there?"

Evans said, "Where is the windmill blade?"

Delmar collapsed on a bent lawn chair and put her hands over her eyes. "Why do things like this always happen to me?"

McCone tapped the deputy's arm, motioned at the refuse bin where we'd seen Delmar toss the thing that at first glance had looked like part of a plane's prop. He went to check, came back shaking his head. "Ms. Delmar, where is it?"

"Oh hell! All right! It's in there." She jerked her head at the shed behind us. "I had to paw through all that junk, scrape paint off everything till I found it. It'll probably never clean up right."

"I'll have to read you your rights," Evans said.

"My rights? Why? I already told you it was an accident. His fault anyway, runnin' out there and attackin' me."

Evans gave up, motioned to his partner to take over. Right off, Delmar started yowling about calling a lawyer.

Evans took McCone and me aside, muttering, "Galway—Farrell—is dead, but *she's* the injured party."

McCone shrugged and said, "Nowadays, it's always the other guy's fault."

"One thing bothers me," Evans said. "This woman's not very bright, and she doesn't strike me as an art expert. What tipped her to who Farrell was?"

"He told her he used to be a famous sculptor under another name."

"But did he tell her what name?"

McCone hesitated, frowning. "I don't know. But he certainly would-n't've told her about the gold." She looked at me, raising her eyebrows.

I shrugged, then spotted the sign advertising recycled merchandise at low prices. "Well," I said, "maybe she's a reader."

"Oh?" From both of them.

"Come on." I headed for the shed where the books were. Maybe I'd come across an old western or two while I was hunting.

Plenty of romances, best sellers, self-help and cookbooks, but no old westerns. On the back wall, though, there was a pictorial set: *Popular Twentieth-Century Artists*. The fourth volume was missing, and when I checked the introductory volume, I found that Number Four was on sculptors. A glance through Number One showed that each article was accompanied by a photo of the individual.

I found the index and flipped to "Farrell, Glenn." There were several notations, but the most interesting was "theft and disappearance." I showed it to McCone and Evans.

"So," McCone said, "Mary Delmar is a reader—at least when she smells a potential profit."

"Yeah, she is. She spotted this set, decided to see if she could find out who Galway actually was. Read about the stolen gold, and figured out what he meant about his art being in his junk."

To my astonishment, McCone hugged me. "Ripinsky, what an absolutely fabulous birthday present!"

I leered down at her. "You like that one, wait till you see what else I've got for you."

She narrowed her eyes at me, then flicked them toward Evans. She's a very private woman, one of the many reasons I love her.

"McCone and I are both pilots." I said to Evans, who was looking quite interested. To McCone I said. "Think airport. Think the Citabria, fueled and ready to go. Think terrific destination."

"Oh?"

I nodded firmly. "Terrific and surprising."

Now, if I could only come up with a terrific surprising flight plan by the time we got back to the Bay Area. . . .

Donald E. Westlake

Now What?

Caper-comedies, film noir, literary satires, private-eye stories, hard-boiled crime stories, mainstream novels, DONALD E. WESTLAKE has written them all, and written them well. His Richard Stark novels about a thief named Parker are unequaled in contemporary hard-boiled fiction. His comic novels stand unrivaled, despite the many, many imitators who worship them. His screenplays, such as *The Grifters,* guarantee sophistication and storytelling mastery. Recently his novels have turned to explorations of societal crimes, such as his wickedly funny examination of corporate downsizing in *The Ax.* His latest book, *The Hook,* takes square aim at both authors and the publishing industry. "Now what?" first appeared in the December 1999 issue of *Playboy.*

Now What?

Donald E. Westlake

Everybody on the subway was reading the *Daily News,* and every newspaper was open to the exact same page, the one with the three pictures. The picture of the movie star, smiling. The picture of the famous model, posing and smiling. And the picture of the stolen brooch. Shaped vaguely like a boomerang, with a larger dark stone at each end and smaller lighter stones scattered between (like stars in the night sky, seen, say, from a cell), even the brooch seemed to be smiling.

Dortmunder was not smiling. He hadn't realized how big a deal this damn brooch would be. With pictures of the brooch in the hands of every man, woman and child in the greater New York metropolitan area, it was beginning to seem somehow less than brilliant that he should smuggle the thing into Brooklyn disguised as a ham sandwich.

Over breakfast (sweetened orange juice, coffee with a lot of sugar, Wheaties with a *lot* of sugar), that concept had appeared to make a kind of sense, even to have a certain elegance. John Dortmunder, professional thief, with his sloped shoulders, shapeless clothing, lifeless hair-colored hair, pessimistic nose and rusty-hinge gait, knew he could if he wished, look exactly like your normal average working man, even though, so far as he knew, he had never earned an honest dollar in his life. If called upon to transport a valuable stolen brooch from his home in Manhattan to a new but highly recommended fence in Brooklyn, therefore, it had seemed to him the best way to do it was to place the brooch between two slabs of ham with a *lot* of mayonnaise, this package to be inserted within two slices of Wonder Bread, the result wrapped in paper towels and the whole carried inside an ordinary wrinkled brown paper lunch bag. It had *seemed* like a good idea.

Only now he didn't know. What was it about this brooch? Why was its recent change of possessor all over the *Daily News*?

The train trundled and roared and rattled through the black tunnel beneath the city, stopping here and there at bright-lit white-tile places that could have been communal showers in state prisons but were actually where passengers embarked and detrained, and eventually one such departing passenger left his *Daily News* behind him on the seat. Dortmunder beat a bag lady to it, crossed one leg over the other and, ignoring the bag lady's bloodshot glare, settled down to find out what the fuss was all about.

300G BROOCH IN DARING HEIST
Lone Cat Burglar Foils Cops, Top Security

Well, that wasn't so bad. Dortmunder couldn't remember ever having been called daring before, nor had anyone before this ever categorized his shambling jog and wheezing exertions as that of a cat burglar.

Anyway, on to the story:

"In town to promote his new hit film, *Mark Time III: High Mark,* Jer Crumbie last night had a close encounter with a rapid-response burglar who left the superstar breathless, reluctantly admiring and out the $300,000 brooch he had just presented his fiancée, Desiree Makeup spokesmodel Felicia Tarrant.

" 'It was like something in the movies,' Crumbie told cops. 'This guy got through some really tight security, grabbed what he wanted and was out of there before anybody knew what happened.'

"The occasion was a private bash for the Hollywood-based superstar in his luxury suite on the 14th floor of Fifth Avenue's posh Port Dutch Hotel, frequent host to Hollywood celebrities. A private security service screened the invited guests, both at lobby level and again outside the suite itself, and yet the burglar, described as lithe, in dark clothing, with black gloves and a black ski mask, somehow infiltrated the suite and actually managed to wrest the $300,000 trinket out of Felicia Tarrant's hands just moments after Jer Crumbie had presented it to her to the applause of his assembled guests.

" 'It all happened so fast,' Ms. Tarrant told police, 'and he was so slick and professional about it, that I still can't say exactly how it happened.' "

What Dortmunder liked about celebrity events was that they tended to snag everybody's attention. Having seen, both on television and in the *New York Post,* that this movie star was going to be introducing his latest fiancée to 250 of his closest personal friends, including the press, at his suite at the Port Dutch Hotel, Dortmunder had understood at once that the thing to do during the party was to pay a visit to the Port Dutch and drop in on every suite except the one containing the happy couple.

The Port Dutch was a midtown hotel for millionaires of all kinds—oil sheiks, arbitrageurs, rock legends, British royals—and its suites, two per floor facing Central Park across Fifth Avenue, almost always repaid a drop-in visit during the dinner hour.

Dortmunder had decided he would work only on the floors below the 14th, where the happy couple held sway, so as not to pass their windows and perhaps attract unwelcome attention. But on floor after floor, in suite after suite, as he crept up the dark fire escape in his dark clothing, far above the honking, milling, noisy red-and-white stage set of the avenue far below, he met only disappointment. His hard-learned skills at bypassing Port Dutch locks and alarms—early lessons had sometimes included crashing, galumphing flights up and down fire escapes—had no chance to come into play.

Some of the suites clearly contained no paying tenants. Some contained occupants who obviously meant to occupy the suite all evening. (A number of these occupants' stay-at-home activities might have been of educational interest to Dortmunder, had he been less determined to make a profit from the evening.)

A third category of suites was occupied by pretenders. These were people who had gone out for an evening on the town, leaving behind luggage, clothing, shopping bags, all visible from the fire escape windows, providing clues that their owners were second-honeymooners from Akron, Ohio who would repay an enterprising burglar's attentions with little more than Donald Duck sweatshirts from 42nd Street.

Twelve floors without a hit. The not-quite-honeymoon suite was just ahead. Dortmunder was not interested in engaging the attention of beefy men in brown private security guard uniforms, but he was also feeling a bit frustrated. Twelve floors, and not a sou: no bracelets, no anklets, no necklaces; no Rolexes, ThinkPads, smuggled currency; no fur, no silk, no plastic (as in credit cards).

OK. He would *pass* the party, silent and invisible. He would segue from 12 up past 14 without a pause, and then he would see what 15 and above had to offer. The hotel had 23 floors; all hope was not gone.

Up he went. Tiptoe, tiptoe; silent, silent. Over his right shoulder, had he cared to look, spread the dark glitter of Central Park. Straight down, 140 feet beneath his black-sneakered feet, snaked the slow-moving southbound traffic of Fifth Avenue, and just up ahead lurked suite 1501-2-3-4-5.

The window was open.

Oh, now what? Faint party sounds wafted out like laughing gas. Dortmunder hesitated but knew he had to push on.

Inch by inch he went up the open-design metal steps, cool in the cool April evening. The open window, when he reached it, revealed an illuminated room with a bland pale ceiling but apparently no occupants; the party noises came from farther away.

Dortmunder had reached the fire escape landing. On all fours, he started past the dangerous window when he heard suddenly approaching voices:

"You're just trying to humiliate me." Female, young, twangy, whining.
"All I'm *trying* is to teach you English." Male, gruff, cocky, impatient.

Female: "It's a pin. Anybody knows it's a pin!"
Male: "It is, as I said, a brooch."
Female: "A brooch is one of them things you get at the hotel in Paris.
For breakfast."
Male: "That, Felicia, sweetheart—and I love your tits—I promise you, is
a *brioche*."
Female: "Brooch!"
Male: *"Bri-oche!"*

Most of this argument was taking place just the other side of the open
window. Dortmunder, thinking it unwise to move, remained hunkered, half-
turned so his head was just below the sill while his body was compressed into
a shape like a pickup's spring right after 12 pieces of Sheetrock have been
loaded aboard.
"You can't humiliate me!"
An arm appeared within that window space above Dortmunder's head.
The arm was slender, bare, graceful. It was doing an overarm throw, not very
well; if truth be told, it was throwing like a girl.
This arm was attempting to throw the object out through the open
window, and in a way it accomplished its purpose. The flung object first hit
the bottom of the open window, but then it deflected down and out and
wound up outside the window.
In Dortmunder's lap. Jewelry, glittering. What looked like emeralds on
the ends, what looked like diamonds along the middle.
Any second now somebody was going to look out that window to see
where this bauble had gone. Dortmunder closed his left hand around it and
moved. It was an automatic reaction, and since he'd already been moving
upward he kept on moving upward, rounding the turn of the landing, heaving up the next flight of the fire escape, breathing like a city bus, while
behind him the shouting began:

Male: "Hey! Hey! Hey! Hey! Hey!"
Female: "Oh, *no! Oh*, no! *Oh, no!"*

Up and over the hotel roof and into the apartment building next door
and down the freight elevator and out onto the side street, a route long
known to Dortmunder. When he at last ambled around the corner onto
Fifth, merely another late-shift worker going home, the police cars were just
arriving in front of the hotel.

• • •

Newspapers tell lies, Dortmunder thought. He read on, to find a description of the thing in his ham sandwich. The things that looked like emeralds were emeralds, and the things that looked like diamonds were diamonds, that was why the fuss. Altogether, the trinket the bride-perhaps-to-be had flung ricocheting out the window last night was valued, in the newspapers, at least, at $300,000.

On the other hand, newspapers lie. So it would be up to Harmov Krandelloc, said to be an ethnic so different from anybody else that no one had yet figured out even what continent he came from, but who had recently set himself up in a warehouse off Atlantic Avenue where it crossed Flatbush as king of the next generation of really worthwhile fences, who paid great dollar (sometimes even more than the usual ten percent of value) and never asked too many questions. It would be up to Harmov Krandelloc to determine what the thing in the ham sandwich was actually worth, and what Dortmunder could hope to realize from it.

But now, on the BMT into deepest Brooklyn, surrounded by newspaper photos of his swag, realizing that the celebrity of its former owners made this particular green-and-white object more valuable but also more *newsworthy* (a word the sensible burglar does his best to avoid), Dortmunder hunched with increasing despondency over his borrowed paper, clutched his brown bag in his left hand with increasing trepidation and wished fervently he'd waited a week before trying to unload this bauble.

More than a week. Maybe six years would have been right.

Roizak Street would be Dortmunder's stop. While keeping one eye on his *News* and one eye on his lunch, Dortmunder also kept an eye on the subway map, following the train's creeping progress from one foreign neighborhood to another; street names without resonance or meaning, separated by the black tunnels.

Vedloukam Boulevard; the train slowed and stopped. Roizak Street was next. The doors opened and closed. The train started, roaring into the tunnel. Two minutes went by, and the train slowed. Dortmunder rose, peered out the car windows and saw only black. Where was the station?

The train braked steeply, forcing Dortmunder to sit again. Metal wheels could be heard screaming along the metal rails. With one final lurch, the train stopped.

No station. Now what? Some holdup, when all he wanted to do—

The lights went out. Pitch-black darkness. A voice called, "I smell smoke." The voice was oddly calm.

The next 27 voices were anything but calm. Dortmunder, too, smelled smoke, and he felt people surging this way and that, bumping into him, bumping into one another, crying out. He scrunched close on his seat. He'd given up the *News*, but he held on grimly to his ham sandwich.

"ATTENTION PLEASE."

It was an announcement, over the public address system.

Some people kept shouting. Other people shouted for the first people to stop shouting so they could hear the announcement. Nobody heard the announcement.

The car became still, but too late. The announcement was over. "What did he say?" a voice asked.

"I thought it was a she," another voice said.

"It was definitely a he," a third voice put in.

"I see lights coming," said a fourth voice.

"Where? Who? What?" cried a lot of voices.

"Along the track. Flashlights."

"Which side? What way?"

"Left."

"Right."

"Behind us."

"That's not flashlights, that's *fire!*"

"What! What! What!"

"Not behind us, buddy, in front of us! Flashlights."

"Where?"

"They're gone now."

"What time is it?"

"*Time!* Who gives a damn what time it is?"

"I do, knucklehead."

"Who's a knucklehead? Where are you, wise guy?"

"Hey! *I* didn't do anything!"

Dortmunder hunkered down. If the car didn't burn up first, there was going to be a first-class barroom brawl here pretty soon.

Someone sat on Dortmunder. "Oof," he said.

It was a woman. Squirming around, she yelled, "Get your hands off me!"

"Madam," Dortmunder said, "you're sitting on my lunch."

"Don't you talk dirty to *me!*" the woman yelled, and gave him an elbow in the eye. But at least she got off his lap—and lunch—and went away into the heaving throng.

The car was rocking back and forth now; could it possibly tip over?

"The fire's getting closer!"

"Here come the flashlights again!"

Even Dortmunder could see them this time, outside the window, flashlights shining blurrily through a thick fog, like the fog in a Sherlock Holmes movie. Then someone carrying a flashlight opened one of the car's doors and the fog came into the car, but it wasn't fog, it was thick oily smoke. It burned Dortmunder's eyes, made him cough and covered his skin with really bad sunblock.

People clambered up into the car. In the flashlight beams bouncing around, Dortmunder saw all the coughing, wheezing, panicky passengers and saw that the people with the flashlights were uniformed cops.

Oh, good. Cops.

The cops yelled for everybody to shut up, and after a while everybody shut up, and one of the cops said, "We're gonna walk you through the train to the front car. We got steps off the train there, and then we're gonna walk to the station. It's only a couple blocks, and the thing to remember is stay away from the third rail."

A voice called, "Which is the third rail?"

"All of them," the cop told him. "Just stay away from rails. OK, let's go before the fire gets here. Not *that* way, whaddya looking for, a barbecue? *That* way."

They all trooped through the dark smoky train, coughing and stumbling, bumping into one another, snarling, using their elbows, giving New Yorkers' reputations no boost whatsoever, and eventually they reached the front car, where more cops—*more* cops—were helping everybody down a temporary metal staircase to the ground. Of course it would be metal, with all these third rails around; it couldn't be wood.

A cop took hold of Dortmunder's elbow, which made Dortmunder instinctively put his wrists together for the cuffs, but the cop just wanted to help him down the stairs and didn't notice the inappropriate gesture. "Stay off the third rail," the cop said, releasing his elbow.

"Good thought," Dortmunder said, and trudged on after the other passengers, down the long smoky dark tunnel, lit by bare bulbs spaced along the side walls.

The smoke lessened as they went on, and then the platform at Roizak Street appeared, and yet another cop put his hand on Dortmunder's elbow, to help him up the concrete steps to the platform. This time Dortmunder reacted like an innocent person, or as close to one as he could get.

A lot of people were hanging around on the platform; apparently, they wanted another subway ride. Dortmunder walked through them, and just before he got to the turnstile to get out of here yet another cop pointed at the bag in his hand and said, "What's that?"

Dortmunder looked at the bag. It was much more wrinkled than before and was blotchily gray and black from the sooty smoke. "My lunch," he said.

"You don't want to eat that," the cop told him, and pointed at a nearby trash can. "Throw it away, why don't ya?"

"It'll be OK," Dortmunder told him. "It's smoked ham." And he got out of there before the cop could ask for a taste.

Out on the sidewalk at last, Dortmunder took deep breaths of Brooklyn air that had never smelled quite so sweet before, then headed off toward Harmov Krandelloc, following the directions he'd been given: two blocks this way, one block that way, turn right at the corner, and there's the 11 paddy wagons and the million cops and the cop cars with all their flashing lights and the long line of handcuffed guys being marched into the wagons.

Dortmunder stopped. No cop happened to be looking in this direction. He turned smoothly around, not even disturbing the air, and walked casually around the corner, then crossed the street to the bodega and said to the guy guarding the fruit and vegetable display outside, "What's happening over there?"

"Let me get you a paper towel," the guy said, and he went away and came back with two paper towels, one wet and one dry.

Dortmunder thanked him and wiped his face with the wet paper towel, and it came away black. Then he wiped his face with the dry paper towel and it came away gray. He gave the paper towels back and said, "What's happening over there?"

"One of those sting operations," the guy said, "like you see in the movies. You know, the cops set up a fake fence operation, get videotape of all these guys bringing in their stuff, invite them all to a party, then they arrest everybody."

"When did they show up?"

"About ten minutes ago."

I'd have been here, Dortmunder thought, if it wasn't for the subway fire. "Thinka that," he said.

The guy pointed at his bag: "Whatcha got there?"

"My lunch. It's OK, it's smoked ham."

"That bag, man, you don't want that bag. Here, gimme, let me—"

He reached for the bag, and Dortmunder pulled back. Why all this interest in a simple lunch bag? What ever happened to the anonymous-workman-with-lunch-bag theory? "It's fine," Dortmunder said.

"No, man, it's greasy," the bodega guy told him. "It's gonna soak through, spoil the sandwich. Believe me, I know this shit. Here, lemme give you a new bag."

A paddy wagon tore past, behind Dortmunder's clenched shoulder blades, siren screaming. So did a second one. Meantime, the bodega guy reached under his fruit display and came out with a fresh new sandwich-size brown paper bag. "There's plastic people," he explained, "and there's paper people, and I can see you're a paper man."

"Right," Dortmunder said.

"So here you go," the guy said, and held the bag wide open for Dortmunder to transfer his lunch.

All he could hope was that no brooch made any sudden leap for freedom along the way. He opened the original bag, which in truth was a real mess by now, about to fall apart and very greasy and dirty, and he took the paper towel-wrapped sandwich out of it and put it in the fresh, crisp, sharp new paper bag, and the bodega guy gave it a quick twirl of the top to seal it and handed it over, saying, "You want a nice mango with that? Papaya? Tangelo?"

"No, thanks," Dortmunder said. "I would, but I break out."

"So many people tell me that," the bodega guy said, and shook his head at the intractability of fate. "Well," he said, cheering up, "have a nice day."

A paddy wagon went by, screaming. "I'll try to," Dortmunder promised, and walked away.

No more subways. One burning subway a day was all he felt up to, even if it did keep him from being gathered up in that sting operation and sent away to spend the rest of his life behind bars in some facility upstate where the food is almost as bad as your fellowman.

Dortmunder walked three blocks before he saw a cab; hang the expense, he hailed it: "You go to Manhattan?"

"Always been my dream," said the cabbie, who was maybe some sort of Arab, but not the kind with the turban. Or were they not Arabs? Anyway, this guy wasn't one of them.

"West 78th Street," Dortmunder said, and settled back to enjoy a smoke-free, fire-free, cop-free existence.

"Only thing," the Arab said, if he was an Arab. "No eating in the cab."

"I'm not eating," Dortmunder said.

"I'm only saying," the driver said, "on account of the sandwich."

"I won't eat it," Dortmunder promised him.

"Thank you."

They started, driving farther and farther from the neighborhood with all the paddy wagons, which was good, and Dortmunder said, "Cabbies eat in the cabs all the time."

"Not in the backseat," the driver said.

"Well, no."

"All's the space we can mess up is up here," the driver pointed out. "You eat back there, you spill a pickle, mustard, jelly, maybe a chocolate chip cookie, what happens my next customer's a lady in a nice mink coat?"

"I won't eat the sandwich," Dortmunder said, and there was no more conversation.

Dortmunder spent the time trying to figure out what the guy was, if he wasn't Arab. Russian, maybe, or Israeli, or possibly Pakistani. The name by the guy's picture on the dash was Mouli Mabik, and who knew what that was supposed to be? You couldn't even tell which was the first name.

Their route took them over the Brooklyn Bridge, which at the Manhattan end drops right next to City Hall and all the court buildings it would be better not to have to go into. The cab came down the curving ramp onto the city street and stopped at the traffic light among all the official buildings, and all at once there was a pair of plainclothes detectives right *there*, on the left, next to the cab, waving their shields in one hand and their guns in the other, both of them yelling, "You! Pull over! Right now!"

Oh, *damn* it, Dortmunder thought in sudden panic and terror, they *got* me!

The cab was jolting forward. It was not pulling over to the side, it was not obeying the plainclothesmen, it was not delivering Dortmunder into their clutches. The driver, hunched very low over his steering wheel, glared straight ahead out of his windshield and accelerated like a jet plane. Dortmunder stared; he's helping me escape!

Zoom, they angled to the right around two delivery trucks and a parked hearse, climbed the sidewalk, tore down it as the pedestrians leaped every which way to get clear, skirted a fire hydrant, caromed off a sightseeing bus, tore on down the street, made a screaming two-wheeled left into a street that happened to be one-way coming in this direction, and damn near managed to get between the oncoming garbage truck and the parked armored car. Close, but no cigar.

Dortmunder bounced into the bullet-proof clear plastic shield that takes up most of the legroom in the backseat of a New York City cab, then stayed there, hands, nose, lips and eyebrows pasted to the plastic as he looked through at this cabbie from Planet X, who, when finished ricocheting off his steering wheel, reached under his seat and came up with a shiny silver-and-black Glock machine pistol!

Yikes! There might not be much legroom back here, but Dortmunder found he could fit into it very well. He hit the deck, or the floor, shoulders and knees all meeting at his chin, and found himself wondering if that damn plastic actually was bulletproof after all.

Then he heard cracking and crashing sounds, like glass breaking, but when he stuck a quaking hand out, palm up, just beyond his quaking forehead, there were no bulletproof plastic pieces raining down. So what was being broken?

Unfolding himself from this position was much less easy, since he was much less motivated, but eventually he had his spine unpretzeled enough so he could peek through the bottom of the plastic shield just in time to watch the cabbie finish climbing through the windshield where he'd smashed out all the glass, and go rolling and scrambling over the hood to the street.

Dortmunder watched, and the guy got about four running steps down the street when his right leg just went out from under him and he cartwheeled in a spiral down to his right, flipping over like a surfer caught in the Big One, as the Glock went sailing straight up into the air, lazily turning, glinting in the light.

It was a weirdly beautiful scene, the Glock in the middle of the air. As it reached its apex, a uniformed cop stepped out from between two stopped vehicles, put his left hand out, and the Glock dropped into it like a trained parakeet. The cop grinned at the Glock, pleased with himself.

Now there were cops all over the place, just as in the recurrent nightmare Dortmunder had had for years, except none of these came floating down out of the sky. They gathered up the former cabbie, they directed traffic and they arranged for the garbage truck—which now had an interesting yellow speed stripe along its dark green side—to back up enough so they could open the right rear cab door and release the passenger.

Who knew he should not look reluctant to be rescued. It's OK if I seem shaky, he assured himself, and came out of the cab like a blender on steroids. "Th-thanks," he said, which he had never once said in that dream. "Th-thanks a lot."

"Man, you are lucky," one of the cops told him. "That is one of the major bombers and terrorists of all time. The *world* has been looking for that guy for years."

Dortmunder said, "And that's my luck? Today I hailed his cab?"

The cop asked, "Where'd you hail him?"

"In Brooklyn."

"And you brought him to Manhattan? That's great! We never would've found him in Brooklyn!"

All the cops were happy with Dortmunder for delivering this major league terrorist directly to the courthouse. They congratulated him and grinned at him and patted his shoulder and generally behaved in ways he was not used to from cops; it was disorienting.

Then one of them said, "Where were you headed?"

"West 78th Street."

A little discussion, and one of them said, "We'll go ahead and drive you the rest of the way."

In a police car? "No, no, that's OK," Dortmunder said.

"Least we can do," they said.

They insisted. When a cop insists, you go along. "OK, thanks," Dortmunder finally said.

"This way," a cop said.

They started down the street, now clogged with gawkers, and a cop behind Dortmunder yelled, "Hey!"

Oh, now what? Dortmunder turned, expecting the worst, and here came the cop, with the lunch bag in his hand. "You left this in the cab," he said.

"Oh," Dortmunder said. He was blinking a lot. "That's my lunch," he said. How could he have forgotten it?

"I figured," the cop said, and handed him the bag.

Dortmunder no longer trusted himself to speak. He nodded his thanks, turned away and shuffled after the cops who would drive him uptown.

Which they did. Fortunately, the conversation on the drive was all about the exploits of Kibam the terrorist—the name on the hack license was his own, backward—and not on the particulars of John Dortmunder.

Eventually they made the turn off Broadway onto 78th Street. Stoon lived in an apartment building in the middle of the block, so Dortmunder said, "Let me out anywhere along here."

"Sure," the cop driver said, and as he slowed Dortmunder looked out the window to see Stoon himself walking by, just as Stoon saw Dortmunder in the backseat of a slowing police car.

Stoon ran. Who wouldn't?

Knowing it was hopeless, but having to try, Dortmunder said, "Here's OK, this is fine, anywhere along here, this'd be good," while the cop driver just kept slowing and slowing, looking for a spot where there was a nice wide space between the parked cars, so his passenger would be able to get to the curb in comfort.

At last, stopped. Remembering his sandwich, knowing it was hopeless, unable to stop keeping on, Dortmunder said, "Thanks I appreciate it I really do this was terrific you guys have been—" until he managed to be outside and could slam the door.

But he couldn't run. Don't run away from a cop, it's worse than running away from a dog. He had to turn and walk, in stately fashion, rising on the balls of his feet, showing no urgency, no despair, not a care in the world, while the police car purred away down West 78th Street.

Broadway. Dortmunder turned the corner and looked up and down the street, and no Stoon. Of course not. Stoon would probably not come back to this neighborhood for a week. And the next time he saw Dortmunder, no matter what the circumstances, he'd run all over again, just on general principle.

Dortmunder sighed. There was nothing for it; he'd have to go see Arnie Albright.

Arnie Albright lived only eleven blocks away, on 89th between Broadway and West End. No more modes of transportation for today; Dortmunder didn't think his nerves could stand it. Holding tight to the lunch bag, he trekked up Broadway, and as he waited for the light to change at 79th Street a guy tapped him on the arm and said, "Excuse me. Is this your wallet?"

So here's the way it works. The scam artist has two identical wallets. The first one has a nice amount of cash in it, and ID giving a name and phone number. The scam artist approaches the mark, explains he just found this wallet on the sidewalk, and the two inspect it. They find a working pay phone—not always the easiest part of the scam—and call that phone number, and the "owner" answers and is overjoyed they found the wallet. If they wait right there, he'll come claim the wallet and give them a handsome reward (usually $100 to $500). The scam artist then explains he's late for an important appointment, and the mark should give him his half of the reward now ($50 to $250) and wait to collect from the owner. The mark hands over the money, the scam artist gives him the second wallet, the one with all the dollar-size pieces of newspaper in it, and the mark stands there on the corner awhile.

"Excuse me. Is this your wallet?"

Dortmunder looked at the wallet. "Yes," he said, plucked it out of the scam artist's hand, put it in his pocket and crossed 79th Street.

"Wait! Wait! Hey!"

On the north corner, the scam artist caught up and actually tugged at Dortmunder's sleeve. "Hey!" he said.

Dortmunder turned to look at him. "This is my wallet," he said. "You got a problem with that? You wanna call a cop? You want *me* to call a cop?"

The scam artist looked terribly, terribly hurt. He had beagle eyes. He looked as though he might cry. Dortmunder, a man with problems of his own, turned away and walked north to 89th Street and down the block to Arnie Albright's building, where he rang the bell in the vestibule.

"Now what?" snarled the intercom.

Dortmunder leaned close. He had never liked to say his own name out loud. "Dortmunder," he said.

"*Who?*"

"Cut it out, Arnie, you know who it is."

"Oh," the intercom yelled, "*Dortmunder!* Why didn't ya say so?"

The buzzer, a more pleasant sound than Arnie's voice, began its song, and Dortmunder pushed his way in and went up to Arnie's apartment, where Arnie, a skinny, wiry ferret in charity cast-off clothing, stood in the doorway. "Dortmunder," he announced, "you look as crappy as I do."

Which could not be accurate. Dortmunder was having an eventful day, but nothing could make him look as bad as Arnie Albright, even normally, and when Dortmunder got a little closer he saw Arnie was at the moment even worse than normal. "What happened to *you?*" he asked.

"Nobody knows," Arnie said. "The lab says nobody's ever seen this in the temperate zones before. I look like the inside of a pomegranate."

This was true. Arnie, never a handsome specimen, now seemed to be covered by tiny red Vesuviuses, all of them oozing thin red salsa. In his left hand he held a formerly white hand towel, now wet and red, with which he kept patting his face and neck and forearms.

"Geez, Arnie, that's terrible," Dortmunder said. "How long you gonna have it? What's the doctor say?"

"Don't get too close to me."

"Don't worry, I won't."

"No, I mean that's what the doctor says. Now, you know and I know that nobody can stand me, on accounta my personality."

"Aw, no, Arnie," Dortmunder lied, though everybody in the world knew it was true. Arnie's personality, not his newly erupting volcanoes, were what had made him the last resort on Dortmunder's list of fences.

"Aw, yeah," Arnie insisted. "I rub people the wrong way. I argue with them, I'm obnoxious, I'm a pain in the ass. You wanna make something of it?"

"Not me, Arnie."

"But a doctor," Arnie said, "isn't supposed to like or not like. He's got that hypocritic oath. He's supposed to lie and pretend he likes you, and he's real glad he studied so hard in medical school so he could take care of nobody but *you*. But, no. My doctor says, 'Would you mind staying in the waiting room and just shout to me your symptoms?' "

"Huh," Dortmunder said.

"But what the hell do you care?" Arnie demanded. "You don't give a shit about me."

"Well," Dortmunder said.

"So if you're here, you scored, am I right?"

"Sure."

"Sure," Arnie said. "Why else would an important guy like you come to a turd like me? And so I also gotta understand Stoon's back in the jug, am I right?"

"No, you're wrong, Arnie," Dortmunder said. "Stoon's out. In fact, I just saw him jogging."

"Then how come you come to me?"

"He was jogging away from me," Dortmunder said.

"Well, what the hell, come on in," Arnie said, and got out of the doorway.

"Well, Arnie," Dortmunder said, "maybe we could talk it over out here."

"What, you think the apartment's contagious?"

"I'm just happy out here, that's all."

Arnie sighed, which meant that Dortmunder got a whiff of his breath. Stepping back a pace, he told him, "I got something."

"Or why would you be here. Let's see it."

Dortmunder took the paper towel–wrapped package out of the paper bag and dropped the bag on the floor. He unwrapped the paper towels and tucked them under his arm.

Arnie said, "What, are you delivering for a deli now? I'll give you a buck and a half for it."

"Wait for it," Dortmunder advised. He dropped the top piece of Wonder Bread on the floor, along with much of the mayo and the top slab of ham. Using the paper towels, he lifted out the brooch, then dropped the rest of the sandwich on the floor and cleaned the brooch with the paper towels. Then he dropped the paper towels on the floor and held the brooch up so Arnie could see it, and said, "OK?"

"Oh, *you* got it," Arnie said. "I been seeing it on the news."

"In the *News*."

"On the news. The TV."

"Oh. Right."

"Let's have a look," Arnie said, and took a step forward.

Dortmunder took a step back. It had occurred to him that once Arnie had inspected this brooch, Dortmunder wouldn't be wanting it back. He said, "The newspaper says that it's worth $300,000."

"The newspaper says Dewey defeats Truman," Arnie said. "The newspaper says sunny, high in the 70s. The newspaper says informed sources report. The news—"

"OK, OK. But I just wanna be sure we're gonna come to an agreement here."

"Dortmunder," Arnie said, "you know me. Maybe you don't *want* to know me, but you know me. I give top dollar. I don't cheat, I am 100 percent reliable. I don't act like a normal guy and cheat and gouge, because if I did, nobody would ever come to see me at all. I have to be a saint, because I'm such a shit. Toss it over."

"OK," Dortmunder said, and tossed it over, and Arnie caught it in his revolting towel. Whatever he offers, I'll take, Dortmunder thought.

While Arnie studied the brooch, breathing on it, turning it, Dortmunder looked in his new wallet and saw it contained a little over $300 cash, plus the usual ID plus a lottery ticket. The faking of the numbers on the lottery ticket was pretty well done. So that would have been the juice in the scam.

"Well," Arnie said, "these diamonds are not diamonds. They're glass."

"Glass? You mean somebody conned the movie star?"

"I know that couldn't happen," Arnie agreed, "and yet it did. And this silver isn't silver, it's plate."

In his heart, Dortmunder had known it would be like this. All this effort, and zip. "And the green things?" he said.

Arnie looked at him in surprise. "They're emeralds," he said. "Don't you know what emeralds look like?"

"I thought I did," Dortmunder said. "So it's worth something, after all."

"Not the way it is," Arnie said. "Not with its picture all over the news. And not with the diamonds and silver being nothing but shit. Somebody's gotta pop the emeralds out, throw away the rest of it, sell the emeralds by themself."

"For what?"

"I figure they might go for 40 apiece," Arnie said. "But there's the cost of popping them."

"Arnie," Dortmunder said, "what are we talking here?"

Arnie said, "I could go seven. You wanna try around town, nobody else is gonna give you more than five, if they even want the hassle. You got a famous thing here."

Seven. He'd dreamed of 30, he would have been happy with 25. Seven. "I'll take it," Dortmunder said.

Arnie said, "But not today."

"Not today?"

"Look at me," Arnie said. "You want me to hand you something?"

"Well, no."

"I owe you seven," Arnie said. "If this shit I got don't kill me, I'll pay you when I can touch things. I'll phone you."

A promissory note—not even a note, nothing in writing—from a guy oozing salsa. "OK, Arnie," Dortmunder said. "Get well soon, you know?"

Arnie looked at his own forearms. "Maybe what it is," he said, "is my personality coming out. Maybe when it's over I'll be a completely different guy. Whaddya think?"

"Don't count on it," Dortmunder told him.

Well, at least he had the $300 from the wallet scam. And maybe Arnie would live; he certainly *seemed* too mean to die.

Heading back to Broadway, Dortmunder started the long walk downtown—no more things on wheels, not today—and at 86th Street he saw that a new edition of the *New York Post* was prominent on the newsstand on the corner. JER–FELICIA SPLIT was the front-page headline. That, apparently, in the *New York Post*'s estimation, was the most important North American news since the last time Donald Trump had it on or off with somebody or other.

What the hell; Dortmunder could splurge. He had $300 and a promise. He bought the paper, just to see what had happened to the formerly loving couple.

He had happened, essentially. The loss of the pin (brioche, brooch) had hit the lovers hard. "It's in diversity you really get to know another person," Felicia was reported as saying, with a sidebar in which a number of resident experts from NYU, Columbia and Fordham agreed, tentatively, that when Felicia had said diversity she had actually meant adversity.

"I remain married to my muse," Jer was quoted as announcing. "It's back to the studio to make another film for my public." No experts were felt to be needed to explicate that statement.

Summing it all up, the *Post* reporter finished his piece, "The double-emerald brooch may be worth $300,000, but no one seems to have found much happiness in it." I know what you mean, Dortmunder thought, and walked home.

Ed McBain

Barking at Butterflies

ED MCBAIN is a rarity in many respects. The 87th Precinct books now span five decades; they are worldwide best-sellers (something few suspense writers can claim); and they have the distinction of being the most imitated books of their time. And not just by other book writers, either. Movies and TV have feasted on the 87ths with chilling and unholy hunger, rarely paying for the privilege of stealing everything but the plumbing. McBain has even remarked sardonically on this thievery in several of his books. McBain is also Evan Hunter, of course, much lauded mainstream writer and powerful teller of urban tales in the realistic tradition of American literature. He is a master's master. "Barking at Butterflies" was first published in *Murder and Obsession*.

Barking at Butterflies

Ed McBain

Damn dog barked at everything. Sounds nobody else could hear, in the middle of the night the damn dog barked at them.

"He's protecting us," Carrie would say.

Protecting us. Damn dog weighs eight pounds soaking wet, he's what's called a Maltese poodle, he's protecting us. His name is Valletta, which is the capital of Malta. That's where the breed originated, I suppose. Some sissy Maltese nobleman must've decided he needed a yappy little lapdog that looked like a white feather duster. Little black nose. Black lips. Black button eyes. Shaggy little pip-squeak named Valletta. Who barked at everything from a fart to a butterfly. Is that someone ringing the bell? The damn dog would hurl himself at the door like a grizzly bear, yelping and growling and raising a fuss that could wake the dead in the entire county.

"He's just protecting us," Carrie would say.

Protecting us.

I hated that damn dog.

I still do.

He was Carrie's dog, you see. She rescued him from a husband-and-wife team who used to beat him when he was just a puppy—gee, I wonder why. This was two years before we got married. I used to think he was cute while she was training him. She'd say, "Sit, Valletta," and he'd walk away. She'd say, "Stay, Valletta," and he'd bark. She'd say, "Come, Valletta," and he'd take a nap. This went on for six months. He still isn't trained.

Carrie loved him to death.

As for El Mutto, the only thing on earth *he* loved was Carrie. Well, you save a person's life, he naturally feels indebted. But this went beyond mere gratitude. Whenever Carrie left the house, Valletta would lie down just inside the door, waiting for her to come home. Serve him a hot pastrami on rye, tell him, "Come, Valletta, time to eat," he'd look at me as if he'd been abandoned by the love of his life and never cared to breathe again. When he heard her car in the driveway, he'd start squealing and peeing on the rug. The minute she put her key in the lock, he jumped up in the air like a Chinese acrobat, danced and pranced on his hind legs when she opened the door, began squealing and leaping all around her until she knelt beside him and scooped him into her embrace and made comforting little sounds to him: "Yes, Valletta, yes, Mommy, what a good boy, oh, yes, what a beautiful little puppyboy."

I used to joke about cooking him.

"Maltese meatloaf is delicious," I used to tell Carrie. "We'll pluck him first, and then wash him real good, and stuff him and put him in the oven for what, an hour? Maybe forty-five minutes, the size of him. Serve him with roast potatoes and—"

"He understands every word you say," she'd tell me.

Damn dog would just cock his head and look up at me. Pretended to be bewildered, the canny little son of a bitch.

"Would you like to be a meatloaf?" I'd ask him.

He'd yawn.

"You'd better be a good dog or I'll sell you to a Filipino man."

"He understands you."

"You want to go home with a Filipino man?"

"Why do you talk to him that way?"

"In the Philippines they *eat* dogs, did you know that, Valletta? Dogs are a delicacy in the Philippines. You want to go home with a Filipino man?"

"You're hurting him."

"He'll turn you into a rack of Maltese chops, would you like that, Valletta?"

"You're hurting *me*, too."

"Or some breaded Maltese cutlets, what do you say, Valletta? You want to go to Manila?"

"Please don't, John. You know I love him."

Damn dog would rush into the bathroom after her, sit by the tub while she took her shower, lick the water from her toes while she dried herself. Damn dog would sit at her feet while she was peeing on the toilet. Damn dog would even sit beside the bed whenever we made love. I asked her once to please put him out in the hall.

"I feel as if there's a *pervert* here in the bedroom watching us," I said.

"He's not watching us."

"He's sitting there *staring* at us."

"No, he's not."

"Yes, he is. It embarrasses me, him staring at my privates that way."

"Your privates? When did you start using *that* expression?"

"Ever since he started staring at it."

"He's not staring at it."

"He is. In fact, he's *glaring* at it. He doesn't like me making love to you."

"Don't be silly, John. He's just a cute little puppydog."

One day, cute little puppydog began barking at *me*.

I came in the front door, and the stupid little animal was sitting smack in the middle of the entry, snarling and barking at me as if I were a person come to read the gas meter.

"What?" I said.

He kept barking.

"You're barking at *me*?" I said. "This is *my* house, I *live* here, you little shit, how *dare* you bark at me?"

"What is it, what is it?" Carrie yelled, rushing into the hallway.

"He's barking at me," I said.

"Shhh, Valletta," she said. "Don't bark at John."

He kept barking, the little well-trained bastard.

"How would you like to become a Maltese hamburger?" I asked him.

He kept barking.

I don't know when I decided to kill him.

Perhaps it was the night Carrie seated him at the dinner table with us. Until then, she'd been content to have him sitting at our feet like the despicable little beggar he was, studying every bite we took, waiting for scraps from the table.

"Go ahead," I'd say, "watch every morsel we put in our mouths. You're *not* getting fed from the table."

"Oh, John," Carrie would say.

"I can't enjoy my meal with him staring at me that way."

"He's not staring at you."

"What do you call what he's doing right this minute? Look at him! If that isn't staring, what is it?"

"I think you're obsessed with this idea of the dog staring at you."

"Maybe because he *is* staring at me."

"If he is, it's because he loves you."

"He doesn't love me, Carrie."

"Yes, he does."

"He loves *you*."

"He loves you, too, John."

"No, just you. In fact, if you want to talk about obsession, *that's* obsession. What that damn mutt feels for you is *obsession*."

"He's not a mutt, and he's not obsessed. He just wants to be part of the family. He sees us eating, he wants to join us. Come, Valletta, come sweet puppyboy, come little Mommy, come sit with your family," she said, and hoisted him off the floor and plunked him down on a chair between us.

"I'll get your dish, sweet babypup," she said.

"Carrie," I said, "I will not have that mutt sitting at the table with us."

"He's not a mutt," she said. "He's purebred."

"Valletta," I said, "get the hell off that chair or I'll—"

He began barking.

"You mustn't raise your hand to him," Carrie said. "He was abused. He thinks you're about to hit him."

"*Hit* him?" I said. "I'm about to *kill* him!"

The dog kept barking.

And barking.

And barking.

I guess that's when I decided to do it.

October is a good time for dying.

"Come, Valletta," I said, "let's go for a walk."

He heard me say "Come," so naturally he decided to go watch television.

"Is Daddy taking you for a walk?" Carrie asked.

Daddy.

Daddy had Mr. Smith and Mr. Wesson in the pocket of his bush jacket. Daddy was going to walk little pisspot here into the woods far from the house and put a few bullets in his head and then sell his carcass to a passing Filipino man or toss it to a wayward coyote or drop it in the river. Daddy was going to tell Carrie that her prized purebred mutt had run away, naturally, when I commanded him to come. I called and called, I would tell her, but he ran and ran, and God knows where he is now.

"Don't forget his leash," Carrie called from the kitchen.

"I won't, darling."

"Be careful," she said. "Don't step on any snakes."

"Valletta will protect me," I said, and off we went.

The leaves were in full voice, brassy overhead, rasping underfoot. Valletta kept backing off on the red leather leash, stubbornly planting himself every ten feet or so into the woods, trying to turn back to the house where his beloved mistress awaited his return. I kept assuring him that we were safe here under the trees, leaves dropping gently everywhere around us. "Come, little babypup," I cooed, "come little woofikins, there's nothing can hurt you here in the woods."

The air was as crisp as a cleric's collar.

When we had come a far-enough distance from the house, I reached into my pocket and took out the gun. "See this, Valletta?" I said. "I am going to shoot you with this. You are never going to bark again, Valletta. You are going to be the most silent dog on earth. Do you understand, Valletta?"

He began barking.

"Quiet," I said.

He would not stop barking.

"Damn you!" I shouted. "Shut up!"

And suddenly he yanked the leash from my hands and darted away like the sneaky little sissydog he was, all white and furry against the orange and yellow and brown of the forest floor, racing like a ragged whisper through the carpet of leaves, trailing the red leash behind him like a narrow trickle of blood. I came thrashing after him. I was no more than six feet behind him when he ran into a clearing saturated with golden light. I followed him with the gun hand, aiming at him. Just as my finger tightened on the trigger, Carrie burst into the clearing from the opposite end.

"No!" she shouted, and dropped to her knees to scoop him protectively into her arms, the explosion shattering the incessant whisper of the leaves, the dog leaping into her embrace, blood flowering on her chest, oh dear God, no, I thought, oh dear sweet Jesus, no, and dropped the gun and ran to her and pressed her bleeding and still against me while the damn dumb dog barked and barked.

He has not barked since.

For him, it must seem as if she's gone someplace very far away, somewhere never even remotely perceived in his tiny Maltese mentality. In a sense this is true. In fact, I have repeated the story so often to so many people that I've come to believe it myself. I told her family and mine, I told all our friends, I even told the police, whom her brother was suspicious and vile enough to call, that I came home from work one day and she was simply gone. Not a hint that she was leaving. Not even a note. All she'd left behind was the dog. And she hadn't even bothered to feed him before her departure.

Valletta often wanders into the woods looking for her.

He circles the spot where two autumns ago her blood seeped into the earth. The area is bursting with fresh spring growth now, but he circles and sniffs the bright green shoots, searching, searching. He will never find her, of course. She is wrapped in a tarpaulin and buried deep in the woods some fifty miles north of where the three of us once lived together, Carrie and I and the dog.

There are only the two of us now.

He is all I have left to remind me of her.

He never barks and I never speak to him.

He eats when I feed him, but then he walks away from his bowl without once looking at me and falls to the floor just inside the entrance door, waiting for her return.

I can't honestly say I like him any better now that he's stopped barking. But sometimes . . .

Sometimes when he cocks his head in bewilderment to observe a floating butterfly, he looks so cute I could eat him alive.

Joyce Carol Oates

The Dark Prince

Long ago somebody dictated that literary fiction and popular fiction were mutually exclusive in every respect. If you were a serious writer and you wrote crime fiction, you usually did so under a pen name. That's changing. Though JOYCE CAROL OATES does employ a pen name (Rosamond Smith), she also publishes a wide variety of crime fiction under the Oates byline as well. Oates is one of the most lacerating, intelligent writers of her generation, and finds in everyday life the stuff of true literature. She is also a master of form. She's invented a number of new ways to structure and write fiction. For all her fame as a literary novelist, she's never quite gotten her due as a crime fiction writer, but with every story she writes, including the following one, that is changing for the better. It was first published in *Ellery Queen's Mystery Magazine,* November issue.

The Dark Prince

Joyce Carol Oates

The power of the actor is his embodiment of the fear of ghosts.
(FROM *The Actor's Handbook* AND *The Actor's Life*)

I guess I never believed that I deserved to live.
The way other people do. I needed to justify
my life every hour. I needed your permission.

It was a season of no weather. Too early in the summer for the Santa Ana winds, yet the harsh dry air blown from the desert tasted of sand and fire. Through closed eyelids you could see flames dancing. In sleep you could hear the scuttling of rats driven out of Los Angeles by the crazed, continuous construction. In the canyons north of the city the plaintive cries of coyotes. There had been no rain for weeks, yet day followed day overcast with a pale glaring light like the inside of a blind eye. Tonight above El Cayon Drive the sky cleared briefly revealing a sickle moon of the moist-reddish hue of a living membrane. *I don't want anything from you, I swear! Only just to say—You should know me, I think. Your daughter.*

That night in early June the blond girl was sitting in a borrowed Jaguar at the side of El Cayon Drive, waiting. She was alone and she appeared to be neither smoking nor drinking. Nor was she listening to a car radio. The Jaguar was parked near the top of the narrow graveled road where there was a fortresslike property, vaguely Oriental in design, surrounded by a ten-foot cobblestone wall and protected by a wrought-iron gate. There was even a small gatehouse but no one was on duty inside. On lower ground, spotlights flooded properties and sounds of laughter and voices lifted like music through the warm night, but this property, at the summit of El Cayon, was mostly darkened. Around the high wall there were no palm trees, only Italian cypresses, twisted by the wind into bizarre sculpted shapes. *I don't have any proof. I don't need any proof. Paternity is a matter of the soul. I wanted just to see your face, Father.*

A name had been given the blond girl. Tossed at her as carelessly as a coin tossed at a beggar's outstretched hands. Eager as any beggar, and unquestioning, she'd snatched at it. A name! His name! A man who'd possibly been her mother's lover in 1925.

Possibly?—probably.

Amid the debris of the past she'd been scavenging. As a beggar too might scavenge trash, even garbage, in search of treasure.

Earlier that night at a poolside party in Bel-Air she'd asked please could she borrow a car?—and several of the men had vied with one another offering her their keys and she was barefoot running, and gone. If the Jaguar was missing for too many hours the "borrowing" would be reported to the Beverly Hills police, but that wasn't going to happen for the blond girl wasn't drunk and she wasn't on drugs and her desperation was shrewdly disguised. *Why, I don't know why, maybe just to shake hands, hello and good-bye if you want it that way. I have my own life of course. I won't be losing anything I'd actually had.*

The blond girl in the Jaguar might have remained there waiting through the night except a private security guard in an unmarked car drove up El Cayon to investigate. Someone in the near-darkened mansion at the top of the hill must have reported her. The cop wore a dark uniform and carried a flashlight which he shone rudely into the girl's face. It was a movie scene! Yet no music beneath to cue if you should feel anxiety, suspense, humor. The cop's lines were delivered flatly so you had no cue from him, either. "Miss? What business do you have here? This is a private road." The girl blinked rapidly as if blinking back tears (but she had no tears left) and whispered, "None. I'm sorry, Officer." Her politeness and childlike manner disarmed the cop immediately. And he'd seen her face. *That face! I knew she'd got to be somebody, someday. But who?* He said, faltering, scratching at the underside of his slightly stubby jaw, "Well. Better turn around and go home, miss. If you don't live up here. These are kind of special folks live up here. You're too young for . . ." His voice broke off though he'd finished about all he had to say to her.

The blond girl said, starting her borrowed car, "No, I'm not. Young."

It was the eve of her twenty-third birthday.

In her purse, the .38-caliber Smith & Wesson she figured now, maybe she'd never use.

Dick Lochte

Rappin' Dog

DICK LOCHTE is the creator of private detective Leo Bloodworth and his precocious teenage assistant Serendipity Dalhquist, who have appeared in two novels, *Sleeping Dog* and *Laughing Dog*. The two novels are excellent studies of modern-day Los Angeles as seen through the eyes of the older Leo and the younger Serendipity. His other series is darkly toned and set in New Orleans, where detective Terry Manion investigates a crime involving his own family in *Blue Bayou* and *The Neon Smile*. Lochte has also proved himself adept at writing the legal thriller, partnering with Christopher Darden on *The Trials of Nikki Hill*. He has been a promotional copywriter for *Playboy* magazine, a film critic for the *Los Angeles Free Press,* and is book columnist for the *Los Angeles Times*. He lives in Santa Monica, California. Whatever he turns to next in his career, there is no doubt that it will be innovative, stylish, and engaging. "Rappin' Dog" first appeared in the anthology *Murder on Route 66.*

Rappin' Dog

Dick Lochte

Go to school,
And play the fool,
You get no help in the cruel world.
Play it smart, get a fast start,
There's an art
To livin' large in the cool world.

The words of rapper B. A. "Big Apple" Dawg reverberated through the unmarked police van. I turned to Mr. Leo Bloodworth, the renowned private investigator, who was sitting next to me and said, "You're playing the fool when you go to school? That's the dumbest advice I've ever heard. The man's a cretin."

"You're preaching to the already converted, Sara," he said, using his own clever diminution of my given name, Serendipity.

The three LAPD detectives in the van, members of an elite team known as the Star Squad, were busy with their surveillance. The leader, a Detective Gundersen, asked, "You getting a good level, Mumms?"

"Just like stereo," Officer Mumms replied. She was a very cool black woman, seated at a table that had been bolted to the floor of the van, studying the various indicators on a tape recorder secured to the table.

"Wire's workin' fine," Detective Gundersen said to our driver. "Give Doggie Boy a honk."

The driver, Detective Lucas, tapped the van's horn twice. He was a rather handsome man with more than a passing resemblance to Mr. John Kennedy, Jr., except that his dark hair wasn't as curly. Detective Gundersen's hair was straight, too, but gray and lay flat on his head like the hair of legendary singer Mr. Frank Sinatra. My grandmother, who is an actress and should know, says Mr. Sinatra's hair wasn't totally his own. Maybe Detective Gundersen's isn't either, but I'd like to think that the Los Angeles Police Department would insist that their officers eschew such nonessential cosmetic touches.

The horn was a code Detective Gundersen had set up with Mr. B. A. Dawg, who was driving a peach-colored Rolls Royce maybe two car-lengths ahead of us on Sunset. It informed him that the transmission was working well and he could stop testing it with his dreadful singsong.

But he didn't stop.

> *Show some sense,*
> *Keep Mr. Pig on the de-fense.*
> *He comes aroun', puts you down,*
> *Expects to find you shiverin' and shakin'.*
> *Take the pledge, use an edge, cut that mutha oinker up into bacon.*

"What the heck's he saying, Mumms?" Gundersen asked.

"You don't wanna know, Herm," Officer Mumms called to him. She smiled at me. "How old are you?"

"Fourteen and a half," I replied truthfully.

"And you don't like rap?"

"Vachel Lindsay is about as far as I go," I said.

"Never heard of her," Officer Mumms said. "But I dig the Dawg man. I hope we can catch the guy messing with him."

Mr. Dawg moved on to another of his ditties, one exploring his total lack of respect for womankind. "He's giving a concert at the Shrine tomorrow night," Officer Mumms said.

"I know," I said.

She leaned toward me and, in a voice loud enough for Mr. Bloodworth to hear, asked, "Your boss like rap?"

Mr. Bloodworth isn't my boss, exactly. Though officially categorized as a "high school student," I am sort of his apprentice, spending my afternoons and some school holidays at his detective agency, mainly observing the art of criminology. I also do a little filing and billing, which I was in the middle of the day before, alone in the office, when the call came in from Ms. Lulu Diamond, Mr. Dawg's manager. If Mr. Bloodworth had been there, he probably would have turned down the job. But he wasn't and so he and I were in the van, sharing an adventure with the members of the Star Squad.

"Does Mr. B. like rap? No," I told Officer Mumms, "rap really isn't his thing. His idea of popular music is 'Moon River.'"

He glared at me with those odd yellow-brown hawk's eyes. "Careful, sis," he said. "You're talking about the late, great Johnny Mercer."

> *Cops, they got the wrong approach,*
> *Like the cockroach,*
> *Crawl around in the dirt,*
> *Gonna meet up with a hero, burn 'em up like Nero, and make 'em face*
> *the big hurt.*

"Jeeze," Detective Gundersen said. "If he don't change the tune, I may wind up killing him, myself."

Mr. Bloodworth sighed.

· · ·

As I said, the big, rawboned sleuth hadn't wanted to get involved with Mr. Dawg at all. But I'd explained to him that because of his recent illness—he'd been felled by a strain of the Outback flu—the month had been a gloomy one, financially speaking. And there was no sign on the horizon of any other ship coming in.

On arriving at Mr. Dawg's suite at the Beverly-Rodeo Hotel, I must admit a certain trepidation on my part, too. The place was filled with an assortment of unpleasant people—loud and arrogant men in expensive baggy gym clothes and silver jewelry, caught up in some football epic on TV and totally ignoring their ladyfriends who, I am sorry to report, were no less anti-social. Nor better dressed.

"Rock and roll trash," Mr. B. muttered to me, and though he was several generations off, his point was well made.

A little pink-cheeked, bespectacled matron in her fifties, her around body covered by a loud Hawaiian muumuu, navigated the crowd gracefully to greet us. "I'm Lulu Diamond," she told us, using a chubby finger to point to the glittering stones embedded in her eyeglass frames.

We exchanged introductions and she asked, "What can I getcha, kid? These bums B. A. calls his friends have cleaned out the portable bar, but I can order up room service."

"I'm fine," I told her.

"You, honey?" she asked Mr. B.

"I'm okay, too," he said, scanning the scene. "I don't see your client."

"He's, uh," she pointed to me and winked, "spending quality time with the missus in the bedroom."

The big detective winced. "Yeah, well, Ms. Diamond—"

"Make it Lulu, big guy."

"Lulu, you think you could pry him loose? We ought to get moving on this, assuming that we're dealing with a real situation."

Lulu frowned and suddenly didn't look so matronly. "B. A. Dawg, with three platinum CDs and the new one going gold after just two weeks, does not have to resort to fake death threats to make headlines."

"I hope not," Mr. Bloodworth said. "Because then we'd be wasting our time."

"I'll go get him," she said.

"There seems to be a lot of violence in the record business," I said, mainly to distract him from the ball game on TV.

"Yeah," he said absently, eyes glazing at the sight of pigskin. "Gangs. Drugs. Good old-fashioned business rivalry. I don't think we're dealing with that here. In fact, I don't know what we're dealing with here."

According to Lulu, Mr. Dawg had received one of those scary notes made up of pasted letters announcing that an organization called the Rap

Tribunal had found him guilty of plagiarism. In his ultimate wisdom, he assumed the sender to be a crank, though he should have realized that anyone who went to all the trouble of clipping and pasting that sort of note surely would not go quietly away.

He'd no sooner disposed of the note when the Tribunal gentleman was on the phone, his voice electronically altered, offering Mr. Dawg a choice. He could donate a portion of the profits from his most popular CD, "Smack Attack," to the poor street people from whom he stole most of his lyrics. Or he could die. The amount requested was $250,000 in $100 bills, to be placed in one of those aluminum suitcases.

He had twenty-four hours to get the money and stand by for further instructions. But if he went to the police, he might as well put a gun to his own head.

That's when Lulu dialed the Bloodworth Agency.

Mr. Bloodworth was falling under the spell of the ball game when I spied Lulu waving to us from an open doorway. "We're being summoned," I said.

Mr. Dawg, a man of thirty or so, was sitting on a rumpled bed. He was wearing leather pants the color of brown mustard. No shoes. No shirt. He was long and thin and very black. His hair was dyed a bright orange. And there were enough pieces of metal embedded in his ears and nose to keep him off of planes for the rest of his life.

"You the fake fuzz?" he asked Mr. Bloodworth.

The sleuth allowed he was.

"Blood-worth. I like that. This your ladyfriend?" Mr. Dawg asked, looking at me.

"Thirty-five years too late for that," Mr. B. said.

"She don't look so young," Mr. Dawg said. "Nasty's only twenty. And she been Mrs. Dawg for two years."

His reference was to the woman seated at the dresser combing her hair. She was nearly as tall as he, and as thin. But there was a languid quality to her, as if she weren't fully awake. I imagine it must have had quite an effect on simpleminded men. She said, "I keep telling you, my name's Nastasia. And it seems like I been with you an eternity, bro."

Mr. Dawg shrugged. "So, you gonna keep me in one piece, Blood-worth?"

"I'll be honest with you, B. A. No one person can guarantee to do that."

"See," Nastasia said. "Told you, Dawgman. Get those cops from last year."

Mr. Bloodworth raised his eyebrows. "What cops would that be?"

"During the tour last year," Lulu said, "we had another little problem when we hit L.A. One of the former members of the Dawg Posse, that's B. A.'s backup, went a little whacko and made some threats. So we called the cops and they sent us these detectives who specialize in dealing with celebrities."

"The Star Squad," Mr. B. said.

"Yeah. That's them," Nastasia said. "Headed up by this old guy and some young dude."

"Young dude was a little too fresh, you ask me," B. A. said.

"You just a crazy man," Nastasia said. "We oughta get those guys back. They didn't take more than a day to pick Walter up and toss his butt into jail."

"It's the way to go," Mr. Bloodworth said. "If you want me to duplicate the level of protection the cops can give you, I'll have to put on a bunch of other operatives. Could cost you as much as ten grand a day."

"That's no good," B. A. Dawg said. "But the man on the phone said no cops."

"They always say that. Cops know how to handle it."

Mr. Dawg snapped his fingers at Lulu and the two of them walked out onto the balcony to discuss the situation.

Nastasia looked me up and down. "What are you playin' at, girl?"

"Beg pardon?"

"What are you doing here?"

"I work with Mr. Bloodworth," I said.

"Yeah? Well, Mr. Blood, here, fits the private eye image, but you, I'd take you for some kinda Spice Girl wannabe."

"Then you'd be making a mistake," I said.

Mr. Dawg and his manager re-entered the room. He snapped his fingers at Mr. Bloodworth. "Cops are in. But I want you to handle it."

"How's that?" Mr. B. asked.

"The cops. I don't like 'em. So I'm payin' you to deal with 'em. Work everything out with them and then tell me."

"Mr. Dawg," I asked, "could it be your former employee, Walter, trying to get your attention again?"

He shrugged. "Walter's crazy enough to do it, I guess."

"Maybe the cops still have a line on him," Mr. Bloodworth said.

"C'mon, tall, blond and rugged," Lulu said to Mr. Bloodworth. "Let's go talk money."

Later, when he and I were driving downtown to Parker Center where the Star Squad offices are located, Mr. Bloodworth said, "Herm Gundersen and I go back a ways. This should be a snap; we'll just let him do all the work."

In point of fact, he and Detective Gundersen had gone through the police academy together. So there was none of the antagonism a private detective sometimes encounters when dealing with lawmen.

"The Dawgman again, huh?" Detective Gundersen said. "Hear that, Lucas?"

Detective Lucas looked up from his desk four feet away. "Who's he pissed off this time?"

"Maybe the same guy you arrested last year," Mr. B. suggested.

The handsome young detective picked up the phone and quickly ascertained that Walter Lipton, the recalcitrant ex-employee, had been released from prison only three weeks before.

"Talk about your likely suspects," Detective Gundersen said. "Well, we'll take over from here, Leo."

"That'd be fine with me, Herm, but Dawg said he'd like us to stick around."

Detective Gundersen hesitated, then smiled. "Sure, buddy. You and the kid are welcome to observe a crack team in action. Lucas, slap on that charming smile of yours and let's show 'em how we handle international celebrities in this man's town."

So we'd "observed" them shooing away the freeloaders at the hotel, setting up the phone taps, arranging for counterfeit bills to be placed in an aluminum suitcase along with a tracking device, and being generally obsequious in the presence of Mr. Dawg, his skinny sullen wife, and Lulu.

To give the Star Squad their due, when the representative of the Rap Tribunal finally called, they certainly leapt into action. Unfortunately, the call had been made on a cellular phone and was therefore untraceable. But at least we had a tape of the conversation and didn't have to rely on Mr. Dawg's rather short attention span.

The gentleman from the Rap Tribunal informed Mr. Dawg that he had thirty minutes to get into his Rolls Royce with the suitcase and drive to a public telephone at an address on Sunset Boulevard. Further instructions would be forthcoming.

So there we were, tagging along, being regaled by the so-called rapmaster's poetic but addled view of life. Suddenly, he stopped mid-rhyme to declare, "Mus' be the place."

He pulled to the curb at a bus stop in front of a sidewalk shop called Café Coffee and got out of the Rolls. The pay phone was just at the edge of the café's patio which was filled with folks satisfying their caffeine fix alfresco.

There were no other spaces, legal or illegal, for the van, so Detective Lucas drove about a quarter of a block past the Rolls and double-parked. Up ahead was an unmarked sedan, stopped in a similar position. Its occupants were four other members of the Star Squad. They were a bit too far away to keep Mr. Dawg in view, but we could see him, resplendent in his powder blue leather jumpsuit, standing at the phone.

"Would you look at the hot babes at that coffee place?" Detective Lucas said. "Damn, I love L.A."

"Keep your roving eye on the Dawgman, huh?" his boss asked.

Thanks to the transmitter taped to Mr. Dawg's chest, we could hear sidewalk noises, the whistle of the wind and, eventually, a ringing phone. "Yeah, it's me," we heard him say. We could not hear the caller at all.

"Hold on," Mr. Dawg said. He reached under the ledge of the booth and removed a small object that had been taped there. "Got it." It was a cellular phone.

Detective Lucas said, "Check out that babe and the guy sitting at the second table over from B. A."

A young African-American couple seemed very interested in Mr. Dawg. In any other city in the free world, it would not seem unusual for people to be gawking at a blond African-American recording star wearing powder blue leather, tearing something from beneath a pay telephone ledge. But this was Hollywood. And none of the other patrons of Café Coffee was giving him a second's notice.

As he hopped back into his Rolls, the couple stood up from their table. The man tossed a few bills down and they both ran for their car.

"What now, Herm?" Detective Lucas asked.

"Wait and watch, lover boy."

Mr. Dawg pulled out into traffic. From our speakers, his voice blared, "Man said he'll call me on the phone, tell me where to go."

The couple got into a little red BMW. When they passed us, heading after Mr. Dawg, Detective Gundersen yelled, "Let's roll."

"I take it neither of those people are the guy who gave Dawg trouble last year," Mr. Bloodworth said.

"Lipton? Naw," Detective Gundersen said. "He's probably manning the phone."

"That's a heck of a bright red car they're using to collect loot," Mr. Bloodworth observed.

"Amateurs," Detective Gundersen sneered. "Mumms, run a check on that license, if you please."

It was blissfully quiet in the Rolls. Mr. Dawg evidently was too caught up in the moment to be thinking about rapping. But Detective Lucas took up the musical slack, humming nervously, oblivious to the scowls being sent his way by his boss.

Mr. Bloodworth picked up on the detective's melody. We listened to their duet for a few minutes, until Detective Gundersen growled, "Could we can the concert?"

Mr. Bloodworth looked at me and shook his head sadly. "You don't like that, you don't like good music," he muttered.

"Another of your Johnny Mercer songs?" I asked.

"Close. Bobby Troup. 'Route 66.'"

He started to recite the lyrics, which sounded to my ears almost like rap, except they were much more whimsical (rhyming "Arizona" with "Winona," for example). The ringing of Mr. Dawg's cellular interrupted him.

We heard the rapper say, "Okay. Make the next turn and head back to the ocean."

The unmarked sedan in the lead must've gotten the message because we saw it head into the left lane just in front of the Rolls. The red Beamer was directly behind Mr. Dawg. We were several cars behind it. "How you doin' on that license check, Mumms?"

"We'll get it when we get it, Herm," she said.

Our little caravan made the turn and continued west on Sunset for about a mile when the cellular rang again. "Okay," Mr. Dawg said, "I turn down Doheny to Santa Monica Boulevard and keep going to the ocean." He was silent for a beat, then added, "Sure, I got the cash. I'm cooperatin'. No, sir, no cops nohow."

Officer Mumms emitted a little chuckle. "Isn't he somethin'?" she asked.

We moved along Santa Monica Boulevard, past the Century City shopping center and on under the San Diego Freeway. Past old movie houses, rows and rows of small businesses, restaurants.

The temperature dropped several degrees when we moved through the seacoast town of Santa Monica. I was starting to smell ocean salt in the air when the phone rang again.

"Right," Mr. Dawg said. "I turn right on Ocean, take the incline to the Coast Highway and keep goin' 'til I see the sign for Topanga Canyon. Then head up the Canyon. Why we going to all this trouble? Lemme jus' give you the damn money. I got me a concert tonight. I . . . Damn, he hung up on me."

Detective Gundersen scowled. "It would've been simpler to have us just stay on Sunset. Why the circle route?"

"Must be making sure the rapman is all by his lonesome," Detective Lucas said.

"Mumms, tell Maclin to press the pedal and go on up Topanga and wait." Detective Maclin was in the lead car. "Lucas, you'd better pull back as far as you can. We don't want to spook those folks in the red car. And, Mumms, can't we find out who the hell they are?"

"Searches take time," Officer Mumms said.

The couple in the red car didn't seem to care if we spooked them or not. They remained on Mr. Dawg's tail up into the Canyon.

My grandmother loves to tell horror stories about gruesome crimes that took place in Topanga back in the 1960s way before I was born, during that odd historic time of social unrest. As we drove through, it didn't look dangerous at all. Just another moderately populated rustic canyon.

Mr. Dawg's phone rang again. This time the instruction was to turn off into Calico Canyon.

Unfortunately, the instruction came too late for the lead car. The Rolls made the turn, followed by the red Beamer. Then, after a considerable distance, us. Detective Maclin and his men were now last in line as we climbed along a small road through the relatively uninhabited, tree-shaded canyon.

Higher and higher we went along the twisting macadam, barely keeping the little red car in sight and not seeing the Rolls at all.

The cellular rang and Mr. Dawg said, rather waspishly. "Okay. I'm stop-pin'. And I'm tossin' the suitcase . . . Now what? . . . You sure I can get out of here goin' up? . . . Okay, you the man."

We rounded a curve and saw the Rolls pulling away.

But the red Beamer had stopped. The male, who'd been driving, got out and was at the side of the road, bending down to pick up the suitcase.

"It's a go-go-go," Detective Gundersen yelled.

"Book'em, Dano," Officer Mumms ordered Detective Maclin.

She, Mr. Bloodworth and I remained in the van. We watched as the six plainclothes policemen ran to the man holding the suitcase. The woman threw open her car door and got out, rushing to her companion.

"LAPD," Detective Gundersen growled. "Drop the money, boy."

"Boy?" the young man shouted back. "Who the hell . . . ?"

Then he made a big mistake. He threw the suitcase at the detective.

Suddenly the other three were on him, pounding him with their fists.

"Jee-zus," Officer Mumms said.

"This is bad news," Mr. Bloodworth said, getting out of the van. "Stay here, Sara."

As he ran toward the melee, Officer Mumms's radio began to squawk and a static-y voice informed us that, according to its plates, the red BMW was licensed to a Mr. and Mrs. Joseph Laurence of Mill Valley.

"Where you goin' girl?" Officer Mumms asked me. "Your boss said stay."

"I took no vow of obedience to him," I told her.

Mr. Bloodworth had pulled one of the detectives off of the young man. And was getting a fist to the side of his head for his trouble.

Screaming at them, the young woman kicked another detective in the shin and received an elbow in the chest that sent her to the ground.

I ran to their car, looked in. Then I quickly opened the driver's door and kept pressing the horn until I had everybody's attention.

"They're tourists," I shouted.

"Huh?" Detective Gundersen said.

"Tourists. From Mill Valley. They've got luggage in the back of their car and highway maps in the front. Look," I held up a pair of Mickey Mouse ears. "They've been to Disneyland."

Officer Mumms had left the van, too. She moved to Mrs. Laurence and was helping her from the ground.

The young man pulled away from Detective Lucas's grip, wiped his bloody nose on his shirt and staggered to his wife.

"You all right, baby?"

"Jus' got the wind knocked out of her," Officer Mumms said.

Mrs. Laurence nodded in agreement.

"You bastards are crazy," Joseph Laurence of Mill Valley said to all of them. "I'm gonna sue your ass off."

"Yeah?" Detective Gundersen said. "First you're gonna have to explain to us crazy bastards what the hell you *tourists* are doing out here with that metal suitcase?"

The young man lost just an inch of attitude. "My wife and I are having a cup of coffee wondering how to spend our last afternoon in L.A. when there's B. A. Dawg, himself, right there on the street. The rappin' rapmaster. So I figure, let's check out what the Dawgman's up to."

"That brings us to the suitcase."

"We're behind the man, see him toss something from his Rolls. I tell my wife, hell, B. A. Dawg may not want whatever that is, but for the rest of us, it's a solid gold souvenir."

Detective Gundersen looked dubious, but he said, "We'll check out your story."

"Check out my story? You sure as hell will. Right after I sue you and everybody else for beating on me and my wife."

The detective shifted his gaze from the battered Laurences and scanned the area. I wondered if he might be checking for a video camera. In a flat voice, he said, "We're pretty sensitive to stalking out here, pal. Got all kind of laws against it. So I'm giving you two choices—you can let us fix up your scrapes and bruises while we're checking out your story. Or you can keep mouthin' off about lawsuits and we'll throw you and the little lady into the tank for stalking and harassing Mr. Dawg."

I hit the horn again.

Everybody looked my way. Detective Gundersen seemed particularly peeved. "What now?" he shouted.

"Speaking of Mr. Dawg, aren't we forgetting something?"

In an absolutely horrific piece of bad timing, from the distance came the unmistakable sound of a gunshot.

Shouting orders for the others to stay with the Laurences, Detective Gundersen ran back to the van, followed by Detective Lucas. And me and Mr. Bloodworth.

Detective Lucas eased around the red BMW, slightly scraping the side of the van on the canyon wall before zooming up the road.

Half a mile or so later, we came upon the Rolls sitting still, its engine purring. I started to open the van door, but Mr. Bloodworth grabbed my arm. The two policemen had their pistols drawn and were searching the area through the van's windows.

Eventually, Detective Gundersen said, "The rest of you stay here."

He slipped from the van and, head moving from side to side like a radarscope, he approached the Rolls. He stopped, turned and stared up the canyon wall, then put his pistol back into its holster. He opened the Rolls's passenger door and bent into the vehicle. A few seconds later, the pale exhaust clouds ceased. Detective Gundersen backed out of the car and, looking at Detective Lucas, made a gun with his thumb and forefinger and pantomimed shooting himself in the temple.

.   .   .

Mr. Bloodworth felt it was his duty to notify the widow Dawg.

But by the time we got to the suite at the Beverly-Rodeo Hotel, the news had already broken. The widow was in black—a lacy, sort of see-through outfit, but definitely black—holding a hankie to her red-rimmed eyes.

She thanked Mr. Bloodworth for doing his best to save her husband's life. Lulu Diamond wasn't quite so forgiving. "I hope you don't expect to get paid for letting poor B. A. take one in the head," she said. "You're lucky I don't sue. Maybe I will."

"You do what you want," he told her. He was feeling very low about the way things turned out.

As we started for the door, Mrs. Dawg called out, "Hey, Mr. Blood, don't listen to her. I'm grateful you did what you could for my husband. You'll get your money. It wasn't your fault the police panicked Walter into shooting B. A."

"It was his fault the bungling cops came into it," Lulu grumbled.

"No. That was my suggestion, Lulu," Mrs. Dawg said. "My fault."

"But when somebody doesn't deliver—"

"Pay the man, Lulu."

"Look, it's my opinion—"

"But it's my money."

Grumbling, Lulu Diamond went to the desk, opened a checkbook and began scribbling on it.

The phone rang and Mrs. Dawg said, "Could you get that, Mr. Blood? I'm not up to phone talk."

Mr. Bloodworth, looking even more uncomfortable than usual, lifted the receiver. "This is, ah, the Dawg suite . . . oh, hi, Herm."

The big detective listened a bit, then his face registered surprise. "Damn. That was fast . . . No kidding. Yeah, I'll tell her. Thanks."

He placed the phone back on its cradle and turned to Mrs. Dawg. "That was the cops, ma'am," he said. "They found the guy who murdered your husband. Walter Lipton."

"Oh?" She said it as though it didn't matter much.

"He put up a fight and they had to shoot him."

"Is he dead?" she asked.

"Uh-huh."

"Too damn bad, huh?" she said and went into the bedroom, closing the door behind her.

Lulu ripped the check from her book, waved it in the air and handed it to Mr. Bloodworth. "You oughta be ashamed to take this."

"Right," Mr. B. said, jerking the paper from her fingers and slipping it into his wallet.

"So they caught and killed the schlemiel who put an end to my meal ticket," Lulu said. "Big friggin' deal."

• • •

"Whew," Mr. Bloodworth said, when we were back in his car. "Tough racket."

As we drove toward the apartment I share with Grams, I opened his glove compartment and began digging through his music tapes. Finally, I found one titled "Kicks on 66, the songs of Bobby Troup."

I slipped it into his cassette player and heard a man with a very pleasant voice sing the title number. "You're right," I told Mr. B., "it's a neat song."

"Troup's a real talent. Used to be married to Julie London."

The name meant nothing to me. "According to the song, Route 66 runs from Chicago to L.A.," I said. "Where is it out here, exactly?"

The big detective scratched his head. "Darned if I know. I think they renamed it or something."

"I'll have to look it up," I said.

"The only thing I have to do is deposit this check," he said. "And hope it clears."

I imagine he must have spent some of it in his dim bars because he seemed a little slurry when he arrived at his apartment at ten that night. I'd been phoning him since four in the afternoon.

"Wha's so 'portant?" he wanted to know.

When I told him, he was silent for a few seconds. Then he said. "Could be a coinc'ence."

"A coincidence? Not likely."

"Hmmm. How can we be sure?"

I gave him a suggestion. I'd been thinking the problem through for five hours.

By the time the detectives, Gundersen and Lucas, arrived at the Beverly-Rodeo Hotel at shortly before eleven, Mr. Bloodworth seemed to have sobered up a bit. The lawmen were totally sober. And angry. "Leo, what the hell is this all about? We found the rifle that killed Dawg in Lipton's apartment. He's been IDed as the purchaser of the cell phone. All that was hanging fire was a checkup on the Laurences. That came in and we are now confident that Lipton was acting alone."

"He's dead," Detective Lucas added. "The case is closed."

"But Mr. Lipton wasn't acting alone," I said. "Someone was working with him, someone who could provide him with Mr. Dawg's suite telephone number, someone who knew that Mr. Dawg was familiar enough with Southern California streets and byways to follow rather cryptic directions."

Detective Gundersen shook his head and turned to Mr. Bloodworth. "Leo, I hope we're not here just because of this kid's fantasies."

"Serendipity's pretty good at this sort of thing," Mr. Bloodworth said. "Let's go on up to the suite. The ladies are waiting for us."

"You bothered that poor woman?" Detective Lucas said. "Interrupted her mourning?"

"She'll rest better when we clean this up," Mr. Bloodworth said, entering the hotel.

On the way up in the elevator, Detective Lucas asked me, "So, who do you think was helping Lipton?"

"Lulu Diamond, of course," I said.

The young policeman raised an eyebrow. "Why 'of course'?"

"She had a strong motive," Mr. Bloodworth said. "I checked in with this guy in New York who's on top of the music business. Says Dawg had feelers out for a new manager. Not only was Lulu going to lose her main client, the insurance policy she's been carrying on his life would be canceled."

"How big's the policy, Leo?"

"Half a mil," Mr. Bloodworth said.

Detective Gundersen let out a low whistle. Detective Lucas looked amazed.

The two women were waiting for us. Not cheerily. Nastasia Dawg sat on the sofa, a wine-colored robe wrapped over what appeared to be a satin nightgown. Lulu was dressed in yet another muumuu, this one with large blood-red flowers against a yellow background.

"Let's get this over with," she said waspishly. "I need my beauty sleep."

"Okay, Lulu," Mr. Bloodworth said, as planned, "these officers are here to arrest you in connection with the murder of B. A. Dawg."

Lulu's mouth dropped. And Nastasia Dawg seemed to shake off her languor for the first time, her eyes saucer-wide.

"You son of a buck," Lulu shouted at Detective Lucas. "You sold me out."

The handsome detective couldn't have been more surprised if Lulu's skin had peeled away exposing a Martian underneath. "Are you nuts?" he wailed.

"Yeah," Lulu said, advancing on him. "Nuts for thinking I could count on you."

"Hold on," Detective Gundersen shouted. "Mrs. Diamond, you're saying Lucas is involved in Dawg's murder?"

"Involved? He planned it."

"She's demented," Detective Lucas whined. "I don't even know her."

"You say that now, you bum," Lulu snarled. "But on the phone it was 'Lulu, honey, it's a perfect plan. I got this nut case Lipton all primed to pull the trigger. He's spent the last year getting crazier and crazier. All we've gotta do is get the rapmeister within fifty yards of him.'"

"This is insane," Detective Lucas protested.

"You located Lipton pretty quick today, Lucas," Detective Gundersen said. "And it was you shot him dead."

The young detective looked from his boss to Lulu to Nastasia.

"Stand up guy, huh?" Lulu said with contempt. She turned to us. "That's how he described himself last year when you cops took care of Walter Lipton the first time."

"You two have been planning this for a year?" Mr. Bloodworth asked.

"His plan," she said. "But I went along. I guess we can forget all about that insurance money now, huh, lover?"

Detective Lucas's hand went for his gun, but Mr. Bloodworth was too fast for him. One punch and the younger man was on the floor and Mr. B. was holding the weapon.

Detective Gundersen looked down at his partner and said, "You have the right to remain silent . . ."

As he worked his way through the Miranda litany, his young detective looked past him, staring at Nastasia Dawg. "Tell 'em," Detective Lucas shouted over the recitation of his rights. "Tell 'em, damnit."

"I don't know what you're talking about, mister," the sultry woman replied.

"I'm talking about *us*."

"You and Lulu?" Nastasia looked genuinely confused. But Mr. Bloodworth and I knew that to be a pose.

"Me and you," the no longer very handsome policeman screamed.

"Man's pathetic," Nastasia said, turning to leave the room.

"Yeah, I guess I am," Detective Lucas said bitterly. "I was dumb enough to fall for that, 'my husband beats me' routine. We had to kill him before he killed her. That's what she got me to believe. Then we'd be in velvet. All that loot. We'd live happily ever after. Just another goddamned pipe dream."

He grabbed Detective Gundersen's arm. "You know I'm not lying to you, Herm," he pleaded. "I wouldn't have done what I did for some ugly fat broad."

Lulu Diamond's eyes narrowed.

"I guess I do know that much about you, Lucas," the older detective said sadly. "Leo, you want to keep him and Mrs. Dawg covered while I phone for somebody to come take 'em away?"

Nastasia sneered at Detective Lucas. "It was a setup. Lulu's working with them, you vain jackass. Why is it I always wind up with fools?"

"Lulu, you were terrific," I said. "You should have been an actress."

"I tried that," she said. "But I never was much good. Guess I was waiting for that perfect role. Thanks for giving it to me, Bloodworth."

"Don't thank me," he said. "It was Sara who wrote the script."

Nastasia turned to me. "Of course, it was you. And tell me, little Spice girl, was it something I said?"

"No. Well, Mr. Dawg did indicate he was jealous of you and Detective Lucas. But, actually, it had more to do with our driving around today. Detective Lucas did something that indicated he knew where we were headed even before Mr. Lipton conveyed that information to Mr. Dawg."

"That's a lie," Detective Lucas said.

"I don't lie," I told him. "When we were traveling on Sunset Boulevard, you knew we would eventually drive out of our way to take Santa Monica Boulevard to the ocean."

"I knew that?" Detective Lucas said. "You need help, kid."

"One of us does. According to the Route 66 page on the Internet, the highway runs along Santa Monica Boulevard and ends at the ocean."

"Yeah. I know that. I once drove 66 all the way from Santa Monica to Albuquerque. So what?"

"So while we were still on Sunset, headed away from the ocean, you started humming Mr. Bobby Troup's famous song. You had Route 66 on your mind at a time when only those who planned Mr. Dawg's murder knew that's where we were headed."

"Another fool, just like B. A.," Nastasia said.

"But with better taste in music," I said. "Unfortunately for you both."

Lia Matera

Dream Lawyer

LIA MATERA brings wit and skepticism to the field of the legal mystery, a subgenre that sometimes takes itself far too seriously. Once a practicing attorney herself, Matera is now a full-time writer whose sardonic take on matters legal and illegal constantly wins her accolades and awards. This isn't to say that her books aren't serious. They are. Her portrayals of the legal system, usually anything but pretty, manage to provoke and expose at the same time. But they also make you laugh. "Dream Lawyer" first appeared in *Diagnosis Dead*.

Dream Lawyer

Lia Matera

Picture this: A cabin in the woods, a hideaway, practically no furniture, just a table and a cot. Nobody for miles around, just me and her. I'm trying to keep her from collapsing, she's crying so hard. Her tin god's up and turned on her.

"She's got a gun there on the table, and I'm not sure what she's thinking of doing with it. Maybe kill herself. So I'm keeping myself between her and it. I'm up real close to her. Even crying doesn't make her ugly, her skin's so fresh. Tell the truth, I'm trying not to get excited. Her shirt's as thin as dragonfly wings, she's all dressed up expecting him. She should be hiding from him, but all day she's been expecting him. She's been dreading him but hoping he'll come, hoping he's got some explanation she hasn't thought of. Except she knows he couldn't possibly explain it away. That's why she's tearing herself up crying.

"She's so beautiful with the light from the window on her hair. But she's talking crazy—what she's going to do now, how she's going to tell everybody. Forgetting the hold he has on her, on all of us, how protected he is and how cool.

"And then . . . in he comes. She shuts up right away, surprised and terrified. I can tell by how stiff she gets, she's hardly even breathing. She's too freaked out to say any more. That's when I notice him there. But he's not paying attention to me. He's looking her over—her crying, the dress-up clothes she has on—and you can see he's making something out of it.

"She looks around like she's going to try to run. Big mistake. He goes cold as a reptile—I've seen it happen to him before. And then he picks up the gun and shoots her right in the face. Just as cold as a snake.

"That was my first thought, that it wasn't the person I knew, it was some . . . life-form, something outside my understanding with its own rules of survival like cockroaches. Because how could he just aim her own gun at her and blow her head off? Without blinking, without a word? After all she meant to him.

"I'm just about dying of shock right there on my feet. Compared to her, I'm nobody to him, nothing, just a bug that rode in on his cuff. Maybe that's why he says, 'I won't kill you. I don't have to.' He starts walking out. At the door he turns. 'If I have to kill you later, I will. But not like this. By inches. You'll see it coming a long way off, Juan. You'll see it coming for miles, so don't look back.'

"That's all. He didn't try to explain anything or change her mind. He didn't say a word to her, not even good-bye. He just killed her like she didn't matter. Like she was a fly and he was a frog. Zap. And then he left.

"By then I could hardly even stand up. I could hardly make my feet move to look closer at her. I wish I never did look. Did you ever have a bee get squashed on your windshield? That's what her head looked like. I wouldn't have expected so many colors of . . . Her face was blown right off except one part where there were still curls caught in a hair clip.

"I could barely keep on my feet much less figure out what to do about it. It was clear she was dead. Or wouldn't want to be saved if she wasn't. So it was no use calling nine-one-one.

"And as to him, well, my God, how was anybody going to believe me? With all his followers and his credentials—who's going to take my word over his? And what did he mean about don't look back? What would he do to me, this reptile-man who could blow away someone that loved him and that probably he loved, too. What would happen to me if I told anybody?

"I wish I could say I was confused over the trauma or something, but I was probably more scared than anything. That's why I left her there. I was too scared to do anything else, just too damn scared. Because I felt like I'd finally seen right inside him and found the devil there. I hit the road and stuck out my thumb, just trying to get some distance, trying to keep myself together.

"You probably know what happened after that. It took the police a while to catch up to him. They were looking for me, too; they knew I was there at the cabin from finding my fingerprints and hairs and like that. When they found me, I could hardly get any words out, I was still so scared. I guess they didn't trust me to stay and testify against him—they put me in custody, in jail. I wanted to get word to him, beg him not to do anything to me, beg him to understand it wasn't my fault, that I'd have shut up and stayed gone if I could. But I knew it was useless.

"When it was his lawyer's turn to do something, she had all these reasons I shouldn't testify. What it came down to was, I couldn't prove it was him and not me that killed Becky. I pointed at him and he pointed at me. And I guess in some legalistic way, we canceled each other out. However the technicalities worked, the jury never heard the whole story. So there was no way for them to figure out the truth, not beyond a reasonable doubt. I don't blame them the way some folks around here do.

"Some people wrote to the newspapers that they should have put me in prison whether I did it or not, because Becky was dead and somebody had to pay. And if it wasn't going to be Castle, it should be me because we were the only ones there in the cabin with her.

"And I can understand how people felt. It makes me sick to know he shot her and got away with it. And her, poor thing, all dressed up in case he was going to melt at her feet, hoping he'd come clean to everybody just to keep her respect. That's the part that hurts the most, that she was good enough to hope so, even with what she knew about him.

"I'd have twisted my life inside out to please a sweet girl like Becky Walker. I cry every time I think about her beautiful gold hair caught in that little clip. I couldn't save her, and I couldn't even get her a little bit of justice. Not even that.

"I tell you, it tears me apart."

The poor man looked torn apart. His natural swarthiness had paled to a sickly yellow. His graying hair was disheveled from finger-raking. His dark eyes, close-set above a hooked nose, glinted with tears. Prominent cheekbones contributed to the starved, haunted look of a survivor.

The walls of his small house were cluttered, even encrusted, with charms of various types. Mexican-made saints cast sad eyes on dried herbs and wreaths of garlic, rusty horseshoes were strung with rabbits' feet, icons of saints hung beside posters of kindly blond space aliens. And everywhere there were gargoyles. Their demon faces scowled down from the rafters, they brooded in corners, squatted on tabletops, leered behind rows of votive candles.

"Did you have a lawyer representing you before or during the trial?" I asked Juan Gomez.

"No."

"When the police questioned you, did they tell you it was your right to have a lawyer present?"

"Yes." He buffed the knees of his worn jeans, rocking slightly. "But what was the point? I was too scared to say what happened, anyway."

"But you feel you need a lawyer now?" Castle had been acquitted of murder: the barn door was open, and the horse was long gone. Unless Gomez wanted some pricey commiseration, there wasn't much I could do for him.

When he nodded, I continued. "I gather this was a big case locally. But I just moved here, so I'm not acquainted with it." Having been fired from yet another law firm, this time for taking a too-strange case as a favor to a friend, I was once again on my own. Just today, I'd unpacked a parcel of business cards reading "Willa Janson, Attorney at Law, Civil Litigation & Criminal Defense." I wasn't turning down anything until I got a little money in the bank.

The move from San Francisco to Santa Cruz had been expensive despite being only seventy-five miles down the coast. And I'd discovered that lawyers in laid-back Hawaii East charged only half the fees of their big-city counterparts.

Now my potential client, whose main selection criterion seemed to be counsel's willingness to make house calls, leaned back in his chair. It was painted white, like the rest of his plain wood furniture, and arranged on duct tape exes on the floor.

"You never heard of the case? You don't know about Sean Castle?" He resumed his anxious rocking.

"No. The name seems familiar." Maybe I'd read about him.

"He's famous for dream research."

"Dream interpretation, that kind of thing?"

"Prophetic dreaming." He continued to look surprised I didn't know. "Sean could lecture seven days a week about dreams and never run out of people wanting more. There's a waiting list for his workshops. He's a brilliant man."

"What does he teach people to do?"

"Recognize the future in their dreams."

I shuddered at the thought. Bad enough to deal with the future when it got here. "What did the dead woman threaten him with? What was she going to expose about him?"

He jerked back as if I'd slapped him. "I can't tell you that."

"I'm sorry?"

"That was up to her." He winced. "It's still up to her. I can't take it away from her."

"But she's dead." Was I missing something?

"A carpet doesn't stop unrolling just because the ground drops out from under it."

"Well, but . . . I don't know where this carpet's going." I did know I'd gone as far as I could with the metaphor. "You say Castle killed her so she wouldn't reveal some secret. And now you feel vulnerable because of it. Maybe you should share the information, if only for your own protection."

"You don't know this because you never met him." Juan looked more than merely earnest. "He means what he says, especially threats."

"You're afraid he'll kill you?" At least that part made sense to me. "Or however he put it."

"I'm not 'afraid' he'll do it, I know he will. Exactly like he said. By inches. It's already started." He watched me glance at the gargoyles. "Gargoyles are demons that switched sides. Because of who they used to be, they can see through any disguise evil puts on—it takes one to know one. They keep evil from coming close, like pit bulls in the yard. That's why they're all over cathedrals."

I glanced uncertainly at the snarling plaster creatures, some winged, some with horns and claws. They were daunting, but pit bulls barked louder.

"You need them when you're sleeping," he added. "You can't stay awake forever."

"No." I continued hastily, "So why do you want a lawyer?" An exorcist, a shaman, a psychic, even an acupuncturist would probably be more useful for counteracting psychological terror. When he didn't respond, I said, "Look, I'm no therapist, but it does seem that Sean Castle is playing on your fears. Manipulating them."

"You'd have to meet him to understand. If he wants something, it happens."

"Okay. But do you need counsel?" He seemed unclear on the demarcation between legal remedies and mythical talismans. And I still had plenty of unpacking to do.

"The lawyer sent me his will."

"He's dead?" I wasn't going to learn Juan Gomez was afraid of a ghost?

"No, he's alive—I'm absolutely sure. So why did his lawyer send me the will? Why does she think *he* lives here? Why did he tell her that? What does it mean?"

"Who's the lawyer?"

"Laura Di Palma." He watched me. "You know her."

"Yes." I don't know what showed on my face. But Di Palma had once cross-examined me in a murder trial. She'd tied me into incoherent knots and invited the jury to scorn my testimony. The experience had been akin to being repeatedly stabbed with an icicle. There was a lingering chill long after the pain subsided. "She didn't explain why she sent the will here? Did she send a cover letter?"

"Just the will. The envelope has her return address."

"Are you named in the will?"

The mention of Di Palma made me more curious than cautious. We shouldn't be discussing this unless and until we agreed I was his lawyer and talked about fees.

"He wants me to take his ashes to Becky's cabin and scatter them there." He blanched just thinking about it.

"You can refuse."

"No, there's a reason he did this. He's trying to tell me something. More than that." He resumed his neurotic rocking. "He's trying to trap me, do something evil to me. I need to figure out what. I need you to talk to his lawyer for me."

"You want me to find out her reasons for sending the will to your address? Or his reasons for wanting you to scatter his ashes?"

"Find out anything, whatever he told her. But don't talk to him yourself." He leaned forward. "Don't put yourself in his line of sight. Don't let him know you're against him. Okay? I have enough on my conscience already."

"Don't worry about me." If I could survive another encounter with Laura Di Palma, I was tough enough to face a mere assassin.

"And her, the lawyer. Be careful of her. Everybody that touches him gets some of the good burned out."

"Di Palma doesn't give him much of a target." I hastened to recover some professionalism. "What I mean is, she can take care of herself."

"No." He shook his head emphatically. "Against him, nobody takes care. You've got to sleep sometime."

I suppressed a smile, imagining Di Palma wrestling with nightmares. If anybody could get a restraining order against Freddy Krueger, it was her. "Why don't you let me take a look at the will?"

He rose and walked to a white velvet box on a whitewashed table. From it he extracted a pair of latex gloves. He put them on, then carried the box over to me.

"Do you want gloves?" he asked. "I have more."

"No, that's okay." I reached into the box and pulled out a manila envelope. The return label was preprinted with Di Palma's law firm address. The envelope was addressed in tidy type to Sean Castle . . . at this address. In block letters above were the words *Juan Gomez* and *c/o*, in care of. "It might just be misaddressed. A clerical error."

"I want to wish it could be so simple!"

I slid the will out. It looked like a Xerox or laser print of a standard-format will. I skimmed a page that distributed property and personal effects among a list of people, none with the surname Castle.

Juan's name appeared in a section about funeral arrangements and disposal of remains. It requested, without embellishment, that Juan take the urn containing Castle's cremains to "the mountain cabin formerly the residence of our mutual friend, Becky" and scatter them there.

I looked up from the will to find Juan standing as hunched and motionless as one of his gargoyles.

"Who owns the cabin he's talking about?" I asked him. "Are they going to want these ashes scattered there?"

"It used to be mine. But I deeded it to Sean so he could put Becky in it. She had to be isolated, and it's pretty far off the beaten path."

"Isolated?"

"That's what Sean said. Now I know what he meant, but then, I didn't think about it. She wanted to live there, so that was that."

"Did she realize it wasn't originally Castle's property? That you were deeding it to him for her benefit?"

He shrugged. "She knew I built it."

I hadn't been his lawyer then; this was none of my business. People signed property over to churches and foundations and gurus every day. Scientologists bought enlightenment one expensive lesson at a time; Mormons tithed inconvenient percentages of their income; my father's favorite guru, Brother Mike, gladly accepted supercomputers.

"Who lives in the cabin now?"

"I don't know. I've never been back. I think of it as empty." He looked wistful. "If only . . . It could have worked out fine for everybody."

I waited, but he didn't elaborate. It certainly hadn't worked out well for the dead woman. Or, apparently, for Juan Gomez.

I returned my attention to the will, one of the first I'd studied since the bar exam. "Aside from being addressed to you care of Sean Castle, it's odd they'd send this out prior to Castle's death. You're sure he's still alive?"

"Yes. I wish he weren't, but I know he is."

"Well, it's not standard practice to distribute a living person's will, not at all. It raises beneficiaries' expectations, and that's unfair all around—the person might change his mind and revise the terms of the will or add a codicil. So I don't know why he'd want this mailed out now. It doesn't promise anything and it invades his privacy. It really might be some kind of mistake."

"He doesn't make mistakes."

"Neither does his lawyer. But a paralegal may have screwed up. Maybe the wrong address in the Rolodex or a misleading scrawl on a Post-it . . . these things do happen." Bad enough Juan had been asked to scatter a murderer's ashes. He shouldn't have to worry about the will containing some hidden threat. "I could find out for you."

"Yes! But be careful. You don't know Sean Castle, you don't know what he does to people."

But I did know Laura Di Palma. And Juan Gomez was a good example of what *she* did to people.

"Willa, it's been years." Di Palma's law partner stood in the waiting room of her office, looking mildly surprised. "Are you still practicing labor law?"

I felt a little guilty saying, "No." I'd gone to law school to join the labor firm of illustrious lefties Julian Warneke and Clement Kerrey. Maryanne More had apprenticed there years before me, going on to the National Labor Relations Board before starting her own firm. But I'd stayed with Julian only two years before the lure of solvency seduced me into an L.A. business firm. I'd done a year of hard time there—despite my efforts to reinvent myself, I'd remained a hippie at heart, valuing my time above money. From a labor point of view, I'd been one sullen wage slave. "I just opened my own firm. Down in Santa Cruz. I'd like to pick up a labor clientele, but I'm barely unpacked."

In fact, that was why I was here now. As long as I was in the city to fetch the last of my boxes, I might as well get in Di Palma's face.

Maryanne nodded. With her smooth chignon and velvet lapels, she looked like a model in a Christmas catalog. "Are you here to see me?"

I glanced at the waiting room's dark wood walls, brocade couches, and Old Master oil paintings. All the place needed was a docent. The decor sure didn't match my impression of Di Palma. I suppose I'd envisioned shark tanks.

"I've been trying to reach Laura Di Palma. I've left several voice-mail messages and I haven't gotten a response. I thought I'd drop in and see if I could catch her."

Maryanne seemed to stop breathing, tensing as if she were listening for something. "I'm sorry, Laura's taken the week off to take care of some family matters. Can I help you?"

"Possibly."

Maryanne nodded slightly, motioning me to follow her down a parqueted corridor. Halfway down, a door labeled "Laura Di Palma" was ajar. In an office splashed with bright colors, a lanky man sat at a glass desk, holding his bowed head. Maryanne sped up, leading me to an office at the end of the hall.

I settled into a wing chair. Jeez, her office looked like a palace library.

"Laura Di Palma sent a copy of a will to Juan Gomez, my client. Among other things, the will asks him to scatter the ashes of her client, Sean Castle. The envelope is addressed to Juan at his house, care of Sean Castle."

Maryanne shook her head slightly. "How odd." Neither of us stated the obvious, that sending the will to someone named in it denied Castle the confidentiality he might reasonably expect. "I assume it was misaddressed, and that she intended to send it to . . . Sean Castle, is it? I'm sorry if your client was disturbed by it."

I sighed. "Disturbed is the least of it. Mr. Gomez worries that Castle gave Ms. Di Palma his address. And he particularly wanted to keep his whereabouts secret from Castle. So I really need to check with Ms. Di Palma and find out what's behind this."

"Well, I can't speak for her. But perhaps I can find out whether it was a clerical error." She looked bothered. Because the office might have to notify Castle? Because she shouldn't have to clean up Di Palma's mess?

"I'd like to talk to Ms. Di Palma myself. My client really needs some assurance that Mr. Castle's not making any kind of veiled threat." After the creepy tale Juan had told, I could use a little reassurance myself. "You know Juan Gomez testified against Castle?"

"I don't know anything about Mr. Gomez. And I really don't know much about Mr. Castle, though I recall Laura represented him last year. But I'll ask her to—" She caught her breath, looking beyond me. "Sandy?" Her tone was bracing.

The lanky man I'd glimpsed in Di Palma's office was now standing in the doorway. A wide mouth and long dimples might ordinarily have been the focus of his thin face. But at this moment, gloom furrowed his brows and narrowed his blue eyes to a wince. He pushed sand-colored hair off his forehead, looking like Gary Cooper in some thirties melodrama.

"Did I hear you mention Laura?" His voice was deep and slightly Southern in inflection. "Anything I can help with?"

Maryanne glanced at me.

He continued standing there, so I said, "I've been trying to get hold of Ms. Di Palma."

The man entered, taking the wing chair beside mine. "About?"

"Sandy, I don't think this is—"

"What about?" he repeated.

"Are you an associate of hers?" I wondered.

"Willa Jansson, Sandy Arkelett. Sandy handles our private investigations." Maryanne's lips remained parted, as if she were on the brink of saying more.

I watched her uncertainly. Arkelett worked for her firm, this should be her call.

Finally, she told him, "Laura apparently sent Sean Castle's will to one of his beneficiaries."

Arkelett's brows rose.

"Juan Gomez. He's my client," I added. "He'd like to know why the will was sent to him. He and Mr. Castle were involved in a case she tried."

"I know Castle. I did the legwork on that case."

"Have you seen him lately? Do you know if the will was sent at his request?"

"Laura didn't tell me about any will." Arkelett was talking to Maryanne now. "You?"

Maryanne shook her head.

"Could it be a phony?" He reached a long arm across the desk as if to take a copy from Maryanne.

"My client didn't want me to make a copy," I explained. I didn't add that he'd nearly come unglued at the prospect of my becoming cursed by it. "It looked like a standard document with a number of bequests. It asks my client to scatter Castle's ashes."

"And it got sent to . . . ?"

"Juan Gomez."

He scowled. "I'll try and get a hold of Castle for you. Do you have a business card?"

I was a little surprised. It would certainly be more usual to contact Di Palma, wherever she was, before going behind her back to question her clients. Nevertheless, I fished two brand new cards out of my bag, handing one to Arkelett and one to Maryanne.

"Law school murders," Arkelett said, reading my card. "You were one of the witnesses."

I felt myself trying to scoot back the heavy wing chair.

"I worked with Laura on that case," he explained.

As the defense investigator, he'd have done a thorough background check of the prosecution's witnesses. He'd have given Di Palma details of my protest-era arrests and my two ghastly months of jail time. God knew Di Palma had gotten her money's worth, rattling my "criminal record" like a saber, using it to hack away at my credibility.

But, as lawyers love to say, that's why she got the big bucks.

Arkelett slipped my card into his pocket, and rose. He left without another word.

Maryanne said, "We'll try to reach Laura for you, of course."

Then she rose, too, resolutely shaking my hand good-bye.

• • •

Arkelett stopped me in the hall outside the suite of offices.

"Look," he said, "I want to ask a favor. I'd like to see Castle's will. Maybe ask your client a couple of questions." He frowned. "Because Laura . . . it wouldn't be like her to screw up. Not on a client matter, anyway."

"What would the will tell you?" And why didn't he just phone Di Palma, wherever she was?

"If you still have the envelope, the date and place it was mailed."

"I could call you with the information."

"I want to look at it myself. In case there's anything else."

Was he expecting blood? A coded scrawl? Juan had made this all seem strange enough. Having a man in a business suit get weird about it was even spookier.

"Some things you need to look at the original," he insisted. "I'd just like to make my own assessment. Take a few minutes of your client's time?" He tilted his head as if to figure me out.

"I don't know—he's a little high-strung." I couldn't resist asking: "Is there a problem? Some reason you're not waiting for Ms. Di Palma?"

He chewed the inside of his cheek. "Laura had to go deal with a . . . a sick cousin." Judging by his face, there was a hell of a lot more to it than that. "And well, we're not sure exactly where that took her. I don't mean to say it's a big deal—she'll be back soon enough. But in the meantime, guaranteed, she'd want me to check this out."

Check out the postmark on Juan Gomez's envelope? No, however Arkelett might try to soft-pedal it, he wanted to know where Di Palma had gone. I backed toward the elevator. Should I help him? If Di Palma wanted him to know her whereabouts, she'd have told him herself.

"I can maybe help your client out," Arkelett persisted. "If he's who I think he is . . ." He looked nonplussed. "Maybe I can help him get his head on straight."

"My client's afraid," I admitted. "Afraid of Castle. He warned me about him several times. And he expressed some concern about Ms. Di Palma, too. So I don't know how he'd feel about seeing you."

Sandy Arkelett leaned closer. I could smell Old Spice on his lean cheeks. "If he wants you present, that's fine. No cost to him—I'll pay you for the hour, okay?"

"I'll see what I can set up." For a fee, I supposed I could fit it into my schedule.

When he opened his door, I said, "How are you Juan? I'm sorry I'm a little early."

As I stepped in, he glanced outside, his grizzled brows rising. I looked over my shoulder. Sandy Arkelett had just pulled up to the curb.

Juan clutched his sweatshirt as if to keep his heart from leaping out of his chest. And I didn't blame him. Just as Arkelett had investigated me when

I'd been a witness against Di Palma's client, he'd doubtless investigated every aspect of Juan's life before Castle's trial. I wondered how Juan would react if Arkelett alluded to any of it.

I closed the door.

"You don't have to do this," I reminded him. "Or, if you like, we can speak to Mr. Arkelett in my office. You don't have to invite him into your home."

"No." Juan's tone was more stoic than his face. "No, I understand what it is to love someone. Someone who's gone."

I'd told him Di Palma was apparently off on some private errand. I'd told him I thought Arkelett was trying to find out exactly where it had taken her. Now Juan had filled in the reason: Arkelett was in love with Di Palma. Maybe Juan was just guessing, but it fit, it made sense.

I looked around the gargoyle-protected room. It was somber with the curtains closed, lighted only with votive candles and a dim table lamp. He must not read much, not in this gloom. But there was no television in sight, either. Did he spend his days praying to the gargoyles leering in flickering candle shadows? "You've met Sandy Arkelett?"

Juan nodded. "He's by her side all the time. He puts himself between her and Castle. You can see that he understands more about Castle than she does. You can see it on his face."

I was a little taken aback. He couldn't have spent much time with Castle and his lawyer. Even his use of the present tense was disconcerting. He seemed to expect me to share some memory or vision.

Sandy Arkelett sighed deeply when Juan opened the door to him. It was a moment before he muttered, "Thanks for seeing me." The worry lines on his long face deepened, lending his words a somber sincerity. "Mind if I come in?"

I admired his thirties-movie silhouette, long and slim in a slightly baggy suit. Even his light brown hair was combed back like Gary Cooper's or Jimmy Stewart's. Di Palma was lucky.

"I was just asking my client if he felt comfortable doing this," I told him.

Juan was flattened against the door, staring at Arkelett.

The detective said, "I won't take but ten minutes of your time, Mr. um . . ." He eyed Juan so intently he seemed to be leaning toward him. "Is it Gomez?"

Juan edged away.

"I know I bring up some hard memories. So I'll make it real short," Arkelett repeated. "But it was a long drive down here—I'd appreciate ten minutes."

"I—I'm sorry. I have nothing against you. On the contrary. I just—"

Arkelett stepped quickly inside. "Thanks," he murmured. "I guess . . . would it be easiest to start with the will?" He glanced at me.

"Do you mind showing Mr. Arkelett the will?"

Juan caught his lower lip between his teeth. He walked to the white box on the white table. Arkelett looked around, his pale brows pinched. I watched Juan put on rubber gloves to open the box and handle the manila envelope inside it.

He brought it to me. Arkelett stepped up behind me, positioned to look over my shoulder.

The envelope was postmarked Hillsdale, CA. Central California, maybe Northern? Like most San Franciscans—former San Franciscans—I'd rarely bestirred myself to explore the outback.

I turned, handing Arkelett the envelope. It had been mailed on the sixteenth. Today was the twenty-second.

Juan reached past me, touching his fingertips to Arkelett's elbow. "Sit down," he said. "On the white pine chair. That's the best one for this. Do you want gloves?"

"No need." Arkelett chewed the inside of his cheek and stared at the postmark.

"Where's Hillsdale?" I asked him.

"North." It seemed to take him extra effort to look away from the word. Then his head lurched as if he were overcompensating. "Below the Oregon border on the coast. Laura's hometown. She started the trip there."

"So she did send it." So much for blaming a paralegal.

Juan hovered near the envelope, latex gloves poised to retrieve it. "Why does it have my address—*my* address with *his* name. How does she know my address?"

Arkelett said, "The firm has it on file."

"My address?" Juan blinked. "But how? Why?"

"You haven't been in contact with Laura lately?"

"No. As a discipline, I try not to think about it. About him. I would never call his lawyer. Never."

Juan was so shaken by the idea that he turned away, touching his hand to the snarling cheek of a candlelit gargoyle. Arkelett watched him.

When Juan turned back, Arkelett continued, "And except for the will, Laura hasn't been in touch with you?"

"Only through Castle. He's very much in touch with me. But not in the way you mean." Juan gestured toward the envelope. "This would be very crude for him. So blunt that at first I thought it was meant as an insult. But I begin to see the layers on top of layers."

"I expect I've stirred up a lot of worries, coming down here like this." Arkelett seemed to be memorizing every millimeter of the envelope. "But I'm just . . ." He glanced at me again. "Just trying to correct an office mistake, that's all. If I possibly can." He extracted the will.

Juan took a stumbling backward step, staring as if Arkelett had shaken out an appendage of Castle's. "I will go, go and . . . leave you for a moment."

He started pushing open the door to another room. Then he turned back to us, trotting to the whitewashed chair and scooting it behind Arkelett, virtually forcing him to sit. He left as if chased out.

Arkelett hunched over the will, giving it his full attention. I stood behind the chair, reading over his shoulder.

Arkelett turned to me. "You don't know much about Castle's trial?"

"Only what Mr. Gomez told me."

He seemed on the verge of saying something difficult. Then, with a shake of the head, "I'm not clear enough on client confidentiality to know how much I can say now." As Di Palma's associate, he was obligated to keep her client matters confidential. "I don't know if Castle's acquittal changes anything. Especially these days, with civil suits getting filed after not-guilty criminal verdicts."

Was he about to admit Castle's guilt? I'd already gathered as much. But he was right, the double-jeopardy rule protected Castle only from criminal reprosecution. It offered no immunity from a civil suit. So it wouldn't do for Arkelett to confirm Castle's guilt. Nevertheless, I was silent, hoping he'd say more.

With a shrug, he continued, "You should read the court documents." A half smile. "And take a look at the arrest report and booking sheet."

Castle must have priors I should know about. Or maybe something in the records supported Juan's fears. Everyone was so damn odd about Castle. I was ready to invest in a few gargoyles myself.

Juan returned then. Arkelett slipped the will back into its envelope.

"Thanks for your time." Arkelett stood slowly. "And thank you, Ms. Jansson. I'm a hundred percent sure Laura's going to phone you first thing when she gets back."

"You'd better find your Ms. Di Palma soon," Juan advised.

Arkelett stopped moving.

"She never understood what Castle is," Juan continued. "She was like a woman with dust thrown in her eyes. When he can blind a woman, he can take her away from anyone. Like he took Becky away from me. He can make her do anything."

Arkelett's face drained of color. "Can you elaborate on that?"

Juan shrugged.

"Are you saying she's in some kind of physical danger?"

"Mental danger, spiritual danger." Juan's eyes glittered.

Arkelett watched him for a moment. "Laura knew what and who she was dealing with—it's not a matter of dust in her eyes. But a lawyer's got to do everything she can for her client. You understand that, don't you? That it was Laura's job to win an acquittal? That's not to say it's necessarily the best result, not even for Castle. Maybe sometimes it's better to put someone away where he can get treatment, even punishment. But from the point of view of the lawyer, she's obligated to go for the gold. That's her pact with the client. Whether it's right in the long run . . . that's for the client to decide, that's for God to know. Laura did her job, that's all. You do understand that?"

Juan stared at his gargoyles. "Yes." His voice was a whisper. "But maybe Becky doesn't understand."

Arkelett handed me the will and walked out.

. . .

Until Juan mentioned them, I don't suppose I'd ever thought about prophetic dreams. But that night, I believed I'd had one.

I dreamed I was sitting in Assistant District Attorney Patrick Toben's no-frills office. Toben was the only local ADA I knew. I'd recently tried a case against him.

In my dream, Toben, dapper and well-groomed as in life, wore a gargoyle print tie. "I called you," he said, "because your business card was found at the crime scene."

At that, I awakened suddenly and fully, convinced Juan Gomez was about to be killed by Sean Castle. My dark bedroom seemed thick with shapes, lurking like Castle's curse. *I'll kill you by inches, Juan. You'll see it coming for miles, so don't look back.*

I sat up, clicking on a lamp. My new place smelled of carpet shampoo and fresh paint. The walls were bare and the corners piled high with boxes. I could hear the clang of metal pulleys on masts at the nearby yacht harbor.

I crawled out of bed, clammy with fear. I pulled a jacket over the sweats I'd slept in, and I slipped into my moccasins. I started toward the door.

I stopped with my hand on the knob. I was still half-asleep, showing a dreamlike lack of impulse control. What excuse did I have for awakening Juan Gomez at this time of night? He was scared enough without having me appear on his doorstep to relate a nightmare.

I took a deep breath. I'd gotten sucked into Juan's world of dreams and curses, complete with medieval gargoyles to protect the sleeping. But I knew better than to elevate mere worries into voodoo, misgivings into prophecies. Sean Castle could manipulate Juan only because Juan had done the psychological and emotional spadework for him. Juan himself had created the pursued, cowering man Castle had vowed to make of him.

Juan said Castle would harm me, too, if he became aware of me. But I could see Juan had it backward. Castle could undermine me only if *I* became aware of *him*, only if I let myself dread what he might do to me. Only if I frightened myself enough to awaken a client in the middle of the night.

I returned to bed and huddled there, trying hard not to imagine gargoyles, claws outstretched, in the shadows beyond the lamplight.

I hugged myself against the seacoast chill, thinking about the tale Juan had told, replaying his words in my mind. Having shared his horror, however briefly, I could move beyond smug pity. It scared me how much that seemed to change his story. Minutes before, I'd been proud of myself for breaking the chain of Juan's superstition. Now I feared the situation was much more complicated than that. How had Juan put it? *I want to wish it could be so simple.*

I considered Sandy Arkelett's reaction to Juan, his worries about revealing a client confidence, his advice that I read the court records and look at the booking sheet. I pondered the fact that Arkelett had recognized my name many years after my testimony, but hadn't recognized Juan's after only a year.

Once again, I jumped out of bed.

I cruised slowly past Juan's house, disquieted to see orbs of candlelight through his sagging curtains. It was nearly four in the morning. I'd hoped for the consolation of finding the place peaceful and dark.

I pulled up to the curb. I'd already promised myself: no debate. If Juan seemed to be stirring, I would knock no matter how foolish I felt. Maybe I had this figured wrong—unlike Di Palma, I made mistakes with disgusting frequency. Even if I was right, it was slim reason to bother Juan in the middle of the night.

But I just couldn't stop worrying about my dream. *Your card was found at the crime scene,* Assistant DA Toben had said.

Maybe it was a blessing not to be as perfect as Di Palma—I was used to apologizing. If I'd worried for nothing, fine, I would simply admit to being an idiot.

I looked over my shoulder as I approached the house. I'd feel like a flake persuading his neighbors I was no prowler.

When I knocked at the door, it opened slightly. Juan had left it unlocked, virtually ajar. Fear crawled up my spine. A man with gargoyles on every horizontal surface wouldn't leave his door open. Not unless he'd given up on protecting himself from Sean Castle. Not unless he'd tired of waiting in agonized dread.

I pushed my way in. "Juan?"

I almost stumbled over an object near the threshold. It was a gargoyle, shattered into lumps and shards of plaster as if dashed against the wall.

Only a few candles glowed, leaving most of the room in shadow. Whitewashed furniture picked up flickers of color from glass votives. There was barely enough light to make out the remains of other gargoyles, their pieces strewn as if in a berserk frenzy. Their cracked demon faces, portions of curling claws, and remnants of reptilian wings covered the floor like macabre carnage.

For a moment, I let myself believe that the large shadow in the corner was another gargoyle, still intact. But I approached it with a knot rising up my throat. I knew it was Juan Gomez, sprawled dead on the floor.

My business card, I noticed, was lying in a pool of blood beside his hand.

Sean Castle had smashed all the gargoyles. Then he'd slashed Juan's wrists with the jagged slivers of plaster. Or perhaps Juan, sure Castle was coming for him, had beaten him to the punch.

Exsanguination was listed as the cause of death. Suicide was presumed, despite the fact that Castle's fingerprints were all over the house.

I spent the rest of the night with the police. Then I went to the office of Assistant District Attorney Patrick Toben. Toben had prosecuted Sean Castle. Now he had the paperwork for this case.

It was only right that he should. My client, I had come to realize, wasn't Juan Gomez, after all. He was Sean Castle.

"Yeah, Sean Castle killed Becky Walker, all right." Toben ran a hand over his neat ginger hair. "Walker was living with Castle in his cabin. We think she freaked out over something he did—probably showing multiple personalities. So he got self-protective and blew her head off. From what you just told me, I guess there was a Juan Gomez inside him watching the whole thing happen. Whatever. By the time we caught up to Castle, he'd ditched the clothes he'd been wearing, gotten rid of the weapon, everything. We just didn't have enough for a conviction. That's how Di Palma played it. You ever seen her in court? Well, then you know. She's good."

"The name Juan Gomez never even came up?"

"Di Palma never let a psychiatrist near Castle. She told us from day one she wasn't going to argue diminished capacity or insanity, nothing like that. She completely removed it as a trial issue, precluding us from examining him ourselves. And from what you tell me now, I can see why. If the psychiatrists labeled him a multiple, we'd have used it against him, we'd have looked for a violent personality or at least suggested the possibility. But our circumstantial case was weak enough that Di Palma stayed away from all of that. She was smart. She must have known, but she let it hang on whether we had enough proof."

I reached out a shaky hand for the coffee Toben had poured me. "When Sandy Arkelett saw Gomez—Castle—I could tell something wasn't right. But I assumed it had to do with Di Palma, with Arkelett trying to find her."

"It's a long drive to look at a postmark," Toben agreed.

"I suppose he just couldn't imagine Di Palma sending a will to a beneficiary by mistake." Sheesh, nobody would take time to check it out if I messed up. "He knew something was wrong."

"Looks like Di Palma didn't screw up, after all." Toben didn't seem very pleased to say so. "I assume Castle had Di Palma write up his will, and that she mailed it to him while she was on the road."

I envisioned Castle receiving the will and writing "Juan Gomez c/o" above the address. He certainly knew how to scare his alter ego. By asking "Juan Gomez" to return to Walker's cabin, Castle was, in essence, making "Juan" assume responsibility, pointing out that he'd been present during the murder, too. Castle was reminding his better half, as it were, that the hand that killed Becky Walker belonged to both of them.

The real question was, had Castle killed "Juan"? Had he taken revenge on his cringing cohabitant? Or had "Juan" rid the world of Castle, killing Becky's murderer the only way he could?

"I should have known something was fishy as soon as I saw Arkelett's reaction to Castle," I fretted again. "He knew the score the minute the front door opened. He knew the problem wasn't with Di Palma, he knew she hadn't made a mistake with the address." I took a swallow of weak coffee. "I was so dense. Even when Arkelett told me to look up the arrest report."

"You'd have recognized Castle's booking photo." Toben tapped a pencil against a file folder.

"Arkelett could have just told me. The photo's a public record." But I knew Arkelett's reluctance involved not the photo but the conclusion to be drawn from it: that Sean Castle had multiple personalities, one of whom was willing to incriminate another. This wasn't an observation to be made by an associate of Castle's lawyer. Not in an era of civil trials following criminal acquittals.

I knew all that. But it didn't take the bitter taste out of my mouth. Maybe I could have done something if I'd figured this out sooner. I wished, not for the first time, that Di Palma and her PI weren't so damned competent.

"We talked to Di Palma this morning." Toben continued. "We tracked her down through an uncle—she's up north. She got real quiet when I told her what happened." His lips curled with disdain. "If she'd have let us do our jobs and put Castle away, he'd be a hell of a lot better off now."

And if Toben had presented a stronger case against Castle, Di Palma would have had to settle for an insanity or diminished capacity defense. But however she might feel about this result, Sandy Arkelett was right. She'd done everything she should for her client. She'd won him his freedom.

Then she'd left it to him to find real justice within himself and with his other selves.

I tried to remember what else "Juan" had told me about Castle. "Was he really a famous dream researcher?"

"Is that what he said?"

"Something about prophetic dreams. He had all those gargoyles to protect him while he slept."

"Sean Castle was the man you met in that little house. Did he look famous to you?"

"No. It's just that . . . I guess on some level, I figured this out while I was sleeping." I refused to attribute more than that to my dream. "I woke up in the middle of the night worrying about it."

"That's why you went over there?"

I nodded. The police had obviously considered my nocturnal call bizarre. Toben probably agreed, but he didn't comment.

He said, "For a living, Castle did a bit of everything. Gardening, roto-rooting, worked at the canneries when they hired extras."

"Castle, gargoyles—I suppose it was just the association of ideas. Gargoyles protect Castles."

"I guess gargoyles aren't protection enough."

"Neither are lawyers, not even the best of them."

Bill Pronzini

Flood

Blue Lonesome and *A Wasteland of Strangers* were two of the most distinguished and original suspense novels of the previous decade. Both were written by BILL PRONZINI, a writer's writer who has written westerns, adventure, dark suspense, and every kind of mystery story there is. Always a pro—and a pro for nearly forty years, at that—Pronzini's work has lately deepened and broadened in its appeal. There is new power and depth in his books, and critics are racing to give him the attention that should have been his long ago. "Flood" first appeared in the April issue of *Ellery Queen's Mystery Magazine*.

Flood

Bill Pronzini

She sat at the upstairs bedroom window watching the river run wild below. Rain lay like crinkled cellophane wrap on the glass, so that everything outside seemed shimmery—distorted the low-hanging, black-veined clouds, the half-submerged trees along the banks, the drift and wreckage riding the churning brown floodwaters. She could hear the sound of the water, a constant thrumming pulse, even with the rain beating a furious tattoo on the roof.

Nearly a week now of steady downpour, a chain of Pacific storms that had lashed northern California with winds up to a hundred miles per hour. It seemed to her that it had been raining much longer, that she could not remember a time when the sky was clear and blue and the sun shone. The rain was *inside* her, too.

When she looked into the mirror, looked into her own eyes, what she saw was a wet, gray, swampy place, a sodden landscape like the one she watched through the window. One in which she was trapped, as she was physically trapped here and now. One from which there seemed to be no escape.

She shivered; it was cold in the room. They had been without heat or power for more than twenty-four hours. The fierce storm winds had toppled trees and power lines everywhere in the region. Roads were inundated and blocked by mudslides, one of them River Road, fifty yards west of their house. Flood stage along these low-lying areas was thirty-two feet; the rising water had reached that mark at eight last night, hours after the evacuation orders had been issued. It must be above forty feet now, at two in the afternoon. All the rooms downstairs were flooded halfway to their ceilings. The last time she'd looked, the car was totally covered and the only parts of the deck still visible were the tops of the support poles for the latticework roof. The roof itself had long since been torn off and carried away.

From the pocket of her pea jacket, as she had several times during the day, she took the ivory scrimshaw bowl. Smooth, round, heavy-bottomed, it fitted exactly the palm of her hand. Her grandfather had carved it from a walrus tusk and done the lacy scrimshawing in his spare time, during the period he'd worked as a mail carrier in Nome just after the Alaska Gold Rush. He'd given it to her mother, who in turn had passed it on to her only daughter. It had been the first thing she'd grabbed to bring upstairs with her when the in-pouring water forced them to abandon the lower floor. It was all she owned of any value, as Darrell so often reminded her.

"You and that damn bowl," he'd said this morning. "Well, you might as well hang onto it. We may need whatever we can sell it for someday. Nothing else of yours is worth half as much, God knows."

She stroked the cold surface, the intricate black pattern. It gave her comfort. Her only comfort in times of unhappiness and stress.

Shadows crawled thickly in the room—moist shadows laden with the brown-slime smell of the river. She found it difficult to breathe, but opening the window to let in fresh air would only worsen the stench. She thought of relighting one of the candles, to keep the shadows at bay, but the unsteady flame reflected off the window pane and made it even harder for her to see out. She was not sure why she wanted to keep looking out, but she did and she had all through the day. Compelled to sit here and watch the rain beat down, the murky, churning water rise higher and higher.

There would be another rescue boat along soon, maybe even one of the evacuation helicopters that were brought in when the floodwaters grew too dangerous for small craft. Rio Lomas, three miles to the east, had been cut off even longer than the River Road homes had, almost a day and a half; by now they would be airlifting evacuees to one of the larger towns inland, at a safe distance from the river. She wished that was where she was, in one of those towns, in an emergency shelter where she could be warm and dry, where the lights were bright and there was clean air to breathe.

Empty wish. Darrell wouldn't leave when the rescuers showed up. No matter how bad things were then, he wouldn't budge. He had refused evacuation in 1986, the worst flood in the river's history, when the waters crested at better than forty-eight feet. They had both come close to drowning that year, forced at the last to sit huddled in the attic crawlspace with the last dozen of his paintings wrapped in plastic sheeting like corpses awaiting burial. He'd refused to leave five years ago as well, the last time before this that the river had overrun its banks and made an island of their home. Stubborn. Fiercely possessive. Yes, and so many other less-than-endearing traits. So *many* others.

She rubbed the scrimshaw bowl and watched the rain slant down, the turmoil of conflicting currents and weird boils and eddy lines in the main channel, the soapy yellowish-white foam that scudded along what was left of the banks.

Why am I here? she thought.

I don't want to be here. I haven't wanted to be here in a long, long time.

The old, tired lament. And the old, tired response to it: I have nowhere else to go. Mom and Pop both gone, Jack blown up by a land mine in Vietnam, no other siblings or aunts or uncles or even a cousin. A few casual friends, but none I can turn to, talk to, count on. Twenty-one years with Darrell, exactly half my life, and the twenty-one before him so far removed I can scarcely remember them. Where would I go? What could I do?

Sudden crashing noise from the far end of the house—Darrell's studio. He'd been drinking all day, and now he had reached the mean, tantrumy stage where he began breaking things. Splintering, tearing sounds reached her ears. He was at his paintings again. Not the better, finished ones. He never destroyed those oils and watercolors, no matter how drunk or frustrated or enraged he became, because they were his "true art"—the ones he believed were the work of an undiscovered, unappreciated genius; the ones he bitterly hoped to sell to summer tourists and the handful of local collectors, so they could pay their bills or at least keep their credit from being cut off altogether. No, his destructive wrath was reserved for the unfinished canvases, his "false starts," and for the unsold riverscapes and still lifes and portraits of eccentric river dwellers that he decided were expendable, not quite up to his own lofty standards.

At first she, too, had believed he was a genius. A great and sensitive visionary. In those early days she had wanted to be an artist herself, at least an artisan. Not painting, nothing so important as that, just the designer and maker of earrings and pendants and other jewelry. She'd felt sure she had the talent to excel at this, but he had convinced her otherwise. Ridiculed and disparaged her efforts until, finally, she'd lost all enthusiasm and given up her work, her dreams, everything except her day-to-day existence as Mrs. Darrell Boyd. But he'd succeeded not only in disillusioning her about her own abilities, but in giving her a true perspective on his as well. He was far less gifted than he considered himself to be, at best a shade or two above mediocre.

The description fit their marriage just as aptly. At best, it had been a shade or two above mediocre. At worst—

Footsteps in the hallway, hard and lurching. She sat rigid, staring out through the rain-wavy glass. Waiting, steeling herself.

"Hey! Hey, you in there!"

She no longer had a name in her own house. She had become *Hey* or *Hey You* or harsh epithets just as impersonal.

"You hear me? I'm talking to you."

"I hear you, Darrell." Slowly she turned her head. He stood slouched in the doorway, shirt mostly unbuttoned and pulled free of his Levi's so that the bulge of his paunch showed. Unshaven, red-eyed, his graying hair a finger-rubbed tangle. She noticed all of that, and yet it was as though she were seeing him the way she had been seeing the storm-savaged river, through a pane of wavy glass. She looked away again before she said, "What do you want?"

"What d'you think I want?"

"I'm not a mind reader."

"What'd you do with it? Where'd you hide it this time?"

"Hide what?"

"You know what. Don't give me that."

"I don't touch your liquor. I never have."

"The hell you never have. There's another fifth, I brought it upstairs myself. What'd you do with it?"

"Look in the storeroom. That's where you put it."

"I know where *I* put it. Where'd *you* put it?"

"I never touched it, Darrell."

"Liar! Bitch!"

She didn't respond. Outside, something swirled past on the cocoa-brown water—a dead animal of some kind, a goat or large dog. She couldn't be sure because it was there one instant, bobbing and partly submerged, and the next it was gone.

"Where's that bottle, goddamnit? I'm warning you."

"In the storeroom," she said.

"That where you hid it?"

"It's been there all along."

"You go find it. Right now, you hear me?"

"I hear you."

"*Now.* Right this minute."

She got to her feet, not hurrying. Without looking at him, she started across the room.

"And put that silly damn bowl away," he said. "Why d'you always have to keep playing with that thing, petting it like it's a fetish or something?"

She slipped the scrimshawed ivory back into her pocket, walked past him into the hallway. Each step was an effort, as if her legs—like the land, like the house itself—had become waterlogged.

The storeroom was between the bedroom and his studio. It had started out as her workspace, but when she'd given up jewelry-making it had gradually evolved into a catchall storage area. Boxes, oddments of furniture, unused canvases crowded it now, along with dust and spiderwebs. When they'd abandoned the lower floor this morning she had brought up as much food as they might need and whatever else could be salvaged, and put it in there. The perishables were on melting ice in the big cooler, the rest scattered on boxes and on the floor. She poked listlessly among the food items and cartons, while he watched from the doorway. It took her less than a minute to find his last fifth of Scotch, more or less in plain sight behind the leg of a discarded table. She picked it up, held it out to him.

He snatched it from her hand. "Don't you ever do that again. Understand? You hide liquor from me again, you'll be sorry."

"All right," she said.

"Make me a sandwich," he said. "I'm hungry."

"What kind of sandwich?"

"What do I care what kind? A *sandwich*."

"All right."

"Make yourself useful for a change," he said, and stalked off with the bottle cradled like an infant against his chest.

She buttered bread, layered ham and processed cheese on top, and then spread mustard on a second slice. Did it all mechanically, taking her time. She put the sandwich on a paper plate and took it to the studio.

He was over by the tall double windows, squinting at one of his older riverscapes—trying to decide whether or not to destroy it, probably. He seemed even more misshapen and indistinct to her now, as if there was more than glass between them, as if she were looking at him underwater. She set the sandwich on his worktable, between the jars of oil paint and the now-open fifth of Scotch, and retreated to the hallway.

The open door to the bathroom drew her. She went inside and close to the medicine-cabinet mirror, but it was too dark to make out her image clearly. She lit a candle and held it up. Her face, like his, seemed water-distorted, and when she peered at it from an inch or so away she could see the rain in her eyes. Behind her eyes. Rain and a turbulent, rising cataract like the one outside.

She snuffed the candle, returned to the bedroom and her seat before the window. Rising, yes. The river's surface was a ferment spotted with debris—clumps of uprooted brush, logs and tree limbs bobbing drunkenly, a fence rail, the shattered remains of a rowboat, a child's red wagon. One of the logs slammed against the side wall of the house with enough force to crack boards before it swirled away.

The rain continued to beat down in gray metallic sheets. The dark waters roared and shrieked like a wild creature caught in a snare, ripping at what was left of its banks, tearing them down and apart in a frenzy. She could *feel* the flood, cold, slimy on her face and the backs of her hands. Smell and taste it, too, rank and primitive.

And still the waters kept rising . . .

Abruptly she stood. On heavy legs, her mind blank, she went out and back to Darrell's studio. He was sitting hunched at the worktable, staring fixedly into a tumbler of whiskey, the sandwich she'd made uneaten and pushed aside. His portable radio was on, tuned to a Santa Rosa station, the voice of a newscaster droning words that had no meaning for her. He did not hear her as she stepped up behind him; he had no idea she was there.

You've never known I was here, she thought. Just that one thought. Then her mind was blank again.

She took out the scrimshaw bowl, held it bottom side up in her hand. She no longer heard the newscast; she listened instead to the roaring and shrieking of the flood. Then, without hesitation, she raised the bowl and brought it down with all her strength on the back of his head.

He didn't make a sound. Or if he did, the raging of the waters drowned it out.

She had no difficulty dragging him across to the window. It was as if, dead or dying, he had become almost weightless. The wind flailed her with rain and surface spume as she raised the sash, hoisted him onto the sill. The river was only a few feet below, all but filling the downstairs rooms; it boiled and frothed, creating little whirlpools clogged with flotsam. She pushed Darrell down into the brown turmoil. There was a splash, and two or three seconds later, no more than that, he wasn't there anymore.

She was seated once again at the bedroom window when the rescue boat appeared. By then, mercifully, it had stopped raining and the floodwaters did not seem to be rising any longer. The worst was over. Everything was still gray and moist and chaotic, but there was a hint of clearing light in the grayness. She was sure of it—light outside and inside, both.

When she saw the boat rounding the bend she opened the window and waved her arms to show the rescuers where she was. They came straight to her at accelerated speed, two men wearing neoprene wetsuits hunched in the stern. She knew both of them; they were volunteer firemen in Rio Lomas.

As they drew alongside one of them called out, "Are you all right, Mrs. Boyd?"

She touched the freshly polished ivory bowl in her pocket. It was not the only thing of value she had; it never had been. "My name is Lee Anne," she said. "Lee Anne *Meeker*. Jewelry-maker."

"Are you all right?"

"Yes, I'm all right."

"Where's your husband?"

"Gone," she said.

"Gone? What do you mean, gone?"

She was not a liar; she told them the literal and absolute truth. "The flood took him," she said. "He was swept away in the flood."

Clark Howard

The Ice Shelf

The short story is arguably the most demanding of all literary art forms, and few people ever master it. CLARK HOWARD is one of the few. While his dozen novels, including *The Hunter* and *Love's Blood*, are all exciting and rewarding books, his short stories display an even greater number of gifts and talents. Two of his stories, "Animals" and "Horn Man," are among the best written by anyone of his literary generation. And the amazing fact is that he continues to work at that level. There is no mistaking a Clark Howard plot—the gritty mood, the hard-pressed protagonist, the breathtaking turn of events—just as there is no mistaking a Simenon or a Chandler or a Ross MacDonald. He is just that good, that unique, that enduring. "The Ice Shelf" first appeared in the September/October issue of *Ellery Queen's Mystery Magazine*.

The Ice Shelf

Clark Howard

The helicopter pilot tapped Patrick Drake's shoulder and pointed downward out the port-side window.

"There it is, Doc. That's the Brandon Ice Shelf."

Drake looked down on a plateau of frozen gravel surrounded on three sides by blue-white glaciers, and on the fourth, three thousand feet below it, by the frigid waters of the Antarctic Circle.

"Little different from Tahiti, huh, Doc?" the pilot said with a wicked grin.

"Little bit," Drake allowed.

"Say, what's a big-shot biologist like you coming up here for, anyway?" the pilot asked. "I thought biologists studied trees and plants and things. Nothing green up here for hundreds of miles."

"Doesn't have to be green," Drake replied. "Biology is the science of life. Any living organism. Doesn't have to be a plant or even an animal. It can be algae, fungus, anything." With one gloved fingertip, he wiped a tiny spot of mold from the instrument panel. "This is alive," he said.

The pilot shrugged dubiously. "Say, did you know there's two women on the team down there? One's about a four, the other's an eight, easy. Trouble is, the eight's married. But not to worry, after you been down there awhile, the four'll start looking like a ten."

Drake suppressed a smile. "I won't be there that long."

"Say, Doc, do the gals in Tahiti really run around topless, like in the movies?"

"Just the ones under thirty," Drake told him.

"Damn!" said the pilot. "What the hell am I doing down here close to the South Pole?" Sighing in disgust, he pointed down again and added, "Well, there's the blockhouse and tent city, Doc. Have you on the ground in about ten minutes."

The International Science Foundation research team was housed in a dozen small thermal tents pitched in a loose circle around a cement-walled Quonset hut with a fiberglass-lined corrugated steel roof. Half of the permanent building held two huge generators fueled by natural-gas tanks behind the structure. The rest of it was divided into a laboratory, offices, storage rooms, and a recreation/dining area with a small kitchen.

When Drake lugged his duffel bag inside and set it down, he was met by a thin woman with stringy, dishwater-blond hair, wearing glasses. "Hi," she said, extending a hand. "Sally Gossett. Welcome to what we call the blockhouse. I have the inside duty today. And I'm the four, in case you're wondering."

"Hello. I wasn't wondering." He shook her hand. "I'm Pat Drake."

"It's an honor to meet you, Dr. Drake." She tilted her head an inch. "Think you can save the project?"

"I'll try. How cold is it out there anyway?"

"We're having a little heat wave. It's twelve."

"Above or below?"

She smiled wryly. "Below. We don't measure above. Take off your gear and come on back to the rec room. I've got coffee on."

Drake zipped off his outer thermal suit and walked back into the rec room wearing threadbare jeans and a brightly flowered Polynesian shirt.

"Didn't have time to shop, huh?" Sally said, eyeing the shirt.

"Didn't have time to change," he explained. "The foundation had the duffel waiting for me in Ushuaia; I imagine there are some more suitable clothes in it." He accepted the mug of coffee she offered. "What's your specialty, Dr. Gossett?" he asked.

"Nematodes," she said. Drake nodded. Microscopic worms in a dry, almost lifeless state of anhydrobiosis. "The others will be in from the field any time now," Sally said. "Didn't the foundation give you a background list on us?" he said.

"It's probably in the duffel with my assignment papers and contract," he said.

Just then the front door opened and two men entered and began shedding their thermals. When they were down to corduroys and flannel shirts, they walked back toward Drake and Sally.

"Looks like the *Bounty* has docked," said one, a round-faced little man who swaggered, but smiled at Drake's shirt.

"Either that, or summer's here at last," replied the other, a big, bearded man who lumbered, but also smiled.

"Edward Latham, ecology," said the shorter one. "It's an honor, Dr. Drake."

"Paul Green, geology," said the bigger man. "Likewise."

Drake shook hands with both of them.

Within the next few minutes, two other members of the expedition returned from their day in the field. Harley Neil, a slight, academic-looking young man, was a glaciologist, and Emil Porter, tall and hawkish, was the team's medical doctor. Bottles of scotch, gin, and vodka were produced and cocktails poured all around in metal cups. The first sips were barely taken when two final people came in and Drake heard a voice say, "Hello, Pat."

He didn't have to turn around to know who it was. The voice was one he had heard dozens of times on lazy mornings and soft rainy afternoons, and hundreds of times in subsequent dreams. Turning, he looked at a pale redhead with freckles going down the front of a scoop-necked sweatshirt, and a set of direct, tawny eyes that, as always, riveted him.

"Claire," he said. "Hello. I had no idea you were up here."

"Didn't the foundation give you a background list?" she asked.

"It's probably in my duffel," he said. "The assignment came up so quickly, I haven't had a chance to look at the specs."

"Pat, this is my husband—" Claire began, but she was not quick enough and the man with her stepped forward without offering his hand and said, "I'm Owen Foster. Biology, same as you. And team leader. I've heard a lot about the famous Dr. Patrick Drake."

"You have me at a disadvantage then, Dr. Foster," Drake said evenly, lowering the hand he had half offered. "I haven't heard of you at all."

A moment of stony silence followed, after which Foster smirked and turned to pour drinks for himself and his wife. Then he looked back at Drake and said, "I take it you're here to rescue us from our inefficiency?"

"I'm here to speed up the schedule if I can," Drake said, "before the expedition funding runs out. If there's a problem with inefficiency, I wasn't told about it. Is there?"

"Perhaps you should determine that for yourself," Foster said, shrugging. "Are you officially taking over the team?"

"My contract and specific assignment are in my duffel," Drake said. "Perhaps I'd better go read it before getting into any details." Quickly swallowing what was left of the gin in his metal cup, Drake looked at Sally Gossett and said, "Since you've got the duty today, how about showing me where I bunk."

"Sure, glad to." Sally put down her own cup, warning, "Nobody touch that."

She and Drake dressed in thermals and she led him outside and across the frozen brown gravel to a small, single-occupancy arctic dome tent with an insulated floor, furnished with a cot, camp chair, small desk, and utility storage wall with drawers. A natural-gas camp stove was already burning.

"Heat and electricity never go off," Sally told him. "Sleeping bag on the cot has quad-flaps, depending on how warm-blooded you are. Snacks, liquor, and other goodies are in the drawers there. Direct phone line connects you to the other tents and the blockhouse; there's a list of numbers next to it."

She paused, out of breath, but managed to get in, "So, where do you know Claire from?"

"University of Minnesota," Drake replied, unzipping his parka. "We were on several projects together over about a four-year period."

"I take it you didn't know she was married to Foster?"

"I didn't know she was married to anybody. She was Claire Dunn when I knew her."

"She still goes by Dr. Claire Dunn," Sally said. "Her husband doesn't like that much; he wants her to be Dr. Claire Dunn-Foster, with a hyphen. I think I should warn you: He's very possessive."

"I appreciate the courtesy," Drake said, "but there's no need for it. I'm up here to do a job and get back home to Tahiti as soon as I can. I have no time for personalities."

"Okay, you're the boss. I think you are, anyway. I'm on duty until nine if you need anything. If not, breakfast is at six. Everybody cooks their own. Except Foster, of course. Claire cooks for him. See you when I see you."

"Thanks, Sally."

When he was alone, Drake opened the duffel and found his assignment packet from the foundation. With the official letter of contract and statement of what he was expected to accomplish was a list of the other members of the expedition and their education and experience backgrounds. Her name was at the top of the alphabetical list: DUNN, CLAIRE MARIE; B.S., UNIVERSITY OF MICHIGAN; M.S., UNIVERSITY OF MINNESOTA; DOCTORATE, UNIVERSITY OF WYOMING. BIOLOGIST. SPECIALTY: WILDLIFE.

Drake shook his head wryly. There was a time, he thought, when that specialty could have been two words instead of one. Wild life. He wondered if she had changed much.

At six the next morning, Drake fried himself sausage and eggs in the block-house, ate breakfast with the entire expedition team, then selected a place where he could face them all, and rose to address them.

"As of today, I am the team leader," he announced, handing Owen Foster an envelope containing a letter relieving him of that responsibility and authority. "I want to make it clear that the reason for this change is not to be interpreted as a reflection of Dr. Foster's competence or capability; rather, because he is one of the two certified ice divers on the team, it is to relieve him of planning and administrative duties to free him up for more diving."

Pouring himself a second cup of coffee, Drake shuffled through a sheaf of papers he had brought over from his tent. "Let's look at an overview of the expedition together and see exactly what it is we're facing here," he suggested. "The purpose of this expedition is to try and determine whether the section of the Antarctic ice sheet known as the Brandon Ice Shelf is, because of global warming, beginning to melt faster than previous melting measurements have indicated. If it is melting faster, then, as all of you know, because the Antarctic ice sheets hold about seventy percent of the Earth's fresh water, the premature melting could mix that fresh water with ocean water and raise sea levels by several feet instead of several inches per year. Such an eventuality would submerge coastlines around the world.

"The governments of the United States, Great Britain, Canada, Sweden, and others are not convinced that this is actually occurring, but are precautionary enough to admit that it *could* be. A coalition of a number of coastal countries has therefore contributed to funding this expedition through the International Science Foundation, which in turn put together a team comprised of the seven of you—and I want to interject here that last night I read all of your backgrounds and qualifications, and I'd like you to know individually and collectively that I have never encountered a better, more qualified scientific team than this one. You are an exceptional group, and if any scientists in the world can prove or disprove this premature-melting theory, it is all of you. I consider it a privilege to be working with you."

There was a big grin from Sally Gossett, a slight sneer from Owen Foster, and an exchange of pleased smiles between the others. Drake continued.

"The problem the expedition currently faces is that of diminishing funds and, consequently, abbreviated time to complete the work and establish findings that will either prove or disprove the premature-melting theory. When the money runs out, the time runs out. So the team either speeds up, works harder, and brings its results in, as they say in the common world of business, under budget, or the team fails, the project is written off, and the world's coastal countries, if our theories are sound, face almost certain future swamping. In the latter instance, we go back to our scientific lives with our individual reputations more than a little tarnished. On the other hand, if we succeed, and if we are correct, somewhere down this icy road may lie a shared Nobel prize for scientific achievement."

On that note, Drake paused, studying the expressions of intense interest and excitement that spread over their faces at the mention of the magic words: *Nobel prize*. Sally's grin faded to a determined line, Claire's brown eyes raised to a compelling stare, even Owen Foster's sneer gave way to something less caustic.

"What do you want us to do, chief?" asked Paul Green, the big, bearded geologist.

"I want everybody to go into ultra-high gear out in the field," Drake said firmly. "Last night I read all of the overview reports on the project to date, and in my opinion this theory is going to be resolved in five ways: studies in the changes in Sally's freeze-dried worms; analysis by you, Paul, of ancient volcano ash that you find trapped between the ice layer and the water beneath it; comparison by you, Claire, of the changes in algae, fungi, and bacteria colonizing damp spaces under lichen layers; and by you, Ed, of microorganisms which, because of possible warming, may now be flourishing instead of merely surviving. And lastly, very importantly, the proofs you four find will be locked in by undeniable evidence of changes in algae now known to be living in microbial mats under the ice shelf itself—and that evidence will be brought up by you, Harley, our glaciologist, and by Dr. Foster, who are the team's ice divers.

"What I want, what this expedition *needs*, is longer hours in the field, more samples collected, more analysis of those samples, and more dives to bring up under-shelf life. In other words, maximum performance from each of you—beginning today."

Owen Foster cleared his throat. "What, may I ask, will be your contribution to this effort, Dr. Drake?"

"I will work alternately with each of you, depending on your daily needs, and will assist and advise when and where I deem it necessary. That answer your question?"

Foster nodded brusquely. "No offense," he said with mock pleasantness. "Just want to be sure you have enough to occupy your time."

Drake saw Claire blush slightly, and ignored it as if he had not noticed. So, he thought, she's told him. He paced back and forth several times, sipping his coffee, then turned to face them again. "Can we do it?" he asked, flatly and finally.

"I sure can," Sally Gossett announced. "The thought of a Nobel prize almost gives me an orgasm."

"We can *all* do it," said big Paul Green.

"Bet your ass we can," seconded little Ed Latham.

Drake turned to Harley Neil, the glaciologist/ice diver. "Any problem on the diving end?"

"Not from me," replied the slight, academic-looking young man. He looked at Foster. "How about you, Owen?"

"I'll carry my weight," Foster assured him.

Emil Porter, the team's medical doctor, spoke up next. "I am obliged to point out, Dr. Drake, that your 'high-gear' schedule involving longer hours out in the elements, more dives under pressurized conditions, and less rest and recreational time, may well affect the health of individual members. Do you understand that it is my responsibility to see that they aren't pushed too far, too hard?"

"Certainly," said Drake. "I was about to address that. I'd like to work with you today on matters of diet, increased vitamins, scheduled hours of relaxation and sleep, and anything else you recommend. I fully appreciate your concerns, Doctor, and am in accord with them."

"Very good," said Porter. "I'm pleased to hear that."

Drake waited a moment, then said, "All right, if there's nothing else, you're all excused to go into the field as previously scheduled by Dr. Foster. Ed, I'll relieve you of block duty so you can also go out. Beginning tomorrow, there will be new schedules posted based on what Dr. Porter and I work out today. Come in at the regular time and we'll have an open discussion session tonight to finalize our new approach. See you all then."

Following a shuffling of feet and rustling of thermals, everyone went out into the stark South Pole day, leaving Drake and the medical doctor behind.

"How do you think it went?" Drake asked candidly.

"Very well," replied Emil Porter. "Very well, indeed."

"I hope they can do it," said Drake. "There's a rough road ahead. It's going to take dedication from every single one of them to accomplish this."

"I believe you'll get that dedication, Dr. Drake, I really do."

Drake smiled slightly and nodded. "Okay, let's you and I go to work."

Drake put in place a new schedule of increased workload that was enthusiastically received by the team members, including grudging acceptance by Owen Foster. In order to show the ex-team leader that he was sincere about his own field performance, he took over dive-technician responsibilities the first day in order to allow Foster and Harley Neil to dive at the same time, instead of one of them always remaining on the surface.

The dive site was about midway out on the ice shelf, a considerable distance from where the frozen gravel ended and an ice plateau began. On three sides of the flat were walls of ice as high as Niagara Falls, while on the open side was a sheer ice wall dropping three thousand feet to Antarctic waters. They were the same walls of ice Drake had viewed from the helicopter. Then, however, it had all looked like a picture postcard. Down here, up close and surrounding, it was more like an awesome, frightening world in which humans did not belong.

A small thermal tent served as dive headquarters, with the dives themselves being accomplished through a circular hole in the shelf that was ten feet in diameter and had been cut, with chainsaws, fourteen feet down to the underside of the shelf, where capped water was met.

"What's the water temperature down there?" Drake asked as he helped the two men dress in dry suits and attach pressure hoses.

"Just below the shelf it's warmer than the air up here," Harley Neil replied. "Naturally, the deeper you go, the colder it gets. I think we've both reached forty below, haven't we, Owen?"

"Just over forty, actually?" said Foster. He studied Drake for a moment. "You're sure you're familiar with this equipment?"

"Positive," Drake assured him. "McCullough pressurizer," he pointed out, "Warren lowering rig, McKee oxygen supply," his finger indicated every apparatus at the site, "cable pulls, generator, backup generator, underwater lantern, electrical batteries, radio intercom. Don't worry, Dr. Foster, I'll get you back up."

As Foster shuffled over to get his dive helmet, Drake said to Harley, "You apprehensive too?"

The young glaciologist grinned. "Not me. I love it below the shelf. I feel at home down there. It's very peaceful. When I die, I'd rather die down there than from cancer or some horror like that up here."

The last place in the world, Drake thought, that this young man looked like he ought to be was in an ice-diving dry suit. Teaching fourth grade somewhere, maybe, but not getting ready to go down a fourteen-foot hole in an Antarctic ice shelf. Drake smiled and patted the younger man on the back.

Foster and Neil dove to forty-four feet that day, found a microbial mat, which was an underwater colony of black algae formed protectively around itself, part of which they scooped up and gathered into break-proof glass tubes to bring back to the surface. It was a successful first-time dive together for the two men, and Drake raised them back to the surface of the shelf without incident.

The following day, Drake worked in the field with big Paul Green, climbing dark, bare crags that rose from the frozen gravel floor to isolated peaks and pinnacles above, to collect rock samples that the bearded geologist praised as if they were nuggets of solid gold.

"Man, look at this little baby," he would say reverently, digging out a rock that had on the underside of its bland gray surface layers of splendid yellow, blue, and orange. "This little sweetheart has been kept cold and dry for a million years, Dr. Drake."

"Call me Pat, please," said Drake. "Good specimen?"

"One of the best I've found," said Green, putting it gently into his waist pack.

On another day, out with Sally Gossett, Drake was moved by the great passion the young woman had for the remote life that was the subject of her work. Using soft tweezers to remove one tiny, curved, yellow bit of microorganism from within a few grains of sandstone, she said almost in a whisper, "Look, Dr. Drake. This tiny fragment of life may be tens of thousands of years old. Can you believe that? It's always hungry, always cold, lives in continuous misery, yet it *survives*."

"Tell me how," Drake asked, although he already was reasonably certain.

"Well," Sally said quietly, "it gets a little bit of natural light every day for an atom of energy, a trace of moisture from the ocean air, and is able to extract an incredibly minuscule bit of mineral from the sandstone for sustenance. And with just that it's able to survive longer than the oldest, strongest tree in any forest in the world."

Drake nodded quietly. This young woman, he thought, was not a four on *any* scale.

After a week, it was clear that the expedition results had increased by a marked percentage, and, according to Dr. Porter, had done so without any adverse health effects on any individual team member. The medical doctor had established a nightly recreation period which required cards, checkers, and trivia games rather than simply sitting around talking while consuming scotch and gin.

"More mental relaxation and less alcohol consumption results in better overall function the next day," Porter explained. He also established a short calisthenics routine before breakfast every morning. "Wakes up the endorphins in the brain that are the foundation for feelings of good physical and mental well-being," he said.

Team members, even Owen Foster, went along with everything the medical doctor suggested. And Drake knew why. The magic spun by Alfred Nobel loomed tantalizingly before them. That and their own professionalism. Still, it almost seemed too easy to him, too smooth. He wondered if it would last. He soon found out.

Drake was alone, working on a routine report to the foundation, when his tent phone rang one night.

"Drake here," he answered.

"Pat, it's Claire. Is it okay if I drop over and talk to you for a few minutes?"

He could not help hesitating before answering, and it gave her the opportunity to reinforce her request.

"It'll be all right, Pat. All the men are in a poker game, and Sally's watching a video movie. Just for a few minutes, Pat, please." She seemed to force a lightness into her voice. "Listen, I promise not to even take off my thermals."

"All right, Claire," he said. "Come on over."

She was there in less than five minutes, out of breath when she removed her hood and face mask, creating old desires in Drake as she shook out her red hair.

"I ran over to turn on the light in Owen's and my tent in case he misses me and looks out the window."

"Claire, I'm not sure this is smart," Drake said, curbing the warm feeling in the pit of his abdomen.

"It probably isn't, but it's necessary, Pat. Look, I'm having a real problem with Owen. He knows about us; our past, I mean. It was stupid, but I told him. I have this thing about honesty in a marriage. I thought he would just consider the past to be the past. But he's becoming more unreasonable and suspicious every day."

"That's ridiculous, Claire. There's no basis for any suspicion. This is the first time I've even been alone with you since I arrived. I've made a point of only doing field and lab work with you when there was another team member present—"

"I know that, Pat. And you know it. But Owen doesn't—not when he's in the water forty or fifty feet under the ice shelf." She put a hand on his arm. "Pat, I'm telling you this for the sake of the project. I know Owen. He's volatile and he's got a short fuse. He could blow up over this and ruin the entire expedition."

With her standing close enough to touch his arm, Drake saw that perspiration had broken on her brow and upper lip.

"Take off your thermals," he said. "If you don't, you'll catch pneumonia when you step back outside."

"Thanks," Claire said with relief, unzipping her sleeves and pant legs to shed the heat-producing outer garb. She sat on the side of the bunk and Drake immediately wished she had taken the camp chair instead. "Listen, can I have one of those little bottles of gin, Pat? I'm very nervous."

He opened a small pantry on the utility storage wall and twisted the top off a jigger-size bottle of Bombay. He was looking around for a clean cup when she took it out of his hand.

"That's okay," she said, and drank it straight from the miniature bottle. When it was down, she smiled and fixed her brownish orange eyes on him in a way that still, after all the years, beguiled him. "Reminds me of when we used to lie in front of the fireplace and sip wine from the same bottle on those icy Sunday afternoons back in Minnesota." Instantly then, her expression became dejected. "God, Pat, whatever happened to us?"

Drake shook his head dismally. "I don't know, Claire. Time passes, people change, life paths turn in other directions." He sat down on the bunk and put an arm around her shoulders. "But you've done all right, Claire. You've got your doctorate and you're married to someone in your field of interest. I must tell you that I've found Owen to be a really exceptional scientist—"

"The only thing Owen is exceptional at," Claire snapped, "is being a world-class son of a bitch." She rose and quickly unbuttoned her flannel shirt. "Would you like to see my bruises, Pat? They're all recent, since you got here. He only hits me on the body so it won't show—"

Drake stood and put his arms around her. "Don't, please, Claire. It's not necessary. I believe you. What can I do to help?"

"I don't know." She shook her head against his chest. "I'm not sure there's anything either of us can do. What is, is. We just have to get through it." Backing away from him, she rebuttoned her shirt and reached for her thermals. "I'd better go, Pat. I'm sorry about this. I just wanted to warn you for the sake of the project." Her eyes softened and she lightly touched his cheek with her fingertips. "I would very much like to see you become a Nobel laureate in science, Dr. Patrick Drake. I would be so proud."

Before he knew it, she was gone, and he was left with the fresh memory of her breasts against his chest. And the thought that they might have bruises on them from the fists of Owen Foster.

The next day, Drake worked with Ed Latham, the swaggering but smiling little geologist. They climbed up to, then out upon, one of the lower promontory glaciers that formed the high walls around the shelf. There, protected by wind panels they put up, they laboriously and methodically used handheld razor rakes to scrape away layer after layer of ice until, about three feet down, they encountered a strain of light rust running parallel to the surface.

"Iron," said Latham. "We're close to something."

Carefully, he scraped past the redness, dismissing it as scientifically worthless, and dug a few more inches until he reached a second strain that was black as tar.

"Ah, this is what we want," he said jovially.

"Ash?" asked Drake.

"Yep. Very old ash. From some ancient volcano that used to be here. It got trapped between the ice layer and the water underneath, and froze so quickly that it's been preserved ever since. Would you hold this collection jar for me, Dr. Drake?"

"Certainly. And call me Pat, please."

After their climb down, and on the walk back, Drake was staring distractedly out at the starkness of the shelf when Latham asked, "So how are we doing, Pat?"

"I'm sorry, what?" Drake said, when Latham's voice got through his reverie.

"I asked how we're doing. You know, the team. Are you okay?"

"Yes, I'm fine. Just a little tired today. We're doing splendidly, Ed. Better than I hoped."

Except, he thought, for those bruises on Claire's body.

When they got back to the blockhouse, they found that the gin and scotch had been broken out early by the rest of the team, who were in an exuberant mood over what Owen Foster had collected under the ice shelf on his dive that day.

"Look at these, Pat!" Sally all but screeched, running to him with an underwater collection tube. "Look what Owen found! Look at the color of these!"

Examining the jar, Drake detected, among a small cluster of black algae, several that were not completely black, but rather bluish black. Where did you find them?" Drake asked.

"It'll all be in my report, Doctor," Foster said with smug aloofness.

Drake, thoughts of Claire's bruises still circulating, took a step forward, eyes narrowing, and said, "Don't get cute with me, Foster, or I'll have you on the next goddamned helicopter out of here. Now where'd you find them?"

"Forty-nine feet down," Foster said tightly, his own eyes darkening in anger. "There's a microbial mat down there that's definitely different from the earlier ones Harley and I have found. It's—I don't know, a *tighter* mat, more closely formed—"

"Maybe to protect this lighter species," Claire offered.

"Protect it from what?" Owen snapped, throwing her an annoyed look.

"From warmth that it's not used to," Sally interjected. "From warmth that it's never felt, and is instinctively frightened of."

"Of course," Drake said, almost speaking to himself. "Warmth coming from far down. So far down that the water is warmer—"

Now Owen Foster's expression became excited. "Because global warming is pushing heavier warm water *under* the ice cap—"

"—and it's gradually working its way upward," Drake finished the thought for him.

"I'll be damned," Ed Latham whispered.

"Me too," agreed Paul Green. The big bear of a man and his smaller friend slapped hands like a couple of basketball players.

A silence came over the group then, only momentary, but as if dictated by some higher plane of feeling that somehow governed them all individually and as a group. It was almost religious, perhaps even divine. For a split instant of time, they were like apostles who suddenly found themselves in the presence of their god.

Finally, Drake stepped over and poured a drink for himself. He raised it in a toast.

"Colleagues," he said, "I think this is our breakthrough."

Drake worked up a new schedule that night, focusing entirely on the latest evidence gathered from Owen Foster's dive. Sally, Claire, and Ed Latham were assigned exclusively to laboratory duty, running full-spectrum tests on the new blue-black algae. Porter, the medical doctor, took over block duty and pitched in to help in the preparation of reports. Foster and Harley Neil increased their diving-schedule depth by decreasing the time spent underwater. Drake and big Paul Green worked together as dive techs to expedite the submersions, decreasing dive prep time, and shuttling fresh samples back to the blockhouse lab.

"Keep a tight rein on the dive times and depths, Pat," Porter cautioned the next morning as the four men prepared to leave for the dive site.

"I will, Emil," Drake assured the tall, hawkish man. "I'm not going to blow this by being overanxious, believe me."

By noon that day, Harley Neil had returned to the surface with more bluish black algae, this sampling containing an even lighter blue cast than the previous day's find.

"How far down?" Drake asked.

"Fifty-two feet," the young diver replied.

When Foster came up a little while later from fifty-five feet, the bluish tint was lighter still. A subsequent dive by both men that afternoon, down to fifty-nine feet, produced for the first time a *greenish* black sample.

"They're getting lighter," Owen Foster said elatedly as he and Harley sat through routine medical exams by Emil Porter at the end of the day.

"Definitely," Harley agreed. "I just wish there was some way we could get around the random gathering and be more selective in what we catch—"

"Maybe there is," Foster said. "Why not each take a second lantern for more light? That way we'll be able to better distinguish color down there."

"But what about the weight? A second lantern, I don't know—"

"We can handle the weight," Foster said confidently.

Drake cut into the conversation, saying, "You may be able to handle it, but I'm not so sure about the generators supplying the power. I don't want them running hot. Let's not rush this, okay?"

Foster glared at him for a moment, then replied grudgingly, "You're the boss, Drake."

"That's right, I am," Drake said evenly.

And if you don't like it, he thought, *try punching me around.*

The next day, Foster and Neil each made two more dives, the first to sixty-two feet, which prompted Emil Porter, who came out to the dive site for samples, to say to Drake, "This worries me, Pat, diving into the sixties like this."

"It's got to be done, Emil," Drake insisted. "The deeper we go, the lighter the algae we find. We've *got* to follow through on this."

"Then shorten the dives," the doctor said. "More depth, less time down. Compensate."

"Okay, okay. I'll try."

But that afternoon, on the second dive, with both men at sixty-five feet, Drake let the dive run a few minutes longer.

"This is risky, Pat," said Paul Green nervously.

"Just keep it to yourself," Drake said shortly. "This has to be up to Owen and Harley, not us or Emil Porter. They know what they can handle down there."

But as it turned out, one of them did not. Even though the afternoon dive produced the best, lightest-green-pigmented algae yet found, it effectively eliminated Harley Neil from dive duty.

"You're grounded," Dr. Porter announced after the evening physical exam.

"What! Like hell I am!" Harley protested.

"I have the medical authority to keep you out of the water," Porter said flatly. "I'm exercising that authority." He turned to Drake. "I warned you, Pat."

"What's the basis for your decision?" Drake asked.

"Blood alkalinity is down, systolic and diastolic pressure both up, there's some ocular expansion, and the beginning of sinus stricture. That enough for you?" Without waiting for an answer, he turned back to Harley. "No alcohol for twenty-four hours, no diving for forty-eight. Then I'll reevaluate you."

"Damn it, this cuts the dive schedule in half!" Harley pounded the side of his fist on the table.

"No, it doesn't," Drake said. "I'll take your place. I'm certified."

Dr. Porter raised one eyebrow skeptically. "How long has it been since you dived?"

"Awhile. But I *am* certified. Radio the foundation if you don't believe me." He bobbed his chin at Neil. "Harley can work as dive tech, can't he?"

"Of course. He can do anything but go under."

"Harley, do you have specs on the dry suits we're using? And a current dive manual?"

"Sure. I'll get them."

The thought of the next day was already generating bursts of apprehension in Drake's mind. He had not dived in a dry suit in more than five years. Any recent diving he had done had been in a wet suit, with scuba gear, in Polynesian and Australian waters. With that kind of history, the smart way to approach the ice-shelf exploration would have been to spend half an hour at twenty feet the first day, forty-five minutes at thirty-five the second, an hour at fifty feet the third, then try a deeper dive. He was going to have to spend about ninety minutes at sixty-plus feet the first day. It was going to be not only arduous but dangerous.

But, he had already decided, it was necessary. If there was going to be an individual Nobel prize for the diver who found the algae that conclusively proved the theory, maybe *he* would be the one to get it.

Later that night, while Drake was carefully reviewing a schematic of the dry suit's valves and attachments, Owen Foster walked into his tent without knocking.

"Just what the hell are you up to, Drake?" he demanded.

"What are you talking about, Foster? And don't you know how to knock?"

"Never mind knocking! And you know damn well what I'm talking about! You set it up with Porter to replace Harley with yourself to make you the lead diver. You want to be the one who brings up the conclusive algae, don't you?"

"That's absurd," said Drake. "I don't care *who* brings it up, as long as the team gets it—"

"Will you guarantee to let me do the deeper dives first?" Foster challenged.

"No, I can't do that." Drake tried to reason with him. "If I see something that's deeper than you are, or deeper than you've been, I have to go for it. This is a scientific endeavor, not some kind of contest, Foster—"

"Yeah, right," Foster snapped. "I suppose you're not trying to impress Claire to get her back either?"

"No, I'm not—"

"I suppose you're going to tell me she hasn't been to your tent since you got here?"

"She came to my tent just to talk. She said she was worried about the project—"

"You're a goddamned liar," Foster said. From under his parka he drew a serrated ice knife and brandished it malevolently. "You listen and you listen good, you son of a bitch. You're not getting my wife, and you're not cheating me out of being the one who brings up the algae sample that proves the warming theory. *I* am going to be the one the scientific world applauds for *that. I* am going to be the one whose name goes into the history books, and *I* am going to be the one on this team who gets an *individual* Nobel prize!"

Drake eyed the knife warily. "You're sick, Foster. You need therapy."

"The only thing I need is for you to stay out of my dive depth tomorrow. I'd gut you right now if I wasn't afraid it would terminate the project. But if you dive past me tomorrow, I swear I'll cut your air hose and let you die down there!"

With that, the enraged man turned and stalked out.

No sooner was Foster gone than Drake's tent phone rang. It was Claire.

"Has he been there?" she asked anxiously.

"Yes, he just left."

"Pat, I'm frightened. He's losing it. It infuriated him that you were diving with him tomorrow instead of Harley. He's afraid that you're going to be the star now, and he'll be just another team member. Listen, can you come and get me?"

"Come and get you?"

"Just to walk with me from the blockhouse to Sally's tent. Everyone else is already gone. Sally's in a two-person tent and said I could bunk with her tonight. She knows that I'm terrified of Owen. Especially since he believes that—well, you and I, you know—"

"I'll be over in ten minutes," Drake told her.

When Drake got over to the blockhouse, Claire was not dressed to leave, as he had known she would not be. Instead, she was in the little kitchen with coffee poured for both of them. Drake zipped off his thermals and sat down with her.

"How in hell did you ever get mixed up with a psycho like Foster?" he asked without preliminary.

Claire shrugged helplessly. "I don't know," she said sadly. "After you and I broke up, I kind of drifted. I was involved with an aeronautical engineer out in California, until I found out that his fifteen-year-old daughter wasn't his daughter at all, but a runaway he had been keeping in his home for over a year as an extra bed partner. Then there was a faculty head in Colorado who got me dangerously into the drug scene before I came to my senses and got out. In Texas there was a wealthy rancher, who was the father of one of my students at the University of Houston, who swore that he and his wife were on the brink of a divorce, but whose wife eventually came to me and threatened to gouge my eyes out with her spurs if I didn't leave her husband alone." She smiled wistfully. "I just couldn't seem to connect with anyone who came up to your standards, Pat, which was what I was trying to do. I wanted very badly to come back to you, I even tried to find you—"

"I didn't know that," Drake said in surprise.

"It's true. I called everyone we mutually knew to locate you. I was going to beg you to give us another chance together. But when I finally found out where you were, you were engaged to somebody named Cindy or something—"

"Wendy."

"—and the two of you had left for Africa on an agriculture project of some kind. So I dropped my desperate quest and started drifting again. When I met Owen, I was down to my last emotion. Unfortunately, I used it on him." Claire rose and turned off the overhead fluorescents, leaving the little kitchen in subdued countertop light. "Do you mind? I have a raging headache." Walking to the room's only window, she pressed a button to electronically raise the thermal shade, and looked out at the ghostly white moonlit night. Drake rose and came over to stand with her.

"So whatever happened to Cindy?" she asked.

"Wendy. She dumped me for a great white hunter. Some guy who worked as a guide for *National Geographic*."

"Did you find anyone else?"

"No," he answered quietly. "I didn't try. By then I knew I couldn't replace you."

They were in each other's arms quickly then, moving in tandem away from the window, to the far end of the counter where the light barely reached, and where she could sit up on the countertop and they could open just enough buttons, just enough zippers, move just enough fabric aside for what they both wanted.

"Don't hold me too tight, Pat," she whispered. "My bruises—"

While they were locked together, her head thrown back, his mouth on her throat, Drake made up his mind to kill Owen Foster under the ice shelf the next day.

The dive site the next morning had an unusually ominous aura about it. The frigid air somehow seemed thinner and more difficult to breathe, the stratocumulus clouds looked low enough to reach up and touch, and during the night some extraordinary wave of heat, the kind of phenomenon unique to Antarctica, had thawed an inch of ice on the surface of the shelf to create a slush in which the scientists had to maneuver about. "This is downright spooky," said big Paul Green, shuddering involuntarily. Along with grounded Harley Neil, he was a dive tech this morning.

"Tell me about it," Harley agreed.

The two men got the dive equipment in place and the generators running, tested everything, then went into the ready tent where Drake and Foster, warily facing each other without speaking, were suiting up. They had everything on except helmet, gloves, and the utility belt which held, on one side, rubber cases containing sample-collection tubes, and on the other, an assortment of small tools to facilitate removing ice or rock in which a microbial mat had been formed by algae for protection.

As the two techs checked each suited diver and helped them on with the belt and gloves, Owen Foster said to them, "I want maximum slack today, beginning at sixty-eight feet. Understand?"

"You don't want to push it, Owen," cautioned Harley. "It won't do the project any good if you end up grounded too."

"Just give me the slack," Foster ordered. "I know what I'm doing."

Harley looked to Drake for approval as team leader. Drake nodded. "Give me the same slack," he told Harley.

Outside, at the lip of the ten-foot dive hole down the fourteen-foot icy cylindrical walls, at the bottom of which the men could see the cerulean water the shelf covered, the techs placed on each diver in turn the heavy, globe-like helmet through which they would receive air and voice communication from the surface. Each diver sat down on an empty equipment crate and waited patiently as his suit was pressurized and the radio reception checked. Several minutes later, they were ready to go.

"Okay," said Harley, "here's the routine but required safety speech. Your dry suits are safe in water of this temperature to a depth of eighty feet. You will have maximum slack of depth plus twenty feet during this dive to accommodate lateral movement only. The suit environment gauges are in the control panel on your left sleeve just below the elbow. When the panel lid is opened, there is an illuminated digital screen on its underside, with command buttons for all functions directly under it. Watch your suit pressure and temperature, watch your heart rate, and watch your depth." He gave each of them a double pat on top of their helmet. "Good luck."

Protocol required that Drake enter the water first. With a powerful underwater lantern secured over his right shoulder, he backed up to the hole and laboriously descended a metal ladder spiked to the inside wall. In less than a minute, his heavy, weighted boots reached the water, and seconds later he hand-walked the final few rungs and submerged.

Owen Foster quickly followed him.

For Pat Drake, being in the water under the ice shelf was like diving back into prehistoric time. He had never been in a body of water that large and that deep, yet devoid of visible, moving sea life. He felt almost as if he were in a synthetic world, a place surreal and unnatural. Inside the diving helmet, his eyes were wide with wonder, his lips parted in silent exclamation. The powerful high-intensity, mercury-metallic iodide incandescence of his lantern, spreading from fourteen inches square to a light the size of a small theater screen twenty feet in front of him, illuminated for him a domain that few humans would ever see. Its terrain, much like that above the shelf, was pitched with crags, crevices, and fissures that once had been above the water and walked on by creatures long extinct, perhaps even scientifically unknown.

Drake's reverie was interrupted by the sudden intrusion of a second shaft of light as Owen Foster descended to the level where Drake was treading with one hand on a protrusion of rock. As Foster glided near him, Drake flipped open the control panel on his sleeve and pressed the blue depth button. The digital screen immediately read: 48. He switched on his radio.

"Harley, this is Drake, reporting both divers at forty-eight. Beginning further descent."

When Foster came into Drake's field of light, Drake saw that he had in his hand the serrated knife he had wielded the previous night when he intruded in Drake's tent. Drake trod backward a little along the rock and held his left hand up, palm out, to indicate that he wanted no trouble. He pointed to Foster, then downward with a thumb, signaling for him to take the lead in the dive. Foster pushed off and began to descend.

At fifty-eight feet, Foster paused for several moments. Drake came down to within a few feet of his depth, but kept well away from him in the lateral distance between them. His mind was racing. *I've got to do this*, he told himself, having now admitted to himself that he wanted Claire back, and that the only way for him to get her was for them to be free of Owen Foster. The previous night, after he and Claire had left the blockhouse and parted, he had gone to sleep thinking how wonderful it had felt being with her again, touching her, loving her. But later, in a nightmarish dream, he had seen her naked body black and blue from her husband's fists, and he had awakened sweating and angry. It was then that he got out of bed and rummaged in the drawers of the utility wall until he found a box of ice nails. Four inches long, their points needle-sharp, they were used on surface ice and rocks, hammered in as hangers for collection vessels. Selecting one of them, he took the cork from an open bottle of wine he had in the tent, cut off an inch of it to push over the nail's point, and had carried it with him to the dive site that morning. When no one was looking, he slipped it into one of the cases on his dive belt, where it now lay.

Drake reported his depth to the surface again, certain that Foster had done the same, then waited while Foster continued his descent. He saw that Foster still had the knife in one hand, and continued to keep a sensible distance between them. Presently he descended to sixty-five feet and began moving his lantern over a small ridge of crags, looking for signs of mat colonization. He knew that Foster, several feet farther down, could see that Drake was holding back to allow Foster first look in the deeper water. *I'll wait*, he thought, *until he finds something worth collecting, until he begins to concentrate on his job, and then I'll drop silently behind him and puncture his suit with the ice nail—*

Suddenly Drake's attention was caught by several dots of color down the wall of the crag. It manifested in the light for only a split instant, but Drake could have sworn it was a very light green, almost lime in hue. Could it possibly have been algae? he wondered. Algae without any blue or black, which were the colors produced by colder water? Squinting, frowning, he moved deeper, closer into the crags. Glancing over, he saw that he was now several feet farther down than Foster, but Foster's light was pointed away from him now, and Foster seemed to be occupied with his own search.

Momentarily dismissing the other diver from his mind, Drake began to carefully examine the crag area where he thought he had seen the light green color. In only a matter of seconds, he had found it: a microbial mat formed by a multitude of millions, perhaps billions, of microscopic organisms that had to have been, because of their light green color, getting a source of *comparative* warmth from somewhere.

This is it! Drake thought excitedly. *This will be enough to keep the project going, to get more money, deeper diving gear, to let us go far enough down to prove the warming theory—*

"Pat, what's your depth?" he heard Harley's voice from the surface.

Drake flipped open his control panel and pressed the depth button.

"Seventy-one."

"That's deep enough," said Harley. "Run a gauge check."

Drake glanced over at Foster. It looked as if he had moved farther away; his light source was about five feet higher and some twenty feet off to Drake's right. Drake ran the gauge test, pressing a sequence of buttons on his sleeve panel.

"Pressure okay," he reported. "Valves okay. Power okay. Everything's fine, Harley."

"Don't go any deeper, Pat."

"Ten-four."

If I hurry, Drake thought, *I can collect this sample, then take care of Foster on the way up.* Looking over, he saw that Foster's light was still in the same place. Quickly unsnapping a collection tube from his utility belt, he used a sand brush to carefully begin moving the light green algae into the tube. When he felt he had enough, he capped the tube and had just attached it back to the belt when he sensed a presence close to him.

Drake turned just as Owen Foster, without his lantern, loomed up in front of him, serrated knife in hand.

Foster moved toward him. Drake backed off and directed the blazing light of his own lantern directly in Foster's face. Inside Foster's helmet, Drake saw his eyes squint blindly. Even so, Foster continued forward and Drake saw his hand come up and slash the water in front of him with the knife. Frantically, Drake fumbled in his utility pack for the ice nail. Again Foster advanced, again the knife slashed. After what seemed like an eternity, Drake found the heavy nail and thumbed off the piece of protective cork he had put over its needle point. But when Foster's knife hewed close to him a third time, he realized that he could not get past it to use the nail without fatally exposing himself. He had hoped to come up on Foster from behind and puncture his dive suit in one of the armpits, where there was less reinforcement; now that plan had been neutralized by the knife and Foster's unexpected aggression. But Drake knew he had to do something—

In desperation, Drake let himself drop several feet and spun to his right, down and away from the hand that held the knife. Reaching out with the nail, he tried to drive it into one leg of Foster's suit, but could not reach it. Foster cut recklessly with the knife again, slashing downward, and this time the blade struck Drake's helmet and twisted out of Foster's hand. Both Foster and Drake watched the knife float as if in slow motion down out of the light path into darkness and disappear.

Foster regrouped quickly from the loss of his weapon, drew his knees up, and maneuvered over Drake until he was behind him, then lowered himself and locked both legs around the neck of Drake's helmet. Their combined weight drove them several feet deeper, but that did not concern Drake; he was too relieved by the knowledge that he now had Foster in an irreversible position of vulnerability. Foster no longer had the knife—but Drake still had the ice nail.

Closing his eyes, thinking about Claire, hating this man above him who had beaten her, Drake reached up with the ice nail and pushed its point smartly through the skin of Owen Foster's dry suit.

There was an immediate reduction of weight on Drake as Foster's suit depressurized and the legs locked around Drake's neck went limp. Drake untangled himself from Foster, working down and a few feet away, then held depth, treading.

"Pat, we're getting a depress warning on Owen!" Harley's urgent voice sounded. "Where is he?"

"I can't see him," Drake lied, "but his light is about thirty feet starboard of me and eight feet above. Want me to go over there?"

"Negative! Stay away from his lines! We're bringing him up!"

"Ten-four."

Reaching up, Drake held onto Foster's feet. He felt tension from above as they tried to pull Foster up, but managed to hold on enough to keep him down. They pulled, he held—for a full minute, until Drake's arms began to give out. Then he let go. *Pull him up*, he thought then. *You're bringing up a dead man.*

Suddenly Drake felt very warm and cozy in his own dry suit, very secure and almost light-headed, now that what he had to do was over. He thought of Claire and the life they would have together, of the Nobel prize he would almost certainly receive—an *individual* prize, too, because *he* would be the one to bring up the first conclusive proof of premature warming. When the expedition was further funded and they got new, deeper dive equipment, he would personally do all the diving; it would be *his* name in the scientific history books—

Almost as if it were a sign, a signal, of his new enthrallment with the future, Drake's peripheral vision picked up something new: a reflection, a gleam, something pinpoint and shiny. It was down five or six feet, over about ten, on the flat facing of an undersea wall. Drake dropped on an angle until he was next to it, and peered out at his finding through the faceplate. His eyes grew wide as they had earlier, but when his lips parted this time it was not in silence.

"I'll be damned," he said aloud.

Inches in front of him was the most beautiful colony of algae he had ever seen. Beautiful yellow algae. Beautiful orange algae. Beautiful *warm* algae. Algae that conclusively proved the expedition's theory.

"Pat, Mayday!" Harley's voice reached Drake again. "Mayday, Pat wake up! What's your depth? Mayday!—"

Drake lazily pressed the depth button on his arm. The digital numbers read: 93.

Seconds later, Drake's lungs turned to ice.

Claire lugged her duffel over to the blockhouse and dropped it just inside the door to take off her thermals. Emil Porter was already there, his own duffel in the same place. They were waiting for the helicopter to return for them, its third trip that morning after taking Ed Latham and Paul Green, then Sally Gossett and Harley Neil, to Ushuaia on two earlier trips. As Claire sat down at one of the card tables, Porter poured a shot of vodka into a cup of tomato juice for her. At the same time, she showed Porter an envelope.

"Sally gave me this before she flew out. Pat left it for me in case anything happened to him under the ice shelf."

"What is it?" Porter asked, sipping his own Bloody Mary.

"A handwritten amendment to a will he has on file back in Minnesota, making me the beneficiary of his foundation dive insurance, and leaving me his beachfront home and laboratory in Tahiti."

Porter raised his eyebrows, impressed. "Well, you said that Pat was as generous and protective as Owen was petty and possessive. Looks like you knew them both pretty well." He tilted his head slightly. "Do you realize what this means, Claire? A million dollars from Owen's dive policy, a million from Pat's, and now the property in Tahiti in addition. You're a wealthy woman."

"Except that I feel a little shabby about what I did to Pat," she confessed.

Porter reached across the table and took her hands. "Don't make a guilt trip out of it, Claire," he said quietly. "What happened to Pat and Owen, they did to themselves. We told a couple of lies: you about having bruises, me about Harley Neil's fitness to dive. We put Pat and Owen under the ice together, that's all. Maybe what happened was over you, maybe it was over a Nobel prize, maybe both. Whatever, it was *their* doing."

From outside came the sound of helicopter rotor blades. Porter rose and gently drew Claire to her feet, pulling her close.

"Look, based on the sample they found on Pat's belt, there'll be a new team up here in thirty days, so our expedition was a success. You and I got what we wanted, each other—plus a lot more, it turns out. Put the past behind you, Claire. Focus on tomorrow. You've waited a long time to be happy again. Enjoy it. With me."

Claire nodded, smiling a slight little smile of solace, and let Porter lead her to the front door to don their thermals.

Moments later, carrying their duffels, they walked together across the great shelf of ice toward the helicopter.

Lawrence Block

In for a Penny

LAWRENCE BLOCK is one of those rare writers who started at the bottom, penning paperback originals, and, through determination, some luck, and enormous growth as a writer, has come to dominate the contemporary mystery scene with two equally popular series. Brooding investigator Matt Scudder, who last appeared in *Even the Wicked,* isn't even a shirttail relative of droll gentleman thief Bernie Rhodenbarr, but they are both rendered with the same style and grace that blesses every book or short story that Larry Block writes. He also has a series character who only appears in short fiction, the philosophic hit man known only as Keller, whose exploits were recently collected in the anthology *Hit Man.* Read him, enjoy him. "In for a Penny" first appeared in the December issue of *Ellery Queen's Mystery Magazine.*

In for a Penny

Lawrence Block

Paul kept it very simple. That seemed to be the secret. You kept it simple, you drew firm lines and didn't cross them. You put one foot in front of the other, took it day by day, and let the days mount up.

The state didn't take an interest. They put you back on the street with a cheap suit and figured you'd be back inside before the pants got shiny. But other people cared. This one outfit, about two parts ex-cons to one part holy joes, had wised him up and helped him out. They'd found him a job and a place to live, and what more did he need?

The job wasn't much, frying eggs and flipping burgers in a diner at Twenty-third and Eighth. The room wasn't much, either, seven blocks south of the diner, four flights up from the street. It was small, and all you could see from its window was the back of another building. The furnishings were minimal—an iron bedstead, a beat-up dresser, a rickety chair—and the walls needed paint and the floor needed carpet. There was a sink in the room, a bathroom down the hall. No cooking, no pets, no overnight guests, the landlady told him. No kidding, he thought.

His shift was four to midnight, Monday through Friday. The first weekend he did nothing but go to the movies, and by Sunday night he was ready to climb the wall. Too much time to kill, too few ways to kill it that wouldn't get him in trouble. How many movies could you sit through? And a movie cost him two hours' pay, and if you spent the whole weekend dragging yourself from one movie house to another . . .

Weekends were dangerous, one of the ex-cons had told him. Weekends could put you back in the joint. There ought to be a law against weekends.

But he figured out a way around it. Walking home Tuesday night, after that first weekend of movie-going, he'd stopped at three diners on Seventh Avenue, nursing a cup of coffee and chatting with the guy behind the counter. The third time was the charm; he walked out of there with a week-end job. Saturday and Sunday, same hours, same wages, same work. And they'd pay him off the books, which made his weekend work tax-free.

Between what he was saving in taxes and what he wasn't spending on movies, he'd be a millionaire.

Well, maybe he'd never be a millionaire. Probably be dangerous to be a millionaire, a guy like him, with his ways, his habits. But he was earning an honest dollar, and he ate all he wanted on the job, seven days a week now, so it wasn't hard to put a few bucks aside. The weeks added up and so did the dollars, and the time came when he had enough cash socked away to buy himself a little television set. The cashier at his weekend job set it up and her boyfriend brought it over, so he figured it fell off a truck or walked out of somebody's apartment, but it got good reception and the price was right.

It was a lot easier to pass the time once he had the TV. He'd get up at ten or eleven in the morning, grab a shower in the bathroom down the hall, then pick up doughnuts and coffee at the corner deli. Then he'd watch a little TV until it was time to go to work.

After work he'd stop at the same deli for two bottles of cold beer and some cigarettes. He'd settle in with the TV, a beer bottle in one hand and a cigarette in the other and his eyes on the screen.

He didn't get cable, but he figured that was all to the good. He was better off staying away from some of the stuff they were allowed to show on cable TV. Just because you had cable didn't mean you had to watch it, but he knew himself, and if he had it right there in the house how could he keep himself from looking at it?

And that could get you started. Something as simple as late-night adult programming could put him on a train to the big house upstate. He'd been there. He didn't want to go back.

He would get through most of a pack of cigarettes by the time he turned off the light and went to bed. It was funny, during the day he hardly smoked at all, but back in his room at night he had a butt going just about all the time. If the smoking was heavy, well, the drinking was ultralight. He could make a bottle of Bud last an hour. More, even. The second bottle was always warm by the time he got to it, but he didn't mind, nor did he drink it any faster than he'd drunk the first one. What was the rush?

Two beers were enough. All it did was give him a little buzz, and when the second beer was gone he'd turn off the TV and sit at the window, smoking one cigarette after another, looking out at the city.

Then he'd go to bed. Then he'd get up and do it all over again.

The only problem was walking home.

And even that was no problem at first. He'd leave his rooming house around three in the afternoon. The diner was ten minutes away, and that left him time to eat before his shift started. Then he'd leave sometime between midnight and twelve-thirty—the guy who relieved him, a manic Albanian, had a habit of showing up ten to fifteen minutes late. Paul would retrace his earlier route, walking the seven blocks down Eighth Avenue to Sixteenth Street, with a stop at the deli for cigarettes and beer.

The Rose of Singapore was the problem.

The first time he walked past the place, he didn't even notice it. By day it was just another seedy bar, but at night the neon glowed and the jukebox music poured out the door, along with the smell of spilled drinks and stale beer and something more, something unnameable, something elusive.

"If you don't want to slip," they'd told him, "stay out of slippery places."

He quickened his pace and walked on by.

The next afternoon the Rose of Singapore didn't carry the same feeling of danger. Not that he'd risk crossing the threshold, not at any hour of the day or night. He wasn't stupid. But it didn't lure him and, consequently, it didn't make him uncomfortable.

Coming home was a different story.

He was thinking about it during his last hour on the job, and by the time he reached it he was walking all the way over at the edge of the sidewalk, as far from the building's entrance as he could get without stepping down into the street. He was like an acrophobe edging along a precipitous path, scared to look down, afraid of losing his balance and falling accidentally, afraid too of the impulse that might lead him to plunge purposefully into the void.

He kept walking, eyes forward, heart racing. Once he was past it he felt himself calming down, and he bought his two bottles of beer and his pack of cigarettes and went on home.

He'd get used to it, he told himself. It would get easier with time.

But, surprisingly enough, it didn't. Instead it got worse, but gradually, imperceptibly, and he learned to accommodate it. For one thing, he steered clear of the west side of Eighth Avenue, where the Rose of Singapore stood. Going to work and coming home, he kept to the opposite side of the street.

Even so, he found himself hugging the inner edge of the sidewalk, as if every inch closer to the street would put him that much closer to crossing it and being drawn mothlike into the tavern's neon flame. And, approaching the Rose of Singapore's block, he'd slow down or speed up his pace so that the traffic signal would allow him to cross the street as soon as he reached the corner. As if otherwise, stranded there, he might cross in the other direction instead, across Eighth Avenue and on into the Rose.

He knew it was ridiculous, but he couldn't change the way it felt. When it didn't get better, he found a way around it.

He took Seventh Avenue instead.

He did that on the weekends anyway because it was the shortest route.

But during the week it added two long crosstown blocks to his pedestrian commute, four blocks a day, twenty blocks a week. That came to about three miles a week, maybe a hundred and fifty extra miles a year.

On good days he told himself he was lucky to be getting the exercise, that the extra blocks would help him stay in shape. On bad days he felt like an idiot, crippled by fear.

Then the Albanian got fired.

He was never clear on what happened. One waitress said the Albanian had popped off at the manager one time too many, and maybe that was what happened. All he knew was that one night his relief man was not the usual wild-eyed fellow with the droopy mustache but a stocky dude with a calculating air about him. His name was Dooley, and Paul made him at a glance as a man who'd done time. You could tell, but of course he didn't say anything, didn't drop any hints. And neither did Dooley.

But the night came when Dooley showed up, tied his apron, rolled up his sleeves, and said, "Give her my love, huh?" And, when Paul looked at him in puzzlement, he added, "Your girlfriend."

"Haven't got one," he said.

"You live on Eighth Avenue, right? That's what you told me. Eighth and Sixteenth, right? Yet every time you leave here you head over toward Seventh. Every single time."

"I like the exercise," he said.

"Exercise," Dooley said, and grinned. "Good word for it."

He let it go, but the next night Dooley made a similar comment. "I need to unwind when I come off work," Paul told him. "Sometimes I'll walk clear over to Sixth Avenue before I head downtown. Or even Fifth."

"That's nice," Dooley said. "Just do me a favor, will you? Ask her if she's got a sister."

"It's cold and it looks like rain," Paul said. "I'll be walking home on Eighth Avenue tonight, in case you're keeping track."

And when he left he did walk down Eighth Avenue—for one block. Then he cut over to Seventh and took what had become his usual route.

He began doing that all the time, and whenever he headed east on Twenty-second Street he found himself wondering why he'd let Dooley have such power over him. For that matter, how could he have let a seedy gin joint make him walk out of his way to the tune of a hundred and fifty miles a year?

He was supposed to be keeping it simple. Was this keeping it simple? Making up elaborate lies to explain the way he walked home? And walking extra blocks every night for fear that the devil would reach out and drag him into a neon-lit hell?

Then came a night when it rained, and he walked all the way home on Eighth Avenue.

. . .

It was always a problem when it rained. Going to work he could catch a bus, although it wasn't terribly convenient. But coming home he didn't have the option, because traffic was one-way the wrong way.

So he walked home on Eighth Avenue, and he didn't turn left at Twenty-second Street and didn't fall apart when he drew even with the Rose of Singapore. He breezed on by, bought his beer and cigarettes at the deli, and went home to watch television. But he turned the set off again after a few minutes and spent the hours until bedtime at the window, looking out at the rain, nursing the beers, smoking the cigarettes, and thinking long thoughts.

The next two nights were clear and mild, but he chose Eighth Avenue anyway. He wasn't uneasy, not going to work, not coming home, either. Then came the weekend, and then on Monday he took Eighth again, and this time on the way home he found himself on the west side of the street, the same side as the bar.

The door was open. Music, strident and bluesy, poured through it, along with all the sounds and smells you'd expect.

He walked right on by.

You're over it, he thought. He went home and didn't even turn on the TV, just sat and smoked and sipped his two longneck bottles of Bud.

Same story Tuesday, same story Wednesday.

Thursday night, steps from the tavern's open door, he thought, *Why drag this out?*

He walked in, found a stool at the bar. "Double scotch," he told the barmaid. "Straight up, beer chaser."

He'd tossed off the shot and was working on the beer when a woman slid onto the stool beside him. She put a cigarette between bright red lips, and he scratched a match and lit it for her.

Their eyes met, and he felt something click.

She lived over on Ninth and Seventeenth, on the third floor of a brownstone across the street from the projects. She said her name was Tiffany, and maybe it was. Her apartment was three little rooms. They sat on the couch in the front room and he kissed her a few times and got a little dizzy from it. He excused himself and went to the bathroom and looked at himself in the mirror over the sink.

You could go home now, he told the mirror image. Tell her anything, like you got a headache, you got malaria, you're really a Catholic priest or gay or both. Anything. Doesn't matter what you say or if she believes you. You could go home.

He looked into his own eyes in the mirror and knew it wasn't true.

Because he was stuck, he was committed, he was down for it. Had been from the moment he walked into the bar. No, longer than that. From the first rainy night when he walked home on Eighth Avenue. Or maybe before, maybe ever since Dooley's insinuation had led him to change his route.

And maybe it went back further than that. Maybe he was locked in from the jump, from the day they opened the gates and put him on the street. Hell, from the day he was born, even.

"Paul?"

"Just a minute," he said.

And he slipped into the kitchen. In for a penny, in for a pound, he thought, and he started opening drawers, looking for the one where she kept the knives.

Honorable Mentions: 1999

I didn't want this list to be mine. I don't like lists of anything compiled by one person. So I asked Phil Reed, chairman of the Edgar Short Story Committee, to give me the stories that they had considered as nominees. I'd like to thank Phil and the committee here very much. As well as the Mystery Writers of America.

—*ED GORMAN*

Allyn, Doug, "Bad Boyz Klub," *Ellery Queen's Mystery Magazine,* December, and *Diagnosis Dead*

———, "Miracles! Happen!" *EQMM,* December

Allyn, Jim, "Ozone Layer," *EQMM,* February

Chittenden, Margaret, "Noir Lite," *EQMM,* January

Collins, Max Allan, "Natural Death, Inc.," *Diagnosis Dead*

Deaver, Jeffery, "Triangle" *EQMM,* March

Ford, G. M., "Clothes Make the Man," *EQMM,* February

Fowler, Earlene, "Blue Time," *Murder on Route 66*

Friedman, Philip, "Dog Days," *Murder and Obsession*

George, Elizabeth, "I, Richard," *Murder and Obsession*

Gorman, Ed, "Angie," *999: New Tales of Horror and Suspense*

Grant, Linda, "Second-Oldest Profession," *Mom, Apple Pie & Murder*

Harvey, John, "Cheryl," *Now's the Time*

———, "Slow Burn," *Now's the Time*

Kahn, Michael, "Bread of Affliction," *EQMM,* September/October

Kaminsky, Stuart, "Confession," *Mystery Midrash*

Kellerman, Faye, "Holy Water," *Mystery Midrash*

LaPierre, Janet, "De Capo," *EQMM,* April

Lehane, Dennis, "Running Out of Dog," *Murder and Obsession*

Leitz, David, "Eye Witness," *Canine Christmas*

Levitsky, Ronald, "Jacob's Voice," *Mystery Midrash*

Mallone, Michael, "Invitation to the Ball," *Murder and Obsession*

Meixell, Steve, "Ivan Ending," *Murderous Intent,* Fall

Oates, Joyce Carol, "Tusk," *Irreconcilable Differences*

Schrier, B. H., "Lin Po and Dragon's Blood," *Alfred Hitchcock's Mystery Magazine,* June

Silverstein, Shel, "Guilty Party" (posthumous), *Murder and Obsession*

Smith, Neville, "Heartache Tonight," *Blue Lightning*

Strong, Marianna, "Last Vigil," *EQMM,* August

Stumpf, Dan, "White Like the Snow," *EQMM,* January

Westermann, John, "Trauma Bells Are Ringing," *New Mystery,* Winter

Weston, Anne, "Girl from Wore Out Canyon," *AHMM,* November

Wheat, Carolyn, *"A Bus Called Pity,"* Mom, Apple Pie & Murder

About the Editor

Ed Gorman has been called "one of suspense fiction's best story-tellers" by *Ellery Queen*, and "one of the most original voices in today's crime fiction" by the *San Diego Union*.

Gorman has been published in magazines as various as *Redbook, Ellery Queen, The Magazine of Fantasy and Science Fiction,* and *Poetry Today*.

He has won numerous prizes, including the Shamus, the Spur, and the International Fiction Writer's awards. He's been nominated for the Edgar, the Anthony, the Golden Dagger, and the Bram Stoker awards.

Former *Los Angeles Times* critic Charles Champlin noted that "Ed Gorman is a powerful storyteller."

Gorman's work has been taken by the Literary Guild, the Mystery Guild, Doubleday Book Club, and the Science Fiction Book Club.